STAR TREK®

THE Q
CONTINUUM

STAR TREK®

THE Q CONTINUUM

Greg Cox

Based on
Star Trek: The Next Generation®
created by Gene Roddenberry

POCKET BOOKS
New York   London   Toronto   Sydney   Singapore

POCKET BOOKS, a division of Simon & Schuster, Inc.
1230 Avenue of the Americas, New York, NY 10020

This book is published by Pocket Books, a division of Simon & Schuster, Inc., under exclusive license from Paramount Pictures.

ISBN: 0-7434-8508-4

First Pocket Books trade paperback edition October 2003

10 9 8 7 6 5 4 3 2 1

Manufactured in the United States of America

These titles were previously published individually by Pocket Books.

For information regarding special discounts for bulk purchases, please contact Simon & Schuster Special Sales at 1-800-456-6798 or business@simonandschuster.com

Acknowledgments

Thanks to John Ordover for conceiving of this trilogy, to Paula Block and Paramount for sanctioning it, to my agent, Russ Galen, for handling the contractual details, and to Carol Greenburg for carefully and fruitfully editing all three volumes. Thanks also to David and Alexandra Honigsberg for bullfighting tips, and to everyone at Tor Books, for letting me restructure my editorial duties so that I could give Q all the time and attention he demanded. And to D. C. Fontana, Gene Roddenberry, and John DeLancie for creating Q and bringing him to life (even though Q insists he created them).

Most of all, though, thanks to Karen Palinko for being the work's first and most rigorous reader, as well as for penning the various sinister ditties that became so much a part of 0's character. *The Q Continuum* is a lot more of a collaboration than it says on the cover.

Q-SPACE

Prologue

Let me back in!
In back me let!

Beyond the wall, he gibbered. Time meant nothing to him. An instant was the same as an eternity; both were merely subjective measures of his isolation and his madness, which began the moment he was cast out of creation and had been taking its toll ever since. His exile had just begun, and it had lasted forever.

It's not fair, he thought, as he had thought since the wall came into being. *Fair is fair, there is there, and here is nowhere, nowhere, no hope. Isn't that so?*

So it is, he answered himself, since he'd had no one else to talk to for as long as long could possibly be. *So, so, so . . . so how could they lock me up like this? Why could they?*

His feverish mind offered an explanation. *Fear. That was their paltry excuse. Mere fear, sheer fear, that's clear.* He cackled at his own cleverness. *Fear, here. Fair, there. Fear is fair.*

No, it is not, he protested angrily. *I never did anything, anything that mattered. Matter isn't anything. No, it isn't, is it?*

Not at all. All is not. Not is now.

Now. Now. Now.

Now, for the first time since his bleak, barbaric banishment began, something new was happening. There was a weakness in the wall, not enough to allow him to slide his way through, at least not yet, but a certain slackening that perhaps foretold an end to his stubborn struggle to get past the wall. He felt a crack, an infinitesimal fracture in the infinite, that he shouted through with all his might.

Me back in let!

Even if the entirety of his being could not pass through the tantalizingly, tormentingly small lesion, he could still send his ceaseless craving back into the realm from which he had been so unjustly cast out, crying out to anyone who might hear his desperate plea.

Back let me in! he demanded.

And a voice answered back.

One

Captain's log, stardate 51604.21
    At Starfleet's request, the Enterprise *has arrived at Betazed to take on Lem Faal, a distinguished Betazoid scientist, and his two children. Under Faal's direction, this ship will take part in a highly classified experiment that, if it is successful, may open up a vast new frontier for exploration.*

"Are you quite sure, Counselor, that you do not wish to visit your family while we are here at Betazed?"

"No, thank you, Captain," Commander Deanna Troi replied. "As it happens, my mother and little brother are off on one of her regular excursions to the Parallax Colony on Shiralea VI, so there's not much point in beaming down."

You didn't have to be an empath to detect an unmistakable look of relief on Captain Jean-Luc Picard's face when he learned that Lwaxana Troi was several dozen light-years away. She knew exactly how he felt; even though she genuinely loved her mother, Troi wasn't too disappointed that there would be no parent-daughter reunion on this particular mission. Surviving a visit with Lwaxana always required a lot of energy—and patience. *Maybe it will get easier someday,* she thought. *And maybe Klingons will become vegetarians, too.*

"That's too bad," Captain Picard said unconvincingly. "Although I'm sure our guest must be anxious to get under way." He glanced toward the far end of the conference room, where a middle-aged Betazoid male waited patiently, reviewing the data on a padd that he held at arm's length from himself. *Must be farsighted,* Troi guessed, a not uncommon condition in Betazoids of a certain age. Lem Faal had striking, dark brown eyes, a receding hairline, and the slightly distracted air of a born academic. He reminded Troi of any number of professors she had encountered during her student days at the university, although, on closer inspection, she also picked up an impression of infirmity even though she couldn't spot any obvious handicap. Wearing a tan-colored civilian suit, he looked out of place among all the Starfleet uniforms. Almost instinctively, her empathic senses reached out to get a reading on the new arrival, only to immediately come into contact with a telepathic presence far more powerful than her own. Becoming aware of her tentative probing, Faal looked up from his data padd and made eye contact with Troi from across the room.

Hello, he thought to her.

Er, hello, she thought back. Growing up on Betazed, she had become accustomed to dealing with full telepaths, even though she felt a bit rusty at mind-speaking after spending so many years among humans and other nontelepathic races. *Welcome to the* Enterprise.

Thank you, he answered. She sensed, behind his verbal responses, feelings of keen anticipation, excitement, anxiety, and . . . something else as well, something she couldn't quite make out. Curious, she stretched out further, deeper until she could almost—

Excuse me, Faal thought, blocking her. *I think the captain is ready to begin the briefing.*

Troi blinked, momentarily disoriented by the speed with which she had been shoved out of Faal's mind. She looked around the conference room of the *Enterprise*-E. The other Betazoid's telepathic comment seemed accurate enough; her fellow officers were already taking their places around the curved, illuminated conference table. Captain Picard stood at the head of the table, opposite the blank viewscreen at the other end of the room, where Faal waited to make his presentation. Decorative windows along the outer wall of the conference room offered an eye-catching view of Betazed's upper hemisphere, an image reflected in the glass panes of the display case mounted to the inner wall. Gold-plated models of great starships of the past hung within the case, including a miniature replica of the lost *Enterprise*-D, her home for seven years. Troi always winced inside a little whenever she noticed that model. She'd been at the helm of that *Enterprise* when it made its fatal crash into Veridian III. Even though she knew, intellectually, that it wasn't her fault, she still couldn't forget the sense of horror she had felt as the saucer section dived into the atmosphere of Veridian III, never to rise again. This new ship was a fine vessel, as she'd proven during their historic battle with the Borg a few months ago, but she didn't feel quite like home. Not yet.

Preoccupied with thoughts of the past, Troi sat down at the table between Geordi La Forge and Beverly Crusher. Will Riker and Data were seated across from her, their attention on Captain Picard. Riker's confidence and good humor radiated from him, helping to dispel her gloomy memories. She shook her head to clear her mind and listened attentively as the captain began to speak.

"We are honored to have with us today Lem Faal, a specialist in applied physics from the University of Betazed. Professor Faal has previously won awards from the Daystrom Institute and the Vulcan Science Academy for his groundbreaking work in energy wave dynamics."

"Impressive stuff," Geordi said, obviously familiar with Faal's work. Troi could feel the intensity of his scientific interest seeping off him. No surprise there; she'd expect their chief engineer to be fascinated by "energy wave dynamics" and like matters.

"Indeed," Data commented. "I have been particularly intrigued by the professor's insights into the practical applications of transwarp spatial anomalies." The android's sense of anticipation felt just as acute as Geordi's. *He must have activated his emotion chip,* Troi realized. She could always tell, which certainly demonstrated how genuine Data's on-again, off-again emotions could be.

"Starfleet," the captain continued, "has the greatest of interest in Professor Faal's current line of research, and the *Enterprise* has been selected to participate in an experiment testing certain new theories he has devised." He gestured toward Faal, who nodded his head in acknowledgment. "Professor, no doubt you can explain your intentions better."

"Well, I can try," the scientist answered. He tapped a control on his padd and the viewscreen behind him lit up. The image that appeared on the screen was of a shimmering ribbon of reddish-purple energy that appeared to stretch across a wide expanse of interstellar space. *The Nexus?* Troi thought for a second, but, no, this glowing band did not look quite the same color as the mysterious phenomenon that had obsessed Tolian Soran. It looked familiar, though, like something she might have seen at an astrophysics lecture back at Starfleet Academy. *Of course,* she realized instantly, *the barrier!*

She felt a temporary surge of puzzlement quickly fade from the room. Obviously, the other officers had recognized the barrier as well. Faal let his audience take in the image for a few seconds before beginning his lecture.

"For centuries," he began, "the great galactic barrier has blocked the Federation's exploration of the universe beyond our own Milky Way Galaxy. It completely surrounds the perimeter of our galaxy, posing a serious hazard to any vessel that attempts to venture to the outer limits of inhabited space. Not only do the unnatural energies that comprise the barrier batter a vessel physically, but there is also a psychic component to the barrier that causes insanity, brain damage, and even death to any humanoid that comes into contact with it."

Troi winced at the thought. As an empath, she knew just how fragile a mind could be, and how a heightened sensitivity to psychic phenomena sometimes left one particularly vulnerable to such effects as the professor described. As a full telepath, Faal had to be even more wary of powerful psychokinetic forces. She wondered if his own gifts played any part in his interest in the barrier.

Faal pressed another button on his padd and the picture of the barrier was replaced by a standard map of the known galaxy, divided into the usual four sections. A flashing purple line, indicating the galactic barrier, circled all four quadrants. "The Federation has always accepted this limitation, as have the Klingons and the Romulans and the other major starfaring civilizations, because there has always been so much territory to explore within our own galaxy. After all, even after centuries of warp travel, both the Gamma and the Delta quadrants remain largely uncharted. Furthermore, the distances between galaxies are so incalculably immense that, even if there were a safe way to cross the barrier, a voyage to another galaxy would require a ship to travel for centuries at maximum warp. And finally, to be totally honest, we have accepted the barrier because there has been no viable alternative to doing so.

"That situation may have changed," Faal announced with what was to Troi a palpable sense of pride. *Typical,* she thought. *What scientist is not proud of his accomplishments?* The map of the galaxy flickered, giving way to a photo of a blond-haired woman whose pale skin was delicately speckled with dark red markings that ran from her temples down to the sides of her throat. *A Trill,* Troi thought, recognizing the characteristic spotting of that symbiotic life-form. She felt a fleeting pang of sadness from the woman seated next to her and sympathized with Beverly, who was surely recalling her own doomed love affair with the Trill diplomat Ambassador Odan. Troi wasn't sure, but she thought she sensed a bit of discomfort from Will Riker as well. A reasonable reaction, considering that Will had once "loaned" his own body to a Trill symbiont. She was relieved to note that both Will and Beverly swiftly overcame their flashes of emotion, focusing once more on the present. *They acknowledged their pasts, then moved on,* the counselor diagnosed approvingly. *Very healthy behavior.*

Worf married a Trill, she remembered with only the slightest twinge of jealousy. Then she took her own advice and put that reaction behind her. *I wish him only the best,* she thought.

"Some of you may be familiar with the recent work of Dr. Lenara Kahn, the noted

Trill physicist," Faal went on. Heads nodded around the table and Troi experienced a twinge of guilt; she tried to keep up to date on the latest scientific developments, as summarized in Starfleet's never-ending bulletins and position papers, but her own interests leaned more toward psychology and sociology than the hard sciences, which she sometimes gave only a cursory inspection. *Oh well,* she thought, *I never intended to transfer to Engineering.* "A few years ago, Dr. Kahn and her associates conducted a test on Deep Space Nine, which resulted in the creation of the Federation's first artificially generated wormhole. The wormhole was unstable, and collapsed only moments after its creation, but Kahn's research team has continued to refine and develop this new technology. They're still years away from being able to produce an artificial wormhole that's stable enough to permit reliable transport to other sectors of the galaxy, but it dawned on me that the same technique, modified somewhat, might allow a starship to open a temporary breach in the galactic barrier, allowing safe passage through to the other side. As you may have guessed, that's where the *Enterprise* comes in."

A low murmur arose in the conference room as the assembled officers reacted to Faal's revelation. Data and Geordi took turns peppering the Betazoid scientist with highly technical questions that quickly left Troi behind. *Just as well,* she thought. She was startled enough by just the basic idea.

Breaking the barrier! It was one of those things, like passing the warp-ten threshold or flying through a sun, that people talked about sometimes, but you never really expected to happen in your lifetime. Searching her memory, she vaguely recalled that an earlier *Enterprise,* Captain Kirk's ship, had passed through the barrier on a couple of occasions, usually with spectacularly disastrous consequences. Starfleet had declared such expeditions off-limits decades ago, although every few years some crackpot or daredevil would try to break the barrier in a specially modified ship. To date, none of these would-be heroes had survived. She remembered Will Riker once, years ago on Betazed, describing such dubious endeavors as "the warp-era equivalent of going over Niagara in a barrel." Now, apparently, it was time for the *Enterprise*-E to take the plunge. She couldn't suppress a chill at the very thought.

"I'm curious, Professor," Riker asked. "Where exactly do you plan to make the test?"

Faal tapped his padd and the map of the galaxy reappeared on the screen. The image zoomed in on the Alpha Quadrant and he pointed at a wedge-shaped area on the map. "Those portions of the barrier that exist within Federation space have been thoroughly surveyed by unmanned probes containing the most advanced sensors available, and they've made a very intriguing discovery. Over the last year or so, energy levels within the barrier have fluctuated significantly, producing what appears to be a distinct weakening in the barrier at several locations."

Shaded red areas appeared throughout the flashing purple curve on the screen. Troi noted that the shaded sections represented only a small portion of the barrier. They looked like mere dots scattered along the length of the line. *Like leaks in a dam,* she thought, finding the comparison somewhat unsettling.

Faal gave her an odd look, as if aware of her momentary discomfort. "These . . . imperfections . . . in the integrity of the barrier are not substantial, representing only a fractional diminution in the barrier's strength, but they are significant enough to recommend themselves as the logical sites at which to attempt to penetrate the barrier. This particular site," he said, pointing to one of the red spots, which began to flash brighter than the rest, "is located in an uninhabited and otherwise uninteresting sector of space. Since Starfleet would prefer to conduct this experiment in secrecy, far from the prying eyes of the Romulans or the Cardassians, this site has been selected for our trial run. Even as I speak, specialized equipment, adapted from the original Trill designs, is being transported aboard the *Enterprise*. I look forward to working with Mr. La Forge and his engineering team on this project."

"Thanks," Geordi replied. The ocular implants that served as his eyes glanced from Data to Faal. "Whatever you need, I'm sure we're up to it. Sounds like quite a breakthrough, in more ways than one."

Troi peered at the spot that Faal had indicated on the map. She didn't recall much about that region, but she estimated that it was about two to three days away at warp five. Neither the captain nor Will Riker radiated any concern about the location Faal had chosen. She could tell that they anticipated an uneventful flight until they arrived at the barrier.

"Professor," she asked, "how similar is the galactic barrier to the Great Barrier? Would your new technique be effective on both?"

Faal nodded knowingly. "That's a good question. What is colloquially known as 'the Great Barrier' is a similar wall of energy that encloses the very center of our galaxy, as opposed to the outer rim of the galaxy. More precisely, the Great Barrier is an *intra*galactic energy field while our destination is an *extra*galactic field." He ran his hand through his thinning gray hair. "Research conducted over the last hundred years suggests that both barriers are composed of equivalent, maybe even identical, forms of energy. In theory, the artificial wormhole process, if it's successful, could be used to penetrate the Great Barrier as well. Many theorists believe both barriers stem from the same root cause."

"Which is?" she inquired.

Faal chuckled. "I'm afraid that's more of a theological question than a scientific one, and thus rather out of my field. As far as we can tell, the existence of the barriers predates the development of sentient life in our galaxy. Or at least any lifeforms we're familiar with."

That's odd, Troi mused. She wasn't sure but she thought she detected a flicker of insincerity behind the scientist's ingratiating manner, like he was holding something back. *Perhaps he's not as confident about his theories as he'd like Starfleet to think,* she thought. It was hard to tell; Faal's own telepathic gifts made him difficult to read.

Sitting beside Troi, Beverly Crusher spoke up, a look of concern upon her features. "Has anyone thought about the potential ecological consequences of poking a hole in the barrier? If these walls have been in place for billions of years, maybe they serve some vital purpose, either to us or to whatever life-forms exist on the opposite side of the wall. I hate to throw cold water on a fascinating proposal, but maybe the barrier shouldn't be breached?"

There it is again, Troi thought, watching the Betazoid scientist carefully. She sensed some sort of reaction from Faal in response to Beverly's question. It flared up immediately, then was quickly snuffed out before she could clearly identify the emotion. *Fear? Guilt? Annoyance? Maybe he simply doesn't like having his experiment challenged,* she speculated. Certainly he wouldn't be the first dedicated scientist to suffer from tunnel vision where his brainchild was concerned. Researchers, she knew from experience, could be as protective of their pet projects as an enraged *sehlat* defending its young.

If he was feeling defensive, he displayed no sign of it. "Above all else, first do no harm, correct, Doctor?" he replied to Crusher amiably, paraphrasing the Hippo-cratic Oath. "I appreciate your concerns, Doctor. Let me reassure you a bit regard-ing the scale of our experiment. The galactic barrier itself is so unfathomably vast that our proposed exercise is not unlike knocking a few bricks out of your own Earth's Great Wall of China. It's hard to imagine that we could do much damage to the ecosystem of the entire galaxy, let alone whatever lies beyond, although the po-tential danger is another good reason for conducting this preliminary test in an un-populated sector. As far as we know, there's nothing on the other side except the vast emptiness between our own galaxy and its neighbors." He pressed a finger against his padd and the screen behind him reverted to the compelling image with which he had begun his lecture: the awe-inspiring sight of the galactic barrier stretching across countless light-years of space, its eerie, incandescent energies rippling through the shimmering wall of violet light.

"Starfleet feels—" he started to say, but a harsh choking noise interrupted his explanation. He placed his free hand over his mouth and coughed a few more times. Troi saw his chest heaving beneath his suit and winced in sympathy. She was no physician, but she didn't like the sound of Faal's coughs, which seemed to come from deep within his lungs. She could tell that Beverly was concerned as well.

"Excuse me," Faal gasped, fishing around in the pockets of his tan suit. He withdrew a compact silver hypospray, which he pressed against the crook of his arm. Troi heard a distinctive hiss as the instrument released its medication into his body. Within a few seconds, Faal appeared to regain control of his breathing. "I apologize for the interruption, but I'm afraid my health isn't all it should be."

Troi recalled her earlier impression of infirmity. Was this ailment, she wondered, what the professor was trying so hard to conceal? Even Betazoids, who generally prided themselves on being at ease with their own bodies, could feel uncomfortable about revealing a serious medical condition. She recalled that Faal had brought his family along on this mission, despite the possibility of danger, and she wondered how his obvious health problems might have affected his children. *Perhaps I should prepare for some family counseling, just in case my assistance is needed.*

Faal took a few deep breaths to steady himself, then addressed Beverly. "As ship's medical officer, Dr. Crusher, you should probably be aware that I have Iverson's disease."

The emotional temperature of the room rose to a heightened level the moment Faal mentioned the dreaded sickness. Iverson's disease remained one of the more conspicuous failures of twenty-fourth-century medicine: a debilitating, degenerative condition for which there was no known cure. Thankfully noncontagious, the disor-der attacked muscle fiber and other connective tissues, resulting in the progressive atrophy of limbs and vital organs; from the sound of Faal's labored breathing, Troi suspected that Faal's ailment had targeted his respiratory system. She felt acute sym-pathy and embarrassment on the part of her fellow officers. No doubt all of them were remembering Admiral Mark Jameson—and the desperate lengths the disease had driven him to during that mission to Mordan IV. "I'm very sorry," she said.

"Please feel free to call on me for whatever care you may require," Beverly stressed. "Perhaps you should come by sickbay later so we can discuss your condi-tion in private."

"Thank you," he said, "but please don't let my condition concern any of you." He held up the hypospray. "My doctor has prescribed polyadrenaline for my cur-

rent symptoms. All that matters now is that I live long enough to see the completion of my work." The hypospray went back into his pocket and Faal pointed again
to the image of the galactic barrier on the screen.

"At any rate," he continued, "Starfleet Science has judged the potential risk of
this experiment to be acceptable when weighed against the promise of opening up
a new era of expansion beyond the boundaries of this galaxy. Exploring the unknown always contains an element of danger. Isn't that so, Captain?"

"Indeed," the captain agreed. "The fundamental mission of the *Enterprise,* as
well as that of Starfleet, has always been to extend the limits of our knowledge of
the universe, exploring new and uncharted territory." Picard rose from his seat at the
head of the table. "Your experiment, Professor Faal, falls squarely within the proud
tradition of this ship. Let us hope for the best of luck in this exciting new endeavor."

It's too bad, Troi thought, *that the rest of the crew can't sense Captain Picard's
passion and commitment the same way I can.* Then she looked around the conference table and saw the glow of the captain's inspiration reflected in the faces of her
fellow officers. Even Beverly, despite her earlier doubts, shared their commitment
to the mission. *On second thought, maybe they can.*

"Thank you, Captain," Lem Faal said warmly. Troi noticed that he still seemed
a bit out of breath. "I am anxious to begin."

This time Troi detected nothing but total sincerity in the man's words.

Two

"The most difficult part," Lem Faal explained, "is going to be keeping the torpedo
intact inside the barrier until it can send out a magneton pulse."

"That's more than difficult," Chief Engineer Geordi La Forge commented. He
had been reading up on the galactic barrier ever since the briefing, so he had a better idea of what they were up against. "That's close to impossible."

The duty engineer's console, adjacent to the chief engineer's office, had been
reassigned to the Betazoid researcher as a workstation where he could complete
the preparations for his experiment. To accommodate Faal's shaky health, La
Forge had also taken care to provide a sturdy stool Faal could rest upon while he
worked. Now he and Geordi scrutinized the diagrams unfolding on a monitor as
Faal spelled out the details of his experiment:

"Not if we fine-tune the polarity of the shields to match exactly the amplitude
of the barrier at the point where the quantum torpedo containing the magneton
pulse generator enters the barrier. That amplitude is constantly shifting, of course,
but if we get it right, then the torpedo should hold together long enough to emit a
magneton pulse that will react with a subspace tensor matrix generated by the
Enterprise to create an opening in the space-time continuum. Then, according to
my calculations, the artificial wormhole will disrupt the energy lattice of the barrier, creating a pathway of normal space through to the other side!"

"Then it's only two million light-years to the *next* galaxy, right?" Geordi said
with a grin. "I guess we'll have to build that bridge when we get to it."

"Precisely," Faal answered. "For myself, I'll leave that challenge for the starship designers and transwarp enthusiasts. Who knows? Maybe a generation ship is

the answer, if you can find enough colonists who don't mind leaving the landing to their descendants. Or suspended animation, perhaps. But before we can face the long gulf between the galaxies, first we must break free from the glimmering cage that has hemmed us in since time began. We're like baby birds that finally have to leave the nest and explore the great blue sky beyond."

"I never quite thought of it that way," Geordi said. "After all, the Milky Way is one heck of a big nest."

"The biggest nest still hems you in, as the largest cage is still a cage," Faal insisted with a trace of bitterness in his voice. "Look at me. My mind is free to explore the fundamental principles of the universe, but it's trapped inside a fragile, dying body." He looked up from his schematics to inspect Geordi. "Excuse me for asking, Commander, but I'm intrigued by your eyes. Are those the new ocular implants I've heard about, the ones they just developed on Earth?"

The scientist's curiosity did not bother Geordi; sometimes his new eyes still caught him by surprise, especially when he looked in a mirror. "These are them, all right. I didn't know you were interested in rehabilitative medicine. Or is it the optics?"

"It's all about evolution," Faal explained. "Technology has usurped natural selection as the driving force of evolution, so I'm fascinated by the ways in which sentient organisms can improve upon their own flawed biology. Prosthetics are one way, genetic manipulation is another. So is breaking the barrier, perhaps. It's about overcoming the inherent frailties of our weak humanoid bodies, becoming superior beings, just as you have used the latest in medical technology to improve yourself."

Geordi wasn't sure quite how to respond. He didn't exactly think of himself as "superior," just better equipped to do his job. "If you say so, Professor," he said, feeling a little uncomfortable. Lem Faal was starting to sound a bit too much like a Borg. Maybe it was only a trick of light, reflecting the glow of the monitor, but an odd sort of gleam had crept into the Betazoid's eyes as he spoke. *I wonder if I would have even noticed that a few years ago?* Geordi thought. His VISOR had done a number of things well, from isolating hairline fractures in metal plating to tracking neutrinos through a flowing plasma current, but picking up on subtle nuances of facial expressions hadn't been one of them.

"Chief!" Geordi turned around to see Lieutenant Reginald Barclay approaching the workstation. Barclay was pushing before him an antigrav carrier supporting a device Geordi recognized from Professor Faal's blueprints. "Mr. DeCandido in Transporter Room Five said you wanted this immediately."

The carrier was a black metal platform, hovering above the floor at about waist level, which Barclay steered by holding on to a horizontal handlebar in front of his chest. Faal's invention sat atop the platform, held securely in place by a stasis field. It consisted of a shining steel cylinder, approximately a meter and a half in height, surrounded by a transparent plastic sphere with metal connection plates at both the top and the bottom poles of the globe. It looked like it might be fairly heavy outside the influence of the antigrav generator; Geordi automatically estimated the device's mass with an eye toward figuring out how it would affect the trajectory of a standard quantum torpedo once it was installed within the torpedo casing. *Shouldn't be too hard to insert the globe into a torpedo,* he thought, *assuming everything is in working order inside the sphere.*

"Thanks, Reg," he said. "Professor Faal, this is Lieutenant Reginald Barclay. Reg, this is Professor Faal."

"Pleased to meet you," Barclay stammered. "This is a very daring experiment that I'm proud to be a part—" He lifted a hand from the handlebar to offer it to Faal, but then the platform started to tilt and he hastily put both hands back on the handle. "Oops. Sorry about that," he muttered.

Faal eyed Barclay skeptically, and Geordi had to resist a temptation to roll his ocular implants. Barclay always managed to make a poor first impression on people, which was too bad since, at heart, he was a dedicated and perfectly capable crew member. Unfortunately, his competence fluctuated in direct relationship to his confidence, which often left something to be desired; the more insecure he got, the more he tended to screw up, which just rattled him even more. Geordi had taken Barclay on as a special project some years back, and the nervous crewman was showing definite signs of progress, although some days you wouldn't know it. *Just my luck,* he thought, *this had to be one of Reg's off days.*

"Please be careful, Lieutenant," Faal stressed to Barclay. "You're carrying the very heart of my experiment there. Inside that cylinder is a mononuclear strand of quantum filament suspended in a protomatter matrix. Unless the filament is aligned precisely when the torpedo releases the magneton pulse, there will be no way to control the force and direction of the protomatter reaction. We could end up with merely a transitory subspace fissure that would have no impact on the barrier at all."

"Understood, Professor," Barclay assured him. "You can count on me. I'll guard this component like a mother Horta guards her eggs. Even better, in fact, because you won't have to feed me my weight in silicon bricks." He stared at the Betazoid's increasingly dubious expression. "Er, that was a joke. The last part, I mean, not the part about guarding the component, because that was completely serious even if you didn't like the bit about the Hortas, cause I understand that not everyone's fond of—"

"That will be fine," Geordi interrupted, coming to Barclay's rescue. "Just put the sphere on that table over there. Professor Faal and I need to make some adjustments."

"Got it," Barclay said, avoiding eye contact with Faal. He pushed the carrier over to an elevated shelf strewn with delicate instruments. The antigrav platform floated a few centimeters above the ledge of the shelf. Barclay's forehead wrinkled with anxiety as he looked up and over the carrier to the controls on the other side.

"Let me just scoot over there to even this out," he said, smiling tightly as he began to walk around the carrier to reach the controls.

As soon as Reg took his first step, time seemed to slow down for La Forge. Geordi watched the rise and fall of Reg's footsteps, the gangly engineer's legs grazing the platform, which he didn't give a wide enough berth. La Forge felt his mouth open and heard his own voice utter the first word of a warning. Slowly, excruciatingly slowly, Geordi watched with horror as Lieutenant Reginald Barclay's left elbow plowed into the corner of the platform. The delicate equipment trembled. Reg jumped away. Geordi instinctively covered his eyes. It was one of the few times he wished that medical science had not restored his sight quite so efficiently.

When he finally gathered the courage to look at the equipment and assess the damage, La Forge thought he might faint with relief. The platform had miraculously righted itself. Time sped up to its normal pace again. He dimly heard Barclay's apologies for the near-disaster, but was more concerned for the Betazoid scientist.

He glanced over at Professor Faal. The scientist's face had gone completely white and his mouth hung open in dumbfounded horror. *Has his disease weakened his heart?* he worried. He hoped not, since Lem Faal looked like he was about to drop dead on the spot. He was shaking so hard that Geordi was afraid he'd fall off his stool. *I wonder if I should call Dr. Crusher?*

"Um," Barclay mumbled, staring fixedly at the floor. "Will that be all, sir?"

Geordi offered a silent prayer of thanks to the nameless gods of engineering. He had not been looking forward to telling the captain how his team managed to completely pulverize the central component of the big experiment. He made a mental note to have Barclay schedule a few extra sessions with Counselor Troi. Some more self-confidence exercises were definitely in order . . . as well as a good talking-to.

"Watch it, Lieutenant," he said, his utter embarrassment in front of Faal adding heat to his tone. "This operation is too important for that kind of carelessness." He disliked having to criticize one of his officers in front of a visitor, but Barclay hadn't given him any other choice. He had to put the fear of god into Reg, and let Professor Faal know he had the situation under control.

At least, that was the plan. . . .

"I don't believe it!" Faal exploded, hopping off his stool to confront Barclay. His equipment might have survived its near miss, but the professor's temper clearly had not. Faal's ashen expression gave way to a look of utter fury. His face darkened and his eyes narrowed until his large Betazoid irises could barely be seen. His entire body trembled. "Years of work, of planning and sacrifice, almost ruined because of this . . . this imbecile!"

Barclay looked absolutely stricken. *Yep,* Geordi thought, *Deanna is definitely going to have her work cut out for her.* Barclay tried to produce another apology, but his shattered nerves left him tongue-tied and inaudible.

"I'm sure that looked a lot worse than it actually was," Geordi said, anxious to smooth things over and calm Faal down before he had some kind of seizure. "Good thing we planned on rechecking all the instrumentation anyway."

Faal wasn't listening. "If you only knew what was at stake!" he shouted at Barclay. He drew back his arm and might have struck Barclay across the face with the back of his hand had not La Forge hastily stepped between them.

"Hey!" Geordi protested. "Let's cool our phasers here. It was just an accident." Faal lowered his arm slowly, but still glowered murderously at Barclay. Geordi decided the best thing to do was to get Reg out of sight as fast as possible. "Lieutenant, report back to the transporter room and see if DeCandido needs any more help. You're off of this experiment as of now. We'll speak more later."

With a sheepish nod, the mortified crewman made a quick escape, leaving Geordi behind to deal with the agitated Betazoid physicist. Fortunately, his violent outburst, regrettable as it was, seemed to have dispelled much of his anger. Faal's ruddy face faded a shade or two and he breathed in and out deeply, like a man trying to forcibly calm himself and succeeding to a degree. "My apologies, Mr. La Forge," he said, coughing into his fist. Now that his initial tantrum was over, he seemed to be having trouble catching his breath. He fumbled in his pocket for his hypospray, then applied it to his arm. "I should not have lost control like that." A few seconds later, after another hacking cough, he walked over to the shelf and laid his hand upon the sphere. "When I saw the equipment begin to tip over . . . well, it was rather alarming."

"I understand perfectly," Geordi answered, deciding not to make an issue of the professor's lapse now that he seemed to have cooled off. What with his illness and all, Faal had to be under a lot of stress. "To be honest, I wasn't feeling too great myself for a few seconds there. I can just imagine what you must have been going through."

"No, Commander," Faal answered gravely, "I don't think you can."

Geordi made two more mental notes to himself: 1) to keep Barclay safely out of sight until the experiment was completed, and 2) to remember also that Professor Lem Faal of the University of Betazoid, winner of some of the highest scientific honors that the Federation could bestow, was more tightly wound than he first appeared.

A lot more.

Interlude

Like most Betazoids, Milo Faal was acutely aware of his own emotions, and right now he was feeling bored and frustrated, verging on resentful. Where was his father anyway? *Probably holed up in some lab,* the eleven-year-old thought, *same as usual. He's forgotten all about us. Again.*

Their guest quarters aboard the *Enterprise* were spacious and comfortable enough. The captain had assigned the Faal family the best VIP suite available, with three bedchambers, two bathrooms, a personal replicator, and a spacious living area complete with a desk, a couch, and several comfortable chairs. Milo fidgeted restlessly upon the couch, already tired of the same soothing blue walls he figured he'd be staring at for the next several days.

So far, this trip was turning out to be just as boring as he had anticipated. He had unpacked all their luggage—with no help from his father, thank you very much—and put his little sister, Kinya, down for a much-needed nap on one of the Jupiter-sized beds in the next room. Monitoring her telepathically, he sensed nothing but fatigue and contentment emanating from his slumbering sibling. With any luck, she would sleep for hours, but what was he supposed to do in the meantime? There probably wasn't another kid his age around for a couple hundred light-years.

In the outer wall of the living room, opposite the couch, a long horizontal window composed of reinforced transparent aluminum provided a panoramic look at the stars zipping by outside the ship. It was a pretty enough view, Milo granted, but right now it only served to remind him how far away he was traveling from his friends and home back on Betazed. All he had to look forward to, it seemed, was a week or two of constant babysitting while his father spent every waking hour at his oh-so-important experiments. These days he often felt more like a parent than a brother to little Kinya.

If only Mom were here, he thought, taking care to block his pitiful plea from his sibling's sleeping mind, lest it disturb her childish dreams. It was a useless hope; his mother had died over a year ago in a freak transporter accident. *Which was when everything started going straight down the gravity well,* he thought bitterly.

Their father, for sure, had never been the same after the accident. *Where in the name of the Second House are you, Dad?* Milo glared at the closed door that led to the corridor outside and from there to the rest of the ship. Sometimes it felt like they had lost both parents when his mother died. Between his illness and his experiments, Dad never seemed to have any time or thought for them anymore. Even when he was with them physically, which wasn't very often, his mind was always somewhere else, somewhere he kept locked up and out of reach from his own children. *What's so important about your experiments anyway? You should be here, Dad.*

Especially now, he thought. Milo knew his father was sick, of course; in a tele-pathic society, you couldn't hide something like that, particularly from your own son. All the more reason why Lem Faal should be spending as much time as possi-ble with his family . . . before something happened to him. *If* something happened, Milo corrected himself. He could not bring himself to accept his father's death as inevitable, not yet. There was always a chance, he thought. They still had time to turn things around.

But how much time?

Milo flopped sideways onto the couch, his bare feet resting upon the elevated armrest at the far end. His large brown eyes began to water and he felt a familiar soreness at the back of his throat. *No,* he thought, *I'm not going to get all weepy.* Not even when there was no one around to see or hear him. Staring across the liv-ing room at the streaks of starlight racing by through the darkness of space, he forced his mind to think more positively.

Flying across the galaxy in Starfleet's flagship had its exciting side, he admit-ted. Every schoolkid in the Federation had heard about the *Enterprise;* this was the ship, or at least the crew, that had repelled the Borg—twice. *This wouldn't be such a bad trip,* he mused, *if only Dad took the time to share it with us.* He could easily imagine them making a real vacation of it, touring the entire ship together, in-specting the engines, maybe even visiting the bridge. Sure, his father would have to do a little work along the way, supervising the most crucial stages of the project, but surely Starfleet's finest engineers were capable of handling the majority of the details, at least until they reached the test site. They didn't need his father looking over their shoulders all the time.

Of course not.

The entrance to the guest suite chimed and Milo jumped off the couch and ran toward the door, half-convinced that his father would indeed be there, ready to take him on a personal tour of the bridge itself. *About time,* he thought, then pushed any trace of irritation down deep into the back of his mind, where his father couldn't possibly hear it. He wasn't about to let his bruised feelings throw a shadow over the future, not now that Dad had finally come looking for him.

Then the door whished open and his father wasn't there. Instead Milo saw a stranger in a Starfleet uniform. An adult human, judging from the sound of his thought patterns, maybe twenty or thirty years old. It was hard to tell with grown-ups sometimes, especially humans. "Hi," he said, glancing down at the data padd in his hand, "you must be Milo. My name's Ensign Whitman, but you can call me Percy."

Milo must have let his disappointment show on his face, because he felt a pang of sympathy from the crewman. "I'm afraid your father is quite busy right now, but Counselor Troi thought you might enjoy a trip to the holodeck." He stepped inside the guest quarters and checked his padd again, then glanced about the room. "Is your sister around?"

"She's sleeping," Milo explained, trying not to sound as let down as he felt. *Humans aren't very empathic,* he remembered, *so I might as well pretend to be grateful. Just to be polite.* "Hang on, I'll go get her."

I should have known, he thought, as he trudged into Kinya's bedroom, where he found her already awake. She must have heard Percy what's-his-name stumble in, he thought. She started to cry and Milo lifted her from the sheets and cradled her against his chest, patting her gently on the back until she quieted. *Dad would never interrupt his work for us,* he thought bitterly, taking care to shield the toddler from his hurt and anger, *not when he can just dump us with some crummy babysitter.*

The holodeck. Big deal. If he wanted to kill time in a holodeck, he could have just as easily stayed on Betazed. And it wasn't even his father's idea; it was the ship's counselor's! *Thanks a lot, Dad,* he thought emphatically, hoping that his father could hear him no matter where he was on this stupid starship.

Not that he's likely to care if he does. . . .

Three

The door to the captain's ready room slid open and Deanna stepped inside. "Thank you for joining us on such short notice, Counselor," Picard said. He waited patiently for her to sit down in one of the chairs in front of his desk, next to Geordi. The door slid shut behind her, granting the three of them a degree of privacy. "Mr. La Forge has informed me of an unpleasant incident involving Lem Faal and I wanted your input on the matter."

Geordi quickly described Faal's confrontation with Lieutenant Barclay to Troi. "It's probably no big deal," he concluded, shrugging his shoulders, "but I thought the captain ought to know about it."

"Quite right," Picard assured him, feeling more than a touch of indignation at the Betazoid scientist's behavior. Granted, Mr. Barclay's awkward manner could be disconcerting, but Picard was not about to let Faal abuse any member of his crew, no matter how prestigious his scientific reputation was. Had Faal actually struck Barclay, he might well be looking at the brig now. "I appreciate your effort to keep me informed," he told La Forge. No doubt Geordi would rather be attending to matters in Engineering, where there was surely much to be done to prepare for the experiment. Picard looked at Deanna. "Counselor, what impression have you formed of Professor Faal?"

Troi hesitated, frowning, and Picard felt a twinge of apprehension. Lem Faal had not struck him as particularly difficult or worrisome. What could Deanna have sensed in the man? Some form of instability? If so, he was concealing it well. "Is there a problem with Professor Faal?" he pressed her.

Her flowing black mane rustled as she shook her head and sighed. "I can't put my finger on anything, but I keep getting a sense that he's hiding something."

"Hiding what precisely?" Picard asked, concerned.

"That's what I can't tell. Unfortunately, Faal is a full telepath, like most Betazoids, which makes him harder to read. To be honest, sometimes I can half-convince myself that I'm only imagining things, or that I'm merely picking up on the normal anxiety any scientist might feel on the verge of a possible failure." She watched Picard carefully, intent on making herself clear. "Then I get another trace of . . . well, something not quite right, something Faal wants to conceal."

"Are you sure," Picard asked, "that you're not simply sensing some deep-rooted anxieties Faal may have about his medical condition? Iverson's disease is a terrible affliction. It can't be easy living with a terminal diagnosis."

"I've considered that as well," Deanna admitted. "Certainly, he has to be troubled by his illness and impending death, but there may be more to what I'm feeling. When he admitted his condition during the briefing, I didn't get the impression that he was letting go of a deeply held secret. He may be concealing something else, something that has nothing to do with his condition."

"What about his family?" Picard asked. He had been less than pleased to read, in his original mission briefing, that Professor Faal was to be accompanied on this voyage by his two children. The devastating crash of the *Enterprise*-D, along with the heightened tensions of the war with the Dominion, had inspired Starfleet to rethink its policy regarding the presence of children aboard certain high-profile starships engaged in risky exploratory and military missions, much to Picard's satisfaction. His own recommendation had come as no surprise; although he had grudgingly adapted to the family-friendly environment of the previous *Enterprise,* he had never been entirely comfortable with the notion of small children taking up permanent residence aboard his ship. Or even temporary residence, for that matter. "How are his children faring on this voyage?"

"Professor Faal has children?" Geordi asked, caught by surprise. "Aboard the *Enterprise?*"

"Yes," Troi said, both intrigued and concerned. "Hasn't he mentioned them to you?"

"Not a word," Geordi insisted. He scratched his chin as he mulled the matter over. "Granted, we've been working awful hard to get the modified torpedo ready, but he hasn't said a thing about his family."

A scowl crossed Picard's face. "The professor's experiment is not without its dangers. To be quite honest, it hardly strikes me as an ideal time to bring one's children along."

"Any time is better than none at all," Troi explained. "At least that's what the family counselors back on Betazed thought. According to Professor Faal's personal file, which I reviewed after our meeting in the conference room, the children's mother was killed less than six months ago. Some sort of transporter accident."

"The poor kids," La Forge said, wincing. Picard recalled that Geordi's own mother had been missing and presumed dead for only a few years now, ever since the *Hera* disappeared along with everyone aboard; it was none too surprising that the engineer empathized with the children's loss.

"Anyway," Troi continued, "it was felt that now was far too soon to separate them from their father as well, especially since his time after the experiment is completed is likely to be so brief."

"I see," Picard conceded reluctantly. He was no expert on child psychology, but he granted that Faal's terminal condition necessitated special consideration where his children were concerned. "No doubt Faal's illness, as well as the recent tragedy involving his wife, imposes a terrible burden on the entire family. Do you think you might be reacting to whatever difficulties he might be having with his children?"

Troi shook her head. "I'm very familiar with parent-child stresses, including my own," she added with a rueful smile. Picard tried hard not to let his own . . . unflattering . . . feelings toward Lwaxana Troi seep over into Deanna's awareness. "Not to mention helping Worf through all his difficulties with Alexander. . . . No, I know what family problems feel like. This is something different." She frowned again, clearly wishing she could offer Picard advice more specific. "All I can say, Captain, is that Faal is more complicated than he appears, and might behave unpredictably."

"By attempting, for example, to strike Lieutenant Barclay?" Picard suggested.

To be fair, he admitted privately, it was Barclay, after all. While he could not condone near-violence against a crew member, Barclay was something of a special case; there were times when Picard himself wondered if Reg Barclay might not be happier in a less stressful environment. The man had his talents, but perhaps not the correct temperament for deep-space exploration.

"For example," Troi agreed. She turned toward La Forge. "Geordi, you've worked more closely with Professor Faal than the rest of us. What are your impressions of him?"

"Gee, I'm not sure," Geordi waffled. "I mean, yeah, he gets pretty intense at times—who wouldn't under the circumstances?—but I don't think he's dangerous or anything, just determined to get the job done while his health is still up to the task. He doesn't talk about it much, but I think his illness weighs on his mind a lot. He's aware that he hasn't got much time left."

"I see," Picard nodded, his irritation at the scientist fading. It was hard not to feel for a man who was facing death just as his life's work neared completion. "Perhaps we should make some allowances for displays of temperament, given the professor's condition." Picard stood up behind his desk and straightened his jacket. Time to conclude this meeting, he decided, and get back to the bridge.

"Faal's reputation is impeccable," he told Troi, thinking aloud. "At the moment, all we can do is keep an extra eye on the professor and try to be ready for any unwelcome surprises." He glanced at the closed door to the bridge. "Counselor, quietly inform both Commander Riker and Lieutenant Leyoro of your misgivings. Mr. La Forge, please keep a careful eye on Professor Faal from now on. We may be worrying unnecessarily, but it's always better to be prepared for any problem that might arise."

"You can count on me, sir," Geordi promised.

"I always do," Picard said, stepping out from behind his desk and gesturing toward the exit. The door slid open and he strode onto the bridge. He nodded a greeting to Commander Riker, who rose from the captain's seat, surrendering it to Picard. "Thank you, Number One," he said. "How goes the voyage?"

"Smooth sailing so far, Captain," Riker reported. He tipped his head at Deanna as she took her accustomed seat beside Picard. Behind them, Geordi disappeared into the nearest turbolift. *Back to Engineering,* Picard assumed.

He settled into his chair, resting his weight against the brown vinyl cushions. All around him, the bridge crew manned their stations; anticipating a straightforward cruise through safe territory, he had chosen to give some of the newer crew members opportunities for valuable bridge experience. On the main viewer at the front of the bridge, stars zipped by at warp five, the maximum speed recommended by Starfleet for non-emergency situations. The familiar hum of ordinary bridge operations soothed his ears. So far, it appeared, their voyage to the edge of the galaxy held few surprises. "No Borg, no Romulans, no space-time anomalies," he commented. "A nice, quiet trip for a change."

"Knock on wood," Riker said with a grin. He glanced around the gleaming metallic bridge. "If you can find any, that is."

"A bit on the dull side, if you ask me," Lieutenant Baeta Leyoro said. The new security officer had joined the ship at Auckland Station. She had previously served aboard the *Jefferson* and the *Olympic* and came highly recommended. Picard had reviewed her file thoroughly before approving her for the post aboard the

Enterprise; the imposing, dark-haired woman had fought in the brutal Tarsian War in her youth, enduring psychological and biochemical conditioning to increase her fighting skills, before leaving Angosia III and joining Starfleet. In theory, the victorious Angosians had, rather tardily, reconditioned its veterans to peacetime, but how effective that reconditioning was remained open to debate; could any treatment truly undo the hardening effects of years of bloody conflict? Picard found Leyoro's personality slightly abrasive, but that was often the case with the best security officers. Aggressiveness, along with a manageable dose of paranoia, seemed to come with the job. *Just look at Worf,* he thought, *or even the late Tasha Yar.*

"On the *Enterprise,*" he replied to Leyoro, "one learns to appreciate the occasional dull patch . . . as long as they're not *too* long."

"If you say so, sir," she said, sounding unconvinced. Her jet-black hair was braided into a long plait that hung halfway down her back. She patted the type-1 phaser affixed to her hip. "I wouldn't want to get too rusty."

"No danger of that, Lieutenant," Riker promised her.

Indeed, Picard thought. On this mission alone, the galactic barrier was nothing to take lightly. The real danger would not begin until they arrived at their destination. "Ensign Clarze," he addressed the pilot at the conn station, a young Deltan officer fresh out of the Academy. "How much longer to the edge of the galaxy?"

Clarze consulted his display panel. Like all Deltans', his skull was completely hairless except for a pair of light blond eyebrows. "Approximately seventy-five hours," he reported promptly.

"Very good," Picard remarked. They were making good time; with any luck, Geordi and Lem Faal should be about ready to commence the experiment by the time they arrived at the barrier. Picard contemplated the viewscreen before him, upon which the Federation's outmost stars raced past the prow of the *Enterprise.* The galactic barrier was still too far away to be visible, of course, but he could readily imagine it waiting for them, marking the outer boundaries of the Milky Way and standing guard over perhaps the most infinite horizon of all. He felt like Columbus or Magellan, prepared to venture beyond the very edge of explored space. *Here there be dragons,* he thought.

A sudden flash of white light, appearing without warning at the front of the bridge, interrupted his historical ruminations. *Oh no,* he thought, his heart sinking. *Not now!*

He knew exactly what that brilliant radiance foretold, even before it blinked out of existence, leaving behind a familiar personage in front of the main viewer. "Q!" Picard blurted. Beside him, Will Riker jumped to his feet while gasps of surprise and alarm arose from the bridge crew, many of whom had never personally encountered the infamous cosmic entity before.

Standing stiffly at attention before them all, Q was costumed even more colorfully than usual. For some reason that Picard could only hope would become evident, their unexpected visitor had assumed the traditional garb of a Royal Guard at Buckingham Palace, complete with a towering helmet of piled black fur and a crisp red uniform adorned with golden buttons and insignia. A white diagonal sash completed the outfit, along with a sturdy iron pike that he grasped with both hands. He held the pike crosswise before his chest, as though barring them from the stars that streaked by on the screen behind him. "Who goes there?" he intoned ominously.

Picard rose from his chair and confronted his bizarrely attired adversary. "What is it, Q? What are you up to this time?"

Q ignored his queries. He kept his expression fixed and immobile, devoid of his customary smirk, like one of the guards he emulated. "What is your name?" he demanded in the same stentorian tone. "What is your quest?"

Picard took a deep breath, determined not to let Q get under his skin the way he invariably did. Even though he had encountered Q on numerous occasions in the past, he had never devised a truly satisfactory strategy for dealing with the aggravating and unpredictable superbeing. The sad fact of the matter, he admitted silently, was that there was really no way to cope with Q except to wait for him to tire of his latest game and go away. No power the Federation possessed could make Q do anything he didn't want to. Picard liked to think that he had scored a moral victory or two against Q over the years, but here Q was again, ready to try Picard's patience and torment the *Enterprise* one more time. *It's been over two standard years since his last escapade,* he thought, remembering the disorienting trip through time that Q had subjected him to the last time he intruded into their lives. *I should have known our luck was due to run out.*

"What is your quest?" Q repeated. He spun the pike upward and rapped the bottom tip of the iron spear against the duranium flooring, producing an emphatic clang that hurt Picard's ears.

"You know full well who we are and why we're here," he declared. "State your business."

Q's frozen features relaxed into a look of weary annoyance. "Some people have no respect for the classics," he sighed in something closer to his usual voice. He clicked his tongue and the pike disappeared in another blinding burst of light. "Really, Jean-Luc, would it have killed you to play along?"

"No games, Q," Picard insisted. "What do you want?"

Q clutched his hands to his heart, feigning a look of aghast horror. "No games? Why, *mon capitaine,* you might as well ask a sun not to blaze or a tribble not to multiply." He glanced at ship's first officer, poised beside his captain. "Oh, do sit down, Riker, you're not impressing anyone with your manly posing. Except maybe the counselor, that is, and even she can see right through you." He snapped his fingers and Riker was suddenly back in his chair, without having moved a muscle himself. He glared at Q with a ferocity that was nearly Klingon in its intensity, while Troi looked like she would rather be anywhere else.

Why me? Picard thought. Q seemed to take peculiar delight in afflicting him. "You don't need to show off your powers to us," he said calmly, making what he knew would be a futile attempt to reason with the vainglorious demigod. "We are fully aware of your capabilities." *And then some,* he added mentally. "I am quite busy with other matters. For once, can't you get straight to the point?"

Q looked back and forth before replying, as if disinclined to be overheard. "Permit me to fill you in on a little secret, my impatient friend. When you can do *anything,* nothing is more boring than simply doing it. Getting there isn't half the fun, it's the whole enchilada." He winked at Picard and a drippy Mexican entrée appeared in the captain's hand. "Care for one?"

Picard handed the enchilada back to Q and wiped his greasy fingers on his trousers. He could feel his blood pressure rising at a rate that would surely distress Dr. Crusher. "No, thank you," he said coldly, his temper ascending toward its boiling point. No matter how many times it happened, he could never get used to being made a fool of in front of his crew.

"Your loss," Q said with a shrug, taking a bite from the snack. "Ah, hot and spicy. Reminds me of a supernova I ignited once." Another thought apparently occurred to him and his looming black hat went away. He casually scratched a tuft of unruly brown hair. "Enough of that. It was starting to itch like the devil."

The greatest challenge in dealing with Q, Picard reminded himself, was keeping in mind just how dangerous he could be. Q's antics could be so ludicrous on the surface that it was easy to forget the very real damage he could cause. Whenever Q appeared, Picard made a point of remembering that Q's idea of fun-and-games had already cost the lives of at least eighteen crew members. Q hadn't killed those men and women himself, of course, but he had been perfectly willing to throw the entire ship into the path of the Borg merely to make a point to Picard. *Never again,* Picard vowed. He'd be damned if he'd let Q sacrifice another human life on the altar of his omnipotent ego.

But how did you impose limits on a god?

Lieutenant Leyoro looked ready to try. She had drawn her phaser on Q the moment he appeared, but, to her credit, she had not attempted anything rash. No doubt she was familiar with Q's history from the ship's security logs. "Captain," she inquired, never taking her eyes off Q, "shall I take the intruder into custody?"

Picard shook his head. Why endanger Leyoro with such a pointless exercise? "Thank you, Lieutenant, but I'm afraid that Q is more like an unwanted guest, at least for the time being."

"Your hospitality simply overwhelms me, Jean-Luc," Q remarked sarcastically before turning his gaze on Lieutenant Leyoro. "I see there have been some improvements made." He sniffed the air. "Could it be I no longer detect the barbaric aroma of the ever-feral Mr. Woof?"

"Lieutenant Commander Worf," Picard corrected him, "has accepted a position on Deep Space Nine."

"And good riddance, I say," Q said. A scale model of Deep Space Nine appeared in front of him, floating at just below eye level. Q stuck the soggy remains of his enchilada onto one of the miniature docking pylons. Tabasco sauce dripped onto the habitat ring. "I visited that dreary place once. What a dump! I couldn't wait to leave." He waved his hand and both the station and the discarded meal vanished.

"That's not the way I heard it," Picard retorted. Naturally, he had carefully studied all of Q's reported appearances throughout the Federation. "According to Captain Sisko's log, he punched you in the jaw and you never came back." He contemplated his own knuckles speculatively. "Hmmm, perhaps I should have simply decked you years ago."

"I'd be happy to take a crack at it," Riker volunteered.

"Oh, please!" Q said, turning his eyes heavenward but taking a few steps backward. "Really, Picard, with all of creation within my reach, why would I ever return to that woebegone sinkhole of a station? They can't even get rid of the voles."

Despite a strong temptation to argue the point, Picard refrained from defending Deep Space Nine. He couldn't expect so flighty a creature as Q to understand all that Benjamin Sisko and his officers had accomplished there over the last several years. He felt a stab of envy, though; Sisko had only the Dominion and the Cardassians to deal with, not a nattering narcissist whose delusions of godhood didn't even have the decency to be delusions. *I wonder if Sisko would be willing to trade the Jem'Hadar for Q?* he thought. Picard would take that deal in a Scalosian second.

"Still, I must congratulate you, Jean-Luc," Q persisted, "in unloading that Klingon missing link. I'm sure he'll fit in perfectly, in a depressingly 'honorable' sort of way, with all the other malcontents and misfits on that station." In the blink of an eye, he teleported from the front of the bridge to the tactical station behind Riker's chair. *"Enchanté, mademoiselle,"* he cooed at Baeta Leyoro, taking her hand and raising it to his lips. "No doubt you have heard nothing but the most extravagant praise of me."

Leyoro yanked her hand back in a hurry. "Listen," she snarled, "I don't care how powerful you're supposed to be. Touch me again and I'll personally send a quantum torpedo up your—"

"Charmed," Q interrupted. He strolled away from the tactical station, taking the long way around the starboard side of the bridge. "Reminds me rather of the late Natasha Yar. Do try to take better care of this one, Jean-Luc."

Picard seethed inwardly. How dare Q make light of Tasha's tragic death? What did an immortal being even know about the pain and loss associated with mortality? "That's enough, Q," he began, barely reining in his anger.

But Q had already discovered another target. He cocked his head in Data's direction. "What? Can it be true? Did I actually detect a pang of genuine grief from your positronic soul when I mentioned the unfortunate Lieutenant Yar?" Q wandered over to Ops and eyed the android quizzically. Data met his frank curiosity with no visible signs of discomfort.

"Perhaps you are referring to the proper functioning of my emotion chip," he suggested helpfully.

"Indeed I am," Q affirmed, carefully inspecting Data's skull. He crouched down and peered into one of the android's synthetic ears. A beam like a penlight shot from Q's index finger. For a second, Picard feared that Q would simply take Data apart to inspect the chip more closely, but then Q straightened up and stepped away from Data's station. "So the Tin Man finally found a heart . . . of a sort."

"That's enough, Q," Picard said forcefully, "and this 'friendly' reunion has gone on long enough. If you refuse to enlighten us as to the purpose of this visitation, then I see no choice but to get on with our business regardless of your presence." He returned to his chair with every appearance of having dismissed Q from his consciousness, then decided to check on the status of Geordi and Lem Faal's efforts to prepare for the experiment. He tapped his combadge. "Picard to Engineer—"

Q would not be so easily dismissed. Picard's badge vanished from his chest, reappearing briefly between Q's thumb and index finger before he popped the stolen badge into his mouth and swallowed. "Delicious," he remarked. "Not quite as filling as freshly baked neutronium, but a tasty little morsel nonetheless."

"Q," Picard said ominously as Riker handed Picard his own badge. "You are trying my patience."

"But, Jean-Luc, I haven't even remarked yet on your spanking new *Enterprise.*" He sauntered around the bridge, running a white-gloved finger along the surface of the aft duty stations and checking it for dust. "Did you think I wouldn't notice that you've traded up?" He wandered over to the illuminated schematic of the *Enterprise*-E on display at the back of the bridge. "Very snazzy and streamlined, but somehow it lacks the cozy, lived-in quality the old place had. Whatever happened to that bucket of bolts anyway? Don't tell me you actually let Troi take the helm?"

Deanna gave Q a withering look, worthy of her formidable and imperious mother, but otherwise declined to rise to Q's bait. "Very well, Q," Picard said, "it's obvious you've been keeping tabs on us. Now if you don't mind, we have an urgent mission to complete." He started to tap his badge once more, wondering if Q would let him complete his call to Geordi.

Of course not.

"Oh, that's right!" Q said, slapping his forehead. "Your mission. However could I have forgotten? That's why I'm here, to tell you to call the whole thing off."

"What?" Picard hoped he hadn't heard Q correctly.

No such luck. "Your mission," Q repeated. "Your big experiment. It's a bad idea, Jean-Luc, and, out of the goodness of my heart, I've come to warn you." With a flash of light, Q transported himself to directly in front of the captain's chair. He leaned forward until his face was only centimeters away from Picard's. He spoke again, and this time his voice sounded deadly serious. "Read my lips, Captain: Don't even think about breaking the barrier."

Then he disappeared.

Interlude

I smell Q, he sniffed. *Q smell I.*

From behind the wall, across the ether, a familiar odor tantalized his senses. Singular emanations, nearly forgotten, impossible to mistake, aroused fragmented flashbacks of aeons past . . . and a personality unlike any other.

Q, Q, that's who, he sang. *Q is back, right on cue!*

Musty memories, broken apart and reassembled in a thousand kaleidoscopic combinations over the ages, exploded again within his mind, sparking a storm of stifled savagery and spite. *It was all Q's fault after all,* he recalled. *False, faithless, forsaking Q.*

He wanted to reach out and wrap his claws around the odor, wring it until it screamed, but he couldn't. Not yet. It was still too far away, but getting closer and closer, too. He flattened himself against the wall, straining impatiently for each new omen of the apostate's approach. A whiff on the cosmic winds. A ripple in space-time. A shadow upon the wall. They all pointed to precisely the same cataclysmic conclusion.

Q is coming. Coming is Q.

And he would be waiting. . . .

Four

How far could he trust Q? That was the question, wasn't it?

Picard brooded in his ready room, having turned over the bridge to Riker so that he could wrestle with the full implications of Q's warning in private. The music of *Carmen,* the original French Radio recordings, played softly in the background. He sat pensively at his desk as Escamillo sang his Toreador's Song, the infectious melody decidedly at odds with his own somber musings. Picard's weary eyes scanned the dog-eared, leatherbound volumes that filled his bookshelves, everything from Shakespeare to Dickens to the collected poetry of Phineas

Tarbolde of Canopus Prime; precious though they were to him, none of the books in his library seemed to offer any definitive solution to the problem of establishing the veracity of an erratic superbeing. At least, he reflected, Dante could be confident that Virgil was telling him the whole truth about the Divine Comedy; the possibility of deceit was not an issue.

So could he believe Q when Q told him that penetrating the barrier was a bad idea? The easy answer was no. Q was nothing if not a trickster. *Mon Dieu,* he had even posed as God Himself once. It was very possible that Q had forbidden the *Enterprise* to breach the barrier for the express reason of tricking them into doing so; such reverse psychology was certainly consistent with Q's convoluted ways. Nor could Picard overlook Q's blatant disregard for the immeasurable value of each human life. *Part of me will never forgive him for that first meeting with the Borg.*

On the other hand, Picard conceded a shade reluctantly, Q's motives were not always malign. When he had briefly lost his powers several years ago, Q had surprised Picard by proving himself capable of both gratitude and self-sacrifice. And every so often Q hinted that he had Picard's best interests at heart. *But,* he thought, *with a friend like Q who needs enemies?* Picard still didn't entirely know what to make of their last encounter; what had truly been the point of that fragmented and disorienting excursion through time? As was too often the case with Q, he had seemed to be both thwarting and assisting Picard simultaneously. The incident frustrated the captain to this day; the more he turned that journey over in his head, the less sense it seemed to make. *It's possible, I suppose, that Q meant well that time around.*

Even Q's most deadly prank, exposing them to the Borg for the first time, had carried a bitter lesson for the future; if not for Q, the Collective might have caught the Federation totally unawares. But who knew what Q's true purpose had been? He could have as easily done so in a fit of pique. Or on a whim.

Whatever his personal feelings toward Q might be, Picard knew he could not dismiss his advice out of hand. He could not deny, as much as he would like to, that Q was a highly advanced being in many respects, privy to scientific knowledge far beyond the Federation's. There might well be some merit to his warning regarding the barrier.

But was Starfleet willing to let the future of humanoid exploration be dictated by a being like Q? That, it seemed to him, was the real crux of the matter. Had not Q himself once declared that the wonders of the universe were not for the timid?

"So I did," Q confirmed, appearing without warning atop the surface of Picard's desk. "How stunningly astute of you to remember, although, typically, you've chosen the worst possible occasion to do so." He shook his head sadly. "Wouldn't you know it? The one time you choose to recall my words of wisdom, it's to justify ignoring my most recent advice."

"I thought such paradoxes were your stock-in-trade?" Picard said, unable to resist such an obvious riposte.

"Touché," Q responded, "or rather I should say, *Olé!"* In fact, he had traded in his guardsman's uniform for the more flamboyant costume of a traditional Spanish matador. A black felt *montera* rested upon his scalp, above his glittering "coat of lights." Golden rhinestones sparkled upon his collar, lapels, and trousers. A thin green tie was knotted at his throat, the chartreuse fabric matching the cummerbund around his waist. A scarlet cape was draped over one arm, although Picard was relieved to see that this would-be bullfighter had left his saber at home.

A strangely appropriate guise for Q, Picard observed, *doubtless inspired by my choice of music.* When he thought about it, Q had much in common with an old-fashioned toreador. Both delighted in teasing and provoking a so-called lesser species for their own sadistic self-glorification. Bullfighting had been banned on Earth since the latter part of the twenty-first century, but Picard doubted that Q cared. "What now?" he demanded. "Why are you here?"

"Votre toast je peux vous le rendre," Q sang in a surprisingly strong baritone, "and one of these days you might seriously think of offering me a drink, but, anyway, it occurred to me that you might be more likely to see reason in private, when you don't have to strut and preen before your subordinates. Fine, I appreciate your prim-itive human need to save face in front of your crew. Now that we're alone, though, be a good boy and turn this ship around. I have faith in you, Picard. Who knows why. I'm sure you can think of a suitably plausible excuse if you put your mind to it."

Picard failed to appreciate Q's backhanded flattery. He listened as patiently as he could, then spoke his mind. "First, before you accuse anyone else of strutting and preening, perhaps you should look in the mirror. Second, I have no intention of abandoning my mission unless you can provide me with a compelling reason to do so. Third, get off my desk!"

Q glanced down at his black rhinestone slippers, located only a few centimeters below Picard's chin. "Picky, picky," he clucked, transporting in a flash to the floor facing the sturdy desk. "There, are you happy now?"

"I am rarely happy when accosted by you," Picard answered, holding up his hand to fend off another volley of insults and repartee, "but I am willing to listen to reason. *Why,* Q? I'm giving you a chance. Tell me *why* we should stay within the barrier?"

"Well, why shouldn't you?" Q shot back, but his heart didn't seem to be in it. He chewed on his lower lip and fumbled awkwardly with the satin cape in his hands while he appeared to wrestle with some inner conflict. He opened his mouth, then hesitated, and for a second Picard had an inkling that Q was actually on the verge of saying something genuinely sincere and heartfelt, perhaps ready for the first time to deal with Picard as one equal to another. Pouring out his soul in the background, Don José, the tragic soldier of Bizet's opera, found himself torn between his duty, his heart, and his pride. Picard leaned forward, anxious to hear what Q had to say.

Then the moment passed, and Q retreated to his usual sarcastic demeanor. "Because I say so," he added petulantly. "Really, Jean-Luc, for once in your incon-sequential blink of a lifetime, listen to me. Don't let your bruised human ego blind you to my superior wisdom."

"I thought I was about to listen to you," Picard stated, more in sorrow than in anger, "and I don't think it was *my* ego that got in the way." He decided to tempt fate by pushing Q even harder. "If it's that important, Q, why not simply send us home with a wave of your hand? We both know you have the power to do so."

"Forgive me, *mon capitaine,*" Q groused, "but perhaps I would prefer not to spend my immortality standing guard over the barrier. I don't want Starfleet sneak-ing back here every time I'm not looking. I know how blindly stubborn and ego-maniacal you mortals are. You're not going to abandon your misbegotten quest unless you think you have some say in the matter."

"Then you must also understand," Picard answered, "humanity's restless urge to explore, to see beyond the next hill." He gestured toward the model starships displayed behind glass on one side of the room, each one a proud reminder of another starship called *Enterprise.* "You're right about one thing. You can turn us back if you want, even destroy this ship if you deem it necessary, but we mortals, as you term us, will not give up that easily. The starships will keep coming, unless you can convince me otherwise."

Q threw up his hands in mock despair. "You're impossible, Picard, thoroughly impossible!" Music soared in the background as the ecstatic citizens of Seville celebrated the coming bullfight. "Well! I'm not about to waste my time here while you're being so pigheaded and primeval, but heed my words, Picard, or you may not live to regret it." He swept his cape off his arm and snapped it with a dramatic flourish. *"Olé!"*

Q vanished, leaving Picard alone with his books and Bizet. *The problem with bullfights,* he reflected soberly, *is that the bull usually ends up dead.*

Five

Despite the hour, the officers' lounge was quite busy. Geordi La Forge spotted Sonya Gomez, Daniel Sutter, Reg Barclay, and several other members of his engineering team seated at various tables around the ship's spacious lounge, trading rumors about Q's most recent appearance, the upcoming assault on the galactic barrier, and other hot topics of discussion. The lights had been dimmed somewhat to give the room more of a murky nightclub ambience, appropriate to the approach of midnight.

Actually, it was a little too dark for his tastes, Geordi decided, so he cyberneti- cally adjusted the light receptors of his optical implants, heightening the visual contrast controls as well. *Ah, that's better,* he thought as Data's gleaming visage emerged from the shadows. Not for the first time, Geordi regretted that the *Enterprise*-D had been destroyed before he got his implants. He would've liked to compare the old Ten-Forward to this new place, yet the switch from his VISOR to the implants made that more or less impossible. The new lounge looked different, all right, but was that because the ship had changed or because his vision had? *Probably a little bit of both,* he guessed.

"It is quite puzzling," Data commented to Geordi. "Spot now refuses to eat her cat food from anything but round plates, even though she has eaten from both round and square plates ever since she was a kitten."

"Cats are just like that," Geordi stated. "Where do you think all those jokes about finicky felines came from? I remember once Alexi, my old Circassian cat, decided that he would only eat if I was eating. Sometimes I'd have to fix myself an extra meal just to get him to finish his dinner. Gained nearly seven kilograms that summer. My parents had to buy me a whole set of clothes for school."

"But it does not make sense, Geordi," Data persisted. Clearly his pet's latest ec- centricity was thoroughly baffling his positronic mind. "Why should square plates suddenly become unacceptable for no apparent reason? What if tomorrow she ran- domly decides that she will only eat from round, *blue* plates?"

Geordi chuckled. "Thank heaven for replicators then." He felt a yawn coming on and didn't bother to suppress it, knowing that the android would not be of- fended. He and Professor Faal had only finished their prep work less than an hour ago, and he really needed to go to bed soon, but Geordi had learned from experience that, after a day of strenuous mental effort and technical challenges, his mind always needed a little time to unwind before he even tried to fall asleep, which is why he had dropped into the lounge in the first place. Besides, he had been eager to pump Data for details on Q's surprise visit to the bridge.

He'd invited Lem Faal to join them, but the Betazoid scientist had politely declined, pleading exhaustion. *Nothing too suspicious there,* he thought, keeping in mind what Deanna thought she had sensed about Faal. No doubt the Iverson's had reduced the professor's stamina to some degree. He wished he had more to report to the captain, either to confirm or refute the counselor's suspicions, but, aside from that brief-but-ugly tantrum after Barclay had almost wrecked his equipment, Faal had been on his best behavior. *Too bad all big-name Federation scientists aren't so easy to get along with.* In his capacity as chief engineer aboard the flagship of the fleet, Geordi had worked alongside many of the most celebrated scientific minds in the entire quadrant, and some of them, he knew, could be real prima donnas. Like Paul Manheim, Bruce Maddox, or that jerk Kosinski. By comparison, Lem Faal struck him as normal enough, at least for a genius dying of an incurable disease.

"Another round of drinks, gentlemen?"

Geordi looked up to see a cheerful, round-faced Bolian carrying a tray of refreshments. His bright blue cheeks were the exact color of Romulan ale.

"Thanks," Geordi answered. "Nothing too strong, though. I've got a lot of work in the morning."

Neslo nodded knowingly. "Just as I anticipated. One hot synthehol cider for you," he said, placing a steaming translucent mug on the table, "and for Mr. Data, a fresh glass of silicon lubricant." Complete with a tiny paper umbrella, Geordi noted with amusement. *I wonder whose idea that was, Neslo's or Data's?* He could never tell what his android friend was going to come up with next, especially now that Data was experimenting with genuine emotions.

The blue-skinned bartender was handing the drink to Data when a flare of white light caught them all by surprise. The rest of the drinks tumbled from Neslo's tray, crashing upon the floor, but no one was watching his mishap, not even Neslo. Every eye in the lounge was drawn to the spot by the bar where the flash burst into existence. Blinking against the sudden glare, and wishing that he hadn't turned up his optical receptors after all, Geordi reacted at once, tapping his combadge and barking, "La Forge to Security. Q is in the officers' lounge!"

Or maybe not. When the light faded, he saw to his surprise that the figure he had expected, Q in all his perverse smugness, was not there. Instead he gazed upon what appeared to be a humanoid woman and a small child. "Fascinating," he heard Data remark.

The woman looked to be about thirtyish in age, slender and tall, with pale skin and a confident air. She was dressed for a safari, with a pith helmet, khaki jacket and trousers, and knee-high brown boots. A veil of mosquito netting hung from the brim of her helmet and she held on to the child's tiny hand while her free hand raised an ivory lorgnette before her eyes. She peered through the mounted lenses and looked about her, seemingly taking stock of her surroundings. She did not appear either impressed or intimidated.

"Well, at least it's a bit more spacious than that other vessel," she commented to the child, quite unconcerned about being overheard, "although what your father sees in these creatures I still can't comprehend."

The toddler, a little boy clad in a spotless white sailor's suit with navy-blue trimming, held an orangish ball against his chest as he searched the room with wide, curious eyes. Geordi, remembering his own little sister at roughly the same age, estimated that the boy was no more than two or three years old. "Daddy?" he inquired. "Daddy?"

Data, as the highest-ranking officer present, approached the strangers. "Greetings," he declared. Geordi rose from his chair to follow behind the android. Bits of glass crunched beneath his feet as he accidentally stepped into a puddle of spilled synthehol and lubricant gel. *Yuck,* he thought as the syrupy mess clung to the soles of his boots.

The crackle of the shattered glasses attracted the woman's attention. "Disgraceful," she said, staring through the lorgnette at the remains of Neslo's meticulously prepared drinks, "leaving sharp edges like that lying around where any child might find them." She lowered the lorgnette and there was another flash of light at Geordi's feet. When he looked down again, the entire mess, both the spilled liquids and the fragments of glass, had completely disappeared. The floor shone as if it had been freshly polished. *Uh-oh,* he thought, *I think I see where this is heading.*

"Children are not customarily permitted in the officers' lounge," Data explained evenly. "I am Lieutenant Commander Data of the Federation starship *Enterprise.* Whom do I have the privilege of addressing?"

Bet I can answer that one, Geordi thought. If the lady was not in fact Q in disguise, then she had to be a relation of some sort. That little trick with broken glass cinched it as far as he was concerned.

The woman looked skeptically at Data, as though noticing him for the first time. "A clockwork humanoid," she observed. "How quaint."

"Robot!" the child chirped happily. "Robot!"

"I am an android," Data volunteered. "And you are?"

"Q," she replied haughtily.

The double doors at the entrance to the lounge snapped open, faster than was usual, and Baeta Leyoro charged into the lounge, brandishing a type-3 phaser rifle. Two more security officers followed hot on her heels, each armed with an equally impressive firearm. "Where is he?" she demanded, searching the room with her eyes.

The security team's dramatic arrival startled the little boy. His ball slipped from his hand, landing with a surprisingly solid thunk and rolling across the floor. Tears poured from his eyes and he let out an ear-piercing wail that Geordi guessed could be heard all over the ship. Lieutenant Leyoro, confronted by a crying toddler rather than Q as she had expected, looked a bit surprised as well. The muzzle of her rifle dipped toward the floor.

"Now see what you've done," clucked the woman who called herself Q. She waved her lorgnette like a magic wand and all three phaser rifles disappeared. Turning her back on Leyoro and the others, she knelt to console the child. "There, there, baby. Those naughty lower life-forms can't hurt you. Mommy's here."

The boy's frightened cries diminished, much to the relief of Geordi's eardrums, replaced by a few quiet sniffles and sobs. The woman's lorgnette transformed instantly into a silk handkerchief and she wiped the child's runny nose. Leyoro stared in amazement at her suddenly empty hands, then eyed the woman with a new wariness. Only Data appeared unfazed by the most recent turn of events.

"Lieutenant Commander?" Leyoro asked the android, keeping her gaze on the woman.

"Permit me to introduce Q," Data replied, but Leyoro did not look satisfied with his answer. The skeptical expression on her face was that of a person who thought someone else was trying to pull a fast one—and was going to regret it if she had anything to do about it.

"I've met Q," she said. "This doesn't look like him."

"I believe," Data elaborated, "that we are encountering another representative of the Q Continuum."

"Well, of course," the woman stated. She lifted the snuffling child and rested his head against her shoulder. "Even a bunch of unevolved primates such as yourselves should be able to figure that out without the help of a mechanical man." She patted the child gently on his back while she glared at the crowd of men and women surrounding her. "I am Q," she insisted.

Another Q, Geordi thought in wonder, *and a baby Q as well!* He hoped that this woman was less irresponsible and more congenial than the Q they were accustomed to. *So far we don't seem to have gotten off to a very good start.*

Hoping to salvage this first-contact scenario, he scurried under a table to retrieve the child's ball. The orange globe was about the size of a croquet ball and heavier than he expected, like a ball of concrete. It also felt distinctly warm to the touch. Shifting to infrared mode, he was surprised to discover that the globe had a core of red-hot, molten ore. *Wait a second,* he thought, increasing the magnification on his optical sensors. A cracked, rocky surface came into view, with odd-looking craters and outcroppings: hills and valleys, mesas and canals, riverbeds, plateaus, and mountain ranges.

"Er, Data," he said, carrying the ball ever more gingerly toward the woman and her child. "I'm not sure, but I think this is a *planet.*"

Even Data appeared a trifle nonplussed by Geordi's announcement. He paused only a second before tapping his combadge. "Captain, I believe we need you in the officers' lounge immediately."

"I'm on my way," Picard answered.

Interlude

Swift as it was, the turbolift ride to the guest quarters felt interminable to Lem Faal. His body was too anxious to rest in the privacy of his own suite, while his mind resented the loss of any of his precious time. He had too much to do, and too little time to do it, to waste precious seconds simply getting from one place to another. The restrictions of mere physicality chafed at him, filling him with bitter anger at the sheer injustice of the universe. *By the Fourth House,* he thought, *I can't even depend on my own pathetic body anymore.*

In fact, his legs ached to shed the burden of supporting his weight. Every day he felt the effects of Iverson's more and more. It wasn't only in his lungs anymore; now the creeping weakness and shortness of his breath had undermined both his strength and his stamina, leaving him ever slower to recover after each new exertion. Working with Chief Engineer La Forge all day had left him exhausted and badly in need of rest. His breath wheezed in and out of his heaving chest, bringing him little in the way of sustaining oxygen. *The experiment has to succeed,* he mused as the turbolift came to a stop. *I can't endure this much longer.*

He staggered out of the lift into the corridor, grateful that none of the *Enterprise* crew were present to witness his debilitated state. The entrance to his quarters was only a short walk away; Faal felt as though he'd trudged across the scorched plains of Vulcan's Forge, through as thin an atmosphere, by the time he got to his door, which slid open at his approach, concealed sensors confirming his identity. Overhead lights came on automatically, illuminating the chambers beyond.

Captain Picard had generously provided Faal and his children with the best accommodations upon the *Enterprise.* The generously appointed suite was a contrast to the cramped Betazoid transports he had traveled on in his youth, in which open space had been at quite a premium. There were some advantages, he reflected, to living in the latter part of the twenty-fourth century. He could only hope that he would somehow live to see the dawn of the twenty-fifth, no matter how unlikely that seemed at this moment.

Despising his own mortal frailty, he sank onto the couch, a sigh of relief escaping his lips despite his determination to defy the ravages of his disease. His breathing remained labored, and his fingers toyed with the hypospray in his pocket. He considered giving himself another dose of medicine, but decided against it; the polyadrenaline helped his breathing, true, but it sometimes kept him awake as well. *I might as well sleep,* he thought. *There's nothing more I can do until the ship nears the barrier.*

He had faith in his technology, but the unexpected arrival of this "Q" character troubled him. Although he had not actually witnessed the mysterious entity's manifestation upon the bridge, La Forge had informed him of some of the ways Q had previously harassed the crew of the *Enterprise.* The engineering chief had taken care to emphasize that Q was more mischievous than dangerous, although Faal suspected La Forge of holding back many of the more alarming details, but his appearance now, on the very brink of the most important experiment of Faal's lifetime, could not bode well. What if Q seriously tried to obstruct the experiment? How could anyone stop him? Faal had heard about creatures like Q before; such supremely powerful energy beings had been known to Federation science since at least the Organian Peace Treaty of 2267. And there were other strange forces at work in the universe, he knew, forces glimpsed only in prophecies and dreams. . . .

Faal felt the hand of destiny upon him. In a way, Q's intervention only confirmed the ailing scientist's conviction that he was on the verge of a breakthrough of apocalyptic proportions. The inexorable tide of evolution carried him forward and he would let no one stop him, not even a godlike being like Q. He shook his fist at the unseen entity, his entire frame trembling with fervor. *Do your worst,* he defied Q. *Greater powers than you propel me and they will not be denied.*

Exhausted by this spontaneous outpouring of emotion, Faal sagged forward, his chin dipping against his chest. Milo and Kinya were away at the *Enterprise*'s child-care center, he recalled. He needed to collect them eventually, of course, but not right away; he didn't have the strength to cope with two demanding youngsters, not the way he was currently feeling. The children were in capable hands. He'd try to sleep a few hours first.

It was a mistake bringing the children on this mission in the first place. He had neither the strength nor the time to look after youngsters and conduct his experiment at the same time. He would have left them behind on Betazed, but the counselors had been too insistent, in their relentlessly compassionate way, to resist. *Perhaps I should have put up more of a fight,* he thought. There was no room for the children in what remained of his life. They would have to learn to get by without him, one way or another. He had to keep his mind and priorities focused on the larger picture; ultimately, mere biological offspring were no substitute for the sort of immortality he sought. Anyone who thought otherwise had not stared into oblivion as hard as he had been forced to.

Shozana would not agree, he suspected, a pang of guilt going almost unnoticed amid his other constant aches and pains, but, in a very real sense, it was his late wife who had brought him to this critical juncture. Her death in that transporter mishap was the defining moment that taught him the true impermanence of physical existence. . . .

There had been no warning at all. Shozana had stepped lightly onto the transporter pad, then turned to wave back at him, her russet hair gleaming in the warm afternoon sunlight that poured through the clear crystal skylights of the public transport station. *See you soon,* she thought to him as a young trans-operator, who looked like he ought to be in school, not behind a control panel, prepared to beam her to a xenobiology conference in the southern hemisphere.

Enjoy yourself, he thought back. *We'll be fine.* There had really been no reason why he had accompanied her to the station that day—it wasn't as if she were leaving on a starship or something—but he had done so anyway. It was a ritual of theirs, one that had always brought them luck before. *Love you,* they thought to each other simultaneously.

Her body evaporated in the golden shimmer of the transporter effect, and he started to leave—until he saw the ashen look on the face of the operator. "What is it? What's happening?" he called out, knowing at once something was wrong, but the panicky youth ignored his cries. His face pale and bloodless, the operator frantically worked the controls while babbling urgently to his counterpart at the other end of the transmission about a "pulsar surge" and "losing the pattern." Faal couldn't follow what the young fool was saying, but the truth hit home with heartbreaking clarity. Shozana was gone. . . .

In the end, there hadn't even been a body to bury. Her signal lost, her flesh and spirit reduced to an entropic stream of disordered particles, Shozana Faal had ceased to exist in the space of a moment. Right then and there, Lem Faal saw the shape of the future. Physical existence was not enough; it was too brief and insubstantial. His own body was disintegrating much more slowly than Shozana's had, but just as inevitably. Soon his pattern, too, would be lost.

An evolutionary breakthrough was required, a transcendent leap to a higher level of being. The old, onerous limitations of the past had to be overcome once and for all. Breaking the galactic barrier was only the first step. . . .

Fatigue overwhelmed his fervent ambitions. Unable to traverse the terrible gulf between the couch and his bedroom, he closed his eyes and collapsed into sleep beneath the bright overhead lights. He twitched restlessly upon the couch, visions of apotheosis filling his dreams.

Six

Aside from the two command officers, La Forge and Data, and Lieutenant Leyoro's security team, the lounge had been largely evacuated by the time Picard arrived. *A wise precaution,* he decided. If this new Q chose to start turning people into frogs right and left, the fewer warm bodies around the better. He took comfort in knowing that, should anything happen to him, Will Riker was safely in charge of the bridge.

Data had brought him up to speed while he took the turbolift from his ready room to the lounge, so he was not surprised to see the woman and the child waiting for him. The woman had a distinctly imperious air about her that reminded Picard far too much of her infuriating male counterpart; he flattered himself that he could have identified her as a Q even if he hadn't been warned in advance. He took note of her unusual costume as well. *No doubt,* he realized, *she thinks she's on an expedition among savages.* The child, whose scream he had indeed heard nine decks away, he spotted sitting cross-legged on a tabletop nearby, playing with his . . . planet?

Picard repressed a shudder at the thought of what this small boy might be capable of. Dealing with children of any sort was never one of his favorite things to do, but an omnipotent child? Wesley was difficult enough on occasion, and he had merely been a prodigy.

Leyoro met him at the door and escorted him to the woman, who scanned him from head to toe with an appraising look. "You must be the one he talks about all the time," she said, mostly to herself. "Luke John, isn't it?"

"I am Captain Jean-Luc Picard of the *Starship Enterprise,*" he informed her. He had no doubt whom the "he" she had mentioned referred to, and couldn't help wondering what Q might have told her about him. *Nothing very complimentary, I'm sure.* "May I ask what brings you here?"

She removed her pith helmet and laid it down on an empty chair. Auburn curls tumbled down to her shoulders, framing her face. If nothing else, she was a good deal more attractive than the usual Q. Her face looked vaguely familiar, but he couldn't place where he might have seen her before.

"I'm looking for my husband," she declared. "Besides, I've always meant to find out why Q finds this primitive vessel so interesting." She glanced around, then shrugged her shoulders. "I must admit, I don't see it yet, but now that we have a family I intend to share more of his interests, however bizarre and unappealing."

"Your husband," Picard repeated, momentarily flummoxed. The only thing more disturbing than the idea of Q married was the realization that he had actually reproduced. *Just what the universe needs,* he thought, *a chip off the old block.* He looked over at the empty bar, wishing Guinan were there. She knew a lot more about the Q Continuum than she usually let on. He generally preferred to respect her privacy regarding her sometimes mysterious past, but he could certainly have used her advice now. *I wonder if I should contact Earth and have her put on a shuttle right away?*

Probably a bit drastic, he decided. *God knows I've coped with the other Q on my own more times than I care to remember.*

"You are correct," he told the woman. "Q was here, a few hours ago, but he has departed."

"Nonsense," she said, looking past him. "He's here, all right. Q," she said firmly, placing her hands on her hips. "Show yourself."

"You called, dearest?" an unmistakable voice rang out, accompanied by a flash of light. Picard spun around to see Q materialize atop the bar counter, stretched out on his side like a model posing for a portrait. He had traded in his anachronistic matador's garb for an up-to-date Starfleet uniform. "Honey, I'm home!"

"This is *not* your home," Picard barked automatically. Q disappeared in a flash, then reappeared next to his alleged spouse. It briefly registered on Picard that this was the first time he had seen Q in the new plum-colored uniforms instituted shortly before the Borg Queen's assault on the Earth. As usual, the sight of Q in uniform seemed grossly inappropriate and offensive.

"Oh, don't be such a sourpuss, Jean-Luc," Q replied. "Allow me to introduce you to my better half, Q." He teleported over to the adjacent table and patted the child on the head. "And this, of course, is little q."

"Daddy!" the boy said gleefully. In his excitement, he forgot to hold on to his "ball," which rolled inexorably toward the edge of the table. With a muted cry of alarm, Geordi La Forge ran over and caught the sphere right as it went over the brink. He let out a sigh of relief and turned toward Picard.

"It doesn't look like an M-class planet," the engineer informed his captain, "but who can be sure?"

"I can," Q stated flatly, taking back the globe from Geordi, who hesitated for a heartbeat before surrendering it. Q grinned and gently shook his finger at the child. "How many times have I told you to be more careful with your toys? Let's put this back into its solar system where it belongs." The orange sphere vanished from sight. "That's a good boy."

This picture of Q as a doting and responsible parent was almost more than Picard could stomach. He didn't know whether to laugh or grimace, so he spoke to the mother instead. "I am happy to meet you," he said diplomatically. "I was unaware that Q had a family."

"Oh, it's a new development," Q explained cheerfully. He snapped his fingers and a rain of white rice descended on the lounge. "We're newlyweds. Isn't it delightful?" The deluge of grain ceased and Q rejoined his bride at her side. "Sorry we couldn't invite you to the ceremony, Jean-Luc, but it was something of a shotgun wedding." He winked at the female Q, as if sharing a private joke with her. A generous assortment of fragrant red roses appeared in the woman's arms. "I'd offer to rethrow the bouquet, but I see that neither the counselor nor Dr. Crusher is present." He raised his hand in front of Picard's face and rubbed his thumb and his index finger together. "Of course, I can always remedy that situation."

"Leave Counselor Troi and the doctor where they are," Picard said more quickly than his pride would have preferred. He didn't know for sure that either Beverly or Deanna was sleeping, but he knew that neither woman would appreciate being yanked from whatever she was doing merely to serve as the butt of one of Q's puerile jokes. He angrily brushed the fallen rice off his uniform while his fellow crew members did the same. Curiously, not a grain appeared to have stuck to either Q.

"Spoilsport," Q said with a scowl. He exchanged a look with his wife. "See what I mean about him?"

The woman gave Picard another frank appraisal. "I still don't understand," she admitted. "He doesn't seem very amusing."

He gave her an affectionate peck on the cheek. "That's because, darling, you've forgotten the ancient, primeval concept of the straight man."

Her eyes lit up. "Oh, now I see it." She blushed and peered at Q through her lashes as if mildly scandalized. "But, Q, that's so . . . carbon-based of you!"

"Isn't it just?" he said, preening. They both tittered slyly at his apparent outrageousness. The child, seeing his parents laughing, started giggling as well, although Picard rather suspected the boy didn't get the joke. He wasn't sure he wanted to either, although he derived a degree of satisfaction and relief from this confirmation that Q was considered something of a reprobate and rascal even among his own kind. The idea of an entire race of godlike beings just as mischievous and troublesome as Q was enough to fill him with utter dread. *I suppose it's too much to hope,* he thought, *that Q will settle down now that he's a husband and a father.*

As often happened with toddlers, the child's attack of the giggles escalated to a full-scale bout of hysterical silliness. He began bouncing up and down on the tabletop, shrieking at the top of his lungs—which sounded like it was in the upper decibel range. Everyone except Data and the elder Q covered their ears to keep out the deafening peals of laughter. The android hurried toward the table, evidently concerned that the boy might fall and hurt himself, but the pint-sized entity Q had christened q slipped from between Data's arms and hurled himself upward, ricocheting off the ceiling and bouncing around the lounge like a rubber ball flung with the force of a particle accelerator. The child struck the floor only centimeters from Picard's feet, then took off at an angle toward Leyoro and the security team. They yelped in unison and dropped to the floor only an instant before q zipped by overhead. Chairs and tables went flying in all directions as q collided with them, and Geordi and Data took cover behind the bar. A bottle shattered and the smell of Saurian brandy filled the lounge, soon joined by the clashing aromas of Gamzain wine and Trixian bubble juice. Q and Q beamed at each other as their hyperactive offspring wreaked havoc throughout the lounge. Picard saw their lips move and, even though he couldn't hear a thing over the child's wild laughter, felt sure they were saying something like, "Isn't he adorable?"

Picard knew he had lost control of the situation, nothing new where any Q was concerned. "Q!" he shouted, not caring which one heard him. "Stop this at once!"

Q conferred with his spouse, who shrugged and nodded her head. He surveyed the chaos, smiled proudly, then clapped his hands. The silence was immediate. Picard noticed the absence of the din a second before he realized that he was no longer in the lounge.

None of them were. Picard looked around in amazement and discovered that he, Data and Geordi, the security team, and all three Qs had been instantaneously transported to the bridge of the *Enterprise.* It was a close call who was the most surprised, the bridge crew or the new arrivals. Riker leaped from the captain's chair, his eyes wide and his mouth open. "Captain!" he exclaimed.

"At ease, Number One," Picard assured him. He cocked his head toward the Q family, knowing that was all the explanation that was required. The baby q now rested securely within his father's arms, while Picard found himself standing between the command area and Ops. Baeta Leyoro rushed over to the tactical console and stood guard over the weapons controls.

Riker got it, untensing his aggressive stance only a little. A newly replicated combadge adorned his chest. "I see," he said, glaring suspiciously at Q. "And the woman and child?"

"Q's wife and heir." Riker's jaw dropped again, and Picard shook his head to discourage any further inquiries. "Don't ask. I'll explain later, if I can." He turned and confronted the omnipotent trio. "Q?" he demanded.

Q, the usual Q, lowered his child to the floor and strolled toward Picard with a look of unapologetic assurance on his face. "I felt it was time for a change in venue," he said, loudly enough for all to hear. Q glanced furtively at his mate, who was inspecting the aft engineering station, and whispered in Picard's ear. "To be honest, that other place reeked too much of *her.*"

"Guinan?" Picard asked aloud. He found it hard to imagine that Q could truly be honest about anything.

"Don't say that name!" Q hissed, but it was too late. The woman glowered at Q the second Picard mentioned the former hostess of Ten-Forward, then huffily turned her back on him. She took her son by the hand and took him on a tour of the bridge.

"I'm going to pay for that," Q predicted mournfully, "and so will you—someday."

Picard refused to waste a single brain cell worrying about Q's domestic tranquillity. Perhaps Q had inadvertently done him a favor in returning them all to the bridge. The best thing he could do now was ignore Q's attempts to distract him and get on with the business of running the *Enterprise.* He took his place in the captain's chair and swiftly assessed the crew assignments. "Mr. Data, please relieve Ensign Stefano at Ops. Mr. La Forge, if you could arrange to send a repair crew to the lounge."

"You needn't bother, Captain," the female Q commented. "Any and all damage has been undone. Your tribal watering hole has been restored to its pristine, if woefully primitive, condition." As an afterthought, she lifted a hand and retrieved her pith helmet from the ether.

"Thank you," Picard said grudgingly. Despite her condescending attitude, which seemed to go along with being a Q, he entertained the hope that this new entity might prove less immature than her mate. *Heaven help us if she's worse,* he thought. "Never mind, Mr. La Forge." He glanced at the chronometer, which read 0105. "You're relieved from duty if you wish."

"If it's all the same to you," Geordi said, crossing the bridge to the engineering station, "I think I'd rather stay here and keep an eye on things."

Picard didn't blame him. How often did they have three omnipotent beings dropping by for a visit? He considered summoning Counselor Troi to the bridge, then rejected the notion; Deanna's empathic powers had never worked on Q and his ilk.

"Besides," Geordi added, "there's still plenty I can do here to get ready for the experiment." He manipulated the controls at his station. "Data, let's double-check to see if the parameters for the subspace matrix have been fully downloaded into the main computer."

"Yes, Lieu—" Data began to answer, but Q interrupted, literally freezing the android in midsentence. He laid his hand on the flight controls and shook his head sadly.

"Jean-Luc, I'm very disappointed with you. I can't help noticing that your little ship is still on course for what you ignorantly call the galactic barrier." He sighed loudly and instantly traded places with Ensign Clarze at the conn. The displaced crewman stood in front of the main viewer, blinking and befuddled. "How about a little detour? I hear the Gamma Quadrant is lovely this time of year." His fingers danced over the conn and the distant stars veered away on the screen. "We could take the scenic route."

Picard didn't know what indignity to protest first. Did Q really think he could cancel their mission just by silencing Data? Riker appeared more worried about the flight controls. He strode over to the conn and dropped a heavy hand on Q's shoulder. "Get out of that seat, Q!"

"Overdosing on testosterone again, Number One," he asked, not budging a centimeter, "or are you merely picking up the slack now that everyone's favorite atavism, the redoubtable Worf, is gone?"

"I'm warning you, Q," Riker said with emphasis. Picard admired his first officer's nerve. Q had them hopelessly outmatched in raw power, but maybe Riker could prevail through sheer force of personality. Stranger things had happened.

"Oh, very well," Q grumbled, rising from the chair. Riker nodded at Ensign Clarze, who gulped once, then resumed his place at the conn. "I hardly wanted to steer this pokey hulk for the rest of eternity." He gave Riker a disgusted look. "I can't believe I ever saw fit to offer you the powers of a Q."

That piqued the other Q's interest. "This is the one?" she asked, her mysterious grudge against Q and Guinan forgotten for the moment. She walked over and circled Riker, then placed her hand over her mouth and tried, not very successfully, to keep from laughing. The baby q mimicked his mother's merriment. "Well, that would have certainly shaken up the Continuum. Small wonder they stripped you of your powers after that."

"Don't remind me," he said sullenly. Caught up in their quarrel, neither Q seemed to notice as the *Enterprise* returned to its previous heading. Picard thanked providence for small favors, but his frown deepened as his gaze fell upon the frozen form of Data. The android officer remained immobile, his mouth open in silent reply to his captain's inquiry.

"Q!" he barked, unwilling to let his first officer take on all the risks of defying Q.

"Yes?" the two elder Qs replied simultaneously.

Picard felt a headache coming on. "You," he specified, pointing at his longtime nemesis. "Restore Mr. Data immediately."

That Q glanced impatiently at the inert android, as though Data were a minor annoyance already dismissed from his mind. "Priorities please, Jean-Luc. We still haven't settled this matter of the barrier."

"Might I remind you, Q," Picard observed, "that Mr. Data once saved your life, at considerable risk to his own existence."

For once, Q looked vaguely taken aback. He gazed back at the android with a chastened expression. "But surely," he blustered, "I have repaid that debt many times over with my invaluable services to this vessel."

"Reasonable people might dispute that point," Picard said dryly. He lifted his eyes to espy the female Q and her child. "Your family is here, Q. Is this really the example you wish to set for them?"

Q peeked back over his shoulder at the woman and the boy. His wife raised a curious eyebrow. The child sucked on his thumb, watching Q with awe and adoration.

"Fine!" he said indignantly. He pantomimed a pistol with his thumb and index finger and pointed it at Data's head. "Bang."

"—tenant," Data finished, coming back to life. He paused and assumed a contemplative expression. "How unusual. There appears to be a discrepancy between my internal chronometer and the ship's computer." He surveyed the bridge until his gaze fell upon the party of Qs. "May I assume that one of our visitors is responsible?"

"Precisely so," Picard confirmed, relieved that Data appeared to be back to normal. "Now then, Mr. Data, you were about to inform Mr. La Forge of the status of a particular computer program."

"Really, Jean-Luc!" Q complained, storming up to the command area. "If I didn't know better, I'd swear you were beginning to take me for granted." He shook a warning finger at Picard. "You really shouldn't do that, you know. You're not the only Starfleet captain I can bestow my attentions on, in this or any other quadrant."

What does he mean by that? Picard wondered, although he was far more concerned with the report from Data that Q seemed so determined to postpone. "I'm sure Captain Sisko would welcome a second round of fisticuffs," he told Q, then turned his attention back to Data. "Please proceed with your report."

Data eyed Q curiously, waiting for a second to see if the impertinent entity would interrupt him a third time, but Q seemed to have given up for the present. Q leaned sideways against a nonexistent pillar, looking rather like a gravity-defying mime, and pouted silently.

"It appears that the program is showing a degree of calibration drift," Data stated. "It is possible that an unknown fraction of the data may have been lost during the start-up routine."

Picard paid little attention to the specifics of the problem, which Data and Geordi were surely capable of resolving, but found it eminently reassuring to hear the business of the ship proceeding despite the presence of their unwanted visitors. Displaying a similar hope that order had been restored, Riker took his place at the starboard auxiliary command station.

"Well," Geordi replied to Data, "that explains the eight percent falloff in AFR ratios I keep seeing." His artificial eyes zeroed in on the engineering monitor as he scratched his head. "There must be a problem in the diagnostic subroutines. Maybe we need to completely recalibrate."

"Captain," Leyoro spoke up, her face grim, "I have to protest any discussion of a top-secret mission in front of these unauthorized civilians." She eyed the Q trio dubiously. "All details of a technological nature are strictly classified."

"As if we would have any interest in your pathetic little scientific secrets," Q said scornfully. "You might as well try to hide from us the secret of fire. Or maybe the wheel."

"Wheel!" the baby q chirped, and began rotating slowly above the floor until his mother set him upright again. Thankfully, he was not inspired to summon fire.

"Your point is well taken, Lieutenant," Picard said, sympathizing with Leyoro's concerns; on one level, it felt more than a little strange to be conducting this discussion in front of a party of intruders. "But I'm afraid that Q is correct in this instance. Realistically, it is doubtful that the Federation possesses any technological secrets that the Q Continuum could possibly covet." Besides, he admitted silently, there was little point in concealing their efforts; Q had proved time and time again that he was supremely capable of spying on them regardless of the time or place. "You may proceed with your work, gentlemen."

"Must they?" Q asked peevishly. "It's all academic anyway. There isn't going to be an experiment."

Geordi did his best to ignore Q. "Now I'm getting a drop-off in the triple-R output," he informed Data. "We might have a bigger problem than the diagnostic subroutines."

"Possibly," Data conceded, "but it could simply be a transtator failure. That would also be consistent with calibration errors of this nature."

"And so on and so on," Q broke in, his voice dripping with boredom. He righted himself until he was perpendicular to the floor once more. "Are you done yet? We have infinitely more important matters to get back to."

Q's offspring, Picard noted, no matter how young he might actually be, seemed to possess a greater reserve of patience than his egomaniacal father. "Mr. Data," he said, "I do not pretend to be intimately acquainted with the finer points of Professor Faal's computer programs. Do you anticipate any difficulties working out these problems prior to our arrival at the barrier?"

"No, sir," Data said. Fortunately, the android did not require sleep like the rest of them, although Data often chose to simulate a dormant state in order to further his exploration of humanity, so Picard had no doubt that Data would work through the night if necessary.

Q yawned, and not from fatigue. "Are we quite through with this dreary business?" he inquired. A nervous-looking Ensign Clarze, who was surely less than eager to be teleported away from his post again, kept his eyes determinedly focused on the screen ahead of him even as Q ambled back to the conn. "Then can I finally prevail upon you to abandon this monumentally misguided exercise? Leave the barrier alone. It is not for the likes of you to tamper with."

Maybe it was exhaustion, maybe it was simply that he had reached his limit, but Picard had suddenly had enough of Q's perpetual snideness and high-handed pronouncements. "Get this straight, Q: I take my orders from Starfleet and the United Federation of Planets, not from the Q Continuum and most especially not from you!"

Q recoiled from Picard's vehemence. "Somebody woke up on the wrong side of the Borg this morning," he sniffed. He raised his eyes unto heaven and struck a martyred pose. "Forgive him, Q, for he knows not what he says. I try to enlighten these poor mortals but their eyes are blind and their ears are deaf to my abundant wisdom." He shrugged his shoulders, dropped his arms to his sides, and turned to his mate. "Honeybunch, you talk to him. Tell him I know what I'm talking about."

The female Q was busy wiping her son's nose, but she looked up long enough to fix her brown eyes on Picard and say, "He knows what he's talking about, Captain." She returned to her son and muttered under her breath, "If only he didn't."

"Big wall!" the toddler interjected, adding his own two cents' worth. "Bad! Bad!" He stamped his tiny foot on the floor and the entire bridge lurched to starboard. Picard grabbed on to his armrests to keep from being thrown from the chair. Data padds and other loose instruments clattered to the floor. Riker stumbled forward, but managed to keep his footing. Baeta Leyoro swore under her breath and shot a murderous glare at Q and his family. Yellow alert lights flashed on automatically all around the bridge. An alarm sounded.

"Now, now," the female Q cooed to her son. "Be gentle with the little spaceship. You don't want to break it." She patted the child on the head and he looked down at his feet sheepishly. Picard felt the *Enterprise*'s flight path stabilize.

He silenced the alarm and ended the yellow alert by pressing a control on his armrest. Although the crisis seemed to have passed, he was unnerved by this demonstration of the baby's abilities. Suppose the child threw a real tantrum? Not even the entire fleet might be able to save them. "Q," he began, addressing the male of the species, "perhaps there is a more suitable location for your son? Children do not belong on the bridge," he said quite sincerely.

"Really?" Q asked. "You gave that insufferable Wesley the run of the place as I recall." He stood on his tiptoes and peered over everyone's heads, as if expecting to find young Wesley Crusher hidden behind a console. Then he lowered his soles to the floor and considered his son. Little q held on to his mother's leg while watching the viewscreen through droopy eyelids. "Still, you may have a point," Q told Picard. "He is looking a trifle bored."

"— — —?" he said to his wife in a language that bore no resemblance to any tongue Picard had ever heard before, one so inhuman that even the Universal Translator was stumped.

"— — —," she replied.

An instant later, the baby disappeared. Picard felt an incalculable sense of danger averted until a new suspicion entered his mind. "Q," he asked warily, "where exactly did the child go?"

Q acted surprised by the question. "Why, Jean-Luc, I understand the *Enterprise* has excellent child-care facilities."

He and the other Q vanished from sight.

Seven

Although entire families no longer lived permanently on the *Starship Enterprise,* Holodeck B could be converted into a children's center to accommodate the offspring of the various diplomats, delegations, and refugees who often traveled aboard the ship. During such times, the holographic center was kept open twenty-four hours a day, to handle the varying circadian rhythms of each alien race as well as to allow for emergency situations. Since alien encounters and other crises could hardly be expected to occur only during school hours, there had to be some place where any mothers and fathers aboard the ship could safely stow their children during, say, a surprise Romulan attack. The last thing anyone wanted was visiting scientists or ambassadors who were unable to assist in an emergency because they couldn't find a babysitter.

Ensign Percy Whitman, age twenty-five, didn't mind working the graveyard shift at the children's center. The Faal children were still living on Betazed time, according to which it was roughly the middle of the afternoon, but they seemed well behaved and remarkably quiet. *That's the nice thing about telepathic kids,* he thought. *They can talk among themselves without disturbing anyone else.* All of which gave him more time to compose his work-in-progress, a holonovel about a sensitive young artist who works nights at a kindergarten for nocturnal Heptarians until he is recruited by Starfleet Intelligence to infiltrate the Klingon High Command.

Tonight the writing was going unusually well. He was already up to Chapter Seven, where the hero, Whip Parsi, fights a duel to the death with the treacherous heir to a hopelessly corrupt Klingon household. "His mighty *bat'leth* sliced through the sultry night air, keening a song of vengeance, as Whip struck back with all the skill and fury of one born to battle," he keyed into the padd on his desk. *Yeah,* he thought, transfixed by his own output, *that's great stuff.* He'd work out the holographic animation later.

A squeal of high-pitched laughter yanked him away from his gripping saga. He looked up from the padd to check on his charges. Everything seemed in order: the two smaller children, roughly two years old in human terms, played happily on the carpeted floor, stacking sturdy durafoam blocks into lopsided piles that inevitably toppled over, while their eleven-year-old brother played a computer game in one of the cubicles at the back of the room. Childish watercolor paintings of stars and planets decorated the walls.

Another meter-high tower of multicolored blocks collapsed into rubble and the toddlers squealed once more. *Nothing to be alarmed about here,* Whitman thought. He started to go back to his masterpiece-in-the-making, then paused and scratched his head. Say, hadn't there been only *one* little tyke before?

He put aside his personal padd and checked the attendance display on the center's terminal. *Let's see* . . . Kinya and Milo Faal. That was one all right, a little Betazoid girl and her older brother. He stood up behind the desk and checked out the smaller children again.

The girl was easy to identify. Her blond curls and striking Betazoid eyes distinguished her from the other gleeful youngster. But where had that child, a brown-haired boy in a white sailor's costume, come from? Had someone dropped off another kid without him noticing? He wasn't aware of any other children visiting the ship, but he was only an ensign; no one told him anything.

Could this be some sort of test or surprise inspection? Maybe the new kid wasn't really here at all but was just a holographic image that had appeared from nowhere while he wasn't looking. He checked out the holographic control display embedded into his desk, but found nothing out of the ordinary.

"Milo?" he called out. Perhaps the eleven-year-old had noticed something. "Did you see anybody come by in the last half hour or so?"

"Uh-uh," Milo grunted rather sullenly, never looking away from his computer game. Whitman suspected that Milo thought he was much too old for the children's center and was taking it out on the babysitter.

"Are you sure?" Whitman asked. It just didn't make any sense. How could there be an extra kid?

"Uh-huh," Milo said, extremely uninterested in anything any grown-up had to say. On the terminal before him, several invading Tholian warships bit the dust in a computer-generated blaze of glory.

Whitman closed his eyes and massaged his temples, growing increasingly agitated by this uncrackable dilemma. The way he saw it, there was no way he could ask anyone for an explanation without looking like a careless and incompetent idiot. His stomach began to churn unhappily. *Maybe if I just keep my eyes shut,* he thought desperately, *and count to ten, everything will go back to normal and I'll have the right number of kids again.*

It was a ridiculous, pathetic fantasy, but it made as much sense as what had already happened so far. He squeezed his eyes shut and counted slowly under his breath. He swallowed hard, then opened his eyes.

Only one toddler sat on the carpet, staring up at the ceiling with unrestrained wonder. Whitman couldn't believe his luck, until he noticed the wobbly stack of blocks rising up in front of him. He craned his neck back and followed the tower of blocks to its top—where he saw the other child, the one in the sailor suit, teetering at the top of an impossibly tall block pile that reached above Whitman's head. The boy's unruly brown hair brushed the ceiling and he giggled happily, completely unfrightened by his precarious perch. The other child clapped her tiny hands together, cheering him on.

"Oh . . . my . . . God," Whitman gasped, unable to believe his eyes. Then he clapped his hands over his mouth, afraid to exhale for fear of bringing down the tower of brightly colored blocks. Across the room, Milo, intent on his one-man war against the Tholian marauders, was oblivious of the miracle.

The baby reached out his hand and two more blocks lifted off the floor and drifted upward into his waiting fingers. Whitman rubbed his eyes and struggled to figure out what was happening. Had something gone wrong with the artificial gravity? Could this be some bizarre holographic malfunction? Stranger things had been known to happen; he'd heard a few horror stories about near-fatal accidents within the old *Enterprise*'s holodecks, like that time a holographic Moriarty had almost taken over the ship. Or when Counselor Troi was nearly gunned down during a Western scenario.

Whitman picked up his padd and dropped it over the desk. The padd fell straight down, just like it was supposed to, so the gravity was working fine. But how then had the little boy managed to erect such a ridiculous structure?

He cautiously snuck out from behind the desk, arms outstretched to catch the teetering toddler if and when he plummeted to the floor. He had to fall soon, Whitman told himself. The ramshackle pile of blocks looked like an avalanche waiting to happen. It could collapse at any second. When it did, would he be able to grab the kid before he crashed to the ground? What would Whip Parsi do at a time like this? He hit the medical emergency alert button, summoning help in advance of the ghastly plunge that was sure to come.

The child continued to stack his blocks. Having run out of room between himself and the roof, the boy blithely turned himself upside down and crawled out onto the ceiling. He began lining up his new blocks in a row across the length of the ceiling while he hung there effortlessly like a fly upon a wall. "Choo-choo!" he burbled.

Whitman suddenly felt very silly holding his arms out. *A gravity screwup,* he thought. *It has to be.* Never mind that he still didn't know how this kid got here in the first place. He was about to contact Engineering when the door whished open and Counselor Troi rushed in. Her hair was disheveled and she looked like she'd come straight from bed, pausing only to throw on a fresh uniform.

"Gee, you're fast," Whitman said, remembering his medical alert from mere moments ago.

"The captain sent me," she explained.

"No security team?" Baeta Leyoro asked, sounding both incredulous and offended.

"That is correct, Lieutenant," Picard confirmed. "I believe that Counselor Troi is better suited to handle this situation." If the infant q had indeed been deposited in the holographic children's center, then Deanna's empathic skills and training were more likely to keep the child under control than a squadron of phaser-wielding security officers, assuming that any of them had even a prayer of stopping q from wreaking havoc aboard the ship. *This is all Q's fault,* he thought angrily. *He simply can't resist making my life difficult.*

Leyoro fumed visibly. The dark-haired security chief abandoned her station at tactical and marched into the command area to face Picard. "Permission to speak frankly, sir?" she requested. Her eyes blazed like a warp-core explosion.

"Go ahead, Lieutenant," he said. With Q and his mate absent for the time being, there might be no better time to hear what Leyoro had to say. Will Riker paid close attention to the irate officer as well, while the rest of the crew carried on with their work, no doubt listening attentively.

She stood stiffly in front of him, her hands clasped behind her back. "With all due respect, sir, I cannot do my job effectively if you keep countermanding my recommendations. If you have no faith in me as your head of security, then perhaps you should find someone else."

Just for a second, Picard wished that Worf had never accepted that post at Deep Space Nine. "Your service record is exemplary," he told her, "and I have a great deal of confidence in you. However, dealing with Q, any Q, is a unique situation that calls for unorthodox approaches, like sending a counselor in place of a security team."

"I believe I am accustomed to coping with unexpected circumstances," she maintained. "In the past, I have smuggled defectors across the Neutral Zone in an uncloaked ship, rescued political prisoners from a maximum-security Tarsian slave labor camp, and even repelled a Maquis raid with nothing more than a single shuttlecraft and a malfunctioning photon torpedo."

Having thoroughly examined Leyoro's file before granting her the post of security chief, Picard knew that she was not exaggerating in the slightest. If anything, she was understating her somewhat colorful (and faintly notorious) history. *Not to mention rebelling against her own government when the Angosian soldiers escaped from that lunar prison colony,* he thought.

Still.

"Despite your varied accomplishments," he insisted, "a Q is unlike any threat that you could have encountered before. Force and shows of force can accomplish nothing where a Q is concerned." He hoped Leyoro would understand what he was saying and not take the matter personally. "This is not about you or your capabilities, but about what a Q can do. Namely, anything."

Leyoro appeared mollified. She relaxed her stance and stopped radiating anger. The furnace in her eyes cooled to a smolder. "So," she asked, "how do you deal with an entity like Q?"

"Lieutenant," he answered, "I've been trying to figure that out for a good ten years now."

Beverly Crusher arrived at Holodeck B only minutes after Troi. Not that any of them really needed to have hurried. The baby q looked quite content to play with his blocks up on the ceiling. Watching him was a disorienting, vaguely vertiginous experience. Troi kept glancing down at the floor to make sure that she wasn't simply looking at a reflection in a mirrored ceiling.

She wasn't.

"Now what do we do?" she asked aloud. "Send a shuttle up there to fetch him?"

"I may have a better idea," Beverly answered, "but first let's get the rest of these kids out of here." At the doctor's suggestion, Percy Whitman began corralling the little Faal girl and herding her toward the door. Troi felt sorry for the poor ensign; she could sense his anxiety and confusion. She had attempted to explain to him quickly about Q and Q and q, but he remained as rattled as before.

"Percy," she whispered as he passed by. "Feel free to drop by my office later if you want to talk about this."

He nodded weakly and gave the tiny Betazoid girl a pat on the back to keep her moving. Enthralled by the astounding spectacle of her peer's visit to the ceiling, the other toddler was not very eager to leave. She started crying, but Percy ssshed her effectively and led her out the door. Sitting upside down above everyone's heads, merrily stringing his blocks across the ceiling, q did not notice his playmate being escorted away. Troi breathed a little easier when the youngest of Professor Faal's children disappeared into the corridor. She had summoned Faal himself to the holodeck, but the scientist could just as easily claim the children outside the chamber, safely away from the baby q's unpredictable activities.

That left only the eleven-year-old at the computer terminal. *Milo,* she recalled from Lem Faal's personal files. She began to inch her way along the edge of the chamber, hoping to sneak the older boy out without attracting q's attention. "Milo," she called in a hushed tone. "Milo?"

Caught up in his game, he had not yet observed any of the oddities taking place nearby, nor did he hear her call his name. Troi admired the intensity of his focus even as she wished that he would lift up his head from the screen for just one moment. She had no idea what the baby q might do to another child if provoked, but she didn't want to find out.

The door to the holodeck was sliding shut behind Ensign Whitman when Lem Faal stormed into the simulated child-care center. His thinning hair was disordered and a heavy Betazoid robe, made of thick, quilted beige fabric, was belted at his waist. "What's this all about?" he said irritably, sounding as if he had been unpleasantly roused from sleep. "What's going on with my children? First, I got an urgent call, then that strange young man out there"—he gestured toward the corridor—"said something about an upside-down baby?" Beverly tried to shush Faal, fearing he'd startle q, but the scientist spotted the child upon the ceiling first. "By the Sacred Chalice," he whispered, taken aback. His red-rimmed eyes widened. His mouth fell open and he gasped for breath.

The situation was getting more complicated by the moment, Troi realized. She had to get both Faal and the remaining child out of here. *"Milo?"* she thought urgently, hoping to reach the Betazoid child on a telepathic level.

"Ha!" the boy shouted in triumph, leaning back in his chair and pumping his fist in the air. "Eat hot plasma, Tholian scum!"

His cry of victory startled q, who evidently forgot about canceling gravity. Durafoam blocks rained upon the floor while the surprised baby dropped like a rock. "Oh no!" Beverly shouted.

Without thinking about it, Troi ran to the center of the room and threw out her arms. Will had always teased her about her total inability to play the ancient Terran game of baseball, but now she relied on every hour she had ever spent practicing in the holodeck to wipe the grin from his face. Her heart pounded. Her breath caught in her throat. Nothing else mattered. There was only the falling baby and the hard metal floor beneath the orange carpeting.

Ten kilograms of quite corporeal child landed in her arms and she breathed once more. She hugged the boy against her chest, taking care not to press her combadge by mistake. For the spawn of two transcendental, highly evolved beings, little q felt surprisingly substantial. Tears sprung from his eyes as Troi shifted her load to make him more comfortable. Memories of her own infant, Ian Andrew, and of holding him much like this, came back to her with unexpected force.

Beverly Crusher rushed to her side, a medical tricorder in her hand.

"Is he all right?" Troi asked her urgently. It felt very strange—and scary—not to be able to sense the baby's emotions. "Was he hurt by the fall?"

"I don't even know if it's possible for him to be hurt," Beverly answered. She began to scan the child with the peripheral unit of her tricorder, then remembered impatiently that conventional sensors were useless where a Q was concerned. She put the tricorder away and examined the boy with her hands. "No swelling or broken bones," she announced after a moment. "I think he's more scared than injured."

The baby's descent, and Troi's spectacular catch, had seized the attention of both Professor Faal and his son.

"Dad?" Milo said, spotting his father from across the room. "What's happening? Where did that baby come from?" Another thought occurred to him and he looked around the simulated child-care facility. "Hey, where's Kinya?"

But Faal was too intent upon the miraculous, gravity-defying infant to answer his son's queries, or even look away from the bawling child in Troi's arms. "I don't understand," he protested, his gaze shifting from q to the ceiling and back again. "Was that some sort of trick?"

"It's a baby Q," Troi volunteered, trying to put a little distance between Faal and Beverly so that the doctor would have more room to work in.

"Q," he whispered, awestruck. Troi didn't like the sound of his breathing, which was wet and labored. She felt glad that Beverly was close by, and not only for the baby's sake. "But it looks so . . . ordinary?"

Milo left his computer game behind and hurried to join his father. He looked completely baffled, but Troi sensed his happiness at his father's arrival. "Q?" he asked. "What's a Q?"

"An advanced life-form," Faal intoned, more to himself than to the boy. He remained intent on the baby Q. "A higher stage of evolution, transcending mere corporeal existence."

"That?" Milo said, incredulous. Troi detected a spark of jealousy within him, no doubt ignited by his father's absorption with the superhuman infant. "It's just a stupid baby."

Did little q understand him? For whatever reason, the baby started crying louder, approaching the earsplitting wail that had earlier resounded throughout the entire ship. "Hush," Troi murmured, rocking him gently, but the child kept crying.

"Hang on," Beverly said, "I bet I have a prescription for that." She reached into the pocket of her blue lab coat and pulled out a cherry-red lollipop. "Here, try this."

The child's cries fell silent the moment he saw the bright red sweet. His pudgy fingers wrapped around the stick and he began sucking enthusiastically on the candy. Troi didn't require any special gifts to sense q's improved spirits.

"The oldest trick in pediatric medicine," Beverly explained with a smile. "I never come to a children's center, holographic or otherwise, without one. Once I got here, I had planned to use it to lure him down off the ceiling." She approached Troi to inspect the baby. "You know, he actually looks a little like Q."

"Try not to hold that against him," Troi said. The sucker had calmed q for a time, but she wondered how long that could last. She didn't mind holding the child for a while, even though she realized that wasn't much of a long-term solution. *He looks so angelic now, it's easy to forget how dangerous he might be.*

Troi hoped the doctor had brought some extra lollipops for later. "You say his mother is much like Q?" Crusher asked.

"So I'm told," Troi answered. She had to admit that she was curious to meet Q's mate. *I guess there really is someone for everyone,* she thought. "At least her ego is supposed to be just as immense."

Professor Faal's interest in the child remained more scientific. He scrutinized the baby like it was a specimen on a petri dish, squinting at the child the closer he got to Troi and the baby Q. Troi was struck by the intensity of his fascination with the child. *Then again,* she recalled, *maybe I've simply become too accustomed to Q and his kind.* She imagined that any scientist would find a Q an irresistible puzzle. "Doctor," Faal said to Crusher, noticing the equipment she was carrying, "might I borrow your tricorder at once."

"It won't do you any good," she warned him, but handed him the instrument. He began scanning q with the tricorder, then scowled in frustration at the (non) readings it displayed. "Dammit, it's not working." At his side, Milo tried to see what his father was reacting to, standing on his tiptoes to peer past his father's arm. Frankly, Troi wished she could somehow persuade Faal to return with Milo to his own quarters, leaving them alone to deal with q, but she suspected it would take wild horses to drag the scientist away from such a unique specimen of advanced alien life.

Beverly considered the child thoughtfully. "It's funny," she said eventually. "I'm kind of surprised that his mother would be willing to leave him alone in the care of a primitive species like us."

"Unless maybe she thought we couldn't possibly do him any harm?" Deanna suggested. "Even if we tried, that is."

"If he's like any other toddler," Beverly said, "then he's perfectly capable of hurting himself by accident." She frowned, disturbed by her own chain of reasoning. Troi could sense her concern growing. "It just doesn't make sense. Why leave a precious child like this with people who completely lack the ability to look after him properly?"

An unexpected burst of light caught them all off guard. "If you must know," said the woman who suddenly appeared in their midst, "I had my eye on him the whole time."

This had to be the female Q, Troi realized. She looked much as the captain had described her, except that now she had assumed the attire of a twentieth-century American tourist on a summer vacation: sandals, pink plastic sunglasses, a large-brimmed hat, and a light cotton sundress with a Hawaiian print design. She held a paper fan in one hand and a flyswatter in the other, both rather gratuitous in the controlled environment of the *Enterprise. Where does she think she is,* Troi wondered, *the Amazon rain forest?* She recognized a bit of baby q in his mother's features, finding this evidence of a family resemblance vaguely reassuring in its similarity to a common, everyday aspect of humanoid parentage.

The woman noticed Troi inspecting her. "Well," she asked acidly, "is my ego as large as you anticipated?"

Troi blushed, recalling her remarks of a few moments ago. She hoped that the woman was equipped with a sense of humor to go with her extraordinary abilities; otherwise Troi might be in serious trouble. "My apologies. I had no idea you were listening."

"Oh, never mind," the Q stated wearily, as if the matter were far too trivial to waste her time upon. "I suppose divinity must resemble egotism to evolutionarily disadvantaged creatures such as yourself." She swept the children's center with a withering stare. To Troi's surprise, Professor Faal stepped backward apprehensively. The Betazoid scientist remained hard to read, but he almost seemed frightened of the female Q. *I guess a harmless baby is one thing,* Troi thought, *but a full-grown Q in her prime is a good deal more intimidating, even for one of the Federation's finest minds.* She reminded herself that Faal, not to mention Milo, were nowhere near as used to encountering the unknown as the crew of a starship. *Especially when she just appears out of nowhere.*

Having surveyed her surroundings, the female Q focused once more on Deanna. "Which one are you?" she asked. "The headshrinker or the witch doctor?"

Any lingering embarrassment Troi might have felt for inadvertently insulting this Q evaporated abruptly. "I am the ship's counselor, Lieutenant Commander Deanna Troi," she declared, "and this is Dr. Beverly Crusher."

"Whatever," Q replied, sounding faintly bored, but her patrician manner softened a bit when her gaze fell upon the child in Troi's arms. The fan and the flyswatter popped out of existence, and she patted his tiny nose with her finger. "Hello, little fellow, have you been having fun among the silly primitives?"

The boy, who was obviously accustomed to his mother appearing from out of nowhere, smiled and showed her his lollipop. "Mama!" he gurgled, and waved the half-eaten sucker in her face. "Yum-yum!"

Troi hoped that his mother approved of giving candy to babies. "That's very yummy, I'm sure," Q said to her child and lifted him from Troi's grasp. The Betazoid counselor willingly surrendered q, her tired arms grateful for the break. She had forgotten how heavy babies could get after a while. Q gave q a tender hug, then looked at the other two women with a marginally more charitable expression on her face. "I suppose I should thank you for tending to my baby as diligently as you were able, not that you can be expected to fully understand the unique needs of such a special and profoundly gifted child, who is, after all, the literal embodiment of the ultimate potential of the Q."

"I wouldn't be so sure of that," Beverly challenged her, understandably annoyed by the woman's attitude. Troi both sensed and shared Beverly's irritation, although Lem Faal, despite his anxiety, seemed to hang on her every word. He couldn't take his eyes off the female Q and her child. "My own son, Wesley, is quite gifted."

"Well, by humanoid standards, perhaps," Q said, distinctly less than impressed.

"Not necessarily," Beverly pointed out. "An entity much like yourself, who called himself the Traveler, judged Wesley worthy of his attention and tutelage."

"The Traveler?" Q asked, sounding intrigued despite herself. She clearly recognized the name. "The Traveler chose *your* son?"

"Exactly," Beverly informed her. Troi could feel her friend's pride in her son, as well as the pain of Wesley's long absence from the *Enterprise.* "I have every reason to believe that he may be on the threshold of entering a higher level of existence."

"For that matter," Troi added, unable to resist joining this game of maternal one-upmanship, "my own son, Ian Andrew, grew up to be a noncorporeal life-form exploring the cosmos."

In fact, the full story was more complicated than that; her son had been an alien entity who had impregnated her with himself in order to learn more about humanoid existence, but she saw no reason to explain all that to this particular Q, who could obviously use being taken down a peg or two. *For her own good, of course,* Troi thought.

The female Q could not believe her ears. Professor Faal looked equally surprised. "Your son," she echoed, "transcending the inherent limitations of matter-based biology? You must be joking."

"Not a bit," Troi stated. "If you doubt either me or Dr. Crusher, you can always consult the ship's logs."

Her son's head resting contentedly on her shoulder, Q subjected Troi and Crusher to more intensive scrutiny than before. "Hmmm," she murmured, mostly to herself, "I think I may be starting to see what Q finds so compelling about you funny little creatures. You may not be as primitive as you appear."

Mother and child both disappeared, leaving the two women, along with Faal and his son, alone in the holographic children's center at roughly three in the morning. Both the holodeck and the ship had survived the visitation intact, although Faal looked as though he had just undergone a religious experience. "I can't believe it. How amazing," he murmured, oblivious of Milo, who tugged on his father's arm but failed to distract the older man from his preoccupation. "Pure energy and power in humanoid form," Faal rhapsodized. "The manifestation—and reproduction—of noncorporeal existence. Animate, anthropomorphized thought!" His breath was ragged, but he didn't seem to notice. He stared inward, poring over his memories for the secrets of the Q's existence. "What did she mean," he asked, "that the child was the embodiment of the Q's potential? Do you think she was implying an even further development in their evolution? Why, the implications are astounding . . . !"

"I think it's getting very late," Troi said simply, uncertain how to respond. Despite all the wondrous events of the last hour, she found she could not ignore the wounded look on Milo's face as his father theorized about the scientific importance of the infant Q. When the other parents, human and otherwise, boasted of their children, she recalled, Faal had not even mentioned his own. Troi could feel the boy's pain. Why couldn't Faal? *Is he unable to sense it somehow,* she wondered, *or does he simply not care?*

Eight

Captain's log, supplemental:
As we approach the outer boundaries of the galaxy, neither Q nor any member of his family has been heard from for several hours. If nothing else, this welcome respite has given both myself and my officers a chance to get some much-needed rest. I anticipate the commencement of Professor Faal's ambitious experiment with renewed optimism and vigor, even as I remain convinced that we have not heard the last of Q.

The galactic barrier shimmered on the viewscreen. Red and purple energies coursed along its length, charging the barrier with enough power to threaten even a Sovereign-class starship. On this side of that incandescent ribbon of light, the

Milky Way Galaxy as they knew it, home to the Federation and the Dominion and the Borg and millions of worlds and races as yet unknown. On the other side, a vast and inconceivable emptiness holding countless more galaxies as large or larger than their own. *This is truly the final frontier,* Picard mused, contemplating the galactic barrier from his chair on the bridge, *one boundless enough to be explored forever.*

"An awesome sight," he commented to Lem Faal. The Betazoid physicist and Geordi La Forge had joined them on the bridge to witness the barrier as it came within visual range of their sensors. Faal stood behind Data's station at Ops, regarding the radiant barrier with open wonder. "I imagine you must be eager to be under way with your experiment," Picard said.

"More than you could ever comprehend," Faal answered. His pale face held a mixture of reverence and ill-disguised rapacity, like King Midas beholding his hoard of gold. "Did you know that the energy that composes the barrier is unlike anything we've ever encountered, aside from the Great Barrier at the galactic core? Why, at first it didn't even register on any of the primitive sensors of the previous century."

"So I gathered," Picard said. He had taken the time to review Starfleet's past encounters with the barrier, particularly the daring voyages of Captain James T. Kirk of that era's *Enterprise,* who had braved the barrier in his flimsy ship not once but *three* times. Kirk had mentioned in his log that the barrier had originally been invisible to every sensor except visual, emitting no conventional forms of radiation nor producing any measurable gravimetric effects. Picard smiled sadly at the thought of Jim Kirk; meeting Kirk himself in the Nexus remained one of the high points of his career. *Too bad he didn't live to see this day. This was exactly the kind of pioneering expedition he loved most.*

"How soon until we're within firing range?" Faal asked. A modified quantum torpedo, holding his crucial apparatus, waited within one of the forward torpedo launchers. Faced with the barrier in all its immensity and enigmatic splendor, Picard found it hard to visualize how any man-made object, no matter how specialized, could hope to make a dent in that heavenly wall. Then again, why would Q warn them to leave the barrier alone unless he actually thought Faal might succeed?

"Approximately three hours, forty-seven minutes, and twelve seconds," Data answered helpfully. He increased the magnification on the main viewer and the image of the barrier expanded to fill the screen.

"Wow," Geordi said, from his seat at the engineering station. "That is impressive." Picard wondered how the barrier appeared to Geordi's optical implants.

"You can say that again," added Riker, who was seated at the starboard auxiliary command station. The first officer was as wide-eyed as the rest of them. "I have to admit, Professor, I don't see any sign of those weak spots you mentioned before."

Faal chuckled at Riker's remark. "Everything's relative, Commander. The fractures are there, you can be certain of it, but even the weakest point in the barrier appears impregnable to the naked eye." He never looked away from the screen, enraptured by the magnified vision of the barrier in all its glory. "Three hours, you say. Captain, could we possibly go a little faster?"

"Only in an emergency," Picard stated. He sympathized with the scientist's impatience, but he failed to see a need to exceed Starfleet's recommended cruising speed of warp five, imposed when it was discovered that higher warp speeds caused ecological damage to the very structure of space. "I'm sorry, Professor, but we should be within range soon enough."

"I understand, Captain," Faal said, accepting the verdict. His fingers toyed with his ever-present hypospray. "I've waited years for this opportunity. I suppose I can wait a few hours more."

Picard was grateful that the scientist did not press the issue. Overall, Lem Faal had been fairly easy to work with so far; could Deanna have been mistaken when she detected some hidden dark side to the man's temperament? He glanced to the left and was reassured to see that the counselor was watching the barrier and not Faal; he assumed this meant that the professor was not radiating any particularly disturbing emotions at present. *Let us hope that she misread Faal initially,* the captain thought. Q and his family were enough of a headache for any voyage. He hardly needed further problems.

"Captain," Data reported, "our external sensors are detecting unusual tachyon emissions."

Picard leaned forward in his chair, responding to Data's unexpected announcement. "From the barrier?"

The golden-skinned android turned to face Picard. "Negative, Captain. I was monitoring radiation levels outside the ship when I noted an intriguing phenomenon. In theory, the ambient radiation should decrease steadily the farther we travel away from the galactic center. However, peripheral sensors on the ship's hull are recording a steadily rising number of subatomic tachyon collisions, and not exclusively from the direction of the barrier."

"I see," Picard answered. He exchanged a quizzical look with Riker. The captain had learned to rely on Data's scientific expertise when dealing with unexpected interstellar phenomena; if the android thought these microscopic collisions with faster-than-light particles were worth mentioning, then they deserved his full attention. "Do the tachyon emissions pose a threat to the ship or the crew?"

"No, sir," Data stated. "The tachyon particles are passing through our deflector shields, but the number of particles would need to increase by approximately 1000.45 orders of magnitude before they constituted a hazard to either organic or cybernetic systems. I was merely calling to your attention an unexpected statistical pattern."

Data didn't sound particularly concerned, Picard noted, but the on-again, off-again nature of the android's emotions often made it hard to gauge his reaction to any given development. When he wanted to be, Data could be as unflappable as a Vulcan high priest, no matter how dire the circumstances. Picard didn't think this was one of those times, though; Data was also capable of conveying a sense of urgency as well, and Picard was not getting that impression from the android officer.

"Is there anything that could account for all this heightened tachyon activity?" Riker asked Data.

"There are only two possible explanations," the android stated. His golden eyes carefully monitored the readouts at the Ops console. "An unusual natural phenomenon, such as a wormhole or quantum singularity, or an artificial tachyon bombardment engineered by parties unknown."

"Artificial?" Leyoro asked.

Data elaborated calmly. "I cannot rule out the possibility that the emissions are being deliberately directed at the *Enterprise.*"

"To what purpose?" Picard asked. He didn't like the sound of this. In theory, only Starfleet Command was aware of the *Enterprise*'s present location.

"That I cannot yet determine," Data responded. "Shall I devote more of the sensor array's resources toward identifying the source of the emissions?"

Picard nodded gravely. "Make it so, and continue to monitor the impact of the tachyons upon the ship." He turned to address Geordi. "Mr. La Forge, is this tachyon surge likely to interfere with your plans for the experiment?"

"We may need to recalibrate our instruments," Geordi answered. "Some of the equipment is pretty delicate." Professor Faal nodded in agreement, and Geordi considered the barrier upon the screen. "Before we release the torpedo containing the magneton generator, I want to launch a class-2 sensor probe into the barrier first, just to see what kind of readings we can get before the probe is destroyed. Then we can fine-tune the settings in the torpedo before we send it into the barrier."

"Professor Faal, is this acceptable to you?" Picard asked.

The scientist sighed impatiently, but nodded his head. "Yes, Captain," he said. "Naturally, I would prefer to go straight to creating the wormhole, but, under the circumstances, sending in a probe first would be a wise precaution. The more accurate our data on the barrier is, the better chance for success."

"Very well," Picard said. "Prepare to launch the probe as soon as we're within range of the barrier."

Confident that Geordi could cope with this new development, he considered Data's suggestion that the tachyons were being purposely directed at the ship. Could they constitute a signal of some sort? "Mr. Data, is there any pattern to the emissions that might suggest an attempt to communicate with us?"

"Negative, sir," the android replied. "I have, in fact, run a statistical record of the tachyon emissions through the Universal Translator without success. The only discernible pattern is one of steady growth, suggesting that the source of the emissions is either growing in intensity and/or drawing nearer to the ship."

"In other words," Riker said, "it could be growing stronger *and* getting closer." He scowled through his beard. "That could be trouble."

Lieutenant Leyoro seemed to feel likewise. "Perhaps we should modify the deflector shields to keep the tachyons out," she suggested. "Maybe by adding more power to the subspace field distortion amplifiers."

"That seems a bit premature," Picard decided after a moment's consideration. Increasing the power of the shields tended to reduce the effectiveness of their scanners. "This doesn't feel like an attack and if it is, it's a singularly ineffective one." He mulled over the possibilities, his arms crossed atop his chest. "Counselor," he asked Troi. "Do you sense anything unusual?"

"No, Captain," she answered. "Nothing from outside the ship. Of course, there are plenty of life-forms out there who don't register on my radar, so to speak. Like the Ferengi, for instance."

"This can't be the Ferengi," Riker quipped. "There hasn't been a price tag attached."

Picard smiled at Riker's joke. "Thank you, Counselor," he said to Deanna. "I appreciate your efforts." He leaned back into his chair and contemplated the viewscreen. *Could this have something to do with our mission?* he wondered. *Is someone trying to sabotage the experiment even before we come within range of the galactic barrier? But why such a subtle approach, employing carefully minute emissions, unless the supposed saboteurs are truly determined to avoid detection?* It seemed unlikely that the Cardassians or their Jem'Hadar allies could get this far into Federation space without someone raising the alarm, but either the Klingons or the Romulans could have slipped a cloaked ship past the borders. Granted, the Klingons were supposedly the Federation's allies once more, but Picard knew better than to trust Gowron too far, especially when there was revolutionary new technology at stake.

And then there were always the more unpredictable factors, like the Tholians or the Gorns. They had been keeping a fairly low profile for the last few decades, but who knew what might draw them out of their isolationist policies?

And, of course, there was Q. . . .

"Captain," Leyoro persisted, "with all due respect, we have to assume hostile intention until we can prove otherwise. Request permission to modulate the shield harmonics to repel the tachyons."

Picard weighed the matter carefully before reaching his decision. "No, Lieutenant, if we start to assume a hostile intent behind every unusual phenomenon we encounter, then our charter to explore the unknown will be severely compromised. For all we know, these harmless emissions may be the first overtures of an entirely new species of being, or evidence of a previously unknown natural phenomenon, and we would do ourselves and our mission a grave disservice if we prematurely cut ourselves off from that evidence out of fear and distrust."

Besides, he thought, sometimes a statistical blip was just that. The universe was all about probabilities, according to standard quantum theory, and if there was one thing he had learned during his long career in Starfleet, it was that the galaxy was big enough and old enough that even the most unlikely probabilities came to pass occasionally.

As if to prove the point, Q appeared upon the bridge. "Scans. Probes. Deflectors," he mimicked. "Don't you ever get fed up with those tired old tricks?" He posed between the captain and Troi, resting his left elbow on the back of the counselor's chair. His standard-issue Starfleet uniform made him *almost* inconspicuous upon the bridge. "I have an idea. Why don't you simply turn around and go home? That would sure catch those pesky tachyons by surprise."

"Go home?" Lem Faal asked anxiously. "Captain, you can't listen to this . . . being!" Picard assumed that Q required no introduction, but noted that Faal appeared more disturbed by Q's opposition to the experiment than by Q's startling entrance. The Betazoid was flushed and trembling at the prospect of watching his plans unravel. Picard heard his weakened lungs laboring strenuously. "You can't cancel the experiment now!"

"I don't intend to," Picard informed the scientist while looking Q firmly in the eye, "not unless our visitor can provide me with a compelling and indisputable reason to do so."

"A reason . . . from this creature?" Faal exclaimed, clearly aghast at the very notion of giving Q a say in the matter. "You can't be serious, Picard. Are you out of your mind?"

"I've often wondered the same thing," Q commented. "You really should consider an insanity defense, Jean-Luc, the next time humanity's on trial."

"This is ridiculous," Faal protested, scurrying toward Picard, but Troi rose and placed a gentle but restraining hand upon the scientist's arm, leaving the captain to deal with the insouciant intruder.

A thought came to Picard and he stared at Q through narrowed eyes. "Do either you or your family, Q, have anything to do with the surge in tachyon collisions we're experiencing?"

"Moi?" The interloper in the Starfleet uniform was the very picture of astonished innocence.

"Vous," Picard insisted, making himself perfectly clear. "Are you responsible for the excess tachyons?"

"Please," Q said, dismissing the notion with a wave of his hand, "I haven't played with tachyons since I was smaller than dear little q. They're far too slow-moving to occupy a mature Q's attention."

"I think you protest a bit too much," Picard said. He remained unconvinced by Q's denials. He knew from experience just how devious Q could be. Why, this very creature had once tried to convince him that Guinan was a deadly threat to the *Enterprise.* What was that name again that Vash had told him that Q had acquired in the Gamma Quadrant? Oh yes, "The God of Lies." *A more than suitable description,* he thought.

Q pursed his lips in mock amazement. "Ooh, a graceful allusion to the mawkish scribblings of a preindustrial mammal. Was that supposed to impress me?" He stared balefully at the captain with a trace of genuine menace in his tone. "Cross my heart, Picard, neither me nor mine have sicced these zippy little particles on you and your ship. You'll have to look elsewhere for the answer to that particular conundrum."

Q vacated the bridge as abruptly as he had arrived, leaving Picard with the unsettling realization that, for once, he actually believed Q was telling the truth.

About the tachyons, at least.

Interlude

"Please state the nature of the medical emergency."

Beverly Crusher was working in her office, checking the crew manifest against the annual vaccination schedule for Rigelian fever while half-listening to the musical score of the new Centauran production of *West Side Story,* when she heard the holographic doctor's voice. *Who the devil turned that thing on?* she wondered. Although she liked to think of herself as open to new ideas and equipment, she still had her doubts about this particular innovation. While the program's medical expertise seemed competent enough, its bedside manner left a lot to be desired.

She found the hologram standing in Ward One, beside a row of empty biobeds. She had given Nurse Ogawa the day off, barring further emergencies. Thankfully, there were currently no casualties recuperating in sickbay. "I'm sorry," he said, more snippishly than Beverly liked, "please rephrase your request."

At first, she couldn't see who he was speaking to. Then she stepped to one side and lowered her gaze. "Yum-yum?" asked the baby q, to the utter bafflement of the emergency medical program. Beverly couldn't help wondering how the child had managed to activate the program in the first place.

"I'm sorry," he replied, "but I am afraid I am not programmed to dispense . . . yum-yums."

"End program," Beverly said with a smirk, feeling more than a little reassured regarding her job security. The hologram vanished as quickly as a Q, and she knelt down to look the child in the face. He wore a miniature version of the Starfleet uniform his father often adopted. "Hello there," she said warmly. "Come for another treat, have we?"

"Yum-yum," he repeated, his current vocabulary less infinite than his potential. He held out a small, pudgy hand.

"Come on," she said, standing up and taking him by the hand. "I think I can take care of this." She led him around the corner to the ship's pediatric unit, which featured a row of smaller biobeds as well as a state-of-the-art intensive care incubator in the center of the facility, beneath an overhead sensor cluster. The room was as deserted as the adult ward. Although no children resided permanently on the *Enterprise*-E, as they had on the previous ship, the pediatric unit was kept ready for any injured youngsters brought aboard during rescue and evacuation efforts; only a few weeks ago, the facility had been filled with the pint-sized survivors of a deadly radiation storm on Arcadia VI. Thankfully, Beverly recalled, all those children had been safely delivered to relatives on Deep Space Seven. The small q did not appear particularly dangerous, but she was glad she didn't have to worry about any underage bystanders during this encounter.

She kept a supply of replicated lollipops in a container in one of the equipment cupboards. Fishing a bright blue sucker from her depleted stock, she offered it to q. "How's this?" she asked. "Do you like uttaberry?"

"Yum!" he said gleefully, popping the candy into his mouth. It occurred to Beverly that q could probably wish his own lollipops into existence, in whatever flavor and quantity he desired, but who knew how the mind of a baby superbeing worked? *Probably just as well that he associates me with sweets,* she thought, *and not castor oil.*

She looked q over; had he been truly as human as he appeared, she would have guessed that he was eighteen to twenty-four months old, but how did one estimate the age of a Q? For all she knew, this harmless-looking toddler could be as old as the pyramids. "So how old are you?" she asked aloud. "One century? Two?"

"Actually, he's only been alive for a couple of your standard years," a voice volunteered from behind her.

Beverly jumped forward and clutched her chest, then spun around to face the female Q, who had just appeared in the nursery.

Something to remember, she told herself. *When the child is present, the mother is never very far away.* The Q's outfit was identical to the doctor's, right down to an exact duplicate of Beverly's favorite blue lab coat. *When in Rome, I guess,* Beverly thought. She waited for a second to steady her breathing, then addressed the woman. "You have to give people a little more warning before popping in like that," she advised. "It's not good for our hearts."

"Really?" the woman said. "I seem to have improved your circulation."

In the best interests of diplomacy, Beverly refrained from comment. "Can I help you?" Beverly asked the female Q. She found it hard to think of her as just Q, although it was probably technically correct to do so; that "name" was all too vividly linked in her mind to another face. Why couldn't this female entity just make life easier for them all and pick another letter in the alphabet?

The Q did not answer her immediately, preferring to stroll around the nursery, running a languid hand over the contours of the small beds and occasionally peeking into the cupboards. The child trailed after her, sucking away at his uttaberry lollipop. "You appear to have a distinct talent for handling small children," she commented to Beverly. The incubator caught her attention and she contemplated it for several seconds, looking quite lost in thought. "Are there many children aboard this vessel?" she asked finally.

"Not at present," Beverly answered. She rather missed the children who had helped populate the old *Enterprise;* it had been a point of pride that she'd known all of them by name.

The female Q drew the little boy nearer and patted him lovingly on his tousled head. "My own son is quite unique: the first child born to the Continuum since we transcended physicality untold aeons ago."

Beverly thought that over for a moment. "What about Amanda Rogers?" she asked, recalling the young Starfleet officer who had discovered that she was actually a Q. "She was born on Earth only a few decades back."

The woman sniffed disdainfully. "That creature was conceived in a primitive, strictly humanoid fashion." She shuddered at the very thought.

Don't knock it if you haven't tried it, Beverly thought, but kept her remark to herself. Still, the Q gave her a peculiar look, as if well aware of Beverly's unspoken sentiments.

If she was, however, she chose to ignore them. "I've observed the individual you mentioned," the Q conceded. "It's a wonder she has any gifts at all, given her atrocious origins. I suppose, however, that the poor creature should not be blamed for the sordid activities of her notorious progenitors. She's more to be pitied, really. It was quite magnanimous of Q to take her under his wing the way he did."

He threatened to kill her, Beverly recalled, wondering if the Q could read that in her mind as well. *Maybe it would be best to change the subject.* "Your son is quite charming," Beverly said. "You must be very proud of him." That certainly seemed like safe ground, she judged. Q or not, few mothers could object to praise of their child.

"He is the future of the Continuum," the female Q stated matter-of-factly. "The first of an entirely new generation of immortals. A true mingling of two divine essences, a future messiah, quite unlike that ignorant urchin you called Amanda Rogers."

Better not let Professor Faal hear you talking like that, Beverly thought. The Betazoid scientist had seemed all too fascinated by the Q child to begin with. She could readily imagine his interest in a genuine "future messiah." He'd probably want to ship the baby straight to his lab on Betazed. *Somehow I don't think his mother would approve of that kind of attention.*

The female Q gazed down at the child, who was content to suck quietly on his treat by his mother's side. Her eyes narrowed and she chewed upon her lower lip as if troubled. "I confess I find the responsibility of motherhood rather . . . daunting."

A-ha, Beverly thought. *Now I get it. Faced with the ancient concept of parenting, which no Q has reckoned with for millions of years, why not come to us humble primitives for our crude but simple wisdom?* She wondered whose idea it really was to drop in on sickbay, the child's or the mother's?

"Don't we all," she confided sympathetically. She couldn't blame the Q for her worries. Every new mother had doubts about her ability to cope with raising a child; how much harder it must be when you're the first of your kind to face that prospect since the dawn of time. Beverly had trouble imagining the devious Q as an innocent Adam—he struck her as more the serpent type—but her heart went out to this nervous new Eve.

She circled around the incubator and took the Q by the hand. The woman flinched at the intimacy, but did not draw away. "You seem to be doing fine," Beverly said. "I know it's scary, but millions of mothers have faced the same challenges and survived. The trick is learning when to say no and when to let them learn from their own mistakes."

"Exactly!" the Q responded, acting amazed and grateful that another living creature understood what she was going through. "Little q has all the power of a Q, but he doesn't know how to use it responsibly." *Like father, like son,* Beverly thought. "I know he needs to explore his potential, but I'm afraid to let him out of my sight for a fraction of a nanosecond."

"You'll get by somehow," she promised. "Just remember to enjoy this time while you have it. I'll tell you the honest truth: the hardest part of having children is letting them go when they're grown. Of course, for all I know, you might not have to worry about that for millions of years."

"Only millions?" the Q said, apparently sincerely. She tugged q nearer to her, sounding both sad and surprisingly human.

"You'll be amazed how fast the time will fly," Beverly cautioned. Part of her still thought of Wesley as the fragile, acutely vulnerable infant she and Jack had brought home so many years ago. "Don't let this time slip by you without taking a moment every now and then to savor the experience. You might tell his father the same thing," she added, feeling generous toward Q for possibly the first time in her life. *Imagine having Q for a dad,* she thought. *The poor kid.*

She hoped he'd take after his mother instead.

"Thank you for your time," the woman said. Beverly tried to remember whether the other Q had ever thanked anyone for anything. The Q squeezed her hand once, then released it. "You know, my darling q's godmother is one of your kind."

A Q with a human godmother? Beverly was intrigued. "And who would that be?"

"Let me see," the woman began, her gaze turning inward as she combed her memory for this apparently insignificant piece of trivia, "I think her name was—"

Nine

Two hours, forty minutes, and only Data knew how many seconds after the *Enterprise* came within sight of the galaxy's edge, Professor Faal and Geordi prepared to launch the sensor probe into the barrier. Although Data had reduced the magnification on the main viewer by several orders of magnitude, the energy barrier filled the screen, bathing everyone on the bridge in its ineffable radiance. *There's something almost mystical about it,* thought Picard, who usually resisted superstitious impulses. He felt much as Moses must have felt when he first beheld the burning bush, or when Kahless drew the original *bat'leth* from the lake of fire.

"Are we far enough away for safety's sake?" he asked. The barrier looked as if it could sweep over them in a matter of minutes, like the largest tsunami in the galaxy.

"I believe so, Captain," Data reported. "As predicted, the barrier yields no harmful radiation or gravitational disturbances. The surrounding space is not affected by the barrier at this distance."

"No evidence of hostile action," Leyoro conceded, looking only a trifle disappointed. "Deflectors at minimum strength."

"No unusual stresses on the hull," Geordi concluded. He looked up in amazement from the engineering monitors to confirm that there actually was a glowing barrier looming before them. "It's like the crazy thing isn't really there."

"Oh, it's most definitely there," Faal whispered avidly, "and more real than any of us has ever been." Turning away from Geordi's monitors, he looked over at Picard, his eyes aglow with anticipation. Picard noticed that he was breathing heavily. "Don't worry, Captain, my artificial wormhole will carve us a safe passage through the barrier, have no fear."

His voice had a fervid tinge that worried Picard. The captain regarded Deanna Troi, who was watching Faal carefully with an apprehensive eye. Faal's outburst during Q's recent visit had given new life to her earlier concerns about the dying scientist's emotional state. Picard frowned, uneasy even though everything seemed to be under control. "How are we doing, Mr. La Forge?" he asked.

"As well as can be expected," Geordi said, his fingers tapping upon the remote controls. Faal, standing behind Geordi, inspected his every move. "The probe should give us the most up-to-date information possible on wave amplitudes within the barrier so we can adjust the shields on the torpedo appropriately. If everything checks out, we should be able to launch the torpedo itself within a few hours." He paused to wipe the sweat from his forehead. "Those tachyon emissions aren't making anything easier, but I think we can work around them."

"There is no question," Faal emphasized, his voice hoarse and strained. Picard was not surprised to see Faal resort to his hypospray once more. Was it only his imagination or was Faal requiring his medication ever more often? "We will make it work," Faal wheezed, "no matter what."

Geordi wandered over to the primary aft science stations, consulting the displays there. "La Forge to Engineering," he said, tapping his combadge. "Begin rerouting the pre-ignition plasma from the impulse deck to the auxiliary intake. We're going to need that extra power to generate the subspace matrix later on." He placed his hands on the control panel. "Permission to launch the probe, Captain?"

Picard held up his hand to delay Geordi. "Just a minute, Mr. La Forge," he said. A nagging concern preyed on his mind. "Mr. Data, has the tachyon barrage continued to accelerate?"

"Slowly but surely," the android affirmed.

"Have you formed any theory concerning the source of the emissions?" Picard asked. The inexplicable nature of the tachyon surge troubled him to a degree. Launching a simple probe was hardly a risky matter, but he disliked doing so while any scientific irregularities remained unaccounted for.

"Some intriguing possibilities have presented themselves," Data stated, "but I am reluctant to venture a hypothesis on such minimal evidence."

"Do so anyway, Mr. Data," Picard instructed, hoping that the resourceful android could cast some light on the mystery. A tenuous explanation was better than none at all. "Which of your working theories presents a cause for concern?"

"An interesting question, sir." Data cocked his head as he considered the issue. "You may find one hypothesis particularly intriguing, although I must emphasize that the evidence supports approximately 75.823 other interpretations."

"Your caveats are duly noted," Picard said. "Go on, Mr. Data."

"Very well, Captain." He manipulated the controls beneath his fingers at superhuman speed, summoning up the relevant information. "Although profoundly weaker in intensity, these persistent emissions are gradually coming to resemble the tachyon probe used by the Calamarain to scan the *Enterprise* on stardate 43539.1."

"The Calamarain?" Riker said, echoing Picard's own reaction as he recalled a cloud of energetic plasma, as large as the *Enterprise*-D or bigger, that had seemed to house a community of gaseous beings possessed of remarkable power. The *Enterprise* had barely survived its first meeting with the Calamarain; if these mounting tachyon emissions had anything to do with those enigmatic beings, then the situation might be more serious than they had first thought.

"Excuse me, Captain," Lem Faal asked, understandably concerned about the effect of Data's theory on his experiment, "but who or what are the Calamarain?"

"An unusual life-form," Picard told him, "that we encountered many years ago. They exist as swirls of ionized gas within a huge cloud of plasma traveling through open space. The Calamarain took hostile action against the *Enterprise,* but their real target was Q himself, who, at that point in time, had lost his powers and taken refuge aboard the ship. Apparently, Q made an enemy of the Calamarain sometime in the past, and they intended to take advantage of his temporary weakness to get their revenge once and for all."

"Can hardly blame them for that," Riker commented. Like most anyone who spent any length of time with Q, the first officer had no great love for the vexatious entity. Picard wondered if the female Q ever felt the same way.

"Agreed, Number One," he said. "Ultimately, Q regained his powers and re-pelled the Calamarain, and that's the last we had heard of them until now." Picard leaned forward in his chair as he considered all the possibilities. "Data, how likely is it that this is the work of the Calamarain?"

Data analyzed the readings on his console. "That is difficult to say, Captain. Their initial scans in our previous encounter consisted of very broad-based emis-sions, registering seventy-five rems on the Berthold scale." Picard nodded, remem-bering vividly the intensity of the alien scan they had experienced years ago: a brilliant deluge of light that had seemed to blot out everything in sight. The Calamarain's first few scans had actually blinded everyone on board momentarily. "These new emissions are far less intense, by several orders of magnitude, but it is a difference of degree, not kind. They may simply be observing us in a more sub-tle and surreptitious manner." Data swiveled in his chair to address Picard directly. "On the other hand, the tachyon surge could also be caused by any number of un-usual natural conditions. It may be that the barrier itself has effects on the sur-rounding space that we are unable to detect at present."

"Last time the Calamarain attacked us because Q was aboard," Riker pointed out. "If the Calamarain are spying on us, and I realize that's a fairly big 'if,' I think we can safely assume that Q is involved somehow."

"That is a plausible assumption," Data agreed.

"What I don't understand," Geordi said, "is why would the Calamarain be in-terested in us now? This is hardly the first time we've hosted Q since that time he lost his powers."

Would that it were so, Picard thought privately. He could've done without that vision of his future self suffering from the effects of Irumodic syndrome.

"They've never come after us the last several times Q showed up," Geordi con-tinued, "and it sure doesn't look like he's been turned into a mortal again."

"Far from it," Baeta Leyoro added with obvious regret. Picard suspected that she would love to get her hands on a powerless and vulnerable Q. *She could prob-ably sell tickets,* he thought.

"We should not jump to assumptions," he stated firmly. "The Calamarain have not been observed in Federation space for over a decade, and our previous encounter with them was several hundred light-years from this vicinity." Picard rose from his chair and looked over Data's shoulder at the readings on the Ops console; a rising line charted the growth of the tachyon effect as it approached a level established by the Calamarain so many years ago. "Still, we should be prepared for any possibility." He turned toward the science station. "Mr. La Forge, when the Calamarain attacked us before, you managed to adjust the harmonics of our deflector shields to provide us with a measure of protection against their tachyon blasts. Please program the ship's computer to do so again should the need arise."

"Yes, sir," Geordi said. "I'll get on that right away."

Picard exchanged a look with Lieutenant Leyoro at tactical. Her eyes gleamed and the corners of her lips tipped upward in a look of much-delayed gratification, but she resisted, with admirable restraint, whatever temptation she might have felt to say, "I told you so."

"Captain Picard," Faal said, "this is all very interesting, but perhaps we should proceed with launching the probe?" He fingered his hypospray anxiously. "I cannot stress how eager I am to attempt the experiment."

"Mr. La Forge?" Picard asked. "Do you require any more time to reprogram the deflectors?"

"No, sir," Geordi reported with admirable efficiency. "The adjusted settings are on call." *Excellent,* Picard thought, glad that they were ready for even the most unlikely of scenarios. Now it was simply a matter of continuing with their mission before Q—or the Calamarain, if they were truly close at hand—could intervene. "You may launch the probe as planned, Mr. La Forge," he stated.

Geordi reached for the launch controls, only to be caught off guard by a blinding flash directly in front of him. For a second, Picard feared that the science station had exploded; then he realized what the flash really entailed. *Blast,* he thought. *Not again!*

Q was back, sitting upon the launch controls, clad in the unearned honors of a Starfleet uniform. Geordi stepped backward involuntarily, and Q peered at him with interest. He took a closer look at Geordi. "Are those new eyes, Mr. Engineer? I can't say they're very flattering, although I suppose it beats wearing a chrome fender in front of your face."

He looked past Geordi and cast a dour eye on the shimmering barrier upon the main viewer. "You disappoint me so, Jean-Luc. I never thought suicide missions were exactly your style." He hopped nimbly off the science console and strolled toward Picard. "Leave the galaxy? Why, you foolhardy humans couldn't put one foot into the Gamma Quadrant without starting a war with the Dominion. What makes you think the rest of the universe is going to be any better?"

"That's enough," Riker said. "The captain has better things to do with his time than listen to you."

Q paid the first officer no heed. "Tell me, Jean-Luc, I know you have a childish fondness for hard-boiled detective yarns." He held out a palm on which a single white egg now balanced upon its end. A caricature of Picard's scowling face was painted on the shell of the presumably hard-boiled egg. "Bit of a resemblance, isn't there?" Q commented. He blew on his hand and the egg wafted away like a mirage. "But haven't you ever paid attention to some of your species' old monster movies?" His voice dropped several octaves, taking on a sepulchral tone. "There are some things that insignificant, short-lived mortals are meant to leave alone." He gave Picard what seemed, for Q, a remarkably sober look, and when he spoke again his voice sounded notably free of irony or sarcasm. "The barrier is one of them, Picard. Trust me on this."

Trust? Q? Of the many surprising and exceptional developments in this highly eventful mission, this suggestion struck Picard as the most unlikely of all. He wasn't sure Q could be direct and honest if his own immortal existence depended on it. "That's not enough," Picard told him. "You need to tell me more than that."

"It's none of your business!" he said petulantly, apparently unable to maintain a sincere appearance for more than a moment or two. "You try to offer a few helpful tips to an inferior organism, but do they appreciate it? Of course not!" He paced back and forth in front of the viewscreen, looking exasperated beyond all measure. "Why can't you simply admit that we Q are older and wiser than you are?"

"Older, certainly," Picard said, "but not necessarily wiser. If you are at all typical of your kind, then the fabled Q Continuum is not above mere pettiness and spite." He rose from his chair and confronted Q. *Let's have this out here and now,* he determined. "As you might imagine, I've given the matter a great deal of thought, and I've come to the conclusion that the Continuum is more fallible and prone to error than you care to admit. Let's look at what we mere mortals have learned about their behavior," he said, ticking his points off on his fingers.

"They put lesser life-forms on trial for the mere crime of not rising to their exalted level, all the while ignoring most of the conventions of due process recognized by supposedly inferior societies. They strip you of all your powers, placing you in mortal jeopardy, after having failed to keep your mischievous excesses under control. Then they reverse their decision and let you run amok through the galaxy again." Q harrumphed indignantly, but Picard showed him no mercy. "According to your own admission, the Continuum summarily executed Amanda Rogers's parents for choosing to live as human beings, left the orphaned child—one of their own—to be raised among we so-called primitive humans, then had the audacity to return years later and threaten Amanda herself with death unless she relinquished her own humanity." He shook his head slowly. "Banishment. Executions. Threats of genocide against less gifted races. These don't strike me as the actions of an advanced and enlightened society. Indeed, I could argue that the Klingons or the Cardassians have a higher claim to social progress."

Q snorted in derision. "Now you're just being ridiculous as well as insulting."

"Am I?" Picard asked, refusing to give any ground. "At least the harsher aspects of their cultures arose from, respectively, a demanding environment and severe economic hardships." He recalled Gul Madred's self-justifying evocations of the famine and poverty that first brought the Cardassian military regime to power generations ago. "Nor are those the only comparisons I could make," he continued, warming to his theme. "The tyranny of the Founders is said to be a response to centuries of Changeling persecution in the Gamma Quadrant, while the militaristic Romulan Empire of the present evolved from an arduous diaspora from ancient Vulcan millennia ago. And who knows what terrible, inexorable forces drove the Borg to first form their Collective?

"But even with the powers of the gods at your disposal, having conquered all the material challenges that trouble humanoid civilizations, the Q Continuum consistently behave in an arbitrary and draconian manner, one better suited to Dark Age despots than the evolved life-forms you claim to be." Picard returned to his chair and faced the viewscreen, his expression stony and resolute. The more he thought about it, the more certain he became that he could not permit Q to deter them from their mission.

"When you say to stay away from the barrier, you are saying that the rest of the universe is not for us. I'm sorry, but with all due respect to your self-proclaimed omniscience, that's not your decision to make." He nodded at Geordi, and when he spoke again his voice was steely in its conviction. "Mr. La Forge, launch the probe at once."

"Yes, sir!" Geordi responded. Keeping one eye on Q, he reached out and pressed the launch controls. Picard looked on as the class-2 probe, looking something like a duranium ice-cream cone, arced away from the *Enterprise,* its trajectory carrying it toward the nearest segment of the galactic barrier. He anticipated that the probe would pass into the barrier in less than ten minutes, beaming back a full spectrum of EM and subspace readings right up to the instant of its destruction, which would probably occur within nanoseconds of its initial contact with the barrier. He heard Lem Faal inhale sharply in anticipation.

"Captain!" Data said emphatically. "Tachyon levels are multiplying at a vastly accelerated rate." He turned to face Picard. "It *is* the Calamarain, sir, and they are approaching rapidly."

"Oh, them again," Q said without much enthusiasm. He had not been nearly so blasé, Picard recalled, when he faced the wrath of the Calamarain without his godlike powers. "Hail, hail, the gang's all here."

Lem Faal eyed Q with alarm, but Picard did his best to ignore Q's inappropriate attempt at humor. Q or no Q, he would not allow the *Enterprise* to be taken by surprise by the Calamarain. "Red alert!" he barked. "Shields up." Crimson warning lights flared to life around the bridge. Lieutenant Leyoro kept her hands poised above the weapons controls, while Riker looked ready to tackle Q if he so much as tried to interfere with Picard's ability to command the ship during this moment of crisis.

Q couldn't have cared less. "Oh dear," he said sourly, "I fear we're going to have to do this the hard way." He stepped between Picard and the viewscreen. "I'm sorry, Jean-Luc, but I can't allow you to be distracted by this minor complication. Too much is at stake, more than you can possibly imagine."

"Blast it, Q," Picard exploded, provoked beyond all patience. This had gone on long enough, and, as far as he was concerned, Q was the unwanted distraction from more pressing matters. "Explain yourself once and for all—the whole truth and nothing but—or get out of my way!"

"Fine!" Q replied indignantly, sounding almost as if he were the injured party. "Just remember, you asked for it."

What does he mean by that? Picard worried instantly, his worst fears confirmed when a burst of light erupted from Q, sweeping over Picard and carrying him away. Blank whiteness filled his vision. His chair seemed to dissolve beneath him. "Captain!" he heard Troi call out, but it was too late.

Deanna—and the *Enterprise*—were gone.

Interlude

"I think her name was—"

The red alert siren sounded, interrupting the female Q just as she was about to divulge the name of baby q's human godmother. Beverly Crusher instantly went into crisis mode. "Excuse me," she said to her visitor as Beverly tapped her com-badge. "Crusher to the bridge. What's happening?"

I was afraid of this, she thought instantly. After their initial briefing on Professor Faal's project, Beverly had reviewed the reports on the original experiments at Deep Space Nine, and discovered that in one of the early trials, the artificial wormhole had collapsed prematurely and produced a massive graviton wave. A plasma fire had broken out aboard the *Defiant* and three people had nearly been killed. In theory, the cause of the collapse—some sort of unexpected reaction between the tetrion field and the shielding on a probe—had been isolated and remedied since that near-disaster, but what if something similar had happened again?

Dire possibilities raced through her mind in the split second it took for the bridge to respond to her page. "The captain has been abducted by Q," Lieutenant Leyoro informed her succinctly; Beverly guessed that Commander Riker was otherwise occupied. "And the ship is about to engage the Calamarain."

"What!" Beverly was shocked by the news. The Calamarain? But they hadn't been heard from in years! Where had they come from all of a sudden? This was the last thing she had expected to hear. And Jean-Luc missing?

"I would prepare for casualties," Leyoro advised. "Do you require any further information or assistance, Doctor?"

Beverly contemplated the female Q and her child. Unlike the doctor, Q's mate evinced no reaction to the startling news. She occupied herself while Beverly was busy by wiping a smear of blue uttaberry flavoring off q's face with the sleeve of her imitation lab coat. "No, I don't think so," Beverly told Leyoro. It sounded like Will and the others had a lot on their hands at the moment; she decided she could handle the Q on her own. "Crusher out."

Her hand fell away from the badge and she confronted the other woman. "Well?" she demanded.

"Well?" the Q echoed, blithe disregard upon her features. She sopped up the last dab of blue from around the child's lips, then lifted him into her arms.

So much for female bonding, Beverly thought. Whatever warm feelings she might have harbored for the Q were washed away by concern for Jean-Luc. "You know what I mean. What has Q, the other Q, done with the captain? Where has he taken him?"

"Am I my Q's keeper?" She gave Beverly what the doctor supposed was intended to be a reassuring smile. "Really, there's no need to be concerned. I'm certain that wherever Q has taken your captain, he has done so for a very good reason."

Beverly didn't find that terribly comforting. "But we need the captain here now. We're on an important mission, and we've just encountered an alien, possibly hostile life-form." She tried a personal appeal. "As one mother to another, can't you do something?"

"Why should I have to do anything?" the woman answered. She took a moment to inspect her reflection in the shining, silver surface of a sealed cupboard, then tucked a few stray curls back into place. "My child is perfectly safe."

"I'm glad to hear it," Beverly shot back, shouting to be heard over the blaring alarm, "but how about the rest of us?"

The female Q shrugged. "The way Q talks, you people live this way every day. If it's not the Dominion or the Borg, it's a temporal anomaly. If it's not an anomaly, it's a warp-core breach or a separated saucer." She smiled indulgently. "I wouldn't want to interfere with your quaint and colorful way of life. It's far more educational for q to see you in your natural environment."

"This is not a field trip!" Beverly protested, despite a growing sense of futility. The original Q had never taken human lives seriously, so why should his mate be any different?

"I beg to differ," the Q said. Then she and her beaming baby boy disappeared without so much as a goodbye.

Beverly feared she knew where the omnipotent pair were heading. Where else would they find a better view of the developing crisis? Before she silenced the alarm and summoned Ogawa and the rest of her emergency personnel, she paused long enough to tap her combadge. "Crusher to the bridge. Expect company."

Ten

William Riker suddenly found himself in command. Before he could react, before he could even rise from his seat, Q vanished from the bridge, taking Captain Picard with him. "Captain!" Deanna called out, but the captain's chair was empty.

For a fleeting second, Riker worried about what might be happening to Captain Picard, but there was nothing he could do for the captain now. The safety of the crew and the ship had to be his number-one priority. *This isn't the first time Q has snatched the captain,* he recalled, *and Q's always brought him back before.* He could only pray that this time would be no exception.

"Scan for any nearby concentrations of ionized plasma," Riker ordered Data. "I want to know the instant the Calamarain come within sensor range." He stood and walked to the center of the command area, quickly considering the problem posed by the Calamarain. They didn't know for sure that the alien cloud-creatures posed a threat to the ship, but he didn't intend to be caught napping.

"Commander," Data stated. "The Calamarain are coming into visual range now."

A great cloud of incandescent plasma drifted between the *Enterprise* and the barrier, obscuring Riker's view of the shimmering wall of energy. The lambent cloud had a prismatic effect, emitting a rainbow's range of colors as it swirled slowly through the vacuum of space. Although the gaseous phenomenon, several times larger than the Sovereign-class starship, bore little resemblance to sentient life as Riker was accustomed to it, looking more like a lifeless accumulation of chemical vapors, he knew that this was the Calamarain all right, an entity or collection of entities capable of inflicting serious harm upon humanoid life if they chose to do so. Riker had no way of knowing if these were precisely the same beings who had menaced them before, but they were clearly of the same breed. "Mr. La Forge," he asked, "how are our shields?"

"They should stand up to them, Commander," Geordi reported. "I've set the shield harmonics to the same settings that worked last time." He double-checked the readouts at the engineering station and nodded at Lieutenant Leyoro, who monitored the shields from her own station at tactical. "Let's just hope the Calamarain haven't changed their own parameters over the last few years."

"I don't understand," Lem Faal wheezed, slowly coming to grips with a radically altered situation upon the bridge. "Where is Captain Picard?" His bloodshot gaze swung from the captain's empty chair to the bizarre alien apparition upon the main viewer. "Commander Riker!" he exclaimed, seizing upon the first officer as his only hope. "You have to stop that entity, drive it away. The probe . . . they could ruin everything!"

"Mr. Mack," Riker barked to a young ensign stationed near the starboard aft turbolift. "Escort Professor Faal to his quarters." He sympathized with the unfortunate scientist, but the bridge was no place for a civilian during a potential combat situation, and Riker didn't need the distraction.

"Commander, you can't do this!" Faal objected, hacking painfully between every word. He looked back at the screen as the young ensign took him by the arm and led him toward the nearest turbolift entrance. "I have to know what's happening. My experiment!"

Ensign Mack, an imposing Samoan officer, stood a head above the stricken Betazoid researcher, and had the advantages of youth and superior health besides, so Riker had every confidence that the ensign would be able to carry out his orders. Soon enough Faal's gasping protests were carried away by the turbolift, and Riker turned his attention to more critical matters: namely, the Calamarain.

He stared at the breathtaking spectacle of the immense, luminescent cloud; under other circumstances he would have been thrilled to encounter such an astounding life-form. *If only there was a way to communicate with them,* he mused, knowing that Captain Picard always preferred to exhaust every diplomatic effort before resorting to force. Unfortunately, the Universal Translator had proven useless the last time they confronted the Calamarain, whose unique nature was apparently too alien for even the advanced and versatile language algorithms programmed into the Translator. "Counselor," he asked Troi, "can you sense anything at all?"

"Aside from Professor Faal's distress?" She closed her eyes to concentrate on the impressions she was receiving. "The Calamarain are more difficult to read. All I'm picking up from them is a sense of rigid determination, a fixity of purpose and conviction. Whatever they are about, they are committed to it without doubt or hesitation."

He didn't like the sound of that. In his experience, an utterly fixed viewpoint could be the hardest to achieve a mutual understanding with. Fanatics were seldom easy to accommodate. He could only hope that the goal the Calamarain were so set upon did not involve the *Enterprise*.

We should be so lucky, he thought doubtfully.

"Commander," Leyoro called out, "the Calamarain are pursuing the probe."

It was true. The scintillating cloud receded into the distance as it abandoned the *Enterprise* in favor of chasing the much smaller projectile. The speed and accuracy of its flight belied any lingering doubts about the cloud's sentience. Through the prismatic ripples of the cloud, he saw the glitter of discharged energy outlining the probe as its protective forcefield struggled to shield it from the attack of the Calamarain. *Why are they doing this?* Riker wondered. *The probe poses no threat to them.*

"The readings from the probe are going berserk," Geordi said. "A massive overload of tachyon emissions." He studied the output at the science station. "Commander, if we could retrieve the probe at this point, examine its hull, we might be able to learn a lot more about the offensive capabilities of the Calamarain."

That may be for the best, Riker thought, taking his place in the captain's chair. It was obvious that the probe was not going to fulfill its original mission within the barrier. "Bring us within transporter range," he ordered. "Mr. La Forge, prepare to lock on to the probe."

"Commander!" Lieutenant Leyoro exclaimed. "That will mean lowering our shields. In my opinion, sir, the probe's not worth risking the ship for."

"If we don't learn more about the Calamarain, we may pay for it later on," he pointed out. "They don't seem interested in us at the moment, only the probe." *Why is that,* he wondered. *The probe came nowhere near them. Why did they go after it?*

The starship soared toward the amorphous, living fog that now held the probe in its grasp. Puzzled, Riker witnessed the coruscating shield around the probe growing weaker and less effective before his eyes. The flaring bursts of power came ever more sporadically while the targeted projectile rocked back and forth beneath the force of the cloud's assault. How much longer could the probe withstand the fury of the Calamarain?

"Shields down," Leyoro reported unhappily.

"I'm trying to lock on to the probe," Geordi said, having transferred the transporter controls to his science station, "but the Calamarain are interfering."

"Deliberately?" Riker asked.

"Hard to say," Geordi answered. "All I know is those tachyon emissions are making it hard to get a solid lock on the probe."

"Do what you can," Riker instructed, "but be prepared to abort the procedure at my command." Leyoro was right to a degree; if the Calamarain showed any interest in coming after the ship itself, they would have to sacrifice the probe and its data.

His combadge beeped, and he heard Dr. Crusher's voice, but before he could respond a white light flared at the corner of his eye. For a second Riker hoped that maybe Q and the captain had returned, then he spotted the female Q and her child sitting behind him on a set of wooden bleachers that had materialized at the aft section of the bridge, blocking the entrances to both of the rear turbolifts. The child now wore an antiquated Little League uniform and baseball cap instead of the sailor suit that had clothed him earlier. His mother wore a matching orange cap and jersey, with a large capital Q printed in block type upon the front of her uniform, as opposed to the lower-case q upon the little boy's jersey. "See," she told q, pointing toward the main viewer, "this is what they call an emergency situation. Isn't it funny?"

The boy laughed merrily and pointed like his mother. " 'Mergencee!" he squealed, bouncing up and down upon the bleachers so forcefully that the timbers creaked.

Riker seldom resorted to profanity on the bridge, but he bit down a pungent Anglo-Saxon expression as he tore his gaze away from the grossly inappropriate tableau that now occupied the bridge. He'd have to deal with the two sightseeing Qs later; right now his attention belonged on the sight of the endangered probe, its shields flashing within the vaporous depths of the Calamarain. Still, he felt less like the commander of a mighty starship than like the ringmaster of a three-ring circus.

"Now, pay attention," the female Q instructed her child. "This is supposed to be educational as well as entertaining." She plucked a pair of red and black pennants from out of the air and handed one flag to little q, keeping the other one for herself as she sat upon the bleachers. The pennants were made of stiff red fabric with the word "Humanoids" embossed on one side. "While your father is occupied elsewhere, let's make an outing of it, assuming the funny humanoids can keep their ship in one piece for that long."

"Pieces!" little q chirped. "Pieces!"

On the screen, a flash of crimson flame erupted from the side of the probe as its hull crumpled beneath the stresses exerted by the Calamarain. "Mr. La Forge?"

Riker asked, guessing that soon there would be nothing left of the probe to salvage.

"I think I've got it," Geordi called out. "Energizing now."

The golden flicker of the transporter effect raced over the surface of the probe, supplanting the futile sparking of its failing forcefield. The probe faded away completely, leaving behind only the spectacular sight of the Calamarain floating 'twixt the *Enterprise* and the galactic barrier.

"One point to the lowly humans," the female Q announced, writing a neon-yellow Arabic number one in the air with her index finger. The fiery numeral hung suspended above the floor for a breath before evaporating. A silver whistle appeared on a cord around her neck. She blew on it enthusiastically, hurting Riker's ears with the shrill sound, before declaring, "Game on!"

The great cloud that was the Calamarain drifted in place for a moment, perhaps unaware at first that its prey had escaped, but then it raced toward the screen, growing larger by the instant. Smoky tendrils reached out for the *Enterprise.* "It's coming after us," Leyoro said.

"Estimate interception in one minute, thirty-two seconds," Data stated.

Riker heard Troi gasp beside him. He wondered if she was feeling the Calamarains' hostile emotions, but there was no time to find out. "Mr. La Forge," he called out. "Is the transport complete?"

"We have it, Commander," Geordi assured him. "It was close, but we beamed it into Transporter Room Five."

"Raise shields," he ordered Leyoro. The incandescent cloud filled the screen before him. Unknown vapors churned angrily, stirring up ripples of ionized gas. He tried to distinguish individuals within the mass of radiant fog, but it was impossible to single out one strand of plasma among the whole. *It's possible,* he thought, *that each Calamarain does not exist as a single entity the way we do. They may be closer to a hive-mind mentality, like the Borg.*

That comparison did nothing to reassure him.

"Already on it," Leyoro said promptly, with a fierce gleam in her cold gray eyes. Riker suspected she was never truly happy except when fighting for survival. A dangerous attitude in the more civilized and peaceable regions of the Federation, but possibly a valuable trait on a starship probing the boundaries of known space. *You can take an Angosian out of the war,* he thought, *but you can't always take the war out of an Angosian.* Not unlike a certain Lieutenant Commander Worf. . . .

The plasma cloud surged over and around the *Enterprise.* Riker felt the floor vibrate beneath his boots as their deflectors absorbed and dispersed some variety of powerful force. A low, steady hum joined the background noise of the bridge, buzzing at the back of his mind like a laser drill digging into solid tritanium. He could practically feel the grating sound chafing away at his nerve endings. *That's going to get real old real fast,* he thought.

"Permission to open fire?" Leyoro asked, eager to return fire. Her survival instincts could not be faulted, Riker knew. They had kept her alive during both the war and the veterans' revolt that came afterward.

He shook his head. "Not yet. Let's not rush into battle before we even know what we're fighting about." Their shields had fended off the Calamarain before. He was confident that they would buy them a little breathing space now.

A jolt shook the bridge, which rocked the floor from starboard to port and back again before stabilizing a moment later. Everyone on the bridge caught their breath, except for the female Q, who cheerily turned to her child and said, "Come to think of it, I believe we may be rooting for the wrong team." The stiff cloth pennants the pair clutched in their hands switched from red fabric to something slick and, in its shifting spectrum of colors, reminiscent of the Calamarain. Riker noted that the lettering on the miniature flags now read "Nonhuman life-forms."

"One point to the Calamarain," she said, blowing sharply on her referee's whistle, "and the score is tied."

Riker refused to be baited, not while his ship was under attack. "Report," he instructed his crew. "What caused that shock?"

"Really, Commander Riker," the female Q chided, "who do you think caused it? The Calamarain, of course. Do you see any other threatening aliens in the vicinity?"

"Just you," Riker said curtly. "Mr. Data, please define the nature of the attack."

"Yes, Commander," Data said, scanning the readouts at Ops. From the captain's chair, Riker could see a string of numerals rushing across Data's console faster than a human eye could follow. "The tachyon barrage emitted by the Calamarain has increased by several hundred orders of magnitude. The intensity of the tachyon collisions is now more than sufficient to fatally damage both the ship and its inhabitants if not for the protection afforded by our deflectors."

"I see," Riker said, none too surprised. The Calamarain had demonstrated the potency of their offensive capabilities the last time they ran afoul of the *Enterprise*. "Mr. La Forge, are our shields holding?"

"For now," Geordi affirmed, "but we can't maintain the deflectors at this level forever."

"How long can we keep them up?" Riker asked. He watched the luminous plasma coursing across the screen, the iridescent hues swirling like a kaleidoscope. *It's strangely beautiful,* Riker reflected, regretting once more that humanity and the Calamarain had to meet as adversaries.

"Exactly?" Geordi said. "That depends on what they throw at us." The circuit patterns upon his implants rotated as he focused on his engineering display. "If they keep up the pressure at this intensity, the shields should be able to withstand it for about five hours. Four, if you want to play it safe."

Good, Riker thought. At least they had time to get their bearings and decide on a strategy. He didn't intend to stay a sitting duck much longer, but it might be in this instance that a judicious retreat was the better part of valor. There was too much unknown about both the Calamarains' motives and their abilities for him to feel comfortable committing the *Enterprise* to an all-out armed conflict. And as for their mission, and Professor Faal's experiment . . . well, that was looking more unlikely by the moment.

"I can do more from Engineering," Geordi offered. "Permission to leave the bridge?"

"Go to it, Mr. La Forge," Riker said crisply as Geordi headed for the turbolift. He looked at Troi and saw that the counselor still had her eyes closed, a look of intense, almost trancelike concentration upon her face. "Deanna?" he asked quietly, not wanting to jar her from her heightened state of sensitivity.

"They're all around us," Troi answered, slowly opening her eyes. "Surrounding us, containing us, confining us. I'm sensing great anger and frustration from every direction, but that's not all. Beneath everything, behind the rage, is a terrible fear. They're desperately afraid of something I can't even begin to guess at."

"How typically vague and ominous," the female Q said from the bleachers, rolling her eyes, to the amusement of her offspring. "Perhaps, young lady, you'd get better results with tea leaves."

"Never mind her," Riker said to Troi. "Thank you, Deanna." He tried to interpret her impressions, but too much remained unknown. How could such powerful entities, capable of thriving in the deadly vacuum of space, possibly be afraid of the *Enterprise?* The very idea seemed laughable, especially when a much more probable suspect sat only a few meters away.

He spun his chair around to confront the anachronistic wooden bleachers and the incongruous duo resting upon them. Riker inspected the female Q. She was an attractive woman, he noted, more so than Q deserved, in his opinion. Remarkably tall, too; it wasn't often Riker met women who were the same height as he, but the individual standing in front of him met his gaze at near eye-level. *She looks almost as imposing as a Klingon woman,* he thought. *Although I guess an omnipotent being can be as tall as she wants.*

"You," he accused. "Are you at the heart of this business? Are the Calamarain afraid of you?"

"Me?" the woman asked. She added ketchup to a hot dog that had not existed a heartbeat before. Neither had the ketchup, for that matter.

"Yes," Riker answered. "The Calamarain tried to kill your husband before. Is it you they fear?"

"They should," she said darkly, then assumed a more chipper expression, "but I'm in a forgiving mood today. No, First Officer, that's not it; the Calamarain have far more to worry about than me and little q these days."

"What do you mean?" Riker demanded. He didn't get the impression the woman was dissembling, unlike the original Q, who always came off as about as sincere as a Ferengi used-shuttle salesman, but who could tell with a Q? As he understood it, this wasn't even her true appearance. "Explain yourself."

The little q reached for his mother's hat, so the female Q amused him by trading their headwear with a snap of her fingers. The oversized hat looked ridiculous on the child's small head, but q giggled happily, his face all but concealed by the drooping brim of the hat.

"About the Calamarain," Riker prompted firmly. Even with their shields defending them from the Calamarain's lethal tachyons, he had no desire to linger in their grasp any longer than necessary. This Q could play the doting mother on her own time. "I'm still waiting for an explanation."

"Such a one-track mind," the Q sighed. "Q is right. You creatures really do need to learn how to stop and smell the nebulas now and again." She tapped the child-sized baseball cap upon her head and it expanded to fit more comfortably. "I'm sure if my husband wanted you to understand about the Calamarain and their selfish grievances, he would have explained it all to you. Mind you, I don't blame him for keeping mum where this whole business is concerned. Kind of an embarrassing anecdote, especially since it was all his fault in the first place."

What in blazes does she mean by that? Riker briefly wished that he had hung on to the supernatural powers Q had granted him years ago, just so he could threaten to kick this other Q off the ship if she didn't start giving him straight answers. "Embarrassing?" he said with deeply felt indignation. "Your husband kidnapped our captain. For all I know, he sicced the Calamarain on us, too. I call that more than 'embarrassing' and I want to know what you intend to do about it, starting with telling us just where Q has taken Captain Picard."

The female Q peered down her nose at Riker. "I'm not sure I approve of your tone," she said icily, placing her hands over baby q's ears. The child, curious, grew a new pair of velvety silver bunny ears out of the top of his scalp, foiling his mother's well-intentioned efforts.

"I don't want your approval," Riker said. The hum of the Calamarain buzzed in his ears, reminding him that he had more important things to do than waste his breath trying to reason with a Q. "I want you to lend a hand, answer my questions, or get off the bridge."

His harsh tone got through to little q, whose childish grin crumpled into tears and sobs. The mother fixed a chilly stare on Riker, who felt his life expectancy shrinking at a geometrical rate. "Well, if that's how you're going to be," she huffed. Without another word, she disappeared from the bridge, taking little q and the bleachers with her.

Well, that's something, he thought, thankful that members of the Q Continuum tended to leave as unexpectedly as they arrived. *For indestructible, immortal beings, they sure seem pretty thin-skinned.* He swiveled his chair around to face the prow of the bridge. On the main viewer, he saw a portion of the Calamarain, its iridescent substance drifting past the window like some lifeless chemical vapor. The roiling gases outside the ship looked more agitated than before. The rainbow colors darkened, the separate fumes clumping together in heavy, swollen accumulations that promised an approaching storm. Flickers of bright electricity leaped from billow to billow, sparking like bursts of lightning through the all-encompassing cloud. Riker felt like they were trapped inside the galaxy's biggest thunderhead. "Deflectors?" he asked, wanting a status report.

"Shields holding," Leyoro informed him, "although I'm detecting an increase in harmful tachyon radiation."

"That is correct," Data confirmed from Ops. "The Calamarain have rapidly raised the intensity of the emissions directed against the ship, possibly in an attempt to penetrate our defenses." He peered intently at the display at his console. "By placing further pressure upon our shields, the amplified nature of the Calamarain's attack reduces our safety factor by 1.531 hours."

"Understood," Riker said, "but we're not going to stick around that long." The captain was missing. The ship was under attack. A prudent departure was definitely in order, he judged. He knew he did not need to worry about leaving the captain behind; Q could find the *Enterprise* anywhere in the universe if he felt so inclined. It seemed a shame to turn tail and run when all they had managed to do so far was misplace Jean-Luc Picard, but there was no compelling reason to continue the experiment in the face of an enemy; it was a pure research assignment after all. The barrier had been around for billions of years. It could wait a little longer. "Mr. Clarze, prepare to go to warp."

"Commander," Lieutenant Leyoro pointed out, "we haven't even tried to strike back at the Calamarain yet. Perhaps we can drive them away with our phasers?"

Riker shook his head. "There's no reason to get into a shooting war, not if we can simply turn around. For all we know, the Calamarain may have legitimate interests in this region of space." He saw Deanna nod in agreement. "Take us out of here, Mr. Clarze."

"Yes, sir," the young Deltan said from the conn, entering the appropriate coordinates into the helm controls. Riker noted a light sheen of perspiration upon the pilot's domed skull; he'd probably never been caught inside a sentient cloud before. *Could be worse,* Riker thought. According to the history tapes, Kirk's *Enterprise* had once been swallowed by a giant space amoeba. "Heading?" Clarze asked.

"The nearest starbase," Riker said, "to report our findings." *Too bad we never got the chance to take on the galactic barrier,* he thought. Still, no experiment was worth risking the *Enterprise,* especially with civilians and children aboard. Starfleet would have to challenge the barrier another day, with or without Professor Faal. It was tragic that the dying scientist had to be thwarted this close to the completion of his final experiment, but the Calamarain had given them no other choice. Who knows? Maybe someday they might even get another chance to establish genuine contact with the Calamarain.

At the moment, though, he found himself more worried about the fact that the viewscreen still held the image of the Calamarain despite his order to go to warp. "Mr. Clarze?"

"I'm trying, Commander!" Clarze blurted, jabbing at the control panel with his fingers. "But something's wrong with the warp engines. I can't get them to engage."

"What?" Riker reacted. If the warp engines were down, the *Enterprise* was in serious trouble. He knew from experience that they could not outrun the Calamarain on impulse alone. He glanced over his shoulder at the crew member manning the aft science station. "Mr. Schultz, what's our engine status?"

"I'm not sure, sir," Ensign Robert Schultz said, peering anxiously at the monitors and display panels at the aft engineering station. "The warp core is still on-line and the plasma injectors seem to be functioning properly, but somehow the warp field coils are not generating the necessary propulsive effect. I can't figure out why."

"That's not good enough," Riker said. Hoping that Geordi had already made it back to Engineering, he tapped his comm badge. "Geordi, this is Riker. What the devil is going on down there?"

"I wish I could tell you," the chief engineer's voice answered, confirming the speed and efficacy of the ship's turbolifts. "We can initiate the pulse frequency in the plasma, no problem, but something's damping the warp field layers, keeping our energy levels below eight hundred millicochranes, tops. We need at least a thousand to surpass lightspeed."

"Understood," Riker acknowledged, remembering basic warp theory. He glanced at Data, wondering if he should pull the android off Ops and send him to assist Geordi in Engineering. *Not unless I absolutely have to,* he decided. "What about the impulse drive?"

"That's still up and running," Geordi stated, "at least for now."

That's something, I suppose, Riker thought, although what he really needed was warp capacity. "Anything you can do to fix the field coils in a hurry?"

"I can run a systems-wide diagnostic," Geordi suggested, "but that's going to take a while. Plus, I've already got half my teams working overtime to maintain the deflectors."

In the meantime, we're stuck here, Riker thought, *with our shields failing and the Calamarain at the door.* "Do what you can, Mr. La Forge." He clenched his fists angrily, frustrated by this latest turn of affairs. It seemed retreat was no longer an option, at least not at present. They might have to fight their way out after all. A strategic notion occurred to him, and he reopened the line to La Forge. "Geordi, have an engineering officer look at the remains of the probe the Calamarain attacked. I want to find out as much as we can about their modes of attack."

"You got it," Geordi promised. "I'll put Barclay on it right away."

Riker experienced a momentary qualm when Reg Barclay's name was mentioned. Deanna insisted that Barclay was making substantial progress, and certainly the man had come in useful when they had to repair Zefram Cochrane's primitive warp vessel back in 2063, but even still . . . Then again, it dawned on him, analyzing the probe was probably less stressful under the circumstances than working on the shields or engines, so the probe and Barclay made a good fit. *I should never have doubted Geordi's work assignments,* he thought. *He knows exactly what his people are capable of.*

Just as Riker knew what a certain android officer could do when the chips were down. "Mr. Data, since we can't get away from the Calamarain, we need to find out what they want. I want you to give top priority to establishing communication with the Calamarain. Perhaps our sensor readings can give you what you need to bring the Universal Translator up to speed. Work with Counselor Troi, if you think she can help. Maybe her nonverbal impressions can provide you with the clue you need to crack their language."

"Yes, Commander," the android replied. He sounded like he was looking forward to tackling the problem. "A most intriguing challenge." He studied the displays at Ops, swiftly switching from one sensor mode to another until he found something. "Counselor Troi," he said after a few moments, "I am detecting a directed transmission from the entity on a narrower wavelength than their tachyon barrage. It may be an attempt at communication. Can you sense its meaning?"

Riker could not see Deanna's face from his chair, but he could well imagine the look of concentration on her face. Even after all these years, her empathic abilities still impressed him, although he could recall more than a few instances when he'd wished that she had not been able to see through him quite so easily. *Like that time on Risa,* he thought.

Deanna Troi shut her eyes, doing her best to filter out the emotions of the crew members present in the conference room as well as, more faintly, throughout the ship. *Speak to me,* she thought to the gaseous mass outside the ship. *Let me know what you're feeling.*

Suddenly, an unexpected "voice" intruded into her thoughts. *You have to talk to the commander,* it urged her silently. *Make him understand. I have to go on with my work. It's vitally important.*

She recognized the telepathic voice immediately. Lem Faal. How desperate was he, she worried, that he would take advantage of her sensitivity like this? *Please,* she told him. *Not now. Please leave me alone.* She needed to have all her faculties focused on the task of reading the Calamarain.

But my work! he persisted. His telepathic voice, she noted, lacked the hoarseness and shortness of breath that weakened his physical voice. It was firm and emphatic, unravaged by disease.

Fortunately, years of dealing with her mother had given her plenty of experience at dispelling an unwanted telepathic presence from her mind. *No!* Faal protested as he felt her squeeze him out of her consciousness. *Wait! I need your help!*

"Leave me alone," she repeated, before banishing him entirely.

"Deanna?" Will Riker asked. Her eyes snapped open and she saw him watching her with a confused, anxious expression. So were Data and Lieutenant Leyoro and the others on the bridge. She hadn't realized she had spoken aloud.

"I'm sorry," she said. "I was . . . distracted."

"By the Calamarain?" the commander asked. She could feel his concern for her well-being.

"No," she answered, shaking her head. She would have to speak to the commander about Faal later; there was something frightening about the scientist's obsession with his experiment, beyond simple determination to see his work completed before death claimed him. First, though, there were still the Calamarain. "Let me try again," she said, closing her eyes once more.

This time Faal did not interfere. Perhaps he had finally gotten the message to keep out of her head. Screening out all other distractions, she opened herself up to the alien emotions seeping into the ship from outside.

They tasted strange to her mental receptors, like some exotic spice or flavor she couldn't quite place. Was that anger/fear or fear/anger or something else altogether? She felt queer impressions suffusing the air around her, like the steady drone of the humming she had heard in the background ever since the cloud had surrounded the ship. They were relentlessly consistent, never quavering or varying in tone or intensity. She couldn't name the feeling, but it was a constant, unchanging, a firm and unshakable conviction/resolution/determination to do what must be done, whatever that might be. She probed as hard as she was able, but the feeling never changed. That was all she could sense, the same inflexible purpose surrounding the *Enterprise* on all sides.

Convinced that she'd heard enough, she opened her eyes slowly, took a few deep breaths, and let the alien emotions recede into the background. "I'm picking up an increased sense of urgency, of alarm mixed with fury," she stated. "There's a feeling of danger, whether to us or from us I can't say." She hesitated for a second, reaching out across the gulf of space with her empathic senses. "I think it's a warning . . . or a threat."

That's a big difference, Riker thought, listening carefully to Deanna's report. *Do the Calamarain want to help us or hurt us?* Judging from the way they'd knocked the probe about earlier, he'd bet on the latter.

"Thank you, Counselor," Data said, comparing Deanna's impressions against his readings and entering the results into his console. "That was quite helpful. I now have several promising avenues to explore."

Could Data really use Deanna's empathic skills as a Rosetta Stone to crack the Calamarain's language? Riker could only wonder how the android was managing to translate Deanna's subjective emotional readings into the mathematical algorithms used by the Universal Translator. Then again, he remembered, Data had knowledge of hundreds, if not thousands, of languages stored in his positronic brain, making him something of an artificial translator himself. *If anybody can do it,* he thought.

"Excuse me, Commander," Leyoro said, "but what's that old human expression again? The one about the best offense . . . ?"

Riker permitted himself a wry smile. "Point taken, Lieutenant. Don't worry, I haven't forgotten our phasers."

Given a choice, he'd rather talk than shoot, but the time for talking was swiftly running out.

Interlude

Bug.

It was buzzing over there, just out of reach. *A shiny, silver bug.* He could see it now, the image refracted through the lens of the wall, deformed and distorted, true, but definitely there. *Itty-bitty little bug, buzzing about on the other side, doing teeny-weeny, buggy little things.*

Busy bug, he crooned. *How fast can you fly? How quick can you die?*

He couldn't wait to swat it with his hungry hand. No, not swat it, he corrected himself. He'd play with it first, teach it tricks, then pull off its wings. *Soon,* he promised, *soon to its ruin.*

Then the bug wasn't alone anymore. A wisp of smoke drifted over to where the bug flitted. *Bug and smoke,* he cursed, his mood darkening. He remembered that smoke, oh yes he did, and remembering, hated. *A joke on the smoke, ever so long ago. Choke on the smoke. Smoking, choking . . . choking the bug!* Through the fractured glass of the wall, he watched as the thin, insubstantial wisp of vapor surrounded the bug. *No! You can't have it!* he raved. *It's mine, mine to find, mine to grind!*

Impatiently, he reached out for the bug and the smoke, unable to wait any longer, forgetting for the moment all that lay between him and his prizes. But his will collided against the perpetual presence of the wall and rebounded back in pain and fury. He drew inward on himself, nursing his injured pride, while the bug and the smoke circled each other just beyond his grasp. *Not now,* he recalled, *not how. But when, when, WHEN . . . ?*

He howled in frustration—and a voice answered. The same voice that had greeted his cries not very long ago. It was a small, barely audible voice, but it sounded faintly louder than it had before, like it was coming from some place not nearly so far away.

(I'm here,) the voice said, *(I'm almost with you).*

WHEN? he pleaded, his own voice sounding like an explosion compared to the other. *WHEN?*

(Soon. There are a few obstacles to overcome, but soon. I give you my word.)

What did it mean by that? The message was too vague, too indefinite, to curb his constant craving to defeat the wall. The bug and the smoke tormented him, teasing him with their pretended proximity. He needed an answer now.

Let me in, he said. *Let you out. Away, away, no more decay. Let me in, again and again.*

(Yes!) the voice affirmed. *(I will make it happen, no matter what.)*

The voice droned on, but he grew bored and stopped listening. The bug captured his attention once more, so small and fragile, but not yet undone by the suffocating smoke. *Buzz, buzz, little bug,* he whispered. *Flitter free while you can.* He assumed the shape of an immense arachnid, stretching out his will in all directions like eight clutching limbs.

A spider is coming to gobble you up. . . .

Eleven

He was no longer on the bridge. A cool white mist surrounded Picard on all sides, obscuring his vision, but the familiar sounds and smells of the bridge were gone, informing him unequivocally that he had left the *Enterprise*. He looked around him quickly and saw only the same featureless fog everywhere he glanced. *The Calamarain?* he wondered briefly, but, no, this empty mist was utterly unlike the luminescent swirls of the living plasma cloud. This place, odorless, soundless, textureless, was more like . . . limbo. He stamped his feet upon whatever surface was supporting him, but the mist absorbed both the force and the sound of his boots striking the ground so that not an echo escaped to confirm the physicality of his own existence. He was lost in a void, a sensation that he remembered all too well.

I've been here before, he thought. *That time I almost died in sickbay and Q offered me a chance to relive my past.* The memory did nothing to ease his concerns. That incident had been a profoundly disturbing, if ultimately illuminating, experience, one that he was in no great hurry to endure again. More important, what about the *Enterprise?* Only seconds before, or so it seemed to him, he had placed the ship on red alert in response to the approach of the Calamarain. "Dammit," he cursed, punching a fist into his palm in frustration. This was no time to be away from his ship!

"Q!" he shouted into the mist, unafraid of who or what might hear him. "Show yourself!"

"You needn't bellow, Jean-Luc," Q answered, stepping out of the fog less than two meters away from Picard. His Starfleet uniform, proper in every respect, hardly suited his sardonic tone. "Although I wish you could have simply listened to me in the first place. You have no idea how strenuously I regret that you forced me to go to such lamentable lengths to convince you."

"I forced you?" Picard responded indignantly. "This is intolerable, Q. I demand that you return me to the *Enterprise* at once."

Q tapped his foot impatiently. "Spare me, Picard. Time is scarce. Just this once, can't we skip the obligatory angry protestations and get on with business?"

"Your business, you mean," Picard said. "My business is on my ship!"

"That's what you think," Q replied. He crossed his arms upon his chest, looking quite sure of himself. "Take my word for this, Jean-Luc. You're not going back to the *Enterprise*—E, F, or G—until we are finished, one way or another. Or don't you trust Riker to keep the ship in one piece that long?"

That's not the point, he thought, but part of him was forced to concede the futility of talking Q out of anything. If there was one thing he had learned since their first meeting in Q's "courtroom" over a decade ago, it was that attempting to reason with or intimidate Q was a waste of time. Perhaps the best and only option was to let the charade play out as quickly as possible, and hope that he could get back to his life and duties soon enough. *Not a very appealing strategy,* he thought, *but there it is.*

He took stock of their surroundings, ready to take on Q's latest game. The empty mist offered no clue as to what was yet to come. "What is this place, Q," he asked, "and don't tell me it's the afterlife."

"Like you'd know it if you saw it," Q said. "You wouldn't recognize the Pearly Gates if you had your pathetic phasers locked on them." He paused and scratched his chin reflectively. "Actually, they aren't so much pearly as opalescent . . . but I digress.

This shapeless locale," he said, sweeping out his arms to embrace the entire foggy landscape, "is merely a starting point, a place between time, where time has no sway."

"Between time?" Picard repeated, concentrating on every word Q said. This duplicitous gamester played by his own arcane rules, he knew, and sometimes doled out a genuine hint or clue in his self-aggrandizing blather. The trick was to extract that nugget of truth from the rest of Q's folderol. "I thought you said earlier that time was scarce."

"By the Continuum, you can be dim, Jean-Luc," Q groaned, wiping some imaginary sweat from his brow. "Sometimes I feel like I'm teaching remedial metaphysics to developmentally stunted primates. Here, let me demonstrate."

Q grabbed hold of the drifting fog with both hands and pulled it aside as though it were a heavy velvet curtain. Picard glimpsed two figures through the gap in the mist, standing several meters away. One was a tall, balding man in a red-and-black Starfleet uniform that was a few years out of style. A lethal-looking scorch mark marred the front of his uniform, above his heart. The other figure was clad in angelic white robes that seemed composed of the very mist that framed the scene. A heavenly light illuminated the second figure from behind, casting a sublime radiance that outlined the robed figure with a shimmering halo. Looking on this tableau, one could be forgiven for assuming that this auroral figure was a veritable emissary from Heaven, if not the Almighty Himself.

Picard knew better. He recognized the figures, and the occasion, instantly. They were himself and Q, posed as they had been when he first confronted Q in this very same mist, shortly after he "died" from a malfunction in his artificial heart. Caught up in their own fateful encounter, the other Picard and Q paid no heed to the onlookers now witnessing themselves at an earlier time. Picard could not hear what his younger self was saying to the younger Q, but he remembered the exchange well enough. There had been a time, after he woke up in sickbay under Beverly Crusher's ministrations, when he had half-convinced himself that he had merely experienced an unusually vivid and perceptive dream, but, in his heart of hearts, which bore no relation to the steel and plastic mechanism lodged in his chest, he had always known that the entire episode had really happened. Even still, it gave him a chill to watch the bizarre occurrence unfold once more.

He was tempted to shout out a warning to his earlier self, but what could he say? "Whatever you do, don't let Q tempt you into changing your past"? No, that would only defeat the entire purpose of that unique, autobiographical odyssey and deprive his other self of the hard-earned insights he had so painfully achieved over the course of that unforgettable journey. He couldn't bring himself to say a word.

"Seen enough?" Q asked. He withdrew his hands and the fog fell back into place, sealing away the vision from the past. "I must say, I seemed particularly celestial there. Divinity looks good on me."

"So you think," Picard retorted, but his heart was not in the war of words. That flashback to his old, near-death experience shook him more than he wanted to admit. "Why show me that?" he asked. "I have not forgotten what happened then."

"You still don't understand," Q said. "That didn't happen before. It's happening now. Here, everything happens now. But when we return to the boring, linear reality you know, the clock hands will resume their dogged, dreary rounds." He held his hands up in front of his face. "Excuse me while I watch my fingernails grow. Let me know when you're through with your futile efforts to comprehend the ineffable."

Picard ignored Q's taunts. Figuring out the rules of this game was the only way he was going to find his way back to the *Enterprise.* "Is that what this is all about? The same routine as before, you're going to make me face up to another chapter of my past?" He couldn't help trying to guess what heartrending tragedy he might be forced to relive. The death of Jack Crusher? That nasty business back at the Academy? His torture at the hands of Gul Madred? *Dear god,* he prayed, *don't let it be my time among the Borg. I couldn't bear to be Locutus once again.* He cast off his fears, however, and faced his opponent defiantly. "You must be getting old, Q," he said. "You're starting to repeat yourself."

To his surprise, Q began to look more uncomfortable than Picard, as though the relentless puppeteer was genuinely reluctant to proceed now that the moment of departure had arrived. "Oh, Picard," he sighed, "how I wish we were merely sightseeing in your own insignificant existence, but I'm afraid it's not your disreputable past we must examine, *mon capitaine,* but my own." He took a deep breath, quelling whatever trepidations he possessed, then gave Picard a devil-may-care grin. "Starting now."

The mist converged on Picard, swallowing him up. For what could have been an instant or an eternity he found himself trapped in a realm of total, blank sensory deprivation—until the universe returned. Sort of.

Where am I? Picard wondered. *What am I?*

There was something wrong with his eyes, or, if not wrong precisely, then different. He could see from three distinct perspectives simultaneously, the disparate views blending to grant him a curiously all-inclusive image that made ordinary binocular vision seem flat by comparison. He searched his surroundings, finding himself seemingly adrift amid the blackness of space. An asteroid drifted by, its surface pitted with craters and shadows, and he glimpsed a blazing yellow sun in the distance, partially eclipsed by an orbiting planet. *I don't understand,* he thought. *How can I be surviving in a vacuum? Am I wearing a pressure suit, or did Q not bother with that?* It was hard to tell; he couldn't feel his arms or his legs. He tried to look down at his body, but all he could see was a bright white glare. What had Q done to him?

"Q!" he shouted, but what emerged from his throat was a long, sibilant hiss. Make that throats, for, to his utter shock, he felt the vibrato of the hiss in no less than three, separate throats. *This is insane,* he thought, struggling not to panic. Over the years, he had almost grown accustomed to being miraculously transported here and there throughout the universe by Q's capricious whims, but he had never been transported out of his own body before—and into something inhuman and strange. "Q?" he hissed again, desperate for some sort of answer.

"Right behind you, Jean-Luc," Q answered. Picard had never been so relieved to hear that voice in his entire life. Somehow, merely by thinking about it, he managed to turn around and was greeted by an astounding yet oddly familiar sight:

A three-headed Aldebaran serpent floated in the void only a few meters away. A trio of hooded, serpentine bodies rose from a glowing silver sphere about which smaller balls of light ceaselessly orbited. The heads, which each resembled Earth's king cobra, faced Picard. Strips of glittering emerald and crimson scales alternated along all three of the snakelike bodies. Three pairs of cold, reptilian eyes fixed Picard with their mesmerizing stare. A threesome of forked tongues flicked from the serpentine faces. "Welcome," the snakes said in Q's voice, "to the beginning."

Of course, Picard thought. Not only did he recognize the triple serpent, an ancient mythological symbol dating back to well before the onset of human civilization, but he recalled how Q had once assumed this form before, at the onset of his second visit to the *Enterprise*. But this time, it seemed, Q had done more than merely transform himself into the fantastical, hydra-headed creature; he had somehow mutated Picard as well. Straining the unfamiliar muscles of his outermost necks, Picard turned his eyes on himself. Even though he had already guessed what he would find, it still came as a terrible shock when he saw, from two opposing points of view, two more serpentine heads rising from the radiant globe that was now his body. For a second, each of his outer heads looked past the central serpent so that Picard found himself staring directly into his own eyes—and back again. The jolt was too much for his altered nervous system to endure and he quickly looked away to see the other hydra, Q, hovering nearby. "So what do you think of your new body, Captain?" he asked. "Tell me, are three heads truly better than one?"

"Good Lord, Q," Picard exclaimed, trying his best to ignore the peculiar sensation of speaking through three sets of jaws, "what have you done?" He had to pray that his unearthly transformation was only a temporary joke of Q's, or else he would surely go mad. Good god, did he now have three separate brains, three different minds to lose?

"Merely trying to inject a note of historical verisimilitude into our scenic tour of my past," Q stated. "Relatively speaking, that is. Understand this, Picard: there is no way your primitive consciousness can truly comprehend what it means to be part of the Q Continuum, so everything I show you from here on has been translated into a form that can be perceived by your rudimentary five senses. It's a crude, vastly inadequate approximation of my reality, but it is the best your mind can cope with." Q drifted closer to Picard, until the transformed starship captain could see the individual scales overlapping each other along the lengths of each extended throat. The flared hoods behind each head puffed up even larger. "Anyway," Q went on, "it seemed more appropriate, and more accurate, to take these shapes during this stage of our excursion, given that the evolution of the humanoid form is still at least a billion years away at this point. In fact, this was one of my favorite guises way back in the good old days, before you overreaching humanoids came down from the trees and started spreading your DNA all over the galaxy."

"Billions of years?" Picard echoed, too stunned at Q's revelations to even register the usual insults and patronizing tone. "Where . . . when . . . are we?"

"Roughly five billion years ago, give or take a few dozen millennia." Q's leftmost head nipped playfully at the head next to it. "Ouch. You know, sometimes I surprise even myself." The central head snapped back while the head on the right continued speaking. "Tell me the truth, Jean-Luc, don't you get tired of Data's painfully precise measurements? How refreshing it must be to deal with someone—like myself, say— who is quite comfortable rounding things off to the nearest million or so."

Picard watched his own heads nervously, unsure when or how he might start turning on himself. There was something horribly claustrophobic about being trapped in this inhuman form, deprived of his limbs and hands and all the normal physical sensations he was accustomed to after sixty-plus years of existence as a human being. He felt a silent scream bubbling just beneath the thin surface of his sanity. "Q, I find this new form . . . very distracting."

It was possibly the greatest single understatement in his life.

"Oh, Jean-Luc," Q sighed, sounding disappointed, "I had hoped you were more flexible than that. After all, you coped with being a Borg for a week or two. Is a tri-headed serpent god all that much harder?"

"Q," Picard pleaded, too far from his own time and his own reality to worry about his pride. "Please."

"If you insist," Q grumbled. "I have important things to show you and I suppose it wouldn't do to have you fretting about your trivial human body the whole time. You might miss something." The triple necks of the Q-serpent wrapped themselves around each other until the three heads seemed to sprout from a single coiled stalk. Picard was briefly reminded of Quetzalcoatl, the serpent deity of the ancient Aztecs. *Quetzalcoatl . . . Q? Could there be a connection?*

He might never know.

"Pity," the triune entity continued, "you hadn't begun to scratch the possibilities of this identity." A flash of light illuminated the darkness for a fraction of a second, and then Q appeared before Picard in his usual form, garbed in what looked like a simple Greek chiton fastened over his left shoulder. A circlet of laurel leaves adorned his brow. Simple leather sandals rested upon nothing but empty space.

Picard's trifocal vision coalesced into a single point of view. Gratefully, he looked down to see his human body restored to him. So relieved was he to have arms and legs again, he barely noted at first that he was now attired in an ancient costume similar to the one Q now wore. He remained floating in space, of course, protected from the deadly vacuum only by Q's remarkable powers, but that was a level of surreality that he felt he could cope with. *Just permit me to be myself,* he thought, *and I'm ready for whatever Q has up his sleeves.*

"Happy now?" Q pouted. He wiggled his fingers in front of his face and scowled at the sight. "I hope you realize what a dreadful anachronism this is. Be it on your head, and you a professed archaeologist!"

"I feel much better, thank you," Picard answered, regaining his composure even while conversing in open space. He glanced down at his own sandaled feet and saw nothing but a gaping abyss extending beneath him for as far as his eyes could see. He was not experiencing a null-gravity state, though; he knew what that felt like and this was quite different. Q was somehow generating the sensation of gravity, so that he felt squarely oriented despite his surroundings. Up was up and down was down, at least for the moment. He fingered the hem of his linen garment, noting the delicate embroidering along the border of the cloth. *God is in the details,* he thought, recalling an ancient aphorism, *or was that the devil?* "What is this?" he asked, indicating the chiton. "Another anachronism?"

"A conceit," Q said with a shrug, "to give a feel of antiquity. As I explained before, and I hope you were paying close attention, this is nothing like what I really looked like at this point in the galaxy's history, but simply a concession to your limited human understanding."

"And the Aldebaran serpent?" Picard pressed. "Was that your true form?"

Q shook his head, almost dislodging his crown of leaves. "Merely another guise, one better suited to a time before you mammals began putting on airs."

"If anyone can be accused of putting on airs," Picard replied, "it's you. You've done little but flaunt your alleged superiority since the time we first encountered you. Frankly, I'm not convinced."

"Yes, I recall your little speech right before we departed the bridge," Q said. "Would you be surprised to know that I share some of your opinions about the more . . . shall we say, heavy-handed . . . tendencies of the Continuum?"

"I know that you've been on the outs with your own kind at least once," Picard answered, "which gives me some hope that the Continuum itself might be rather more mature and responsible." It dawned on him, not for the first time, that almost everything he knew about the rest of the Q Continuum had come from Q's own testimony, hardly the most reliable of sources. He resolved to question Guinan more deeply on the subject, if and when he ever had the opportunity. "Well?" he asked, surveying this desolate section of space. On the horizon, the eclipsing planet no longer passed between himself and the nearest sun, permitting him an unobstructed view of the seething golden orb, which he registered as a typical G-2 dwarf star, much like Earth's own sun. It was a breathtaking sight, especially viewed directly from space, but he was not about to thank Q for letting him see it. "Why are we here?" he demanded. "What is it you wish to show me?"

"The beginning, as I said," Q stated. With a wave of his arm, he and Picard began to soar through the void toward the immense yellow sun. The hot solar wind blew in his face as the star grew larger and larger in his sight. It was a thrilling and not entirely unpleasant experience, Picard admitted to himself. He felt like some sort of interstellar Peter Pan, held aloft by joyous spirits and a sprinkling of pixie dust.

"Picture yourself in my place," Q urged, "a young and eager Q, newly born to my full powers and cosmic awareness, exploring a shiny new galaxy for the first time. Oh, Picard, those were the days! I felt like I could do anything. And you know what? I was right!"

At that, they plunged into the heart of the roaring sun. Picard flinched automatically, expecting to be burnt to a crisp, but, as he should have known, Q's omnipotence protected them from the unimaginable heat and brilliance. He gaped in awe as they descended first through the star's outer corona as it hurled massive tongues of flame at the surrounding void, not to mention, Picard knew, fatal amounts of ultraviolet light and X-rays. Listening to the constant crackle and sizzle of the flames, he could not help recalling how the *Enterprise* had nearly been destroyed when Beverly, in command while he and the others were being held captive by Lore, had flown the ship into another star's corona in a daring and ultimately successful attempt to escape the Borg. Yet here he was, without even the hull of a starship to shield him against the unleashed fury of the sun's outer atmosphere.

Next came the chromosphere, a thin layer of fiery red plasma that washed over Picard like a sea of hot blood, followed by the photosphere, the visible surface of the sun. Picard had thoroughly studied the structure of G-2 stars at the Academy, of course, and subjected hundreds of stars to every variety of advanced sensor probe, but none of that had prepared him for the reality of actually witnessing the surface of a sun firsthand; he gawked in amazement at churning energies that should have been enough to incinerate him a million times over. Not even the legendary lake of fire within the Klingon homeworld's famed Kri'stak Volcano compared to the raging inferno that seemed to consume everything in sight except him and Q.

Despite Q's protective aura, Picard felt as if he were standing naked in a Vulcan desert at high noon. Sweat dripped from his forehead while rivers of perspiration ran down his back, soaking the simple linen garment he wore. *Humidity on the surface of a sun?* It was flagrantly impossible; he had to assume that Q had inflicted this discomfort on him purely for the sake of illusion. Picard was none too surprised to note that Q himself looked perfectly cool and comfortable. "I get the idea, Q," he said, wiping more sweat from his brow and flinging it toward his companion. Tiny droplets evaporated instantly before reaching their target. "It's very hot here. Do you have anything less obvious to teach me?"

"Patience," Q advised. "We've barely begun." He dabbed his toe in the boiling gases beneath their feet and Picard felt whatever was supporting him slip away. He began to sink even deeper into the bright yellow starstuff. A mental image of himself being dipped into hot, melted butter leaped irresistibly to the forefront of his consciousness. Reacting instinctively, he held his breath as his head sank beneath the turbulent plasma, but he needn't have bothered; thanks to Q, oxygen found him even as he drowned in the sun.

They dropped through the photosphere until they were well within the convection zone beneath the surface of the sun. Here rivers of ionized gas, not unlike those that composed the Calamarain, surged throughout the outer third of the sun's interior. Picard knew the ambient temperature around him had to be at least one million degrees Kelvin. They dived headfirst into one of the solar rivers and let the ferocious current carry them ever deeper until at last, like salmon leaping from white water, they broke through into the very heart of the star.

Now he found himself approaching the very center of a stellar furnace that beggared description. Here untold amounts of burning hydrogen atoms, transformed into helium by a process of nuclear fusion, produced a temperature of more than fifteen million degrees Kelvin. Not even the warp core aboard the *Enterprise* was capable of generating that much heat and raw energy. The visual impression Picard received was that of standing in the midst of a single white-hot flame, and the heat he actually felt was nearly unbearable. Every inch of exposed skin felt raw and dry and sunburned. Acrid chemical fumes stung his eyes, nose, and throat. The crackle of the spurting flames far above him gave way to a constant pounding roar. Overall, the intense gravitation and radiation at the solar core were so tremendous that they practically overwhelmed his senses, and yet somehow he was still able to see Q, who looked rather bored until his eyes lit on something *really* interesting. "Look, there I am," he announced.

Brushing tears away from his eyes, Picard stared where Q was pointing, but all he could see was a faint black speck in the distance, almost imperceptible against the dazzling spectacle of the core. They flew closer to the point of darkness and soon he discerned an individual figure sitting cross-legged in the middle of the gigantic fusion reaction. He seemed to be toying with a handful of burning plasma, letting the ionized gas stream out between his fingers. "Another golden afternoon," Q sighed nostalgically, seemingly oblivious of Picard's intense discomfort. "How young and inexperienced I was."

Picard coughed harshly, barely able to breathe owing to the caustic fumes and searing heat. The choking sounds jarred Q from his reminiscing and he peered at Picard dubiously. "Hmm," he pronounced eventually, "perhaps there is such a thing as too much verisimilitude." He snapped his fingers, and Picard felt the awful heat recede from him. He gulped down several lungfuls of cool, untainted air. It still felt warm all around him, but more like a sunny day at the beach than the fires of perdition. "I hope you appreciate the air-conditioning," Q said, "although it does rather spoil the effect."

The effect be damned, Picard thought. He was here as an abductee, not a tourist. He gave himself a moment to recover from the debilitating effects of his ordeal, then focused on the individual Q had apparently brought him here to see. *A young and inexperienced Q?* This he had to see.

Picard flew close enough to discover that the figure did indeed resemble a more youthful version of Q, one not yet emerged from adolescence. To his surprise, something about the teen reminded Picard of Wesley Crusher, another wide-eyed young prodigy, although this boy already had a more mischievous twinkle in his eye than Wesley had ever possessed. "Portrait of the artist as a young Q," Picard's companion whispered with a diabolical chuckle. "Beware." As he and Picard looked on, the young man, dressed as they were in the garb of ancient Greece, isolated a ribbon of luminous plasma, stretching it like taffy before imbuing it with his own supernatural energies so that it shimmered with an eldritch radiance that transcended conventional physics. He pulled his new creation taut, then flung it free. The fiery ribbon shot like a rubber band toward the ceiling of the core and soon passed out of sight. "I had forgotten about that!" Q marveled. "I wonder whatever happened to that little energy band?"

With a start, Picard remembered the inexplicable cosmic phenomenon that had driven Tolian Soran to madness—and, in more ways than one, claimed the life of James T. Kirk. Surely Q couldn't be claiming to have created it during an idle moment in his boyhood, could he? "Q," he began, shocked and appalled at the implications of what he suspected, "about this energy band?"

"Oh, never mind that, Jean-Luc," Q said, dismissing the question with a wave of his hand. "Do try not to get caught up in mere trivia."

Only Q could be so blasé, Picard thought, about the genesis of a dangerous space-time anomaly, and so negligent as to the possible consequences of his actions. He opened his mouth, prepared to read Q the riot act, when the boy came up with a new trick that rendered Picard momentarily speechless. Miniature mushroom clouds sprouted from the teen Q's fingers and he hurled them about with abandon, paying no heed to either Picard or the older Q. A toy-sized nuclear blast whizzed by Picard, missing his head by a hair. "Can he see us?" Picard asked, ducking yet another fireball.

"If he wanted to, of course," Q answered. A nuclear spitwad passed through him harmlessly. "But he has no reason to even suspect we are here, so he doesn't."

I suppose that makes sense, Picard thought. He could readily accept that the older Q was more adept at stealth and subterfuge than his youthful counterpart. He wondered if Q felt the least bit uncomfortable about peeking in on his past like this. "Aren't you at all tempted," Picard asked, "to speak to him? To offer some timely advice, perhaps, in hopes of changing your own past?"

"If only I could," Q said in a surprisingly melancholy tone. Picard was disturbed to see what appeared to be a genuine look of sorrow upon his captor/companion's face. *What kind of regrets,* Picard mused, *can plague such as Q?*

The moment passed, and Q regained his characteristic smugness. "You're not the only species, Jean-Luc, that worries incessantly about preserving the sanctity of the timeline. If changing one human life can start a historical chain reaction beyond any mortal's powers to predict, imagine the sheer universal chaos that could be spawned by tampering with a Q's lifetime." He shuddered, more for effect than because of any actual chill. "Remind me to tell you sometime about how your own Commander Riker owes his very existence to a momentary act of charity by one of my contemporaries. It's quite a story, although completely irrelevant to our present purposes."

Picard hoped that Q was exaggerating where Will Riker was concerned, but he saw Q's point. Various ancient theologians throughout the galaxy, he recalled, had argued that even God could not undo the past. It was comforting to know that Q recognized the same limitation, at least where his own yesterdays were concerned.

Picard took a closer look at the adolescent figure not too far away. "What is he . . . you . . . doing now?"

Before their eyes, the teen Q rose to his feet, dusted some stray solar matter from his bare knees, and stretched out his arms. Suddenly he began to grow at a catastrophic rate, expanding his slender frame until he towered like a behemoth above his older self and Picard. He seemed to grow immaterial as well, so that his gargantuan form caused nary a ripple in the ongoing thermonuclear processes of the star. Soon he eclipsed the great golden sun itself, so that its blazing corona crowned his head like a halo. His outstretched hands grazed the orbits of distant solar systems.

"I don't understand," Picard said. "How can we be seeing this? What is our frame of reference?" The gigantic youth loomed over them, yet he was able to witness the whole impossible scene in its entirety. He tore his gaze away from the colossal figure to orient himself, but all he could see was the sparkle of stars glittering many light-years away. Somehow they had departed from the sun completely without him even noticing. "What is this place? Where are we now?"

"Shhh," Q said, raising a finger before his lips. "You must be quite a pain at a concert or play, Picard. Do you always insist on examining the stage and the curtains and the lighting before taking in the show?" He quietly applauded the boy's grandiose dimensions. "Just go with it. That which is essential will become clear."

I hope so, Picard thought, feeling more awestruck than enlightened. *There must be some point to this, aside from demonstrating that Q was as flamboyant and egotistical in his youth as he is in my own time.*

The boy Q inspected his own star-spanning proportions and laughed in delight. It was an exuberant laugh, Picard noted, but not a particularly malevolent one. Picard was reminded of the optimistic, idealistic, young giants in H. G. Wells's *The Food of the Gods,* a novel he had read several times in his own boyhood. Most unexpectedly, he found himself liking the young Q. *Pity he had to grow into such a conceited pain-in-the-backside.*

"I was adorable, wasn't I?" Q commented.

Is that what he wants me to know? Picard thought. *Merely that he was once this carefree boy?* "Even Kodos the Executioner was once a child," he observed dryly. "Colonel Green is said to have been a Boy Scout."

"And Jean-Luc Picard built ships in bottles and flew kites over the vineyards," Q shot back. "Evidence suggests that he may have briefly understood the concept of fun, although some future historians dispute this."

Picard bristled at Q's sarcasm. "If this is some misguided attempt to reawaken my sense of fun," he said indignantly, "might I suggest that your timing could not be worse. Snatching me away while my ship is in jeopardy is hardly conducive to an increased appreciation of recreation. Perhaps you should postpone this little pantomime until my next scheduled shore leave?"

Q rolled his eyes. "Don't be such a solipsist, Jean-Luc. I told you before, this isn't about you. It's about me." His head tilted back and he stared upward at the Brobdingnagian figure of his younger self. "Look!" he exclaimed. "Watch what I'm doing now!"

Without any other warning except Q's excited outburst, the teen Q began to shrink as swiftly as he had grown only moments before. His substance contracted and soon he was even smaller than he had been originally, less than half the height of either Picard or the older Q. But his process of diminution did not halt there, and he quickly became no larger than a doll. Within seconds, Picard had to get down on his knees, kneeling upon seemingly empty space, and strain his eyes to see him. The boy Q was a speck again, as he had been when Picard had first spied him across the immeasurably long radius of the solar core. A heartbeat later, he vanished from sight. Picard looked up at the other Q, who had a devious smile on his face. "Well?" Picard asked, frustrated by all this pointless legerdemain. "He's gone."

"*Au contraire, mon capitaine,*" Q said, waving a finger at the puzzled human. "To Q, there is no zero," he added cryptically. "Let's go see."

In a blink, Picard was somewhere else. It was a strangely colorless realm, a shapeless world of stark black and white without any shading in between. The utter darkness of space had been supplanted by an eerie white emptiness that seemed to extend forever, holding nothing but flying black particles that zipped about ceaselessly, tracing intricate patterns in the nothingness. A slow-moving particle arced toward Picard and he reached out to pluck it from its flight. The black object streaked right through his outstretched hand, however, leaving not a mark or a tingle behind, leaving Picard to wonder whether it was he or the particle that was truly intangible.

He hoped it was the particle. Certainly, he thought, patting himself for confirmation, he felt substantial enough. He could hear his own breathing, feel his heart beating in his chest. He felt as tangible, as real, as he had ever been.

But where in all the universe was he now?

Total silence oppressed him. There were no sounds to hear and no odors to smell. Not even the limbo where Q had first transported him, with its swirling white mists, had seemed quite this, well, vacant. For as far as his eyes could see, there were only three objects that seemed to possess any color or solidity: himself, Q, and a now-familiar young man cavorting among the orbiting particles. Picard watched as the adolescent Q did what he had not been able to do and caught on to one of the swooping particles with his bare hands. Compared with the youth, it looked about the size of a type-1 phaser and completely two-dimensional. It dangled like a limp piece of film from his fingertips.

Picard looked impatiently at the Q he knew. "What are you waiting for? Explain all this, or do you simply enjoy seeing me confused and uncertain?"

"There is nothing simple about that joy at all, Jean-Luc, but I suppose I do have to edify you eventually. This," he said grandly, "is the domain of the infinitesimal. What you see buzzing about you, smaller than the very notion of sound or hue, are quarks, mesons, gluons, and all manner of exotic subatomic beasties. Or rather, to be more exact, they are the *possibilities* of micro-micro-matter, discrete units of mathematical probabilities following along the courses of their most likely speeds and directions. Whether they actually exist at any one specific time or place is open to interpretation."

"Spare me the lecture on quantum theory," Picard said, doing his best not to sound impressed. He hated to give Q the satisfaction of watching him play the dumbstruck mortal, but, if Q was in fact telling the truth about their present location, if they were actually existing on a subatomic level, then it was hard not to marvel at the sights presented to him. "Is that really a quark?" he asked, pointing to the young Q's immaterial plaything. The boy was peering into the thin black object as if he saw something even smaller inside it.

"Cross my heart," his older self said, "an honest-to-goodness quark, not to be confused with that grasping barkeep on you-know-where."

Picard had no idea whom Q was referring to, and he didn't really care. Perhaps the greatest challenge posed by Q, he reflected, was to see past his snideness to the occasional tidbits of actual revelation. Picard took a moment just to bask in the wonder of this uncanny new environment, one never before glimpsed by human eyes. It was sobering to think that, ultimately, everything in existence was composed of these phantom particles and their intricate ballet.

" 'The cloud-capped towers, the gorgeous palaces, the solemn temples, the great globe itself,' " he recited, recalling his precious Shakespeare. " 'Yea, all which it inherit, shall dissolve; and like this insubstantial pageant faded, leave not a rack behind. We are such stuff as dreams are made on.' "

"My goodness, Picard," Q remarked, "are you moved to poetry?"

"Sometimes poetry is the only suitable response to what the universe holds for us," Picard answered. The essential building blocks of matter darted around him like flocks of birds on the wing. "This is fascinating, I admit, but I fail to see the relevance to your earlier warnings and prohibitions. What has this to do with my mission to the galactic barrier?"

"More than you know," Q stated. An hourglass materialized in his hands and he tipped it over, letting the sands of time pour down inexorably. "Keep watching. Here's where things start to get messy."

The boy Q held the quark up in front of him, like a scrap of paper, then thrust his arm into the quark up to his elbow. His hand and lower arm disappeared as if into a pocket-sized wormhole. He dug around inside the quark for a moment, the tip of his tongue poking out of the corner of his mouth in his concentration, until he seized hold of something and yanked it back toward his body. It looked to Picard like he was turning the quark inside out.

Instantly, the entire submicroscopic realm changed around them all, becoming a sort of photo-negative version of its prior self; Picard looked about him to see a dimension of total blackness, lightened only by flying white particles. Black was white and white was black and the young Q gazed goggle-eyed at what he had wrought. "I don't understand," Picard said. "What's happening?"

"Quiet," Q shushed him, his gaze fixed on his younger self, who was whooping and hollering in triumph. He appeared very pleased with himself, unlike the curiously somber Q standing next to Picard. Clearly, this memory held no joy for Q, although Picard could not tell why that should be so. *Am I missing something?* Picard wondered.

"Q!" a booming Voice exploded out of the darkness, startling both Picard and the adolescent Q, but not, conspicuously, the Q Picard was most accustomed to. He knew exactly what was coming.

"WHAT HAVE YOU DONE?" the Voice boomed again.

The boy glanced about guiltily, dropping the now snow-white quark like a hot potato. He struck Picard as the very portrait of a child caught with his hand in the proverbial cookie jar. The inverted quark flopped like a dead thing at the boy's feet, and he tried to kick it away casually, but it stuck to the sole of his sandal. "Um, nothing in particular," he replied to the Voice, trying unsuccessfully to shake the quark from his foot. "Why do you ask?"

"YOU KNOW WHY. YOU ARE TOO YOUNG TO TRIFLE WITH ANTI-MATTER. WHY HAVE YOU DEFIED THE EDICTS OF THE CONTINUUM?"

The Voice sounded familiar to Picard, although its excessive volume made it hard to identify. *Where have I heard it before?* he thought. *And what was that about antimatter?* He surveyed his surroundings another time; was all of this actually antimatter? He was used to conceiving of antimatter as a fairly abstract concept, something tucked away at the heart of warp engines, safely swaddled behind layers of magnetic constriction. It was difficult to accept that antimatter was all around him, and that, contrary to the fundamental principles of physics, no explosive reaction had resulted from his contact with this realm. Antimatter, in any form, was intrinsically dangerous. Small wonder the rest of the Continuum frowned on the young Q's impulsive experiments.

Sheepishness gave way to defiance as the teen Q realized there was no way to escape the blame. "It's not fair!" he declared. "I know what I'm doing. Look at this!" He snatched the telltale quark from his foot and waved it like a flag. "Look all around! I did this—me!—and nothing got hurt. Nothing important, anyway."

"THE WILL OF THE CONTINUUM CANNOT BE FLOUTED."

Without any fanfare, the quantum realm reversed itself, returning to its original monochromatic schema. Once again, inky particles glided throughout a blank and silent void. "I liked it better the other way," the boy Q muttered to himself. Picard glanced at his companion and saw that the older Q was quietly mouthing the same words.

"YOU MUST BE DISCIPLINED. YOU ARE REQUIRED TO SPEND THE NEXT TEN MILLION CYCLES IN SOLITARY MEDITATION."

"Ten million!" the boy protested. "You have to be joking. That's practically forever!" He flashed an ingratiating smile, attempting to charm his way out of hot water. "Look, there's no harm done. How about I just promise not to do it again?"

"THE JUDGMENT OF THE CONTINUUM CANNOT BE QUESTIONED. TEN MILLION CYCLES."

"But I'll be ancient by then!" the young Q said.

"Ouch!" his future self responded.

"MAKE IT SO," the Voice declared, and Picard suddenly realized whom the Voice reminded him of. *Me. The Voice sounds like me.* Was that why Q had always delighted in provoking him, he speculated, or was the similarity merely an unusually subtle joke on Q's part? Either way, it appeared obvious that Q had developed a grudge against authority figures at a very early age.

"Just you wait," the boy vowed bitterly, more to himself than to his oppressor. "One of these days I'll show you what I can really do, you wait and see."

"THE TEN MILLION CYCLES BEGIN NOW," the Voice stated, apparently unimpressed by the youth's rebellious attitude. *Do I really sound that pompous?* Picard had to wonder. *Surely not.*

Staring sullenly at his feet, the young Q vanished in a twinkle of light. Picard could not tell if he had transported himself willingly or if he had been yanked away by the Continuum. He supposed it didn't matter much.

"Believe me, Jean-Luc," Q said, gazing mournfully at the spot his earlier self had occupied, "when I was that young, ten million cycles really did feel like an eternity."

Picard found it hard to sympathize, especially when he was being held against his will while the *Enterprise* faced unknown dangers. "Was this extended flashback really necessary?" he asked. "It comes as no surprise to learn that you started out as a juvenile delinquent."

"Says the man who was nearly expelled from Starfleet Academy—twice," Q replied. "And we're not done yet." He flipped over the hourglass once more, reversing the flow of sand. "This was only the beginning."

There's more? Picard thought. How much longer did Q intend to keep him away from his ship? "No more," he began to protest, but his angry words were swallowed up by another flash of supernatural light, leaving the quarks to continue alone their endless and invisible pavanes.

He was on his way again—to only Q knew where.

Interlude

Lieutenant Reginald Barclay did his best to ignore the ceaseless hum of the Calamarain as he inspected the battered probe, but that was easier said than done. He was all too aware that the steady drone in the background emanated from the same entities, called the Calamarain according to Chief La Forge, that had inflicted the damage he was now evaluating. If they could do this to the molded duranium-tritanium casing, what could they do to ordinary human flesh and blood?

Barclay shuddered, glad that no one was present to witness his attack of nerves. Sometimes his imagination was just a little too vivid for his own peace of mind, even if Counselor Troi tried occasionally to convince him that his rich imagination could be a source of strength rather than a liability, provided he managed to control it rather than the other way around. Unfortunately, that was about the only eventuality he couldn't imagine.

And who wouldn't be worried, now that the captain was missing, too? Abducted by Q, from what Chief La Forge said. Barclay had a great deal of faith in Captain Picard's ability to keep the ship intact despite the numerous—too numerous, as far as Barclay was concerned—hazards encountered in deep space, but how could the captain extricate them from this crisis if he wasn't even aboard? It was enough to make even a Klingon nervous . . . maybe.

The probe, plucked from the Calamarain's grasp moments before its imminent destruction, rested on the floor of Transporter Room Five. Approximately four meters in length, it was a conical, metallic object with a bulbous, multifaceted head constructed of triple-layered transparent aluminum. The matte black finish of the probe was scorched and dented while the once-transparent head, resembling the eye of an enormous insect, appeared to have been partially melted by whatever forces had assailed the probe. The formerly clear sensor windows had clouded over, turning opaque and milky. A fissure along the right side of the cone revealed a sliver of charred circuitry beneath the ruptured hull.

A full-color, three-dimensional picture of a similar crevice opening up along the length of the *Enterprise* itself forced its way into Barclay's mind, but he pushed it away as fast as he could. *That's the way,* he told himself. *Just focus on the job.* He scanned the probe with his tricorder, detecting no significant residual radiation, before gingerly laying his hands on the blasted surface of the mechanism. To his surprise, it felt slightly warm to the touch, despite having been beamed in straight from the cold of interstellar space. He consulted his tricorder again and observed that the metals composing the hull remained agitated at an atomic level, although the degree of ionic activity was swiftly falling off as the disrupted matter restabilized. He recorded the data into the memory of the tricorder and charted its progress for several seconds. The forced acceleration of the atoms within the alloy, along with the resulting stresses of its molecular bonds, were consistent with the sort of tachyon overload La Forge had suggested he look out for. Tachyons definitely seemed to be the Calamarain's weapons of choice, but what kind of harm could they impose on Federation technology, not to mention innocent Starfleet officers?

Convinced that he had learned as much as he could from the torn and toasted exterior of the probe, he proceeded to the next stage of the autopsy, wincing slightly at the more alarming connotations of that term. First, he confirmed that the deuterium microfusion propulsion unit at the rear of the probe was indeed deactivated; fortunately, class-2 sensor probes were not equipped with warp capacity, so he didn't have to worry about any loose particles of antimatter poking a hole into reality as he knew it. Next, using a delicate phaser scalpel, he peeled off a section of the burnt outer casing, exposing the intricate navigational and sensory apparatuses within.

The probe's innards did not look much better than its supposedly protective sheath. Most of the circuitry was fused and useless now. Still, he chipped the carbon scoring away from one of the output ports and plugged a palm-sized data-retrieval unit into the central memory processor in hope of rescuing whatever scraps of information might have survived the tachyon barrage. *There's probably not much left,* he thought glumly, *but here goes nothing.*

Unexpectedly, the retrieval unit whirred to life at once and began humming almost as loudly as the Calamarain themselves. "Hey!" he said out loud to the empty transporter room. Maybe the internal damage wasn't as bad as it looked.

He waited until the unit had recorded all available data onto an isolinear chip, then began dissecting the entire mechanism, methodically extracting the co-processors one at a time, scanning every component with his tricorder to record the extent of the damage (if any), then moving on to the next one. It was slow, laborious work and Barclay soon found himself wishing that Chief La Forge had been able to spare another engineer to assist him at the task.

Not that he was all too eager to return to Engineering, not while there was still a chance he might run into Lem Faal again. That distinguished and ever-so-intimidating scientist still gave him dirty looks every time Barclay had to come by Faal's temporary workstation to check with Mr. La Forge about something or another. *I can't believe I almost wrecked the pulse generator,* he thought, reliving those awful, endless seconds for the one thousandth time. His cheek still burned where Faal *almost* hit him. Barclay knew that he had completely thrown away any chance he had of taking part in the historic experiment, even assuming the Calamarain let the operation proceed as planned. *Another wasted opportunity,* he thought, the latest in a long string of self-administered wounds to his Starfleet aspirations. Counselor Troi insisted that his reputation among his peers wasn't nearly as bad as he feared, but sometimes he wondered if she was just being nice.

At times like this, he thought, his mind wandering somewhat, it was very tempting to sneak away to the nearest holodeck and escape from the stress and humiliations of the real world. Perhaps he could relive some of his greatest holovictories, like defeating Baron Diabolis in Chapter Twenty-Three of *The Quest for the Golden Throne* or outwitting Commander Kruge before the Genesis Planet completely self-destructed. The latter was one of his proudest moments; after seventy-three tries, he'd actually managed to save Spock without sacrificing the original *Enterprise,* which was even better than the real Kirk had been able to do. Perhaps next time he could save David Marcus, too. . . .

No, he thought, shaking his head to clear his mind of past and future fantasies. He had worked too hard to get a handle on his holodiction problem to backslide now, especially when Chief La Forge and the others were depending on him. He refocussed all his concentration on the job at hand, using the phaser scalpel to separate two fused coprocessors, then gently pulled a melted chip out of its slot.

A glint of blue flame peeked out from beneath the slot and Barclay scooted backward on his knees, half-expecting the entire probe to explode in his face like a defective torpedo. When nothing of the sort occurred, he crept back toward the probe, his tricorder outstretched before him. *Funny,* he noted; the tricorder wasn't reporting any excess heat or energy.

There was definitely something there, though: an incandescent blue glow that seemed to come from somewhere deeper within the inner workings of the perhaps-not-totally lifeless probe. Not entirely trusting his instruments, Barclay held up his open palm in front of the mysterious radiance. His skin didn't detect any heat either, but he thought he felt a peculiar tingling along his nerve endings. He might be imagining the sensations, he reminded himself, painfully aware of his own tendency toward hypochondria. He still remembered, with excruciating accuracy, that time last month when he paged Dr. Crusher in the middle of the graveyard shift, thoroughly convinced that he was dying from an accidental overdose of genetronic radiation and in immediate need of massive hyronalyn treatments, only to discover that there was nothing wrong with him except a slight case of heartburn. Maybe it was best, he concluded, to reserve judgment on the whole question of whether he was really feeling something or not.

But what was causing that glow? It wasn't very intense, more like the bioluminescent gleam of a Rigelian firefly, but he couldn't account for what might be producing the light. *Wait a sec,* he thought, a hypothesis forming in his mind. Maybe bioluminescence was precisely what he was looking at. Excitement overcoming his trepidations, he reached down with both hands and pried out an entire shelf of singed isolinear coprocessors, then looked back eagerly into the cavity he had exposed. There, beneath the discarded rows of coprocessors, was the source of the lambent blue sheen: the newfangled bio-gel packs that were rapidly becoming the next generation of Starfleet data-processing technology. The organic memory cells, designed to accelerate the transfer and storage of information from the probe's sensors, looked surprisingly undamaged compared with the rest of the probe's entrails; they were laid out in a sequence of finger-sized sacs connected by semipermeable silicate membranes that appeared to have remained intact despite the pummeling endured by the probe. Now that the preceding layer of circuitry had been removed, he could see that all of the gel packs were imbued with the same strange, unaccountable incandescence that had first attracted his attention.

Even though the bio-organic technology was relatively new, having been introduced on the ill-fated *U.S.S. Voyager* before that ship ended up in the Delta Quadrant, Barclay knew the packs didn't ordinarily glow this way; they were intended to store information, not energy. Something must have happened to them during the probe's interrupted voyage to the barrier. *You know,* he thought, *the light from the packs kind of looks like the glow of the galactic barrier.*

Inspiration struck him like the blast of a holographic disruptor beam (set well within conventional safety parameters). He quickly scanned the gel-filled sacs to confirm that the curious glow was not an aftereffect of a tachyon overload. This had nothing to do with the Calamarain then, and perhaps everything to do with the probe's brief proximity to the barrier itself.

According to the latest scientific theories, which Barclay had studiously reviewed before getting kicked off the wormhole project, the energies that composed the galactic barrier were largely psychokinetic in nature. He had not programmed his tricorder to scan for any psionic traces before, but now he recalibrated the sensor assemblies to detect emanations along the known psychic frequencies and checked out the probe again.

Voilà, he thought, feeling much as he had when he found the (holographic) lost Orb of the Prophets; there they were, distinct pockets of psionic energy contained within the shining gel packs. Obviously, the bio-neural material within the packs had somehow absorbed small quantities of psionic energy from the barrier. *Is that why the Calamarain attacked the probe,* he wondered. It was even possible that the borrowed psionic power had helped protect the organic components of the probe from the Calamarain's tachyon bombardment.

This is amazing, he thought. Who knew what the full implications of his discovery might be? He couldn't wait to tell Mr. La Forge. Even the thought of facing Professor Faal again didn't seem as daunting as before, at least in the abstract. He double-checked his tricorder readings one more time, then headed for the exit. "Wow," he murmured to himself, proud of his accomplishment and wondering if this heady feeling was what Mr. La Forge or Commander Data felt whenever they made some startling scientific breakthrough. Reality, he discovered, could be even more satisfying than a holodeck.

Who would have thought it?

Twelve

The storm was well and truly upon them.

The wrath of the Calamarain could be felt all over the bridge, much more viscerally than before. The unremitting hum of the plasma cloud had grown into the rumble of angry thunder that battered the ears of everyone aboard. On the main viewer, lightning arced across the prow of the saucer section, striking violently against the forward deflector shields. Riker gritted his teeth as the impact slammed him back into his seat. Sparks flew from the tactical station behind him, singeing the back of his neck, and he spun his chair around in time to see Léyoro snuff out the flames with her bare hands. "Shields down to fifty-one percent," she reported, rerouting the deflector readings through the auxiliary circuitry even as she extinguished the last white-hot spark beneath the heel of her palm.

Riker scowled at the news, the smell of burning circuitry irritating his nostrils. Their defenses were almost halfway down already, and they hadn't even begun to fight back. Hell, they still didn't know why they were under attack. "What in blazes did we do to provoke this?" he asked out loud.

"I am afraid I cannot yet determine that, Commander," Data answered from his station at Ops, "although I believe I am making progress in adapting the Universal Translator to the transmissions from the Calamarain." Deanna stood at the android's side, between Ops and the conn, her hands cupped over her ears in a futile attempt to screen out the roar of the thunder. How could she be expected to sense anything, Riker thought, in the middle of a tempest like this? "The counselor's impressions are proving quite informative," Data stated nonetheless.

"How much more time do you need?" Riker asked. Given a choice, he'd rather talk with the Calamarain than engage them in battle, but the *Enterprise* couldn't take this pummeling much longer. There was only so long he was willing to turn the other cheek.

"That is difficult to estimate," Data confessed. "The intensity of the barrage is now such that it is extremely problematic to filter out what might be an attempt at communication, much like trying to listen to a whistled melody in the midst of a hurricane."

"Give me your best guess," Riker instructed.

Data cocked his head to one side as he pondered the problem. "Approximately one-point-three-seven hours," Data concluded after only a few seconds of contemplation. "As a best guess," he added.

"Thank you, Mr. Data," Riker said, although he would have preferred a significantly smaller figure. At the rate the storm outside was eating away at their shields, the *Enterprise* might not last another hour, unless they started giving as good as they got. *Who knows?* he thought. *Maybe the Calamarain are like the Klingons, and only respect aliens who fight back.*

Then again, he reminded himself, it took the Federation close to a hundred years to come to terms with the Klingon Empire. . . .

A new thunderbolt rocked the ship, tilting the bridge starboard. Next to Data, Deanna staggered and grabbed on to the conn station to maintain her balance. Riker felt a shudder run along the length of the bridge, and possibly the entire starship, before their orientation stabilized. "We have damage to the starboard warp nacelle," Ensign Schultz reported from the aft engineering station.

"Casualties reported on Decks Twelve through Fourteen," another officer, Lieutenant Jim Yang, called out from the environmental station. "No fatalities, though."

Not yet, Riker thought grimly.

"Commander," Leyoro spoke up, echoing his own thoughts, "we can't wait any longer."

"Agreed," Riker said, hitting the alert switch on the command console. He regretted that yet another first-contact situation had to lead to a show of force, but the Calamarain hadn't given them any other choice except retreat. *Let's see what happens when we bite back,* he thought. "All crew to battle stations."

Baeta Leyoro, for one, was raring to go. Her white teeth gleamed wolfishly as she leaned over the tactical controls. "All weapons systems primed and ready," she announced. "Awaiting your command."

"Start with a midrange phaser burst," he ordered. "Maximum possible dispersal." The wide beams would weaken the burst's total force, but Riker saw no obvious alternative. *How the hell,* he thought, *do you target a cloud?*

"Yes, sir!" Leyoro said, pressing down on the controls. Phaser arrays mounted all along the ship's surface fired at once, emitting a unified pulse that spread out from the *Enterprise* in every possible direction. On the screen, Riker saw the pulse emerge as a wave of scarlet energy that disappeared into the billowing, churning mass of the Calamarain. He wasn't sure, but he thought the turbulent cloud became even more agitated when and where it intersected with the phaser burst. The roiling gases swirled furiously, throwing off electrical discharges that crackled against the *Enterprise*'s shields. A clap of thunder rattled Riker all the way through to his bones.

"I sure felt that," he said, raising his voice to be heard over the din. "The question is: did they feel us?" He peered over at Deanna, who had taken her seat beside him the minute he sounded the battle alert. "Any response from out there?"

Deanna shook her head. "I'm not sure. I don't think so. They're already so upset, it's hard to tell."

He nodded. *In for a penny,* he thought, *in for a pound.* "Another burst. Increase phaser intensity to the next level." There was no turning back now. He hoped he could avoid actually killing one or more of the Calamarain, but their alien nature made it impossible to gauge the ultimate effect of the phaser beams. He had no intention of going to maximum strength before he had to, but, one way or another, he was going to make these strange, bodiless beings think twice about attacking this ship.

"Here goes nothing," Leyoro muttered as she fired again. A second burst of directed energy, even more dazzling than before, met the fury of the Calamarain. Once again, it was absorbed into the accumulated plasma almost instantaneously.

The cloud's reaction was just as immediate.

With a howl even louder than any Riker or the others had heard before, the Calamarain shook the *Enterprise* savagely. Riker held on tightly to the armrests of the captain's chair while keeping his jaw firmly set to avoid biting down on his tongue. All about the bridge, crew members bounced in their seats, their minds and bodies jangled by the brutal quaking. Even Data appeared distracted by the disturbance; he looked up from his console with an impatient expression upon his golden face, as if he were anxious for the shaking to cease so he could continue with his work. Riker knew just how he felt.

Mercifully, the worst of the battering subsided after a few moments, although the sentient tempest still raged upon the screen and the thunder reverberated ominously behind every buzz and beep from the bridge apparatus. Riker felt his temples begin to pound in concert with every resounding peal. He searched the bridge to make sure that no one had been injured seriously, then looked back at Deanna. The counselor's face was pale, her eyes wide with alarm.

"They felt that," she gasped. Obviously, she had shared at least a part of the Calamarain's pain.

"I got that impression," he said.

Barclay had hoped that Mr. La Forge would be alone when he reached Engineering, but no such luck. The first thing Barclay saw as soon as he got off the turbolift was the chief engrossed in a heated discussion with Lem Faal, who was the last person Barclay wanted to run into right now. The red alert signals flashing all around the engineering section only added to his trepidation, as did all the busy Starfleet officers hard at work in response to the alert.

Engineering was abuzz with activity, much more so than usual. Every duty station was manned, sometimes by more than one individual. His fellow engineers shouted instructions and queries back and forth to each other as they hastily adjusted and/or monitored illuminated instrumentation panels all along Engineering. Yellow warning signals blinked upon the tabletop master systems display, indicating problems with at least half a dozen vital ship systems, while a whole team of crew members, led by Sonya Gomez, clustered around the towering warp engine core, carefully manipulating the enclosed matter/antimatter reaction. Ordinarily, Barclay could have expected a friendly greeting upon entering Engineering, but at the moment his colleagues were too intent upon their assigned tasks to take note of his arrival. Even Lem Faal seemed too busy with Chief La Forge to spare Barclay another dirty look.

Maybe this isn't the best time, Barclay thought, his previous enthusiasm cooling in the face of the irate Betazoid scientist. He wanted to talk to Mr. La Forge about his discovery in Transporter Room Five, but the chief looked like he had his hands full with the red alert, not to mention Professor Faal. The visiting scientist was obviously upset. He held on to a duranium pylon for support while he argued with La Forge. "I don't understand," he said. "We can't cancel the experiment now. It's ridiculous."

"We're under attack," La Forge pointed out, looking past Faal at the cutaway diagram of the *Enterprise* on the master situation monitor, his attention clearly divided between Faal and the ongoing crisis. "It's a shame, but I'm sure Commander Riker knows what he's doing." He started to turn away from the irate physicist. "Now, you'll have to excuse me while I see what's the matter with our warp engines. You should go back to your quarters."

"This is more than a shame," Faal objected, a faint whistle escaping his throat with every breath. La Forge had discreetly briefed the engineering team on the physicist's medical problems, and Barclay felt sorry for the man despite the bad blood between them. Iverson's disease, like all manner of illnesses and medical threats, terrified Barclay. Even though he knew Iverson's disease was caused by a genetic disorder and was by no means contagious, listening to Faal's tortured breathing still gave him the creeps.

"I've devoted years to this project. It's my last hope for . . . well, I suppose you'd call it immortality." His knuckles whitened as he held on to the pylon with what looked like all his strength. "Your Commander Riker has no right to make this decision. I'm in charge of this experiment. Starfleet specifically told your captain to cooperate with my experiment!"

La Forge shrugged impatiently. "I don't know much more than you do, but I know we can't pull this off in the middle of a combat situation, especially with the captain missing." He hurried over to the master systems display, where Ensign Daniel Sutter stepped aside to permit La Forge access to the primary workstation. La Forge continued to speak to Faal as he simultaneously ran a diagnostic on the graviton polarity generators. "Maybe the Calamarain will go somewhere else and we can try again. Or maybe you'll have to try another section of the barrier."

"No," Faal said, following closely behind La Forge. He sounded ever more sick and distraught. "This is the ideal location. All our sensor readings and calculations prove that. We have to break through the barrier now. I might not get another chance. I don't have much time left. . . ."

Barclay was getting tense just listening to this conversation. He seriously considered turning around and coming back later. *But what if the way the bio-gel packs in the probe absorbed some of the barrier's energy turns out to be important?* He'd never forgive himself if the *Enterprise* got destroyed and it was all his fault; it was bad enough that he'd infected the entire crew with that mutagenic virus a couple of years ago. *Don't live in the past,* Counselor Troi always told him. *Show people what you're capable of.*

Mustering up all his courage, Barclay stepped closer to the chief and Faal. The Betazoid genius spotted him approaching and gave him a murderous look; clearly, he hadn't forgotten the incident with the pulse generator. Or forgiven.

"Excuse me, sir," Barclay said to La Forge. He could feel Lem Faal's baleful glare burning into the back of his neck. "But when you've got a moment, I'd like to talk to you about something I found in that probe you asked me to look at."

La Forge sighed, as if the rescued probe was just one more thing for him to worry about. Barclay immediately regretted bringing it up. "Can this wait, Reg?" he asked with a slight edge of irritation in his tone. "There's an emergency with the warp engines *and* the deflectors."

"Yes. No," he answered. "I mean, I don't know."

Professor Faal lost his patience entirely. "What are you doing, wasting time with this idiot?" Saliva sprayed from his mouth as he gasped out the words. "This is intolerable! I want to speak to Commander Riker!"

Before La Forge could respond, a tremendous clap of thunder echoed through Engineering, drowning out even the constant thrum of the warp core. The floor swayed beneath Barclay's feet and he found himself stumbling down a sudden incline that hadn't existed an instant before, bumping awkwardly into no less than Professor Faal himself. *Just kill me now,* he thought.

La Forge frowned as the floor gradually leveled out again. "This isn't good," he said. Circuit patterns rotated in his ocular implants as he concentrated on the tabletop display, taking stock of the situation. "I can't waste any more time with this. Reg, make sure the professor gets back to his quarters okay, then head back here. We'll talk about the probe later." Without a backward glance, he stalked across Engineering toward the warp core, issuing orders as he went. "Sutter, divert impulse power to the subspace field amplifiers. Ortega, keep an eye on the EPS flow. . . ."

Why me? Barclay thought, left alone with Lem Faal. *Couldn't someone else—anyone else—escort Faal? He already hates me enough.* But La Forge was in charge; he had to keep his eyes on the big picture. "Yes, sir," Barclay said dutifully, if less than enthusiastically. "Please come with me."

Faal ignored him entirely, chasing after Geordi. "You can't do this, La Forge," he said, his wheezing voice no more than a whisper. "The barrier is bigger than some pointless military exercise. We can't lose sight of that. The experiment is all that matters!"

But La Forge, determined to inspect the warp engine power transfer conduits, would not be distracted. "Reg," he called out, exasperated, "if you could take care of this?"

I can't let Mr. La Forge down, Reg thought, taking Faal gently but firmly by the arm. "Please come along, Professor." Part of him felt guilty about bullying a sick man; another part was greatly relieved that Faal wouldn't be able to put up much resistance.

Physically, that is. The scientist's vocal indignation showed no sign of abating. "Let go of me, you incompetent cretin! I insist on seeing Commander Riker."

Barclay had no idea where Riker was. On the bridge, he assumed, coping with the latest ghastly emergency. *There you go again,* he chastised himself, *leaping to the worst possible conclusion.* But he couldn't help it. The flashing red alert signals and blaring sirens ate away at his nerves like Tarcassian piranha. A dozen nightmarish scenarios, ranging from an uncontrolled plasma leak to a full-scale Q invasion, raced through his mind. He tried to dismiss his fears as irrational and unfounded, but with only partial success. *An angry Q could do anything,* he thought, *anything at all.* Still, he somehow managed to get the professor away from La Forge and into the turbolift. *Let me just get Faal stowed away safely. Then I can report my findings on the probe.* "Which deck are your quarters on?" he asked.

"Seven," Faal said grudgingly, still visibly incensed. Unable to stand upright on his own, he had to lean back against the wall of the lift. Something wet and clotted gurgled in his lungs. Barclay tried not to stare at the silver hypospray Faal removed from his pocket. *It's not contagious,* he kept reminding himself. *It's not.*

The turbolift came to a stop and the doors whooshed open, revealing an empty corridor leading to the ship's deluxe guest quarters, the ones reserved for visiting admirals and ambassadors. *Nothing but the best for the winner of the Daystrom Prize,* Barclay thought, wondering how much larger the suite was than his own quarters on Level Eleven. "Here we are," he announced, grateful that Faal had not raised more of a fuss once they left Engineering. *I'll just drop him off, then hurry back to Mr. La Forge.* He still needed to tell the chief about the psionic energy the probe had picked up.

"Just give me a minute, Lieutenant," Faal said. His hypospray hissed for an instant, and the debilitated scientist grabbed on to the handrail for support. His chest rose and fell slowly as he choked back a rasping cough. Barclay looked away so as not to embarrass the professor.

The next thing he knew a pair of hands shoved him out of the lift compartment into the hall. Surprised and befuddled, he spun around in time to see the doors sliding shut in front of his face. For one brief instant, he glimpsed Faal through the disappearing gap in the door. The Betazoid grinned maliciously at him. The doors came together and the lift was on its way.

Oh no! he thought. He immediately called for another lift, which arrived seconds later, and he jumped inside. *I can't believe I let him do that. I can't even keep track of one sickly Betazoid.* He didn't know how he was ever going to look Geordi La Forge in the eyes again. *Just when I thought I was really on to something, what with the probe and all, I have to go and do something like this!*

"Destination?" the turbolift inquired when Barclay didn't say anything at first. The prompt jogged his mind. Where could Professor Faal have run off to? Back to Engineering? Boy, was Chief La Forge going to be annoyed when Faal showed up to pester him again. "Engineering," he blurted, and the lift began to descend. *Maybe I can still stop him before he gets to Mr. La Forge.*

But, wait, he recalled. Hadn't Faal kept demanding to see Commander Riker? Suddenly, he knew what the professor's destination had to be.

The bridge.

"Stop. Cancel previous order. Take me to the bridge. Nonstop."

Please let me get there before Faal can bother the commander too much.

"Fire phasers again," Commander Riker ordered. "Take us up another notch, Lieutenant."

"With pleasure, sir," Leyoro said. A burst of high-intensity phaser beams leaped from the emitter arrays to sting the alien cloud-creatures enclosing the *En-*

terprise. As before, the Calamarain reacted with a thunderous roar that caused the starship to rock like an old-fashioned sailing vessel adrift on a stormy sea.

The floor of the command area rolled beneath Riker's feet as yet another tremor jarred the bridge, reminding him forcibly of the Great Alaskan Earthquake of 2349. *Back on Earth,* he thought, *that would have been at least a five-point-two.* Thank heavens the *Enterprise*-E had been constructed as soundly as it had; otherwise, he'd be expecting the roof to cave in at any moment.

His mind swiftly reviewed the situation. They had hurt the Calamarain with that last phaser burst, but not enough, apparently, to make the vaporous aliens let go of the ship; frothing, luminescent fog still filled the screen of the main viewer. So far, it seemed, all they had done was make the Calamarain even more angry. *That's progress, I guess,* he thought, wondering briefly what Jean-Luc Picard would do in these circumstances before pushing that thought out of his mind. The captain was gone. Riker had to rely on his judgment and experience, as he had many times before. "Tactical status?" he inquired.

"Shields at forty-six percent," Leyoro briefed him. "Phasers armed and ready. Quantum torpedoes locked and loaded."

Riker acknowledged her report with a nod. He wasn't sure what good the torpedoes would do against a living cloud of plasma, especially one located at such close quarters to the *Enterprise,* but it might be worth finding out. "Ensign Berglund," he ordered the officer at the primary aft science station, "locate the area of maximum density within the Calamarain cloud formation."

Ordinarily, he'd assign Data a task like that, but he didn't want to divert the android's concentration from his work with the Universal Translator. Sondra Berglund, a blond Canadian officer with a specialty in advanced stellar spectroscopy, could handle the job just as well with the sensors assigned to her science console. *If we're going to target anywhere,* he decided, *we might as well aim for the highest concentration of Calamarain.*

"Um, I'm afraid that would be us," she reported after a few seconds. "The plasma is most dense around the *Enterprise* and diminishes in volume and intensity the farther the distance from the ship."

That was no good then, Riker realized. He had a vivid mental image of hundreds, if not thousands, of gaseous Calamarain swarming over and around the Sovereign-class starship. *They're ganging up on us, all right,* he thought, *and pounding on the walls.* There was no way he could detonate a quantum torpedo against the Calamarain while the ship remained at the heart of the cloud; they'd be caught within the blast-hazard radius. For all they knew, the matter-antimatter reaction set off by a standard torpedo could harm the *Enterprise* more than the Calamarain. He'd have to hold back on the torpedoes until he put some distance between the ship and its noncorporeal adversaries.

On the main viewer, riotous swells of ionized gas convulsed between the ship and open space. Riker didn't remember the cloud looking anywhere near this stirred up the first time the *Enterprise* encountered the Calamarain several years ago. He still didn't understand what they had done to agitate the amorphous entities. Q wasn't even aboard anymore!

His temples throbbed in time with the thunder outside. His gaze darted over to Deanna, who looked like she was having an even harder time. Her eyes were shut, her face wan and drawn. He assumed she was still in touch with the Calamarains' pain and anger, and it tore at his heart to see her under such strain. Between the tumult on the bridge and the damage they had inflicted back on their foes, Deanna was getting lambasted from both sides.

Hold on, imzadi, he thought. *No matter what happens next, this can't go on much longer.*

Her lids flickered upward and she met his eyes. A thin smile lifted her lips. Riker knew that even if his actual words hadn't gotten across to her, his message definitely had. There was a Klingon term, he recalled, for such an instance of wordless communication in the midst of battle, but what exactly was the word again? *Tova'dok.* That was it, he recalled. He and Deanna were sharing a moment of *Tova'dok.*

Their private communion did not last long. With renewed ferocity, the unleashed power of the Calamarain slammed into the ship, causing the bridge to lurch to port. Behind him, at the engineering station, Ensign Schultz lost his balance and tumbled to the left, smacking his head into the archway over a turbolift entrance. Berglund hurried to assist him.

"Everyone okay back there?" Riker called out over the crashing thunder.

"I think so," Schultz answered. Riker glanced back over his shoulder to see a nasty cut on the young man's scalp. A trickle of blood leaked through his fingers as he held his hand to his head. Undaunted, Schultz headed back to his post. Riker admired his spirit, but saw no reason to risk the ensign unnecessarily.

"Report to sickbay, mister," Riker ordered. "Berglund, take over at engineering." The overhead lights dimmed momentarily, more evidence of the duress imposed on the ship by the Calamarain; Ensign Schultz wasn't the only resource on the *Enterprise* that had been knocked out of commission.

"Shields at forty-one," Leyoro updated him as Schultz took the turbolift from the bridge. Riker wished he could have sent someone with the wounded ensign to ensure that he got to sickbay, but he couldn't spare anyone from the bridge while they remained besieged by the Calamarain.

"Understood," he said. No warp engines. Minimal shields. And, so far, no significant damage to the Calamarain. Their situation was getting worse by the moment. "Data, how are you doing on that translator?"

Data looked up from his computations. "Significant headway has been made; in fact, I believe I have identified a specific wave pattern that translates to something close to an expression of pain." His voice acquired a regretful tone. "Unfortunately, I estimate that I still require as much as one-point-two-zero hours before I can reliably guarantee actual communication with the Calamarain."

That might not be good enough, Riker thought.

Before he could open his mouth, though, he heard the turbolift whish open behind him. At first, he thought it might be Robert Schultz, stubbornly refusing to abandon his post, but then he heard the impassioned voice of Professor Faal. "What's happening?" he asked frantically. "What are you doing?"

Damn, Riker thought. This was the last thing he needed. Deanna looked distressed as well by the Betazoid scientist's unexpected arrival. He peeked at Deanna, recalling her concerns about the doctor's stability and motives. She raised one hand before her face, as if to fend off the disruptive emotions emanating from Faal. *No surprise there,* Riker thought. He imagined that the professor was throwing off plenty of negative feelings.

A moment later, the turbolift doors opened again, revealing an abashed Reg Barclay. "I'm s-sorry, Commander," he stammered, his Adam's apple bobbing nervously, "but the professor insisted, sort of." His eyes bulged and his jaw fell open as his gaze fell upon the frothing plasma storm upon the main viewer.

"Yes," Faal seconded. His face was flushed, his wild brown eyes crazed with anxiety. "I have to talk to you, Commander. It's more important than you can possibly realize."

"Commander?" Leyoro asked, still determined to engage the enemy despite the lack of any tangible results. The nonstop reverberations of the Calamarain rolled over the bridge like a series of sonic booms. The red alert signals flashed like beacons in the night.

Riker decided to get the confrontation over with; Faal wasn't going to like what he had to say, but perhaps he could be made to see reason. He rose from the captain's chair to face the celebrated physicist. Faal's body was trembling so hard that Riker feared for his health. The man's breathing was shallow and rapid, and he seemed to be having trouble standing; Faal tottered unsteadily on shaky feet. Riker's hand drifted over his combadge, ready to summon Dr. Crusher if necessary.

"I regret to inform you, Professor, that I've made the decision to abandon the experiment due to hostile activity on the part of the Calamarain." He saw no reason to alarm the doctor by detailing the full particulars of their danger; instead, he reached out to brace up the ailing scientist. "I'm sorry, but that's the only prudent choice under the circumstances."

Faal batted Riker's arm away. "You can't do that!" he snapped. "It's completely unacceptable. I won't hear of it. The captain's orders came straight from Starfleet Command." A fit of coughing attacked Faal, bending him all the way over. Faal dosed himself with his ubiquitous hypospray, then staggered over to the empty chair Riker usually occupied and collapsed down onto it. "The barrier," he gasped. "That's all that matters."

The floor beneath Riker's boots tilted sharply, nearly knocking him off balance. Lightning flashed through the storming plasma cloud upon the main viewer, the glare of the thunderbolt so bright that it overloaded the safety filters on the screen and made him squint. "The Calamarain seem to disagree."

"Then destroy them!" Faal urged from the chair, squinting at the control panel in front of him as if he were determined to launch a volley of photo torpedoes himself. Wet, mucous noises escaped from his lungs. "Disintegrate them totally. This is a Federation starship. You must be able to dispose of a pile of stinking gases!"

Riker was shocked by the man's bloodthirsty ravings. "That's not what we're here for," he said forcefully, "and that's not what this ship is about." He pitied Faal for his failing health and frustrated ambitions, but that didn't condone advocating genocide. "Mr. Barclay, return Professor Faal to his quarters."

"No!" Faal wheezed. He tried to stand up, but his legs wouldn't support him. Barclay hurried around to Faal's side, but Faal just glared at him before shouting at Riker again. "I won't go! I demand to be heard!"

"Shields down to thirty-four percent," Leyoro interrupted. "Shall I call Security to remove the professor?"

"Do it," Riker ordered. Lieutenant Barclay, wringing his hands together, looked like he wanted to sink through the floor. Riker turned his back on both the irate scientist and the embarrassed crewman. He had more important things to deal with.

Like saving the *Enterprise*.

Thirteen

Cool night air blew against Picard, chilling him. Far beneath him, moonlight from no less than two orbiting satellites reflected off the shimmering surface of a great expanse of water. *Where am I?* he thought, trying to orient himself.

He and Q were no longer in the subatomic realm they had exited only a heartbeat before, that much was certain. Without even knowing where he truly was, he could tell that this was more like reality as he knew it. The coolness of the breeze, the taste of the air, the comforting tug of gravity at his feet, all these sensations assured him that he was back in the real world once more. But where and, perhaps more important, when?

He quickly took stock of his surroundings. He, along with Q, appeared to be standing on some sort of balcony overlooking a precipitous cliff face that dropped what looked like a kilometer or so to the still black waters of an enormous lake or lagoon. The balcony itself, as green and lustrous as polished jade, seemed carved out of the very substance of the cliff. As Picard leaned out over the edge of a waist-high jade railing, intricately adorned with elaborate filigree, he saw that similar outcroppings dotted the face of the precipice, each one packed with humanoid figures, some looking out over the edge as he was, others dining comfortably at small tables as though at some fashionable outdoor café. A sense of excitement and anticipation, conveyed by the hubbub of a hundred murmuring voices, permeated the atmosphere. Picard got the distinct impression that he and Q had arrived just in time for some special occasion.

Jade cliffs. Two moons. A gathering of hundreds in caves dug out of the face of a great, green cliff. The pieces came together in his mind, forming a picture whose implications left him reeling. *"Mon dieu!"* he gasped. "This is Tagus III. The sacred ruins of the ancient cliff dwellers!"

"Well, they're not exactly ruins at the moment, Jean-Luc," Q said casually, "nor are they really all that ancient." Picard's self-appointed tour guide sat a few meters behind him at a circular table set for two. Q sipped a bubbling orange liquid from a translucent crystal goblet and gestured toward the empty seat across from him. A second goblet rested on the jade-inlaid tabletop, next to a large copper plate on which were displayed strips of raw meat, swimming in a shallow pool of blue liquid that could have been sauce or gravy or blood for all Picard knew. He didn't recognize the delicacy, nor did he expect to if this alien time and place was truly what it appeared to be.

The jade pueblos of Tagus III, he marveled, *as they must have been nearly two billion years ago.* He had studied them for years, even delivered the keynote speech at an archaeological conference devoted to the topic, but he had never expected to witness them in person, let alone in their original condition. The Taguans of his own time had strictly forbidden any outsiders to visit the ruins, keeping them off-limits to archaeologists and other visitors ever since the Vulcans conducted their own ill-fated dig on the site over a decade before. The ban had frustrated a generation of scholars and historians, including Picard himself, for whom the celebrated ruins remained one of the foremost archaeological mysteries in the Alpha Quadrant. Possibly the oldest evidence of humanoid civilization in the galaxy, at least prior to the groundbreaking and still controversial work of the late Professor Richard Galen, the ruins on Tagus III had provoked literally millennia of debate and speculation. Before the Taguans decided to deny the site to offworlders, there had been at least 947 known excavations, the first one dating back to 22,000 years ago, almost 18,000 years before the rise of human civilization on Earth. The legacy of the ancient beings who first made their mark on this very cliff had puzzled and intrigued the galaxy since before human history began.

And here he was, visiting in the flesh a wonder of immeasurable age that he had read about ever since he was a small child in Labarre. Picard recalled that once before Q had offered to show him the secrets of Tagus III, the night before Picard was to speak at that prestigious archaeological conference. Seldom had he ever been so tempted by one of Q's insidious propositions, although he had ultimately found the strength to reject Q's offer, both out of respect for the Taguans' deeply held convictions and his own habitual suspicions as to Q's true motives. He'd be lying to himself, however, if he didn't admit just how enticing the prospect of actually setting foot on the site had been.

Now that he really was here, he could not resist trying to absorb as many sights and sounds as he was able. No matter the circumstances of his arrival, and despite his compelling desire to return to his ship as expeditiously as possible, the archaeologist in him could have no more turned away from this once-in-a-lifetime opportunity than the starship captain could have accepted a desk job at the bottom of a gravity well. He had to witness all there was to see.

Besides, he rationalized, the Taguans' twenty-fourth-century mandate against visiting aliens would not go into effect for a couple of billion years or so. . . .

He took a closer look at the people crowding the balconies beside and below him. Whether the Taguans of his own time were actually descended from those who had left their presence marked upon these cliffs, as they steadfastly maintained, or whether they represented a subsequent stage of immigration or evolution, as suggested by the findings of the Vulcan expedition of 2351, was a question greatly debated in the archaeological community. Indeed, it was this very issue that had inspired the modern Taguans to close off the ruins to outsiders, in an attempt to protect their vaunted heritage from the "lies and fallacies" of non-Taguan researchers.

Judging from what he saw now, it appeared that the Vulcans were correct after all. The Taguans he knew were characterized by turquoise skin and a heavy layer of downy white fur. In contrast, the figures populating this historical vista, clad in revealing silk garments of diverse hues, looked quite hairless, with smooth, uncovered flesh whose skin tones ranged from a pale yellow to a deep, ruddy red. Their faces were remarkably undifferentiated from each other, bearing only the essential basics of humanoid features, without much in the way of distinguishing details. Two eyes, a nose, a mouth, a vague suggestion of lips and ears. The vague, generalized visages looked familiar to Picard, but it took him a moment to place them.

Of course, he realized after a quick search through his memory. The inhabitants of ancient Tagus bore a distinct resemblance to the unnamed humanoids who had first spread their genetic material throughout the galaxy some four billion years before his own era. He well remembered the holographic image of the original, ur-humanoid who had greeted him at the completion of his quest to finish the work of

Professor Galen. Could it be that the people of the jade cliffs were the direct descendants of those ancient beings who had indirectly contributed to the eventual evolution of the human race, the Klingons, the Vulcans, the Cardassians, and every other known form of humanoid life? If so, then the ruins on modern-day Tagus were even more important than he had ever believed.

A thought occurred to him, and he turned from the railing to address Q, who took another sip from his goblet. "Why aren't they noticing us?" Picard asked. He explored his own very human features with his hand. They felt unchanged. Looking down, he felt relieved to see that his Grecian garments had been replaced by his familiar Starfleet uniform. "We must stand out in the crowd. In theory, Homo sapiens has not even evolved yet."

"To their eyes, we look as they do," Q explained. He drained the last of his drink, then refilled the cup simply by looking at it. "Given your own limited ability to adapt to new forms, I'm letting you stick with the persona you're accustomed to. I hope you appreciate my consideration."

"But this is what the ancient Taguans looked like?" Picard asked, gesturing at the crowds swarming over the cliff face.

"Actually, they called themselves the Imotru," Q stated, "but, yes, this is no illusion or metaphor. Aside from you and I, you're seeing things exactly as they were." Q's face remolded itself until he looked like another Imotru. Only the mischievous glint in his eyes remained the same. "See what I mean?" He blinked, and his customary features returned.

The peal of an enormous gong rang across the night, and a hush fell over the scene as the buzz of countless conversations fell silent. Picard could feel a sense of acute expectation come over the scene, drawing him back to the railing overlooking the great lake. Something was obviously about to happen; the teeming throng of Imotru assembled along the cliff were waiting eagerly for whatever was to come.

A spark of light way down upon the surface of the lagoon caught his attention. Picard heard a hundred mouths gasp in anticipation. A moment later, a string of torches ignited above the black, moonlit water, their flames reflected in a series of mirrors arranged around the torches, which formed a hexagonal pattern, cordoning off an open stretch of water, about seventy meters across, in the direct center of the dark lake. The polished mirrors reflected the light inward so that this single swatch of rippling water was illuminated as if by the afternoon sun, while the rest of the lagoon remained cast in shadow. A single swimmer, holding aloft the glowing brand she must have used to light the torches, floated amid the brightly lit pool she had created. With a dramatic flourish, she doused the brand to a smattering of cheers and stamping feet.

Was that it? Picard thought, peering down at the lighted hexagon demarcated by the torches and mirrors. Based on the crowd's reaction, he suspected not. There was still that keen sense of anticipation in the air, an almost palpable atmosphere of mounting excitement. Somehow he knew that what he had just witnessed was merely a prelude, not the main event.

Most of the assembled Imotru, he observed, were now looking upward, eagerly searching the moonlit sky for . . . what? An image from an ancient jade bas-relief, meticulously reproduced in the Federation database, popped into his head just as a thrilling possibility presented itself. *No,* he thought, disbelieving his own good fortune, *surely we couldn't have arrived in time for that!*

A roar rose from the crowd. Dozens of seated Imotru leaped to their feet, including Q, who joined Picard by the railing. "Look up, Jean-Luc," he whispered. "Here they come."

Picard needed no urging. He strained his eyes to spot the sight that had electrified the assemblage, the sight whose true nature he could scarcely bring himself to believe. *It must be them,* he thought. *It couldn't be anything else, not here in this place and time.*

Sure enough, his eyes soon discerned a flock of winged figures on the horizon, soaring toward them. The Imotru cheered and stomped their feet so heavily that Picard feared for the safety of the jade balconies, even though he knew that some of them had endured even into the twenty-fourth century. He found himself stamping his own boots, caught up in the fervor of the crowd. The winged figures drew ever nearer, much to the delight of the onlookers upon the cliff. "They've been gliding for two full days," Q commented, "since taking flight from the peak of Mount T'kwll."

Picard no longer doubted what he was about to behold. He could only marvel at the amazing twist of fate that had granted him this unparalleled chance to see a timeworn legend made flesh. "The fabled Sky Divers of Tagus III," he whispered, his voice hushed. If this was no mere trick of Q's, then he was about to make the most astounding archaeological discovery since Benjamin Sisko found the lost city of B'hala on Bajor.

Within moments, the fliers were near enough that he could see that, as he had hoped, they were in fact dozens of youthful Imotru men and women, borne aloft by artificial wings strapped to their outstretched arms. Silver and gold metallic streamers trailed from their wrists and ankles, sparkling in the moonlight. Were the wings made of some unusual gravity-resistant substance, Picard wondered, or were the Imotru lighter than they appeared, perhaps gifted with hollow bones like birds? Either way, they presented a spectacular sight, silhouetted against the twin moons or glittering in the night like humanoid kites.

The Sky Divers soared overhead, swooping and gliding in complex feats of aerial choreography. Each flier, he saw, gripped a shining blade in one hand, just as they did on the fragmentary bas-relief Picard now recalled so well. Despite the graceful ballet taking place above, his gaze was invariably drawn back to the dark waters at the base of the cliff—and the lighted regions within the radiance of the torches and mirrors. He felt his heart pounding, knowing what had to come next. His eyes probed the rippling surface of the lake, hunting for some sign of what lurked beneath. *Perhaps that part of the legend is just a myth,* he thought, unsure whether to feel disappointed or relieved. Professor Galen, he recalled, had theorized that the Sky Divers were no more than a symbolic representation of cultural growth and entropy.

Then it began. A single flier, chosen through some process Picard could only guess at, used his silver blade to sever the straps binding him to his wings while the crowd below bellowed its approval. The shed wings drifted away aimlessly, slowly spiraling down like falling leaves, as the young Imotru plunged toward the water below with frightening speed.

Trailing golden ribbons behind him, the diver splashed headfirst into the lake below, landing squarely within the brightly lit boundaries of the hexagon. On a hundred balconies, Imotru whooped and stamped wildly. Things had clearly gotten off to a good start as far as the crowd was concerned. Down in the hexagon, the triumphant diver kicked to the surface and impulsively embraced the lone swimmer who had waited there. His joy and exuberance were obvious to Picard even from more than a kilometer away.

One by one, following some prearranged signal or sequence, more gliders fell from the sky. The second diver used her arms and legs to guide her descent, also landing safely within the torch-lit target zone. The audience cheered again, although slightly less wholeheartedly than they had before. Still, the woman joined the other two Imotru in their celebration, splashing happily within the golden glow of reflected light.

The third diver looked less fortunate, his downward trajectory carrying him away from the charmed hexagon. Too late, he threw out his arms and legs, striving to alter his course, but his efforts were in vain. The entire crowd held its breath, and, for a second or two, Picard feared the young man would be scorched by the dancing flames of the torches.

Before he came within reach of the flames, however, an enormous serpentine head broke the surface of the black waters and snapped at the falling youth. Water streamed off its scaly hide and a slitted yellow eye fixed on the falling youth. A forked, sinuous tongue, larger than a man's arm, flicked at the sky. Ivory fangs flashed in the moonlight and Picard saw a splash of azure blood burst from the diver before both predator and prey disappeared beneath the waves churned up by the creature's shocking appearance.

Just like on the jade artifact, Picard thought, saddened but not too surprised by what had transpired. Apparently the myth of the Sky Divers was all too true, up to and including the Teeth of the Depths. *So much for mere symbolic interpretations,* he thought.

And still the gliders cut their wings free, undeterred by the grisly fate of their cohort. Toward the waiting lake they dropped like Icarus, some attempting to steer their falls, others simply trusting to fate. Looking carefully, Picard saw more reptilian heads rising from the murky waters outside the protective torches, drawn no doubt by the scent of blood and the splashing of the defenseless bodies. Only within the illuminated hexagon did the divers appear to be safe. Those who hit the water within its confines floated merrily, crowing and cavorting as only those who have barely escaped death can rejoice. Those who plummeted beyond the light of the torches were quickly dragged under by the voracious predators.

"The trick," Q said casually, as though discussing some minor athletic competition, "is to miss the flames and the snapping jaws. The faster the fall, the greater the risk—and the glory." He applauded softly, whether for the divers or the serpents Picard was afraid to guess. "Like I told you a few years back, they really knew how to have fun here back in the good old days." Wandering back toward the table, Q plucked a strip of raw meat from the copper plate and tossed it over the edge of the balcony. As Picard watched aghast, similar scraps flew from balconies all around him, so it looked like it was raining blue, bleeding strips of meat. "The treats are to distract the snakes from the divers," Q explained, "or to incite the snakes to an even greater frenzy. I can't remember which."

Rather than watch the fierce serpents claim their prey, Picard focused on the jubilant survivors within the hexagon. "They're safe now," he said, "but how will they escape from the lake?"

"Oh, the snakes are strictly nocturnal," Q told him. "They'll be able to swim to shore in the morning, after what will undoubtedly be the greatest night of their lives."

Picard was unable to tear his gaze away from the barbaric spectacle. Before his eyes, what seemed like an unending string of young people gambled with their lives, some joining the riotous celebration within the six-sided sanctuary, others torn asunder by the hungry serpents. To cope with the awful and awe-inspiring pageant, he forced himself to think like an archaeologist. "What is this?" he asked. "A religious sacrifice? An initiation rite? A means of population control?" Turning away from the rail, he confronted Q. "What in heaven's name is the purpose of this appalling display?"

"Don't be so stuffy, Jean-Luc," Q said, offering Picard a strip of meat dripping with blue gore. Picard refused to even look at the edible. With a sigh, Q tossed it off the balcony himself. "They do it for the thrill. For the sheer excitement. It's all in fun."

Picard tried to grasp the notion. "You're saying this is simply some form of sports or theater? A type of public entertainment?"

"Now you're getting closer," Q confirmed. "Think of the matadors or bull dancers of your own meager history. Or the 'Iwghargh rituals of the Klingons. With a slightly higher body count, of course."

It was almost too much to digest. Deep in thought, Picard pulled out a chair and sat down opposite Q. "This is fascinating, I admit, and, you're right, no worse than various bloodthirsty chapters of early human history. The gladiatorial violence of the Roman coliseums, say, or the human sacrifices of the ancient Aztecs. I can't say I regret having viewed this event. Still, seeing it in person, it's hard not to be appalled by the profligate waste of life."

"But you short-lived mortals have always taken the most extraordinary and foolish risks to your brief existences," Q said. "Diving off cliffs, performing trapeze acts without a net, flying fragile starships into the galactic barrier . . ."

Q's coy reference to the *Enterprise* jolted Picard, yanking the status of his ship back into the forefront of his consciousness. Never mind this time-lost scenario, what was happening to Riker and his crew back in his own era, and how soon was this game of Q's likely to end? "Is that why we're here?" he asked, thinking that perhaps he had seen through Q's current agenda. "It seems rather a roundabout way to make your point."

"If only it were that easy," Q replied, "but that diverting little entertainment out there is far from the most important event transpiring at this particular moment in time. Permit me to call your attention to that individual dining on that balcony over there." Q pointed past Picard at a jade outcropping located several meters to the left, where he saw a solitary Imotru watch in fascination as the Sky Divers tempted fate with their death-defying descents. "Recognize him?"

What? Q's question puzzled Picard. How could he be expected to recognize a being who had died billions of years before he was born? "He's Imotru, obviously, but beyond that I don't see anything familiar about him."

Q looked exasperated. "Really, Picard, you can be astonishingly dim sometimes." He rolled up his sleeves and extended both hands toward the figure on the other balcony. He wiggled his fingers as if casting a spell. "Perhaps this will make things easier."

Wavy brown hair sprouted from the Imotru's shining skull, but he appeared not to notice. His features remolded themselves, becoming more human in appearance, even as he continued to observe the divers as if nothing were happening. His eyebrows darkened, his lips grew more pronounced, until Picard found himself staring at a very familiar acquaintance, albeit one still clad in Imotru garb. "It's you," he said to Q. "You were disguised as an Imotru."

"I'm disguised every time we meet," Q pointed out. "Surely, you understand that my true form no more resembles a human being than it does an Imotru."

So we're still exploring Q's own past, Picard realized. Examining the scene, he saw that the other Q looked noticeably younger than the Q who had brought him here, although not nearly as youthful as the boyish Q who had toyed with antimatter in the micro-universe. This Q had left adolescence behind and seemed in the first full flush of adulthood, however those terms applied to entities such as Q. He appeared utterly riveted by the grisly extravaganza put on by the Imotru, lifting a scrap of blue meat from his plate and nibbling on it experimentally while his eyes tracked each and every plunge. The expression on his face, Picard discerned, looked wistful and faintly envious.

"This was the first time I had ever seen anything like this," the older Q said, "but not the last. I came every year for millennia, until their civilization crumbled, the Imotru gradually succumbed to extinction, and the Sky Divers became nothing more than a half-forgotten myth." He watched himself watching the divers. "But it was never quite the same."

"Did you always come alone?" Picard asked. It occurred to him how seldom the young Q seemed to interact with others of his kind. *When I was his age, relatively speaking,* he thought, *I thrived on the company of my friends: Marta, Cortin, Jenice, Jack Crusher . . .*

"Funny you should mention that, Jean-Luc," Q responded, throwing their last shred of blue meat to the serpents. He snapped his fingers and both he and Picard were gone before the bloody scrap even reached the water.

Interlude

The red alert alarms did not go off in the guest quarters, so as not to panic unnecessarily any civilian passengers, but Milo Faal did not need to see any flashing colored lights to know that something was happening. He could sense the tension in the minds of the crew, as he could see the raging plasma storm outside his window and feel the tremors every time the thunder boomed around them.

Milo did his best not to look or think afraid in front of his little sister. Kinya was too young to understand all that was occurring. The little girl stood on her tiptoes, her nose and palms glued to the transparent window, captivated by the spectacular show of light and sound. Milo couldn't look away from the storm, either. He stood behind Kinya with one hand on the arm of a chair and the other one on his sister's shoulder, just in case she lost her balance, while he tried to figure out what was going on.

Most of the crew members whose thoughts he latched on to did not know much more than he did about the churning cloud outside, but he got the idea from some of them that the cloud was actually alive. Did that mean the storm was shaking them around on purpose? He could not repress a shudder at the thought, which transferred itself empathically to Kinya's tiny frame, which began to tremble on its own, even if the little girl was not consciously aware of the source of the anxiety. "Milo," she asked, looking back over her shoulder, "what's wrong?"

"Nothing," he fibbed, but another sudden lurch said otherwise. A half-completed jigsaw puzzle, featuring a striking illustration of a Klingon bird-of-prey, slid off a nearby end table, the plastic pieces spilling onto the carpet. Milo had spent close to an hour working on the puzzle, but he barely noticed the undoing of his efforts. He had more important things to worry about.

Where are you, Dad? he called out telepathically. Lightning flashed on the other side of the window, throwing a harsh glare over the living room. *Dad?* he called again, but his father might as well have been back on Betazed for all the good it did.

Taking Kinya by the hand, and stretching his other arm out in front of him to break any falls, he led her across the living room toward the suite's only exit. If his father would not come to them, he thought, then he was getting pretty tempted to go find their dad. The *Enterprise* was a huge ship, he knew, but it couldn't be too hard to locate Engineering, could it? Anything was better than just sitting around in the quaking guest quarters, wondering what to do next.

He and Kinya approached the double doors leading outside, but the heavy metal sheets refused to slide apart. "Warning," the voice of the ship's computer said. "Passengers are requested to stay within their quarters until further notice. In the event of an emergency, you will be notified where to proceed."

Milo stared in disbelief at the frozen doors. *In the event of an emergency . . . ?* He glanced back at the seething mass of destructive plasma pounding against the hull. If this wasn't an emergency, then what in the name of the Sacred Chalice was it? And how come Dad wasn't stuck here, too?

"Dad?" Kinya picked up on his thoughts. "Where's Daddy, Milo?"

I wish I knew, he thought.

Fourteen

It took Picard a second or two to realize that he and Q had relocated once again, although none too far. The jade cliffs remained intact. The Sky Divers continued their daring plunges to salvation or doom. Even the cool of the evening breeze felt much the same as before. Then he observed that their vantage point had shifted by several degrees; they now occupied another balcony, one perched about ten or eleven meters above their previous locale. "I don't understand," he told Q. "Why have we moved? What else is there to see here?"

"Ignore the floor show," Q advised, "and look at the audience." He lifted an empty saucer from the table and set it glowing like a beacon in the night, using it as a spotlight to call Picard's attention to one specific balcony below them. There Picard saw once more the solitary figure of the youthful Q, enraptured by the life-and-death drama of the ancient Imotru ritual. Before Picard could protest that he had already witnessed this particular episode in Q's life, the beam shifted to another balcony, where Picard was stunned to see both himself and the older Q watching the younger Q intently. "Look familiar?" his companion asked. Speechless, Picard could now only nod numbly. *What is it about Q,* he lamented silently, *that he so delights in twisting time into knots?*

But Q was not finished yet. The spotlight moved once again, darting over the face of the cliff until it fell upon a young Imotru couple dining on a balcony several meters to the right of Picard and Q's new whereabouts. Or at least they looked like Imotru; the harsh white glare of the searching beam penetrated their attempt at camouflage, exposing them to be none other than the young Q one more time, as well as a female companion of similarly human appearance. "It's you," Picard gasped, "and that woman." Although noticeably younger than Picard recalled, the other Q's companion was manifestly the same individual who had recently visited the *Enterprise,* two billion years in the future.

Picard's mind struggled to encompass all he was confronted with. Counting the smirking being seated across from him, there were, what, *four* different versions of Q present at this same moment in time? Not to mention at least two Picards. He kneaded his brow with his fingers; as captain of the *Enterprise,* he had coped with similar paradoxes before, including that time he had to stop himself from destroying the ship, but that didn't make them any easier to deal with. The human mind, he was convinced, was never designed with time travel in mind.

Still, he had no choice but to make the best of it. "What are you and she doing over there?" he asked, contemplating the couple highlighted by the glow of the spotlight.

"If you're referring to my future wife," the Q at his table said, "her name is Q." He beamed at the oblivious couple. "As for what is transpiring, can't you recognize a romantic evening when you see one?"

"I'm not sure I'm prepared to cope with the concept of you dating, Q," Picard said dryly. "Why are we here? Is it absolutely imperative that I share this moment with you?"

"Trust me, Jean-Luc," Q assured him, "all will become clear in time." Another goblet of liquid refreshment occupied the center of the table. Q finished off a cup of orange elixir, then placed the crystal goblet on the tabletop between him and Picard. He tapped the rim of the cup, producing a ringing tone. "Let's listen in, shall we?"

A pair of voices rose from the cup, as though the goblet had somehow become some sort of audio receiver. The voice of the younger Q was unmistakable, although surprisingly sincere in tone. Picard heard none of the self-satisfied smugness he associated with the Q of his own time.

He (eagerly): "Isn't it amazing? Didn't I tell you how wondrous this is? Primitive, corporeal life, risking everything for one infinitesimal moment of glory. Look, the snakes got another one! Bravo, bravo."

She (faintly scandalized): "But it's so very aboriginal. You should be ashamed of yourself, Q. Sometimes I wonder why I associate with you at all."

He (disappointed): "Oh. I was sure you, of all Q's, would understand. Don't you see, it's their very primitiveness that makes it so moving? They're just sentient enough to make their own choices, decide their own destinies." He stared gloomily into his own cup. "At least they know what they want to do with their lives. Nothing's restraining them except their own limitations as a species."

She (conciliatory): "Well, maybe it's not entirely dismal. I like the way the moonlight sparkles on the reptiles, especially when their jaws snap." She placed a hand over his. "What's really bothering you, Q? You're young, immortal, all-powerful . . . a touch undisciplined, but still a member of the Continuum, the pinnacle of physical and psychic evolution. What could be better?"

He (wistful): "It's just that . . . well, I feel so frustrated sometimes. What's the good of having all this power, if I don't know what to do with it? Merely maintaining the fundamental stability of the multiverse isn't enough for me. I want to do something bold, something magnificent, maybe even something a little bit dangerous. Like those foolish, fearless humanoids out there, throwing themselves into gravity's clutches. But every time I try anything the least bit creative, the Continuum comes down on me like a ton of dark matter. 'No, no, Q, you mustn't do that. It's not proper. It's not seemly. It violates the Central Canons of the Continuum. . . .' Sometimes the whole thing makes me sick."

For a second, Picard experienced a twinge of guilt over eavesdropping on the young Q's this way. It felt more than a little improper. Then he remembered how little Q had respected his own privacy over the years, even spying on his romantic encounters with Vash, and his compunctions dissolved at a remarkable rate.

She (consoling, but uncertain): "Every Q feels that way at times." A long pause. "Well, no, they don't actually, but I'm sure you do." She made an effort to cheer the other Q up, looking out at the plummeting Imotru. "Look, two reptiles are fighting over that skinny specimen over there." She shuddered and averted her eyes. "Their table manners are utterly atrocious!"

He (appreciative, aiming to lighten the mood): "You know, I don't think you're half as shocked as you make yourself out to be. You've got an unevolved streak as well, which is why I like you."

She (huffily): "There's no reason to be insulting." She spun her chair around and refused to look at him.

He (hastily): "No, I didn't mean it that way!" Materializing a pair of wineglasses out of thin air, along with a bottle of some exotic violet liqueur, he poured the woman a libation and held it out to her. Glancing back over her shoulder, her slim back still turned on Q, she inspected the gift dubiously. Q plucked a bouquet of incandescent yellow tulips from the ether. "Really, Q, you know how much I respect and admire you."

She (ominously, like one withdrawing a hidden weapon): "Just me?"

He (uncomfortably): "Um, whatever do you mean?"

She (going in for the kill): "I mean that cheeky little demi-goddess out by Antares. Don't think I didn't hear about you and her commingling on the ninth astral plane. I am omniscient, you know. I wasn't going to mention it, presuming I was above such petty behavior, but since you think I'm so unevolved . . . !"

He (defensive): "What would I be doing on the ninth astral plane? This has to be a case of mistaken cosmology. It wasn't me, it was Q. Why, I barely know that deity."

She (unconvinced): "And a fertility spirit, no less! Really, Q, I thought you had better taste than that."

He (desperate): "I do, I do, I promise. I was only trying to broaden my horizons a bit, explore another point of view. . . ." He offered her a strip of succulent meat. "Here, why don't you try feeding the serpents?"

She (chillingly): "I think I want to go home."

Picard laughed out loud. It was almost worth traveling back in time to hear Q put on the spot like this. "That reminds me," he said to the Q sitting across from him, "back during that business in Sherwood Forest, you gave me quite a bad time about my feelings for Vash. You described love as a weakness, and berated me constantly about being 'brought down by a woman,' as I believe you put it." He cocked his head toward the quarreling couple on the next balcony. "I must confess I find your own domestic situation, both here and back on the *Enterprise,* more than a little ironic."

"Don't be ridiculous," the older Q retorted. "You can't possibly compare your farcical mammalian liaisons with the communion, or lack thereof, between two highly advanced intelligences. They're entirely different situations."

"I see," Picard said skeptically, contemplating the scene on the adjacent balcony, where the female Q had just conspicuously turned her back on her companion. "As we ridiculous mammals like to say, tell me another one."

The voices from the goblet argued on, lending more credence to Picard's position. He savored the sound of the younger Q losing ground by the moment.

He: "Fine, go back to the Continuum. See if I care!"

She: "You'd like that, wouldn't you? More time to spend with that pantheistic strumpet of yours. No, on second thought, I'm not going anywhere. And neither are you."

He: "Try and stop me."

She: "Don't you dare!"

Picard eyed Q across the jade tabletop. "Advanced intelligences, you said? I am positively awestruck by your spiritual and intellectual communion. You were quite correct, Q. This excursion is proving more illuminating than I ever dreamed."

"I knew this was a bad idea," Q muttered, a saturnine expression on his face. "I could hardly expect you to sympathize with the perfectly excusable follies of my youth."

Picard showed him no mercy. "I have to ask: what did your ladyfriend over there think of your short-lived partnership with Vash?"

"That?" Q said dismissively. "That lasted a mere blink of an eye by our standards. It was nothing. Less than nothing even." He shrugged his shoulders, remembering. "She was livid."

More livid than she sounds now? Picard wondered. That was hard to imagine.

He: "I should have known you wouldn't appreciate any of this. None of you can."

She: "Maybe that's because the rest of us are perfectly happy being Q. But if that's not good enough for you, then I don't belong here either."

With an emphatic flash, the female Q vanished from the scene, leaving the young Q just as alone as his even younger counterpart a few balconies below. "Our first fight," an older Q explained, "but far from our last."

The abandoned Q looked so dejected that, despite Picard's well-earned animosity toward the being sitting opposite him, he felt a touch of sympathy for the unhappy young Q. "No one understands," he muttered into his cup, completely unaware that his private heartbreak was being transmitted straight to Picard's table. "Just once, why can't I meet someone who understands me?"

His older self looked on with pity and regret. "I believe you mortals have a saying or two," he observed, "about the danger of getting what you wished for." He sighed and pushed the talking goblet away from him. "Too bad you wouldn't coin those little words of wisdom for another billion years or so."

A moment later, the balcony was empty.

Fifteen

Lem Faal was not about to leave the bridge quietly. "I'm warning you, Commander Riker, you'll regret interfering with this operation. My work is my life, and I'm not going to let that go to waste because of a coward who doesn't have guts enough to fight for our one chance to break through the barrier."

"Perhaps," Riker answered, losing patience with the Betazoid physicist despite his tragic illness, "you should worry more about the safety of your children and less about your sacred experiment."

Summoned by Lieutenant Leyoro, a pair of security officers flanked Faal, but the scientist kept protesting even as they forcibly led him toward a turbolift. Claps of thunder from the Calamarain punctuated his words. "Don't lecture me about my children, Riker. Sometimes evolution is more important than mere propagation."

What exactly does he mean by that, Riker wondered. Surely he couldn't be saying what Riker thought he was implying? *Faal's starting to make my dad sound like father of the year.* Even Kyle Riker, hardly the most attentive of parents, never seemed quite so eager to sacrifice his children's well-being on the altar of his overweening ambition. Riker refused to waste any further breath debating the man. If it weren't for the failure of the warp engines, they would have already been long gone by now, whether Faal liked it or not.

The turbolift doors slid shut on Faal and his grim-faced escorts. Riker breathed a sigh of relief. "Mr. Barclay, please take over at the engineering station." Riker wasn't sure what precisely Barclay had to do with Faal's unexpected arrival on the bridge, but now that Barclay was here he might as well replace the injured Schultz.

Faal had no sooner left, however, when a blinding flare at the prow of the bridge augured the sudden return of the baby q. A second flare, instants later, brought the child's mother as well. "Sir?" Barclay asked uncertainly.

"You have your orders, Lieutenant," Riker said, aggravated by yet more unwanted visitors. When had the bridge of the *Enterprise* turned into the main terminal at Spacedock? "Can I help you?" he asked the woman in none too hospitable a tone. *Blast it, I was hoping we'd seen the last of these two.*

The toddler stared wide-eyed at the swirling colors of the Calamarain as they were displayed on the main viewer. "Frankly, I was in no hurry to revisit this ramshackle conveyance," the woman said disdainfully, "but little q insisted. He simply adores fireworks. Perhaps you could fire your energy weapons again?"

"Our phasers are not here to entertain you!" Leyoro snapped, offended by the suggestion. She took her weapons very seriously.

Riker didn't blame her. This was no laughing matter, although he hardly expected a Q to appreciate that. Things kept getting worse, no matter what they tried. A crackle of lightning etched its way across the screen, throwing off discharges of bright blue Cerenkov radiation wherever the electrical bursts intersected with the ship's deflector shields. The rattle of thunder was near-constant now; it almost seemed to Riker that the persistent vibrations had been with them forever. His determined gaze fell upon the female Q and her child. *Hmmm,* he thought. Both Barclay and Geordi seemed to find the malfunction in the warp nacelles pretty inexplicable. Well, he could think of few things more inexplicable than a Q.

He rose from his chair and strode toward the woman. "There wouldn't be any fireworks at all if we weren't dead in the water," he accused. "Is this your doing?"

"You mean your petty mechanical problems?" she replied. "Please, why would I want to go mucking about with the nuts and bolts of this primitive contrivance?" A Calamarain-generated earthquake shook the bridge, and q squealed merrily. "We're simply here as spectators."

Riker considered the female Q. Since her previous visit to the bridge, she had discarded her antique sports attire for a standard Starfleet uniform, as had the little boy. He wondered briefly what they had done in the interim. Did infant Q's require naps? More important, why would this Q want to prevent the *Enterprise* from leaving? The other Q had done nothing but encourage them to turn back.

"Maybe so," he conceded. It was entirely possible that the Calamarain were responsible for the failure of the *Enterprise*'s warp drive, in which case it was even more urgent that they find a way to communicate with the cloud-beings. "But you must know something about Captain Picard. What has your husband done with him?"

"Oh, not that again!" she said in a voice filled with exasperation. "First the doctor, now you. Really, can't you silly humanoids do without your precious captain for more than an interval or two? You'd think that none of you had ever flown a starship on your own."

"We don't want to do without the captain," Riker insisted, ignoring the woman's ridicule. She was sounding more like her mate every minute. "Wherever Q has taken him, he belongs here, on this ship at this moment."

The woman made a point of scanning the entire bridge, as if looking for some sign of Captain Picard's presence, then returned her attention to Riker. "That doesn't seem to be the case," she said with a smirk.

"Shields down to twenty-seven percent," Leyoro reported. A few meters away from Leyoro, a small electrical fire erupted at the aft science station. Ensign Berglund jumped back from the console just as the automatic fire-suppression system activated. A ceiling-mounted deflector cluster projected a discrete forcefield around the flickering blaze, simultaneously protecting the surrounding systems from the flames and cutting off the fire's oxygen supply. Within seconds, the red and yellow flames were snuffed out and Berglund cautiously inspected the damage.

At least something's working right, Riker thought, grateful that the fire had been taken care of so efficiently. Now if he could only get the warp nacelles functioning again . . . ! *Maybe if we shoot our way out of here,* he thought, *without holding anything back?* "Lieutenant Leyoro, target the phaser beam directly in front of us, *maximum* intensity." He had held back long enough; the Calamarain needed to learn that they could not threaten a Starfleet vessel without risking serious repercussions. "If you can disengage from contact with the enemy, Counselor, now would be the time to do it."

Deanna nodded back at him, acknowledging his warning. "Just give me a second," she said, closing her eyes for a heartbeat or two, then opening them once more. "Okay, I'm as prepared as I'll ever be."

"Fire when ready, Lieutenant," Riker ordered. He glared at the turbulent vapors upon the viewer. "I want to see the stars again."

"My feelings exactly," Leyoro agreed. A neon-red phaser beam ploughed through the seething chaos of the Calamarain, cutting an open swath through the iridescent vapors. Riker winced inwardly, hoping he was not burning through scores of Calamarain individuals. *Am I killing separate entities, or merely diminishing the mass of the whole?* He would have to ask Deanna later; right now he didn't want to know. Beside him, Troi bit down on her lower lip as the beam seared past swollen clouds filled with angry lightning, and gripped her armrests until her knuckles whitened; obviously, she had not been able to cut herself off entirely from the emotions of the Calamarain.

"Ooh!" q exclaimed, pointing enthusiastically at the screen. He stuck out his index fingers like gun muzzles, as little boys have done since the invention of firearms across the universe, and red-hot beams leaped from his fingertips to sear two burning holes in the visual display panel. Riker jumped out of his seat to protest, terrified that the playful child would create a hull breach beyond the screen. *Blast it,* he thought. *This is the last thing I need right now.*

Thankfully the female Q was on top of things. With a snap of her fingers, she squelched the child's imitative phaser beams and repaired the damage to the main viewer. "Now, now, darling," she cooed to the boy, "what have I told you about pointing?" Thus chastened, q meekly hid his tiny hands behind his back.

Blast it, Riker thought angrily. The last thing he needed right now were the two Q's and their antics, even though he seemed to be stuck with them. He sank back into the captain's chair and concentrated on the *Enterprise*'s efforts to carve out an escape route. As he had requested, Riker soon saw the welcoming darkness of open space at the far end of the tunnel the phasers had cut through the Calamarain. *Now there's a sight for sore sensors,* he thought. "Straight ahead, Mr. Clarze. Full impulse."

"Yes, sir!" the pilot complied, sounding more than anxious to leave the sentient thunderstorm behind. Riker was gratified to see the distant stars grow brighter as the unscratched viewscreen transmitted images from the ship's forward optical scanners. *Here goes nothing,* he thought, crossing his fingers. Once they were clear of the clouds, perhaps their warp engines would function again.

"Riker to Engineering," he barked, patting his combadge. "Prepare to engage the warp drive at my signal."

"Acknowledged," Geordi responded. "We're ready and willing."

But the Calamarain would not release them so easily. Thick, viscous vapors flowed over and ahead of the ship's saucer section, encroaching on the channel before them. Lightning speared their shields repeatedly, giving them a rough and bumpy ride. To his dismay, Riker saw their escape route narrowing ahead, the gathering cloud front eating away at that tantalizing glimpse of starlight. "Keep firing!" he urged Leyoro, despite an almost inaudible whimper of pain from Deanna. *Hang on,* he told her wordlessly, lending her whatever support his own thoughts could provide. *We're almost out.*

A single scarlet beam shot from the saucer's upper dorsal array. Two hundred and fifty linked phaser emitter segments contributed to the awesome force of the beam, striking out at the enveloping throng of the Calamarain. On the screen, heavy accumulations of ionized plasma steamed away beneath the withering heat of the phaser barrage.

And still the furious cloud kept coming. Despite the unchecked power of the *Enterprise*'s phasers, a roiling flood of incandescent gas poured over them as fast as Leyoro could boil it off with her phasers, if not faster. Riker couldn't help being amazed by the sheer immensity and/or quantity of the creature(s) pursuing them; even on full impulse, it was taking several moments to fly clear of them. He felt like he was trying to outrace an animated nebula.

The choppiness of their headlong flight increased every second. Riker was thrown from one side of the chair to the other as he struggled to ride out the violent squall. There was no way he could have shouted out any additional orders even if he had wanted to; it would have been like trying to converse during the downward plunge of a roller coaster. His stomach rushed up into his throat as the *Enterprise* executed a full 360-degree barrel before stabilizing, more or less, on an even keel.

Additional fires broke out around the bridge, more than the automated system could cope with. Smoke and the smell of burning plastic tickled Riker's nose. At the operations console, Data dealt with a small blaze swiftly and effectively by opening a flap in his wrist and spraying the flames with some of his own internal coolant. Other crew members followed his example, more or less, by resorting to the hand-held fire extinguishers stored beneath each console. Riker took pride in the bridge crew's performance; they had coped with the outbreak of electrical fires without even a single command from him. *You can't beat Starfleet training,* he thought.

Through it all, the baby q appeared to be having the time of his life. He squealed happily as the *Enterprise* careered through the gap in the Calamarain at close to the speed of light. Defying gravity, the boy turned somersaults in the air, occasionally blocking Riker's view of the screen. *Enjoy this ride while you can,* he thought, *because we're not doing this again.*

The child's mother just shook her head in obvious disdain. "Barbaric," she muttered. "Utterly barbaric."

Sorry we couldn't provide a smoother trip, Riker thought sarcastically. Frankly, the female Q's low opinion of the ship was the least of his concerns.

Instead, his attention was focused on the rapidly shrinking opening ahead of them. He could barely see the stars now, only a small black hole in the substance of the Calamarain that looked scarcely large enough for the Sovereign-class starship to squeeze through. *C'mon,* he thought, *faster, faster,* spurring the *Enterprise* on with his mind even though he knew that they could not possibly accelerate any further without their warp capacity. Would they make it through the gap before it closed entirely? It was going to be close.

Ultimately, the ship tore through the advancing edges of the tunnel, leaving frayed tendrils of glowing mist behind it. Staring at the main viewer, Riker saw a vast expanse of interstellar space, bisected briefly by their own crimson phaser beam before Leyoro ceased fire. For the first time in hours, he could no longer hear the discordant thunder of the Calamarain, although that blessed silence would not last long unless they left their gaseous foes far behind them. Riker didn't need to see the input from the rear sensors to know that the Calamarain had to be hot on their heels.

"Riker to La Forge," he ordered, hoping that the damping effect on their warp engines did not extend beyond the boundaries of the Calamarain. "Give me everything you've got."

Sixteen

Years of beaming to and from the *Enterprise* had accustomed Picard to instantaneous travel. Even so, the ease and speed with which Q switched settings remained disconcerting.

The jade cliffs were gone, replaced by crumbling gray ruins that seemed to stretch to the horizon. Toppled stone columns, cracked and fractured, leaned against massive granite blocks that might once have composed walls. Dry gray powder covered the ground, intermixed with chips of broken glass or crystal. Gusts of wind blew the powder about, tossing it against the desolate landscape, while the breeze keened mournfully, perhaps longing for the bygone days when the ancient structures had stood tall and proud. No sign of life, not even vermin, disturbed the sere and lonely ruins.

What is this place? Picard wondered. That which he saw about him reminded him of what was left of the Greek Parthenon after the Eugenics Wars, except on a vastly larger scale. Piles of stone debris blocked his view in most every direction, but he could tell that the original structure or structures had been huge indeed. The ruins seemed to extend for kilometers. He looked upward at an overcast sky, through which a cool, twilight radiance filtered. If ever a ceiling had enclosed any part of the ruins, no trace of it remained, except perhaps in the hundreds of tiny crystal shards that sparkled amid the dust.

Picard blinked against the wind as it cast the sand into his face, and he stepped behind the shattered stump of a colossal stone column for shelter from the gritty powder. The climate felt different from Tagus III: the air more dry, the temperature cooler, the gravity slightly lighter. He suspected he wasn't even on the same planet anymore, although his and Q's latest destination seemed M-class at least. "Where are we now?" he asked Q, who stood a few meters away, heedless of the wind-blown powder. He was getting damned tired of asking that question, but there seemed to be no way around it. He was merely a passenger on this tour, without even the benefit of a printed itinerary. "And when?"

"Don't you recognize this place?" Q challenged him. He kicked the gray powder at his feet, adding to the airborne particulates. "Surely, a Starfleet officer of your stature has been informed of its existence? We're still a couple million years in the past, to be fair, but this particular locale looks much the same in your own tiny sliver of history."

Intrigued despite himself, Picard inspected his surroundings, searching for some clue to his present whereabouts. The sky above was no help; the heavy cloud cover concealed whatever constellations might have been visible from the surface. He contemplated the truncated column before him, running his hand over its classic Ionic contours and leaving a trail of handprints in the dust. The wandering aliens who had once posed as gods to the ancient Greeks had left similar structures throughout the Alpha Quadrant; this could be one of any of a dozen such sites discovered since Kirk first encountered "Apollo" close to a century ago, or another site as yet uncharted by Starfleet. Was Q about to claim kinship to those ancient Olympians who had visited Earth in the distant past? Picard prayed that wasn't the case. The last thing he wanted to do was give Q credit for any of the foundations of human civilization. *If I had to pick Q out of the Greco-Roman pantheon, though,* he thought, *I'd bet a Ferengi's ransom that he was Bacchus or maybe Pan.*

None of which gave him a clue where in the galaxy he was.

"Stumped?" Q asked, savoring the mortal's perplexity. "Do let me know if this is too difficult a puzzle for your limited human mind."

Picard opened his mouth to protest, to ask for more time, then realized he had fallen into playing Q's game. *The fewer minutes we waste, the sooner I'll return to*

my ship. "Yes, Q," he admitted freely. "I'm at a complete loss. Why don't you illuminate me?" *And with all deliberate speed,* he added silently.

Q scowled, as if irked by Picard's ready surrender, but he wasn't ready to abandon the game just yet. "Perhaps a slight alteration in perspective will refresh your
memory."

Picard felt an abrupt sense of dislocation. His surroundings seemed to rush
past him and, in the space of a single heartbeat, he found himself standing elsewhere within the same ruins. He staggered forward, dizzy from the rush, and
braced himself against a fragment of a fallen wall. *I think I like Q's usual telepor-
tation trick better,* he thought, steadying himself until the vertigo passed. He lifted
his gaze from the gravel at his feet—and spotted *it* at once.

What from the side had appeared to be just more jutting granite rubble was
now revealed to be a lopsided stone torus about three meters in diameter. Its asym-
metrical design looked out of place among the scattered evidence of ancient archi-
tecture. Green patches of corrosion mottled its brownish gray surface, although
the torus appeared more or less intact. Q waved at him through the oblong opening
at the center of the torus, but Picard was too stunned to respond. Suddenly, he
knew exactly where he was.

"The Guardian," he breathed in awe. He had never seen it in person, but, Q was
correct, he was of course familiar with its history. More precisely known as "the
Guardian of Forever," it was the oldest known artifact in the universe, believed
to date back at least six billion years. Since its discovery by the crew of Kirk's
Enterprise, the Guardian had been the subject of intensive study by Starfleet yet had
remained largely an enigma. Picard glanced about him at the dilapidated stone ruins
that surrounded the Guardian; archaeological surveys conducted in his own century
had proven conclusively that the crumbling masonry was little more than a million
years old. The Guardian predated the other ruins by countless aeons, having already
been incalculably ancient before the temples or fortresses that rose up around it were
even conceived. *Here,* he thought, *was antiquity enough to daunt even Q . . . perhaps.*

But its age was not its only claim to fame. The Guardian, he recalled, was more
than merely an inanimate relic of the primordial past. Although it appeared inactive now, it was supposedly capable of opening up a doorway to any time in history, past or future. Picard briefly wondered if he could use the portal to return to
his own era without Q's cooperation, but, no, that was probably too risky. More
likely he would simply strand himself upon an unknown shoal of time with no
more appealing prospect than to hope for rescue at Q's hands. *Better to stay put for
the time being,* he concluded. Matters had not grown that desperate yet.

Brushing the clingy powder from his palms, Picard shielded his eyes with one
hand while he scanned the vicinity. He and Q appeared to be the only beings alive
in the ruins, excluding the Guardian, which was said to possess at least a pseudo-
life of its own. "Shouldn't we be expecting your younger self any time now?" he
asked Q. At this point, Picard felt he had a fairly good idea of the nature, if not the
purpose, of their extended trek through time. "That is why we're here, I assume."

"A brilliant deduction, Jean-Luc," Q said, his sarcastic tone belying his words.
"Even Wesley could have figured that out by now." He strutted across the rubble-
strewn plain toward Picard, skirting around the Guardian. "But I'm afraid you're
mistaken. My irrepressible earlier incarnation is not coming. He's already here. He's
been here all along, only not in any form you can perceive." He pointed at a solitary

cornerstone that had survived beyond the edifice it had once supported. "Cast your eyes over there while I adjust the picture for the metaphysically impaired."

In a blink, another Q, looking not much older than the one who had been so taken by the bloody spectacle at the jade cliffs, appeared, sitting cross-legged atop the great granite block. His chin rested upon the knuckles of his clasped hands as he stared moodily into the empty space within the Guardian. Clad in a stark black sackcloth robe that struck Picard as ostentatiously severe, he presented an almost archetypal portrait of disaffected youth, trapped on the cusp between adolescence and maturity. "A rebel without a cosmos," the older Q recalled, climbing marble steps that no longer led to anything recognizable. He swept the top step free of dust and sat down a few meters away from Picard. "I really had no idea what to do with myself back then."

Some of us still don't know what to do with you, Picard thought, refraining from saying so aloud lest he initiate another pointless war of words. The lighting itself had changed when the young Q became visible, throwing deep red and purple shadows upon the angst-ridden youth and his barren backdrop. Tilting his head back, Picard saw that the sky was now filled with an astonishing display of surging colors that put Earth's own aurora borealis to shame. Flashes of vibrant red and violet burst like phaser fire through what only moments before had been a dull and lifeless canopy. The dazzling pyrotechnics reminded Picard of the legendary firefalls of Gal Gath'thong on Romulus, but the pulsating, vivid hues above him were, if anything, even more luminous. "What's happening?" he asked Q. "Where did . . . that . . . come from?"

"Now you're seeing as a Q sees," the other explained. "What you call the Guardian produces ripples in space-time that extend far beyond this planet's atmosphere. Think of them as fourth-dimensional fireworks," he suggested breezily.

The young Q seemed unimpressed by the unparalleled light show unfolding overhead. His gaze fixed straight ahead, he yawned loudly. A listless forefinger traced the outline of the Guardian in the air, and a miniature replica of the stone torus materialized out of nothingness, hovering before his face. Q examined his creation without much enthusiasm. "At least our ancestors *made* things," he muttered sulkily.

Atop the immense cornerstone, young Q twirled his index finger and the model Guardian rotated for his inspection. He thrust the single digit into the tiny orifice of his toy and watched sullenly as it disappeared up to the bottom knuckle. Apparently unsatisfied by this diversion, he retrieved his finger, then dispatched the replica back into the ether with a wave of his hand. Leaping impatiently to his feet, his simple sandals kicking up a flurry of dust, he confronted the genuine Guardian. "Show me something!" he demanded.

"WHAT DO YOU WISH TO BEHOLD?" the Guardian asked, hundreds of centuries before it ever spoke to Kirk or Spock, its sonorous voice echoing off the accumulated wreckage of its former housing. An inner light flashed with each syllable of its query, rendering the weathered surface of the portal momentarily translucent. Scientists still debated, Picard recalled, whether the Guardian actually possessed sentience or merely a highly sophisticated form of interactive programming. Was it more or less alive, he wondered, than his ship's computer, the fictional characters that came to life in a holodeck, or even Data? That was a question better suited to philosophers, he decided, than a timelost Starfleet captain.

"Anything!" the young Q cried out in boredom. "Show me anything. I don't care."

"AS YOU WISH," the Guardian replied. A pristine white mist began to descend from the upper arch of the great torus, filling the vortex at its center. Through the falling vapor, Picard glimpsed images appearing, rushing swiftly by like a holonovel on fast-forward. Visions of the past, Picard wondered, or of untold ages to come? Despite the haze produced by the mist, the procession of images summoned up by the Guardian looked more real and tangible than any he had ever seen on a conventional viewscreen. Picard felt he could reach out and touch the people and places pictured therein, then remembered that he probably could. Gaping in amazement, he tried to capture each new vision as it played out before him:

A tremendous explosion cast immeasurable quantities of matter and energy throughout creation; vast clouds of gas collapsed until they ignited into nuclear fire; drifting elemental particles clumped together, forming moons and planets, asteroids and comets; single-celled organisms swam through seas of unimaginable breadth and purity; limbless creatures flopped onto the land and almost instantly (or so it appeared to Picard) evolved into a bewildering variety of shapes and sizes; humanoids appeared, and nonhumanoids, too, creatures with tentacles and feelers and antennae and wings and fins, covered with fur and feathers and scales and slime. Civilizations rose up and collapsed in a matter of seconds; for an instant, Picard thought he spotted the ancient D'Arsay in their ceremonial masks and rites, and then the cascade of history rushed on, leaving them behind. Machines were born, sometimes surpassing their makers, and fragile life-forms dared the void between worlds in vessels of every description, leaving their tracks on a thousand systems before shedding their physical forms entirely to become numinous beings of pure thought. There were the Organians, Picard realized, and the Metrons and the Thasians and the Zalkonians and the Douwd . . .

"No, no," Q exclaimed, not content with the ongoing panorama of life and the universe. "I've seen all this before! I want to see something else. I want to *be* somewhere else."

"WHERE DO YOU WISH TO JOURNEY?" The Guardian flashed its willingness to convey Q wherever he desired.

The black-garbed youth stamped his foot impatiently, sending yet another fissure through the massive block beneath him. "If I knew that, I wouldn't be here in the first place, you pretentious doorframe." He hopped off the stone, raising a cloud of gray powder where he landed, and approached the Guardian. "Show me more," he commanded. "Show me what's new, what's different!"

"Here we go," his older self sighed. He rose to his feet and took Picard by the elbow, leading him over to just behind where young Q now stood. "Get ready," he warned Picard, his words unheard by the youth only a few centimeters away, who quivered with unfocused energy.

Again? Picard thought, readying himself for another change of venue. He'd been on whirlwind tours of the Klingon Empire that had moved at a more leisurely pace.

Within the Guardian, images zipped past so speedily that he could barely keep up with them. He caught only quick, almost subliminal fragments of random events, of which only the smallest fraction could he even begin to identify: a mighty sailing ship sinking beneath the waves, a glistening Changeling dissolving into a golden pool, a dozen Borg cubes converging on a defenseless world, a shuttlecraft crashing into a shimmering wall of light . . .

"What now?" Picard asked, unable to look away from the rapid-fire parade of images. "What does he intend to do?"

"Stick a pin in a map," his companion stated. "Entrust his future to the fickle whims of chance." He shrugged apologetically. "It seemed like the only thing to do at the time."

The young Q glanced back over his shoulder, and, for a second, Picard thought they had been exposed. But the youth was merely giving the lifeless ruins one last look before taking a deep breath, closing his eyes, crossing his fingers, and hurling himself forward into the mist-draped opening of the time portal. Picard had only an instant to register the young Q's disappearance before the other Q's hands shoved him roughly from behind, propelling him straight into the waiting maw of the Guardian of Forever.

Seventeen

According to standard Starfleet guidelines, it took zero-point-three-five seconds to go from impulse flight to warp travel. According to Riker's chronometer on the bridge, Geordi and his engineering crew did it in zero-point-two.

It wasn't nearly fast enough.

Riker felt a momentary surge of acceleration that trailed off almost immediately as the Calamarain hit them from behind like the front of a hurricane. The ship's inertial dampers were tested to the limit as its propulsive warp field collapsed instantaneously, causing the vessel to skid to a halt through friction with the cloud's billowing mass. The storm enveloped them at once, much to the delight of little q, who clapped his tiny hands in synch with the thunder.

Riker was considerably less amused. *Dammit,* he thought. *It's not fair!* He was no Betazoid, but he could practically feel the distress and disappointment permeating the bridge. Baeta Leyoro swore and slammed a fist into her open palm. Lieutenant Barclay poked at the engineering controls rather frantically, as if hoping to reverse their readings. Only Data appeared unaffected by the dashing of their hopes of escape, looking preoccupied with his repairs to the operations console. "Let me guess," Riker said bitterly. "No more warp drive."

Barclay swallowed nervously before confirming the awful truth. "I'm afraid not, Commander. Something's interfering with the field coils again."

"If this is typical of your expeditions," the female Q sniffed, "it's a wonder that you humans ever got out of your own backwoods solar system."

If we'd known the likes of you were waiting for us, Riker mused, *we might have had second thoughts.* Outwardly, he disregarded the Q's needling, preferring to address the problem of the Calamarain, who at least refrained from waspish gibes. He was starting to wonder, though, whether this was truly a new entity at all, or if the original Q had simply had a sex change. Granted, he had already seen both Q and his alleged mate at the same time, but somehow he suspected that materializing in two places simultaneously was not beyond Q's powers.

"Shall I go to impulse, sir?" Ensign Clarze asked.

Riker gave the matter a moment's thought. Was there any way they could outrace the Calamarain? Given that they had previously encountered the cloud-creatures in an entirely different sector several years ago, he could only deduce that the Calamarain were capable of faster-than-light travel on their own, assuming that these were indeed the very same entities that had attacked Q aboard the *Enterprise* during the third year of their ongoing mission. Certainly, the storm had managed to keep pace with them at impulse speed.

"No, Mr. Clarze," Riker declared evenly. They were running low on options, but he was determined to maintain a confident air for the sake of the crew's morale. "Well, Mr. Data?" Riker asked, addressing the android. "It's looking like you're our best hope at the moment."

If all else failed, he thought, he would have to order a saucer-separation maneuver, dividing the *Enterprise* into two independent vessels. The Calamarain appeared to clump together as one cohesive mass; possibly they could not pursue two ships at the same time. In theory, he could distract the sentient cloud with the battle section while the majority of the crew escaped in the saucer module. Naturally, he would remain aboard the battle bridge until the bitter end—and hope that Captain Picard eventually returned to command the saucer.

Apparently tired of standing upon the bridge, the female Q and her little boy had, without even thinking of asking anyone's permission, occupied Riker's own accustomed seat, to the right of the captain's chair. The child sat on his mother's lap, sucking his thumb and watching the main viewer as if it were the latest educational holotape from the Federated Children's Workshop. Riker didn't waste any breath objecting to the woman's brazen disregard of bridge etiquette and protocol. Why bother arguing decent manners with a Q? *I wonder how long they'll choose to stick around if I have to separate the saucer,* he wondered. *Would they transfer to the battle bridge as well, and stay all the way to the ship's final annihilation?*

Before he sacrificed one half of the *Enterprise,* however, along with the lives of the bridge and engineering crew, Riker intended to exhaust every other alternative, which was where Data came in.

And the Universal Translator.

"I believe I have," Data stated, "successfully developed a set of algorithms that may translate the Calamarain's tachyon emissions into verbal communication and vice versa, although the initial results may be crude and rudimentary at best."

"We don't want to recite poetry to them," Riker said, "just call a truce." He stared grimly at the luminescent fog stretching across the main viewer. Jagged bolts of electricity and incessant peals of thunder rocked the ship. "Say hello, Mr. Data."

The android's fingers manipulated the controls at Ops faster than Riker's eye could follow them. "I am diverting power to the primary deflector dish," he explained, "in order to produce a narrow wavelength tachyon stream similar to those the Calamarain appear to use to communicate. If my calculations are correct, our tachyon beam should translate as a simple greeting."

"I hope you're right, Data," Riker said. "It would be a shame if we accidentally insulted them by mistake."

"Indeed," Data replied, cocking his head as if the possibility had not previously occurred to him, "although it is difficult to imagine how we could conceivably make them more hostile than they already appear to be."

You've got a point there, Riker admitted, given that the Calamarain had spent the last several hours dead set on shaking the *Enterprise* apart. The sharp decline in the strength of the ship's deflector shields testified to the force and severity of the Calamarain's assault. *Perhaps now we can finally learn why they attacked us in the first place.*

"Greeting transmitted," Data reported. The tachyon emission was invisible to the naked eye, yet Riker peered at the viewer regardless, looking for some sign that the Calamarain had received their message. All he saw, though, were the same churning mists and flashes of discharged energy that had besieged the *Enterprise* since before the captain disappeared.

Troi abruptly sat up straight in her chair. "They heard us," she confirmed, her empathic senses once more linked to the Calamarain. "I feel surprise . . . and confusion. They're not sure what to do."

"Good work, Mr. Data," Riker said, hope surging inside him for the first time in nearly an hour, "and you too, Deanna." Was he just deluding himself or had the oppressive thunder actually subsided a degree or two in the last few moments? They weren't out of the woods yet, but maybe the Calamarain had stopped hammering them long enough to contemplate Data's greeting. *Go ahead,* he thought to his amorphous foes. *Think it over some. Give us another chance to make contact!*

"Commander," Data alerted him, "short-range sensors detect an incoming transmission from the Calamarain, using the same narrow wavelength they applied earlier."

Hope flared in Riker. Thanks to Data, they still had a prayer of turning this thing around. *Too bad Captain Picard isn't here to speak with the Calamarain. He's probably the best diplomat in Starfleet.* "Put them through, Mr. Data."

"Yes, Commander," Data said. "Our modified translator is interpreting the transmission now."

A genderless, inhuman voice emerged from the bridge's concealed loudspeakers. The voice lacked any recognizable inflections and sounded as though it were coming from someplace deep underwater. "We/singular am/are the Calamarain," it stated.

"I apologize for the atonal quality of the translation," Data commented, "as well as any irregularities in syntax or grammar. Insufficient time was available to provide for nuance or aesthetics."

"This will be fine," Riker assured him. "Can the computer translate what I say into terms the Calamarain can understand?"

"Affirmative, Commander," Data said. "You may speak normally."

Riker nodded, then took a deep breath before speaking. "This is Commander William T. Riker of the *Starship Enterprise,* representing the United Federation of Planets." He resisted an urge to straighten his uniform; the Calamarain were not likely to appreciate any adjustment in his attire, even if they could see him, which was unlikely. Their senses were surely very different from his own. "Do I have the honor of addressing the leader of the Calamarain?"

There was a lag of no more than a second while Data's program translated his words into a series of tachyon beams; then that chilling voice spoke again. "We/singular speak from/for the Calamarain," it said in its muffled, watery tones.

What precisely did it mean by that? Was more than one individual addressing him at once, Riker wondered, or was it merely a verbal conceit, like the royal "we" once employed by Earth's ancient monarchs? Or could it be that the Calamarain genuinely possessed a collective consciousness like the Borg? He repressed a shudder. Anything that reminded him of the Borg was not good news. Riker decided to take the speaker at its word, whoever it or they might be.

"We come in peace," he declared, going straight to the heart of the matter. "Why have you attacked us?"

After another brief pause, the eerie voice returned. "Mote abates/attenuates. No assistance/release permitted. Stop/eliminate."

What? Riker gave Data a quizzical look, but the android could do nothing but shrug. "I am sorry, Commander, but that is the closest translation," he said.

"Deanna?" Riker whispered, hoping she could decipher the Calamarain's cryptic explanation.

"I sense no deception," she said. "They are quite sincere, very much so. Whatever they're trying to tell us, it's very important to them." She bowed her head and massaged her brow with both hands, clearly striving to achieve an even greater communion with the enigmatic aliens. "Beneath their words, I'm picking up that same mixture of fear and anger."

Why would the Calamarain be afraid of us? Riker couldn't figure it out. If the events of the last hour or so had proved anything, it was that the *Enterprise* could not inflict any lasting harm on the Calamarain. *If only I knew what they meant,* he thought. "I don't understand," he said, raising his voice. "What do you want of us?"

"Preserve/defend mote," the Calamarain insisted obscurely.

Interlude

What is that? the spider asked. *That is what?*

Something was there, on the other side, that he could not quite identify, something at the center of it all. The smoke surrounded the bug, and the bug surrounded *It,* but what was *It,* glowing within the entrapped insect like a candle in a skull? Sparking like a quark in the dark?

There was something Q-ish about it, but different, too. Not the Q, nor a Q, but flavored much the same. *It is new,* the spider realized with a shock. *Newer than new. Q-er than Q.*

New . . . For the first time it occurred to the spider to wonder how much might have changed, there on the other side. But that would depend on how long he'd been outside, wouldn't it, and that would be . . . ? *No! Not! No!* His mind scuttled away from the question, unable to face the answer that loomed just past his awareness.

Change, change, he chanted, calming himself. *Change on the range into something quite strange.* Change could be good, especially his own. He could make changes, too, and he would, yes indeed, just as soon as he could.

Everything changes, and will change even more. . . .

Eighteen

Someone was singing in the snow.

Picard had little time to orient himself. An instant ago he had inhabited the arid ruins encircling the Guardian of Forever. Now he seemed to be located amid a frozen wasteland, his boots sinking into the icy crust, cold and distant stars shining in the dark sky far above him. The rime-covered plain stretched about him in all directions. Like Cocytus, he thought, the ninth and lowest level of hell. His breath misted before him, but he did not feel in any danger of freezing to death.

Q's work, no doubt. The cold, dry air felt chill against Picard's body, nothing more. *Very well then,* he thought, disinclined to question his lack of hypothermia. He had more important mysteries to solve, like where was that infernal singing coming from?

The voice, rich and resonant, carried through the glacial cold:

> *"She was a kind-hearted girl, a lissome fair daughter,*
> *Who always declined the gifts that I brought her. . . ."*

Still unaware of his two humanoid observers, the young Q looked similarly intrigued by the robust voice crooning through the frigid air. Deterred not at all by the forbidding landscape, he trudged across the frosty tundra in search of the source of the melody. Picard and the older Q followed closely behind him, sometimes stepping in his sunken footprints. Starlight trickled down through the endless night, but not enough to truly light their way. Defying logic and conventional means of combustion, Q whipped up a torch, which he held out in front of him. Lambent red flames flickered above his fist, casting an eerie crimson glow upon their frozen path. The sleeves of Q's charcoal robe flapped slowly in the biting winter wind, and Picard found himself wishing that Starfleet uniforms came complete with gloves and a scarf. Although no new snow fell from the cloudless sky, the breeze tossed loosely packed white flakes into the air, making vision difficult. The icy bits pelted his face, melting against his reddened cheeks and brow.

> *"But pity's the thing, so I begged for cool water,*
> *And then led her away like a lamb to a slaughter. . . ."*

They marched for several minutes, during which time Picard observed the utter absence of any signs of animation. Nothing moved upon or above the ice except the windblown particles of snow. Picard wondered if any form of life existed beneath the permafrost, such as that found in Antarctica. Perhaps, if he could place this planet by means of the constellations overhead, it might be worth bringing the *Enterprise* by to check? Then he recalled that all of this was taking place millions of years in the past. Any life-forms that might exist here and now would most likely be long extinct when he returned to his own time. *For all I know, this entire planet and star system may not even exist in the twenty-fourth century.*

The soles of his boots crunched through the snow. No, he knew instinctively, there was no life here. This was a dead place, devoid of vitality, empty of possibility. Save for the singing voice, and the soft hiss of the burning torch, the icy plain was locked in silence. *Much like the old Klingon penal colony on Rura Penthe,* he mused, *known to history as the "aliens' graveyard."* Surely, that icebound planetoid could have been no more bleak and inhospitable than this.

> *"Like a lamb to slaughter, yes, like a lamb to the slaughter. . . ."*

The echoing refrain grew louder as they neared its origin. Soon Picard spied the figure of a man, human in appearance, sitting upon a granite boulder covered by a thick veneer of frost. He appeared larger than either Q, and his stout frame was draped in heavy clothing that looked as though it had seen better days yet nonetheless retained a semblance of faded glory. His heavy fur coat was frayed around its sleeves and along its hem while his high black boots were scuffed and the heels worn down to the sole. Rags were wrapped around his hands and boots to hold on to his heat, and a ratty velvet scarf protected his throat. A wide-brimmed hat, drooping over his brow, and tattered trousers completed his outfit, giving him an archaic and faintly dispossessed air.

"Who is this?" Picard asked. "I don't recognize him."

"Of course not," Q retorted impatiently. "Your ancestors weren't even a gleam in creation's eye yet."

It wasn't that foolish an observation, Picard thought, considering the timelessness of Q and his ilk. "Is this what he genuinely looked like," he asked his guide, wanting to fully understand what he was witnessing, "or are we dealing in metaphor again?"

"More or less," Q admitted. "In fact, he resembled a being not unlike a Q, whose true form would be patently incomprehensible to your limited human senses."

So this is your interpretation of how he first appeared to you, Picard thought. *He must have made quite an impression.* Although worn and ragged, the stranger presented an intriguing and evocative figure. Singing to himself, he was engaged in what looked like a game of three-dimensional solitaire. Oversized playing cards were spread out on the snow before him, or floated in fixed positions above the mud-slick ground, arranged in a variety of horizontal, vertical, and diagonal patterns. He looked engrossed in his game, meticulously shifting cards from one position to another, until the flickering, phosphorescent light of Q's torch fell upon the outermost row of cards. He looked up abruptly, fixing gleaming azure eyes on the young Q, his face that of a human male in his mid-forties, with weathered features and heavy, crinkly lines around his eyes and mouth. "Say, who goes there?" he said, sounding intrigued rather than alarmed.

Q faltered before the stranger's forthright gaze, taking a few steps backward involuntarily. "I might ask you the same," he retorted, his brash manner failing to conceal a touch of obvious apprehension. He thrust out his chest and chin to strike a less nervous pose.

"You must understand," his older self whispered in Picard's ear, "this was the first time since the dawn of my omniscience that I had encountered anything I didn't understand. A little healthy trepidation was only natural under the circumstances."

Picard was too entranced by the unfolding scene to respond to Q's excuses. "Well said!" the stranger laughed lustily. "And you're more than welcome, too. I was starting to think I was the only preternatural deity stuck in the middle of this irksome Ice Age."

"W-who are you?" Q stammered. Fog streamed from his lips; another artistic touch, Picard guessed, courtesy of the other Q. "What are you?"

"Call me 0," he said, doffing his hat to reveal unruly orange hair streaked with silver. "As to where I'm from, it's no place you've ever heard of, I promise you that."

"That's impossible," young Q said indignantly, his pride stung. "I'm Q. I know everything and have been everywhere."

"Then where are you now?" the stranger asked.

The simple question threw Q for a loop. He glanced around, feigning nonchalance (badly), and seemed to be searching his memory. Taking his own inventory of their surroundings, Picard noted a trail of deep, irregularly paced footprints stretching away in the opposite direction from the way they had come. As far as he could see, the tracks extended all the way to the horizon. How long, he wondered, has the stranger been wandering through this wintry Siberian wasteland?

"Er, I'm not sure," Q confessed finally, "but I'm quite certain it's no place worth remembering. Otherwise, I would recognize it at once, as I would your own plane of origin."

The individual who called himself 0 did not take offense at this challenge to his veracity. He simply chuckled to himself and shook his head incredulously. "But there's *always* someplace else, no matter how far you've been. Some unknown territory beyond the horizon, across the gulf, or hidden beneath a hundred familiar layers of what's real and everyday. There has to be someplace Other or why else do we roam? We might as well just plant ourselves in one cozy cosmos or another and never budge." He clapped his gloved, rag-swaddled hands together, and a curved glass bottle, filled with an unknown liquid of pinkish tint, appeared in his grasp. He wrenched the stopper from the spout and spit it onto the hoarfrost at his feet. Roseate fumes poured from the mouth of the bottle.

"For myself," he said, after taking a swig from the carafe, "I don't much care whether you believe me or not, but if I'm not from the parts you know, then where did this come from? Answer that."

He offered the bottle to Q, who looked uncertain what to do. "How do I know you aren't trying to poison me?" he said, striving for a light, jokey tone.

0 grinned back at him. "You don't. That's the fun of it." He shoved the bottle at Q. "Come now, eternity's too short not to take a chance now and then. Caution is for cowards, and for those who lack the gaze and the guts to try something new."

"You really think so?" Q asked. Despite his earlier misgivings, he was clearly curious about the rakish stranger. It struck Picard that 0's professed philosophy was a far cry from the conservative limits imposed on the young Q by the Continuum.

"I *know* so," 0 declared. He wagged the bottle in front of Q's face, then started to withdraw it. "But maybe you don't agree. Perhaps you're one of those timid, tentative types who never do anything unexpected. . . ."

Impulsively, Q grabbed the carafe by its curved spout and gulped down a sizable portion of the bottle's contents. His eyes bugged out as the drink hit his system like a quantum torpedo. He bent over coughing and gasping. "By the Continuum!" he swore. "Where did you find that stuff?"

0 slapped Q on the back while deftly retrieving the bottle from Q's shaking hand. "Well, I'd tell you, friend," he said, "but then you don't believe in places you've never laid eyes on."

Next to Picard, across the ice from the young Q and his new acquaintance, an older-but-arguably-wiser Q confided in the starship captain. "It's true, you know," he said, a wistful melancholy tingeing his voice, "I've never tasted anything like it ever again. I've even tried re-creating it from scratch, but the flavor is never quite right."

Only Q, Picard thought, *could get nostalgic about something that happened millions of years in the past.* Still, he thought he could identify with some of what Q was experiencing. He felt much the same way about the *Stargazer,* not to mention the *Enterprise*-D.

By now, the young Q had recovered from the effects of the exotic concoction. "That was fantastic!" he blurted. "It was so . . . different." He said that last word with a tone of total disbelief, then regarded the stranger with new appreciation. "I don't understand. How did you get here, wherever here is? And are there others like you?"

0 held up his hand to quiet Q's unleashed curiosity. "Whoa there, friend. I'm glad you liked the brew, but it seems to me you have the advantage on me. Where are you from, exactly?" His icy blue eyes narrowed as he looked Q over. "And what's this Continuum you mentioned a couple moments ago?"

"But surely you must have heard of the Q Continuum?" Q said, all his misgivings forgotten. "We're only the apex of sentience throughout the entire . . . I mean, the *known* . . . multiverse."

"You forget, I'm not from around your usual haunts," 0 said. "Nor have I always been camped out in this polar purgatory." He swept his arm to encompass his arctic domain. "A bit of a wrong turn there, I admit, but that's what happens sometimes when you strike out for parts unknown. You have to accept the risks as well as the rewards." He regarded Q with a calculating expression, brazenly assessing the juvenile superbeing. Picard didn't like the avid gleam in the stranger's eyes; 0 seemed more than simply curious about Q. "Perhaps you'd care to show me just how you got here?"

His game abandoned, 0 began to sweep his playing cards together, combining them into a single stack. Picard peeked at the exposed faces of the cards, and was shocked to see what looked like living figures moving about in the two-dimensional plane of the cards. The suits and characters were unfamiliar to him, bearing little resemblance to the cards used in *Enterprise*'s weekly poker games, but they were definitely animated. He spotted soldiers and sailors, balladeers and falconers and dancing bears among the many archetypes represented upon the metal cards, and apparently crying out in fear as 0 shuffled them together. Although no sounds escaped the deck, the figures shared a common terror and state of alarm, their eyes and mouths open wide, their arms reaching out in panic. "What in heaven's name," Picard started to ask Q, but 0 patted the cards into place, then dispatched the deck to oblivion before Picard could finish his question. Snow-flecked air rushed in to fill the empty void the stack of cards had formerly occupied.

Had the young Q noticed the unsettling nature of the cards? Picard could not tell for certain, but he thought he discerned a new wariness entering into the immature Q's face and manner. Or maybe, he speculated, 0 simply seemed a shade too eager to uncover Q's secrets.

"How I got here?" young Q repeated slowly, displaying some of his later self's cunning and evasiveness. "Well, that's a terribly long and complicated story."

"I've got time," 0 insisted. He clapped his hands and another ice-coated boulder appeared next to his own. He gestured for Q to take a seat there. "And there's nothing I like better than a good yarn, particularly if there's a trace of danger in it." He looked Q over from head to toe. "Do you like danger, Q?"

"Actually, I think I should be going," Q stated, taking a few steps backward. "I have an appointment out by Antares Prime, you see? Q is expecting me, as well as Q and Q."

His retreat was short-lived, for 0 simply rose from his polished stone resting-place and advanced on Q, dragging his left leg behind him. His infirmity caught the young Q by surprise, freezing him in his tracks upon the tundra; Picard guessed he'd never seen a crippled god before. "Not so fast, friend," 0 said, his voice holding just a trace of menace, a hint of a threat. "As you can plainly see, I can't get around as quickly as I used to." He leaned forward until his face was less than a finger's length from Q, his hot breath fogging the air between them. "Don't suppose you know an easy exit out of this oversized ice cube, do you, boy?"

Picard struggled to translate what he was witnessing into its actual cosmic context. "His leg," he asked Q. "What is the lameness a metaphor for?"

"Just what he said," Q answered impatiently, unheard by the figures they observed. "Must you be so bloody analytical all the time? Can't you accept this gripping drama at face value?"

"From you, never," Picard stated. He refused to accept that an entity such as 0 appeared to be would actually limp, at least not in a literal human sense.

Q resigned himself to Picard's queries. "If you must know, he could no longer travel at what you would consider superluminal speeds, at least in the sort of normal space-time reality you're familiar with." He directed Picard's gaze back to the long-ago meeting upon the boreal plain. "Not that I fully understood all that at the time."

"Can't you leave on your own?" the young Q asked, apparently reluctant to divulge the existence of the Guardian to the stranger. Picard admired his discretion, even if he doubted it would last. He knew Q too well.

"Sort of a personal question, isn't it?" 0 shot back indignantly. "You're not making light of my handicap, are you? I'll have you know I'm proud of every scrape and scar I've picked up over the course of my travels. I earned every one of them by taking my chances and running by my own rules. I'd hate to think you were the kind to think less of an entity because he's a little worse for wear."

"Of course not. Not at all!" Q replied and his older self groaned audibly. His perennial adversary, Picard observed, was not enjoying this scene at all. He shook his head and averted his eyes as his earlier incarnation apologized to 0. "I meant no offense, not one bit."

"That's better," 0 said, his harsh tone softening into something more amiable. "Then you won't mind if I hitch a ride with you back to your corner of the cosmos?" He flashed Q a toothy grin. "When do we leave?"

"You want to come with me?" the young Q echoed, uncertain. Events seemed to be proceeding far too fast for him. "Er, I'm not sure that's wise. I don't know anything about—I mean, you don't know anything about where I come from?"

"True, but I'm looking to learn," 0 said. He tapped the large rock behind him with the heel of his boot and both boulders disappeared, leaving the frozen plain devoid of any distinguishing features. "Trust me, there's nothing more to be seen around here. We might as well move on."

When did they become "we," Picard wondered, and the young Q might have been asking himself the same question. "I don't know," he murmured, lowering his torch to create a little more space between him and 0. "I hadn't really thought—"

"Nonsense," 0 retorted. His robust laughter produced a flurry of mist that wreathed his face like a smoking beard. He threw his arm around Q's shoulders, heedless of the youth's blazing torch. "Don't tell me you're actually afraid of poor old me?"

"Of course not!" Q insisted, perhaps too quickly. Picard recognized the tone immediately; it was the same one the older Q used whenever Picard questioned his superiority. "Why should I be?"

Next to Picard, the older Q glowered at his past. "You fool," he hissed. "Don't listen to him."

But his words fell upon literally deaf ears. Breaking away from 0, the younger Q snuffed out his torch in the snow; then, displaying the same supreme high-handedness that Picard had come to associate with Q, he traced in silver the oddly shaped outline of the time portal. "Behold," he said grandly, as if determined to impress 0 with his accomplishment, "the Guardian of Forever."

0 stared greedily at the beckoning aperture, and Picard did not require any commentary from the older Q to know that the younger was on the verge of making a serious mistake. Picard had not reached his advanced rank in Starfleet without learning to be a quick judge of character, and this 0 character struck him as a bold, and distinctly evasive, opportunist at the very least. In fact, Picard realized, 0 reminded him of no one so much as the older Q at his most devious. "You should have trusted your own instincts," he told his companion.

"Now you tell me," Q grumped.

Nineteen

Preserve the mote? What the blazes did that mean?

Riker's fists clenched in frustration. This was like trying to communicate with the Tamarians, before Captain Picard figured out that their language was based entirely on mythological allusions. *We rely too damn much on our almighty Universal Translator,* he thought, *so we get thrown for a loop when it runs into problems.* He signaled Data to switch off the translation program while he conferred with the others. " 'Preserve/defend mote,' " he echoed aloud. "What mote are they talking about? A speck of spacedust? A solitary atom?" Could this refer to some primal metaphor, such as the Tamarians employed? What was that old quote about "a mote in your eye" or something?

Or, looking at it from a different angle, couldn't "mote" also be used as a verb? Yes, he recalled, an archaic form of the word "might," as in "So mote it be." Preserve might? Preserve possibilities? Riker's spirit sagged as he considered all the diverse interpretations that came to mind.

"Maybe they don't mean mote," Leyoro suggested, "but moat, as in a circle of water protecting a fortress."

Spoken like a security officer, Riker thought, but maybe Leyoro was on to something here. A moat, a ring of defense . . . *Of course,* he realized. "The barrier. The Calamarain don't think in terms of solids, like walls or fences. To them, the galactic barrier is a big moat, circling the entire Milky Way!"

"That is a most logical conclusion," Data observed. "As you will recall, they first attacked when the probe attempted to enter the barrier."

" 'Moat abates/attenuates,' " Troi said, repeating the Calamarain's original pronouncement. "Perhaps they're referring to the weaknesses in the barrier that Professor Faal detected."

"That makes sense," Riker declared, convinced they had found the answer. He would have to remember to commend Lieutenant Leyoro in his report, assuming they all came out of this alive. "They're protecting the barrier from us. 'No assistance/release permitted.' Maybe that means they don't want us to escape—or be 'released' from—the galaxy."

That sounds just presumptuous enough to be right, he thought. Lord knows this wouldn't be the first time some arrogant, "more advanced" life-form had tried to enforce limits on Starfleet's exploration of the universe. Just look at Q himself, for instance. It was starting to seem like the Calamarain had a lot in common with the Q Continuum. He glanced sideways at the strange woman and child seated at his own auxiliary command station. She appeared to be flipping through a magazine titled simply *Q*, materialized from who-knows-where, while q watched the tempest visible on the viewscreen. The other Q, he recalled, had warned the captain not to cross the barrier. Could it be that Q and the Calamarain had been on the same side all along?

"This might not be the most judicious occasion to argue the point," Data stated with characteristic understatement.

"Shields down to twenty-one percent," Leyoro confirmed.

Riker saw the wisdom in what they were saying. As much as he resented being dictated to by a glorified cloud of hot gas, he was perfectly willing to withdraw from the field of battle this time, provided that the Calamarain could be persuaded to release the *Enterprise* long enough to let them go home. "Put me through to them again," he instructed Data.

"This is Commander Riker to the Calamarain," he said in a firm and dignified manner. "We respect your concerns regarding the . . . moat . . . and will not tamper with the moat at this time. Please permit us to return to our own space."

The entire bridge, he knew, waited anxiously for the aliens' response. With any luck at all, they would soon be able to abort their mission with no fatalities and only minimal damage to the ship. *That's good enough for me,* he thought. Any first-contact situation where you could walk away without starting a war was at least a partial success in his book. Besides, for all they knew, the Calamarain had a legitimate interest in the sanctity of the galactic barrier. That was something for the scientists and the diplomats to work out in the months to come, if the Calamarain proved willing to negotiate.

Right now, he mused, *I just want to bury the hatchet so we can concentrate on finding the captain.*

Then the voice of the Calamarain spoke again, crushing all his hopes: *"Enterprise* is/was chaos-haven. Deceit/disorder. No permit trust/mercy/escape. Must preserve/enforce moat. *Enterprise* is/to be dissipated."

"I do not think they believed you, Commander," Data said.

"I got that impression, Data," Riker affirmed. There was no audible menace in that uninflected voice, but the essence of its message was clear. The Calamarain did not trust them enough to let the ship go free. "Guilt by association," he realized. "All they know about us is that we've harbored Q in the past, shielding him from their retribution. That's what they mean by 'chaos-haven.' They think we're accomplices."

Now, there's a bitter twist of fate, he thought. *Will the* Enterprise *end up paying the price for Q's crimes?*

"I don't get it," Ensign Clarze said, scratching his hairless dome. "What do they mean, dissipated?"

Baeta Leyoro translated for the younger, less experienced crewman. "Destroyed," she said flatly. "They intend to destroy the entire ship."

"Touchy creatures," the female Q remarked, sounding quite unconcerned about the starship's imminent obliteration. "I never much cared for them."

Riker was inclined to agree.

Twenty

The oblong portal shimmered beneath the ice-cold sky. Young Q had not summoned the entire stone framework of the Guardian to 0's Arctic realm, but merely the aperture itself, which hovered above the frozen tundra like a mirage. The same white mist began to seep from the portal, turning to frost as it came into contact with the surface of the snow-covered plain; through the fog, Picard glimpsed the dusty ruins from which they had entered this glacial waste.

"Come along, Picard," Q instructed, heading for the spuming portal. "What transpires next is best witnessed from the other side."

Picard followed without argument. In truth, he would be happy to leave the barren ice behind; even with Q's powers to protect him from the cold, he found this frigid emptiness as desolate and dispiriting as Dante must have found the frozen lake of sinners at the bottom of the Inferno. Still, he had to wonder what was yet to occur. Was the young Q actually going to introduce 0 to Picard's own universe even with everything they didn't know about the mysterious entity? Picard, for one, would have liked to know a lot more about what precisely 0 was—and how he came to be stranded amid the drifting snow.

"Après vous," the older Q said to Picard, indicating the frothing aperture. Holding his breath involuntarily, Picard rushed through the fog, and found himself back among the dusty wreckage of the ancient ruins surrounding the Guardian of Forever, beneath a sky transformed by luminous time ripples. Moments later, his all-powerful guide emerged from the gateway as well. He joined Picard a few meters away from the Guardian. Their uniforms, Picard noted with both surprise and relief, were totally warm and dry despite their recent exposure to snow and ice. "Now what?" the captain asked.

"Now," Q said glumly, "you get a firsthand view of one of my more dubious achievements."

"One of many, I imagine," Picard could not resist remarking.

"Don't be ill-mannered, Jean-Luc," Q scolded. "I'm reliving this for your benefit, don't forget."

So you say, Picard thought, although he had yet to deduce what exactly Q's youthful exploits, millions of years in the past, had to do with himself or the *Enterprise,* unless 0 or his heirs somehow posed a threat in his own time. That seemed unlikely given the enormous stretches of time involved, but where Q and his sort were concerned, anything was possible.

"Here I come," Q stated, as his younger self indeed leaped out of the mist. The callow godling spun around on his heels and looked back the way he had come. Picard was unable to interpret the apprehensive expression on his face. Was the young Q worried that 0 would not be able to follow him through the portal—or that he would?

"Couldn't you have simply closed the door behind you?" Picard asked the other Q.

"Why, Captain," Q answered, looking aghast at the very suggestion, "I'm shocked that you would even propose such a cowardly ploy. That would have hardly been honorable of me, and, as you should know by now, I always play fair."

That's debatable, Picard thought, but saw no reason to press that point right now. Peering past both Q's, he spotted the silhouette of 0's stocky frame appearing within the foggy gateway. He held his breath, anticipating the stranger's arrival, but then something seemed to go wrong. Travel through the Guardian had always been instantaneous before, but not for 0 apparently. He strained against the opening as though held back by some invisible membrane. Reality itself seemed to resist his entrance. "Help me," he called out to Q, a single arm stretching beyond the boundaries of the portal. "For mercy's sake, help me!"

The older Q shook his head dolefully, but his earlier incarnation wavered uncertainly. He stepped forward to grip 0's outstretched hand, then hesitated, chewing his lower lip and wringing his hands together. "I don't know," he said aloud.

Perhaps responding to his indecision, the Guardian itself weighed in with its own opinion. "CAUTION," it declared, "FOREIGN ENTITY DOES NOT CONFORM TO ESTABLISHED PARAMETERS FOR THIS PLANE."

"Q!" 0 cried, his face pressed furiously against the membrane, his voice distorted by the strain. "Help me through, will you? I can't do it without you."

"CAUTION," the Guardian intoned. "THE ENTITY DOES NOT BELONG. YOU CANNOT INTERFERE."

"Don't listen to it, Q," 0 urged. His words came through the portal even if his physical form could not. "You can make your own rules, take your own chances. You and me, we're not the kind to play it safe. What's the good of living forever if you never take a risk?"

For a second, Picard entertained the hope that 0 would not be able to break through the unseen forces that held him back. Unfortunately, the Guardian's solemn warnings had exactly the opposite effect on the young Q as intended. "No one tells me what to do," the youthful Q muttered, and in his defiant tone Picard heard uncounted centuries of resentment and stifled enthusiasm, "not Q, not the Continuum, and especially not some moldering keyhole with delusions of grandeur."

Leaving all his doubts behind, he leaped forward and grasped 0's wrist with both hands. "Hold on!" he shouted. "Just give me a second!"

"ENTRY IS DENIED," the Guardian proclaimed. "INTERFERENCE IS NOT PERMITTED."

"Oh, be quiet," 0 urged it, eliciting a bark of laughter from his young, would-be liberator. His face flattened against the invisible barrier that barred his way, 0 kept pushing forward, gaining a millimeter or two. "You can do it, Q. I know you can!"

"You're quite right," Q said, grunting with effort. "I *can* do anything. And I will." Digging his heels into the dusty ground, he pulled on 0's arm with all his might. Perspiration speckled his brow and the veins on his hands stood out like plasma conduits. Picard tried to imagine the cosmic forces at work behind this facade of human exertion. Despite his better judgment, he had to admire the young being's tenacity and determination. Too bad they weren't being applied to a less questionable purpose. . . .

Smoke poured from the Guardian as it sought to restrain the stranger from beyond, defying the combined strength of both Q and 0. For a few fleeting instants, Picard could actually see the membrane, stretched over 0's thrusting head and shoulders like a layer of adhesive glue and glowing with white-hot energy so intense it made his eyes water. A network of spidery black cracks spread rapidly over the luminescent surface of the membrane and then, with a crash that sounded like a thousand stained-glass windows collapsing into broken shards, the barrier winked out of existence and 0 came tumbling onto the rubble-strewn ground, knocking Q onto his back.

"What was I thinking of?" the older Q said, looking on mournfully. "Would you have ever guessed I could be arrogant, so rash and presumptuous?"

Picard refrained from comment, more interested in observing the ongoing saga than in engaging in more fruitless banter with Q.

The young Q, exhilarated by his triumph, leaped to his feet, the back of his robe thoroughly dusted with gray powder. He looked no more frosted than Picard or his older counterpart. "Let's hear it for Q," he gloated, shaking his fist at the defeated Guardian, "especially this Q."

0 rose more slowly. Panting and pale, he clambered onto shaky legs and inspected his new surroundings, scowling somewhat at the obvious evidence of age and decay. "Looks like this locality has seen better days," he said darkly. "Please tell me this seedy cemetery is *not* the celebrated Q Continuum."

"What, this old place?" Q replied. He appeared much more confident now that he was back on familiar ground. "The Continuum exists on a much higher level than this simple material level." He laughed at the other's error. "You have a lot to learn about this reality, old fellow."

"No doubt you'll be happy to show me around," 0 said slyly. He stretched his limbs experimentally, looking mostly recovered from the duress of his transition. His bones cracked like tommyguns in a Dixon Hill mystery. "Ah, but it's good to breathe warm air again, and see something beside that endless, infernal ice." He limped over to Q. "Where to next, young man?"

"Next?" Q scratched his head. His plans had obviously not proceeded that far. Now that 0 had arrived safely, Q looked uncertain what to do with him. "Well, um, there's kind of an interesting spatial anomaly a few systems away. Some entities find it amusing." He pointed toward a distant patch of turbulent, rippling sky. "See, over by those quasars there, just past the nebula." He tugged on the fabric of his robe to shake off some of the dust. "Race you there?" he proposed.

"Sounds good to me," 0 agreed, "but I'm afraid it's been a long time since I moved faster than a sunbeam, at least through plain, ordinary space." He gave his bad leg a rueful pat. "I don't suppose a bright young blade like you knows any convenient shortcuts in this vicinity?"

"A shortcut?" Q mulled the matter over while 0 looked on expectantly, far too keenly for Picard's liking. Bad enough that Q had let this unknown quantity into reality as he knew it, he didn't want young Q to give 0 free rein throughout the physical universe. Alas, inspiration struck Q, much to Picard's dismay. "The Continuum itself is the ultimate shortcut, linking every time and place in a state of constant, ineffable unity. I'll bet you could use the Continuum to go anywhere you pleased."

"There's an idea!" 0 crowed, slapping Q on the back. "That's positively brilliant. I knew I could count on you." Beneath the silent gaze of the Guardian, 0 circled the young and relatively inexperienced Q like a lion that had just separated an antelope from the herd. "Now then," he said in an insinuating manner, "about this Continuum? I can hardly wait to lay my eyes on such an auspicious establishment." He limped across the arid landscape, conspicuously favoring his weaker leg. "If you don't mind giving me a lift, that is."

"I suppose," Q answered absently, "although I could as easily transport us straight to the anomaly."

"Time enough for that later," 0 assured him, an edge in his voice belying the courteous phrasing. Was the young Q aware, Picard wondered, of just how intent the stranger was on his goal? 0's single-mindedness was obvious enough to Picard, even if his full motives remained obscure. "The Continuum first, I think."

"Oh yeah, right," Q mumbled, looking around the forlorn ruins. "I suppose there's no reason to stick around here anymore." He cast a guilty, sidelong glance at the brooding edifice of the Guardian, perhaps only now wondering if he really should have heeded the ancient artifact's warnings. "Unless you'd like to look around here some more? There's a nearly intact temple over on the southern continent that was built by some of my direct organic precursors."

"The Continuum will do just fine," 0 insisted. He stopped limping around the other being and lowered his head to look Q directly in the eye. "Now if you please."

Q shrugged, apparently deciding not to cry over spilled interdimensional membranes. "Why not?" he declared, and Picard felt an unaccountable chill run down his spine even though he knew that all of these events had transpired millions of years before his own time. "Get ready to feast your senses on possibly the pinnacle of existence, a plane of reality never before glimpsed by anyone but Q." He summoned an expectant drumroll from the ether. "Q Continuum, here we come!"

Picard saw a wily smile creep over 0's weather-beaten visage an instant before both Q and his new friend departed the abandoned ruins in a single burst of celestial light. He and the older Q were left alone amid the crumbling pillars and shattered stones. "Now what?" Picard asked his self-appointed travel director, although he suspected he knew what was coming next.

Q shrugged. "Whither they goest, we goest." He smirked at Picard. "I'd tell you to hold on to your hat, but I guess Starfleet doesn't go in for snappy headgear." He subjected Picard's new uniform to a withering appraisal. "Pity. One should never underestimate the effectiveness of a stylish chapeau."

"Enough, Q," Picard barked. "You may be immortal, but I am not. Let's get on with this, unless you're afraid to show me just how big a fool you made of yourself."

Q glared at him murderously, and for one or two long moments Picard feared that perhaps he'd finally pushed Q too far. His body tensed up, half-expecting to be hurled into a supernova or transformed into some particularly slimy bit of protoplasm. *Just so long as he leaves the* Enterprise *alone,* Picard resolved, prepared to meet his fate with whatever dignity he could muster.

Then, to his surprise, the choler faded from Q's face, replaced by what looked amazingly like a moment of sincere reflection. "Perhaps you're right," he admitted after a time, "and I am stalling unnecessarily." He shook his head sadly. "I'm not particularly enjoying this trip down memory lane."

Picard almost sympathized with Q. With atypical gentleness, at least where Q was concerned, he suggested they continue their journey through the past. "It's a truism with humanity that those who do not learn from the past are doomed to repeat it. Perhaps, in your case, reliving your history is the only way we can both learn from it."

"Oh, that's profound, Picard," Q said, regaining some of his usual hauteur. "Very well, let's be on our way, if only to spare me any more of your pedantic clichés."

Why do I even try to treat him like a sane and reasonable being? Picard asked himself silently, but his justifiable irritation could not derail his mixed excitement and alarm at the prospect of actually visiting the Q Continuum for the first time. What could it possibly be like? He couldn't begin to imagine it. Even translated into human analogues, as it would surely have to be, he envisioned a wondrous, transcendent realm surpassing the Xanadu of Kublai Khan or fabled Sha Ka Ree of Vulcan myth and legend. As Q swept them away from the decaying ruins with a wave of his hand, Picard closed his eyes and braced himself for the awesome glory to come.

The reality was not what he expected. He opened his eyes and looked upon . . . a customs station? He and Q stood on a stretch of dusty blacktop that led up to a simple gate consisting of a horizontal beam that blocked further passage on the roadway. A rickety wooden booth, apparently staffed by a single guard, had been erected to the right side of the gate. A barbed-wire fence extended to both the east and the west, discouraging any unauthorized attempts to evade the gate. A sign was mounted beneath the open window of the booth, printed in heavy block lettering: YOU ARE NOW ENTERING THE Q CONTINUUM. NO PEDDLERS, VAGRANTS, OR ORGANIANS ALLOWED.

A golden sun was shining brightly overhead, although it seemed to be reserving its warmest beams for the other side of the fence. Picard lifted a hand to shield his eyes from the glare and peered past the barbed wire. As nearly as he could tell, the Q Continuum looked like an enormous multi-lane freeway with more loops, exits, and on-ramps than seemed physically possible. Elevated roadways doubled back on each other, then branched off at dozens of incompatible angles. *Mass transit as designed by M. C. Escher,* Picard thought, astounded by the sight.

"What were you expecting, Shangri-La?" Q asked, enjoying Picard's gawk-eyed befuddlement.

"Something like that," he admitted. *I suppose this imagery makes a certain amount of sense, given the younger Q's description of the Continuum as a shortcut that spanned the known universe.* He could readily believe that this stupendous tangle of thoroughfares connected any conceivable location with everywhere else.

Assuming you got past the gate, of course.

That appeared to be the challenge facing 0 and Q's previous self at this moment. Not far away from where Picard and Q now resided, the young Q and his newfound acquaintance stood before the barricade as the customs official emerged from his booth, clipboard in hand. He was a stern, officious-looking individual wearing a large copper badge upon his khaki-colored uniform. A sturdy truncheon dangled from his belt. Picard was irked but not too surprised to note that this functionary bore a marked resemblance to himself. *Come off it, Q,* Picard thought. *Surely I don't look that humorless?*

The guard scrutinized 0 with a scowl upon his face. "You're not Q," he stated flatly.

"You can say that again," 0 proclaimed, unabashed, "but I'd be grateful if you'd let me trod your fine road. Young Q here tells me it's the swiftest way around these whereabouts."

He clapped Q on the back, sending Q staggering forward toward the guard. Looking on from less than five meters away, Picard noted that the youth had traded his monkish black robe for something closer to what 0 wore, minus the rags and tatters, naturally. He now wore boots, breeches, and a heavy fur coat. *Just what Q needed,* Picard thought sarcastically, *a disreputable role model.*

The guard gave Q a disapproving glance, then inspected his clipboard. "State your name, species identification, planet or plane of origin, and the nature of your business in the Continuum."

0 rolled his eyes, seemingly unimpressed by this display of authority. "Are you sure you don't want my great-great-grandmother's genetic code as well?" he asked dryly. Sighing theatrically, he launched into his recitation. "0's the name, my species is special, my origin is elsewhere, and my business is none of yours. Is that

good enough, or would you care to arm-wrestle for it?" He shook off his shaggy greatcoat and rolled up his sleeve. Right behind him, the young Q placed a hand over his mouth to muffle an attack of giggles.

The guard looked considerably less amused by 0's flippancy. His scowl deepened and he lowered his clipboard to his side. "Where are you from," he asked, and Picard somehow sensed he was speaking for the whole of the Q, "and why should we permit you access to the Continuum?"

0 retrieved his coat from the pavement and threw it over his shoulder. "Well, the where of it is a long story that depends a lot on who's telling it. Let's just say I was once quite a mover and shaker a good ways from here, but I'm afraid that my able accomplishments were not always appreciated by those that should have known better, so it came to pass that the time was right for me to set off for greener pastures." He leaned forward and brushed some of the dust from his boots before straightening his spine, adjusting his hat, and addressing the guard. "As for why you should allow me safe passage through your local stomping grounds, aside from basic hospitality, that is . . . why, this peerless young paragon will vouch for me."

"Is this true?" the guard demanded of Q. He didn't seem to regard the young entity as much of a paragon.

Q gulped nervously, wilting under the guard's censorious stare. He looked to 0 for support and was greeted by a conspiratorial wink. The newcomer's boldness rubbed off on Q, who squared his shoulders and glared back at the guard defiantly. "Certainly!" he announced. "0's word is good enough for me. What's with this siege mentality anyway? We could do a lot worse than open our borders to new ideas and exotic visitors from foreign lands."

0 beamed at him. "That's telling 'em, friend." He poked the guard's badge with his finger. "You should listen to this young fellow if you've got any sense under that shiny, shorn scalp of yours."

That was uncalled for, Picard thought.

"So be it," the guard decreed. "This entity is permitted within the Continuum—on the understanding that you, Q, take responsibility for him."

"They expected *you* to be the responsible one?" Picard remarked, arching an ironic eyebrow. "Why do I get the impression this was a horrendous mistake?"

The older Q averted his eyes from the scene before them. "For a lower life-form, you can be annoyingly prophetic sometimes."

Caught up in his newfound bravado, the young Q didn't hesitate a bit. "Agreed," he said grandly. "Raise up the gate, my good man."

"Well done," 0 whispered. He doffed his wide-brimmed hat and plopped it onto Q's head. Grabbing his erstwhile sponsor by the elbow, he dragged his bad leg toward the barricade and the vast interdimensional highway beyond. Picard looked on as the guard retreated to his booth. Moments later, the horizontal beam tilted upward until it was perpendicular to the road, and the newly united fellow travelers strode into the future, embarking on the endless highway for destinations unknown.

"So tell me, Q," 0 asked as his voice receded into the distance, "have you ever considered the fundamental importance of *testing* lesser species . . . ?"

Interlude

Where is Q, the spider hissed. *Q is where?*

His stench was all over the bug over there, but not Q himself. Beneath the smelly smoke, it reeked of Q. Q had been with it, or would be, or should be. What did it matter when? Not at all, not for Q. Never for Q.

Damn you Q, you damn me, damn Q, damn me! He remembered it all now. Q was to blame, Q and all those other Q, parading their pompous, prejudiced, pitiless power throughout perpetuity. There were too many Q to count, far too many to be allowed to exist, but that could be remedied, given the chance. *Hew the Q. Hew Q too. Rue, Q, rue! Your day is through!*

The scent of Q set the spider salivating. Its avaricious arms scraped at the wall, greedy to grab, keen to consume. *Where are you now, Q, my old Q. What have you been doing all this time? What has time done to you and to me and to we. Have you ever thought of me? You should have, yes, you should.*

The time was coming. The voice had promised. Soon.

Q will pay. All the Q will pay. Q and Q
QQQQQQQQQQQQQQQQQQQQQQQQQQQQQQQQQQQQQQQQQQQQQQQQQQQ
QQQQQQQQQQQQQQQQQQQQQQQQQQQQQQQQQQQQQQQQQQQQQQQQQQQ
QQQQQQQQQQQQQQQQQQQQQQQQQQQQQQQQQQQQQQQQQQQQQQQQQQQ
QQQQQQQQQQQQQQQQQQQQQQQQQQQQQQQQQQQQQQQQQQQQQQQQQQQ
QQQQQQQQQQQQQQQQQQQQQQQQQQQQQQQQQQQQQQQQQQQQQQQQQQQ
QQQQQQQQQQQQQQQQQQQQQQQQQQQQQQQQQQQQQQQQQQQQQQQQQQQ
QQQQQQQQQQQQQQQQQQQQQQQQQQQQQQQQQQQQQQQQQQQQQQQQQQQ
QQQQQQQQQQQQQQQQQQQQQQQQQQQQQQQQQQQQQQQQQQQQQQQ . . .

Q-ZONE

Prologue

Soon, he cackled. Sooner. Soonest.

Behind the wall, he watched with keen anticipation as lesser life-forms, no more than a bug or a wisp of smoke to him, buzzed about on the other side. Only the wall, the wretched wall that had kept him out for longer than his muddled memory could even begin to encompass, kept him from reaching forth and swatting both bug and smoke away. Tendrils of his contorted consciousness capered spiderlike against the edge of the wall, scraping away at the boundaries of his banishment. He couldn't touch the other side just yet, but he could watch and wait and wonder about what he would do when the wall, the wicked and wearying wall, finally came down.

Very soon, he singsonged, *soon soon soon.* The wall would crumble. The voice had promised him so, that teensy-tiny voice from the other side. It was difficult to conceive how such a paltry piece of protoplasm could possibly undo that which had held him back for so long, but he had hope and reason to believe. Already he sensed that the wall was weaker than before, minute faults and fissures undermining its primal, protracted permanence. All it needed was one good push from the other side and a gap would be formed, the gap he needed to break through. *And then . . . and then what time has done to the galaxy will be nothing compared to what I'll do to all those stars and planets and people.* He flexed his tendrils in his eagerness to be free once more. *Yes, that's right, all the things I'll do . . . to Q and Q and Q.*

There was only one thing that worried him. What if someone silenced the other voice before it fulfilled its promise? And not just anyone someone, but Q. That Q, the quisling Q, the Q who could never, ever be trusted. *I can smell you, Q.* His stench was all over the shiny silver bug on the other side. It stank and perhaps could sting. *Stink, stank, sting, bee,* he chanted to himself. *You can't stop me. Q can't escape me.*

Soon could not come soon enough. . . .

One

Ship's log, stardate 51604.3, First Officer William T. Riker reporting.

Captain Picard is missing, abducted by the capricious entity known as Q. We can only pray that Q will return the captain unharmed, although time has taught us that Q is nothing if not unpredictable.

The captain's disappearance cannot have come at a worse time, as the Enterprise is under attack by the gaseous life-forms whom Q calls the Calamarain. Although Lieutenant Commander Data has succeeded in adapting our Universal Translator to the Calamarain's inhuman language, allowing us a degree of communication with them, we have thus far failed to win their trust. They have rendered our warp engines inactive and will not permit us to retreat, so we must persuade them otherwise. Speed is imperative, as our time is running out.

To complicate matters, we have a number of potentially disruptive guests aboard the ship. Chief among them are a mysterious woman and boy who claim to be Q's mate and child. Like Q himself, these individuals treat the ship and its crew as mere toys for their amusement. Furthermore, they appear unwilling or unable to inform us where Q has taken Captain Picard.

Equally uncooperative is Professor Lem Faal, a distinguished Betazoid physicist, whose ambitious attempt to breach the immense energy barrier surrounding our galaxy has been interrupted by the unexpected arrivals of both the Q family and the Calamarain. Dying of an incurable disease, and obsessed with completing his work in the time remaining to him, Faal has vigorously challenged my decision to abort the experiment in light of the unanticipated dangers we now face. While I sympathize with the man's plight, I cannot allow his single-minded determination to endanger the ship further.

Indeed, according to what we have gathered from the Calamarain, our first effort to dare the barrier was the very event that provoked the Calamarain's wrath, thus threatening us all with destruction. . . .

The storm raged around them. From the bridge of the *Enterprise*-E, Commander William Riker could see the fury of the Calamarain on the forward viewscreen. The massive plasma cloud that comprised the foe, and that now enclosed the entire Sovereign-class starship, had grown increasingly turbulent over the last few hours. The sentient, ionized gases outside the ship churned and billowed upon the screen; it was like being trapped in the center of the galaxy's biggest thunderhead. Huge sonic explosions literally shook the floor beneath his feet, while brilliant arcs of electrical energy flashed throughout the roiling cloud, intersecting violently with their own diminished shields. The distinctive blue flare of Cerenkov radiation discharged whenever the shield repelled another bolt of lightning from the Calamarain, which was happening far too often for Riker's peace of mind.

With the captain absent, his present whereabouts unknown, Riker was in command, and fighting a losing battle against alien entities determined to destroy them. *Not this time,* he vowed silently, determined not to lose another *Enterprise* while Jean-Luc Picard was away. Once, in that cataclysmic crash into Veridian III, was enough for one lifetime. *Never again,* he thought, remembering the sick sensation he had felt when that grand old ship had slammed into its final port. *Not on my watch.*

Their present circumstances were precarious, though. Warp engines down, shields fading, and no sign yet that the Calamarain were willing to abandon their ferocious attack on the ship, despite his sincere offer to abandon the experiment and retreat from the galactic barrier—on impulse if necessary. Diplomacy was proving as useless as their phasers, even though Riker remained convinced that this entire conflict was based solely on suspicion and misunderstanding. *Nothing's more tragic than a senseless battle,* he thought.

"Shields down to twenty percent," Lieutenant Baeta Leyoro reported. The Angosian security chief was getting a real baptism by fire on her first mission aboard the *Enterprise.* So far she had performed superlatively, even if Riker still occasionally expected to see Worf at the tactical station. "For a glorified blast of bad breath, they pack a hell of a punch."

Riker tapped his combadge to initiate a link to Geordi in Engineering. "Mr. La Forge," he barked, "we need to reinforce our shields, pronto."

Geordi La Forge's voice responded immediately. "We're doing what we can, Commander, but this tachyon barrage just keeps increasing in intensity." Riker could hear the frustration in the chief engineer's voice; Geordi had been working nonstop for hours. "It's eaten up most of our power to keep the ship intact this long. I've still got a few more tricks I can try, but we can't hold out indefinitely."

"Understood," Riker acknowledged, scratching his beard as he hastily considered the problem. The thunder and lightning of the storm, as spectacular as they looked and sounded, were only the most visible manifestations of the Calamarain's untempered wrath. The real danger was the tachyon emissions that the cloud creatures were somehow able to generate and direct against the *Enterprise.* Ironically, it was precisely those faster-than-light particles that prevented the ship from achieving warp speed. "What about adjusting the field harmonics?" he asked Geordi, searching for some way to shore up their defenses. "That worked before."

"Yeah," Geordi agreed, "but the Calamarain seem to have learned how to compensate for that. At best it can only buy us a little more time."

"I'll take whatever I can get," Riker said grimly. Every moment the deflectors remained in place gave them one more chance to find a way out. "Go to it, Mr. La Forge. Riker out."

He sniffed the air, detecting the harsh odor of burned circuitry and melted plastic. A few systems had already been fried by the relentless force of the aliens' assault, although nothing the auxiliary backups hadn't been able to pick up. The Calamarain had drawn first blood nonetheless, while the starship crew's own phasers had done little more than anger the enraged cloud of plasma even further, much to the annoyance of Baeta Leyoro, who took the failure of their weapons personally.

This is all Q's fault, Riker thought. Captain Picard had shielded Q from the Calamarain several years ago, and apparently they had neither forgotten nor forgiven that decision. It was the *Enterprise*'s past association with Q, he believed, that made the Calamarain so unwilling to trust Riker now when he promised to abort Professor Faal's wormhole experiment. Tarred by Q's bad reputation . . . talk about adding insult to (possibly mortal) injury!

For all we know, he mused, *the Calamarain might have sound reasons for objecting to the experiment. If only they could be reasoned with somehow!* He glanced over at Counselor Deanna Troi, seated to his left at her own command station. "What are you picking up from our stormy friends out there?" he asked her. The seriousness in his eyes belied the flippancy of his words. "Any chance they might be calming down?"

Troi closed her eyes as she reached out with her empathic senses to probe the emotions of the seething vapors that had enveloped the ship. Her slender hands gently massaged her temples as her breathing slowed. No matter how many times Riker had seen Deanna employ her special sensitivity, it never failed to impress him. He prayed that Deanna would sense some room for compromise with the Calamarain. All he needed was to carve one chink in the other species' paranoia and he was sure he could find a peaceful solution to this needless conflict.

Blast you, Q, he thought bitterly. He had no idea what Q had done God-knows-when to infuriate the Calamarain so, but he was positive it was something stupid, infantile, and typically Q-like. *Why should he have treated them any differently than he's ever treated us?*

Riker's gaze swung inexorably to the right, where an imperious-looking auburn-haired woman rested comfortably in his own accustomed seat, a wide-eyed toddler bouncing on her knee while she observed the ongoing battle against the Calamarain with an air of refined boredom. Mother and child wore matching, if entirely unearned, Starfleet uniforms, with the woman bearing enough pips upon her collar to outrank Riker if they possessed any legitimacy—which they most definitely did not. The first officer shook his head quietly; he still found it hard to accept that this woman and her infant were actually Q's wife and son. Frankly, he had a rough time believing that any being, highly evolved or otherwise, would willingly enter into any sort of union with Q.

Then again, the female Q, if that's what she truly was, had enough regal attitude and ego to be one of Q's relations. *A match made in the Continuum,* he thought. She seemed content to treat the imminent annihilation of the ship and everyone aboard as no more important than a day at the zoo, which was probably just how she regarded the *Enterprise.* At least the little boy, whom she called q, appeared to be enjoying the show. He gaped wide-eyed at the screen, clapping his pudgy little hands at each spectacular display of pyrotechnics.

I'm glad somebody's having a good time, Riker thought ruefully. *I suppose I should be thankful that I don't have to worry about the kid's safety.* The two Qs were probably the only people aboard the *Enterprise* who weren't facing mortal danger. *Who knows?* he wondered. *They may even be at the heart of the problem.* Could the Calamarain tell that Q's family was on the ship? That couldn't possibly reflect well on the *Enterprise.*

"I'm sorry, Will," Troi said, reopening her eyes and lowering her hands to her lap. "All I can sense is anger and fear, just like before." She stared quizzically at the iridescent plasma surging across the viewer. "They're dreadfully afraid of us for some reason, and determined to stop us from interfering with the barrier."

The barrier, Riker thought. It all came back to the galactic barrier. He could no longer see the shimmering radiance of the barrier on the forward viewer, but he knew that the great, glowing curtain was only a fraction of a light-year away. For generations, ever since James Kirk first braved the galactic barrier in an earlier *Enterprise,* no vessel had ventured into it without suffering massive casualties and structural damage. Professor Faal had insisted that his wormhole experiment would have no harmful effect on the barrier as a whole, but the Calamarain definitely seemed to feel otherwise. They referred to the barrier as the "moat" and had made it abundantly and forcefully clear that they would obliterate the *Enterprise* before they would permit the starship to tamper with it. *I need to find some way to convince them that we mean no harm.*

That might be easier accomplished without any Qs around to cloud the issue, he decided. "Excuse me," he said to the woman seated to his right, ignoring for the moment the sound of the Calamarain pounding against the shields. He was unsure how to address her; although she claimed her name was Q as well, he still thought of her as *a* Q rather than *the* Q. "I'm afraid that the presence of you and your child upon the *Enterprise* may be provoking the Calamarain, complicating an already tense situation. As the acting commander of this vessel, I have to ask you to leave this ship immediately."

She peered down her nose at him as she might at a yapping dog whose pedigree left something to be desired. One eyebrow arched skeptically. For a second or two, Riker feared that she wasn't even going to acknowledge his request at all, but eventually she heaved a weary sigh. "Nonsense," she said, in a tone that reminded him rather too much of Lwaxana Troi at her most overbearing. "The Calamarain wouldn't dare threaten a Q. This is entirely between you and that noxious little species out there."

Riker rose from the captain's chair and looked down on the seated woman, utilizing every possible psychological advantage at his disposal. She didn't look too impressed, and Riker recalled that, standing, the woman was nearly as tall as he was. "That may be so," he insisted, "but I can't afford to take that risk." He tried another tack. "Surely, in all the universe, there is someplace else you'd rather be."

"Several trillion," she informed him haughtily, "but dear q is amused by your little skirmish." She patted the boy's tousled head indulgently.

Don't think of her as a godlike superbeing, Riker thought as a new approach occurred to him. *Think of her as a doting mom.* His own mother had tragically died when he was very young, but Riker thought he understood the type. "Are you certain it's not too violent for him?" he asked, trying to sound as concerned and sympathetic as possible. "Things are likely to get messy soon, especially once our shields break down. It's not going to be pretty."

The woman's brow furrowed at his words. It appeared the potential grisliness of the crew's probable demise had not crossed her mind before. She glanced around her, checking out the various fragile humanoids populating the bridge. Outside, the tempest bellowed its intention to destroy the *Enterprise* and all aboard her. As if to make Riker's point, the ship pitched forward, slamming Lieutenant Leyoro into her tactical console. Her grunt of pain, followed by a look of stoic endurance, did not escape the female Q's notice.

Riker felt encouraged by her hesitant silence. *This might actually work,* he thought. "You know," he added, "I cried my eyes out the first time I read *Old Yeller.*"

The woman gave him a blank look; apparently her omniscience did not extend to classic children's fiction of the human species. Still, the basic idea seemed to get across. She cast a worried look at her son. "Perhaps you have a point," she conceded. Resignation settled onto her patrician features. "Too much mindless entertainment cannot be good for little q . . . even if his father can't get enough of your primitive antics."

With that, both mother and child vanished in a flash of white light that left Riker blinking. He breathed a sigh of relief, settling back into the captain's chair, until q reappeared upon his own knee. "Stay!" he yelped boisterously. For a superior being from a higher plane of reality, q felt solid enough and, if Riker could trust his own nostrils, in need of a fresh diaper beneath his miniature Starfleet uniform.

Riker groaned aloud. *Good thing the captain's still missing,* he thought, for the first and only time since Picard's abduction. The captain, it was well-known, had even less patience with small children than his first officer. *Now what do I do with this kid?* he wondered, looking rather desperately at Deanna for assistance. Despite their otherwise dire circumstances, the counselor could not resist a smile at Riker's sudden predicament.

Mercifully, the female Q materialized in front of Riker and lifted the toddler from his knee. "Come along, young q," she scolded gently. "I mean it." She tapped her foot impatiently upon the floor, giving Riker just enough warning to avert his eyes before the pair disappeared in another blinding flash of light.

He waited apprehensively for several seconds thereafter, holding his breath against the likelihood of another surprise reappearance. Had Q and q really left for the time being? He did not delude himself that the *Enterprise* had seen the last of either of them, let alone their mischievous relation, but he'd gladly settle for a temporary respite if it gave him enough time to settle matters with the Calamarain. *Just what we needed,* he thought sarcastically. *Three Qs to worry about from now on.*

Deanna broke the silence. "I think they're gone, Will."

"Thank heaven for small favors," he said. Now, if only the Calamarain could be disposed of so easily! "Mr. Data, activate your modified translation system. Now that our visitors have departed, let's try talking to the Calamarain one more time."

"Understood, Commander." The gold-skinned android manipulated the controls at Ops. After much effort, Data had devised a program by which humanoid language could be translated into the shortwave tachyon bursts the Calamarain used to communicate, and vice versa. "The translator is on-line. You may speak normally."

Riker leaned against the back of the captain's chair and took a deep breath. "This is Commander Riker of the *U.S.S. Enterprise,* addressing the Calamarain." In truth, he wasn't exactly sure whom he was speaking to. *Give me a face I can talk to any day,* he thought. "I'm asking you to call off your hostile actions toward our vessel. Speaking on behalf of this ship, and the United Federation of Planets, we are more than willing to discuss your concerns regarding the . . . moat. Let us return to our own space now, and perhaps our two peoples can communicate further in the future."

I can't get more direct than that, Riker thought. He could only hope that the Calamarain would realize how reasonable his offer was. *If not, our only remaining option may be to find a way to destroy the Calamarain before they destroy us,* he realized. A grim outcome to this mission, even assuming their foe could be extinguished somehow.

"They've heard you," Troi reported, sensing the Calamarain's reaction. "I think they're going to respond."

"Incoming transmission via tachyon emission," Data confirmed. He consulted his monitor and made a few quick adjustments to the translation program.

An eerie voice, devoid of gender or human inflections, echoed throughout the bridge. Riker decided he preferred the computer's ordinary tones, or even the harsh cadence of spoken Klingon.

"We/singular remain/endure the Calamarain," it intoned. "Moat is sacred/essential. No release/No escape. Chaos waits/threatens. Enterprise brings/succors chaos. Evaporation/sublimation is mandatory/preferable."

Riker scowled at the awkward and downright cryptic phrasing of the Calamarain's message. Unfortunately, Data didn't have nearly enough time to get all the bugs worked out of the new translation program. *It will have to do,* he resolved. Throughout human history, explorers and peacemakers had coped without any foolproof, high-tech translating devices. Could the crew of the *Enterprise* do any less?

When the Calamarain talked of "chaos," he guessed, they referred to Q and his kind. Frankly, he couldn't blame the Calamarain for mistrusting anyone associated with Q; that devilish troublemaker wasn't exactly the most sterling character witness. As for "evaporation/sublimation," he feared that term was simply the cloud creatures' way of describing the forthcoming destruction of the *Enterprise,* sublimation being the chemical process by which solid matter was reduced to a gaseous state. *Who knows?* he thought. *Maybe the Calamarain think they're doing us a favor by liberating our respective molecules from the constraints of solid existence.*

He didn't exactly see things their way. "Listen to me," he told the Calamarain, hoping that his own words weren't getting as badly garbled as theirs. He strove to keep his syntax as simple as possible. "The beings known as the Q Continuum are not our allies. We do not serve the Q."

In fact, he recalled, Q had also warned Captain Picard to stay away from the galactic barrier

"Chaos within/without," the Calamarain stated mysteriously. "Chaos then/now/to come. No/not be/not again. Excess risk/dread. No *Enterprise*/no be."

That doesn't sound good, Riker thought, *whatever it means.* He refused to give up, boiling his intended message down to its basics. "Please believe me. We will not harm you. Let us go." *Even our shaky translator can't mangle that,* he prayed.

The Calamarain responded not with words but with a roar of thunder that rocked the bridge. Riker felt his breath knocked out of him as the floor suddenly lurched to starboard, nearly toppling him from the captain's chair. Troi gasped nearby and fierce bolts of electrical fire arced across the viewscreen. At the conn, Ensign Clarze struggled to stabilize their flight path; sweat beaded on his smooth, hairless skull. Behind Riker, Lieutenant Leyoro held on to the tactical podium for dear life while the rest of the bridge staff fought to remain at their stations. Only Data looked unfazed by the abrupt jolt. "The Calamarain are not replying to your last transmission, Commander," he reported. The android inspected the raging tempest on the screen. "At least not verbally."

Troi released her grip on her chair's armrests as the floor leveled. The din of the Calamarain's attack persisted, though, like a ringing in Riker's ears and a constant vibration through his bones. "I sense great impatience," she informed him. "They're through with talking, Will."

"I got that impression," he said. He looked around the bridge at the tense and wary faces of the men and women depending on his leadership. *Wherever you are, Captain,* he thought, *I hope you're faring better than us.*

Two

"Now where are we?" he asked. "And when?"

Captain Jean-Luc Picard, late of the *Starship Enterprise,* looked around as he found himself drifting in deep space. An astounding abundance of stars surrounded him on all sides, more than he had ever seen from a single location before. Just by twisting his neck from side to side, he could spot an astonishing variety of stellar phenomena: giant pillars of dust and gas rising up into the starry void, great globular clusters filled with millions of shining blue suns, supernovas spewing light and matter in their violent death throes, nebulas, quasars, pulsars, and more. Craning his head back, he saw above him what looked like the awesome spectacle of two enormous clouds of stars colliding; huge glowing spirals, streaked with shades of blue and scarlet and bedecked with countless specks of white-hot fire, merged into an amorphous mass of luminescence large enough, Picard guessed, to hold—or destroy—several million solar systems. Were any of those worlds inhabited? he wondered, hoping despite all appearances that some form of sentient life could survive the tremendous cosmic cataclysm transpiring overhead. Then Q drifted between Picard and the fusing stellar clusters, completely spoiling the view.

"Quite a show, isn't it?" Q remarked, floating on his back with his interlocked hands cradling the back of his head, his elbows extended toward the sky. Like Picard, he wore only a standard Starfleet uniform, his omniscience protecting them both from the vacuum. "You should have seen it the first time."

Impressive, yes, Picard agreed silently, but where exactly, in space *and* time were they now? As he floated in the void, he considered all that he saw around him. Judging from the sheer density of stars in sight, he theorized that he and Q were either very close to the galactic core of the Milky Way or else sometime very distant in the past, when the expanding universe was much smaller, and the interstellar distances much shorter, than they were in his own time. Or both, he realized.

"When is this?" he asked Q again. At the preceding stop on Q's tour, Picard had found himself millions of years in the past. He could only speculate what era Q had brought him to now, just as he could only ponder what devious reason Q had for abducting him in the first place. Besides Q's own perverse amusement, that is. "I demand an explanation."

"One would think you would have learned by now, *mon capitaine,*" Q replied, "that your demands and desires are quite irrelevant where I am concerned." He assumed a standing posture a few meters away from Picard. "For what it's worth, though, we are presently a mere one million years before your home sweet home in the twenty-fourth century." A polished bronze pocketwatch materialized in Q's palm and he squinted at its face. "Hmmm. We seem to be a few minutes early."

"Early for what?" Picard asked. At every previous stop, they had observed the activities of Q's younger self. Yet they appeared to be very much alone at the present, with only a surplus of stars to keep them company. *A million years ago,* he thought, both amazed and aghast. *Even if I knew where Earth was among those distant stars, the first human beings will not stand erect for another five hundred thousand years. Here and now, I am the only living* Homo sapiens *in the entire universe.* It was a terrifying thought.

"For them," Q answered as a sudden flash of white light attracted Picard's eyes. The light flared and died in an instant, leaving behind two humanoid figures striding across the empty void as though they were walking upon a level pathway. They approached him and Q at a brisk pace, coming within ten or fifteen meters of where Picard floated beside Q. Paradoxically, he thought he heard footsteps, despite the utter absurdity of any sound existing in the vacuum. *Then again,* he thought, *with Q, nothing is impossible.*

He recognized both figures from earlier points in Q's past. One of them was Q himself, albeit a million years younger than the self-centered and thoroughly irritating individual who had kidnapped him only hours before. This was a more youthful Q, he had learned, one at the very onset of his mischievous career. Would that the Continuum had curbed him way back here, Picard thought, knowing better than most just how insufferable Q would become in the many millennia ahead. *I don't know what's scarier,* he mused, *a more juvenile Q or a one closer to the Q I know.*

The other figure made Picard even more uneasy. He called himself 0, as in nil, and he claimed to be an explorer from a far-off dimension unknown even to the Continuum. Picard, who considered himself a quick judge of character, found 0 quite a shady customer. *Back on the* Enterprise, he thought, *I wouldn't trust him within a light-year of my starship.* Picard was quick to remember that everything he now saw had been "translated" by Q into terms his human mind and senses could comprehend. That being the case, Picard had to wonder what more-than-human characteristics were represented by 0's weathered features and stout frame, and how much the older Q's memories may have colored his anthropomorphized portrait of the roguish stranger. From what preternatural first impression came the devilish gleam in the man's azure eyes, the cocksure set of his toothy grin, or the swagger in his stride? Picard could tell 0 was trouble at first glance; so why couldn't the Q of this era? Just who or what *was* 0? Falstaff to the young Q's Prince Hal, Picard speculated, falling back as ever on his beloved Shakespeare, or something a good deal more sinister? *If nothing else, I'm accumulating valuable insights into the early days of the Q Continuum.* He just hoped that he would someday be able to return to his own ship and era so that he could report all he had learned back to Starfleet, where the Q were justly regarded as one of the universe's most intriguing mysteries—and potential threats.

As before, neither 0 nor the younger Q were aware of Q's and Picard's presence. Much like Scrooge and his ghostly visitors, Picard thought, when they spied on the likes of Bob Cratchit or Fezziwig.

0 sang boisterously as he trod the spaceways with Q:

> *"There was a young lad whose bold virility,*
> *brought him some pains in a court of civility."*

The attire of the new arrivals, Picard noted, had changed significantly since 0's first appearance in this universe. This came as no surprise; throughout Picard's trek through time, the clothing of those he observed had evolved more or less along Earth's historical lines. An artistic conceit, according to Q, intended to convey a sense of antiquity, as well as the gradual passage of time, to the likes of Picard, who had to wonder whether the concept of clothing even applied to the Q in their true form. *How much of this is real,* he mused, *and how much simply stage dressing on the part of Q?*

He might never know.

> *"On posh settees with pinky out,*
> *He found not much to chat about."*

At present, 0 and the young Q affected the fashions of eighteenth-century Europe, some one hundred thousand millennia before the real thing. Both figures wore stylish velvet suits, 0's a rich olive green, while Q preferred periwinkle blue. Their long coats were open in front to expose rosy damask vests from which ruffled shirt tops peeked. Black silk cravats were tied around their necks and each man wore a short brown wig, tied in the back, atop his head. Polished black shoes with gleaming metal buckles clicked impossibly against the emptiness of space, beneath white wool stockings that were held up by ribbons tied above the knee. They might have been two fine gentlemen out for a night on the town, Picard observed, except that, in this instance, that town was the known universe of a million years ago.

0's singing voice was as gravelly as ever, and more enthusiastic than melodious:

> *"But on darkened nights, 'hind tavern gates,*
> *He discovered he had lots of mates!"*

Wrapping up his raucous ditty, he laughed and slapped young Q on the back. "Boldness!" 0 declared. "That's the ticket. Follow your instincts and never mind what the fainthearted say." His raspy voice held a trace of an accent that Picard couldn't place; certainly it was nothing resembling the captain's native French. 0's crippled left leg dragged behind him as he hiked beside Q, expounding on a topic he had mentioned before. "Take the fine art of testing, say. Determining the ultimate limits and potential of lesser species under controlled conditions. That's a fine and fitting vocation for beings like us. Who better than we to invent curious and creative challenges for our brutish brethren?"

"It sounds fascinating," young Q admitted. "I've always been intrigued by primitive life-forms, especially those with a crude approximation of sentience, but it never occurred to me to intervene in their humble existences. I've simply observed them in their natural environments."

"That's fine for a start," 0 said, "but you can't really understand a species unless you've seen how they respond to completely unexpected circumstances—of the sort that only we can provide. It's an engrossing pastime for us, entertaining as well as educational, while providing a valuable service to the multiverse. Only by testing baser breeds can they be forced to transcend their wretched routines and advance to the next level of existence." 0 lifted his gaze heavenward as he extolled this lofty agenda. "Or not," he added with a shrug.

"But doesn't meddling with their petty lives interfere with their natural evolution?" Q asked. Picard's jaw nearly dropped at the sight of Q making the case for the Prime Directive. *Now I've seen everything,* he thought.

"Nature is overrated," 0 insisted. "We can do better." A gold-framed mirror appeared out of nowhere and 0 held it out in front of him so that it captured the reflection of both him and Q. "Take you and me, say. Do you think our far-seeing forebears would have ever evolved to this exalted state if they'd worried about what nature intended? Of course not! We've overcome our base, bestial origins, so it's only fitting that we help other breeds do the same—if they're able."

"And if they're not?" Q asked.

0 dispatched the mirror to oblivion, then shrugged. "Well, that's regrettable when it happens, but you can't groom a garden without doing a little pruning now and then. Extinction's part of the evolutionary agenda, natural or not. Some portion of those beneath us are going to flunk the survival test whether we help them along or not. We're just applying a little creativity to the process."

Picard recalled the older Q's periodic attempts to judge humanity and felt a chill run down his spine. Was this where Q acquired his fondness for draconian threats? If so, he thought, then 0 had a lot to answer for.

"That's true enough, I suppose," the young Q said, listening attentively and occasionally nodding in agreement. To Picard's dismay, 0's lessons appeared to be sinking in. "I take it you've done this before?"

"Here and there," 0 admitted with what Picard regarded as characteristic vagueness. "But you don't need to take my word for it, not when you can experience for yourself the rich and restorative rewards of such pursuits. And there's no time like this moment to begin," he enthused, giving Q a hearty slap on the back while simultaneously, Picard noted, changing the subject from his past to the present. "Now, where are these peculiar people you were telling me about?"

Young Q pointed at the colliding star clusters overhead. Lace cuffs protruded from the deep, turned-back sleeves of his velvet coat. "Look!" he urged 0, and Picard was surprised by the infectious good humor in the youth's tone, so different from the sour sarcasm of his older self. "Here they come."

Picard looked where indicated. At first he saw nothing but the same breathtaking panorama he had viewed before, the luminous swirls of stars and radiant gas coming together into one resplendent pageant of light and color, but as he gazed further a portion of the colossal spectacle seemed to detach itself from the whole, growing ever larger in comparison as it hurled across the void toward the assembled immortals, plus Picard. The strange phenomenon devoured the incalculable distance between them, coming closer and closer until he recognized the incandescent cloud of seething plasma.

"The Calamarain," Picard breathed in astonishment, never mind the lack of any visible atmosphere. And one million years in the past, no less! He never would have imagined that the Calamarain were so old. Were these the very same entities who had been approaching the *Enterprise* before, at the very moment that Q had snatched him away, or were these merely their remote ancestors? Either way, who could have guessed that their kind dated back to so distant an era?

Then again, he reflected, the late Professor Galen's archaeological studies had revealed, with a little help from the captain himself, that humanoid life existed in the Milky Way Galaxy as far back as four billion years ago, and Picard had recently seen with his own eyes humanoid beings on Tagus III two billion years before his own time, so why should he be surprised that gaseous life-forms were at least one million years old? Picard shook his head numbly; the tremendous spans of time encompassed by his journey were almost too huge to conceive of, let alone keep track of. *It's too much,* he thought, trying to roll with the conceptual punches Q kept dishing out. *How can one mortal mind cope with time on this scale?*

The massive cloud that was the Calamarain, larger and wider across than even a Sovereign-class starship, passed within several kilometers of Picard, 0, and the two Qs. Iridescent patterns dazzled along the length and breadth of the cloud, producing a kaleidoscopic array of surging hues and shades. "So these are them?" 0 said, the wrinkles around his eyes deepening as he peered at the huge accumulation of vapors. "Well, they're sparkly enough, I'll give them that." His nostrils flared as he sniffed the vacuum. "They smell like a swamp, though." He limped nearer to the border of the cloud. "What say we start the testing with them, see how adaptable they are?"

"Er, I'm not sure that's a good idea," young Q answered, lagging behind. One of his high stockings came loose and he tugged haplessly at its neck. Next to Picard, his older self sighed and shook his head sadly. "The Coulalakritous are fairly advanced in their own right, only a few levels below the Continuum, and they aren't exactly the most sociable of creatures."

"Coulalakritous?" Picard whispered to his own Q, lowering his voice out of habit even though neither 0 nor the young Q could hear him.

"The name changed later," he said, shrugging his shoulders. "Be reasonable, Jean-Luc. It's been umpteen thousand years, after all. How often do you think of your precious France as Gaul?"

Picard decided not to argue the point, choosing instead to concentrate on the scenario unfolding before him. So this was indeed where Q first acquired his insidious inclination for "testing" humanity and other species. *Many thanks, 0,* he thought bitterly; if the mysterious entity did nothing else, this alone was enough to condemn him in Picard's eyes.

"Wait," young Q called out, hurrying to catch up with his companion as 0 continued to advance toward the sentient plasma cloud. "I told you, they don't approve of visitors."

"And you're going to let that stop you?" 0 challenged. He chuckled and stirred the outside of the cloud with a meaty finger. Thin blue tracings of bioelectrical energy ran up his arm, but he only cackled louder. "All the more reason to shake up their insular existence and see how they react. You'll never learn anything if you worry about what the subject of your experiment wants. Let the tested dictate the terms of the test and you defeat the whole point of the exercise."

"I don't know," young Q said, hesitating. Picard thought he saw restraint and good sense warring with temptation and unchecked curiosity on the callow godling's face. *I know which side I'm betting on,* he thought, calling upon over ten years of personal experience with the older Q.

"Come on, friend," 0 egged him on. "Surely we didn't come all this way just to gawk at these cumulus critters from out here. Where's your sense of adventure, not to mention scientific inquiry?"

Restraint and good sense went down in flames as the young Q's pride asserted itself. "Right here!" he crowed, thumbing his chest. "Who are these puffed-up piles of hot air to decide where a Q should come and go? To blazes with their privacy!"

"There's the Q I know!" 0 said proudly, and Picard, looking on silently, had to agree. 0 jabbed his protégé in the ribs with his elbow. "For a second there I thought you might be one of those stuffed shirts from the Continuum." His face assumed a mock-serious expression that endured for only an instant before collapsing into a mischievous grin. "Between you and me, friend, you're the only one of your lot with any fire or fission at all, not to mention a sense of humor."

"Don't I know it!" young Q said indignantly. He backed up to take a running leap into the glowing cloudmass. "Last one into the Coulalakritous is a—"

0 grabbed Q's collar as he ran by, only moments before the impetuous super-being dived headlong into the sentient plasma. "Not so fast," he counseled Q, con-fusing his duly appointed guardian. "No reason to go barging in there, especially if this phosphorescent fog is as inhospitable as you give me to believe." A crafty smile creased his face. "I say we infiltrate them first. The testing is always more ac-curate if the tester's hand remains concealed, especially at the beginning."

Showing his true colors, Picard thought. Alas, the starstruck young Q failed to make the connection between 0's plan to deceive the Coulalakritous and the way 0 had already inveigled his way into Q's trust—and, through him, the Continuum.

"Just follow my lead, young Q, and keep your wits about you." Like a genie re-turning to his bottle, 0 dissolved into a pocket of phosphorescent mist indistinguish-able from that which composed the Coulalakritous. He/it hovered for a second outside the immense cloud, then flowed tailfirst into the billowing vapors as though sucked in by some powerful pumping mechanism. The young Q gulped nervously, looking back over his shoulder as if contemplating a hasty retreat, but soon underwent the same transformation and followed his would-be mentor into the mass of plasma. Picard made an attempt to keep track of the two new streams of gas, but it was like trying to discern an individual splash of liquid within a restless ocean. From where Picard was floating, 0 and young Q were completely lost within the Coulalakritous. Their metamorphosis surprised him at first, but the logic behind it was readily appar-ent. *If Q assumes human form when he tests humanity, I suppose it only follows that he and 0 would disguise themselves as gases before testing the Coulalakritous.*

"Hard to imagine I was ever so suggestible," the older Q commented, but Picard felt more apprehensive than nostalgic. His heart sank as he guessed what was coming next.

"We're going after them, aren't we?" he asked, resigned to yet another bizarre and disorienting experience. *At least I might learn something that could help the* Enterprise *in my own time,* he consoled himself, assuming his ship had indeed en-countered the Calamarain in his absence. It dawned on him that he had no idea how much time might have passed upon the *Enterprise* while he was away. Had the Calamarain threatened the ship once more? What was happening to Riker and the others?

"You know me so well, Jean-Luc," Q said. He snapped his fingers and a sudden hot flush rushed over Picard as, before his eyes, the very atoms of his body sped up and drifted farther apart, their molecular bonds dissolving at Q's direction. He held his hand up before his face just in time to see the hand become insubstantial and semitransparent, like a ghost in some holodeck fantasy. His fingers fluttered like smoke rising from a five-year-old's birthday cake, merging and coalescing into a single continuous stream of radiant mist. His arm quickly went the way of his digits and, before he knew it, Picard saw within his field of vision only the outer limits of the man-sized accumulation of gas he had become.

How can I see without eyes? he marveled. *How can I think without a brain?* But the Calamarain, or the Coulalakritous, or whatever they were called at this place and time, proved that consciousness could exist in this form, so he could, too, it seemed. The galaxy looked the same as it had before, the overflowing cornucopia of stars around him shining just as brightly. He felt a strange energy suffusing his being, though, like the tingle of static electricity before it was discharged. Strange new senses, feeling like a cross between hearing and touch, detected waves of power radiating from the Coulalakritous. The charge of the larger cloud tugged on him like gravity, drawing him toward the seething sea of vapor. Picard surrendered to the pull, uncertain how he could have fled even if he had wanted to. Despite his resignation, a sudden sense of misgiving increased as the great cloud filled the horizon. He felt a surge of panic welling from somewhere deep inside him, and realized that it stemmed from his memories of being immersed in the group-mind of the Borg Collective. If he had still possessed a physical body, he would have trembled at the prospect of losing his individuality once again.

Another shimmering cloudlet drifted a few meters away, on a parallel course toward the Coulalakritous. Lacking a mouth or any other features, it nonetheless addressed him in Q's voice. "Be of stout heart, Picard. You're going where no vaporized human has ever gone before."

Then the stars were gone and all Picard could see or hear or feel was the overwhelming presence of the cosmic cloud all around him. It was a maelstrom of surging currents and eddies, carrying him along in their wake. A million voices hummed around him, yet, to his vast relief, he discovered he could still isolate his own thoughts from the din. Snatches of conversation, too many to count, beat upon his new inhuman senses, almost deafening him:

. . . *the Principal Intent of Gravitational Fixities are to perpetuate Substance along Graduated Hierarchies . . . until fuller Thou art, tarry and ask Myself again . . . to the Inverse, the Singular Attributes of Transuranic Essentials plainly denote . . . Solitary Pygmy Suns forever desired before Paired Twins . . . no, Thou mistakes My Supposition grossly . . . ever should the Whole of Thoughtful Souls arrive at Concord and Harmony . . . much does Myself long to behold Such . . . never in Tenfold Demi-Spans shall That come to pass . . . should Thou refuse to merge Thy Vitality with Thy Fellows, Thou cannot rightly anticipate that They shall merge Thine with Thou . . . Our Hours were Exemplary in the Time Before . . . was a Unique Instance, not a Tendency of Import or Duration . . . I dreamed I was a Fluid . . . wherefore do We journey? . . . entreat Succor for Myself, My Ions lose Their Galvanism . . . Thou ever avers Such! . . . the Pursuit of Grace takes precedence over Mere Beauty . . . do Thou fancy that Quasars have Spirits? . . . I dispute That resolutely . . . no, pray regard the Evidence. . . .*

Mon Dieu, Picard thought, spellbound by the unending torrent of communication, which struck him as being somewhere halfway between a Vulcan mind-meld and late-night debates at Starfleet Academy. As far as he could tell, the Coulalakritous did not possess a single unified consciousness like the Borg, but rather were engaged in incessant dialogue with each other. Could it be, he speculated, that this sentient cloudmass represented some form of absolute democracy? Or perhaps they had a more academic orientation, like an incorporeal university or seminar. He wondered how this incredible forum compared with the Great Link of the Changelings, as described in Odo's intelligence reports from Deep Space Nine. The so-called Founders were liquid while the Coulalakritous were gaseous, but how different did that make the two species? From the point of view of a former solid, he mused, both seem equally amorphous . . . and astounding. He could only hope that someday he would have the opportunity to compare the experiences with Odo himself. No doubt Worf or Miles O'Brien would be happy to introduce them.

"Annoying, aren't they?" Q's voice piped up from somewhere nearby. "They never shut up and they never tire of debating each other. Small wonder they don't want to communicate with any other intelligences; they're too busy arguing with themselves."

Picard looked for Q, but all he saw was the ceaseless motion of the Coulalakritous. It seemed a minor miracle that he could hear Q at all over the cacophonous buzz of the cloud-creatures' conversation. *These aren't really sound waves at all,* he considered, recalling a Starfleet theory that the Calamarain communicated by means of tachyon emissions. *Am I actually "hearing" tachyons now?*

The ambient heat within the cloud was intense, but his new form did not find it uncomfortable. Of course, he realized. The Coulalakritous would have to generate their own internal heat, and in massive quantities, to avoid freezing solid in the cold of space. Some sort of metabolic chemical reaction, he wondered, or controlled nuclear fusion? Either way, he suspected that his ordinary human body would be incinerated instantly by the volcanic temperature within the cloud. Instead, the ionized gases merely felt like a sauna or hot spring. Remarkable, Picard thought, savoring the experience despite other, more pressing concerns. The more he listened, the more he thought he could isolate individual voices by their tone or timbre. There were diverse personalities alive within the collective boundaries of the plasma cloud: long-winded bores, excited explorers, passionate visionaries, skeptics, cranks, poets, philosophers, fussbudgets, free thinkers, reactionaries, radicals, and scientists. He could hear them all, and the only thing they all seemed to have in common was that they savored debate and discussion. *There's so much we could learn from these beings,* Picard thought.

Q sounded substantially less awestruck. "If I live to be another eternity, I'll never understand why I found this nattering miasma so interesting in the first place." Picard could hear the impatience in his tone. "If you're quite through with your adolescent sense of wonder, perhaps you'd care to pay attention to the carefree antics of my younger self and his dubious acquaintance. That *is* why we're here, you know."

"Where are they?" Picard asked, genuinely at a loss.

"Can't you hear them?" Q responded. "Why, they're right over there."

Not only could Picard not distinguish 0 and the other Q from the rest of the maelstrom, he couldn't even see Q. No doubt the Coulalakritous could tell each other apart visually, he thought, but he could barely make sense of what he was hearing, let alone seeing. Even though he was beginning to distinguish one voice from another, he could hardly pinpoint two specific individuals in this gaseous Tower of Babel. The sights and sensations remained far too alien. "Over there? Pay attention?" he said, incredulous. "I don't even know what I am anymore."

"Complain, complain. Is that all you can do, Jean-Luc?" Q said. "I knew I should have brought along Data instead. At least he can listen to more than one sound at once and still comprehend what he's hearing." He sounded sorely ill-used. "Very well, I suppose I have to do *everything* around here."

All at once, the overpowering rustle of impassioned discussion surrounding him receded further into the background, to the extent that he could now isolate the distinctive voices of both 0 and the younger Q. The two counterfeit

Coulalakritous became visible as well, acquiring a silvery metallic glow that set them apart from the other sentient gases swirling through the vast gaseous community. Shapeless and inhuman, they reminded Picard of globules of liquid mercury. He assumed that the silver tinting was for his benefit alone; presumably both the Coulalakritous and the trespassing immortals were unaware of the change. The argent glow had to be out of phase, too, lest he and the older Q's presence be exposed. To Picard's slight annoyance, he observed that his obnoxious traveling companion had not bothered to make himself visible as well. *It's just like Q,* he fumed, *to put others at a disadvantage, especially me.*

"Happy now?" the indistinguishable Q asked. He might have been anywhere around Picard. "Do try to concentrate, Jean-Luc. I don't want to have to relive this a third time just for your sake."

Conveniently, the silver puffs of vapor were not far away, although Picard found it hard to estimate precise distances within such an atypical environment. They were certainly within listening range. He felt slightly uncomfortable eavesdropping this way, even on a Q, but he had to concede that it was preferable to having to deal with 0 and the other Q directly. Every Starfleet captain knew a little espionage was necessary now and then.

"Is this all they do?" 0 inquired out loud. His cloud, Picard noted, was larger than the younger Q's, and streaked with dark metallic shadings that were almost black in places. "Why, they're nothing but talk! Rancid and rubbish, all of them." He clearly did not approve.

"Well, they're said to have traveled extensively throughout the galaxy," his companion offered. At the moment, the youthful Q resembled a glistening dust devil, whirling madly with speed and energy to burn. "And they never forget anything, or so I'm told."

"Tell me about it," the older Q said dryly, possibly recalling the Calamarain's undying vendetta against him.

"Can they travel faster than a ray of sunlight?" 0 asked, and Picard could readily imagine the calculating expression on the old rogue's face. If 0 still had a humanoid face, that is.

"Why, sure! How else would they get around?" Q said cheerily, then remembered 0's inability to travel at warp speed except through the Continuum. "Er, nothing personal, I mean. I forgot about your . . . well, there's more to godhood than zipping from here to there in a hurry." The spinning cloud turned pink with embarrassment at his faux pas. "Why rush when you have all of eternity, right?"

This really was a long time ago, Picard realized. It was hard to imagine the Q of the twenty-fourth century being embarrassed by anything, let alone a tactless remark. *More's the pity,* he thought.

"Calm down, friend. No offense taken," 0 insisted. "This old wanderer's well aware of his present limitations. It's hardly your fault, Q." An edge of bitterness colored his words and Picard recalled the crippled leg 0 possessed in his human guise. "Blame instead those meddling miscreants who banished me here in the first place. Contemptible curs!"

"But I thought you came here of your own choosing," the Q-cloud said, taken aback by the sudden malevolence in 0's tone, the spin of its miniature eddies slowing anxiously.

"So I did!" 0 asserted, regaining his usual robust air. "Who says otherwise?"

"But, I mean, you . . ." Q stammered. Picard had to admit to himself that he found this Q's discomfort rather satisfying; it was good to see Q off balance for once, even if Picard had been forced to travel countless centuries in the past to witness the occasion.

"Yesterday's news," 0 insisted. "Moldy memories better off forgotten." The silver mist that was 0 cruised along the perimeter of the plasma cloud. Picard found he could follow him by focusing his attention in that direction. "Let's get on with the business of testing this talkative tempest. Here's an idea: Suppose we try to herd this cloud in one direction or another. Put some wind in our sails, so to speak."

"Er, what exactly would that prove?" Q asked.

"Why, nothing less than whether the Coulalakritous are capable—and worthy—of controlling their own destiny. If the likes of you and I have the power to change their course at will, then plainly they're not as highly evolved as they should be." He emitted the tachyon equivalent of a low chuckle. "And, as an added bonus, I acquire my own personal porters. What do you say, Q? Do you think we can do it?"

Mon Dieu, Picard thought, shocked by the cold-blooded ruthlessness of 0's suggestion. *He's thinking of enslaving the Coulalakritous, to harness them as a means of faster-than-light transportation for himself!* It was a blatant violation of the Prime Directive, not to mention basic morality. The voices around him belonged to a sentient people, not beasts of burden. Did the young Q comprehend the full horror of what his companion was advocating? Picard wondered. Was this the telltale moment that would lift the scales from his (metaphorical) eyes?

Apparently not. "I don't know," young Q said. "I've never really considered the matter before."

"Of course not," 0 said readily. "Why should you, a healthy young Q like yourself?" The silver mist, with its darker undertones, oozed sinuously around the glowing pocket of gas that now embodied the young Q. "For us that have a wee bit of trouble getting around, though, this notion merits a closer look. After all, much as I enjoy your company, you don't want to have to chauffeur me around the cosmos indefinitely, do you?"

"That's what I promised the Continuum," Q said, sounding as if the full implications of that commitment were just now sinking in.

"So you did," 0 assented, "and for sure you meant it at the time." The volume of the dark silver gas began to increase dramatically, spreading out in all directions around the outer surface of the entire cloud. "Still, it can't hurt to explore other options now. You wanted to test another species, right? Trust me, this is as good a way as any."

"Wait. What are you doing?" The Q-mist started to churn anxiously within the confines of the elder entity's substance but found itself hemmed in, unable to move. "Stop it!"

"Just blasting two planets with one asteroid, that's all," 0 stated as his dark silver stain permeated the nebulous borders of the Coulalakritous, enclosing the cloud within his own gaseous grip. "Nothing to be alarmed about, at least not for you and me. The cloud, on the other hand . . . well, they might have cause for concern."

This is monstrous, Picard thought, sickened by 0's shameless attempt to place an entire community of intelligent beings under his control. If he understood the situation correctly, 0 meant to turn the Coulalakritous into the interstellar equivalent of galley slaves, yoked into transporting 0 throughout the galaxy at warp speed. He had to remind himself that, whatever happened next, everything he was witnessing now had already taken place from the perspective of his own era, was incredibly ancient history in fact, predating the very birth of humanity, none of which made it any easier to watch. "Why didn't you do something?" he challenged the older Q, wherever he was.

"It was too new," Q apologized from somewhere behind Picard. *"I* was too new. 0 sounded like he knew what he was doing. How was I supposed to know whether it was a reasonable experiment or not?"

"How could you not have?" Picard answered angrily. Humanity had already learned that such exploitation of another intelligent species was unconscionable, and human history was only a nanosecond in the lifetime of Q if his most grandiose claims were to be believed. "What's so hard to understand about slavery?"

"Ever ridden a horse, Picard?" Q retorted. "Ever bred bees for honey? Believe me, you're a lot closer to a horse or a bug than I was to the Coulalakritous, even back then. Don't be so quick to judge me."

"These are not horses!" the captain said. Indignation deepened his voice. "And they are most certainly not insects. I've heard them, felt them, experienced at least a fragment of their existence—and so have you."

"I've listened to you, too, Picard," Q said, materializing before Picard in his usual guise. He pinched the fabric of his uniform. "Contrary to my appearance, that doesn't make me human, or even a humanitarian."

Picard would have shaken his head in disgust had he still possessed humanoid form. *I don't know why I should be so surprised,* he thought. *Q has never shown any consideration for "lesser" species before, and it seems he was always that way.*

By now the taint of 0 had spread all over the exterior of the cloud community. It thickened and solidified, enclosing the Coulalakritous within a thin, silvery membrane that began to squeeze inward, forcing the assembled gases (including Picard) to flow only in the direction 0 had chosen. But his efforts to take the reins of the cloud did not go unnoticed.

The perpetual buzz of a million voices fell silent for an instant, thousands upon thousands of discussions interrupted simultaneously, before the dialogue started up again with a new and more urgent tone:

what is This? . . . What Now transpires? . . . Make It cease! . . . Fearful am I . . . I cannot touch the Outside! . . . Nor I . . . Nor I . . . hurts Myself . . . crushing . . . so Cold . . . losing Vitality . . . cannot move . . . cease . . . cease NOW! . . .

It was hideous. Within seconds, 0 had reduced an ageless, living symposium to panic. Picard heard the shock and dismay in the cries of the entire assemblage. He longed for the *Enterprise,* whose powerful phasers might be able to surgically peel 0 away from the Coulalakritous, but his ship was many millennia away. *If only I could do something to help these people!*

0 laughed boisterously, drowning out Picard's frustrated craving to stop him. The membrane squeezed harder and Picard felt the compressed gases press in on him from all sides but one, propelling him forward against his will. "Wait," he protested, not understanding why he should be feeling any pressure at all. "I thought we were out of phase with this moment in time."

"Poetic license," Q explained, his humanoid shape unaffected by the pressure. "I want you to get the full experience."

In other words, Picard realized, Q was generating the sensation himself, to simulate conditions within the besieged cloud of plasma. Picard was less than grateful. *I could have easily done without this much verisimilitude.*

The Coulalakritous fought back. Overcoming their initial consternation, the voices began to come together with a single purpose:

... cease ... halt the Adversary ... Our Volition is Our Own ... Our Will is United ... cease crushing Us ... hurts ... disregard the Torment ... shall not yield ... persevere, do not cease stirring, All of We ... Halt the Cold ... do not be Fearful ... Ours is the Heat of Many is ... must be Free ... persevere ... Together We can break free ... Together We ... together ... Flashes of lightning sparked along the inner skin of the membrane 0 had become. *... Together ... Together ... Together ...*

"Are you indeed?" 0 mocked them, his voice emerging from the membrane so that he seemed to be speaking from all directions at once. "All unanimity aside, I believe I have the upper hand at the moment," he said, demonstrating his point by constricting the enclosed gases further. Picard lost sight of the Q-mist as, poetic license or not, he felt his substance stretched and prodded by the pressure being exerted on the cloud community. Because his senses were distorted by his unlikely new form, it felt like a scream and sounded like heavy gravity. Claustrophobia gripped him now that he could no longer flow freely through the great cloud, and he marveled at how quickly he had grown accustomed to his gaseous state. At least he was used to being contained within a skin of flesh; he could only imagine how unbearable this captivity must be to the Coulalakritous. *If only I could do something,* he thought, *but I'm not even really here ... I think.*

The cloud-beings did not submit readily to 0's will. The atmosphere surrounding Picard warmed dramatically, transforming into a cauldron of superheated gases, as they expanded outward against the pressure of the membrane. The swirling maelstrom of sentient vapors increased in fury, gaining strength and intensity by the moment. Picard had a sudden mental image of being in the middle of—no, being *part of*—an old-fashioned steam engine of colossal proportions. *Perhaps,* he thought hopefully, *0 has underestimated the Coulalakritous.* After all, they surely hadn't endured into the twenty-fourth century, eventually evolving into the Calamarain, by being defenseless. He cheered on their efforts, wishing he could add his own determination, out of phase as he was, to the struggle.

... Together ... break free ... Together ... break free ... Together ... break free ... Together ... break free ... Together ...

Slowly, the tide appeared to turn. The cloud swelled against the membrane, spreading it ever thinner around an expanding volume of ionized and agitated gas. "Beasts! Brutes! Upstarts!" 0 cursed them, but his voice faded in volume as his width approached infinitesimal. Within the cloud, fierce currents tossed Picard around like a cork upon the waves. "Blast you," 0 raged, barely audible now. "Give up, why don't you? Surrender!"

Then, like an overinflated balloon, the membrane that was 0 came apart and the victorious Coulalakritous rushed through the gap to freedom. "Time to switch seats for a better view," the older Q commented, and Picard abruptly found himself outside the cloud, looking on from a distance. The gigantic fog, even larger and more diffuse than before, loomed ahead of him, so attenuated that Picard could glimpse stars and nebulae through it. The Coulalakritous wasted no time contracting back to their original proportions, growing opaque once more. A second later, a stream of silver mist was forcibly ejected from the vaporous community. "Not my most digni-fied exit," Q commented, watching his younger self spew forth from the interior of the Coulalakritous, "but I like to think I've improved since. You must concede that I've always managed to depart the *Enterprise* with more than a modicum of style."

"I have always savored your exits," Picard couldn't resist replying, "more than any other aspect of your visits." Now that they had left the plasma cloud behind, they had both resumed human form. Picard was relieved to look down and see his body once more. Given a choice, he discovered he preferred floating adrift in space to squeezing in among the Coulalakritous.

"Ho, ho, Jean-Luc," Q said darkly, hanging upside down in relation to Picard. "Very droll. It would be too much to expect, I suppose, any sign of gratitude for showing you glimpses of a higher reality."

"Not when your motive has always seemed to be more about your own self-aggrandizement than my enlightenment," Picard answered.

"My self can't possibly be more aggrandized," Q stated, "as I thought you would have understood by now." He looked away from Picard at what remained of 0, hovering about a dozen meters away. "Watch closely, *mon capitaine*. Here's where things get *really* interesting."

Reduced to a severed string of silver-black film, 0 rapidly reconstituted him-self, assuming the same human form he had affected before. His craggy face was flushed with anger and his once-fine clothes were charred and seared around their edges. Smoke rose symbolically from the anomalous male figure suspended in the vacuum of space; Picard could not tell whether the fumes emanated from 0's gar-ments or his person. Beyond a doubt, 0 looked irritated enough to spontaneously combust at any moment.

His companion and guardian, the young Q, metamorphosed from mist to humanoid appearance, then strolled across the void toward 0. His attire was less battle-scarred than the other's, Picard noted, perhaps because Q had not attempted to subdue the Coulalakritous. Nervously eyeing his cohort's affronted demeanor, he seemed inclined to laugh the whole business off as an inconsequential lark. "Well, it appears we've worn out our welcome, and then some," he remarked flip-pantly. "Their loss, then. It's hardly the first time a lesser species has failed to ap-preciate a superior life-form."

"Nor would it be the last," his older self added, with a pointed look at Picard.

"On that you and I can agree," Picard shot back, feeling singularly unapprecia-tive at the moment.

The young Q's attempt at levity failed to assuage 0's ire. "They can't do this!" he snarled, his previously jovial mask slipping away to expose a visage of unmis-takable indignation. "I won't be banished again, not by their sort." His pale blue eyes glittered like icy gems, reflecting the luminous shimmer of the Coulalakritous. "Never again," he swore. "Never, I say!"

Taken aback by 0's pique, young Q squirmed uncomfortably, uncertain how to deal with his friend's temper. "But didn't they pass your test?" he asked. "You tried to harness them. They wouldn't let you. I thought that was the whole point of the endeavor."

"They cheated!" 0 barked. "Just like the others. And if there's one thing that I never abide, it's a cheater. Remember that, Q, if you remember nothing else. Never allow cheaters to make a travesty of your tests."

"Cheated how?" Q asked, looking genuinely puzzled. "Did I miss something? As I much as I loathe admitting my ignorance, I am rather new at this, so I suppose it's possible I missed a subtlety or two. Perhaps you can explain what precisely they did wrong?"

If 0 was listening at all to Q's prattle, he gave no sign of it. He glared at the incandescent majesty of the Coulalakritous with undisguised hostility. He took a deep breath, inhaling some manner of sustenance from the ether, and appeared to be drawing on a hidden reserve of strength. The smoky gray fumes rising from his scorched garments entwined about each other and, from Picard's vantage point nearby, 0's human facade appeared to flicker slightly, giving Picard brief, almost subliminal glimpses of another, more inhuman form. He received an impression of something dark and coiled, surrounded by a blurry aura of excess limbs or tendrils. Or was that only an illusion created by the twisting spirals of smoke? The more he watched, the more Picard became convinced that what he saw was no mere trick of smoke and starlight, but a genuine glimpse of another aspect of the enigmatic stranger. Picard's Starfleet training, along with years of experience in dealing with diverse life-forms, had taught him not to judge other beings by their appearance; nonetheless, he could not repress a shudder at this transitory look behind 0's customary persona. Indeed, he reflected, it was the very indistinctness of the images he perceived that made them far more eerie and unsettling than a clear and distinct depiction of the alien would have been. Picard found his imagination all too eager to fill in the blanks in this fractional, impressionistic portrait of 0's true nature. *I knew there was more to him than met the eye,* he thought. *Why couldn't Q see that?*

Power radiated from 0 like a gust of chilling wind. Picard felt the passage of the energy upon his face, stinging his cheeks, yet the power was not directed at him but at the imposing presence of the Coulalakritous. What could 0 do to such magnificent entities? Picard wondered. Had not the Coulalakritous already demonstrated their ability to defend themselves?

Yet, to his horror, he beheld the huge plasma cloud begin to shrink beneath 0's assault, its expansive volume diminishing by the second. The billowing gases slowed and thickened, the swirling eddies coming to a halt. Picard was only mildly surprised to discover that he could still hear the varied voices of the Coulalakritous crying out in distress, their words slurred and winding down like a malfunctioning recording:

no . . . nooo . . . noooo . . . not . . . anewwww . . . ceasssse . . . sooooo . . . cooooold . . . stopppppp . . . traaaaaap . . . noooooo . . . essssscaaaaaape . . . ceasssssse . . . at . . . onccccccce . . . ceassssssse . . . freeeeeezzzing . . . helppppppp . . .

"Yes, stop!" young Q seconded anxiously. "You don't need to do this, 0. Whatever they did, they're not worth our attention, let alone your peace of mind." His gaze darted back and forth between 0 and his imploding target. "Er, you can stop anytime now, anytime at all. . . ."

The enraged immortal paid no heed to either Q or the Coulalakritous. His hatefilled eyes protruded from their sockets while phantom tentacles wavered in and out of reality around him. A trickle of saliva dripped from the corner of his mouth as he ground his broad white teeth together. All his effort and concentration were aimed without exception at the intangible community that had possessed the audacity to elude his control. 0 raised his arms, an action echoed by a blur of black extensions, and coruscating scarlet energy flashed about his extended fingertips.

The cloud of plasma had already contracted to at least one-third its original size. It no longer looked truly gaseous in nature, but more like a mass of steaming, semiliquid slush. Then the slush congealed further, sucking in the last retreating wisps of vapor and turning a dull, ugly brown in hue. Picard had a horrifying mental image of an oppressed prisoner being crammed into a box far too small for him, as he watched, helpless to intervene, while 0 forced the entire awesome accumulation of gas-beings ever closer to a solid state.

. . . *Weeeeeee willlllllll nottttttttt forrrrrgettttttt* . . . the Coulalakritous vowed, their separate voices finally merging into one before falling silent entirely. Where only moments before had existed an incandescent cloud of blazing plasma, there now remained only a dense, frozen snowball, indistinguishable from any of a billion comets traversing the dark between the stars. *If they registered on the* Enterprise's *sensors in this state,* Picard guessed, *we wouldn't give them a moment's thought.* Were the Coulalakritous still conscious and aware of their utter paralysis? Part of Picard prayed that they were not.

Yet 0 was not satisfied. His beefy hands curled into grasping claws, he brought them closer together above his head, as if literally squeezing the onetime cloud between his palms instead of merely empty space. His phantasmal other self, superimposed upon his humanoid shell, shadowed his every move. Less than a kilometer away from 0, the inert chunk of ice that was the Coulalakritous kept on being compressed by invisible forces, its crystalline surface cracking and collapsing inward beneath the crushing power exerted by the vengeful immortal. How far did 0 intend to take this? Picard wondered, aghast. Until the very atoms that composed the Coulalakritous fused together, igniting a miniature supernova? Or was 0 able and willing to compress his victims' mass to so great a density that the Coulalakritous would be reduced to a microscopic black hole, a pinprick in reality from which they could never escape? Was such a horrendous feat even possible?

Young Q appeared to fear something along those lines. "I think that's enough, 0," he announced with unexpected firmness. With a burst of pure energy, he placed himself between 0 and his prey, grunting involuntarily as he felt the force of 0's unchecked ire. The flesh upon his face rippled and grew distorted, like that of an old-time astronaut enduring tremendous G-forces, and his bones crunched together noisily as he shrunk into a slightly squatter, more compact Q, losing at least a centimeter of height. He held his ground, though, and 0's attack rebounded upon its source, staggering the older entity and sending him stumbling backward through empty space. *Q to the rescue?* Picard marveled, more than a little startled by this atypical display of altruism. *I mean, of all people . . . Q?*

"What?" 0 was as taken aback by Q's actions as Picard. "Are you out of your all-knowing mind?" he bellowed, visibly dismayed by the young Q's defiance. His ruddy face grew even more crimson. A vein along his left temple throbbed rhythmically like a pulsar. "Get out of my way, or I swear I'll . . . I'll . . ."

Q flinched in anticipation of the other's wrath, but no explosion, verbal or literal, followed. Perhaps caught off guard by his own angry words, 0 faltered, falling mute even as the flailing, insubstantial tendrils that enshrouded him withdrew into some private hiding place deep within his person. He turned his back on Q and the two invisible onlookers while he struggled to regain his composure. "0?" the young Q inquired anxiously.

When the stranger, his clothes still smoldering from his first battle with the

Coulalakritous, faced them again, no trace of animosity could be found in his expression. He looked contrite and abashed, not to mention exhausted by his exertions. Perspiration plastered his damp curls to his skull. "Forgive me, friend, for losing my temper that way. I shouldn't have raised my voice to you, no matter how vexed that malodorous miasma made me."

"Never mind me," Q responded, stretching his body until he regained his usual dimensions. He looked back over his shoulder at the solidified chunk of Coulalakritous tumbling through the void, its momentum carrying the frigid comet slowly toward them. "What in the name of the Continuum have you done to them?"

0 paused to catch his breath before replying. Freezing the gas-beings had obviously taken a lot out of him. All the blood had drained from his face, leaving him drawn and pale. Lungs heaving, he bent forward, hands on his knees, and stared at his shoes until his color returned. "That?" he inquired, short of breath. "A mere bit of thermodynamic sleight-of-hand, and nothing those cantankerous clouds didn't have coming to them." He limped across the vacuum until he hovered only a few meters away from his fretful protégé. "You have to understand, Q, that in any tests there must be penalties for failure, and for deliberate cheating, or else there's no inducement to excel. It looks harsh, I know, but it's the only way. Lesser lights are not going to submit to our tests out of the goodness of their hearts. They seldom comprehend, you see, the honor and the opportunity being bestowed upon them. You need to *motivate* them, and sometimes that means having the gumption to apply a sharp poke when necessary."

"But the Coulalakritous?" Q asked, sounding baffled. "What exactly did they—"

"Things didn't go off quite as I planned there," 0 interrupted, striking a conciliatory tone. "To be honest, I underestimated how out of practice I am, and how inexperienced you are." He saw Q bristle at the remark and held up his hand to fend off the younger being's objections. "No criticism intended, friend, merely a statement of fact. I'm the one at fault for dropping us both into the deep end before we were ready. Perhaps we should round up some able assistance before trying again." He scratched his chin thoughtfully as the approaching ball of ice, roughly the size of a Starfleet shuttlecraft, barreled helplessly toward the location where he and Q just happened to be standing. "Yes, extra hands, that's the ticket. And I know just the right reinforcements to enlist in our cause. . . ."

"Reinforcements?" Q asked, seconds before the frozen Coulalakritous would have collided with the two humanoid figures. Neither seemed particularly concerned about the oncoming comet. "Who do you mean?"

"Wait and see," 0 promised. With a casual wave of his hand, he deflected the course of the tumbling mass of petrified plasma and sent it hurling off at a forty-five-degree angle from him and his companion. "Follow me, Q. You won't be disappointed." He vacated the scene in a flash, taking the young Q with him. Left behind, Picard watched as the victimized Coulalakritous receded into the distance. The closest star, the nearest possible source of warmth, was countless light-years away.

"It took them a couple millennia to thaw out again," Q whispered in his ear. He glanced down at the bronze pocketwatch in his hand. "Not that they learned anything from the experience. They're still just as ill-mannered as before."

Picard was appalled. Small wonder the Calamarain had been eager to exact their revenge on Q back in the twenty-fourth century. "That's all you have to say about it?" Picard demanded, offended by Q's cavalier tone. "An entire species frozen into suspended animation for heaven knows how long, and you have the audacity to complain about their manners? Didn't this atrocity teach you anything? How could you not have realized how dangerous this 0 creature was?"

"Oh, don't overdramatize, Jean-Luc," Q replied, a tad more defensively than usual. "Perhaps I was a trifle blind, in an omniscient sort of way, but ultimately it was a mere prank, nothing more. A trifle mean-spirited, I concede, but there was no real harm done, not permanently. In the grand cosmic scheme of things, our ionized friends were merely inconvenienced, not actually injured in any way that need concern us here." He shrugged his shoulders. "Can I help it if the Calamarain didn't see the funny side of it?"

"If what I witnessed just now was nothing more than a prank," Picard declared indignantly, "then I shudder to think what you would consider genuine maliciousness."

Q gave Picard a smile that chilled the captain's blood. "You should," he said.

Three

"Reg?" Deanna asked between two claps of thunder. "Are you feeling all right?"

Riker glanced over his shoulder at Barclay, who was manning the primary aft science station. The nervous lieutenant was looking a bit green, possibly from the constant shaking caused by the assault of the Calamarain. Despite the best efforts of the *Enterprise*'s inertial dampers, the bridge continued to lurch from side to side, a far cry from the usual smooth ride. The rocking sensation reminded Riker of an Alaskan fishing vessel he'd served on as a teen, but surely it wasn't bad enough to make anyone nauseous, was it?

Barclay started to reply, then clapped both hands over his mouth. Riker rolled his eyes and hoped the queasy crewman would not have to bolt for the crew head. Barclay was a good man, but sometimes Riker wondered how he ever got through the Starfleet screening process. Behind the command area, Baeta Leyoro snorted disdainfully.

"That will be enough, Lieutenant," Riker instructed her. Maintaining morale under such arduous conditions was hard enough without the crew sniping at each other, even if he half sympathized with the security chief's response. "How are our shields holding up?"

"Sixteen percent and sinking," Leyoro responded. She glared at the tempest upon the viewscreen.

Riker nodded grimly. They needed to find some way to retaliate. He would have preferred a more peaceful resolution to this conflict, but they were rapidly running out of options. Unfortunately, conventional weapons had thus far proven ineffective against their attacker; phasers had not discouraged the Calamarain, whose close quarters to the *Enterprise* precluded the use of quantum torpedoes. Maybe, he mused, the Calamarain required a more specialized deterrent.

Lightning flashed across the viewscreen, and an unusually violent shock wave rocked the bridge, interrupting Riker's thoughts and slamming him into the back of the captain's chair. His jaw snapped shut so suddenly he narrowly avoided biting off the tip of his tongue. To his left, he heard Deanna gasp in alarm, but whether she was reacting to the sudden impact or the Calamarain's inflamed emotions he couldn't begin to guess. At the conn, Ensign Clarze stabbed at his controls in a desperate effort to stabilize their flight but met with only mixed results. The floor beneath Riker's feet pitched and yawed like a shuttle going through an unstable wormhole. Even Data had to strain to keep his balance, digging his fingertips into the armrests of his chair. *We can't take much more of this,* he thought.

As if to prove the point, Riker felt his stomach turn over abruptly. *Oh, no,* he thought. He identified the sensation at once, even before he spotted a puddle of spilled coolant, released during an earlier impact, lifting off from the floor and floating through the air, forming an oily globule only a few meters away. "We have lost gravity generation throughout decks one through fourteen of the saucer section," Data confirmed.

At least we didn't lose the entire network, Riker thought. The ship's internal gravitation system was divided into five overlapping regions; from the sound of it, they had lost gravity in about half of the saucer. In theory, the entire battle section of the ship, including Engineering, still had gravity, but for how much longer? This latest technical mishap provided an eloquent testament to the Calamarain's offensive capabilities. It took a lot to take out the gravity generators; even with a total power loss, the superconducting stators that were the heart of the graviton generators were supposed to keep spinning for up to six hours. He couldn't remember the last time he had experienced zero gravity anywhere aboard the *Enterprise,* except in the holodecks, where reduced gravity was sometimes employed for recreational purposes.

Starfleet training included zero-G exercises, of course, but Riker could only hope that the rest of the crew didn't feel as rusty as he did. The last time he'd actually done without gravity had been during his short-lived flight on Zefram Cochrane's *Phoenix,* and that had hardly been a combat situation, at least from his perspective. Even the most primitive shuttle had come equipped with its own gravity for the last hundred years or so. *We're not used to this anymore,* he worried, wishing he'd scheduled more zero-G drills before now.

Still, the bridge crew did their best to adjust to the new conditions. Keeping a watchful eye on the drifting coolant, Clarze ducked his hairless dome out of its way. Deanna's hair, already shaken loose by the previous jolts, snaked Medusa-like about her face, obscuring her vision, until she neatly tucked the errant strands back into place. Behind and above the command area, a scowling Baeta Leyoro had lost contact with the floor and begun floating toward the ceiling. Executing an impressive backward somersault, she grabbed the top of the tactical podium with both hands, then pulled her body downward until she was once more correctly oriented above the floor. "Get me some gravity boots," she snapped at the nearest security officer, who rushed to fulfill the command.

Following standard procedure, Riker clicked his chair's emergency restraining belt into place, and heard Deanna doing the same. The hovering blob of spilled coolant wafted dangerously near Data's face, and Riker anticipated a gooey mess, but the air purification system caught hold of it and sucked the viscous mess into an intake valve mounted in the ceiling, just as similar valves cleared the atmosphere of the ashes and bits of debris produced by the battle. *Thank goodness something's still working right,* Riker thought. "Ensign Berglund," he addressed the young officer at the aft engineering station, "any chance we can get the gravity back on-line?"

"It doesn't look good," she reported, holding on tightly to a vertical station divider with her free hand. "I'm reading a systemic failure all through the alpha network." She perused the readouts at her console avidly. "Maybe if they try reinitializing the entire system from main engineering?"

Riker shook his head. He didn't want Geordi and his people concentrating on anything except keeping the shields up and running. "Gravity is a luxury we'll just have to do without for a while." Easier said than done, he realized. Humanoid bodies were simply not designed to function without gravity, especially so suddenly; pretty soon, Barclay wouldn't be the only bridge member seasick. He tapped his combadge. "Riker to Crusher. I need a medical officer with a hypospray full of librocalozene right away."

"Affirmative," Beverly replied. She didn't ask for an explanation; Riker realized sickbay must have lost gravity as well. "Ogawa is on her way."

By foot or by flight? Riker wondered, grateful that the turbolifts did not require gravity to operate properly. "Thank you, Doctor." Glancing around the bridge, he saw that Leyoro's security team was already distributing magnetic boots from the emergency storage lockers to every crew member on the bridge, starting with those standing at the aft and perimeter stations. The Angosian lieutenant stomped her own boots loudly on the floor as she regained her footing. "Good work," he told her tersely, indicating her team's rapid deployment.

"Standard procedure," she replied, shrugging. "I figure we're better off facing these stupid BOVs with our feet firmly on the ground."

"BOVs?" Riker asked. He didn't recognize the term, presumably a bit of slang from the Tarsian War.

Leyoro flashed him a wolfish grin. "Better Off Vaporized," she said.

That might be a bit redundant in this case, he thought, considering the gaseous nature of their foes. He appreciated the sentiment, though; he was getting pretty tired of being knocked around himself. But what could you do to an enemy who had already been reduced to plasma? That was the real problem, when you got down to it. Explosions and projectiles weren't much good against an undifferentiated pile of gases. The Calamarain had already blown themselves to atoms, and it hadn't hurt them one bit.

A partial retreat was also an option, he recalled. True, they couldn't outrun the Calamarain on impulse alone—that much he knew already—but maybe they could find a nebula or an asteroid belt that might provide them with some shelter from the storm, interfere with the Calamarain's onslaught. "Mr. Clarze," he barked, raising his voice to be heard above the thunder vibrating through the walls of the starship. "Is there anything nearby that we could hide behind or within?" Such a sanctuary, he knew, would have to be within impulse range as long as their warp engines were down.

The Deltan helmsman quickly consulted the readouts on his monitor. "Nothing, sir," he reported glumly, "except the barrier, of course."

The barrier, Riker thought, sitting bolt upright in the chair. Now, there's an idea!

The gravity was out, his little sister was crying, and Milo Faal didn't know what to do. Ordinarily weightlessness might have been kind of fun, but not at the moment. All the loud noises and shaking had upset Kinya, and none of his usual tricks for calming her were working at all. His eyes searched the family's quarters aboard the Enterprise in search of something he might use to reassure the toddler or distract her, but nothing presented itself; Kinya had already rejected every toy he had replicated, even the Wind Dancer hand puppet with the wiggly ears. The discarded playthings floated like miniature dirigibles throughout the living room, propelled by the force with which Kinya hurled each of them away. Not even this miraculous sight was enough to end her tantrum. "C'mon, Kinya," the eleven-year-old boy urged the little Betazoid girl hovering in front of him, a couple of centimeters above the floor. Milo himself sat cross-legged atop a durable Starfleet-issue couch, being careful not to make any sudden movements while the gravity was gone; as long as he remained at rest he hoped to stay at rest. "Don't you want to sing a song?" He launched into the first few verses of "The Laughing Vulcan and His Dog"—usually the toddler's favorite—but she refused to take the bait, instead caterwauling at the top of her lungs. Even worse than the ear-piercing vocalizations, though, were the waves of emotional distress pouring out of her, flooding Milo's empathic senses with his sister's fear and unhappiness.

An experienced Betazoid babysitter, Milo was adept at tuning out the uncontrolled emanations of small children, but this was almost more than he could take. "Please, Kinya," he entreated the toddler, "show me what a big girl you can be."

Such appeals were usually effective, but not this time. She kicked her tiny feet against the carpet, lifting her several centimeters above the floor. Milo leaned forward carefully and tapped her on the head to halt the momentum carrying her upward. Kinya howled so loudly that Milo was surprised the bridge wasn't calling to complain about the noise. Not that Kinya was just misbehaving; Milo could feel how frightened his sister was, and he didn't blame her one bit. To be honest, Milo was getting pretty apprehensive himself. This trip aboard the *Enterprise* was turning out to be a lot more intimidating than he had expected.

Since their father was missing, like always, and no one else would tell them what was going on, Milo had eavesdropped telepathically on the crew and found out that the *Enterprise* was engaged in battle with a dangerous alien life-form. *And I thought this trip would be dull,* Milo recalled, shaking his head. He could use a dose of healthy boredom right now.

A thick plane of transparent aluminum, mounted in the outer wall of the living room, had previously offered an eye-catching view of the stars zipping by. Now the rectangular window revealed only the ominous sight of swollen thunderclouds churning violently outside the ship. He wasn't sure, but, judging from what he had picked up from the occasional stray thoughts, it sounded like the clouds actually *were* the aliens, no matter how creepy that was to think about. The billowing vapors reminded Milo of an electrical tornado that had once frightened Milo when he was very young, during a temporary breakdown of Betazed's environmental controls. His baby sister was too small to remember that incident, but the thunder was loud and scary enough to make her cry even louder each time the clouds crashed together.

Please be quiet, he thought at the toddler. His throat was sore from emotion, so he spoke to her mind-to-mind. *Everything will be okay,* he promised, hoping he was thinking the truth. *There, there. Ssssh!*

Kinya listened a little. Her insistent bawling faded to sniffles, and Milo wiped his sister's nose with a freshly replicated handkerchief. The little girl was still scared; Milo could sense her acute anxiety, like a nagging toothache that wouldn't go away, but Kinya became semi-convinced that her big brother could protect her. Milo was both touched and terrified by the child's faith in him. It was a big responsibility, maybe bigger than he could handle.

If only Mom were here, he thought for maybe the millionth time, taking care to block his pitiful plea from the other child. But his mother was dead and nothing would ever change that, no matter how hard he wished otherwise. And his father might as well be dead, at least as far as his children were concerned.

Despite his best efforts, Kinya must have sensed his frustration. Tears streamed from a pair of large brown eyes, gliding away into the air faster than Milo could wipe them, while her face turned as red as Klingon disruptors. His sister hovered about the carpet, surrounded by all the drifting toys and treats. Kinya grabbed a model *Enterprise* by its starboard warp nacelle and began hammering the air with it, frustrated that she could no longer reach the floor with it. Tossing the toy ship aside, she snatched the Wind Dancer puppet as it came within her grasp and twisted its ears mercilessly. Kinya managed to abuse the toys without missing a note in her tearful ululations. Milo wanted to borrow two cushions from the couch to cover his own ears, but even that wouldn't have been enough to block out her outpouring of emotion. *It's not fair,* he thought angrily. *I shouldn't have to deal with all this on my own. I'm only eleven!*

Then, to his surprise and relief, he sensed his father approaching, feeling his presence in his mind only seconds before he heard his voice in the corridor outside. His father was very irate, Milo could tell, and seemed to be arguing with someone, speaking loudly enough to be heard through the closed steel door of the guest suite. *Now what?* he wondered.

"This is intolerable!" Lem Faal insisted as the door slid open. He was a slender, middle-aged man with receding brown hair, wearing a pale blue lab coat over a tan suit. "Starfleet Science will hear about this, I promise you that. I have colleagues on the Executive Council, including the head of the Daystrom Institute. You tell your Commander Riker that. He'll be lucky to command a garbage scow after I'm through with him!"

Milo was amazed. Ever since Mom died, his father had been distant, distracted, and, okay, irritable sometimes, but Milo had never heard him go all Klingon at another adult like this. What could have happened to upset him like this? Looking beyond his father, he spotted a security officer standing outside the doorway, holding on to his father's arm. Both men wore standard-issue gravity boots, and Milo wondered if the gravity had gone out all over the *Enterprise.* "I'm sorry, Professor," the Earthman said, "but, for your own safety, the commander thinks it best that you remain in your quarters for the time being." Milo sensed a degree of impatience within the officer, as if he had already explained his position several times before.

"But my work," Faal protested as the officer firmly but gently guided him into the living quarters. Milo hopped off the couch and launched himself toward his father for a closer look at what was going on. "You have to let me go to Engineering. It's vital that I complete the preparations for my experiment. All my research depends on it. My life's work!"

Because of his illness, Faal looked much frailer than his years would suggest. His whole body trembled as he railed against the unfortunate guard. Nearing the doorway, Milo slowed his flight by bouncing back and forth between facing walls. He winced every time he heard his father wheeze; each breath squeaked out of his disease-ravaged lungs.

"Maybe later," the officer hedged, although Milo could tell, as his father surely could, that it wasn't going to happen. The guard let go of Faal's arm and stepped back into the corridor. "There are extra boots in the emergency cupboards," he said, nodding in Milo's direction. "I'll be out here if you need anything," he said. "Computer, seal doorway. Security protocol gamma-one."

"So I'm under house arrest, is that it?" Faal challenged him. He grabbed the edge of the door and tried to stop it from sliding shut. "You dim-witted Pakled clone, don't you understand what is at stake? I'm on the verge of the greatest breakthrough since the beginning of warp travel, an evolutionary leap that will open up whole new horizons and possibilities for humanoids. And your idiotic Commander Riker is willing to sacrifice all that just because some quasi-intelligent gas cloud is making a fuss. It's insane, don't you see that?"

"I'm sorry, sir," the officer said once more, maintaining a neutral expression. "I have my orders." Faal tried to keep the door open, but his enfeebled fingers were no match against the inexorable progress of the steel door. His hands fell away as the door slid shut, shielding the unfortunate officer from further scorn.

Gasping for breath, the scientist leaned against the closed doorway, his chest heaving. His fruitless tirade had obviously cost him dearly. His face was flushed. His large brown eyes were bloodshot. He ran his hand anxiously through his hair, leaving stringy brown tufts jutting out in many different directions. Milo could feel his father's exhaustion radiating from him. Even with no gravity to fight against, it wore Milo out just watching him. "Are you all right, Dad?" he asked, even though they both knew he wasn't. "Dad?"

In a telepathic society, there was no way Milo's father could conceal his illness from his children, but he had never really spoken to them about it, either. Milo had been forced to ask the school computer about "Iverson's disease" on his own. A lot of the medical terminology had been too advanced for him, but he had understood what "incurable" meant, not to mention "terminal."

His father reached into the pocket of his lab coat and produced a loaded hypospray. With a shaky hand, he pressed the instrument against his shoulder. Milo heard a low hiss, then watched as his father's breathing grew more regular, if not terribly stronger. None of this came as a surprise to the boy; he had asked the computer about "polyadrenaline," too. He knew it only offered temporary relief from his father's symptoms.

Sometimes he wished his father had died in that accident instead of his mother, especially since Dad was dying anyway. This private thought, kept carefully locked away where no one could hear, always brought a pang of guilt, but it was too strong to be denied entirely. *It's just so unfair! Mom could have lived for years. . . .*

At the moment, though, he was simply glad to have his father back at all. "Where have you been, Dad?" he asked. He grabbed the doorframe and pulled himself downward until his feet were once more planted on the carpet. "The ship keeps getting knocked around and everything started floating and Kinya won't stop crying and I hear the ship is being attacked by aliens and we might get blown to pieces. Do you know what the aliens want? Did anyone tell you what's going on?"

"What's that?" his father replied, noticing Milo for the first time. He breathed in deeply, the air whistling in and out of his congested chest, and steadied himself. "What are you talking about?"

"The aliens!" Milo repeated. Fortunately, their father's arrival had momentarily silenced the toddler, who teetered on tiny legs before lifting off from the floor entirely. "I know it's not polite to listen in on the humans' thoughts, but the alarms were going off and the floor kept rocking and I could hear explosions or whatever going off outside and you were nowhere around and I just had to know what was happening. Have you seen the battle, Dad? Is Captain Picard winning?"

"Picard is gone," Faal said brusquely. A plush toy kitten drifted in front of his face and he irritably batted it away. "Some insignificant moron named Riker is in charge now, someone with no understanding or respect for the importance of my work." He seemed to be talking to himself more than to Milo. "How dare he try to stop me like this! He's nothing more than a footnote in history. A flea. A speck."

This was not the kind of reassurance Milo hoped for and needed from his father. *He's worried more about his stupid experiment than us,* he realized, *same as always.* He tried to remember that his father was very sick, that he wasn't himself these days, but he couldn't help feeling resentful again. "What happened to the captain?" he asked anxiously. "Did the aliens kill him?"

"Please," his father said impatiently, dismissing Milo's questions with a wave of his hand before creeping slowly toward his own bedroom. "I can't deal with this right now," he muttered. "I need to think. There has to be something I can do, some way I can convince them. My work is too important. *Everything* depends on it. . . ."

Milo stared at this father's back in disbelief. He didn't even try to conceal his shock and sense of betrayal. How could Father just ignore him at a time like this? *Never mind me,* he thought, *what about my sister?* He looked over his shoulder at Kinya, who was watching her father's departure with wide, confused eyes. "Daddy?" she asked plaintively.

Lightning flashed right outside the living room, followed by a boom that sounded like it was coming from the very walls of the guest suite. The overhead lights flickered briefly, and Milo saw the forcefield reinforcing the window sparkle on and off like a toy Borg shield whose batteries were running low. The momentary darkness panicked the toddler. Tears streaming from her eyes and trailing behind her like the tail of a comet, Kinya bounced after her father, arms outstretched and beseeching. *I know how she feels,* Milo thought, breathing a sigh of relief as Faal grudgingly plucked the tearful girl from the air. "About time," Milo murmured, not caring whether his father heard him or not.

But instead of clasping Kinya to his chest, the scientist kept the whimpering child at arm's length as he handed Kinya over to Milo, who was momentarily surprised by how weightless she felt. "By the Chalice," his father wheezed in an exasperated tone, "can't you handle this?" The model *Enterprise* cruised past his head, provoking a disgusted scowl. "And do something about these blasted toys. This is ridiculous." He glanced over Milo at the tempest beyond the transparent window. "They're just clouds. How can clouds ruin all my plans?" he mumbled to himself before disappearing into his private bedchamber. An interior doorway slid shut, cutting him off from his children

The total absence of gravity did nothing to diminish the anger and disillusionment that crashed down on Milo in the wake of his father's retreat. Without warning, he found himself stuck with a semi-hysterical sibling and a murderous rage he could scarcely contain. *No,* he thought emphatically. *You can't do this. I won't let you.*

Summoning up as much psychic energy as he could muster, he willed his thoughts through the closed door and straight into his father's skull. *Help us, please,* he demanded, determined to break through the man's detachment. *You can't ignore us anymore.*

For one brief instant, Milo sensed a tremor of remorse and regret within Lem

Faal's mind; then, so quickly that it was over even before Milo realized what had happened, an overpowering burst of psychic force shoved him roughly out of his father's consciousness. Mental walls, more impervious than the duranium door sealing Faal's bedroom, thudded into place between Milo and his father, shutting him out completely.

Unable to comprehend what had just occurred, Kinya blubbered against her brother's chest while, biting down on his lower lip, Milo fought back tears of his own. *I hate you,* he thought at his father, heedless of who else might hear him. *I don't care if you're dying, I hate you forever.*

On the bridge, six levels away, Deanna Troi felt a sudden chill, and an unaccountable certainty that something very precious had just broken beyond repair.

Still looking slightly green, Lieutenant Barclay nevertheless stood by his post at the science station. His long face pale and clammy, he awkwardly clambered into the magnetic boots he found waiting there. Judging from his miserable expression, the only good thing about the total absence of gravity upon the bridge was that it couldn't possibly make him any sicker.

Riker barely noticed Barclay's distress, his attention consumed by the daring but risky stratagem that had just presented itself to his imagination. "Mr. Data," he asked urgently, "if we did enter the galactic barrier, what are the odds the Calamarain would follow us?"

"Will!" Deanna whispered to him, alarmed. "Surely you're not thinking . . ." Her words trailed off as she spotted the resolute look on Riker's face and the daredevil gleam in his eyes. "Are you sure this is wise?"

Maybe not wise, but necessary, he thought. The Calamarain were literally shaking the *Enterprise* apart; the failure of the gravity generators was only the latest symptom of the beating they had been taking ever since the cloud-creatures first attacked. Even if Data managed to invent some ingenious new way of fighting back against the Calamarain, they would never be able to implement it without some sort of respite. At that very moment, an ear-shattering crash of thunder buffeted the ship, tossing the bridge from side to side with whiplash intensity. Duranium flooring buckled and a fountain of white-hot sparks erupted only a few centimeters from Riker's boots. Feeling the heat upon his legs, he drew back his feet instinctively even as a security officer, Caitlin Plummer, hurried to douse the blaze with a handheld extinguisher. Startled cries and exclamations reached Riker's ears as similar fires broke out around the bridge. With only one foot securely embedded in his gravity boots, Barclay hopped backward as his science console spewed a cascade of orange and golden sparks. His shoulder bumped into Lieutenant Leyoro, who drove him away with a fierce stare that seemed to frighten him even more than the flames. "E-excuse me," he stammered. "I'll just stand over here if you don't mind. . . ."

Despite the tumult, Data promptly responded to Riker's query. "Without a better understanding of the Calamarain's psychology, I cannot accurately predict their behavior should we penetrate the barrier."

Of course, Riker reprimanded himself, *I should have guessed as much.* "What about us? How long could we last in there?"

Data replied so calmly that Riker would have bet a stack of gold-pressed latinum that the android had deactivated his emotion chip for the duration of the crisis. "With our shields already failing, I cannot guarantee that the ship would survive at all once we passed beyond the event horizon of the barrier. Furthermore, even if the *Enterprise* withstood the physical pressures of the barrier, the overwhelming psychic energies at work within it would surely pose a hazard to the entire crew."

"What about Professor Faal's plan?" he asked, grasping at straws. "Can we try opening up an artificial wormhole through the barrier, maybe use that as an escape route?" It would be ironic, Riker thought, if Faal's experiment, the very thing that had ignited this crisis, proved to be their ultimate salvation. Still, he was more than willing to let Faal have the last laugh if it meant preserving the *Enterprise*. Lord knows he didn't have any better ideas.

Data dashed his hopes, meager as they were. "The professor's theory and technology remain untested," he reminded Riker. "Furthermore, to initiate the wormhole it would be necessary to launch the modified torpedo containing the professor's magneton pulse emitter into the barrier, but there is a ninety-eight-point-six-four percent probability that the Calamarain would destroy any torpedo we launch before it could reach the barrier." Data cocked his head as he gave the matter further thought. "In any event, even if we could successfully implement the experiment, there is no logical reason why the Calamarain could not simply follow the *Enterprise* through the wormhole."

Damn, Riker thought, discouraged by Data's cold assessment of his desperate scheme. The first officer was willing to gamble with the ship's safety if necessary, but there was no point in committing suicide, which seemed to be what Data thought of Riker's plan. *Never mind the wormhole,* he railed inwardly, *I should have tried entering the barrier earlier, when our shields were in better shape.* But how could he have known just how bad things would get? Why wouldn't the Calamarain listen to reason?

Turbolift doors slid open and Alyssa Ogawa rushed onto the bridge, a full medkit trailing behind her like a balloon on a leash. Gravity boots kept her rooted to the floor. "Reporting as ordered, sir," she said to Riker.

"Thank you, Nurse," he answered. "Please give everyone on the bridge, except Mr. Data, of course, a dose of librocalozene to head off any zero-G sickness." He glanced behind him where Barclay was still keeping a safe distance from both the smoking science console and Lieutenant Leyoro. "You can start with Mr. Barclay."

"Ummm, I'm allergic to librocalozene," Barclay whimpered, clutching his stomach. "Do you have isomethozine instead?"

Ogawa nodded and adjusted the hypospray.

Riker repressed a groan. He didn't have time to deal with this. "Do Ensign Clarze next," he advised Ogawa. The last thing he needed was a queasy navigator. As the nurse went to work, he returned his attention to Data.

"One further consideration regarding the barrier," the android added. "Starfleet records indicate that the danger posed by the barrier's psychic component increases proportionally to the telepathic abilities of certain humanoid species." He looked pointedly at Troi. "Please forgive me, Counselor. I do not mean to alarm you, but it is important that Commander Riker fully comprehend what is at risk."

"I understand, Data," she said, not entirely concealing the anxiety in her voice.

So do I, Riker thought. If he did dare to brave the barrier, Deanna would almost surely be the first casualty. *Not to mention Professor Faal and his children,* he realized. They were from Betazed, too, and, being fully Betazoid, even more telepathically gifted than Deanna. Flying into the barrier would surely doom the children. Could he actually give that command, even to save the rest of the crew?

"Do whatever you have to, Will," Deanna urged him. "Don't worry about me."

How can I not? he asked her silently, already dreading the pain of her loss. But Deanna was a Starfleet officer. In theory, she risked her life every time they encountered a new life-form or phenomenon. He couldn't let his personal feelings influence his decision. *If only I could switch off my own emotion chip,* he thought.

"Shields down to twelve percent," Leyoro announced. She didn't remind Riker that time was running out. She didn't need to. Working briskly and efficiently, Ogawa pressed her hypospray against Leyoro's upper arm, then moved on to Deanna. Riker hoped she wasn't wasting her time; if their shields collapsed entirely, they'd all have a lot more to worry about than a touch of space sickness. *Too bad we can't inoculate the crew against a tachyon barrage.*

Frustration gnawed at his guts. "Blast it," he cursed. "We can't stay here and we can't risk the barrier. So what in blazes are we supposed to do?"

To his surprise, a tremulous voice piped up. "Excuse me, Commander," Barclay said, "but I may have an idea."

Four

"I don't understand," the young Q said. "What are we doing back here? I mean, it's a fascinating site, but I thought you'd seen enough of it."

Looking on, quite unseen, Picard wondered the same. He found himself once more facing the legendary alien artifact known as the Guardian of Forever, as did 0 and young Q. The immeasurably ancient stone portal looked exactly as it had the first time Q had brought him here: a rough-hewn torus, standing five meters high at its peak and surrounded by crumbling ruins of vaguely Grecian design. It was through this portal, he recalled, that the young Q had first drawn 0 into reality as Picard knew it.

> *"Never again my plans gone astray,*
> *Never again my life locked away,*
> *Never again to die,*
> *Never again, say I. . . ."*

0 sang softly to himself in a voice little more than a whisper; the song seemed to have special meaning to him. Could it refer, Picard wondered, to the recent debacle with the Coulalakritous? The stranger's archaic garments, he observed, no longer bore the scars of that confrontation. 0 limped across the rubble-strewn wasteland until he was directly in front of the Guardian. "Listen to me, you decrepit doorway," he addressed it, placing his hands upon his hips and striking a defiant pose. The shifting winds blew swirls of gritty powder around his ankles. "I'm not fond of you and I know you don't approve of me, but you're in no position to be picky about whom you choose to serve. I'm stronger now than when last we met, and getting more like my old self with every tick of the clock." He bent over and lifted a fist-sized chunk of dusty marble from the ground, then held it out before him. The solid marble burst into flames upon his palm, but 0 did not flinch from the fiery display, continuing to hold the burning marble until it was com-

pletely incinerated. When nothing was left but a handful of smoking ashes, he flung the smoldering residue onto the ground between him and the portal. "I trust we understand each other."

"I COMPREHEND YOUR MEANING," the Guardian said, its stentorian voice echoing off the fallen marble columns and shattered temples around it. "WHAT AND WHERE DO YOU DESIRE TO BEHOLD?"

0 glanced back at the young Q, who sat upon a set of cracked granite steps several meters behind his companion, looking confused but intrigued. "I knew I could make this antiquated archway see reason," he told Q with a conspiratorial wink, "and the question's not where, but whom." Turning back toward the portal, he opened his mouth again, but what next emerged from his lips bore no resemblance to any language Picard had ever heard, with or without access to a Universal Translator. Indeed, he didn't seem to *hear* the words so much as he felt them seeping into his skin, burrowing directly into some primordial back chamber of his brain. He looked away from 0, back at Q's earlier self, and saw that the youth appeared just as baffled as Picard.

"What sort of language is that?" Picard asked the older Q standing beside him. He placed his hands over his ears, but the sounds—or whatever they were—still penetrated his mind. "What is he saying?"

Q shrugged. "I didn't know then," he said in a fatalistic tone, "and I don't know now. A call to arms, I imagine, or maybe just a list of names and addresses." He leaned against a tilted marble column and shook his head sadly. "What's important is, they heard him."

"Who?" Picard demanded, shouting in hopes of drowning out the unsettling effect of 0's inhuman ululation. It didn't work, but Q managed to hear him anyway.

"Them," he said venomously. He pointed past the imperious figure of 0 to the open portal itself. As before, a thick white mist began to stream from the top of the archway, spilling over onto the arid ground at 0's feet. Peering through the haze, Picard saw a procession of historical images rushing before his eyes like a holonovel on fast-forward. The races and cultures depicted were unfamiliar to him, and Picard was extraordinarily well versed in the history of much of the Alpha Quadrant, but, as one image gave way to another at frightening speed, he thought he could begin to discern a recurring theme:

Larval invertebrates emerge from silken cocoons and proceed to devour their insectile parents. Adolescent humanoids, covered in downy chartreuse feathers, riot in the streets of an elegant and sophisticated metropolis, toppling avian idols and putting ancient aeries to the torch. A lunar colony declares its independence, unleashing a devastating salvo of nuclear missiles against its homeworld.

Generational conflict, Picard realized, seizing on the common thread. *The new violently destroying the old.*

0 stretched out his hand toward the portal, beckoning with his fingers, and a figure emerged from the haze, stepping out from the parade of matricidal and patricidal horrors to assume form and definition outside the portal. He was a silver-haired humanoid of angelic demeanor, resplendent in shimmering amethyst robes that billowed about him from the neck down. A sea-green aura surrounded him, blurring his features somewhat, and, despite his humanoid mien, he failed to achieve any true solidity, resembling a glimmering mirage more than an actual being of flesh and blood. He did not look particularly dangerous, but Picard sus-

pected that first impressions might be deceptive, especially where any confederate of 0's was concerned.

"Gorgan, my old friend," 0 greeted him, lapsing into conventional speech. "It's been too long."

"Longer for you, I suspect, than for any other." Gorgan's deep voice echoed strangely among the barren ruins, sounding artificially amplified. He tipped his head deferentially, revealing an immaculate silver mane that swept back and away from his broad, expansive brow. Beneath the greenish glow, his face seemed pinkish in hue. "I am at your service, my liege."

0 accepted the other's expression of fealty without question. "We have plenty to discuss, but stand aside now while I round up more of our comrades from departed days."

Gorgan stepped away from the portal, seemingly content to await 0's convenience, but the young Q was incapable of such patience. "Wait just one nanosecond," he called out, springing up from the battered stone steps. "I'm not so sure about this. I agreed to accept responsibility for you, not . . . whoever this is." He gestured toward Gorgan, who regarded him with what looked like wry amusement. The newcomer's apparent lack of concern about Q's identity and objections only rankled the youth further. "I insist you tell me what in the Continuum you think you're doing."

"I'm not thinking anything," 0 said brusquely. "I'm doing it, and never mind the Continuum." He reached out once more for the portal and there was a momentary flicker within its aperture as the Guardian appeared to shift its focus. A flustered Q, having clearly lost control of the situation, stumbled hesitantly toward 0. Despite his evident unease, he also appeared consumed by curiosity. "Don't worry so much," 0 reassured him. "I promise you won't be bored."

"You can say that again," the older Q remarked gloomily.

Visions from the past or future cascaded beneath the arch of the Guardian, capturing the attention of both the young Q and Picard. Although Gorgan's face remained benignly serene, an avid gleam crept into his eyes as he watched the historical vistas unfold:

Tribes of fur-clad savages hurl rocks and sharpened bones at each other amid a primeval forest. Mighty armies clash on battlegrounds awash in turquoise blood, the ring of metal against metal echoing alongside the cries of the wounded and the dying. A fleet of sailing ships sinks beneath the waves of an alien sea, their wooden masts and hulls torn asunder by blazing fireballs flung by catapults upon the shore. Mechanized steel dreadnoughts roll through the blasted rubble of an embattled city while bombs fall like poisonous spores from the smoke-choked sky, blooming into flowery displays of red-orange conflagration. In the hazardous confines of a teeming asteroid belt, daring star pilots flying sleek one-man vessels wage a nerve-wracking, hyperkinetic, deep-space dogfight, executing impossible turns as they fire coruscating blasts of pure destructive energy at enemy spacecraft performing equally risky maneuvers; the eternal night of space lights up like the dawn for a fraction of a second every time a sizzling beam strikes home or a brazenly fragile ship collides with an asteroid that got too close.

Picard had no difficulty identifying the theme of this grisly pageant. *War,* he realized, appalled by the sheer bloody waste of it all even as he was struck by the foolhardy courage of the combatants. *War, pure and simple.*

Called forth from the billowing fog, another entity emerged from the time portal. Even more so than Gorgan, however, this being lacked (or perhaps declined) human form, manifesting as a flickering sphere of crimson energy spinning fiercely about two meters above the ground, casting a faint red radiance on the dust and debris below. No sound emerged from the sphere, nor did its passage produce so much as a breeze to rustle the gritty powder it glided over. Whatever this entity was, it seemed even more immaterial than the gaseous Coulalakritous, consisting like Gorgan of undiluted energy, not matter at all. *Much like the energy being who impregnated Deanna Troi several years ago,* Picard recalled, *or perhaps the entity who possessed me during the Antican-Selay peace negotiations.* Indeed, Starfleet had discovered so many noncorporeal life-forms over the last couple of centuries that Picard sometimes wondered if sentient energy was actually as common throughout the galaxy as organic life had proven to be. Judging from their appearance, both Gorgan and this new entity provided support for such a supposition.

"Hello again, (*)," 0 said to the shimmering sphere, and Picard hoped he would never need to pronounce that name himself, if that was in fact what the energy creature was called. "Welcome to a whole new arena, billions upon billions of new worlds, all waiting for us."

If (*) responded to 0, it did not do so in any form Picard could hear. Instead it simply spun silently in the air, undisturbed by the errant gusts of wind that blew perpetually throughout the ruins. Moving away from the Guardian, it passed straight through a solid marble column, emerging unchanged from the other side of the truncated masonry. Perhaps at 0's direction, it joined Gorgan at the sidelines, hovering a few centimeters above the robed man's head. The crimson glow of (*) overlapped with the other's greenish aura, yielding a zone of brown shadows between them.

Stalled halfway between the steps and 0, the young Q inspected the rotating sphere with interest, then remembered his doubts about this entire procedure. "See here, 0, I can't just stand by while you conduct all this . . . unauthorized immigration. I don't know a thing about these entities you're so blithely importing into my multiverse." He strode forward and laid a restraining hand upon 0's shoulder. "Can't you at least tell me what this is all about?"

"All in good time," 0 said gruffly. Looking back over his shoulder, he glowered at Q with enough menace to make the younger being withdraw his hand and step backward involuntarily. Q gulped nervously, his eyes wide and uncertain. His gaze fixed on his would-be mentor, he failed to notice Gorgan and (*) advancing on him with deliberate, predatory intent. A cruel smile appeared on the humanoid's lips while the glowing sphere rotated faster in anticipation. Gorgan's features shifted behind his luminous aura, growing subtly more bestial. The threat of violence, metaphysical or otherwise, hung over the scene, although Picard could not tell how much the young Q was aware of his present jeopardy. All his anxious wariness seemed directed at 0 and what he might do next. Picard found himself in the odd position of sympathizing with Q, even though, intellectually, he recognized that the young Q could not possibly suffer irreparable harm at this point in history since he had to survive long enough to afflict Picard in the future. *Unless,* he reluctantly acknowledged, *Q is about to throw another blasted time paradox at me.*

To Picard's surprise, and the young Q's relief, 0 abruptly switched modes, adopting a more congenial attitude. His eyes no longer intimidated and his voice grew more ingratiating. Temporarily turning his back on the Guardian, he strove to allay Q's reservations while, unseen by Q, Gorgan and (*) quietly retreated to their earlier posts. "Unauthorized immigration? Really, Q, that doesn't sound like you. You weren't so cautious and conservative when you rescued me from that loathsome limbo, or when you so eloquently argued my case before the Continuum. As I recall, you stated pretty boldly that the Continuum could use some fresh blood and new ideas. Well, here they are," he said, an arm sweeping out to indicate (*) and Gorgan. "Don't tell me you've changed your mind now."

"Well, no. Not exactly," Q replied. He glanced over at Gorgan, who graced him with a beatific smile entirely unlike the one he had affected while stalking Q from behind. "It's just that this is somewhat more than I had in mind."

"You wanted the unknown," 0 reminded him. "You wanted to have an impact on the universe, bring about something new."

"Yes, but . . ." Q stammered. "These beings . . . who are they exactly? What do they want?"

"To help us, of course," 0 asserted, "in our grand and glorious campaign to elevate the standards of sentient life throughout this galaxy. What else?" He beamed at the specter and the sphere lurking on the periphery of the discussion. "I know these faithful fellows from days gone by and can vouch for them wholeheartedly. That must be good enough to overcome any dismal doubts you might have? After all, you vouched for me."

"I suppose," Q said dubiously. He looked from 0 to the mysterious pair and back again, perhaps realizing for the first time that he was distinctly outnumbered. He sighed and squinted at the fog streaming out of the time portal. "But how much new blood exactly were you planning to extract from that thing?"

"Just one more old acquaintance," 0 promised, grinning at Q's gradual acquiescence. "Then, trust me, we'll have all the support we need to embark on any crusade we choose . . . for the good of this entire reality, naturally." He called upon the newcomers to back up his claim. "Isn't that so, fellows? You're with us through thick and thin, aren't you?"

"Absolutely," Gorgan purred. Something about his manner brought an old phrase to Picard's mind: First thing we do, let's kill all the lawyers. "I look forward to continuing our work in this brave new dimension, as I also anticipate getting to know this fine young entity."

His bodiless cohort merely hung in the air, its crimson radiance pulsing like a heartbeat. Picard found it hurt his eyes to stare at (*) for too long. *That's enough to give one a headache,* he thought. Not a pleasant prospect, this far from sickbay.

"You know," the older Q commented. "I never did warm to those two, especially that sanguinary fellow spinning like a pinwheel over there. No sense of subtlety whatsoever. You should have seen what a slaughterhouse he made of Cheron later on."

Cheron? Picard vaguely remembered an ancient civilization that was supposed to have destroyed itself via racial warfare some fifty thousand years before his own century. Was Q implying that this extradimensional visitor would eventually be responsible for the extinction of an entire species?

"Of course, I still run into them now and again," Q continued. "Now, *that's* awkward, I must tell you. Of course, they usually have the sense to go scurrying off into some miserable, insignificant corner of the cosmos whenever they sense me drawing near. And good riddance, I say."

"What are you saying, Q?" Picard asked, disturbed by the implications of Q's remarks. "That these beings still exist in our own era?"

"Your own era," Q corrected him archly. "I refuse to be tied down to any specific time or place, present attire notwithstanding." He tugged on the gray jacket of his imitation Starfleet uniform, straightening its lines. "Besides, let's not get too far ahead of ourselves, shall we? We can handle the historical footnotes later. There is still more to be seen here," he instructed Picard. "Behold."

Now flanked by Gorgan and (*), Q's younger self stood by helplessly, torn between anxiety and anticipation, as 0 advanced on the Guardian for what he had vowed would be the last time. Once more that eldritch keening flowed from 0's mouth, invoking another cavalcade of frightful images within the open maw of the portal:

An untamed tornado ravages a cultivated landscape, destroying vast orchards of alien fruit and tossing dome-shaped farms and storage facilities into the fevered sky along with the graceful reptiles who tended to the land. An earthquake rips through the heart of a populous community, the tremors opening up gaping chasms that swallow up entire parks and buildings. A majestic chain of volcanos erupts after centuries of dormancy, spewing ash and fire into the heavens and spilling torrents of plutonic lava onto half a continent, instantly reducing a thriving nation, thick with citizenry, into a smoking wasteland. Oceans of water pour from enormous clouds as a flood of biblical proportions sweeps over one unfortunate world; the deluge swiftly drowns every living thing that walked or crawled or slithered upon the surface, the evolution of millennia lost beneath the swelling sea.

These were no mere rebellions or self-inflicted wars, Picard recognized, not simply conflicts between sentient and sentient, but unequal struggles pitting mortal beings against the awesome power of nature at its most destructive. Unprovoked catastrophes: what ancient historians and jurists once labeled "acts of God."

With eerie appropriateness, what came next through the portal was nothing less than a veritable pillar of fire. Composed entirely of dancing scarlet flames, it snaked horizontally through the steaming gateway, then rose upward like a rearing serpent to achieve a height of over fifty meters above the desolate ruins. Picard felt the heat of the blazing column upon his face and he had to tilt his head back to spy the apex of the looming inferno, which he estimated to be at least two meters in diameter. Was this colossal torch truly an intelligent entity like the others Q had drawn from the portal? he wondered. It was hard to see it as anything other than an incredible thermal phenomenon, but Picard guessed that was not the case.

"As you have summoned Me, so have I come," the tower of flame proclaimed, confirming the captain's assumption. Its voice was nearly as sonorous as the Guardian's, although a touch more human in tone, having a firm yet paternal quality. "Let worlds without number prepare for My Judgment and tremble at My Wrath."

0 laughed out loud at the flaming column's words. "You don't need to put on such lofty airs on my account. I've known you too long for that." He strolled casually around the circumference of the pillar, heedless of the blistering heat radiating from it, clucking at its awesome dimensions. "Maybe you could see your way clear to taking on a more . . . approachable appearance." He shook his head wearily. "It's like talking to a bloody forest fire."

"Let it be as you request," the tower answered, sounding slightly miffed. "Many are My Faces. As numerous as the stars are the manifestations of My Glory."

"Someone thinks highly of himself," the older Q said snidely. "Or should that be Himself?"

Picard was too engrossed by the fiery pillar's sudden transformation to acknowledge Q's remark. Before his gaping eyes, the huge column of swirling flame contracted into the shape of a man, then rapidly cooled to the consistency of human flesh. The newborn figure stood a few centimeters taller than 0 and was sheathed in gleaming armor of solid gold. His stern features were adorned by a flowing, snow-white beard; Picard found himself reminded of the face of Michelangelo's famous portrait of Moses, and was momentarily disappointed that He wasn't actually carrying two inscribed stone tablets. The thought occurred to him that such Old Testament imagery, including the pillar of fire itself, still lay countless aeons in the future. "Q—" he began.

The elder Q held up his palm. "Before you ask . . . no, this is not how I, as a Q, perceived 0's motley band of recruits. Instead this is how they would appear—and will appear—to humanoids such as yourself, according to your own rudimentary senses."

I suspected as much, Picard thought. As the young Q approached the forbidding new arrival, the captain wished he could fully understand how this latest visitor appeared to Q's earlier self. *If only I could see through Q's metaphors to what is actually happening.*

"Excuse me," young Q said to the armor-clad stranger. "Who are you?"

"I am The One," He replied, His arms crossed stiffly atop His chest.

"The One?" inquired Q, who was after all only *a* Q.

"He invented monotheism," 0 explained with a shrug. "Indulge Him." He raised his voice to address the entire gathering. "Old friends and comrades, call me 0 now, for I've put the pitfalls and purgatory of the past behind me. I offer you an opportunity to do the same. There are dazzling days ahead, I promise you!" Throwing an arm over Q's shoulder, he spun the youth around so hard that the toes of Q's boots were dragged through the dust and debris. "Now let me introduce to you our proud patron, as well as our native guide to these parts, my good friend and rescuer . . . Q."

The three from the portal spread out around Q and 0, then drew in closer, surrounding the young Q, who, from where Picard was standing, seemed to be not so much basking in the attention as trying with visible effort to maintain a cocky and confident air despite the fact that, 0's flattery notwithstanding, he had rather quickly gone from being 0's all-knowing host and chaperon to ending up as the newest and junior member of a well-established group where everyone knew each other, and their actual agenda, much better than he did. "So," he said breezily, ducking out from under 0's arm while trying to slip unobtrusively out between Gorgan and The One, "how long have you fellows known 0?"

"Long enough," Gorgan asserted, pressing in upon Q and blocking his escape. The more Picard listened to it, the more Gorgan's voice seemed to be generated artificially rather than through the normal action of lungs and vocal cords. The shimmering stranger was only simulating humanity, and not entirely successfully. "Long enough to know where our best interests lie. And yours."

"Be strong in My Ways," The One added, "and you shall surely prosper. Falter, and your days shall be filled with sorrow." He laid his hand upon Q's shoulder, and the young godling flinched instinctively, stumbling backward into the hovering presence of (*). His body fell *through* the glowing sphere, receiving what looked like some manner of jolt or chill. Emerging behind (*), Q gasped and continued to fall until he landed in a sitting position upon the ground, his limbs trembling and his eyes and mouth wide open. The palpitations quickly subsided, but Q's expression remained dazed.

"Watch yourself," 0 warned him. He took Q by the hand and helped him to his feet. His associates kept their distance this time, granting the jittery Q a bit more personal space. "There's nothing to be skittish about. We're all on the same side here." The deep lines carved into 0's weathered visage stretched to accommodate his toothy grin. "Stick with us, Q, and we'll have a fine time, you'll see. This great, gorgeous galaxy will never be the same."

"Skittish? Me?" Q said loudly, pulling together a semblance of self-assurance. "I'm nothing of the sort." He brushed the clingy dust from his trousers with elaborate indifference. "I'm simply unaccustomed to so much like-minded company. I've always been something of a lone wolf within the Continuum."

"And a black sheep, too, I think," 0 surmised. "No use denying it; it's as obvious as the smug somnambulism of the other Q. Well, you're not alone anymore, my friend. Rest assured, you're one of us now."

"Lucky me," the older Q observed from within the shadow of a tilted Doric column.

"Fallen in with a bad crowd, have we?" Picard said. He shook his head, feeling a tad disillusioned that the errors of Q's youth would prove to be so mundane. "It's an old story, Q."

"Older than you know," Q stated, "and more serious than you can possibly imagine."

How so? Picard wondered. Examining the scene, he noted that, beyond the congregation of superbeings, the Guardian of Forever had fallen still and silent. The last thin ribbons of mist dissipated into the atmosphere of the lonely setting while the empty aperture at the center of the Guardian offered only a view of the fallen temples on the other side of the portal. It appeared that whatever intelligence inhabited the Guardian had taken 0 at his word that there would be no further corridors opened between this reality and whatever distant realm 0 and his cohorts originated from. Just as well, Picard concluded. Judging from the older Q's ominous remarks, these four would prove dangerous enough.

He peered at the new arrivals. Something about them, particularly Gorgan, struck a chord in his memory, but one he couldn't quite place. He felt certain that he had never personally encountered any of these entities before, but perhaps he had reviewed some record of their existence. The buried memory teased him, and he wished he had immediate access to the *Enterprise*'s memory banks. Perhaps something from Starfleet records, maybe even from the logs of one or more of the earlier *Starships Enterprise*. "Gorgan," he muttered. "Where have I heard that name before?"

"Stardate 5029.5," Q volunteered helpfully. "In and around the planet Triacus. Before your time, of course, but I believe one of your predecessors had an unpleasant encounter with the ever-insinuating Gorgan. One James T. Kirk, to be exact." Q rested his chin upon the knuckles of one hand, striking a meditative pose. "Speaking of which, one of these days I really should go back a generation or so before your birth and see if Starfleet captains were always as humorless as you are."

Don't even think about it, Picard thought vehemently. Kirk and his crew had run into enough challenges during their long careers without the added aggravation of coping with Q. Meanwhile, he searched his memory for details regarding the original *Enterprise*'s contact with Gorgan. He dimly recalled several incidents in which Kirk's crew faced powerful beings along the lines of Q and 0. Was Gorgan the one who hijacked the *Enterprise* using some brainwashed children, or the one who turned out to be Jack the Ripper? Given the rampant generational strife in the images preceding Gorgan's entrance, he guessed the former.

"What about that one?" Picard asked, pointing to the spinning globe of crimson light. He asked partly out of curiosity, partly to distract Q from his alarming notion of visiting the twenty-third century.

"I believe your Starfleet database refers to it as the 'Beta XII-A entity,' named for the rather forgettable world where your kind first made its acquaintance." Q scowled at the shining energy creature. "A deceptively innocuous name, in my opinion, for so bloody-minded a presence."

Beta XII-A, Picard memorized dutifully. That, too, sounded familiar, although Starfleet had charted too many planets for him to pinpoint its location and history immediately, not without Data's total recall. He resolved to research the matter thoroughly if and when Q deigned to return him to the *Enterprise.* "And what of the final entity?" he asked Q. "The one who calls himself The One?"

Q rolled his eyes. "What do I look like, an information booth? All will become clear in time, Jean-Luc. Rather than subject me to this plodding interrogation, you would do better to observe what transpires *now.*" He diverted Picard's attention back to the curious assemblage several meters away.

0 had just finished recounting his and Q's recent altercation with the Coulalakritous to Gorgan and the others. "Looking back," he admitted, "we should have started off with a more underdeveloped breed of subjects, the sort less capable of violating the spirit of the test." He paced back and forth through the broken masonry, dragging his bad leg behind him. "Yes, that's the idea. We need to be more selective next time. Choose just the right specimens. Advanced enough to be interesting, naturally, but not evolved enough to skew the learning curve." He stopped in front of the young Q and eyed his designated host and guardian expectantly. "This is your neck of the woods, my boy. Any likely candidates come to mind?"

Q looked grateful to occupy center stage again. The one advantage he had over the others was his superior knowledge of this particular reality. "Let me think," he said, scrunching up his face in concentration. His foot tapped impatiently in the dusty gravel as he looked inward for the answer. A second later, his face lighted up as an idea occurred to him; Picard half-expected a lightbulb to literally materialize over the young Q's head, but, to his relief, no such absurdity occurred. "There's always the Tkon Empire," he suggested.

Picard could not have been more startled if the young Q had suddenly proposed a three-week debauch on Risa. *The Tkon Empire,* he thought numbly, transfixed by shock and a growing sense of horror. *Oh my God. . . .*

Five

"Come again?" Riker asked.

"It's true," Barclay insisted. "I examined the probe that we sent toward the galactic barrier, the one we transported back to the ship after the Calamarain attacked, and I discovered that the bio-gel packs in the probe had absorbed some psychokinetic energy from the barrier itself, partially protecting them from the Calamarain's tachyon bursts." He waved a tricorder in Riker's face, a little too close for comfort. "It's all here. I was going to report back to Mr. La Forge about what I found, but then Professor Faal insisted on coming to the bridge, and I had to follow him, and then you assigned me to the science station after Ensign Schultz was injured—"

Riker held up a hand to halt the uncontrolled flood of words pouring from Barclay's mouth. Sometimes, in his own way, the hapless officer could be just as long-winded as Data used to be, and as slow to come to the point. Riker took the tricorder from Barclay and handed it off to Data for analysis. "Slow down," he ordered. "How can this help us now?"

He wasn't just being impatient; with the Calamarain pounding on the ship and their shields in danger of collapsing, Riker couldn't afford to waste a moment. To be honest, he had completely forgotten about that probe until Barclay mentioned it, and he still wasn't sure what relevance it had to their present circumstances. As far as he was concerned, their entire mission concerning the galactic barrier had already been scrapped. His only goal now was to keep both the ship and the crew intact for a few more hours.

"The *Enterprise*-E has the new bio-gel packs, too," Barclay explained, "running through the entire computer processing system, which is directly linked to the tactical deflector system." He leaned against the back of the captain's chair and closed his eyes for a moment. Riker guessed that the lack of gravity upon the bridge was not helping Barclay's shaky stomach any.

"Sit down," he suggested, indicating the empty seat where the first officer usually sat when he wasn't filling in for the captain. Barclay sank gratefully into the chair, his magnetic boots clanging against the floor as he moved. "All this bio-organic technology is still pretty new to me," Riker admitted. The first Starfleet vessel to employ the new organic computer systems, he recalled, had been the ill-fated *U.S.S. Voyager*, now stranded somewhere in the Delta Quadrant. Hardly the most promising of pedigrees, even though its bio-gel packs were hardly responsible for *Voyager*'s predicament. "What does this have to do with the current situation?"

"Oh, the bio-gel is wonderful stuff," Barclay declared, scientific enthusiasm overcoming nausea for the moment, "several orders of magnitude faster than the old synthetic subprocessors, and easier to replace." Riker sensed a lecture coming on, but Barclay caught himself in time and cut to the chase. "Anyway, if the ship's bio-gel packs absorb enough psychokinetic energy from the barrier, maybe we can divert that energy to the deflectors to protect us from the barrier itself. In effect, we could use part of the galactic barrier's own power to maintain our shields. Like a fire wall, sort of. It's the perfect solution!"

"Maybe," Riker said, not yet convinced. The *Enterprise* was a lot bigger and more complicated than a simple probe. Besides, if any crew member was going to pull a high-tech rabbit out of his or her hat, Riker would have frankly preferred someone besides Reginald Barclay. *No offense,* he thought, *but where cutting-edge science is concerned I have a lot more faith in Data or Geordi.* He turned toward Data. "Is this doable?" he asked the android.

"The data Lieutenant Barclay has recorded is quite provocative," Data reported. "There are too many variables to guarantee success, but it is a workable hypothesis."

"Excuse me, Commander," Alyssa Ogawa said as she came up beside him. Riker felt the press of a hypospray against his forearm, followed by the distinctive tingle of medicinal infusion. Even though he had not suffered any negative effects from the zero gravity yet, he derived a twinge of relief from the procedure. One less thing to worry about, he thought.

"Shields down to ten percent," Baeta Leyoro stated, continuing her countdown toward doom. A rumble of thunder and a flash of electrical fire accented her warning. The jolt shook the tricorder free from Data's grip and the instrument began to float toward the ceiling. Data reached for the tricorder, but its momentum had already carried the tricorder beyond his reach. "Hang on," Leyoro said, plucking her combadge from her chest. She hurled the badge like a discus and it spun through the air until it collided with the airborne tricorder. The force of the collision sent both objects ricocheting backward toward their respective points of origin. Leyoro snatched the badge out of the air even as the tricorder soared back toward Data's waiting fingers. "Just a little trick I picked up on Lunar V," she said, referring to the penal colony where she and the other Angosian veterans had once been incarcerated.

Remind me not to play racquetball with her, Riker thought. *Or a game of domjot, for that matter.*

"Sir, we're sitting ducks here," she said. "We have to *do* something, and fast."

Riker made his decision. "Let's risk it," he declared, rising from the captain's chair. "Data, you and Barclay do whatever's necessary to set up the power feed between the bio-gel packs and the deflectors. Contact Geordi; I want his input, too. See what he can do from Engineering. His control panels may be in better shape than ours. Ensign Clarze, set course for the galactic barrier."

"Yes, sir!" the young crewman affirmed, sounding eager to try anything that might liberate them from the Calamarain. *I know how you feel,* Riker thought.

He cast an anxious look at Troi, seated to his left. "Deanna, I want you and every other telepath aboard under medical supervision before we get too near the barrier. Report to sickbay immediately and remind Dr. Crusher of the potential psychic hazards of the barrier. Nurse Ogawa, you can accompany her." He tapped his combadge. "Riker to Security, escort Professor Faal and his entire family to sickbay at once." He almost added "red alert," then remembered that the ship had been on red alert status ever since the Calamarain first appeared on their sensors. *Too bad we don't have an even higher level of emergency readiness,* he thought, *specifically for those occasions when we jump from the frying pan into the fire.*

Riker's eyes met Deanna's just as she and Ogawa entered the turbolift. For an instant, he almost thought he could hear her voice in his mind, through the special bond they had always shared. *Take care,* her eyes entreated, then the turbolift doors slid shut and she was gone.

Good enough, he thought, turning his attention back to the task before him. There had never been any need for grand farewells between them. Each of them already knew that should anything happen to either one, the other would always remember what had existed between them. They were *imzadi,* after all.

On the viewscreen, Riker caught a glimpse of starlight as the prow of the *Enterprise* pierced the outer boundaries of the Calamarain. He felt surprisingly heartened by the sight of ordinary space after long hours spent in the opaque and angry fog. Then the front of the gigantic plasma cloud overtook them, snatching away that peek at the stars. "The Calamarain are pursuing us," Leyoro stated.

"Can we shake them?" he asked.

"Not at this rate," Clarze called back from the conn. "I'm at full impulse already."

No surprise there, Riker observed. *We already knew they were fast.* "Very well, then," he said defiantly, determined to bolster the crew's morale. "Let them come along with us. I want to know just how far they're willing to take this."

With any luck, he thought mordantly, *they're not half as crazy as we are.* With all eyes glued to the viewscreen, watching for the first light of the barrier as the starship zoomed head on for the absolute edge of the galaxy, Riker inconspicuously crossed his fingers and hoped for the best. *I can't believe I'm really staking the* Enterprise *on some far-fetched scheme from Reg Barclay, of all people!* This was not one of Barclay's holodeck fantasies, this was real life, about as real as it gets.

And, possibly, real death as well.

"But this isn't the way to Engineering!" Lem Faal gasped.

"I told you, sir, you and your family have been ordered to sickbay." The security officer, Ensign Daniels, kept a firm grip on the scientist's arm as he herded Faal and the children through the corridors of the starship. Milo clomped down the weightless halls in magnetic boots several sizes too large for him, cradling Kinya in his arms. He sensed that the large human crewman was rapidly losing patience with the boy's father. "Please hurry, sir. Commander Riker's orders."

Milo hurried after the two adults. His father struggled to free his arm from Daniels's grip as, wheezing with every breath, he tried to convince the crewman to let him go to Engineering instead. *What was he planning to do with us,* Milo wondered bitterly, *just dump us on the poor ensign or drag us along to his shipboard laboratory?* Probably the former, he guessed. Two children would just be in the way in Engineering, the same as they always seemed to be in the way where their father was concerned. Resentment seethed in the pit of his stomach. Concern for their future, and anxiety over their safety, only slightly diluted the bile that bubbled and boiled within him every time he thought of his father's gross abandonment of them. *Even now,* he brooded sullenly, *he's more worried about his precious apparatus than us.*

Red alert lights flashed at every intersection, emphasizing the urgency of their fast-paced march through the *Enterprise.* Ensign Daniels didn't know or wouldn't explain why they had to go to sickbay in such a rush, but obviously it was some sort of emergency. *Are they expecting us to get sick? Are the aliens winning the fight? Are we going to die?* Milo gulped loudly, imagining the worst, but tried not to look afraid in front of his little sister. He had to act brave now, for her sake, even though his whole body trembled as he visualized a dozen different ways for the cloud-monsters to kill him. *What if we have to evacuate the ship?* The galactic barrier, he knew, was a long way away from the nearest Federation colony. *Will the clouds let us escape in peace?*

At least Kinya was weightless, too. Even still, his arms were getting tired from holding Kinya this whole hike and his legs weren't feeling much better. *It still takes effort to move this much mass,* he realized. "Are we almost there?" he asked Ensign Daniels. His voice only cracked a little.

"Almost," the security officer promised. They rounded a corner and Milo saw a pair of double doors on the left side of the hall. A limping crewman, a Tellarite from the look of him, staggered toward the doors from the other end of the corridor, clutching a wounded arm against his chest. Blood leaked from a cut on his forehead and scorch marks blackened the sleeves of his uniform. One tusk was chipped, and his hoof-shaped boots clicked at an irregular pace against the steel floor. A rush of pain from the injured officer hit Milo before he had a chance to block it. His hands stung vicariously from the man's burns. He felt a phantom ache where his tusk would have been had he been a Tellarite. He closed his eyes and pushed the stinging sensations away.

Kinya, who had been sobbing and squirming as Milo carried her, fell still at the sight of the wounded crewman. She tightened her grip on his shoulders. The Tellarite really looked like he'd been through a war. Even Milo's father was quieted, at least for the moment, by this open evidence of the battle being waged, his indignant remarks to Ensign Daniels trailing off in mid-insult. Seeing his father act so subdued and reasonable, Milo had to wonder how long it would last. Not long enough, he guessed.

The double doors opened automatically at the Tellarite's approach, offering Milo his first look at sickbay. His instant impression was one of crowded, constant activity. Between the wounded and those treating them, there had to be over a dozen people in the medical facility, many of them strapped onto biobeds whose monitor screens reported on the vital signs of each patient. Despite the packed conditions, however, everything seemed to be under control. The activity was fast, but not frenzied; health workers in magnetic boots shouted queries and instructions to each other, but nobody was panicking. Sickbay worked like a machine, with a dozen moving pieces working in perfect coordination with each other. Polished steel instruments flew from hand to waiting hand. Ensigns with handheld suction devices efficiently cleared the atmosphere of floating fluids, ash, and fragments of cloth. Was it always so busy, he wondered, or only during emergencies?

The doors stayed open for Milo and his party. Ensign Daniels led the way and gestured for the rest of them to follow. Remembering the pain he had absorbed from the Tellarite, Milo clamped his mental shields down hard before stepping inside.

The air had a medicinal odor that he had learned to associate with sterilization fields, and the overhead lights were brighter than elsewhere on the ship. They made their way carefully into a hive of ceaseless motion that adjusted to their presence and flowed around them as easily as a mountain stream circumvents the rocks and other obstacles in its path. A levitating stretcher bumped into Milo's shoulders and he caught an alarming glimpse of a severed antennae taped to the stretcher next to the unconscious body of a wounded Andorian crew member. *Can they reattach that?* he wondered, turning around quickly so that his sister wouldn't see the grisly sight. He heard a frightened whimper from the little girl.

The doctor attending to the Andorian, a tall man with a bald dome, glanced down at the children and rolled his eyes. "Marvelous," he muttered sarcastically. "Children, no less. We'll be getting cats and dogs next." Curiously, Milo did not detect irritation from the man, or any other emotion; it was almost like he wasn't really there.

Looking around, Ensign Daniels spotted Dr. Crusher deeper inside the facility, directing her medical team like a general on a battlefield. "Doctor!" he called out, weaving through the throng. "I have Professor Faal and his family."

A nurse rushed up and handed Dr. Crusher a padd. A report on one of the patients, Milo assumed. She glanced at it quickly, tapped in a few modifications, then handed it back to the nurse, who hurried away to see to the doctor's instructions. Dr. Crusher took a deep breath before focusing on the security officer and his charges. "Good," she said. "I've been expecting them." She nodded at Milo's father. "Give me just a second, Professor, then follow me." Her sea-green eyes surveyed the room. "Alyssa, take over triage until I get back. Make sure the EMH looks at those radiation blisters on Lieutenant Goldschlager, and tell Counselor Troi to join me as soon as she finishes up with Cadet Arwen." She took custody of Faal's arm from the security officer. "Thank you, Ensign. If you're not needed elsewhere, we can really use an extra pair of hands. Contact Supply and tell them to beam another load of zero-G plasma infusion units directly to sickbay. We can't replicate them fast enough."

"Yes, Doctor," Daniels promised. "First thing."

"Come with me, Professor," the doctor said, leading them away from the main crush of the medical emergency ward to an adjacent facility, where they found a row of child-sized biobeds as well as what looked like a high-tech incubator unit. The pediatric ward, Milo realized unhappily. He felt like a patient already and he hadn't even been injured yet. "Here, let me help you with her," Dr. Crusher said to him, bending over to lift Kinya from his grateful arm, which he stretched until its circulation returned. Kinya squalled at first, but the doctor patted her on the back until she got used to her new address. "That's a good girl," she cooed, then wiped her own forehead with her free hand. "Thank you for coming, Professor. We're in a crisis situation here, obviously, but I want to make sure you and your family are properly cared for."

"Never mind that," Faal said. His face looked flushed and feverish. The effects of weightlessness, Milo wondered, or something more serious? "What's this all about, Doctor? I demand an explanation."

Dr. Crusher glanced down at Milo, then decided to choose her words carefully. "To elude the Calamarain, Commander Riker has decided to take the *Enterprise* into the outer fringe of the barrier. He believes that our engineers have devised a way to provide us with some protection from the barrier, but it seemed wisest to place all telepaths under direct medical observation." She nodded toward the listening children. "I don't think I need to explain why."

She didn't need to. Milo knew how dangerous the galactic barrier could be, especially to anyone with a high psionic potential; just because he resented his father's work didn't mean he hadn't paid attention to what his parents had hoped to accomplish. Even humans, who were barely telepathic at all by Betazoid standards, sometimes had their brains fried by the barrier, and now the *Enterprise* was taking them right into it! Milo shuddered at the thought. The battle with the clouds—with the *Calamarain,* he corrected himself—had to be going badly if Commander Riker was desperate enough to fly into the barrier instead. *We should have never left Betazed,* he thought. *We're all going to die!*

His father sounded just as upset by this turn of events, although for different reasons. "But he can't," he exclaimed, "not without my wormhole." His chest heaving, he leaned against the central incubator and groped for his hypospray. "That's the whole point. That's why we're here."

"Right now Commander Riker is primarily concerned with the safety of the ship," another voice intruded. Milo sensed Counselor Troi's arrival even before he saw her framed in the entrance to the kid's ward. She walked toward the other two adults, taking care to step around Milo. "I can assure you, Professor, that the commander has considered every possibility, including your wormhole theory, and he truly believes that he is acting in the best interests of everyone aboard, including your children."

"But he's not a scientist," Faal wheezed. The hypospray hissed as it delivered a fresh dose of polyadrenaline to his weakened body. "What does he know about the barrier and the preternatural energies that sustain it?"

The counselor tried her best to calm him. "Commander Riker may not have specialized in the hard sciences, and certainly not to the extent you have, but he's consulted with some of our best people, including Commander La Forge, and he and Lieutenant Commander Data and Lieutenant Barclay feel tha—"

"Barclay?" Faal exploded, his voice sounding perceptibly stronger than seconds ago, and Milo felt Troi's heart sink. He didn't know who Barclay was, but the counselor instantly realized that she had made a mistake in mentioning his name. "Do you mean to tell me that my own extensive research into the barrier and its effects is being trumped by the scientific expertise of that clownish incompetent? By the Holy Rings, I've never heard such lunacy."

"Please, Professor," Dr. Crusher said firmly. "There is no time to debate this. The decision has been made and I need to prepare you and your family before it's too late." She gestured toward one of the kid-sized biobeds. "What I'd like to do is set our cortical stimulators on a negative frequency in order to lower the brain activity of you and the children to a more or less comatose state during the period in which we are exposed to the psionic energy of the barrier. The same for you, Deanna," she added. "Along with the extra shielding devised by . . . Data and Geordi . . . that should be enough to protect all of you from any telepathic side effects."

She sounded very certain, but Milo could tell she wasn't nearly as confident as she pretended to be. Didn't she know she couldn't fool a Betazoid? Maybe the doctor and the counselor should actually listen to his father. Despite his failings as a parent, Milo figured his father probably knew more about the barrier than anyone in the Federation.

Lem Faal sure thought so. "This is so ridiculous I can't even begin to describe how insane it is," he insisted, returning his hypospray to the inner pocket of his jacket. "It was bad enough when Riker just wanted to retreat from the barrier, but to go forward into it without even attempting my experiment . . ."

"Perhaps you should worry less about your experiment and more about your children," the doctor said heatedly. Milo sensed her anger at his father's skewed priorities. She lowered Kinya onto one of the miniature biobeds. His sister sat sideways on the bed, her small legs dangling over the edge. "According to Starfleet conventions, I don't require your consent to protect your family during a red alert, but I do expect your cooperation. Deanna, please escort the professor back to the adult ward. Have Nurse Ogawa find biobeds for both you and Professor Faal. I'll be with you in a few minutes, after I've prepared the children."

Counselor Troi laid her hand on the man's arm, but Milo's father had exhausted his patience as well. He reached out unexpectedly and snatched Dr. Crusher's combadge off her lab jacket. "Mr. La Forge," he barked, speaking into the shiny reflective badge, "this is Lem Faal. Generate the tensor matrix at once and prepare to launch the magneton generator. This is our last chance!"

Geordi's voice emerged from the badge, sounding understandably confused. "Professor Faal? What are you doing on the com? Has Commander Riker authorized this?"

"Geordi, don't listen to him!" Dr. Crusher tried to grab the badge back from Faal, but the obsessed scientist batted her hand away impatiently.

"Forget about Commander Riker," he shouted, the badge only centimeters away from his face. Saliva sprayed from his lips.

"We're so close, we have to try it. Anything else would be insane."

"You're out of line, Professor," Geordi told him emphatically, "and I'm busy. La Forge out."

"No!" he shouted into the badge, even though the connection had already been broken off. "Fire the torpedo, blast you. You have to fire the torpedo!"

A hypospray hissed as Dr. Crusher applied the instrument to his left shoulder. "Dad!" Milo cried out as his father stiffened in surprise. His face went slack as his eyelids drooped and he sagged backward into the doctor's waiting arms.

"Don't worry," she assured Milo. "I just prescribed him an emergency tranquilizer. He'll be fine later." With the counselor's help, she guided his father's limp body out of the pediatric ward into the primary facility. An Octonoid crewman with both his lower arms in slings hopped off a biobed to make room for Faal.

Despite the narcotic, the scientist's anxiety did not abate entirely. Although his eyes remained shut, his lips kept moving, driven by a powerful sense of urgency that not even the tranquilizer could quell. Standing next to the biobed, his ears turned toward the unconscious man, Milo could barely make out his father's delirious whispers. "Help me . . . we're so close . . . you can't let them stop me . . . please help me."

Who is he talking to? Milo wondered. *Me?* "I don't know how to help you, Dad. I don't know what I can do."

"You mustn't blame yourself for any of this, Milo," Counselor Troi told him, placing a comforting hand upon his shoulder. He could sense her sincerity and concern, as well as an underlying apprehension concerning Lem Faal. "Your father has simply been under a lot of stress lately."

That's one way of putting it, he thought, some of his resentment seeping through. He wondered if the counselor, who was only half Betazoid, could tell how angry he got at his father sometimes.

"We should hurry," Dr. Crusher said, interrupting his moment with the counselor. She glanced at Lem Faal's sleeping form and breathed a sigh of relief. "I want to get the children put under first," she explained to Troi, "then I can look after you and Professor Faal."

Unsure what else to do, Milo followed the two women back into the pediatric ward, where he watched Dr. Crusher tend to Kinya. His little sister squirmed and cried at first—watching her father collapse had upset her once again—but the doctor put her to sleep with a sedative, then stretched the toddler out on the biobed. Retrieving a pair of compact metallic objects from a pocket in her lab coat, she affixed the shiny gadgets to Kinya's small forehead. "These are only cortical stimulators," she told Milo while simultaneously checking the readings on the display panel mounted above the bed. Milo didn't know what she was looking for, but she appeared satisfied with the readings. "They won't hurt her, I promise."

"I know," Milo said. "I believe you." In some ways, Dr. Crusher reminded him of his mother. They both always seemed to know what they were doing, and they didn't talk down to him. He appreciated that.

"Too bad Selar transferred to the *Excalibur,*" she commented to Troi as she made a final adjustment to the devices attached to Kinya's head. "Vulcans are supposed to be resistant to the barrier's effects, despite their telepathic gifts. No one really knows why, although there are any number of theories."

Milo was too worried about everything else to get interested in how Vulcan brains worked. At the doctor's direction, he climbed onto the empty bed across from Kinya's. From where he was sitting, he could see his father sleeping in the next ward over. To his surprise, he saw his father's face twitching, the fingers of his hand flexing spasmodically. Lem Faal looked like he was waking from a nightmare. *How long is that tranquilizer supposed to keep him down anyway,* Milo wondered, *and should I alert the doctor and the others?*

Counselor Troi must have sensed his uncertainty because she turned and followed his gaze to where his father rested fitfully. Her eyes widened as Faal's entire body convulsed, then sat up suddenly. Running his hand through his disordered hair, he shot darting glances around the sickbay like a hunted animal searching desperately for an escape route. His bloodshot eyes were haunted and a thin string of saliva dribbled from his lower lip. Milo scarcely recognized his father.

"Beverly!" Troi called out, attracting the doctor's attention. The counselor rushed toward the open doorway between her and the adult ward. "Please, Professor, you have to stay where you are. We're getting closer to the barrier. The doctor has to prepare you."

At her mention of the barrier, Faal's wild eyes filled with purpose. Gasping for breath, he lowered himself off the bed and started to stagger across the crowded sickbay toward the exit. Caught up in their own emergencies, the various nurses and patients paid little attention to the gaunt, determined-looking Betazoid making his way through the maze of bodies and medical equipment. Milo hopped off his own bed and hurried after Troi, watching her pursue his father. "Milo, wait!" Dr. Crusher called to him, but he didn't listen to her.

Younger and healthier than the dying scientist, Counselor Troi quickly caught up with Faal and grabbed his elbow from behind. "You have to stay here," she repeated urgently. "You're not safe."

Faal spun around with a snarl, a glint of silver metal flashing between his fingers. Milo recognized the object immediately: his father's ubiquitous hypospray, loaded with polyadrenaline.

No, Milo thought, disbelieving. *He wouldn't!*

But he did. Amid all the noise and activity, he couldn't hear the hypospray hiss when his father pressed it against her throat, but he saw her mouth open wide in surprise, watched her face go pale. It happened so fast there was nothing anyone could do to stop him. She clutched her neck instinctively, releasing her hold on Faal, and swayed dizzily from side to side, her gravity boots still glued to the duranium floor. She started hyperventilating as the polyadrenaline hit her system, huffing rapidly in short, ragged breaths. Her eyes glazed over and the veins in her throat throbbed at a frightening pace. Milo guessed that her heart, her lungs, and her entire metabolism had gone into overdrive, burning themselves out. She was swaying so wildly that she surely would have hit the floor if not for the absence of gravity.

"Deanna!" Dr. Crusher shouted. To Milo's relief, the doctor shoved her way past him to attend to her friend. Taking Troi's pulse with one hand, she immediately administered some sort of counteragent via her own hypospray. The antidote took effect almost instantly; Milo was glad to see Troi's breathing begin to slow. She looked like she was stabilizing now, thanks to Dr. Crusher's prompt response. *Praise the Holy Rings,* Milo thought, grateful that his father had not actually killed the counselor.

Lem Faal had not lingered to view the consequences of his actions, or to wait for a security officer to show up. Peering through the bustle of sickbay, Milo spotted his father disappearing through the double doors that led to the corridor outside. Milo chased after him, his oversized boots slowing him down more than he liked. Still occupied with the stricken counselor, Dr. Crusher did nothing to stop him from threading his way toward the exit. The doors swished open in front of him and he was free of sickbay when an unexpected hand grabbed onto his collar, dragging him back into the ward. "And where do you think you are going, young man?" a voice said sternly.

It was the bald-headed doctor, the one who didn't register on Milo's empathic senses. He eyed Milo dubiously, keeping a firm hold on the boy's collar. "I'm afraid no one is released from sickbay until they've been given a clean bill of health by a qualified health care professional."

"But my father!" Milo said, looking frantically at the exit as the doors slid shut again.

"First things first," the doctor insisted. "We'll deal with your father's appalling breach of protocol later. First we need to return you to the pediatric ward."

Milo had a vision of cortical stimulators being applied to his forehead and tried to free himself from the doctor's grip. *What's going to happen to my dad if I'm out cold?* All the doctors and nurses were too busy to bring his father back to sickbay before the ship entered the barrier. *It's up to me to save Dad,* Milo thought. "Let me go!" he yelled, but the bald doctor only tightened his grip. He was surprisingly strong.

"No!" Dr. Crusher ordered the other physician. With one arm wrapped around Counselor Troi to steady her, the ship's chief medical officer had clearly taken notice of Milo's near escape. "Don't let him get away," she instructed her colleague.

"I wouldn't dream of it," he replied archly, "even if my behavioral parameters included dreaming." Milo wasn't sure what he meant by that, but the doctor sure wasn't letting go of him anytime soon. He was about to give up when the whole sickbay shook like a malfunctioning turbolift. *The cloud monsters,* Milo guessed. *They must be trying to stop the* Enterprise *from going into the barrier.*

"Crusher to Security," the doctor said, tapping the badge on her chest. Obviously, she intended to send Security after Milo's father. The badge emitted a high-pitched whine, however, which was clearly not what Dr. Crusher had expected. "What the devil? There's something wrong with the com system."

The overhead lights flickered and, to Milo's surprise, so did the doctor holding his collar. *He's a hologram,* the boy realized, taking advantage of the doctor's momentary instability to break free and run for the exit. "Stop!" the hologram cried, and tried to seize Milo again, but his immaterial fingers passed uselessly through the fleeing child. "You haven't been discharged yet!" He glanced back at Dr. Crusher, then shrugged helplessly. "Don't look at me. *I'm* not responsible for unexpected power fluctuations. This is all Engineering's fault."

Milo barely heard the holo-doctor's excuses. As the sickbay doors whished shut behind him, he found himself confronted with a three-way intersection—and no sign of his father. *He can't have gone far,* he thought, silently blaming the hologram for slowing him down, *but which way did he go?* Milo searched telepathically for his father, but could not sense his presence anywhere. *He must be blocking me out,* he realized. Frustrated, he tried to guess where his father would want to go next.

Engineering, of course, and his equipment. Hadn't he tried to convince Ensign Daniels to take him to Engineering in the first place? Milo scanned the adjacent corridors for the nearest turbolift entrance, then raced down the left-hand hallway. Maybe he could still catch his father before . . . what? Milo had no idea what exactly he hoped to accomplish. He only knew that he had to do *something* before his father did anything terrible to himself.

Or someone else.

Six

Glevi ut Sov, Empress of Tkon, awoke one morning in the second year of her reign, during the latter days of the Age of Xora, with a feeling of unaccountable unease. There was a wrongness afoot, if not with her, then with the empire she hoped to rule wisely and well for many decades to come. Rising to a sitting position upon the couch, propped up by numerous soft cushions, each embroidered with the sacred emblem of the Endless Flame, she listened carefully to the silence of the early morning. Had any alarm or summons disturbed her dreams, calling her to cope with one emergency or another? No, the quiet of her private chambers was quite unbroken. Nothing had roused her except her own premonitions.

Hooves pawing the ground. . . . A fragment of a dream flashed through her memory. *Curved horns stabbing at the sky.* For an instant she could almost recall the entire dream, but then the memory slipped away, banished from her consciousness by the dawn of waking. What had she been dreaming again?

She rubbed her golden eyes with the back of her hand, wiping away the dried residue of slumber, stretched luxuriously, and deftly lowered her bare feet into a pair of fur-lined slippers resting on the floor. She could have commanded any number of attendants to help her rise and prepare for her duties, but she preferred to look after herself. Soon enough today, affairs of state would demand her attention for the remainder of her waking hours; for now, the beginning of each day remained her own.

The subdued night glow of the opaque crystal walls faded automatically as elegant chandeliers flooded the chambers with light, highlighting the intricate colored patterns of the antique Taguan carpet upon the floor. The empress paid little attention to the ornate designs of the rug, which had been in her family since her great-grandfather's time. Her shadow preceded her as she stepped away from the couch, the hem of her silk gown trailing upon the carpet. A translucent screen, upon which was printed a copper representation of the flame emblem, descended silently from the ceiling, sealing off the imperial bedchamber from the forefront of her quarters. Her desk, carved from the finest D'Arsay teak, awaited her, as did her favorite chair.

The outer rooms felt chilly this morning. "Warmer," she stated simply, "by, oh, seven and a half grades." Her technologists assured her that someday soon it would no longer be necessary to actually speak aloud to their homes and offices; the new psi-sensitive technology now being developed in labs throughout the empire would allow one to direct any and all instrumentality by thought alone. She frowned at the notion, not entirely sure she liked the idea of her palace knowing what she was thinking.

Yawning, she sat down in her chair. The room was already feeling warmer and more comfortable, but, despite the reassuring tranquillity of her chambers, she could not shake the ominous mood with which she had woken. She searched her memory, trying to bring to light any disturbing dream that might have left her spirit troubled, yet no such nightmare came to mind. As far as she recalled, her sleep had been soothing and unruffled until the very moment she came awake.

From where, then, had come this persistent sense of impending danger? "Show me the city," she said to the smooth, crystalline wall facing her and, like a window opening upon the world outside the palace, a panoramic view of a sprawling metropolis appeared on the wall, providing the empress with a live image of Ozari-thul, capital city of the great world Tkon, center of the Empire of the Endless Flame.

Resting her chin in her palm, she gazed out upon the city, her city, seeing nothing that would account for her anxious presentiments. Ozari-thul at dawn looked nearly as placid as her chambers, the vast majority of the city's twelve million inhabitants not yet stirring from their homes. Graceful towers, winding like crystal corkscrews, pierced the morning sky, while ribbons of interlocking roadways guided a few scattered vehicles on postnocturnal errands throughout the city. The blazing sun rose to the south, and she could not help noticing how much larger and redder it seemed now than it had in the not-so-long-ago days of childhood. That so swollen a sun should actually be *cooler* than it had once been struck her as paradoxical, but her scientists assured her that was indeed the case, and certainly the changing weather patterns of the last few years had borne their theories out.

Is that it? she wondered. Was her knowledge of the geriatric sun's eventual fate coloring her perceptions of the morning? That seemed unlikely. She had known about the long-term threat posed by their sun for years now, since even before she assumed the throne after her mother's death. Besides, the empire's finest scientists all agreed that the expansion of the sun, as that familiar yellow orb evolved into what the physicists called a red goliath, would not engulf the homeworld, as well as the rest of the inner planets, for several centuries. More than time enough for the Great Endeavor to come to their rescue—or was it?

She felt a stab of hunger, prompting her to ask for her breakfast, which instantly materialized on her desk: a beaker of hot tea and a plate of toasted biscuits, with *susu* jam and just a dab of imported Bajoran honey. Frankly, she would have liked more honey, but it wasn't worth the scolding she would receive from the court nutritionists, who fretted about the foreign sweeteners in the delicious amber spread. It was her duty, after all, to keep her mind and body fit, although she sometimes wondered what was the good of being empress if she couldn't even have an extra dollop of honey now and then.

A tinted crystal disk was embedded in the top of the teak desk. Washing down a tiny bite of biscuit with a sip of moderately spiced tea, she gazed at the disk and called up the most recent report on the progress of the Great Endeavor. Dates and figures scrolled past her eyes; as always, she was impressed by the sheer, unprecedented scale of the project, as well as the enormous expense. To literally move the sun itself out of the solar system, then to replace it with a younger star taken from an uninhabited system light-years away . . . had any other species *anywhere* ever attempted such a feat? Only to preserve Tkon itself, the sacred birthplace of their people, would she even dream of undertaking so colossal an enterprise. Small wonder her nerves were jittery.

And yet . . . according to this report, the Endeavor was proceeding on schedule and only slightly over budget. If necessary, she would bankrupt the imperial treasury to save the planet, but that drastic a sacrifice did not seem to be called for at present. Work was continuing apace on the solar transporter stations, their prospective new sun had not yet displayed any serious irregularities, and everything appeared to be in order. If all went according to plan, they would be ready to attempt the substitution within her lifetime. The Endeavor was no more risky today than it had been the day before, so why did she feel so perturbed?

With a word or two, she cleared the crystal viewing disk and called for her first minister. The image of an older man, seen from the waist up, appeared at once within the crystal. From the look of him, Rhosan arOx had already been at work for an hour or so. A ceremonial cloak of office was draped over his shoulders and his graying hair was neatly groomed. His cheeks had a healthy violet hue, which reassured her more than she wanted to admit. *He looks like he can manage affairs for many more years,* the empress thought, *just as he did for Mother.* "Good morning, Most Elevated," he said. "How can I help you?"

"Nothing too urgent," she replied, reluctant to burden him with her indistinct worries. "I was merely interested in . . . well, the state of the empire."

The vertical slits of his pupils widened their golden irises. "If I may take the liberty of asking, is something troubling you, Most Elevated?"

He's still as perceptive as he ever was, she thought. "It is most likely nothing," she assured him. "I feel . . . fretful . . . this morning, for no apparent reason. The foolish fancies of an inexperienced empress, most likely."

"I doubt that," he said promptly, "but I will be happy to allay your cares by informing you what I know." His gaze dropped to the surface of his own desk; over the last several months, he had taken over an increasingly larger share of her executive duties, freeing her to concentrate on the Great Endeavor. "Let's see. Labor negotiations with the Diffractors' Guild are dragging on, the United Sons and Daughters of Bastu are protesting the latest interplanetary tariffs, the Organians turned back our envoy again, and some fool politician on one of the outer worlds—Rzom, I believe—is refusing to pay his taxes, claiming the Great Endeavor is, quote, 'a sham and a hoax,' end quote, making him redundant as well as a damn idiot." Rhosan looked up from his data display. "Just the usual headaches, in other words. Nothing that should cause you excess concern."

"I see," the empress said, her tea and biscuits getting cold. "Thank you for your concise summary of the issues at hand. I don't believe any of the matters you mentioned could be the source of my thus far baseless apprehensions. Please forgive me for disturbing your work with such a nebulous complaint."

"It was no trouble," he insisted. "I hope I was able to put your mind to rest."

"Perhaps," she said diplomatically. "In any event, you may return to your numerous other responsibilities." Governing an empire of seven trillion inhabitants was no small task, as she well knew. "I shall see you later today, at the Fathoming Ceremony."

"Until then," the first minister acknowledged, dipping his head as she closed the connection. The crystal disk went blank. *If only I could dismiss my qualms so easily,* she mused. None of the routine difficulties Rhosan had alluded to justified the sense of dread that cast an inauspicious cloud over each passing moment. She raised her teacup to her lips, hoping the warmth of the tea would dispel the chill from her soul, but knowing in her heart that there was no easy balm for the doubts and fears that afflicted her.

A design etched onto both cup and plate caught her eye. The Endless Flame, ancient symbol of the empire since time immemorial. In olden days, she recalled, now lost in the haze of myth and legend, her primal ancestors were said to have been prophets, mystics, and seers. Their visions, according to archaic lore, had proven instrumental in the founding of the dynasty. Those distant days were long departed now, and subsequent rulers had required no such oracular prowess to guide the empire, but she couldn't help wondering, amid the miraculous technology of their modern age, if the blood of seers still flowed through her veins. Would her eldest forebears have recognized this seemingly inexplicable anxiety, this puzzling tremor in her psyche and spirit?

A single shard of memory lodged in her mind, less than a heartbeat in duration. A barely recalled sliver of a dream about . . . hooves?

Something *terrible* was coming, of that she was convinced.

"Comfortable, confident, trapped by tradition, enamored of their own hallowed history, and drunk with delusions of destiny," 0 sneered at the mighty Tkon Empire. "They're perfect, Q! I couldn't have chosen any better."

Five attentive entities, plus two more whose presence was unknown to the others, watched the planet Tkon spin beneath them, no larger than a toy globe compared to the scale on which Q and the others currently manifested themselves. From their lofty vantage point, several million kilometers above the world where the young empress dwelt, they could see a swarm of satellites, artificial and otherwise, orbiting the central planet. Tkon was the fourth planet in its system, and its influence spread outward in an expanding sphere of imperial hegemony that encompassed colonies on both the inner and outer worlds of its own solar system as well as distant outposts lit by the glow of alien stars. Tkon's defenses, based on those same satellites, colonies, and outposts, were formidable enough to discourage aggression from the barbarian races who lurked beyond the outermost reaches of the empire. 0 and his cohorts, on the other hand, couldn't have cared less about Tkon's vast military resources.

"Actually," the young Q said, "I've always considered the Tkon a civilizing factor in this region of the galaxy." He was starting to regret suggesting the Tkon Empire in the first place. What kind of testing did 0 have in mind? Nothing too severe, he hoped. "Their accomplishments in the arts and sciences, although aboriginal by our standards, naturally, are laudable enough on their own terms. I'm particularly fond of the satirical profile-poems of the late Cimi era—"

"Q, Q, Q," 0 interrupted, shaking his head. "You're missing the point. It's these creatures' primitive progress that makes them the ideal test subjects for our experiments. Where's the sport in testing some backward species that can barely split an atom, let alone synthesize antimatter? That would be a total waste of our time and abilities." He scowled at the thought before turning his mind toward brighter prospects. "These Tkon, on the other hand, are just perfect. Not too primitive, not too powerful. They're hovering at the cusp of true greatness, waiting for someone like us to come along to push them to the next level . . . if they're able."

"Precisely," Gorgan agreed. He licked his lips in anticipation. "I can already see some intriguing possibilities for them."

"*In* them," Q corrected, assuming the other was referring to the Tkon's potential as a species.

Gorgan shrugged. "As you prefer."

"They have grown overproud and must be humbled," The One pronounced. "They must drink bitter waters before they face My Judgment."

(*) merely flashed through pulsating shades of crimson, awaiting 0's command. A Tkon starship, en route to the eleventh planet in the home system with a crew complement of one thousand two hundred and five, approached the gathered immortals. Although traveling over twenty times the speed of light, it seemed to Q to be crawling toward them, and not much larger than an Organian dovebeetle. Despite, or perhaps because of, the difference in scale between the gleaming vessel and the immaterial onlookers, the ship remained unaware of Q and the others even as it came within their proximity. It glided between Q and 0, who nonchalantly reached out and swatted the miniature spacecraft away, sending it tumbling through space and into the hard red radiance of (*).

Moments later, as Q reckoned time, (*)'s influence caused a bloody mutiny to erupt aboard the ship, leading ultimately to a helix drive explosion that blossomed into a firefly flash of blue-green before dimming into nothingness. (*) glowed a little brighter afterward, savoring its snack.

It had happened so quickly, from this celestial point of reference, that Picard could scarcely keep up with all that was happening, let alone grasp its meaning. "That ship," he murmured. "All those lives . . ."

"A matter of no importance," Q insisted, "a tiny teardrop of tragedy before the deluge. You mustn't let yourself be distracted by such marginalia. The fate of an empire, and more, is at stake."

Picard nodded grimly, unable to speak. He knew full well what was coming, and Q was right: The destruction of a single starship was next to nothing compared to the apocalypse ahead.

"You have to admit," 0 said to the young Q, the tiny starship already forgotten, "the Tkon still have a long way to go before they're remotely comparable to us, or even that fetid fog we first ran into."

"I don't know," Q responded, the bright tiny spark that had been a spacecraft still imprinted on his metaphysical retinas. Intellectually, he liked the idea of helping lesser life-forms evolve; it certainly beat the unending boredom the Continuum provided in such dispiriting quantities. Primitive species had often proved more unpredictable, and therefore more entertaining, than his fellow Q . . . with the possible exception of Q herself. On the other hand, when it came to actually visiting trials and tribulations on a harmless little species like the Tkon, who had worked so hard to achieve their own modest triumphs . . . well, he found it seemed vaguely unsporting. "They seem to be doing fairly well on their own," he observed.

"Fairly well?" 0 echoed. He laughed so loud that Q found himself blushing without really knowing why. "They're nowhere close to transcending fourth-dimensional existence, let alone achieving true cosmic consciousness. Why, they still require a massive infrastructure and social hierarchy just to satisfy their crude physical needs." He rolled his eyes and raised his hands in amazement. "You can't let yourself get sentimental about your subjects, no matter how cute and comical they are. Face the facts, Q. At this rate, it will take them a couple of eternities to catch up with us, if they even last that long, which I sincerely doubt. They've gotten smug, complacent, convinced that they're sitting at the top of the evolutionary ladder. They have no more incentive to evolve further, which means they're just short of total stagnation. They need to be reminded that there are bigger forces in the universe, sublime mysteries they haven't even begun to unravel."

"So be it," The One seconded, nodding His bearded head ponderously. His golden armor clanked as He crossed His arms atop His chest, the metallic ringing resounding across five dimensional planes and creating unaccountable subspace vibrations that caused technicians to scratch their heads in confusion throughout the entire empire. "Let it be written."

"If testing these beings is indeed on the agenda," Gorgan pointed out, "we should do so swiftly." He gestured toward the flaming thermonuclear globe at the center of the Tkon's solar system. "That old sun is clearly on its last legs."

Q glanced at the orb in question, seeing at once that Gorgan was correct. The sun of Tkon, a standard yellow star of no particular distinction aside from its use-fulness to the Tkon, had almost depleted its store of hydrogen atoms. Soon enough, the helium in its core would begin fusing into carbon, eventually causing the star to swell into a bloated red caricature of its former self, and, from the look of things, swallow up all of the inner planets, including Tkon. "Seems to me," he suggested, "that the Tkon have challenges enough already without us adding to their difficulties."

"Which is why this is exactly the right time to test them," 0 insisted, looming over the endangered world like a constellation. "Now is the defining moment of their existence. Can they remain focused on the big picture despite their trivial everyday concerns, not to mention whatever ingenious obstacles we place before them? Will they perish with their star, abandon their homes for distant shores, or achieve the impossible in the face of impediments both natural and supernatural?" He rubbed his palms together eagerly. "It should be a fascinating experiment!"

"Er, what kind of impediments did you have in mind?" Q found himself look-ing backward over his shoulder, half-expecting to find the entire Continuum look-ing on in disapproval. *If they had any idea what 0 has in mind . . . !* To his surprise, he discovered that the danger of incurring his peers' censure only made 0's plans all the more irresistible. There was an undeniable, if vaguely illicit, thrill in defy-ing propriety this way. If only there was some way to scandalize the Q and the oth-ers without inconveniencing the Tkon too much.

"Why, whatever we feel like," 0 stated readily. Q envied his reckless, carefree attitude. "You don't want to plan these things too much beforehand. You need to leave yourself room to improvise, to invent and elaborate. It's as much an art as a science." He gestured toward the solar system at their feet. "Go ahead," he urged Q. "It was your idea. It's only fitting you take the first shot. Indulge yourself. Employ that extraordinary imagination of yours. Give their tiny, terrestrial, time-bound minds something to really think about."

Q gathered his power together, feeling the creative energies crackle in his hands. *This is it,* he thought, *This is my chance.* A peculiar sense of . . . suspense? tension? . . . percolated within him. It was a strange, but not altogether unpleasant sensation. After all this time, after countless aeons spent waiting for the opportu-nity to show what he could do, what if he couldn't think of anything? What if he made a mistake or, worse yet, committed some ghastly cliché that just made 0 and the rest think less of him? He felt the pressure of the others' expectant gaze, sa-vored an unprecedented fear of failure, then took a deep if figurative breath, ab-sorbing inspiration from the ether. "Suppose," he said tentatively, not quite committing himself, "I miraculously extended the life span of their sun by another four billion years?" Easy enough, he thought; all that was required was a fresh infusion of elemental hydrogen into the star's core. "That would come as a real stunner to them, wouldn't it? What do you think they will do with all that extra time? How will their society and institutions react? It should make for an informative experiment, don't you think?"

0 sighed and rubbed his brow wearily. Gorgan and The One shook their heads and stepped backward, placing a bit more distance between them and Q, who could tell at once that his suggestion had not been well received. *Hey, don't blame me,* he thought indignantly. *It was my first try, after all.*

"You're missing the point," 0 explained. "That's no test; that's a *gift."* He spit out the word as if it left a bad taste in his mouth. "Four billion extra years? What's that going to teach them—or us, for that matter? Progress, even survival itself, must be earned. Challenges are to be overcome. Benevolence is for babies."

Q's ears burned. Was 0 calling him a baby? Why, he was almost seven billion years old! "Can't the unexpected come in positive forms as well as negative?" he argued. "Isn't a species' reaction to miraculous good fortune as significant, as educational and edifying, as the way they cope with adversity?"

"On some abstract, intellectual level perhaps," 0 said grudgingly, "but take it from me, Q, it's a lot more boring, for the tested and tester alike. What would you rather do, watch the Tkon cope with the ultimate issues of life or death, or simply feed them a few cosmological crumbs now and then, watching from afar as they scurry around in gratitude?" He yawned theatrically. "Frankly, I have better things to do than watch you dote on an undeserving warren of underdeveloped, overpopulated vermin. Where's the sport in that?" He paced back and forth across the sector, his footsteps creating deep impressions in the fabric of space-time that would someday be charted by the first Verathan explorers, five hundred thousand years later. "Come on, Q. Surely you can do better than that. What's it going to be?"

"I don't know," Q blurted, feeling both embarrassed and resentful. "I'm not sure." Why was 0 making this so hard? *It's not fair,* he thought. *The Continuum is forever badgering me about going too far; now 0 is unhappy because I won't go far enough.* He wanted to *do* something, but not necessarily *to* anyone.

"Listen to me, Q," 0 entreated. "This is what you've always wanted, a chance to use your innate abilities the way they were always meant to be used. Don't censor yourself before you even begin. Don't hold back. Show the Tkon, and the rest of the multiverse, what you're really made of. Put the fear of Q into them!"

Well, not fear exactly, Q thought. Still, 0 had a point. Realistically, there was no way to make an impact on the universe without affecting the Tkon or some species like them. He couldn't balk now, not if he was really serious about joining 0 in his campaign. Despite his qualms, he felt a tingle of excitement, a sneaky thrill that was only heightened by the sense that he was getting away with something he shouldn't. "All right," he declared, "let's start with something silly and see where we go from there."

Without warning, thousands upon thousands of plump, juicy red *vovelles,* a Tkon fruit not unlike a tomato, poured from the sky above the great city of Ozarithul. The succulent deluge pelted the streets and rooftops of the capital, leaving a wet, pulpy mess wherever the falling fruits came to rest. The fruits exploded upon impact with masonry or flesh, spraying everyone and everything with sloppy red debris. The people of the city, the great and the lowly alike, ran for shelter, then stared in awe and amazement at the inexplicable phenomenon. Slitted golden eyes blinked in disbelief while psionic announcements urged the citizens to remain calm. "Not bad," 0 pronounced. "A bit adolescent, but okay for a start."

Q was delighted by the results of his opening move. He laughed out loud as a ceremonial parade down the heart of the city was reduced to pandemonium by the unnatural downpour, sending both marchers and onlookers scrambling, already dripping with raw seed and juice, slipping and sliding in the gory remains of thousands of skydiving fruits. The high priestess of the Temple of Ozari, her immaculate white robes and headdress splattered with pulp, tried futilely to finish the Ritual of Ascension until an overripe *vovelle* cut her off in the midprayer. But not everyone found the bizarre fruitfall an ordeal or an offense; small children, exhilarated by the marvelously messy miracle, ran squealing through the streets, scooping up handfuls of pulverized fruit innards to hurl at each other, giggling deliriously as the gooey redness ran through their hair and down their faces.

Q was just as gratified and amused. All that tremendous chaos, and all because of him! Whyever had he waited so long to play this game? One whimsical notion, and he had affected the lives of millions, maybe even billions, of other beings. This was a day that neither he nor the Tkon Empire would ever forget, and he was just getting warmed up. Why, he could do anything now, anything at all. A million outrageous possibilities popped into his mind. He could bring the colorful gods and monsters of Tkon mythology to life, or make their entire history flow backward. He could imbue an ordinary Tkon with a fraction of Q-power and see what happened next, or turn himself into a Tkon for a time. He could make them speak exclusively in limericks or sign language or Ionian pentameter. He might even change the value of *pi* throughout the entire empire or lower the speed of light; just imagine the divine confusion and merriment that would ensue! The possibilities were as infinite as his imagination. He could hardly wait to get started.

But suppose he got carried away? The thought materialized within his mind as unexpectedly as the fruits bombarding Ozari-thul, surfacing from some surprising core of responsibility at the locus of his being. The possibilities at hand were almost too unlimited. For the first time, Q was frightened by his own omnipotence.

The rain of *vovelles* halted abruptly, leaving a puzzled population to gaze quizzically at the now-empty sky. They peeked out nervously from beneath archways and covered pavilions, half-expecting the fruits to return in greater numbers, perhaps accompanied by icemelons and *susu* as well. Automated sanitation systems began clearing away the slippery debris. Awe and wonder gave way to feverish speculation and debate as news of the bizarre incident immediately spread to every corner of the empire. Despite a full imperial investigation, however, including the subatomic and electromagnetic scrutiny of over five thousand barrels of *vovelle* pulp, plus countless hours of careful analysis and ontological theorizing, no satisfactory explanation was ever provided, nor did the empress and her people come close to guessing the truth—until much later.

"What's the matter, Q?" 0 asked. "Why have you stopped?" He must have known from the look on Q's face that the young godling was not merely gearing up for some newer and greater escapade. "Is there a problem?"

"It's nothing," Q said, unable to meet the other's eyes; he didn't want to admit to any second thoughts. What kind of rebel was he if he got squeamish about a mere harmless jest? They'd think he was a coward, afraid of upsetting the

Continuum. "I was simply concerned about the long-term ecological impact of all those plummeting succulents." The excuse sounded feeble even to his own ears. "It's just that I want to pace myself, not use up all my creativity on the first evolving life-form that catches my eye."

"But you were only getting warmed up," 0 told him. "That was nothing but a schoolboy prank. Not that I don't like a good joke as much as the next all-powerful life-form, but don't you want to try something, well, more serious?"

"Maybe later," Q said. It was tempting to play with the Tkon again, try out some of his new ideas, but he didn't want to be pushed into anything he was uncomfortable with by simple peer pressure alone. *If I wanted to just go along with the crowd, I could have stuck with the Continuum. I'm only going to do what I want to do—just as soon as I figure out what that is.*

"I see," 0 answered. He looked disappointed in Q, but refrained from any further criticism. "Well, why don't you sit this one out while Gorgan and the others show you how it's done." He nodded at his companions, who began to descend and disperse to the far-flung borders of the Tkon Empire, their very substance shrinking and growing more compact as they accommodated themselves to the mortal plane of their respective targets. Soon they appeared to be no larger than the individual denizens of the worlds they had each selected, but appearances, in this case, were extremely deceiving. "They'll just soften them up for us," 0 told Q. "You and I, maybe we can deliver the coup de grâce later on, after our friends have had their fun." He strolled over to Q and rested his celestial frame upon an invisible chair. "You'll like that, Q. The final test. The exam to end all exams. That's what makes it all worthwhile, you'll see."

"Really?" Q asked, too keyed up to sit. He watched the receding forms of Gorgan, (*), and The One with mixed emotions. Part of him, the part that had thoroughly enjoyed raining overripe fruit upon the palaces of Ozari-thul, wished he was going with them. Another part, from which his trepidations had emerged, waited nervously to see what sort of stunts Q's old acquaintances were intent on. "What kind of final test?" he asked.

"Later," 0 promised. "For now, just sit back and enjoy the show."

I'll try, Q thought, settling back into a comfortable curvature of space-time, adjusting the gravity until it fit just right and resting his head against a patch of condensed dark matter. He had to admit, in spite of his occasional reservations, there was something exceptionally stimulating about not knowing what was going to happen next.

Seven

Galactic barrier, here we come, Riker thought as the *Enterprise* came within sight of the perilous wall of energy. He wasn't looking forward to justifying this decision to Captain Picard, in the unlikely event that they ever met again. Two empty chairs flanked the captain's seat; with Picard away and Deanna off in sickbay, the command area felt even lonelier than usual.

"There it is," Ensign Clarze called out unnecessarily. Even through the stormy chaos of the Calamarain, the luminous presence of the barrier could be perceived, shining through the temperamental clouds like a searchlight through the mist and throwing a reddish purple radiance over the scene upon the viewer. *Let's hope that it's not luring us on to our destruction,* Riker thought. At maximum impulse, they would be within the barrier in a matter of moments.

"Steady as she goes, Mr. Clarze," he instructed. A loose isolinear chip, its casing charred by the explosion that had liberated it from a broken control panel, drifted between Riker and the viewscreen, pointedly reminding him that the gravity had gone the way of most of their shields. *Thank heaven we still have life-support,* he thought, *after the beating we've taken.* He suspected that the old *Enterprise*-D, as durable as she was, would have already succumbed to the Calamarain's assault. *We upgraded just in time.*

"Shields at eight percent," Leyoro reported. Small wonder that the ship felt like it was shaking itself apart. The Calamarain, perhaps becoming aware of Riker's desperate strategy, threw themselves against the hull and what remained of the deflectors with the same relentless ferocity they had displayed for hours now. *Don't they ever get tired,* he thought, *or is that just something we solids have to put up with?*

"Data. Barclay. Where's that extra energy?" He smacked his fist against the arm of the chair. "We need those shields."

"Scanning for it," Barclay said from the aft engineering station. Now that the pressure was on, the nervous crewman seemed to find a hidden reserve of professionalism, or maybe he was just too busy to be frightened. *This had better work,* Riker thought, drawing comfort from the fact that Geordi had looked over Barclay's findings and seconded Data's technical evaluation of the plan. *That's as much as I can ask for, given our lousy situation.* "Yes," Barclay reported, "I think I'm reading something now. The bio-gel packs are being energized by the proximity of the barrier. I'm picking up definite traces of psionic particles."

Lightning crashed across the prow of the saucer section, and sparks spewed from the engineering station, the electrical spray gushing toward the ceiling instead of raining upon the floor as they would have under ordinary gravitational conditions. It looked like a geyser of fire. Barclay had no choice but to step back from the sparking console while he waited for the emergency circuits to shut down the geyser. "Commander," he said, chagrined, "I can't monitor the bio-gel packs anymore."

Terrific, Riker thought bitterly. "Data, take over from your station. Divert whatever energy we've absorbed to the shields immediately." *It will have to be enough.*

"Yes, Commander," Data acknowledged, his synthetic fingers flying over the control panel faster than any human eye could follow. "Initiating energy transfer now."

Here goes nothing, Riker thought. Everything depended on Barclay's wild scheme.

"Shields back up to seventy percent," Leyoro reported in surprise; Riker didn't think she was the sort to believe in miracles. "The readings are very peculiar. These aren't like any deflectors I know, but they're holding."

And just in time, Riker thought as the ship plunged into the barrier. He braced for the impact, wondering briefly if it was even possible for the ship to be knocked about more than the Calamarain had done. The light radiating from the viewer grew brighter and for an instant he believed he saw the Calamarain flash strangely, their vibrant colors reversed like a photographic negative. Then the whole screen whited out, overloaded by the incredible luminosity of the barrier. The hum of the

Calamarain, and the thunder of their aggression, vanished abruptly, replaced by a sudden silence that was almost as unnerving. It was like going from a battlefield to a morgue in a single breath, and creepy as could be.

"Commander," Leyoro exulted, "the Calamarain have withdrawn. They can't stand the barrier!" She let out a high-pitched whoop that Riker assumed was some sort of Angosian victory cry. A breach of bridge protocol, but forgivable under the circumstances. He felt like cheering himself, despite the eerie quiet.

But, having shed the Calamarain at last, could they survive the barrier? He hoped that their adversaries, in choosing the better part of valor, had not proven wiser than the *Enterprise*. "Mr. Clarze," he commanded, "come to a full stop." He didn't want to go any deeper into the barrier than they had to, let alone face whatever dangers might be waiting on the other side, with the ship in the shape that it was. "Leyoro, how are our new and improved shields holding up?"

The deathly hush of the barrier had already spread to the ship; the lights of the bridge dimmed, then went out entirely, leaving only the red emergency lights and the glow from the surviving consoles to illuminate the stations around him. The familiar buzz of the bridge faded as lighted control panels flickered before falling dead. The forward viewer was useless, the screen blank. They were flying blind, more or less.

"Sufficiently, I think," Leyoro allowed. "The readings are difficult to interpret; the psychic energy bombarding the ship is the same energy that is maintaining our shields, which makes them hard to distinguish from each other."

"How much longer can we stay here?" he asked, cutting straight to the crux of the matter. He felt a dull ache beneath his forehead, and recalled that Kirk had lost close to a dozen crew members on his trip through the barrier, their brains burned out by some sort of telepathic shock. He suddenly wondered if his decade-long psychic bond with Deanna could have left him peculiarly vulnerable to the telepathic danger of the psychic energy now surrounding the ship. *Lord only knows what it's doing to my frontal lobes,* he thought, *even through our shields.*

Leyoro shook her head, unable to answer his question. Her glee over eluding the Calamarain had given way to concern over their present status. He saw her grimace in pain, then massage her forehead with her fingers. *Never mind my brain,* he thought, *what about Leyoro's?* It had not occurred to him before that her modified nervous system, permanently altered by the Angosians to increase her combat readiness, might put her at risk as well.

He looked to Barclay and Data instead. "How long?" he asked again, wondering if the real question wasn't how long they *could* stay within the barrier, but how long they dared to.

"It is impossible to state with certainty," the android informed him. "As long as the bio-gel packs continue to draw psychic power from the barrier, we should be safe, but we must allow for the possibility that these unusual energies, which the bio-gel packs were never designed to accommodate, may burn out the packs at any moment, in which case our situation would become significantly more hazardous."

"Um, what he said," Barclay confirmed, twitching nervously. Paradoxically, his self-conscious mannerisms had returned as soon as the immediate danger passed. *He works best under pressure,* Riker guessed. *The less time he has to fret about things, the better he copes.*

"Understood," he said. "Good work, both of you. Contact Commander La Forge and tell him to start repairing the damage done by the Calamarain. Top priority on the shields; with any luck, we can get our conventional deflectors up and running before these new bio-gel packs burn themselves out."

"What about the gravity, sir?" Barclay asked. Despite the anti-nausea treatment from Nurse Ogawa, he still looked a little green around the gills. Simple spacesickness, or was Barclay's cerebrum also taking a beating from the barrier? Riker recalled that the engineer's brain had been artificially enhanced once before, when the Cytherians temporarily increased his intelligence. Barclay's IQ had returned to normal eventually, but it was conceivable that he could have picked up a little heightened telepathic sensitivity in the process. *Data may be the only crew member aboard who is entirely immune to the effect of the barrier,* Riker realized.

Riker shook his head in response to Barclay's query. "Shields first, then the warp drive. We'll just have to put up with weightlessness a little longer." To keep up morale, he allowed himself an amused grin. "Think of it as a vacation from gravity."

"Now that we're free of the Calamarain's damping influence," Leyoro pointed out, "the warp engines may be operative again."

That's right, Riker thought, immediately tapping his combadge. "Geordi, we're inside the outer fringes of the barrier, but the Calamarain have retreated. What's the status of the warp engines?"

"Not good, Commander," Geordi's voice stated, exerting its own damping influence on Riker's hopes. "I don't know if it was the Calamarain or the barrier or both, but the warp nacelles have taken an awful lot of damage. It's going to take several hours to fix them."

Blast, Riker thought, not too surprised. As he recalled, the barrier had knocked out Kirk's warp engines, too, the first time he dared the barrier. Plus, when you considered all the pounding they had received from the Calamarain's thunderbolts, and with minimal shields there at the end, he figured he should be thankful that at least the com system was working. "Go to it, Mr. La Forge. Riker out."

"It may be just as well, Commander," Data commented. "It is impossible to predict the consequences of going to warp within the barrier itself. I would be highly reluctant to attempt such an experiment without further analysis of the unknown energies that comprise the barrier."

Except that that may be a risk we have to take, Riker thought, *especially if the Calamarain are waiting for us right outside the barrier.* "What about those angry clouds we just got rid of?" he asked Leyoro. It was possible that the Calamarain, assuming the *Enterprise* destroyed by the barrier, may have left for greener pastures. "Any sign they're still hanging around out there?"

"I don't know, sir," Leyoro said unhappily; it was obvious that the security chief did not like having to keep disappointing her commander. Just as obviously, her head was still bothering her. She rubbed her right temple mechanically, while a muscle beside her left eye twitched every few seconds. "The barrier is so intense it's overwhelming our sensors. They can't detect anything past it."

So we're blind, deaf, and numb, Riker concluded. The big question then was what was more dangerous, staying inside the barrier or facing the Calamarain? *We already know we can't beat the Calamarain as is,* he thought, *so our best bet is to stay put until Geordi can get the warp drive working again, then try to make a quick escape.* He surveyed the bridge, inspecting the faces of his crew, and was glad to see that all of them, including Barclay, seemed fit enough for action. He considered sending Leyoro to sickbay for a checkup, but there was a host of people aboard, all of them in danger; he couldn't afford to start relieving officers just because they might have a suspicious headache. His own head was throbbing now, but none of his people looked like they were ready to keel over.

Yet.

Eight

During the fifth year of the reign of the empress, on an unusually chilly summer night in the largest city on Rzom, the eleventh planet in the primary solar system of the Tkon Empire, a young man stood on the wide crystal steps leading to the front entrance of the imperial governor's mansion and exhorted the crowd that had gathered in the spacious and well-lit plaza to hear him speak. A life-sized statue of the empress, carved from the purest Rzom marble and posed heroically atop an elegant pedestal at the center of the plaza, looked on in silence.

"Why," he asked the onlookers rhetorically, "should we pay exorbitant taxes, wasting the resources of a lifetime, just to preserve an overcrowded old world millions of miles from here, whose time has come?"

About a third of the crowd, most the same age as the speaker, cheered his words enthusiastically, while others muttered among themselves or cast angry yellow stares at the youth upon the steps. A contingent of five safeties, clad in matching turquoise uniforms, flanked the crowd, watching carefully for the early signifiers of a brewing disturbance. The faces of the safeties were fixed and expressionless, displaying no response to the young man's fervent oratory. Pacification rings waited patiently on the fingers of each safety's hand, linked to sophisticated neutralization equipment embedded in the very walls and pavement of the city. So far, there had been no cause to employ the rings, but the safeties remained alert and ready. Nervous faces, perhaps even the governor's, peered through the curtained windows of the palace, viewing the drama from behind the safety of reinforced crystal walls.

"That world is our birthplace," a woman shouted indignantly from the forefront of the crowd. From the looks of her, she was a governmental functionary of approximately the sixth echelon, whose reddish hair was already turning silver. A disk-shaped emblem melded to the collar of her insulated winter mantle proclaimed that she had voluntarily donated more than her allotted share to the Great Endeavor.

The young man's partisans among the crowd, students mostly, greeted the woman's passionate outburst with jeers and laughter. Emboldened by their support, the speaker on the steps hooted as well. "I wasn't born there and neither were you," he shot back, winning another round of cheers from his contemporaries. Despite the chill of the evening, on a world little known for its warmth, his vermilion cloak was open to the wind and flapping above his shoulder as he spoke. His ebony locks were knotted in the latest style. "I'm proud to say that I was born here on Rzom—and to Hades with decrepit Tkon!"

Many of the older spectators clucked disapprovingly and shook their heads. "You should be ashamed of yourself," the aging functionary said. "You don't deserve the blessings of the empire!"

One crystal step above and behind the youthful firebrand, unobserved by either his supporters or detractors, nor by the watchful eyes of the vigilant safeties, Gorgan watched with pleasure as the public debate grew more heated. *It's always so easy,* he thought, *pitting the young against the old. This new plane is no different than any other realm.*

The graying woman's admonition was seconded by others in the audience. This time those rallying around her matched the volume of the young people's catcalls and derisive glee. "That's right," another man yelled. He looked like an archivist or invested myth reader. "Go live among the barbarians if that's what you want. Real Tkon know that the homeworld is worth any sacrifice."

The open show of opposition seemed to rattle the leader of the dissidents, who stepped backward involuntarily, passing effortlessly through the immaterial form of Gorgan, who casually eased to one side for a bit more personal space. The proud young Rzom faltered, momentarily at a loss for words, but Gorgan came to his rescue, whispering into the youth's ear in a voice only his unconscious mind could hear.

"Blessings? What blessings?" the speaker demanded, parroting the words that flowed so easily from Gorgan's lips. "Over fifteen percent of the empire's adult laborers are devoted to the empress's misguided Endeavor, and over twenty-seven percent of the entire imperial budget! All to keep the inner planets from meeting their natural fate. Can you imagine what else could have been done with all that time and treasure, the advances we could have achieved in art, science, medicine, exploration, and social betterment? The finest minds of a generation are being squandered on a grandiose exercise in sentimentality and nostalgia." His voice grew bolder and more confident as Gorgan fed him subliminal cues. "Our ancestors had the courage to physically leave Tkon generations ago; we should have the courage to let go of it spiritually at long last. Let's work together to enhance the future, not preserve the past!"

"Hear, hear!" cried a young woman, barely past adolescence, her emerald tresses knotted so tightly that not a single strand blew freely in the wind. "Tell them, Jenole!"

The man beside her, wearing the indigo crest of a licensed commerce artist, gave her a contemptuous sneer. "Spoiled whelp," he muttered, loud enough for her to hear. Throughout the assembled throng, individuals eyed their neighbors skeptically and began clustering into hostile pockets of two or more, placing physical as well as ideological distance between themselves and those who disagreed with them. Soon the crowd had parted into two hostile camps, glaring at each other and shouting slogans and insults at their fellow citizens. Even the acutely disciplined safeties began to let their masks of neutrality slip, betraying their inclinations and allegiances with a slightly downturned lip here, an arched eyebrow or furrowed brow there.

Marvelous, Gorgan thought, delighted to see the people turning on themselves, splitting apart along generational lines. *Just marvelous.* It was his curse and his glory that he could only achieve and wield power through the manipulation of others, but that restriction was of little import when such creatures as these proved so easy to beguile.

"And what of the trillions of inhabitants of the inner worlds?" the older woman challenged the youth. "Are you prepared to cope with the countless refugees the dying sun will send stampeding in our direction? Not to mention the loss of our history, the end of all archaeological research into the distant past, the utter destruction of sites and natural wonders hallowed by millions of years of striving and civilization?" She paused for breath, then turned around to face the divided assemblage. "Don't future generations deserve a chance to gaze upon the sacred shore of Azzapa? Or walk in the footsteps of Llaxem or Yson?" She held out her hands to the crowd, pleading for their understanding. "Don't you see? If we let Tkon and the other worlds be destroyed, then we're cutting out the very heart of the culture we all share."

Gorgan was disturbed to see uncertainty upon the faces of some of the younger members of the audience. He scowled at the aging bureaucrat whose words appeared to be striking a nerve in listeners both young and old. *She's making too much sense,* he brooded. *Something has to be done.*

Leaving the leader of the dissidents to his own devices, Gorgan glided down the steps toward the woman, the hem of his voluminous gown leaving no trail upon the polished surface of the steps. He crept silently to her side until his face was only a finger away from her ear. *You don't stand a chance,* he whispered. *You're too old. Your time has passed.*

Higher upon the crystal steps, the youth called Jenole attempted to regain the mob's attention, along with the loyalty of his followers. "Tkon's no heart. It's just a planet, a big rock in the endless null . . . like a hundred million other worlds." He thumped a fist against his chest, raising his voice to heighten the impact of his impassioned declaration. "The real heart of the empire is right here! On Rzom, and inside us all!"

His fellow students cheered in unison, some of them a bit less robustly than before, drawing murderous looks from the opposing camp. The narrow gazes of the safeties arced back and forth between the students and their critics, watching both sides carefully. The silicon rings on their fingers glinted beneath the elevated lights of the plaza, which cast a gentle, faintly violet radiance over all that transpired.

"But that doesn't *mean* anything," the functionary protested, responding to Jenole's shouted claim to the heart of the empire. She tried to match his fiery intensity, but found her will and energy fading. *It's no use,* a voice at the back of her mind whispered, sounding very much like her own. *There's no point, you've already lost.* Despite several layers of insulated fabric to protect her from the winter, she felt a chill work its way into the marrow of her bones. *Tkon is doomed. Nobody cares. The sun is dying and so are you. . . .*

Still, she tried to rally her spirits, fighting against the despair and hopelessness that descended over her like a suffocating fog. "No, you don't understand. We have a choice." She could barely hear her own words over the insidious voice inside her skull *(It's a lost cause),* but she struggled to force her argument out through her lips. "We can either run from the disaster or prevent it. Diaspora or deliverance."

"What's that?" her opponent seemed to bellow at her. "Speak up. We can't hear you."

Sadness shrouded her like a heavy net, dragging her down. "What do you want?" she murmured. *There is no hope.* Her chin sagged against her chest as her gaze dropped to the uncaring steps below. *They'll never learn.* "Why won't you listen? We have a choice. It doesn't have to happen. . . ."

She receded back into the crowd, as if drawn by some inexorable gravitational force, leaving Gorgan alone and triumphant upon the lower steps. *Despair is a powerful weapon,* he gloated, *especially for those already feeling the tug of entropy upon their bodies and souls.* He contemplated the victor of the debate, standing tall before the imposing edifice behind him, blithely incognizant of the alien influences that had driven his critic from the field. *Arrogance, too, has its uses. With both tools at my disposal, I can sever any bond, tear asunder any union, and work my will on the scraps that remain.*

One of those scraps, clad in a cloak as florid as his oratory, trumpeted his cause to the entire plaza. "You see, the rightness of our position cannot be denied! Down with the musty memory of Tkon. The future belongs to the new age of Rzom!"

His peers took up his cry, but at the fringes of the crowd people began to drift away. The older citizens in particular, having lost their most vocal advocate, seemed to lose interest in the confrontation. One by one, they turned away, shrugging dismissively. It was cold out, after all, and they had better things to do. Beneath their crisp, spotless uniforms, the coiled muscles of the safeties geared down to an only slightly lessened state of readiness.

Gorgan noticed the difference and, noticing, frowned. The situation had plateaued too soon and now ran the risk of inspiring nothing more than empty rhetoric. He could not settle for mere words, no matter how inflammatory. It was time to up the stakes, accelerate the conflict to the next level. He eyed the safeties, so self-assured in their authority, and smirked in anticipation of what was to come. *You have no idea what awaits you.*

He did not need to draw any nearer to the cocksure youth standing astride the top steps to project his new suggestions into such a willing mind. He rode the momentum he had already brought about to egg the self-infatuated student leader on to greater heights of rebellion.

"Friends, allies, brothers and sisters in arms," Jenole called out, the regal facade of the governor's palace looming behind him. "Listen to me. We need to send a message to everyone who has tried to force down our throats their Great Endeavor." He spat out the name as if it were an obscenity. "To the governor, to the selfish cowards back on Tkon, and even to the empress herself."

Leaping onto the uppermost step, beneath the carved crystal archway of the grand entrance, he aimed an accusing finger at the statue of the empress upon her pedestal. "There she is," he hollered, "the architect of this entire insane enterprise."

Not far away, but separated from this moment and place by a phase or two of reality, a time-lost starship captain flinched at the word "enterprise" as he heard it translated into his own tongue. The name reminded him of dangers and responsibilities he was not being allowed to face. "Q," he began.

"Sssh," Q hushed him, watching 0 and his younger self watching Gorgan watching the Rzom. "Pay attention, Jean-Luc. You may find the modus operandi quite instructive. I certainly did."

"Let's show the galaxy that we mean what we say," the Rzom youth continued, "that we refuse to blindly worship the past. Down with that monument to folly. Down with the empress!"

Incited by their spokesman, the mob of students rushed the statue, climbing onto the pedestal and throwing their weight against the marble figure. Horrified by this attempt at vandalism, a few of the older citizens tried to intervene, placing themselves between the statue and the next wave of demonstrators, but they were quickly shoved aside by the overexcited students. Fists were raised and angry words exchanged, prompting the safeties to take action at last. "Attention," the senior safety announced, her voice artificially amplified by a mechanism planted against the base of her throat. "Step away from the statue at once. This gathering is declared a threat to public order and is hereby terminated. All citizens are directed to refrain from further debate and to exit the plaza in an orderly fashion."

The safety's instructions chastened a fraction of those assembled, who froze sheepishly in their tracks, then began to slink away; lawlessness did not come easily to people who had known decades of peace and stability. But the majority of the students, whose memories were shorter and whose law-abiding habits were less deeply ingrained, ignored the safety, continuing to clamber over the marble monument like Belzoidian fleas swarming over an unguarded piece of cake, while shouting and cheering uproariously. They appeared to be having the time of their lives, much to the delight of Gorgan. Tools that enjoyed their work always performed better than those who had to be grudgingly forced to their tasks. He nodded approvingly as a jubilant young Rzom started swinging back and forth from the outstretched arm of the sculpted empress.

The senior safety, on the other hand, scowled grimly at the sight. She had been afraid of this; the disturbance had already escalated too far, too fast. Choosing not to waste time with any further warnings, she sent a silent electronic signal to her fellow safeties, then aimed the ring on her left forefinger at the youth hanging from the statue's arm.

A beam of directed energy, fluorescently orange, leaped from the ring, targeting the would-be vandal, who instantly disappeared from sight. The safety smiled in satisfaction, knowing that the reckless youth had been painlessly transferred to a holding facility at headquarters several city blocks away. Not for the first time, she wondered how safeties had ever managed before transference technology became so convenient; she could just imagine the incredible nuisance of having to physically subdue and transport each offender before placing them into a cell.

Around the plaza, each of the five safeties used their rings to thin out the crowd of students attacking the monument. As expected, the mere sight of their friends being deleted from the scene was enough to discourage several of the students, who backed away from the statue and each other, clearly unwilling to spend the night in a pacification cell, and probably not too eager to explain to their parents and tutors exactly how they ended up there. The senior safety permitted herself a sigh of relief; for a few seconds there, she had worried that she'd waited too long before attempting to dispel the agitated crowd. Now, though, the situation seemed to be coming under control.

But the student leader, not to mention Gorgan, would not surrender so easily. Urged on by his anonymous muse, Jenole entreated his followers to carry on their crusade in the face of the safeties' resistance. "Don't give up!" he cried out. "This is our moment, our chance to demonstrate once and for all that we will not be herded into submission, that we can take control of our destiny no matter who stands against us!"

His words had an impact on his peers, who kept storming the statue even as their fellow rebels disappeared left and right. Cracks formed in the marble surface of the monument, branching out from each other like twigs on a tree branch. An ominous scraping noise emerged from the base of the statue, where the empress's sculpted feet met the pedestal below. Beams of light picked off the demonstrators as they climbed out onto the arms and shoulders of the statue, but new bodies replaced those that vanished almost as quickly as their predecessors were transferred away. "That's right!" Jenole encouraged them from the top of the steps. "Don't let them break our spirits with their cowardly ploys. Show them that the future belongs to us!"

"Doesn't he ever run out of breath?" the senior safety muttered to herself. Turning away from the besieged monument, she directed both her ring and her attention at the students' ringleader, who presented quite an inviting target as he posed before the palace, his garish red cloak flapping in the wind. With any luck, deleting that loudmouthed boy would suck the wildfire out of the rest of the protestors.

No, Gorgan thought, shaking his head slowly. He would not allow the furor he had created to be so readily extinguished. As the safety took aim at Jenole, Gorgan summoned his power by clenching his fists and pantomiming a pounding motion with his hands, tapping one fist upon the other with a steady, deliberate rhythm. Without even realizing he was doing it, Jenole mimicked the gesture, pounding his own fists together in time with his unseen mentor just as the transference beam locked on to him.

Nothing happened.

To the safety's astonishment, Jenole remained where he stood, defying her attempt to relocate him. She blinked and tried again, with equally nonexistent results. The safety did not understand, and Jenole looked a bit bewildered as well; neither of them had ever known a safety's equipment to malfunction before. Only Gorgan, his upper hand silently hammering the fist below, greeted this new complication with aplomb. *The surprises are only beginning,* he promised.

The confused safety wagged her hand from the wrist up, hoping she could somehow shake her ring back into life. When that proved futile, she sent a private audio transmission to the two nearest safeties. A lighted visual display sewn into her right sleeve instantly informed her of their ranks and identity numbers. "One-one-two-eight, six-seven-four, target subject at top of steps immediately. Priority *Skr'zta.*"

Responding without hesitation, two uniformed figures, previously facing the endangered statue, swiveled at the waist and directed beams of cadmium light at Jenole. Either ray, the senior safety knew, would communicate his coordinates to the central processor, initiating the transference. The outspoken student gulped visibly as the twin beams intersected upon his chest right above his heart, but he continued to make that peculiar pounding gesture, for reasons neither he nor the safeties truly understood.

Whatever he was doing was obviously working. The other safeties exchanged baffled looks as Jenole persisted in striking a dramatic pose overlooking the plaza, despite the best efforts of three safeties—and advanced Tkon technology—to remove him. Now it was the senior safety's turn to swallow nervously, flinching involuntarily as one of the empress's marble arms broke away from her body, plummeting onto the tiled floor of the plaza to shatter into two pieces. With her pacification ring rendered unaccountably impotent, the safety felt like she had lost her own arm as well. "Get the safeties," Jenole instructed the other dissidents. "Their rings are useless now. Don't let them stop us!"

That those last two statements were mutually contradictory did not bother any of the students, who divided their efforts between toppling the now-mutilated statue and assailing the safeties, who suddenly found themselves outnumbered and unarmed. No safety had carried any physical weapons for years; why bother when any implement that might be needed could be summoned instantaneously by means of their rings? All at once, the senior safety found herself longing for an old-fashioned meson rifle—or even a big stick.

She tried to summon reinforcements, only to discover that the communicator at her throat had gone as dead as the silicon ring on her finger. Gritting her teeth, she tried to will the ring back into operation, but the accursed thing couldn't even produce a faint orange glow anymore. Its failure—impossible, inexplicable—left her with no hope of quelling the disturbance, let alone protecting herself. A tide of shrieking students, intoxicated with the heady bouquet of insurrection, flooded over her. She felt frenzied hands grabbing her, tugging at her ring, nearly breaking her finger in the process. The ring slipped free, scraping her knuckles red, and the crowd tossed her aside. She went stumbling across the floor of the plaza, falling onto her knees and barely throwing her hands out in time to stop her face from hitting the hard ceramic tiles.

A moment later, there was a ghastly wrenching noise, as the statue was torn from its pedestal and its heavy weight crashed to the ground, shaking the tiles beneath her palms and knees. A marble head bearing a marble crown rolled across the plaza until it came to a rest only a few arm's lengths away from the shaken safety. Its features, once beautiful and serene, were now chipped and gouged, looking up at the night sky with only the scarred vestiges of its former grace.

The empress had fallen.

"Yes!" Jenole crowed to the students below him, Gorgan perching behind him like a shadow. "No one in the empire can ignore us now!" His victorious compatriots hooted and howled in jubilation, letting the battered safeties creep away to safety. A blond-haired girl danced atop the empty pedestal while her friends in the crowd tossed fragments of the shattered statue among themselves, claiming pieces as souvenirs.

"That's right, celebrate!" Someone tossed Jenole the head of the empress, which he held aloft triumphantly, his golden eyes aglow, his cheeks flushed with excitement. "We've won. The night is ours." His gaze swept over the throng of ecstatic students, making certain he had their full attention. "But this is just the beginning." Gorgan's lips moved soundlessly and the words emerged from Jenole's throat, his voice alive with passion and commitment. "But this is just the beginning. There's an industrial transfer station only a few blocks from here, down by the River Hessari, where thousands of cauldrons of pure *tmirsh* are marked for delivery to the Great Expenditure. Raw material, torn from our planet and our people, never to return!"

The rioters booed and shouted profanities. Gorgan felt his power grow with the crowd's intensity. This was just like the old days, before 0's downfall. *This time it will be different,* he vowed. *No one can hinder us.*

"Those cauldrons belong to us," Jenole declared, "and I say they're not going anywhere. Now is the time for us to take back our destiny." He dropped the defaced marble head and let it roll awkwardly down the steps into the crowd, eliciting a full-throated hurrah from his peers. "Those cauldrons are waiting for us," he asserted, pointing past the plaza toward the riverfront. "Are you with me?"

The crowd's response was both overwhelming and inevitable. Any possible opposition had either fled in retreat or succumbed to the revolutionary fever. Unwilling or unable to defy the mob, the governor remained locked inside his mansion, while fresh safeties, summoned no doubt by observers within the palace, cordoned off the plaza, reluctant to engage the demonstrators until the mystery of their equipment's failure could be adequately explained.

But there was no time for answers. Running down the steps, taking them two at a time, Jenole set off a stampede of eager and unthinking young men and women streaming toward the far end of the plaza—and the line of turquoise figures who waited to halt their progress. Seen from above, as Gorgon levitated above the fray, the rampaging students resembled a surging sea, their knotted tresses bobbing like waves driven by a storm.

The newly arrived safeties never stood a chance. A deluge of amok Rzom youth crashed against them, meeting only inactive technology, and broke through their ranks, pouring into the city streets and shattering the quiet of the evening with their chants and cries and uninhibited laughter. The gates of the transfer station presented even less resistance than the cordon around the plaza. The night shift stepped back, frightened and uncomprehending as their sons and daughters tore through the unguarded facility, wreaking havoc on data files and delicate apparatus, shoving fragile exports off transporter platforms and stasis units alike, then converging on the preservation dome where materials allocated for the Great Endeavor were kept until needed.

The pillar of steam that rose from the River Hessari as countless units of molten *tmirsh* were dumped into its rushing amethyst currents could be seen from one end of the city to another. Some said, and they were correct, that the gigantic plume of heated vapor was even witnessed by imperial satellites in orbit around Rzom, who transmitted the image instantaneously to the empress herself.

Gorgan basked in the satisfaction of a job well done. He had planted the seed. Now it was up to his allies to nurture and cultivate the crop.

Until it was time for the harvest.

Nine

In the tenth year in the reign of the empress:

The imperial fleet waited just past the asteroid belt that divided the inner worlds of the Tkon Empire, including Tkon itself, from their rebellious siblings beyond the belt. At the prime-control of the scout ship *Bastu,* at the forward tip of the formation, Null Pilot Lapu Ordaln stayed attuned to his long-distance surveyors and wondered if he could ever possibly be ready for what was to come.

A battle such as was about to take place had not been fought since the Age of Xora, innumerable generations ago. Indeed, it was practically unheard-of to have this many vessels in the void at one time; safe and effective travel by transference had largely rendered nullcraft obsolete, except for exploration and warfare. The average citizen had not needed to ride a rocket from one planet to another since his grandfather's time, at least until recently, when the present crisis brought commerce and contact between the empire and the rebel worlds to a halt. "Hellwings," he cursed aloud. Why couldn't Rzom and the other outer planets simply go along with the Great Endeavor like the rest of the empire? What in Makto's name had driven them to mount this insane rebellion, putting everyone at risk? Rend it all, he had friends on Rzom, even a cousin or two. Why, then, this senseless war?

To be fair, sages and opinionators still argued about who had truly started the war, the empire trying to quell uprisings on the outer worlds, or the rebels encroaching on imperial space to sabotage the Great Endeavor. *Never mind who began it,* he told himself, trying to ready his spirits for the confrontation ahead. *Our job now is to end it, one way or another.*

He glanced around the habitation bulb of *Bastu,* exchanging a glance with his subpilot, Nasua Ztrahs, strapped into her own control less than an arm's length away. Aside from them, no other living creature breathed within the bulb; all of the vital functions of the vessel, including attack and defense modes, were operated by the ship itself, with its organic pilots ready to override the thinking chips only in the event of some genuinely unforeseen circumstance. One pilot was practically superfluous; a subpilot to take over if the prime was disabled was an extra level of redundancy, dictated as much by tradition as by cautious calculation. Besides, Ordaln thought bitterly, if there wasn't some flesh and blood at stake, how could you call it a war?

There. Here they come. The ship's surveyors detected the approach of the enemy armada, alerting the null pilot at the speed of thought. Funny, it still felt wrong to think of Rzom as the enemy. Defensive systems came to life all around the bulb as the cerebral imager projected three-dimensional graphics of the oncoming ships directly into his mind. He heard Ztrahs suck in her breath and knew that she had received the same input. Testing the imager compulsively, as if every component of *Bastu* had not already been checked out by imperial shipwrights, he confirmed that he could switch back and forth at will between a subjective ship's-eye view of the battle to an objective, omniscient overview of the entire conflict. He was relieved to note that, just as their informants had reported, the imperial ships outnumbered their rebel counterparts at least three to one. *We'll make short work of them,* he thought, *no matter how bloody a business it proves to be.*

"For Tkon and the empress," he said, loud enough for Ztrahs to hear. It was a null pilot's job to maintain proper morale, even for a crew of two.

"For Tkon and the empress," she answered back, her voice tense but controlled. It dawned on Ordaln that she probably had friends and relations on the other side, too.

Then the first of the enemy vessels was upon them. . . .

Almost, (*) thought hungrily. The clash it had been waiting for was only instants away. At the moment, it sensed more dread than anger among the participants, more apprehension than aggression, but that would change once the fighting started. Hate would come to the fore, and then (*) would feed.

And feed well.

Holding the enemy within their sights, monitoring each other's advance to the tiniest degree, neither side took notice of a flickering sphere of crimson energy spinning fiercely less than a light-year away, emitting a faint red radiance that failed to register on either imperial or rebel sensors. (*) also observed the disparity in strength between the two forces, and resolved to address that problem soon enough. It held no favorites in the coming contest, only a determination that both victory and defeat be forestalled for as long as possible. Only the war itself mattered; the fury and strife were their own reward.

The imperial fleet fanned out in three dimensions, assuming a pyramid formation with its point aimed straight at the heart of the rebel armada, which responded by angling outward and away from their center, forming a sideways funnel whose open mouth expanded as if to swallow the advancing pyramid. For a brief moment, as the forward end of the armada spread out like concentric ripples upon the surface of a pond, it looked like the larger, imperial fleet might pass through the opposing forces without even engaging the enemy, but the imperial pyramid flattened out abruptly as the warships that comprised its base raced to intersect the circumference of the gigantic, empty loop the invading armada had become. All along the periphery of both fleets, imperial and rebel ships rushed headlong at each other, unable to evade direct confrontation any longer.

Not even (*) could tell which side fired first. As swiftly and nigh simultaneously as if a switch had been activated, bursts of incandescent energy jumped from ship to ship to ship, linking hundreds of nullcraft in an intricate and ever-shifting lattice of red and purple beams of light that knitted the edges of both fleets to each other, locking them into a taut, violently twisting tapestry that only total defeat or victory could rip apart. Projectile weapons, powered by their own destructive energies, carried the battle deeper into the masses of the opposing forces, arcing through the void to hurl themselves at inhabited vessels several hundred times larger than the unmanned missiles that perished in sacrificial blazes against the hulls of their targets. The narrowing space between the contending fleets filled with fire and debris.

Despite heavy shielding on the part of both adversaries, the furious exchange of armaments claimed its first casualties within minutes. Unscratched, untested void fighters, subjected to dozens of assaults from above and below, succumbed to destruction and/or decompression. Transitory flashes of unfettered plasma strobed the battle lines, sparking anguish and desire for revenge among the surviving combatants. Abstract political differences suddenly became deadly personal as pilots on both sides dived and ducked amid the chaos, striking back with every tactic and weapon at their command. More ships fell before the inferno, leaving the remaining ships ever more intent on exacting retribution.

(*) savored the unleashed hate and fury of the volatile humanoids within their metallic conveyances. Its only fear was that the hostilities would terminate too soon, before it had drained every last drop of sustenance from the unsuspecting mortals. Avidly, it examined the ongoing encounter, subjecting the entire battle to its keen and far too experienced analysis. How best, it meditated, to prolong the conflict?

Ironically, the ships, large and small, that comprised both fleets were virtually identical in design, not surprising considering that not long ago they had indeed composed a single unified force, before time and trouble outpaced their common ancestry. Only carefully guarded meson signatures kept allied vessels from firing upon each other in confusion. (*) rotated thoughtfully, seeing all the possibilities.

For the first few minutes, Lapu Ordaln found himself at the still, silent center of the storm. The Rzom nullcraft had all darted away to the perimeter, leaving behind an empty hole at the core of their formation. He experienced a moment of private relief at this momentary respite, even though he knew he couldn't allow the rebels to evade him this easily. If fortune was with Tkon, his comrades behind him would halt the enemy's advance long enough for *Bastu* to reverse course and catch up with the fight.

"Let's go get them," he stated decisively, while psionically urging his ship to switch to pursuit mode. *Bastu* executed a flawless crescent turn that sent them speeding toward the action, which, as the imager showed him, had already begun. In his mind's eye, he saw the fighting flare up at the outskirts of the rebel armada, then work its way inward, zigzagging through the rapidly intermeshing fleets like spidery cracks fragmenting a sheet of ice. The meson tracking system functioned perfectly, tracing imperial ships in blue and rebel vessels in red. To his dismay, he watched as, one at a time, graphics both blue and red vanished neatly from the display.

We could be next, he realized, feeling a bitter resentment toward the Rzom lunatics who had brought them all to this sorry pass. He wanted to look away, but the cerebral imager made that impossible. The more he squeezed his eyelids shut, the more clearly he saw the deadly conflagration that was drawing him closer by the second, like a charged particle to a blazing atomic core. He braced his back against the gravity cushion and tugged on the straps of his harness to make certain they were secure. *Bastu* was coming within range of its weapons capacity, not to mention close enough to draw fire from the enemy. Time to kill or be killed. Thank Ozari that the ship actually did the targeting, sparing him and Ztrahs that awful responsibility.

Without warning, the red and blue outlines marking each nullcraft disappeared from the display. His eyes opened wide in surprise, but the image remained the same. Suddenly there was no way to distinguish imperial ships from the rebels, friend from foe. *Bastu*'s attack systems froze even as the ship plunged into the melee, the thinking chips paralyzed by this unexpected loss of crucial data.

"Lapu?" his subpilot asked, confusion evident in her tone. Obviously she was receiving the same inadequate display from the imager.

"Reinitialize the entire system," he replied. "Do whatever you can to get the accursed thing up and running again. Quickly." In the meantime, he realized with a start, he would have to take over control of the weapons from the ship. He was fighting this war for real.

But what good could he do? *Bastu* weaved effectively through the crowded null-space, avoiding collisions with the other warships, but Ordaln did not know what else could be done. He couldn't just fire blindly; given the relative size of the fleets, he was more likely to hit one of his own ships than a rebel. "Lapu—I mean, Pilot Ordaln!" Ztrahs reported within moments, visibly aghast. "It's not just us. It's everyone, us and the enemy both. Nobody's markers are working."

How was that possible? A solar flare? A transreal anomaly? Ordaln didn't even try to figure it out; he was a pilot, not a techner. Instead his mind instantly grasped the strategic implications of what had happened; all at once, the empire's numerical superiority had become a liability. Without the meson tags, the rebels had better odds of hitting their enemies than he did.

"They did it on purpose!" he blurted, blood pounding in his temples as the truth struck him with the force of orbital acceleration. What manner of crazed, reckless ploy was this? Fighting in the dark like this might get them all killed. Didn't so many lives, Tkon or Rzom, mean anything to them? "They're insane, all of them! Fanatics!"

But he wouldn't let them get away with it. . . .

Yes, (*) approved, basking in the renewed waves of enmity suffusing the sector. The warriors of the inner planets would not overcome those of the outer worlds so easily now. Their frustration fed their animosity, feeding (*), just as the desperation of all concerned only heightened the intensity of their violent passions. This was more than mere nourishment now; it was an exquisite delicacy.

(*) spun silently in the depths of space, lapping up the hate that spilled like blood. Best of all, it had not yet approached the very peak of its feeding cycle. The more the organic specimens hated, the stronger (*) grew, and the stronger it became, the better it could fan the flames of the conflict, toying with the minds and matter below it to yield ever greater rewards.

As it did now.

* * *

Rzom trash. It was all their fault.

Another shudder shook the habitation bulb as *Bastu* came under attack again. Ordaln unleashed a volley of concentrated plasma bolts at the nearest vessel, not caring terribly whether it hailed from Tkon or Rzom or any of the other worlds that had been dragged into this stinking bloodbath. They had attacked him, that was enough, so he emptied his arsenal at them, then waited for the pulse cannons to recharge.

Tkon can still win, he realized, *even with everyone shooting randomly. We can triumph by attrition, when the last rebel craft has been reduced to null-dust.* He just had to stay alive until then, and the best way to do that was to fire at anything that came within range of his weapons. "Blast them all, and let Ozari take Their pick," he growled, his throat bubbling over with bile. He launched a brace of cobalt missiles at a suspicious-looking scout ship at sixty degrees, and was gratified to see it spiral away in flames. "Isn't that right, Nasua?"

The subpilot was dead, killed by a jagged piece of silicon crystal that had broken through the habitation bubble during the last missile strike. Ordaln wasn't worried. She wouldn't be dead much longer. Already both pilot and bulb were repairing themselves, the crystal shard retracting back into *Bastu*'s internal mechanisms, the pierced plasteel shell of the bulb knitting itself shut miraculously. Time almost seemed to be running in reverse as the gaping wound in Ztrahs's throat closed, leaving not even a scar behind. Ordaln watched, unsurprised, at the way the color came back into her expression. Her lifeless golden eyes blinked, then looked back at him. "They killed me again?" she asked, sounding more annoyed than distressed.

"Yes," he replied curtly. It was nothing new; they had each been killed a couple of times already. But Ozari would not let them die, it seemed, as long as the fight continued. Their wounds healed magically, their ship kept repaired, their weapons perpetually replenished . . . what more proof did they need that the fates were on their side? This had become a holy war, and Ordaln was more than happy to wipe the rebel dirt from existence, no matter how many times he had to die. He'd had friends among the Rzom, sure, and family, too, but they were nothing to him now, not anymore. All that mattered was winning the war, which meant destroying the enemy once and for all.

He launched more missiles, one in every direction, confident that no matter how many he fired, there would always be more. He was glad that he had taken control of the weapons himself. It was more satisfying this way. "Die, rebels, die!" he chanted, and Ztrahs joined in, laughing maniacally. "Death to the Rzom!"

And the battle went on and on. . . .

Ten

In the fiftieth year of the reign of the empress:

Far from the stresses of work or war, a photon wave engineer named Kelica udHosn stretched out upon a leased solo lifter and went fishing for birds. Elsewhere in the empire, there was strife and nullfleets were clashing, but not here on Wsor, deep in the heart of the inner worlds, between sacred Tkon and the dying sun. Kelica's shallow float drifted several lengths below a billowing bank of swollen tangerine clouds. A thin line of polynitrated filament stretched upward from the reel in her left hand to somewhere deep within the cloud directly overhead. A minus-grav hook, baited with a piece of raw *ewone*, waited for any unwary avians who might be lured by the glistening magenta pulp.

To be completely up-front about it, Kelica didn't care if she caught a plump galebird or not. This was the first vacation she'd had from the Great Endeavor in what felt like a radioactive half-life and it was enough simply to waft through the sky on the gentle wind currents, the clouds above her, the rolling umber hills of the Maelisteen countryside far beneath. Yes, this was exactly what she needed after seven months of balancing and rebalancing the light index ratios for the proposed solar transference. For Ozari's sake, the tired old sun wasn't going to flare out anytime this week. The Great Endeavor could do without her for a few days.

She rolled onto her side and took a sip of the spicy nectar in the juiceskin beside her. An elevated calciate ridge, about a hand's breadth high, ran along the perimeter of her oblong lifter, preventing her from tumbling off its padded surface carelessly, even though she kept her emergency floater belt on just in case. She gazed out at the breathtaking scenery available to her from her lofty vantage point; aside from another float on the horizon, she had the whole sky to herself. That was the great thing about Wsor: As one of the innermost planets, the war with the outer worlds had barely touched it so far. Peeking over the edge of the safety ridge, she saw Proutu Mountain rising to the southeast, its snowcapped peak reflected in the glassy surface of Lake Vallos. A few small pleasure rafts, looking like discarded wood shavings from this high up, nestled atop the lake, prompting her to wonder why anyone would still go fishing the old-fashioned way when they could go trolling through the clouds instead.

Lazy minutes passed without a single tug on her line, and Kelica began to feel just the tiniest bit bored. Closing her eyes and activating the implant at the base of her brain, she tapped into the psi-network, her mind scanning the local emanations for something interesting.

People of Wsor, turn away from your sin and arrogance. Pay heed to The One who stands in judgment above you all. The days of your folly are numbered. Great is The One who comes from beyond. . . .

What was this, some kind of crazy religious wavecast? Might be good for a giggle or two, she decided as she adjusted her sun-warmed limbs against the cushions and took another sip of the nectar. The float coasted south toward the mountain, blown along by a cooling breeze.

. . . unto you and yours shall the overweening pride of your ancestors be held to account, even unto the end of days. Repent of your wayward paths, for The One will brook no impiety nor disrespect. Yea, even if no more than one soul shall turn away from The One, then all shall be punished. Many will fall before His Wrath, and those that live through the first chastisement will surely long for the sweet release of death. . . .

Okay, okay, Kelica thought. She got the message, which was exhausting its novelty value at amazing speed. Who would actually want to listen to this blather? She searched for something else on the adjacent psi-bands.

. . . and the signs of His Judgment shall be written among the elements. Fire and water shall be His Rod and His Scourge, just as the rocks below and sky above. . . .

Huh? How did she get this again? She tried another neural frequency.

. . . and there shall be neither peace nor mercy, neither pardon nor deliverance. . . .

For the first time, she began to feel slightly nervous. The demented rantings seemed to be all over the psi-scape, supplanting even the imperial news and weather wavecasts. She even tried accessing some of the more popular erotic transmissions, but to no avail. The apocalyptic warnings were everywhere, and expressly where they didn't belong.

Fall upon your knees and pray for salvation, but it shall not be forthcoming. The time for redemption has passed. Now comes The One and His Anger is great. . . .

It must be a psychological propaganda offensive, she realized, but how had the Rzom insurrectionists succeeded in hijacking the entire psionic network? And did they really expect modern-minded Tkon to fall for all this pompous mumbo-jumbo?

A yank upon her hand reminded her of her fishing line, which she had completely forgotten. Automatically she began reeling the taut filament in, too preoccupied by the unsettling wavecast to even wonder what she had caught. She was only planning to let the bird go anyway. She liked snaring the pretty birds, but saw no point in letting them suffer afterward. That was just pointless cruelty.

A deafening boom came without warning, the shock wave rocking the small lifter and tossing her backward against the cushions. Her elbow collided with the juice-skin, squirting nectar onto her side. Grabbing the safety ridge with her free hand, she pulled herself up to a sitting position and looked with amazement to the south.

The top of Proutu Mountain wasn't there anymore. Instead of the white-frosted peak she had admired only minutes before, a tremendous explosion of smoke and ash as large as the mountain itself gushed from an open crater, spewing flame and red-hot magma. Rivers of glowing lava poured over the jagged rim of the crater, racing the swiftly melting snow down the side of the mountain—no, the volcano!—and flooding into the wide-open reservoir of the lake, where a gigantic wall of steam rose into the air, obscuring her view of the mountain itself. The once-placid surface of the lake churned and bubbled, turning into an enormous cauldron of boiling mud and water.

Proutu had erupted. But that was impossible; the mountain had been extinct for aeons. All the travel data said so. And there hadn't been any signs or indications. No preliminary tremors, no geothermal disturbances. No warning at all, except:

Behold His Justice, and tremble. Look upon the retribution of The One and know that the harrowing has just begun. . . .

"Sacred Ozari," she whispered. This couldn't be happening, but it was. Her ears still ached from that first cataclysmic detonation. A noxious odor, like sulfur or *macrum,* teased her nostrils. Ignoring the sticky wetness of the nectar spilling onto the floor of the float, she retained the presence of mind to press down with her thumb upon the release switch of her fishing reel, slicing through the filament and setting the unseen avian free. Then she looked back down at the frothing lake beneath her. None of the tourist rafts had overturned yet, but dead fish were floating to the surface by the hundreds, turning the murky waters into a grotesque, colossal bouillabaisse.

. . . nothing shall be spared, neither the beasts of the field, nor the swimmers in the deep. . . .

Fortunately, the initial shock wave had sent her gliding away from the volcano. Thank . . . someone . . . that she hadn't been any closer to the mountain when it blew. She started to activate the auto-recall on the lifter, intending to get back to the launch center as quickly as possible, when she remembered the other float she had glimpsed earlier. Could that poor individual possibly have survived?

Holding the float in place by mental control, she peered back into the roiling fog of smoke and steam. The acrid smell was getting stronger by the moment; she could feel it stinging at the back of her throat. "Hello!" she called out hoarsely. "Is there anybody there?" There was no point scanning for a psychic cry for assistance; that malevolent sermon, which sounded like pure gloating now, was still raving across every psi-band, swamping everything else. She could hear that harsh, unforgiving voice bellowing inside her skull, no matter how hard she tried to shut it out. She shut down her implant entirely, but somehow the voice still came through.

. . . from the lower regions shall His Vengeance come. As blazing as an inferno is the sting of His Whip. . . .

Cupping her palm over her nose and mouth in a fruitless attempt to keep out the increasingly corrosive fumes, she squinted with teary eyes into the opaque black smoke. *I can't wait any longer,* she thought. *I have to turn back.*

Then she heard it.

"Help me!" a strident voice cried out from behind the curtain of fog. It was a man's voice, steeped in terror. "Somebody help me!"

Kelica hesitated, unwilling to steer her own float into that lightless, tenebrous murk, but unable to abandon the desperate stranger lost in the dark. "Help, help me, please!" he screamed again, coughing loudly afterward. He sounded like he was choking.

To her relief, the prow of the other lifter poked from the sooty depths of the spreading smoke, pulling the rest of the craft behind it. That surge of hope was quickly replaced by fear when she saw that the unlucky air-fisher was no longer safely inside his craft, but was instead dangling by his fingertips from the edge of the float. "Don't panic," she whispered to herself, remembering the multiple safety measures built into the floater belt around his waist. He couldn't fall to his death if he tried. It was scientifically impossible. Of course, that was what they had said about Proutu erupting, too.

As the stalks fall before the scythe, so shall the unrighteous fall before The One. Nemesis is He, the leveler of nations, the purifier of worlds. . . .

Both man and floater were blackened with ash. Sooty tears ran like rivulets down his cheeks, streaking his face. "Just let go," Kelica called out, worried about colliding with the other lifter. They probably wouldn't hit hard enough to do any damage, but she didn't feel like taking chances. "Activate the minus-grav switch, and I'll come by and pick you up."

He tried to reply, but all that escaped his throat was a raspy cough. He nodded, though, and closed his eyes, mentally willing the belt into readiness. His straining fingers let go of the float—and he fell like a stone.

What! She couldn't believe it. The belt should have held him aloft. Why hadn't it worked? Her mouth hung open, too shocked to even breathe, while she watched the shrinking figure drop toward the boiling lake. *It's still all right,* she remembered. *The emergency transfer will kick in any second now, the moment he hits trigger velocity, transporting him back to the center and canceling his downward momentum.* She waited anxiously for the falling man to disintegrate into quantum particles.

It never happened. She stared in horror as he plummeted into the lake, the splash of his impact lost amid the churning chaos of the reservoir. Kelica gasped, sucking in air at last, only to choke on the caustic smoke. Panic set in, spreading through her like a fever. She had to get out of here now! *Back,* she ordered the lifter, grateful that she didn't have to breathe the word aloud. The fumes were getting worse, making her sick.

. . . and the kingdom of the air shall crumble, and the waters of life made into slaying venom. . . .

"Shut up, shut up," she snapped, pressing her hands against her ears. This was a nightmare. It couldn't be real. "Stop it. I don't want to hear it."

. . . and the orchards will be as deserts, and the skies as lifeless as the void. . . .

Something rough and feathery smacked against her head, then rebounded onto the sticky floor of the float. It was an adult galebird, its eyes glassy and immobile, its beak locked open in silent protest. She didn't need to feel for its hearts to know it was dead. The fumes, she realized. The gases from the volcano were killing the birds.

. . . from the meager to the mighty, from the lowly to the lords of the spheres, none shall escape The One. . . .

More downy bodies struck the lifter. They were falling by the dozens now. She held up her hands to shield her head as the shallow float teetered beneath the force of the avian downpour. The stricken birds began to pile up all around her, some of them still alive, their crimson wings weakly flapping, and a new fear struck her: What if the weight of the birds overloaded the capacity of the float? This was only a solo lifter!

Frantically, she started bailing out the bottom of the float, throwing the dead and dying birds over the side as fast as she could manage, heedless of the new feathered bodies slamming into her head and shoulders, buffeting the tiny craft while she wheezed for breath amid the suffocating smoke. But despite her frenzied efforts, the front of the float tipped downward alarmingly, throwing her forward onto her hands and knees among the grisly carpet of dead birds, their tiny bones crunching beneath her weight.

. . . for the greatest of the great is but a mote of foulness in the sight of The One, as the most flawless of gems is but a rough and coarsened stone in the face of His Glory. . . .

She wanted to flee the lifter, jump free of the float, but fright kept her frozen in place. What if her belt didn't work, either? She tried to activate either the minus-grav or the transfer alert, thinking at the belt so hard that her brain hurt, but nothing happened. She remained tethered by gravity to the foundering lifter, even as it began to spiral irresistibly toward the scalding water below, picking up speed as it carried her inexorably toward annihilation.

. . . thus shall perish the heretics and apostates, the blasphemers and nonbelievers, for I am The One, the alpha and omega, your beginning and your end. . . .

The last thing she saw, before the terrifying acceleration rendered her mercifully unconscious, was something almost too incredible to believe, even in the middle of a waking nightmare. It was the bottom half of the mountain where, impossibly, insanely, the flowing lava had carved a single word into the granite side of the mountain, like an artist affixing his signature to his latest masterpiece.

It was the ancient Tkon symbol for the number one.

Eleven

"Ah, I love the luster of lava atop lesser life-forms," 0 rhapsodized. "Between you and me, Q, The One can be a bit overbearing at times, not to mention utterly humorless, but you have to admit that He puts His All into His Work."

"I spied a lush morsel on a banquet so vast," he chanted in his customary singsong fashion,

> *"That I wanted my fill as 'twere my last,*
> *Among this spread that was all I could wish,*
> *Never before had I seen such a dish,*
> *Oh, never before had I seen such a dish."*

The length and breadth of the Tkon Empire was spread out between them like a colossal game board. At the moment, the planet Wsor occupied the spotlight of 0's attention, which passed through the spinning globe and projected onto an adjacent plane of reality a magnified view of the volcanic devastation currently demolishing the southern continent, much as a lesser entity might use a holographic monitor. Rivers of molten lava, rendered several quadrillion times larger than life, oozed across the intangible screen, casting a crimson glow upon 0's grinning features as he levitated above the game board, being careful to keep the soles of his buckled shoes off the solar system below. Superimposed upon the magma, like a ghostly double image, were the stern and unforgiving features of The One. "Didn't I tell you this only got better?" 0 asked.

"It's certainly dramatic enough, I suppose," Q answered. He hung upside down on the reverse side of the board, his knees wrapped around a stretch of sturdy quantum filaments while his head dangled only a light-year or so above (or below, depending on your orientation) the diverse worlds of the empire. To be honest, he was starting to get distinctly disgusted, but it struck him as impolite to say so. 0's confederates had been at work for some time, at least half a century by Tkon standards, and yet all their games, no matter how creatively conceived, seemed to arrive at the same conclusion: lots of death and devastation and screaming. Which had a certain crude shock appeal at first, granted, until it became unpleasant and monotonous. *Frankly,* he thought, *I'd appreciate a little comic relief at this point, maybe even a nice romantic interlude.* He avoided 0's gaze as he let his mind wander. *I wonder what Q is doing right now?*

"About time you thought of me," his sometime girlfriend and future wife replied indignantly, flashing onto the scene. She stood just out of reach, oriented along the same axis as Q, so that he found himself staring directly into her kneecaps. "I was starting to wonder if I was going to cross your mind anytime before the heat death of the universe."

Q somersaulted off his invisible trapeze, landing on his feet in front of Q. Arms crossed atop her chest, she fixed a pair of dubious eyes upon him. Her auburn tresses fell across her shoulders, less elegantly coifed than they would be aboard the *Enterprise*-E six hundred millennia from now, but the arch of her eyebrow was no less haughty.

Despite her forbidding expression and body language, Q was glad to see her. Where was the fun of embarking on a bold new adventure if there was no one around to show off for? 0 and his pals didn't count; they were part of the experiment, and too experienced in this kind of thing to be either impressed or shocked by Q's role in the proceedings. *I need an audience,* he decided, and he couldn't think of anyone better than Q.

"Well?" she demanded, her face as frozen as absolute zero.

Apologies were only embarrassing, he decided. Better to simply brazen this one out. "Q! Great to see you! Come to join the fun?"

"Hardly," she said scornfully, shaking her head.

"Say, who have we here?" 0 called out. In a blink, he joined them on the opposite side of the game board. The projected scenes of volcanic havoc disappeared from view. "Aren't you going to introduce me to your fine female friend, Q?"

"Oh, right," Q muttered, slightly discomfited by the reality of having to deal with both 0 and Q at the same time. They each came from completely different slices of his existence, engaged separate aspects of his personality. It was like trying to be two different people at once. "0, this is Q. Q, this is 0. He's not from around here."

"So I hear," she said icily, regarding the stranger with all the warmth and affection she might lavish on a Markoffian sea lizard before turning her back on him. "I need to talk to you, Q . . . alone."

0's face darkened ominously at the female Q's not terribly subtle snub, reminding Q a little too much of how he had looked right before he flash-freezed the Coulalakritous. Then 0 saw Q watching him, and his expression lightened, assuming a more amiable mien. "Of course," he agreed readily. "Far be it from me to intrude upon such a charming young couple. The last thing you two need is a crusty old chaperon such as myself. If you'll excuse me, m'dear, I'll be stepping out for a while." Tipping his head at the female, he opened a doorway into another continuum, then stepped halfway through. "Don't be all day, Q," he warned, lingering for a moment between dimensions. He cast a glance at the expanse of the Tkon Empire as it waited beneath their feet. "The best is still to come. Mark my words, you haven't seen anything yet."

The doorway closed behind him, disappearing along with 0. *I wonder what he has in mind,* Q thought, intrigued by his new friend's cryptic promises. More apocalyptic destruction, or something more interesting? He looked forward to finding out.

His significant other didn't seem curious at all. "Finally," she huffed. "I thought he'd never leave." She surveyed the game board skeptically, as if she half-expected to find 0's muddy footprints all over the unsuspecting empire. "All right, Q, what's this all about?"

"Er, what do you think it's all about?" Not the most brilliant retort he had ever come up with, but perhaps it might buy him enough time to think of something more clever. How best to present the situation to her anyway, and precisely what sort of reaction did he hope to elicit? It was hard to say, especially when he had mixed feelings himself about what The One and his associates were doing to the Tkon.

"Don't get coy with me, Q," she warned. "The Q told me all about the disreputable gypsy vagabonds you've been hanging around with. Really, Q, I thought you had better taste than to fraternize with entities so . . . parvenu."

Ordinarily, he found her impeccable snobbishness delightfully high-handed, but not when it was turned against him. Who was she to pick out his friends for him, as if he lacked the judgment and maturity to choose his own company? It was insulting, really. "You don't know anything about them," he said defensively, "and neither do the Q. I'll have you know that 0 and the others bring a fresh new perspective to this part of the multiverse. I may not agree with everything they're about, but I would certainly never dismiss their ideas out of hand simply because they're not part of our own boring little clique. *I* have an open mind, unlike certain other Qs I might name."

A pair of ivory opera glasses appeared in her hand, and she glanced down at the sprawling interstellar empire beneath them. As she inspected the goings-on there, she shared what she saw with Q. A montage of moving images unfurled before his eyes, all taken from the daily lives of the present generation of Tkon: battle-weary soldiers crawling through the trenches of some Q-forsaken tropical swamp, a hungry child wandering lost amid the rubble of an obliterated city, angry rioters shouting through a hastily erected forcefield at uniformed troops, priceless manuscripts and ancient tapestries hurled onto a bonfire by chanting zealots, a spy on trial for her life before a military tribunal, even an assassination attempt on the life of the empress.

"Is this what you call a fresh perspective, a bold new idea: making life miserable for a tribe of insignificant bipeds?" She snapped the lorgnette shut with a flick of her wrist, terminating the picture show. "It's as tedious as it is tragic. Why don't you just peel the scales off an Aldebaran serpent while you're at it? Or pull the membrane off an amoeba?"

"At least they're doing something," Q pointed out, not entirely sure how he ended up defending 0's mysterious agenda, but too irritated to care. "They take an interest in matters outside the rarefied atmosphere of your precious Continuum. True, this sort of hands-on approach can get a bit messy, but it's no worse than the ghastly foolishness that developing species always inflict on themselves anyway. Remember those divers throwing themselves into the jaws of monsters back on Tagus? They turned themselves into fish food voluntarily, just for the sake of a primitive ritual, so what's wrong with sacrificing a few million more to a good end? Their tiny lives are measured in micro-nano-aeons, after all."

"Is that so?" she answered. "Who are you trying to convince, me or yourself?"

Good question, he thought, although he wasn't about to admit it. "I don't need to convince you of anything. I'm perfectly capable of making my own decisions."

"Particularly when they're the wrong ones. . . . Oh, don't make that face at me. This is more important than your wounded male ego." Her expression softened a tad as she tried one more time to get through to him. "Listen to me, Q. We've known each other ever since we've been able to manipulate matter and recite the pledge of omniscience at the same time. We learned how to parse the lesser atomic force together. Trust me when I say that I'm only looking out for your best interests here. Forget about this 0 character and his low-life confederates. I promise I won't think any less of you if you come away with me now."

"And then what?" Q asked, less heatedly than before. Although touched by her concern, he wasn't ready to surrender just because she had started firing roses instead of ammo. "Am I supposed to just creep back to the Continuum with my hypothetical tail between my legs, to sit back meekly with folded hands while the great big universe goes by?" He struggled to make her understand. "Don't you see? I can't give up now. This is the first time I've ever taken a risk, done something with my immortality. I'm not a kid anymore. It's high time I hold to my guns, stand by my mark, draw a line in the ether, and all that decisive stuff. Right or wrong, I have to see this through to the end, no matter what. It's the only way I'll ever find out who I really am."

"But this isn't about you," she protested. "It's about 0 and his crazy games. He's just using you."

"Maybe so," Q agreed, "but he can't take advantage of me without my cooperation. That's my choice to make, so, you see, it really does come back to me."

She sighed and shook her head sadly. "If you don't know who you truly are, then you're the only intelligence in the Continuum who doesn't. You're stubborn and unpredictable, Q. A volatile catalyst in the never-ending chemical reaction that is creation, the spice in the primordial soup. You have all the verve and vitality of the cosmos and not one iota of common sense." She dropped her opera glasses into the glowing red sun at the center of the Tkon Empire and watched as they bubbled and melted away. "And I suppose that's why I'm never going to be able to convince you to do the sane and rational thing and listen to me for once."

"No," Q confirmed, "although you wouldn't be you if you didn't keep trying now and then." Beyond that, he wasn't sure how to respond to her spontaneous description of him. *I kind of like that bit about the spice,* he thought, more than a little flattered, *although I could have done without the commentary on my common sense, or lack thereof.* "Thanks a lot, I guess."

"Good-bye, Q," she said before transporting away. "Don't say I didn't warn you." *Why should I,* he reflected, *when I know you'll always be there to remind me?*

Young Q gazed ruefully at the empty space that his highly significant other had occupied only milliseconds before, seemingly saddened by her departure. Theirs had been a bittersweet parting, at best. "Just wait," he promised the starry blackness beside him. "We'll look back at this and laugh someday."

"Not to worry, lad," a bombastic voice assured him. 0 materialized in the space the female had vacated. He looked much happier now that the distaff Q was gone. "She'll come around eventually, see if she doesn't." He threw back his head and chuckled heartily. "Women! They're the same in every reality. Why, the stories I could tell you!" He gave Q a solid punch in the shoulder that sent him stumbling sideways. "But I don't need to teach a strapping young rooster like you about the fairer sex, do I? I imagine you've got a girl in every solar system or my name isn't 0!"

Several meters away, unseen and unheard by either participant in this one-sided discussion, Jean-Luc Picard groaned aloud. "I can't believe you actually fell for all this phony masculine camaraderie," he told the Q standing beside him.

"Cut me some slack, *mon capitaine,*" he said. "I was barely seven billion years old. What did I know about the ways of extra-dimensional executioners?"

"Executioner?"

"Just watch the show, Jean-Luc," Q advised sourly, "before I regret bringing you here in the first place."

Twelve

Lem Faal felt like an ullafish fighting its way upstream. As he staggered down the seemingly endless corridors of the *Enterprise* in search of Engineering, pockets of uniformed crew members kept streaming past him on the way to sickbay, getting in his way. *Idiots,* he cursed. Didn't they realize he had more important things to do than let them pass by in their pointless attempts to preserve their own insignificant existences? Immortality was within his grasp, but these blinkered Starfleet buffoons were doing their best to obstruct him, especially that pigheaded fool Commander Riker.

Wheezing painfully, he slowed long enough to brace himself against a sturdy duranium wall. He could feel the constant hum of the Calamarain vibrate through the metal. His lungs felt like they were wrapped in barbed wire, and the corridor seemed to swim before his bloodshot eyes. He reached for his hypospray, then remembered that he had emptied its contents into Counselor Troi, feeling a flicker of guilt at having treated a fellow Betazoid so badly. *I had no choice,* he rebuked his conscience. *They were going to put me in stasis, shut down my brain just when I need it most. There was nothing else I could do. I* had *to get away.*

The barrier was all that mattered, and the voice in his mind beckoning to him from beyond the great wall. That voice had promised him life, plus knowledge and power beyond mortal understanding. *Come soon,* the voice whispered even now. *Soon, sooner, soonest. Soon, come soon. Closer to me, closer to you, closer . . .*

All he had to do was create the wormhole, break through the barrier to the other side. Then he would be saved, would be spared from his own terrifying mortality. He would never stop, never cease to be, as Shozana had when she had disappeared before his very eyes.

Your eyes are my eyes are yours. View you, view I . . .

He closed his eyes, seeking relief in the darkness for just a second. Odd . . . he could barely remember his wife's face now; all he could see was the column of energized atoms she had become when the transporter malfunctioned. *I shall become pure energy, too,* he thought, *but in a different, more transcendent way.*

"Sir, are you all right? Can I help you?"

Coming closer, closer coming, closer . . .

He opened his eyes and saw the concerned face of a minor Starfleet officer, a Benzite from the looks of him. Puffs of essential gases escaped from the respiratory device positioned beneath his nostrils. Faal noted a large orange bruise upon his bluish green forehead. "What?" the scientist asked. He could barely hear the officer's words over the voice calling out to him, growing stronger and louder the nearer they came to the barrier.

The wall divides us, the wall is nigh . . . deny the wall, and hopes are high . . . heigh, heigh, heigh!

The more clearly he heard the voice, the more enigmatic its words became. It spoke in riddles, as sacred oracles have always done, but Faal had deciphered its message from the beginning. Eternal life and enlightenment waited beyond the galactic barrier.

The wall is nigh, the wall deny . . . heigh, high hope, heigh.

"You don't look well, sir," the Benzite said. "I'm on my way to sickbay." He held a sleeve that was stained with whatever Benzites used for blood. Tiny droplets peeled off the torn fabric and floated in the weightless corridor. "Can I help you there?"

"No," Faal wheezed. He shook his head, then regretted it; the motion caused the floor to spin beneath his feet even faster than before. It took all his concentration to make his tongue move the way it had to, say the words the Benzite needed to hear. "The wall is . . . I mean, I have to get to Engineering. Mr. La Forge needs me," he lied.

Closer to the wall, closer to the All . . .

The Benzite looked dubious. He assessed Faal's heaving chest and trembling limbs. "Are you sure, sir? No offense, but I don't think you're in any shape to assist anyone."

Why won't he leave me alone? Faal thought desperately. Every moment he was kept away from his goal was a torture. *Closing on the wall, or is the wall closing on you, closing the door . . . ?* He wanted to hurl the overly solicitous officer away, consign him to oblivion, but instead he had to waste precious moments allaying the concerns of this nonentity. *Close, closing, closer . . .* "I'm all right," Faal assured him, forcing himself to smile reassuringly. "I'm not injured, just a little closer . . . that is, just a little ill. It must be the weightlessness."

"Oh, right." The Benzite nodded his head. "I wouldn't know. Benzites don't get nauseous."

"You're very fortunate, then," Faal gasped. *Come closer to me closer to you, soon, sooner, soonest.* "But I'll be close . . . fine . . . if I can just make it to a turbolift."

"We're at red alert, sir," the Benzite pointed out helpfully. "The turbolifts are only for emergency use."

"This *is* an emergency, you dolt!" He couldn't hide his impatience any longer. The ship was approaching the barrier. He had to get to Engineering, launch the torpedo containing the magneton generator, force La Forge to initiate the subspace matrix, create the artificial wormhole, liberate the voice. . . . There was so much to do in so little time, and this blue-skinned, gas-sniffing cretin would simply not let him be. "The voice is calling me. I have to go!"

Soon, sooner. Come to the wall, come soon . . .

Lurching forward, away from the duranium bulkhead, he grabbed the Benzite's wounded arm and shoved it roughly. The crewman's blood felt slick and greasy against his palm, but the Benzite emitted an inarticulate croak and crouched over in pain, gasping so hard that the fumes wafting from his respirator dissipated before reaching his nostrils. *Serves you right,* Faal thought vindictively.

More Starfleet personnel came around the corner ahead, a man and two women, in scorched gray uniforms. Faal breathed a sigh of relief that they had not arrived in time to see him accost the Benzite. "He's hurt badly," he blurted hastily, pointing back at the breathless Benzite. "Hurry. Please help him." He pushed his way past them, urging them onward, then hurried around the corner until they were out of sight. *Hurry, hurry, hurry . . . come soon come.* If fortune was with him, the Benzite wouldn't be able to speak clearly for a few more moments, giving him time to get away.

The time is nigh, the wall is high, defy the nigh high wall . . . try!

The barbed wire tore at his lungs with every breath and his heart was pounding alarmingly, but he refused to let his debilitated physical state slow him down. He was more than this decaying shell of crude flesh and bone. His mind could overrule the limitations of his treacherous body and soon would be able to do far more than that. *I'm coming,* his mind called to the voice beyond the wall, the voice that had summoned him all the way from Betazed, enticed him away from his children and his deathbed. *Do not forsake me. I will bring down the wall. I will, I swear it.*

Closer to the wall, closer . . . closer . . .

He was tempted to shed the cumbersome gravity boots and simply soar down the hall, but, more realistically, he feared losing control of his momentum, at worst ending up becalmed in the air out of reach of any convenient wall or ceiling. What did he know about maneuvering in zero-G? He was a scientist, not an athlete. No, it was safer just to walk on his own two feet, no matter how weary they were.

Feel you closer, closer you feel me closer . . .

A turbolift entrance beckoned to him from the end of the corridor. Shallow breaths whistling from his diseased lungs, he propelled himself down the last few meters until his hands smacked against the sliding metal doors—which refused to open. "Let me in!" he demanded, pounding on the doors with his fists. The blood of the Benzite left a sticky stain on the painted surface of the door.

A dismayingly calm voice, which he had come to know as the ship's computer's, responded promptly, "The turbolifts are not currently available to unauthorized personnel. Civilian passengers should report to either sickbay or their quarters."

He let out a moan of despair. It was just as the Benzite had foretold. Intellectually, he understood the reasoning: Starfleet didn't want people to become trapped in the turbolifts while the ship was under attack. But what did that matter when his very future was at stake? It was all the Calamarain's fault, he realized. *You should have warned me about them,* he accused the voice.

Smoke, it answered obscurely. *Nothing but smoke to choke and choke.*

Faal didn't understand. If not for the lack of gravity, he would have slumped to the floor. Instead he let his magnetic boots anchor him to the floor as his exhausted frame swayed from left to right. He listened to the thunder of the Calamarain booming against the ship, and cursed the day he ever heard the name *Enterprise.* He would sooner have stayed on Betazed, helpless and dying, than endure the infinite frustration of coming so close to salvation, only to be stopped in his tracks by a balky turbolift.

No smoke in the wall, none at all, none at all . . .

Then, as the voice foretold, the thunder fell silent. The metal doors beneath his palm ceased to vibrate in unison with the alien hum. *The Calamarain,* he realized instantly, *they're gone.* Which meant, he deduced almost as quickly, that the *Enterprise* must have just entered the barrier.

Into the wall, closer to the All . . .

A sense of awe, mixed with dread and anticipation, passed through him only a heartbeat before his entire body was jolted by an intense psychic shock that raced through his nervous system, electrifying him. His spine and limbs stiffened, his arms stretched out at his sides. Tiny traceries of white energy linked his splayed fingers like webbing. His muscles jerked spasmodically and his eyes glowed with silver fire. Although no one was around to see it, the scientist flickered in and out of reality, transforming into a photonegative version of himself and back again. The pain in his lungs, the aching exhaustion in his joints vanished at once, driven out of his awareness by the supernatural vitality coursing through his body. *It's the power of the barrier,* he realized, *filling me, transforming me.*

But more than just mindless energy was pouring into his brain, expanding his mind. He sensed a personality as well, or at a least a fragment of one, the same personality that had called to him for so long, promised him so much. *Yes . . . feel you closer, so close so closer . . . yes.* The voice brushed his soul, like the delicate touch of a spider's leg, and another identity, older and vastly more powerful, met and melded with his own. For one brief millisecond, Faal's self reeled with fear, protective of his unique individuality, but then it was submerged beneath the alien memories and sensations that seemed inextricable from the power he now possessed, the voice that was possessing him. *You are I are you, view I, view you . . .*

The face of that strange, meddling entity, Q, appeared in his memory, now bringing with it a sense of anger, of long-simmering hatred, that he had not previously known. *Q, cursed Q, treacherous Q . . . what will we do, to Q and Q and Q . . . ?*

Frantic to hang on to some trace of what he was, Faal tried again to visualize his wife's face, but instead all he could see was that other Q, the female one with the astounding child, the child of the Q. The power of the barrier, and the voice beyond, flooded his synapses, setting off a cascade of memories that the power seemed to sort through at will, picking and choosing according to its own unfathomable agenda. *Yes, yes,* he thought, no longer capable of distinguishing his own desires from those of the voice, *the child is the future, the child is our future, in the future the child. . . .*

Unable to cope any further with the forces at work within, Faal blacked out, his sagging limbs floating limply above the floor while dreams of apotheosis brought themselves to life.

Close, so close. . . .

Where is he? Milo wondered. He was lost and couldn't find his father anywhere. He had tried to take a turbolift, hoping to catch up with his dad at Engineering, only to discover that they had all shut down during the emergency. In theory, that meant his father was stuck on this level, too, but this ship was so huge, with so many corridors and intersections to choose from. To be honest, Milo wasn't sure he could find his way back to sickbay if he tried. *Dad!* he called out with his mind. *Come back!*

He couldn't sense his father's thoughts anywhere, no matter how hard he concentrated. It was like his father had cut himself off completely from the rest of the world, or at least from his son. *I don't even know who he is anymore,* Milo thought. The father he knew, the one he remembered from before, never would have attacked the counselor like that.

Milo stomped down another hallway, feeling clumsy in his oversized magnetic boots. Maybe he *should* try to find sickbay; Dr. Crusher and Counselor Troi had been very insistent about using the cortical stimulator on him before the ship entered the galactic barrier. Thank the Sacred Chalice that Kinya was safe at least, even if he and Father were in danger. His throat tightening, he wondered who would take care of her if . . . something happened . . . to his father and him. *Aunt Mwarana would take care of her, I guess.*

A crew member, rushing down the corridor toward him, spotted Milo and slowed to a stop. "Hello?" she said. "What are you doing wandering around at a time like this?"

"Um, I'm looking for my father," he mumbled. How could he begin to explain how crazy his father had become, what he had done to poor Counselor Troi? "I think he was going to Engineering, but I'm not sure if he got there."

The woman hesitated, chewing on her bottom lip, torn between her own urgent errand and the plight of the boy. He could sense her indecision and concern. She reached a decision quickly, though, just like a Starfleet officer. "My name is Sonya Gomez, and I was on my way back to Engineering from sickbay anyway." Milo noticed a foam cast around her left wrist and sensed some residual soreness from the injury. "Why don't you come along with me and we'll see if your father is there? If not, I'm sure we can spare someone to see you back to your quarters."

"Okay," Milo said. He sure couldn't think of a better plan. Gomez held out her hand, and Milo accepted it gratefully. She began to lead them down the corridor in the same direction he had just come when she suddenly stopped and cocked her head. A quizzical expression came over her face. Milo felt a surge of optimism within her heart.

"Hey, listen to that," she said. "The thunder's stopped."

She's right, Milo thought. He would have said so, except for the blazing fire that ignited inside his skull. His small frame convulsed unexpectedly, like he was being electrocuted. He heard Sonya Gomez shouting in alarm from somewhere very far away. She shook his shoulders, but he couldn't feel it, not like he could feel the fire as it poured from his brain into the rest of his body, causing his entire body to tingle and twitch.

His eyes rolled upward and he lost consciousness, but instead of falling into blackness, all he found waiting for him was a brilliant purple light.

Thirteen

Glevi ut Sov, Dowager Empress of Tkon, awoke early one morning during the dawning of the Age of Makto, in the eightieth year of her reign, troubled by the shadows of unremembered dreams. She no longer slept as well as she once had. A symptom of her advanced age, she wondered, or of the increasing precariousness of the times? Her reign had been a turbulent one, marked by civil war and catastrophe, although she remained steadfast in her conviction that the Great Endeavor was worth any sacrifice she and the empire had endured. *Only my conscience does not plague me,* she thought.

Unlike her decrepit body, her private chambers had changed little over the decades. Skilled artisans had successfully concealed any evidence of the damage inflicted by the earthquake of seven years ago, or by the bomb that had failed to assassinate her only a few months before. She permitted herself a defiant smile; sometimes her stubborn ability to survive impressed even her. *They'll not get rid of me that easily,* she vowed, not for the first time.

She kneaded her weary eyes with skeletal knuckles, wishing she could clear her mind as readily. What had that dream been about anyway? The memory lurked at the back of her awareness, just beyond her reach, but the feeling remained, a sense of alarm mixed with inspiration, as if she had finally isolated the root cause of all that disturbed her suffering empire. There *was* a root cause, of that much she felt certain; over the last several decades, as she had assiduously studied reports from all over the empire, she had grown convinced that there was a reason for the numerous, often seemingly unrelated adversities that had rocked the foundations of their society for all these many years, a reason that sometimes seemed to lurk just beyond the awareness of her consciousness. Perhaps this latest dream held the key to an answer she already knew deep within her soul.

She knew better than to chase the memory, however. Dreams were like fish: The harder you tried to hold on to them, the more slippery they seemed to be. If it was important, it would come back to her in time. After all, she wasn't planning to die right away, at least not today.

Doing her best to ignore the creaking noises that, perversely, her hearing remained keen enough to detect, she carefully lowered her feet into the well-worn slippers on the floor. Despite the incessant appeals of her attendants, she still refused to let anyone help her aged bones rise. As long as she could stand, however shakily, on her own two feet, so, she was convinced, would the empire. It was a silly superstition, but she held to it nonetheless.

The chambers lighted slowly, as was her preference these days. She took a moment to steady herself, then reached out and grasped the sturdy walking stick propped against the wall by her couch. A polished quartz rendition of the Endless Flame emblem topped the stick. Her shadow, now much thinner than she might like, waited patiently for her to begin their daily trek to her venerable desk. With a sigh, she obliged the shadow by putting one foot before the other. The soles of her slippers squeaked as she shuffled across the floor.

As ever, the outer rooms felt too cold for comfort, so she gave the chamber a mental command to increase the temperature by at least ten grades. That she could effect such a change merely by thinking it still amazed her; out of habit, she often spoke aloud to her palace, much to the whispered amusement of the younger members of her court.

A finger unconsciously stroked the base of her skull where, beneath her snow-white hair and delicate skin, her personal psi-transmitter had been implanted. All her physicians and technologists swore to her that she couldn't possibly feel anything from the implant. You won't even know it's there, all the brilliant young geniuses insisted; everybody has one these days. No doubt they knew what they were talking about, but she was positive she felt an itching at the back of her neck sometimes, not to mention a faint buzzing in her ears. *Maybe I'm just imagining it,* she thought, *just like I imagined whatever I dreamed last night.*

Placing her stick against the side of the desk, she sat down in her chair, grateful for the extra heat that was already flooding the chamber. She supposed she could just keep the heat going continuously, so that the chambers would always be warm right from the start, but that struck her as extravagantly wasteful, especially during wartime. Given all the sacrifices she had demanded of her people over the years, all the resources poured into the Great Endeavor despite every crisis that had threatened to derail it, the least she could do was cope with a bit of chill upon waking, especially when she suspected that a good part of the cold was simply her aging metabolism taking its time to come up to speed each morn.

She directed a thought at the freshly restored wall across from her and the city presented itself to her once more, lifting her spirits. Ozari-thul still rose proudly beneath the ruddy glow of dawn. True, many towers were under repair while wary imperial fliers patrolled the skies above them, but the heart of Tkon still beat as soundly as her own, the people going about their business even in the face of terrorism and sabotage. The scarlet sun confessed its mortality every day, yet the time was swiftly approaching when the slow death of that ancient orb would no longer endanger the worlds and people now within its radiance. *I cannot betray their confidence in me,* she thought. *The Great Endeavor must be completed.*

A twinge of hunger interrupted her musings and, in response, her breakfast appeared atop the desk. The biscuits and jam were tempting, and to blazes with what her doctors said about the honey, but she pushed the tray aside for the moment. Something, perhaps the lingering influence of that elusive dream, compelled her to check on her empire first.

Gazing down upon the tinted crystal disk, newly replaced after the bombing, she retrieved the latest bulletins. As usual, it made for depressing reading. New fighting along the intermediate orbits. Two more ships lost and a nebular mining station fallen to the rebels. Demonstrations and work stoppages throughout the inner worlds, even rumors that the governor of Wsor was secretly trying to negotiate a separate peace with Rzom in exchange for neutrality in the war. A devastating jungle fire on the fourth moon. Mass suicides among the commerce artists. A blight on this season's crop of *tamazi,* plus an outbreak of melting fever in the provinces of Closono-thul. Intelligence reports on a new millennial cult calling for the preordained destruction of Tkon. Flooding along the canals on Dupuc. A massacre on the second moon of a planet she had never heard of before.

On and on it went. Disasters. Combat. Epidemics. Accidents. Atrocities. Raids. Carnage. Fatalities. Revolts. Armed incursions . . . bad news from every corner of the empire, loyal or otherwise. The only consolation was that the rebels seemed to be hurting just as much, which was cold comfort indeed; despite close to a generation of internecine conflict, she still thought of the outer planets as under her protection, even if she had to fight to save them from themselves. The war itself had turned into one long, bloody stalemate in which neither side could gain any lasting advantage over the other. Was that the fault of her generals, she wondered, or were there other factors at work?

A piece of her dream flashed across her consciousness, almost too quickly to identify. Something about a captive beast . . . and spears? She reached for it, but it slipped away as quickly as it came. *Patience,* she counseled herself. *Let it come at its own speed.* She had learned to trust her dreams over the course of her lifetime, much as her visionary ancestors must have. *Don't force it. Wait.*

The image felt oddly familiar, though, as if she had dreamed it before, perhaps many times before, without ever remembering it. *Until now,* she thought, *to some degree.*

Turning her attention away from ephemeral fragments of the night before, she lifted a biscuit, generously drenched in honey, to her lips, then put it down again. "Too late," she sighed. The endless litany of dire news reports had killed her appetite.

She stared again into the disk, looking for some sign of a pattern, of a common thread linking all the disparate hardships tormenting her people. There was a link, she suddenly felt convinced. Her dream had told her so, even if she couldn't yet recall how it went. Perhaps the answer lay, she thought, in those *other* reports, the ones that didn't appear to make sense at all, that hinted in fact at the supernatural.

These strange, unexplainable incidents had been part of the bulletins for years, although often hidden in the margins or between the lines. Usually described as "apocryphal" or "unconfirmed," they had remained eerily consistent over the decades: accounts of dead soldiers rising up to fight again, of carefully maintained technology failing without cause, of storms and hurricanes birthed without warning out of clear skies and tranquil seas, of all manner of impossible occurrences taking place despite every precept of logic and science, just like that rain of *vovelles* that had fallen upon the city so many years ago, when she was barely more than a child. *I haven't thought of that for ages, but I suppose that's when it all started to go wrong.* A vision of swollen, overripe spheres of fruit pelting themselves against her windowpane, making wet, smacking noises while their juices ran like rivulets of blood down the transparent glass, surfaced from the dusty recesses of her memory. *It's almost as if some higher power were playing with us, testing us. . . .*

At once, her dream came back to her, more vivid than before. She saw a great horned animal at bay, its hooves pawing the ground, its curved ivory horns stabbing the air above its massive head. Its fur was dark and matted, except for a white patch upon its brow in the shape of a flame. Three masked figures, and two more farther back in the shadows, had the beast cornered, prodding it with long sharp sticks that drew blood wherever they pierced the animal's shaggy hide, but never enough to inflict serious injury on the beast. The wounds were like pinpricks, intended not to kill but only to torture and enrage. Maddened, the poor creature frothed at the mouth and blew steam from its snout, roaring its helpless fury even as the bloody spears came at it again and again.

Then, finally, when the beast could offer no further resistance, the masked tormentors laid down their spears and stepped aside, making way for the fourth figure to advance toward the vanquished animal, a shining silver blade resting in his grip. This fourth figure, to whom the others seemed to defer, wore no mask, but she could not discern his features no matter how hard she tried. All she could see was the light reflecting off the burnished sheen of the blade as he raised it high above the beast's drooping head. The fifth figure came forward finally, reaching out as if to stop the bearer of the sword, but he had waited too long. There was no more time, and the blade came sharply down—

The empress came back to her chambers with a start, one hand jerking forward and knocking the breakfast tray over the edge of the desk. Crystalline plates and teacup crashed onto the carpet, splintering into dozens of tiny shards and soiling the Taguan carpet with a mixture of tea, crumbs, and honey. She gave the mess only an instant's thought, disintegrating the broken meal and transferring it away, before clearing the disk and contacting her new first minister. The head and shoulders of a middle-aged Tkon came into focus. *He looks more like his father every day,* the empress thought, recalling another trusted first minister from many years ago. "Most Elevated," he addressed her. "I'm delighted to hear from you. I have excellent news regarding the Great Endeavor. I believe we may be ready to commence the solar transference in a matter of weeks."

His words cheered her spirits, momentarily dispelling the pall cast by her premonitions. Never mind the dark wonders alluded to in the reports, the true miracle was that the Great Endeavor had proceeded toward completion despite all the calamities of the last seventy-odd years. It had required constant pressure from the throne to keep the massive project on track, but perhaps soon her persistence would be rewarded and the empire preserved. *I will die happy,* she thought, *even if we can accomplish no more than that.*

She could not allow such hopeful musings, however, to distract her from her current purpose. "Those are fine tidings indeed," she told him, "but let us speak of another matter. I want you to arrange an imperial address to be sent out simultaneously across the entire empire, including those regions currently in revolt. I assume we have the capacity to transmit my words into even Rzom and the other outer planets?"

Fendor arOx looked uncomfortable. "Well, yes, actually, although we've taken pains not to let the rebels know that we still had the means to do so. It's a hidden advantage we've been holding in reserve."

"A wise decision," she assured him. *He's as prudent as his father, too.* "But the time has come to employ that advantage. I wish to speak to my fellow Tkon, all of them. And as soon as possible." The memory of her dream, of that spectral blade slashing down, chilled her in a way no heated chamber could hope to overcome. She knew now that this very nightmare had been haunting her sleeping hours for more years than she cared to estimate, only now escaping into the clear light of day. "I feel very strongly that the future of the empire is at stake."

* * *

"By Q, I think she's got it," Q rejoiced, encouraged by what he saw transpiring in a private chamber in the imperial palace on the homeworld of the empire. He felt certain that the Tkon, as embodied by their elderly empress, were rising to the challenge posed by 0's colleagues. "I have to admit, I was getting a bit nervous there," he informed 0, "but it looks like they're going to pass our test after all, and with flying colors no less." He smiled paternally, pleased with himself for having selected the Tkon in the first place. "I always knew they had it in them."

0 frowned, looking curiously dissatisfied with the hopeful omens so prized by the younger entity. "We'll see about that," he muttered.

"My friends and neighbors," the empress began, "I speak to you today not as a ruler to her subjects, nor as a conqueror to her foes, but as one mortal being to another."

Eschewing the grandeur of her illuminated throne, she sat behind her old wooden desk, clad in a simple but elegant white robe. With what she prayed was unmistakable symbolism, she lifted her sardonyx scepter before her, crowned by the sacred emblem of the Endless Flame, and deliberately placed it aside. Her well-lined face, serene in its composure, faced the glowing crystal screen that the first minister assured her would transmit her voice and image to every planet, moon, null station, and vessel that had ever sheltered the far-flung children of Tkon.

"I have put the trappings of power and authority away because the issue that faces us now is far greater than any political differences, no matter how serious or legitimate. Believe me when I tell you that I have come to the astounding but certain conclusion that our entire species is being tested by awesomely powerful alien beings crueler and more merciless than any god or demon imagined by our common ancestors. No other explanation can account for the ceaseless array of troubles, both natural and preternatural, that we have all been subjected to for as long as a generation."

She paused to give her listeners time to absorb all she had told them, growing all the more convinced that she was doing the right thing. Now that she was finally giving voice to the nameless fears that had haunted her dreams, she felt that the tide was turning in her favor at last. Recognizing their true enemy, the secret genesis of all their woes, was the essential first step toward restoring the safety and happiness the empire had once provided to all its citizens, great and small.

"A startling proposition? That it is, yet I am confident that if you will examine our recent history with this understanding in mind, you will realize I speak the truth. We have all been provoked and tormented almost beyond the level of endurance, and must now rise above these hardships to prove that the better part of our natures, that which truly makes us a people, can withstand any test and emerge triumphant in the end, deserving of and ready for an even more glorious future."

So far, so good, she thought, buoyed by the conviction and sincerity behind everything she had shared with her people. Now came the tricky part, as she moved from abstract generalities to tangible reality. She took a deep breath, praying that minds throughout the empire would not slam shut when they heard what she said next.

"I do not think it was a coincidence that this testing came upon us at the same time that the sun which has brought warmth and light to our worlds now nears its

end. Was there ever a time when our people faced a greater challenge, a more elemental test of our worthiness to grow and go on?" Placing her hands beneath the
surface of her desk, she cupped her fingers in a traditional solicitation of good fortune. "Many of you have opposed the Great Endeavor, questioned its practicality
and expense. I respect your opinions on this subject, and admire the courage and
determination with which you have defended your beliefs. But I say to you now
that the time for fighting is over. For better or for worse, all preparations for the
Great Endeavor have been completed. The work has been done, the riches have
been spent, the time and trouble have become a fixed part of our history; all that
remains is to reap the rewards of decades of striving.

"This, I believe, is the ultimate test of our species and our sanity. Let us not
permit the hostilities that have divided us to blind us to opportunity before us.
Whether or not you have opposed the Great Endeavor, surely there is no reason we
should hesitate to spare our solar system from the sun's inevitable expansion now
that we have the means to do so. A new sun, brought here to replace our dying star,
can only benefit us all."

She leaned forward, placing the hopes of a lifetime into her voice. "I now call
for an immediate cessation of all hostilities throughout both the Tkon Empire and
the Rzom Alliance. As proof of my sincerity, I vow in the name of Ozari to abdi-
cate my throne and grant independence to each of the outer worlds upon the successful completion of the Great Endeavor." *There,* she thought. *I said it.* She could
just imagine Fendor and the rest of her ministers gasping in surprise. *I hope their
hearts will survive the shock.*

"Now is our moment, our one great chance to put the conflicts and tragedies of
the past behind us and prove to whatever beings have engineered our misfortunes
that the children of Tkon cannot be defeated. I ask you all, as one who wants only
the best for friend and foe alike, to consider my words and look deeply into your
souls for all that is wise and caring, for, as surely as our sun is fading but our
people shall endure, *they* are watching us."

Fourteen

"I must say, you've lasted longer than I expected you to."

Preceded by a flash of white light that briefly dispelled the shadows from the
dimly lit bridge, the female Q materialized in Deanna's accustomed seat. Baby q
was draped over her shoulder as she gently patted his back.

As if I didn't already have a headache, Riker thought, repressing a temptation
to groan. "Can I help you?" he said harshly, hoping that she'd take a hint and leave,
but knowing in his heart that the universe couldn't be that generous.

Q ignored the sarcasm, not to mention Riker's hostile glare. "Yes. Hold on to
q . . . carefully, of course." Without waiting for Riker's consent, she lifted the infant
off her shoulder and handed him to Riker, who held the baby at arm's length, uncertain what to do about him. Even with the gravity off line, it went against his instincts to simply let go of the seemingly fragile youngster. "That's better," she said,
taking a moment to stand up and adjust her ersatz Starfleet uniform. "Even the
most devoted of mothers, which I am, needs a break every now and then."

I do not *have time for this,* Riker thought, as q, unhappy with his new location, began to squirm in the first officer's grip. The *Enterprise* remained becalmed within the uncertain shelter of the galactic barrier, hiding out from the Calamarain, while Geordi and his crew raced against time to get the warp engines repaired before their psionically amplified shields failed. Or before the psychic energy of the barrier, despite the shields, started frying their brains more than it already had. "The *Enterprise* is not a daycare center," he said indignantly, rising to his feet and thrusting the baby back at his mother, who gave him a dirty look before she accepted the child. To his relief, q quieted as he nestled back into his mother's arms; the last thing Riker needed was an omnipotent temper tantrum. "Why are you here and what do you want?" he demanded of the female Q.

"You needn't be so ill-mannered," she said huffily. Riker noticed that, despite the conspicuous absence of anything resembling gravity boots upon the woman's feet, she had no difficulty navigating within the weightless environment. Data observed her with curiosity, Lieutenant Leyoro glowered, and Barclay gulped, while the remainder of the bridge crew took pains to get out of her way as she strolled effortlessly, casually inspecting the charred remains of the mission ops monitor station and ducking her head to avoid a floating piece of torn polyduranide sheeting. "My, you have managed to make a mess of things, haven't you?"

"Sir?" Leyoro asked. She patted the phaser on her hip as she eyed the intruder; she no doubt realized that firing on the female Q would be a futile effort, but felt compelled by duty to make the offer. Riker shook his head, noticing again how tense and under strain Leyoro looked. Her face was pale, her jaw clenched tightly shut. Her free hand held on to the tactical platform so tightly that her knuckles were as white as her face. Her left eye twitched periodically. More than the rest of them, she seemed to be suffering from the telepathic flux of the barrier. *Too bad the Angosian doctors who revved up her nervous system,* he thought, *never considered the long-term consequences of their tinkering.*

"Stand down, Lieutenant," he told her, "and report to sickbay." He hoped Doctor Crusher could do something for her, even if it meant putting her into a coma like Deanna.

"What?" she said, succeeding in sounding incredulous despite a slight quaver in her voice. "Commander, I can't abandon my post at a time like this."

"We're not fighting anyone now," he said firmly. "This is an engineering crisis. Besides, you're no good to me as a casualty." He glanced around the bridge for a workable replacement, briefly considering Data before deciding that the android was more valuable at Ops. "Ensign Berglund, take over at tactical, and keep an eye on those shields."

"Yes, sir," the young Canadian woman said, stepping away from the auxiliary engineering station. Riker recalled that she had held her own during that phaser battle on Erigone VI. Leyoro let Berglund take tactical, but lingered nearby, looking like she might want to argue the point with Riker. He hoped she wouldn't.

"Do you always reshuffle your subordinates like this?" the female Q asked, completing her circuit of the bridge and returning to the command area. "Or are you simply taking advantage of the captain's absence to put your own stamp on things?"

Riker refused to be baited. "Why have you come back?" he asked.

"Dear little q was getting bored waiting for his father to return from his errand with your Captain Picard," she explained, "and matters didn't seem quite as . . . tumultuous . . . as before."

In other words, Riker thought, *we're more likely to drop dead quietly, thanks to the psychic radiation from the barrier, than be blown to bloody pieces by the Calamarain.* Apparently the former was more appropriate for family viewing.

"Besides," she continued, "I admit to some mild curiosity as to how this little outing of yours will turn out. Q always said I should take more of an interest in the affairs of inferior life-forms, and now that we're a family I want to make a point of sharing his hobbies."

Is that all there is to it? Riker scratched his beard, wondering. *Another frivolous whim by a typically irresponsible Q, or is there more to her reappearance, maybe some hidden agenda at work?* The other Q, the usual Q, had been very vocal in his objections to the idea of the *Enterprise* having anything to do with the galactic barrier; in fact, it had been Captain Picard's determination to carry out Lem Faal's experiment that had apparently provoked Q to abduct Picard. Now that the *Enterprise* had actually entered the barrier, perhaps Q's mate really wanted to keep a closer eye on them.

She needn't have bothered, he thought. He had no intention of implementing Professor Faal's wormhole experiment except as an extremely last resort; there were too many dangers and unforeseen factors involved. His only priority now was to save their passengers, the crew, and the ship, in that order. *But maybe,* it occurred to him, *there's another way to do that.*

"Since you have nothing better to do," he said to Q, "perhaps you can lend us a hand?"

"Oh?" she replied, one eyebrow raised skeptically.

Riker took a deep breath before elaborating upon his suggestion. To be honest, he felt very uneasy about dealing with a Q, let alone becoming indebted to one, but he couldn't ignore the fact that the capricious entity standing before him, blithely burping her baby, had the ability to return the entire ship to the safety of the nearest starbase—or anywhere else, for that matter—in less than a heartbeat. He would be derelict in his duty to the crew if he didn't at least try to turn that fact to their advantage.

"Excuse me, Commander," Data interrupted, "but you should be aware that I am detecting pockets of concentrated psionic energy within the ship. Level twelve of the saucer section."

"Sickbay?" Riker asked at once. *Are Deanna and the others in danger?* He remembered that Faal and his family had also been sent to sickbay.

Data consulted his readings. "I do not believe so, Commander, but nearby."

"Send a science team to investigate," he instructed, then turned back toward the female Q. Data's report had only increased his resolution to find a safe way out of the barrier and past the Calamarain, even if it meant asking a favor of Q's spouse.

According to some of the preliminary reports coming out of the Gamma Quadrant, *Voyager* had run into a Q or two; he wondered if Captain Janeway had ever tried to persuade Q into returning her ship to the Alpha Quadrant, and if so, why she had failed?

"Look," he said, flashing his most ingratiating smile, the one that had charmed ladies from one quadrant to the other, "you and I both know that this ship is in trouble. We also know that you can change that in an instant." He watched her expression carefully, but could discern nothing more than a certain bemused curiosity on her part. "For old times' sake, and out of respect for this ship's long friendship with Q"—*I can't believe I'm saying this,* he thought—"why don't you relocate the *Enterprise* to a more congenial environment, where we'll be in a better position to offer you the full hospitality of the ship? I promise you, at the moment you're not seeing us at our best."

She smiled mercilessly. "Please don't take offense, Commander, but a mud hut with room service is not significantly more attractive than a mud hut without such amenities." She shifted the baby to her other shoulder as she considered Riker's proposition. A tiny mouthful of milk or formula oozed from the child's lips to hang messily in midair. "Upon reflection, I think I am content to remain where we are. Do feel free, though, to pilot your little vessel as you see fit . . . under your own power, of course."

Thanks a lot, he thought sarcastically, not yet willing to take no for an answer. "Our options are somewhat limited at present, but why stay here? If you want to understand Q's interest in humanity, why not return us to the heart of the Federation? Or even Earth itself?" *A reasonable question,* Riker thought, but their visitor seemed to feel otherwise.

"I am hardly obliged to justify my decisions to you," she declared, elevating her chin to a more aristocratic angle. "My reasons are my own, and none of your concern."

Not when they may be the only thing standing between this crew and obliteration, he mused, unswayed by her imperious attitude. The only question was, how best to overcome her objections, whatever they might be? *Why would she want to stay here in the first place?*

A sudden suspicion struck him, flaring to life through the slow, steady ache that threatened to muddy his thinking: Could it be that this entire episode, with the Calamarain and the barrier and Picard's disappearance, was simply another one of Q's convoluted "tests," with the female Q in on the scam? Certainly it wouldn't be the first time that Q threw them into a life-threatening predicament without even bothering to explain the rules of the game.

Then again, he warned himself, trying to figure out Q's ultimate motives was a good way to drive yourself insane. Maybe he had no choice but to accept the female Q's protests at face value. He opened his mouth to respectfully but emphatically press his point when a high-pitched scream of pain caught him by surprise.

He spun around as fast as his magnetic boots would permit to see Baeta Leyoro doubled over, halfway between the tactical station and the nearest turbolift, clutching her head in her hands. Only the total absence of gravity kept her from collapsing to the floor in a heap.

Her eyes squeezed shut, her mouth hanging open, she groaned like she was dying.

Interlude

Soon. Sooner. Now.

Everything was happening at last. Time, which had been an endless moment for more than an eternity, was now rushing by like an unchecked flood, bringing new surprises and changes washing past him from the other side.

The smoke had blown away, at least for now, and the shiny, silver bug had burrowed into the wall, like a pest eating away at its persistent, perpetual, punishing permanence. Not enough to let him back into the galaxy just yet, not quite, but that long-awaited hour was getting sooner and closer.

Close, closer, closest. The wall is high, but the time is nigh.

Already a tiny portion of his being, a mere fragment of his fearless and fathomless fabulousness, had merged with the little voice from the other side, the voice that now resided within the silver bug within the wall. He was part of the voice now, as the voice was part of him, and together they would tear a hole in the wall large enough to let the rest of him, in all his splendor and ingenuity, back into the realm that the Q had denied him.

Damn you, Q. Damn Q, you.

Only Q remained unaccounted for. His stench lingered about the shiny bug, but his essence was elsewhere. But wherever Q was, Q was up to no good, for no good ever came from Q, only cowardice and betrayal. Good for nothing, that was Q.

Except, perhaps, for the child. Q was not within the bug, but his mate was and their spawn. The voice, that infinitesimal voice from beyond, had shown him the child, the child of Q. The child was something different, a merging of Q and Q into something quite new, something that had not existed when last he trod that glittering galaxy. The child was the future.

And, wait and see, the future belongs to me. . . .

Fifteen

The smoldering red sun of Tkon was ready to move. Surrounding the cooling orb was the largest matter-transference array ever constructed in the memory of the universe, a spherical lattice of sophisticated technology several times greater in diameter than the star itself, painstakingly constructed by the finest minds in the Tkon Empire over the course of a century. It was a staggering feat of engineering so immense that it impressed even Q, especially when he considered that this stunningly audacious project had been conceived of and executed by mere mortal beings immeasurably less gifted than either he or 0.

"Look at that," he crowed, pointing out the massive structure that surrounded the crimson sun like a glittering mesh cage. "Can you believe they actually pulled it off, despite everything that Gorgan and the others did to disrupt their little civilization? I don't know about you, but I think they deserve a round of enthusiastic applause."

"They haven't done it yet," 0 said darkly. His heavy brows bunched downward toward the bridge of his nose as he glowered at the caged sun. His beefy fists clenched at his sides.

Funny, Q thought. *You'd think he would be proud of how well this test turned out, especially after that embarrassment with the Coulalakritous.* But he was too elated to fret overmuch over his companion's unexpectedly sour mood. *Perhaps this is simply a case of post-testing melancholia, perfectly understandable under the circumstances.* "Oh, but they're almost finished. The empress even got that cease-fire she was asking for. See, there's a delegation from Rzom at the palace at this very moment, on hand to witness the historic event along with representatives from the entire sector. Even as we speak, that sparkly gadget of theirs is mapping the star, absorbing all the facts and figures they'll need to convert it into data, then beam it to that empty patch over there." He pointed to a singularly lifeless section of space beyond the borders of the empire: a perfect dumping ground for obsolete stars. "And see," he enthused further, stepping across the sector, crossing light-years with each stride before coming to a halt a couple of paces short of an incandescent yellow sun encased in a vast transference lattice identical to the one containing Tkon's dying sun, "here's the bright and shiny new star, good for another five billion years or so, that they're going to put in the old one's place." He took a few steps backward to take a longer view, scratching his jaw contemplatively. "Hmmm. I suppose relocating that star does spoil the aesthetic design a bit, but I guess I can get used to it."

He strolled back toward 0, chatting all the way. "And the timing! Think of it. They're going to have to beam the new sun into place less than a nanosecond after the old one disappears, just to minimize the gravitational effects on the whole system. A pretty tricky operation for a species still mired in linear time, don't you think?"

One of these aeons, he decided, *I'm going to have to bring Q back to this moment so she can see it for herself. And she thought this was going to turn out badly!*

"Oh, they're cunning little creatures, there's no question of that," 0 agreed, his eyes fixed on the caged red fireball around which the Tkon Empire still orbited, at least for a few more moments. "Cunning and crafty, in a crude, corporeal kind of way." A cross between a sneer and a smirk twisted the corners of his lips. "For all the good it will do them."

Q blinked in surprise. "What do you mean by that?" he asked. "They won, fair and square."

"Don't be naive, Q," 0 said impatiently. "This isn't over yet." He clapped his hands together, producing a metaphysical boom that set cosmic strings quivering as far as a dozen parsecs away. In response, three spectral figures emerged from the celestial game board that was the Tkon Empire. They started out as mere specks, almost as infinitesimal as the empress and her peers, but rapidly gained size and substance as they rejoined 0 and Q on a higher plane. "My liege," Gorgan addressed 0 somewhat apologetically, "is it time already? I feel there is so much more we could do. In truth, I was just warming up."

"They are a stiff-necked people," The One confirmed, the worlds of the empire reflected in the gleaming golden plates of His armor, "slow to repent, deeply wed to their infamy."

(*) said nothing, spinning silently above their heads, resembling nothing less than the swollen red sun of Tkon. Q wasn't sure, but he thought the glowing sphere looked fuller and brighter, more *sated,* than before. Or perhaps it was simply more hungry than ever.

"I was thinking maybe a children's crusade," Gorgan suggested, "starting with the youngest of their race. . . ."

0 shook his head. "You've done enough, all of you, although hardly as much as I might expect." Gorgan drew back, dipping his head sheepishly; his angelic features seemed to melt beneath the flickering light of (*), growing coarser and more lumpish in response to 0's implied criticism. Even The One appeared slightly abashed. The radiant halo framing his bearded, patriarchal features dimmed until it

was barely visible. "You've bled the beast," 0 admitted grudgingly. "Now it's time for me to administer the final stroke."

He knelt above the fenced-in star, then thrust his open hand into the very core of the sun, his wrist passing immaterially through the steel and crystal framework the Tkon had so laboriously erected around the star. "Wait!" Q shouted. "What are you doing?" The young superbeing rushed forward, determined to stop 0 from doing whatever the older entity had in mind. *This isn't fair,* he thought. *Not to the Tkon, and not to me.*

0 glanced over his shoulder, undaunted by the sight of the agitated Q running toward him. "Grab him," he said brusquely, and Gorgan and The One obeyed without hesitation. Q felt four hands take hold of him from behind, pulling his arms back and pinning them against his spine. His feet kicked uselessly at the space beneath him, unable to propel him onward as long as the others maintained their grip.

"Pardon me, boy," Gorgan said with exaggerated politeness. He twisted Q's wrist until the captive winced in pain. "I'm afraid we can't allow you to interfere at this particular juncture."

"That which must be, must be," The One agreed, holding on tightly to Q's right arm and shoulder. "Such is it written in the scriptures of the stars."

"No!" Q yelled. "You have to let me go. I said I'd be responsible for him. I'm responsible for all of this!" He tried to free himself by changing his shape, his personal boundaries blurring as his form flowed from one configuration to another so quickly that an observer would have glimpsed only fleeting impressions of a three-headed serpent, coiled and twisting, whose triune bodies merged into that of a salt vampire, wrinkled and hideous, the suckers on his fingers and toes leeching the Q substance from his captors before they withdrew into the flat, leathery body of a neural parasite, flapping toward the empty space overhead, his stinger lashing at the others even as it became the ivory horn of a shaggy white mugato, who flexed his primitive primate muscles against his restraints, which resisted even the corrosive hide of a Horta, capable of boring through the hardest rock—but not through the metaphysical clutches of the others.

"Stop it! Let me go," he shouted, now a poisonous scarlet moss, a thorny vine, a drop of liquid protomatter, a neutron star. . . . "This isn't what I wanted." He jumped from tomorrow to yesterday, backward and forward in time, by a minute, by a day, by a century. He shifted from energy to matter and back again, multiplied himself infinitely, turned his essence inside out, and twisted sideways through subspace. Yet whatever he did, no matter how protean his metamorphoses, how unlikely and ingenious his contortions, his captors kept up with him, holding him tighter than an atom clung to its protons. *They can't do this to me,* he fumed, tears of rage and frustration leaking from his eyes whenever he had eyes. *I'm a Q, for Q's sake!*

But Gorgan and The One were formidable entities in their own rights. Together, and assisted perhaps by the unholy energies of (*), they were enough to drag the struggling Q safely distant from where 0 now toyed with the Tkon's sun. "Sorry about this, friend," 0 said, watching Q's futile efforts to liberate himself with open amusement. "It's for your own good. Obviously, you still have a lot to learn about the finer nuances of testing. Most importantly, you must never let vain little vermin like these get the better of you; it only means that you didn't make the standards stringent enough to begin with. Remember this, Q," he said, shaking a finger on his free hand pedantically. "If the test isn't hard enough, *make it harder.* That's the only way to ensure the right results."

He's insane, Q realized suddenly, wondering how he had missed it before. *I was so blind.* Defeated, he reassumed his original form, sagging limply between Gorgon and The One, only their constant restraint holding him upright. "What are you doing?" he whispered, fearful of the answer.

0 shrugged. "Nothing much. Just speeding things up a mite. Take a look."

All around the star, the metallic lattice began to glow with carefully controlled energy. The Tkon were beginning the transference. In the throne room of the imperial palace, beneath a majestic stained-glass dome commemorating a thousand generations of the Sov dynasty, the aged empress, no more than a fragile wisp of her former self, but with eyes still bright and alert, gratefully accepted a tiny goblet of honey wine from her faithful first minister as they gazed in rapture at the culmination of the Great Endeavor to which she had devoted her life and her empire. Throughout the solar system and beyond, trillions of golden eyes watched viewscreens large and small, and the citizens held their breath in anticipation of the miracle to come.

But within the heart of the dying sun, a darker miracle was taking place. The last of the star's diminishing supply of hydrogen fused rapidly into helium, which fused just as quickly into carbon, which fused in turn into heavier elements such as oxygen and neon, chemical processes that should have taken millions of years occurring in the space of a heartbeat. The heavy elements continued to fuse at an unnatural rate, producing atoms of sodium and magnesium, silicon, nickel, and so on, until the star began to fill with pure, elemental iron. The dense iron atoms resisted fusion for an instant, but 0 exerted his will and forced the very electrons orbiting the nucleus of the iron atoms to crash down into the nucleus, initiating a fatal chain reaction that should not have taken place for several million more years.

"Stop," Q whispered hoarsely, knowing what was to come. The star was still at the center of the empire!

On null stations positioned around the lattice, and in control rooms manned by expert technologists, jubilant anticipation turned into panic as painstakingly calibrated instruments, tested and refined for decades, began delivering data too impossible to believe. The star was changing before their eyes, aging millions of years in a matter of seconds, turning into a ticking time bomb with an extraordinarily short fuse. "What is it? What's happening?" asked the empress in her throne room as the countdown to the planned solar transference suddenly came to a halt, and puzzled ambassadors and governors and wavecasters and war tenors and sages exchanged baffled and anxious looks. "I don't understand," she began, putting down her goblet. "Has something gone wrong?"

Her primary scientific adviser, psionically linked to the project's control center, blanched, his face turning as white as milk. "The sun . . ." he gasped, too shocked to even think of lowering his voice, "it's fluxing too fast. Much too fast. It's going to destroy us all."

"Why?" the empress demanded, leaning forward on her throne. "Was it something we did? Did the Endeavor cause this?" She grasped for some solution, the proper course of action. "What if we halt the procedure?"

"No," the trembling adviser said, shaking his head. "You don't understand. We couldn't do this. Nothing could do this. It's impossible, I tell you. This can't be happening."

It's him, she realized. *The figure from my dream. The executioner with the sword. His wicked game is coming to its end.* After all their struggles, all the glory of their ancient past and the hardships of her own generation, could their entire future be extinguished so abruptly and with so little compassion? It seemed unthinkable, and immeasurably unjust, but somehow it was so. How could they contend against a vicious god?

"We did our best," she whispered to her people in their final moments. A single tear ran down her cheek. "Let that always be remem—"

She never finished that sentence. The red sun, rushing through its death throes at 0's instigation, expanded in size, swallowing and incinerating all the inner planets of the system, including fabled Tkon. 0 jumped back from the ballooning star, scrambling away like a man who has just lit a firecracker. Gorgan, The One, and (*) retreated as well, dragging Q with them. All of them knew that the sudden expansion was only the beginning.

An instant later, the star collapsed upon itself, its entire mass imploding, raining back upon the stellar core, which then exploded again in a spectacular release of light and heat and force that dwarfed, by countless orders of magnitude, all the energy it had previously emitted over all the billions of years of its long existence. For one brief cosmic second, it shone brighter than the rest of the Milky Way Galaxy put together, including what would someday be called the Alpha Quadrant. The flare could be seen beyond the galactic barrier itself, glowing like the Star of Bethlehem in the skies of distant worlds too far away to be reached even at transwarp speed.

Thanks to 0, the Tkon's sun had become a supernova, only moments before they hoped to say farewell to it forever.

Sixteen

Jean-Luc Picard watched in hushed silence as the entire Tkon Empire was destroyed for all time. He was horrified, but not surprised. After the *Enterprise*'s encounter with the ancient Tkon portal on Delphi Ardu, Picard had reviewed the archaeological literature on the Tkon Empire, so he knew all about the supernova that eventually annihilated their civilization. He had never guessed, however, that Q had played any part in that disaster. *I've always wondered,* he thought, *how a culture capable of moving stars and planets at will could be destroyed by a predictable stellar phenomenon. Now I know.*

It was one thing, though, to read about the extinction of a people in a dry historical treatise; it was something else altogether to witness the tragedy with his own eyes, share the lives of some of the individuals involved. His throat tightened with emotion. He blinked back tears. Trillions of fatalities were just a statistic, he reflected, until you were forced to realize that every one of those trillions was a sentient being with dreams and aspirations much like your own.

He had to wonder what humanity would do, four billion years hence, when Earth's own sun faced its end. *Will we display the prescience and the resolve that the Tkon achieved in the face of their greatest challenge? Will we seize the chance for survival that was so cruelly snatched away from the Tkon at the last minute?* He prayed that generations of men and women yet unborn would succeed where the Tkon so nobly failed, and thanked heaven that a similar crisis would not face the Federation in his lifetime.

Or would it? The Tkon's sun had ultimately detonated millions of years before its appointed time, thanks to the preternatural influence of beings like Q. What was to stop such creatures from doing the same to Earth's sun, or any other star in the Alpha Quadrant? He glanced at the familiar entity beside him, presently honoring the death of the Tkon with an uncharacteristic moment of silence, and was newly chilled by the terrifying potential of Q's abilities. *Q has threatened humanity with total obliteration so many times,* he thought, *that I suppose I should not be too shocked to discover that he has been involved in carrying out just such an atrocity, no matter how indirectly.* It was easy to think of Q as simply a prankster and a nuisance. The supernova blazing before them bore awful testament to just how dangerous Q and his kind really were.

"It's not a total loss, you know," Q said finally. "Supernovas such as that one are the only place in the universe where elements heavier than iron are created. Ultimately, the raw materials of your reality, even the very atoms that make up your physical bodies, were born in the heart of an awesome stellar conflagration such as we now behold. Who knows? There may be a little bit of Tkon in you, Jean-Luc."

"Small comfort to the trillions who perished, Q," Picard responded. The face of the Tkon empress, both as a lovely young woman and as the fine old lady she became, was still fresh in his memory. *She came so close to saving her people.*

"Try to take the long view, Picard." Q squinted at the luminous ball of light that had consumed the Tkon Empire; it was like staring straight into a matter/antimatter reaction. "All civilizations collapse eventually. Besides, there are still traces of the Tkon floating around the galaxy, even in your time. Artifacts and relics that attest to their place in history."

"Like the ruins on Delphi Ardu," Picard suggested. He wished now that he had visited the site himself, instead of sending an away team. Riker had been quite impressed by what he had seen of the Tkon's technology and culture.

"Just to name one example," Q said. "Then there's this little toy." He wandered away from the nova, past what had been the Tkon's home system, until he came upon a golden star, about the size of a large tribble, encased within what looked like a wire framework. A few lighted crystal chips, strung like beads upon the wire lattice, blinked on and off sporadically. *Of course,* Picard recalled, *the sun the Tkon had intended to beam into their system, and the gigantic transporter array they constructed to do so.* "It's still there," Q stated, "forgotten and never used. If I were you, Picard, I'd find it before the Borg or the Dominion do." He gave the relic a cursory glance. "Not that this has anything to do with why we're here, mind you."

Picard saw an opportunity to press Q on his motives. "Very well, then. If the destruction is so very insignificant, on a cosmic scale, they why *are* we here? What's the point?"

"Isn't it obvious?" Q asked, sounding exasperated. He turned and spoke to Picard very distinctly, pronouncing each word with patronizing slowness and clarity. "This isn't about the Tkon. It's about *him.*"

The blinding flash of the supernova dazzled Q right before the shock wave knocked him off his feet. He tumbled backward, the force of the explosion wrenching him free of Gorgan and The One, who were equally staggered by the blast. Q scrambled to his feet, several light-years away from the nova, then stared slack-jawed at what 0 had wrought. The light and the impact may have hit him already, but the psychological and emotional effect of what had happened was still sinking in.

A series of lesser shock waves followed the initial explosion, shaking the space-time continuum like the lingering aftershocks of a major earthquake. Q tottered upon his heels, striving to maintain his balance, while some detached component of intellect wondered absently how much of the star's mass remained after the detonation; depending on the mass of the stellar remnant, Tkon's sun could now devolve into either a neutron star or a black hole. He watched in a state of shock as, in the wake of the supernova, the collapsing star shed a huge gaseous nebula composed of glowing radioactive elements. The gases were expelled rapidly by the stellar remnant, expanding past Q and the others like a gust of hot steam that left Q gasping and choking. Cooling elemental debris clung to his face and hands like perspiration. "Ugh," he said, grimacing. He'd forgotten how dreadful a supernova smelled.

The radioactive nebula expanded past Q, leaving him a clear view of all that remained of the huge red orb that had once lighted an empire. The stellar remnant had imploded even further while he was blinded by the noxious gases, achieving its ultimate destiny. He couldn't actually see it, of course, since there was literally nothing there except a profound absence, but he knew a black hole when he saw one. He could feel its gravitational pull from where he was standing, pulling at his feet like an undertow. Was this void, this empty black cavity, all that was left of the Tkon empress and all her people?

It's all my fault, he thought. *This wasn't supposed to happen.*

He turned on 0 in a rage. "How could you do that? They were winning your stupid game, then you changed the rules! A supernova, without any warning? How in creation could they possibly survive that?"

His henchmen, no longer jarred by the explosion of moments before, began to converge on Q once more, but 0 waved them away. Now that the deed was done, he appeared more than willing to face the young Q's anger. He wiped the stellar plasma from his hands, then straightened his jacket before addressing Q's objections. "Now, now, Q. Let's not get too worked up over this. You clearly missed the point of this exercise. I was simply testing their ability to cope with the completely unexpected, and isn't that really the only test that truly matters? Any simple species can cope with civil disorder or minor natural disasters. That's no guarantee of greatness. We have to be more strict than that, more stringent in our standards." He tilted his head toward the black hole a few parsecs away, assuming a philosophical expression. "Face facts, Q. If your little Tkon couldn't handle something as routine as an ordinary supernova, then they wouldn't have amounted to much anyway."

"He sounds just like you," Picard observed.

"You must be joking." Q looked genuinely offended by the suggestion, although thankfully more appalled than annoyed. "Even so dim a specimen as yourself must be able to see the fundamental difference between me and that . . . megalomaniacal sadist and his obsequious underlings."

"Which is?" Picard asked, pushing his luck. In truth, he had a vague idea of where Q was going with this, but he wanted to hear it from Q's own lips.

"I play fair, Jean-Luc." He held out the palms of his hands, beseeching Picard to understand. "There's nothing wrong, necessarily, with tests and games, but you have to play fair. Surely you'll concede, despite whatever petty inconveniences I may have imposed on you in the past, that I have always scrupulously held fast to the rules of whatever game we were playing, even if I sometimes found myself wishing otherwise."

"Perhaps," Picard granted. He could quibble over Q's idea of fairness, particularly when competing against unwilling beings of vastly lesser abilities, but allowed that, with varying degrees of good sportsmanship, Q had let Picard win on occasion. *At least that's something,* he thought, feeling slightly less apprehensive than he had mere moments ago. "And 0?" he prompted. "And the Tkon?"

Q made a contemptuous face. "That was no test, that was a blood sport."

His younger self could not yet articulate his feelings so clearly. Distraught and disoriented, he wavered in the face of 0's snow of words. 0 sounded so calm, so reasonable now. "But you killed them all," he blurted. "What's the good of testing them if they all end up dead?"

"An occupational hazard of mortality," 0 pointed out quite matter-of-factly. "You can't let it get to you, Q. I know it's hard at first. Little helpless creatures can be very appealing sometimes. But trust me on this, the testing gets easier the more you do it. Isn't that right, comrades?" The other entities murmured their assent, except for (*), who maintained his silence. "Pretty soon, Q, it won't bother you at all."

Q thought that over. The idea of feeling better later was attractive, offering the promise of a balm for his stinging conscience, but maybe you were supposed to feel a little bad after you blew up some poor species' sun. *Is this what I want to do with my immortality?* he wondered. *Is 0 who I really want to be?*

"Let me ask you something," he said at last, looking 0 squarely in the eye. He knew now what he needed to know. "Aside from the Coulalakritous, has any species—anywhere—ever survived one of your tests?"

0 didn't even bother to lie. The predatory gleam in his eyes and the smirk that crossed his face were all the answer Q required.

It was the beginning of the first Q war. . . .

Q-STRIKE

Prologue

Let the ending begin. Begin the end of eternity. . . .

It was finally happening. After endless, empty aeons of exile, his liberation was at hand. Balls were rolling. Gears were turning. A shiny, silver key had inserted itself into the eternal lock and now awaited only a flick of the wrist to open wide the gate and let him back into that vast array of suns and planets and moons and swirling nebulae from which he had so long been barred.

Turn the key. Set me free. Free me, me, me!

Time, too much time, had taken its toll on the orderly procession of his thoughts, but not his infamous ingenuity and enthusiasm. He could scarcely wait to make his mark on the galaxy once more, teach it the true meaning of terror and torment. He'd pick up right where he left off—before Q spoiled everything.

All due to Q, and Q and Q, too.

Already a tiny portion of himself, the merest sliver of his soul, had slipped into a crack in the wall, merging with one of the crude and contemptible creatures there, peering out through its obsolete ocular apparatus, while the rest of him snapped and scratched impatiently at the primordial partition that had defied him for longer than his scattered mind could begin to encompass, but not for very much longer. *He is the key. The key is me. The key to set me free.* He had seen things through the primitive eyes of his avatar within the wall, seen the child of Q and Q, the child of the future.

My future. Mine! he roared at the silent wall, while spider legs of extended thought capered and clawed and craved release. *Hear me Q? Hear me here . . . and now.* He probed for further cracks in the wall, shouted into the flickering fissures.

Now the end has begun. Begin the end of Q. . . .

One

Ship's log, stardate 51604.3, First Officer William T. Riker reporting.

Captain Picard remains missing, transported away by Q, who alone knows when and if the captain will return to the Enterprise. *In his absence, I have barely managed to preserve both the ship and the crew, despite the best efforts of the gaseous life-form known as the Calamarain.*

Our situation remains grave. To escape the Calamarain, we have taken refuge within the outer fringes of the galactic barrier. Although our shields, modified to absorb psychokinetic energy from the barrier itself, protect us from the worst of its effects, we cannot remain immune to the destructive force of the barrier indefinitely. Already the more telepathically sensitive members of the crew are experiencing discomfort and even pain from the excess of psychic energy composing the barrier and now surrounding the ship.

Due to damage inflicted by both the Calamarain and the barrier, our warp engines are inoperative, and we have lost artificial gravity in large portions of the saucer section, including the bridge. I can only hope that we can complete the most needed repairs before we are forced to exit the barrier and reenter our galaxy, perhaps to face the Calamarain again.

Lieutenant Baeta Leyoro's pain-racked cry echoed throughout the bridge. If not for the lack of gravity, she would have surely collapsed to the hard duranium floor; instead the stricken security officer levitated in midair, her body doubled over in agony as the psychic flux of the barrier set her synapses on fire. A plait of black hair rose from her scalp, swaying like a cobra about to strike. A heart-wrenching whimper escaped her lips, squeezing out from between tightly clenched teeth.

Riker blamed himself. *I should have sent her to sickbay immediately, the moment I realized that her augmented nervous system made her uniquely vulnerable to the barrier.* Instead he had waited until it was too late, with the result that she had succumbed to her seizure halfway between her post and the turbolift. But now was no time to second-guess himself. "Beam her directly to sickbay," he ordered, then slapped the combadge on his chest. "Riker to Dr. Crusher. Lieutenant Leyoro requires emergency care. Expect her at once."

Even as he warned Beverly of the incoming patient, a shimmering silver glow enveloped the floating, fetal form of Leyoro. *Thank heavens the transporters are still working,* Riker thought, relieved that Leyoro could benefit from that technology at least, even if their jury-rigged deflectors, experimentally altered by Lieutenant Barclay and Data, had not been enough to protect her. The scintillating twinkle of the transporter effect shone even brighter amid the dimly lit bridge, where only flashing red alert signals provided any illumination at all. Even the blue tracking lights that routinely ran along the floor of the bridge had been snuffed out by the abuse the *Enterprise* had sustained over the last several hours.

Riker's own head throbbed in sympathy with Leyoro; he suspected that his long-standing telepathic bond with Deanna had increased his sensitivity as well, weakening his brain's defenses against the psychic barrage. Swollen veins pounded beneath his temples and brow, although the ache was not yet fierce enough to make him abandon his post. *My brain will have to explode first,* he vowed defiantly, his jaw set squarely beneath his black beard. He nodded grimly as Leyoro vanished in a cascade of sparks that swiftly evaporated before his eyes.

"Got her," Beverly's voice confirmed via his combadge. "Crusher out."

Convinced that Leyoro's fate now rested in the capable hands of the ship's medical officer, Riker leaned forward in the captain's chair and turned his attention to other pressing matters. A brilliant violet glow emanated from the forward viewscreen, catching his eye. Overloaded by the immeasurable radiance of the galactic barrier, the screen had initially gone dead upon their entry into the mysterious wall of energy. Now the screen flared back to life, but only to show a brighter form of blankness, filled from top to bottom by an undifferentiated display of pure luminosity. The glare from the screen pierced his eyes. "Someone dim the main viewer," he instructed gruffly.

"Affirmative, Commander," Data responded. Seated at Ops, the gold-skinned android manipulated the controls at his station. Scorch marks along the console's polished metal casing testified to the rigors of their recent battle against the Calamarain, as did numerous other scars all around the bridge. A fragment of torn polyduranide sheeting drifted past Riker's face, free from the downward pull of gravity, and he batted it away with a wave of his hand. On the screen, the phosphorescent effulgence of the galactic barrier faded to a more subdued but equally uninformative gleam. "Is that acceptable, Commander?" Data inquired calmly.

"That will do, Mr. Data," Riker said. The sooner they put the barrier behind them, the better. He tapped his combadge again. "Riker to La Forge. What's our warp status?"

Geordi's voice answered him from Engineering, sounding more than a little harried. "We've patched up the plasma-injection system, but the warp-field coils in the starboard nacelle still need a lot of work. We're talking another hour at least."

"Understood," Riker acknowledged. There was no need to urge La Forge to hurry; the engineering chief knew full well how shaky their shields were compared with the awesome power of the barrier. *The devil of it is,* Riker thought, *we don't even know* why *the Calamarain attacked us in the first place, even though it obviously had something to do with the barrier.* Were the gaseous entities still waiting for the *Enterprise* outside the wall? Riker didn't want to find out until he knew the ship could make a quick escape at warp speed. *With any luck, the Calamarain will have given us up for dead the moment we flew into the barrier.*

"I certainly hope you're not planning to sit here forever," said a voice to his left, belonging to a tall, auburn-haired woman who had usurped Deanna's seat in the command area. Her tone could be described as patronizing at best, contemptuous at worst. "As impressive and mystifying as our surroundings must appear to creatures of your ilk, I'm afraid I grew accustomed to such spectacles several millennia ago." She raised an impeccably manicured hand to her mouth in an only partially successful attempt to stifle a yawn. "Can't you *do* something just to liven things up a bit?"

The woman in question, balancing a sleepy toddler upon her knee, was reportedly Q's wife and the mother of his child, two propositions that frankly boggled Riker's mind whenever he cared to think of them, which definitely wasn't now. "If we're not sufficiently entertaining for you, you're more than welcome to leave," he informed her. Ever since she had refused to use her Q-like omnipotence to rescue the *Enterprise* from its current predicament, let alone enlighten him as to what Q had done with Captain Picard, he had resolved not to let either her or her child distract him from his duty.

"Don't be ridiculous," she said haughtily. The pips on the collar of her fake Starfleet uniform identified her (inaccurately) as a five-star admiral. *Typical,* Riker thought; from what he had seen so far, the female Q's ego was easily a match for her husband's. "I told you before, I intend to find out what precisely my esteemed spouse and partner finds so intriguing about this primitive vessel, no matter how excruciatingly tedious that task proves to be. Besides," she added, smiling indulgently at her small son, clad in equally counterfeit Starfleet attire, "little q enjoys your aboriginal antics."

"Ant-ticks!" q burbled happily. He waved a pudgy little hand, and a parade of tiny insects suddenly appeared on the floor of the command area, marching single file past the elevated captain's chair and across the top of Riker's gravity boots. Despite his determination to ignore Q's visiting relations as much as possible, the first officer had to suppress a shudder at this reminder of the seemingly harmless infant's abilities. Such amazing power in the hands of a child was enough to send a chill down a Vulcan's spine. *Like the original Q isn't immature enough,* he thought.

Naturally, q's mother was charmed by her offspring's naive misunderstanding. "Oh, isn't that adorable?" she said. Propelled by the motion of their miniature limbs, the insects began to lift off from the floor, adding to the ash and debris in the air. Fortunately, the female Q scooped up the floating bugs with a net she materialized from nowhere, then consigned both the net and its chittering contents to oblivion. "I'm sorry, dearest," she explained to the child, patting him on the head, "but our present surroundings are barbaric enough without any additional infestations."

Baby q objected strenuously to the sudden disappearance of his playthings. He scrunched up his face and let out an earsplitting squall while simultaneously kicking his little legs. His tantrum shook the entire bridge, which lurched from side to side, nearly throwing Riker out of his chair. Behind him, he heard Ensign Sondra Berglund, who had replaced Leyoro at tactical, stumble awkwardly in her heavy magnetic boots. "That's enough," he barked at the female Q. "He's your child. Do something about him."

To his surprise, the woman actually looked abashed, as if she feared the child's behavior reflected poorly on her parenting skills. "Now, now," she cooed to q in a soothing tone, "you can play with your funny arthropods another time." Accompanied by a brief flash of white light, an enticing *jumja* treat appeared in q's balled-up fist. Not surprisingly, the delectable glop-on-a-stick successfully distracted q, who abandoned his uproar in favor of sucking energetically on the sugary confection. "There," his mother said approvingly. "Isn't that better?"

Although the candy calmed the child, it also made something of a mess. Riker already spotted sticky handprints all over Troi's customary seat. Deanna herself was currently in sickbay, under the care of Dr. Crusher. He allowed himself a moment of concern regarding Deanna's safety, praying that the doctor's efforts had protected Deanna, with her empathic sensitivity, from the barrier. *Be well,* imzadi, he thought.

Deanna's Betazoid gifts rendered her unusually susceptible to the concentrated psionic energy surrounding the ship, as were their civilian passengers: Professor Lem Faal of Betazed, and his two children. As full telepaths, the Faal family were probably more at risk than anyone else aboard the *Enterprise*. For that reason, he had ordered all three Betazoids, along with Deanna, to sickbay before they even entered the barrier. He'd hoped that precaution would be enough to keep their guests safe, but, insanely, Faal had caused a disturbance in sickbay, attacking Deanna and escaping with his son. Even now, security was searching for the missing patients.

I knew Faal was upset about his experiment being called off due to the unexpected attack of the Calamarain, but I never expected him to resort to violence. Thank heavens, Deanna wasn't seriously harmed, Riker thought, *or I'd be tempted to beam him to the Calamarain myself.*

At tactical, Ensign Berglund had regained her footing. "Shield strength is fluctuating, Commander," she reported, "by variances of twenty percent and more." Her eyes never left the display panel. "I'm doing my best to stabilize the deflectors, but it's not working."

Riker glanced quickly at Lieutenant Reginald Barclay, now positioned at the secondary aft science station. It had been Barclay's idea to divert telekinetic energy from the barrier to the ship's shields by way of the organic bio-neural gel packs in the *Enterprise*'s computer system, a hastily improvised tactic that had proven successful . . . so far.

"The gel packs are still absorbing energy from the barrier," Barclay assured Riker, gulping nervously, "but it's hard to quantify. I had to reroute the monitoring program to science two after the engineering station exploded." He cast a wary look at the charred remains of the main engineering console, only a few stations away. "The gel packs were never intended to serve as batteries for psychic energy, so there are no established parameters to judge their efficiency."

"This is correct, Commander," Data confirmed. He had carefully evaluated Barclay's preliminary findings earlier, as had Geordi La Forge. "Prolonged exposure to the barrier is causing a significant percentage of bio-neural circuitry to incinerate. At present, energy absorption exceeds extinction by a rate of approximately forty-seven-point-three-four percent, averaged over the duration of our stay in the barrier, but at any given moment the quantity of energy available to the deflector array can vary dramatically, just as Ensign Berglund reports."

Riker nodded. "Let me know the instant the scale tips the other way. Ensign Clarze," he instructed the young Deltan crewman at the conn, "set a course that takes us straight out of the barrier in the shortest possible time. When we go, I want to leave here in a hurry."

"Yes, sir," Clarze said. Riker had been impressed by the way the inexperienced ensign had kept his cool during this crisis, coping with both the hostile activities of the Calamarain as well as the always unsettling caprices of Q and his kin. He resolved to make a note of this the next time he and Deanna completed their personnel evaluation reports, assuming any of them came out of this alive. He gazed at the lambent glow of the main viewer. Somewhere beyond that incandescent haze, the Milky Way waited for them, as did, perhaps, an angry and homicidal mass of sentient plasma.

Where are the Calamarain? Riker brooded. *And, just as importantly, where is Captain Picard?*

Two

Six hundred thousand years ago:

"What have you done??"

The booming voice came without warning, reverberating through space-time and startling five celestial figures, in addition to two more who looked on anonymously from a slightly different phase of reality. Jean-Luc Picard, late of the *Starship Enterprise,* stood amid the starry vastness of space, accompanied by Q, his self-appointed guide on this forced excursion through galactic prehistory, and watched, as through a one-way mirror, as Q's younger self faced the consequences of his fateful alliance with the malicious cosmic entity who called himself 0, as well as with 0's trio of malevolent cronies.

Like 0 and the others, Picard presently existed on a sublimely magnified scale, such that stars and planets were no more than ball-sized spheres of matter and burning gas in comparison. His gaze encompassed parsecs of open space, and yet that stern and unforgiving voice seemed even larger than himself. Picard cast a speculative glance at Q, then lifted his eyes heavenward. "The Q Continuum, I presume?"

"Just so," Q affirmed. Clad in the latest Starfleet uniform, he gestured toward his younger self, standing a few light-years away. More than a hint of melancholy tinged his ordinarily sarcastic voice. "In truth, I wasn't too surprised, even then. I could hardly expect the Continuum to overlook the small matter of a premature supernova, not to mention the total destruction of a major spacefaring civilization."

Still saddened by the tragedy, Picard looked back over his shoulder at the lifeless void that was all that remained of the mighty Tkon Empire, destroyed by 0 in a fit of pique after his underlings failed to subvert its civilization. Where once a sophisticated and admirable people, numbering in the trillions, had spread their culture throughout their solar system and beyond, achieving heights of technological wizardry exceeding those of the Federation, the detonation of their sun, brought on abruptly by 0's supernatural puissance, had extinguished nearly every trace of their existence, leaving only a few scattered ruins on distant outposts to mark their passing. Picard could still feel the relentless tug of the black hole the Tkon's sun had become. Invisible to his naked eye, even in this transfigured state, the dense gravitational vortex pulled on him like an undertow, so that Picard found himself leaning forward to counter its attractive force. *What was done to the Tkon,* he mused, *was a crime of interplanetary proportions.*

Now, it seemed, as detective Dixon Hill might put it, the time had come to face the music. . . .

"I'm s-sorry," the younger Q stammered, staring up at the source of the bodiless voice. His fine attire, which had resembled that of an eighteenth-century European dandy, several hundred millennia ahead of its time, transformed at once into a coarse and uncomfortable sackcloth robe. "I never meant for this to happen."

In fact, Picard recalled, the young Q had played little part in the annihilation of the Tkon, had even attempted to stop 0 once he realized what the other was up to, but to no avail. At worst, he had been only an unwilling accessory to genocide, not that this seemed to have spared Q's conscience much. After all, if not for Q's recklessness and gullibility, 0 and his unholy associates would have never gained entry to this reality in the first place. Q had promised to take responsibility for 0 when he rescued the mysterious wayfarer from some extradimensional wasteland. 0 in turn had welcomed three lesser entities into Q's reality, making Q responsible by extension for the depredations of these sinister beings, who now faced judgment beside Q and their ruthless sponsor. Picard wondered how much the other Q would hold the young Q to his original promise.

"WHAT HAS BEEN DONE CANNOT BE UNDONE."

Young Q flinched beneath every syllable, just as his older counterpart winced in sympathy. The mature Q was clearly troubled by this peek at his ignominious youth, but made no effort to intervene in what transpired. Even the Q, Picard observed with a certain relief, drew the line when it came to tampering with the past; not even the gods could erase yesterday, no matter how much they might want to. *Q obviously survived this occasion,* he inferred, *or else he would have never been able to torment me in the future.* He shook his head. *Lucky me.*

"It all started out as a game," young Q tried to explain, pleading for understanding with outstretched hands, "a simple test of their resourcefulness. . . ."

"That's enough, boy," 0 interrupted harshly. Unlike Q, he saw no need to discard his anachronistic finery. His stylish velvet suit, olive green in hue, looked even more elegant and ostentatious next to Q's penitent gray robe. The buckles on his polished black shoes shone like silver, while one ruffled sleeve, Picard noted, was scorched from when he had thrust his merciless hand into the heart of the Tkon's murdered sun. "We've no need to justify ourselves to their sort."

"But it's the Continuum," Q pointed out, while his older self mouthed the very same words. This incident was obviously imprinted deeply in the later Q's memory. "They've come for us. They know what we've done."

"Stiffen your spine, I say, and shut your mouth." 0 limped across the vacuum and rested a meaty hand upon Q's shoulder. His three henchmen, whom Q knew as Gorgan, (*), and The One, clustered behind him, letting their leader face the judgment of the Continuum. "We're all in this together, Q. There's no backing out now."

"YOU," the stentorian voice targeted 0, sounding not unlike Picard's own resonant timbre. "YOU AND YOUR FAMILIARS DO NOT BELONG HERE. YOU MUST BE CAST OUT FOR ALL TIME."

"I've heard that before," 0 said with a chuckle, then glared at the sky with icy blue eyes. He placed his hands on his hips and thrust out his wide chin. His raspy voice held not a note of regret or repentance. "How dare you judge any of us, you pontificating pests? What do you know of the noble art of testing developing species, forcing them to prove their potential and worthiness to survive? Of the guile and glory of pushing lesser life-forms to their ultimate limits and beyond? What have you ever done that can match what we have accomplished, you cautious Continuum? We're better than the lot of you!"

"0!" young Q whispered frantically to his former role model and mentor. Once 0's insolent disregard for the authority of the Continuum had thrilled and delighted the callow superbeing, but that was before 0 had gotten him into real trouble. Before Tkon. Picard could only imagine how tempted the elder Q must have been to warn his younger self of impending events.

"Don't hide behind these sonorous sound effects," 0 challenged the bodiless voice. "Face us in person, preternatural deity to preternatural deity, if you've got the guts and gumption."

"YOU ARE NOT WORTHY TO LOOK UPON THE Q. YOU SHALL BE BANISHED FROM THIS REALM."

"Do your worst," 0 dared the Continuum. Taking a deep breath, he seemed to call upon his full strength, just as he had when he froze the Coulalakritous into a solid mass. A flickering aura formed around his humanoid guise, along with a vague impression of another, less substantial form superimposed upon his anthropomorphic persona.

Once before, another half a million years in the past, Picard had beheld this shadowy other aspect of 0. As then, the images were indistinct and almost subliminal in nature, and all the more ominous for their tantalizing and suggestive elusiveness. Try though he did to discern the actual shape of 0's alter ego, Picard caught only transitory glimpses of whipping tendrils that extended beyond the boundaries of 0's human form like the unfurled wings of some alien raptor. *That which is only half-seen is all the more troubling to the imagination,* he reflected; although Picard had often conversed comfortably with alien beings who varied dramatically from the humanoid model, what he spied of 0's other form sent a chill through his body. *Or maybe it is just the implication of deliberate deception that is so unnerving.* What other secrets might 0 be hiding?

Whatever his shape or origins, 0 remained a force to be reckoned with. Even separated from the scene by one degree of existence, Picard felt the power radiating from 0, stinging his exposed face and hands like a freezing wind. "Stand fast," he called out to Q and the others, his gravelly voice rising to a thunderous roar. "These censorious charlatans don't know whom they're dealing with! If we stick together, we can withstand any foe."

But the cumulative force of the Continuum struck like disruptor fire from a Romulan warbird, dispersing 0's ectoplasmic tentacles and sending him staggering backward into Gorgan and The One. Gorgan's voluminous robes and flowing white locks, suffused as ever by a faint greenish aura, flapped like hung laundry in a hurricane while The One's gleaming metal armor protected him only slightly better. His stern and bearded visage blinked in the face of the attack, the flesh of his face pulled tightly against the skull beneath. Hovering above their heads, the glowing crimson sphere that was (*) was stretched into a faint, translucent oval by the concussive force directed against them. "Do your worst!" 0 bellowed, ribbons of smoke rising from his seared garments. "I'll not surrender, never again!" Pressing forward, dragging his lame left leg behind him, he clenched his fists and hurled blasts of pyrotechnic energy at his unseen foes. Blazing fireballs arced like meteors across the heavens, exploding into scarlet bursts of light and heat so bright that Picard was forced to look away.

"Eyes front," the Q beside him said. "I wouldn't want you to miss anything."

Picard squinted into the glare. Not for the first time, he wondered what Q's purpose was in showing all this to him. *What have these fantastically ancient events to do with my own life and times?*

If 0's fiery assault had any effect on the Continuum, Picard saw no sign of it. 0 was powerful, no doubt, but he was only one where the Continuum represented the collective might of who knew how many. Of his lackeys, only The One rose to his defense. "Bow not to false gods!" He declared, flinging one thunderbolt after another after 0's fireballs. His austere, patriarchal features could've been carved from the hardest Cardassian granite; even His long, forbidding beard was stiff and un-yielding. "Feel the sting of My Righteous Fury."

Despite the aid of The One, 0 began to lose ground. Battered by the irresistible force of the Continuum, the murderer of the Tkon Empire was forced to retreat once more, spewing a trail of blinding conflagrations behind him. Young Q felt the wrath of the Continuum as well. He tumbled head over heels, nearly rolling away from 0 and the others before 0 reached out and grabbed on to Q's forearm, digging his fingers into Q's metaphysical flesh. "I'll never yield, never I say," the stranger gasped, squinting his eyes against the impact of the Continuum's offensive, "but even the most courageous combatant knows when to retreat. Time to flee to fight again, Q. Get us away from here!"

"What?" The beleaguered young godling looked uncertain. Wringing his hands nervously, he looked back and forth between 0 and the direction from which the Q's attack emerged. *Can he see his fellow Q?* Picard wondered. *Does he know too well how angry they must be?* The Continuum had punished Q before, he recalled, for follies far less consequential than this. "I don't know what to do," the youth said. "I'm not sure."

"Don't run, you fool," the later Q whispered to his young self, who, alas, could not hear the voice of experience speaking. "You're only making it worse."

"Run!" 0 urged him. He tossed away his stylish brown wig, exposing his own reddish hair, tied in the back. His black silk cravat had come undone, dangling loosely around his neck. "We have to flee, Q, now. Or are you prepared to take the blame for what happened to the late, lamented Tkon Empire?" His crippled leg dragged behind him, reminding Picard that 0 was unable to travel faster than light without Q's assistance. "Are you ready to pay for my crimes?"

"But it wasn't my fault," Q whimpered. His face was contorted by fear and distress. Tears leaked from his eyes. "Not all of it, not really."

"Are you so sure of that?" 0 asked, showing him no mercy. "Are you certain that the high-and-mighty Q Continuum will see things the same way? From what I've seen so far, they're not the forgiving type." A devilish grin stretched across his broad, ruddy face. "They'll deal with you most harshly of all, I'll wager."

"YOU CANNOT OVERCOME US," the voice of the Continuum intoned. "SUBMIT TO BANISHMENT OR RISK DESTRUCTION."

"Don't do it," the older Q said, shaking his head mournfully.

"Now's the time," 0 spat through clenched teeth. "I can't hold them off any longer."

He's going to panic, Picard realized, only a heartbeat before the young Q let out an inarticulate howl and swept he, 0, and the rest of their infamous party away in a flash of white light. Picard found himself alone in deep space except for the continuing presence of the Q he was accustomed to. The rest of the Continuum remained invisible to his senses.

"You don't need to say anything, Picard," his companion said. "I know when I've made an ass of myself."

> *"Got a fine young maid,*
> *Her dowry's paid,*
> *My fortunes made,*
> *My plans are laid,*
> *I'll sit awhile in shade. . . ."*

Young Q shook his head in disbelief. 0 sounded altogether too pleased with himself for someone who had called down the judgment of the Continuum upon them all. How could he sing at a time like this? *I'm a fugitive,* he realized, *and an immortal one. My life is over and it won't ever end.*

Dejected, he sat upon the ground, his knees drawn up beneath his chin. The ground itself consisted of solid dilithium, its crystalline surface worn smooth by the ceaseless passage of the dense metallic liquid that enveloped Q and his partners in crime. The metallic sea, which covered the entire surface of the polished, planet-sized mass of dilithium, extended for hundreds of thousands of kilometers overhead before eventually segueing into an even vaster expanse of swirling helium and hydrogen vapors blown by hurricane-force winds exceeding five hundred kilometers an hour. The buried core of this gas giant, upon which they now resided, located in what would someday be called the Detrian system, had been one of his favorite hiding places when he was a child; it was like being on the yolk of an enormous egg, shielded from prying eyes by several layers of liquid and gaseous shell. He had told no one about it, not even 0, but never had he dreamed that he would someday use it to hide out from justice. *This isn't the way it was supposed to happen,* he grieved.

"Maybe we should turn ourselves in," he suggested, looking up from the polished surface of the core. He could no longer bear to stare at his own guilty reflection. "Perhaps the Continuum will show mercy if we surrender freely."

0 did not respond to his suggestion, but instead kept on singing, missing only a beat or two in the melody, as the lyrics took a peculiar turn:

> *"Woe to those who are afraid,*
> *I've never looked kindly upon being betrayed. . . ."*

Why is he looking at me? Q thought nervously. 0 was just singing, that's all. "You don't know the Continuum like I do," he insisted. "They can actually be quite reasonable on occasion. I'm sure if we explain ourselves, show them how matters simply got out of hand, we could expect some leniency."

> *"I venture I'd be quite dismayed. . . ."*

Several meters away, skating blithely over the slick crystal plane, 0 laughed out loud at the end of his song. He retied his unfurled cravat as he coasted over the solid dilithium. "You've a lot to learn about being a rebel, my naive young friend. Rule Number One: Never surrender. Isn't that right, fellows?"

The other entities clustered nearby. The One had formed Himself an impressive-looking dilithium throne in which He sat rather too regally, Q thought, for One who had so recently been forced to flee for His liberty. Gorgan looked significantly more agitated, pacing back and forth behind The One's throne, the hem of his amethyst robe brushing the ground. His immaterial form shimmered, looking slightly less solid than a hologram. Silent as ever, (*) hovered in the flowing currents of the metal sea, casting a bloodred radiance over the entire scene.

"Isn't that right?" 0 repeated loudly, a dangerous edge in his voice. Bubbles streamed from his lips, ascending toward the gaseous atmosphere far, far above.

"Oh yes, certainly," Gorgan piped up unctuously. As always, his voice had a peculiarly unnatural echo, as if it were generated artificially by a being whose lips and lungs were merely simulcra of the real things. "No surrender at all," he insisted.

The One sat immobile upon His throne, His upper limbs resting upon sculpted armrests. His golden plate armor, medieval in style, showed no sign of rust or corrosion, despite the liquid nature of this undersea hiding place. "The final battle is not yet fought. My Might will endure unto the last."

"That's more like it," 0 said gruffly, sliding toward Q. "An occasional reversal is to be expected when you're living boldly. I warned you there'd be danger, Q. That's the price you pay for taking chances."

They were not entirely alone. Eyeless, segmented, cylindrical life-forms, evolved to survive the incredible pressure of the gas giant's lower depths, swam through the molten dilithium, instinctively giving 0 and the others a wide berth. *They're smarter than I was,* Q thought, envying the primitive creatures. "Is that what we're doing?" he asked. "Living boldly? Being rebels?" He stared glumly at the horizon, where the solid dilithium met the aqueous sky, refusing to look at 0. "So why do I feel like some wretched criminal on the run?"

0 glared down at him. "All right then, let's have this out here and now. What are you so morose about? The Tkon? Ephemeral creatures whom the universe will never miss. A million years from now? They'll be completely forgotten, while we go on forever. They should be thankful they attracted our attention. At least we'll remember the fine sport they provided. That's a better legacy than most such mortals can expect."

"Sport?" Q jumped to his feet, practically shouting in 0's face. Blind eels, their sinuous bodies covered by iridescent scales, swam away in alarm. "They didn't stand a chance. It wasn't fair."

"What does fair have to do with it?" 0 held his ground. "Of course the outcome is always the same. They're just animals after all. Crude, corporeal creations fit only to provide us with a bit of diversion. It's the *style* with which such savage species are dispatched that matters, Q. You have to learn to appreciate the elegance of extinction, the deft and delicate dance of destruction."

"You blew up their sun! You call that delicate?" The angry words came gushing out of him in a flood of bubbles. He couldn't have held the accusations back if he wanted to. "I saw you, 0. I was there. You weren't concerned with style. You were just angry at the Tkon because they beat Gorgan and the others at their own morbid little games. They beat *you*—and you killed them for it."

"They were creatures!" 0 spat angrily. "Why can't you understand that? Creatures like that *can't* beat beings like us. It's impossible by definition." He sneered scornfully at Q. "Don't waste my time crying over the poor, unfortunate Tkon. I know what your real problem is. You're afraid. For the first time in your puerile, immature existence, you've stepped outside the boundaries set by that hidebound Continuum of yours, and now you want to go scurrying back in search of forgiveness." He made a clucking sound with his tongue. "I thought you were braver than that, but maybe you're just another timid little Q after all."

"That's not true," Q shot back, but with less certainty than with which he had spoken for the Tkon.

"Isn't it?" 0 asked. "Where's the Q who pulled me through the Guardian of Forever, and the devil with the consequences? I thought you wanted to be different from your conservative brethren. I thought you wanted to make your mark on the multiverse, maybe even give the rest of the Continuum a much-needed jolt or two. I thought you wanted adventure and excitement and glory."

"I did. I do. I . . . I . . ." He didn't know what he wanted anymore.

"That's not what it looks like to me. One little scolding from the other Q and suddenly all your revolutionary zeal and ambition collapses like a chronal wave in a transtemporal field." Without warning, 0 shoved Q hard enough to knock the younger entity off his feet. Q landed with a bump onto the ground, his flailing limbs churning up the viscous fluid surrounding him, creating short-lived eddies in the flowing dilithium. "See," his assailant taunted, "a little pressure and you fall right over. You can't even stand up for your own convictions."

Is that true? Q wondered, sprawled upon the glossy surface of the core. *Am I merely afraid of getting caught?* He was afraid of what the Continuum might do certainly, and with good reason, but was that all he felt at this moment? Maybe 0 was right and wrong at the same time, at least where Q was concerned. *This is absurd,* he thought angrily, too disgusted by himself and this entire situation to even bother climbing to his feet again. *I'm a Q. I know all there is to know. So how come I can't even figure myself out?*

"What I didn't realize, in the greenness of my youth," the later Q said from a few meters (and one plane of reality) away, "was that I had far more options than simply 0 or the Continuum. There were an infinite number of ways I could amuse myself, and scandalize my fellow Q, without throwing my lot in with 0 and his motley band." A deep-dwelling eel, taking a long detour around the five fugitives, passed through the older Q's torso as though he wasn't there. "As you must have noticed, *mon capitaine,* I've hardly required assistance to make your humdrum life more interesting."

Picard decided to let that remark pass. He'd exchanged enough repartee with Q to last him a lifetime. He was rather more interested in finding out what happened next to the younger version of Q, who seemed to be digging himself a deeper and deeper hole with each new development. Although there was little love lost between himself and the usual Q, Picard could not help sympathizing with the star-crossed youth at 0's feet. He knew too well how easily an inexperienced, impetuous novice could get in over his head, wincing inwardly as he recalled that long-ago incident at the Academy when his headstrong folly had nearly cost him his Starfleet career before it had truly begun. *Too bad there's no Boothby to counsel young Q at this crucial crossroads,* he reflected, *only 0 and his unsavory compatriots.*

"You're looking unusually pensive, Jean-Luc, even for you." Q plucked a couple of unsuspecting eels from the adjacent reality and began tying them into knots, much like a traditional children's performer turning balloons into animals. An instant later, he presented Picard with a tangle of alien organisms twisted into a miniature replica of the *Enterprise.* "Hit a nerve, have we?"

Picard scowled, unhappy to be reminded that his ship was facing danger without him. The Calamarain had only just come within range of Data's sensors when Q snatched him away from the bridge. Although he had complete confidence in Will Riker to command the *Enterprise* in his absence, he found it deeply disturbing not to know how his ship was faring several hundred thousand years from now. "Are you quite sure that you are the more mature Q?" he said acidly as he took the quivering memento from his guide. As gently as possible, Picard tried to extricate the abused eels from their forced contortions. It was like trying to untangle a plate of writhing *gagh*.

"Touché, Jean-Luc," Q said, looking pleased to have provoked a response from Picard, "but do not confuse adult whimsy and irreverence with juvenile misbehavior." He gestured toward his younger incarnation, awash in difficulties and confusion. *"I* would never get into such an embarrassing fix."

"Except you did," Picard pointed out. Successfully liberating the knotted eels from each other, he released them to swim away as quickly as their long, segmented bodies could carry them. He wondered if they would ever find their way back to their own phase of existence. "That troubled boy is you."

"Please!" Q rolled his eyes in exasperation. "Is an oak tree the same as an acorn? Is a silicon nodule no different than a Mother Horta? He is then. I am now." He shrugged his shoulders. "Granted, at the moment now *is* then, but that's another matter altogether."

Picard endured a familiar frustration. *Why do I even try conversing with him?* He contemplated the younger Q once more. If anything, Q had gotten even more vexing and impossible to deal with over the intervening aeons.

Intent upon their own ongoing drama, neither young Q, nor the bad company into which he had fallen, had noticed the abrupt disappearance of two eels from the murky ocean enclosing the planet's solid core. Instead 0 focused all his formidable personality upon the fallen form of Q. "Well?" he demanded. "What's it going to be? Are you going to sit there, stewing in childish self-pity and remorse, or are you ready to take on the Continuum and anyone else who tries to stop you from fulfilling your true potential? Think carefully, Q. Your destiny depends on what you do next."

Before the young entity could answer, an intense white flare illuminated the metal sea, overpowering (*)'s incarnadine glow. For an instant, the nocturnal depths of the gas giant were suffused with the brightness of a sunny afternoon. "It's the Continuum!" Q shouted, his voice torn between alarm and relief. "They've found us!"

Three

The readings on her medical tricorder shocked Dr. Beverly Crusher. As she scanned Lieutenant Leyoro's brain with the handheld peripheral sensor, the display screen on the tricorder reported alarming levels of bio-neural energy. The stricken security officer's cerebral cortex was being drowned in neurotransmitters, accelerating her synaptic activity at a dangerous rate. *She can't survive much more of this,* Crusher realized.

Leyoro's unconscious body had been beamed directly onto the primary biobed from the bridge. A surgical support frame was clamped over her torso to provide cardiovascular support and even emergency defibrillation if necessary. Crusher kept a close eye on her patient's vital signs and basic metabolic functions, as reported on the monitor mounted above the bed. To her distress, the heightened electrical activity within Leyoro's brain was causing inflammation and spasms all along her artificially augmented nervous system. Leyoro's limbs twitched uncontrollably until Crusher programmed the SSF to provide a steady intravenous infusion of benzocyatzine to inhibit the muscular contractions. Thankfully, the equipment did not require gravity to function effectively. The muscular relaxant merely took care of one symptom, though; treating the root cause of her condition was going to be a lot trickier.

I'm dealing with too many unknowns here, Crusher thought, frustrated. There was little reliable documentation on the telepathic shock sometimes induced by the galactic barrier, primarily because all attempts to cross the barrier had been explicitly banned for close to a century because of that very danger. Furthermore, there was too much she didn't know about the specific neurological modifications the Angosian military scientists had performed on Leyoro during the Tarsian War. Leyoro's medical records were on file, as were the examinations Crusher had performed years ago on Roga Danar, another victim of Angosian biochemical tampering, but that hardly prepared her to treat this unexpected interaction between the barrier's psychic energies and Leyoro's heightened neurology. This was a one-of-a-kind medical emergency.

Fortunately, sickbay had calmed some now that the battle with the Calamarain was over for the time being. Most of the casualties from that conflict had been treated and discharged already, except for a few of the more serious cases, which were currently under the watchful care of the EMH. Crusher shook her head in disbelief; she never thought she'd be grateful for having that supercilious hologram around. Maybe he had his uses after all, even if his bedside manner still left a lot to be desired. Too bad, though, that Selar had transferred to the *Excalibur.* Vulcans were supposed to be immune to the barrier's effects.

She glanced over quickly at the adjacent biobed, where Deanna Troi rested in an artificially induced coma, a set of cortical stimulators blinking upon the Betazoid officer's forehead. Crusher had placed Troi in a coma herself, lowering her brain activity, in hopes of protecting the empathic counselor from the same telepathic overload that was killing Leyoro. So far, judging from the display above Troi's biobed, it seemed to be working; Deanna's synaptic levels were well within the acceptable range for an adult Betazoid of her age and telepathic ability, even though her metabolism was only gradually recovering from the overdose of polyadrenaline she had received from Lem Faal's hypospray.

I'm still shocked by what he did, she thought, remembering the scientist's startling attack on Deanna. *I knew he was agitated about his experiment, not to mention his terminal disease, but I never thought he'd go so far as to assault a crew member rather than abandon his project.* She had not seen Faal since he fled the sickbay after injecting Troi with the polyadrenaline, nor did she know what had happened to Faal's young son, Milo, who had taken off after his father. As Betazoids and full telepaths, both Faal and the boy were also in severe danger from the psychic effects of the barrier. She had sent a security officer in search of them, and informed the bridge of the disturbance, but so far security had not returned either Lem Faal or Milo. *For all I know, they could be worse off than Leyoro right now.*

The security chief's neurotransmitters continued to rise. An agonized moan escaped her lips. Crusher knew she had to try something—anything—before Leyoro suffered permanent brain damage or worse. It was too late to use a cortical stimulator to induce a coma the way she had with Deanna; Leyoro's condition had to be stabilized before Crusher could even attempt to shut her brain down in that fashion. Tapping on the touch-sensitive controls of the surgical clamshell, she added four hundred milligrams of triclenidil to the intravenous infusion. It was a dangerous ploy; the triclenidil would enhance Leyoro's natural defenses, but might also enhance the psionic sensitivity that had rendered her vulnerable in the first place. She wished she could risk an analgesic as well, maybe hyrocortilene or metacetamine. The poor woman sounded like she was in agony, but Crusher couldn't take the chance that further medication might produce a dangerous counterreaction to the chemicals she had already administered to Leyoro.

Thank goodness the little girl is safe at least. Alyssa Ogawa was watching over Lem Faal's youngest child, Kinya, over in the emergency pediatric unit, where the Betazoid child slept in a coma similar to Deanna's. Crusher knew the nurse would call her instantly if Kinya showed any symptoms at all of neurological distress.

Crusher gripped the steel supports of the SSF as she watched for the slightest improvement in Leyoro's brain chemistry. *Come on, Baeta,* she silently urged her patient. *Help me here.* Overhead the sensor cluster hummed quietly as it scanned Leyoro with a full array of diagnostic tools. Crusher's heart leaped as she saw the production of neurotransmitters within Leyoro's cerebral cortex begin to level off. "Yes!" she whispered. The triclenidil was working! Leyoro was a long ways from out of the woods yet, but at least she had a chance. Crusher cautiously administered another hundred milligrams and crossed her fingers.

The entrance to sickbay slid open and three more crew members rushed in, carrying the unconscious bodies of Lem and Milo Faal. She recognized Ensign Daniels, the security officer she sent in search of the missing patients, along with Ensign Gomez from Engineering and Lieutenant Sumi Lee from Science. "Dr. Crusher, over here," the EMH called out. The holographic MD was already helping Ensign Daniels get Lem Faal's limp body onto the nearest empty biobed. For once, Crusher was thankful that the gravity was out; it had to make transporting the two bodies easier.

"Keep an eye on Lieutenant Leyoro at Bed One," she instructed the EMH, racing toward the new arrivals. The heavy magnetic boots made her feel slow and clumsy. "Let me know if her brain activity increases by any factor."

"Understood," he said, without any of his usual sarcasm or grousing. Apparently even a hologram knew when there was no time for a bad attitude. He headed straight for Leyoro, his image flickering only for a second during a brief but worrisome power fluctuation. The lack of gravity did not slow him at all.

"I found him by a turbolift, sprawled on the floor," Ensign Daniels informed Crusher as she checked Lem Faal's vital signs. He was still alive, thank heavens, but unresponsive. He seemed to be whispering, having a feverish conversation with himself, but she strained to make out what he was saying.

"The wall . . . the wormhole . . . must bring down the wall. . . ."

To her slight surprise, his breathing sounded fine; the last time she had seen Faal he had been gasping for breath, his weakened lungs succumbing to the wasting effects of Iverson's disease.

"The boy was with me," Ensign Gomez explained as Crusher shifted her attention to the supine eleven-year-old form of Milo Faal, whom Gomez and Lee had lowered onto the next biobed. "He had gotten lost somehow, and I was escorting him back to sickbay when he suddenly clutched his head and collapsed." The memory brought on a shudder. "It was very strange. There was some sort of bizarre optical effect, maybe an X-ray discharge. For just a second, he looked like a photo-negative version of himself; then, in a flash, he looked normal again. I tried to wake him, but he was out cold. Then Lieutenant Lee found us."

The science officer nodded. "Lieutenant Commander Data had sent me to investigate a pocket of concentrated psionic energy he had detected from the bridge."

Crusher didn't like the sound of that. "Did you find the source of that energy?"

"Yes." Lee waved a standard tricorder in the direction of both Lem Faal and his son. "It's them."

"What do you mean?" Crusher asked. Milo's vital signs were encouraging, too. Neither of the Betazoids appeared to have been affected as severely, or in precisely the same way, as Baeta Leyoro.

Lee hesitated before answering, double-checking the display on her tricorder. "I can't be sure. Ensign Breslin is still scanning the corridors for any residual traces, but it seems like these two people have each absorbed a portion of the barrier's energy."

Is that even possible? Crusher wondered. *And what sort of effect could it have on them?* This was different from what had happened to Leyoro; that had been a severe neurological shock, potentially fatal, but still subject to medical understanding and treatment. But this . . . science couldn't even explain what the barrier was, let alone how that mysterious energy could sustain itself within an ordinary humanoid brain. She initiated a full diagnostic scan of both patients' brains, while placing Professor Faal under restraint, just in case he awoke on his own. She didn't want another violent episode like before.

The results of the scans were puzzling. The monitors above both father and son reported accelerated brain activity, but without the adverse side effects that had endangered Leyoro. It was as if their respective cerebellums were rapidly evolving and adapting to accommodate the greater demands being placed on them by the explosion of synaptic activity. The very structures of their brains were being reconfigured before her eyes. Even stranger, the sensors recorded *two* distinct sets of brain waves coexisting within Lem Faal's mind, as though one personality had been superimposed upon another. *Like during a Vulcan mind-meld,* she thought, remembering a similar dual pattern in a recent study from the Vulcan Science Academy.

Some form of psychic possession? Crusher speculated. She'd seen stranger things during her years aboard the *Enterprise,* and it might explain a lot about the scientist's increasingly erratic behavior. But who or what could be possessing Faal? The Calamarain or something else entirely? There was always Q, of course, but somehow this didn't feel like his style.

Taking a more hands-on approach to the examination, she gently reached out and raised one of Lem Faal's eyelids, wanting to check on his pupils. She let out a gasp, startling the three other crew members, as she was met by an unexpected sight. Faal's once-brown eye now glowed with an eerie white light that stared up at her, suffused with what had to be the energy of the galactic barrier itself.

"Oh my God," she whispered.

Four

The brightness faded and the fugitives, as well as Picard and the elder Q, were surrounded by four new individuals, clad in the intimidating armor of Roman legionnaires. Picard recognized the female Q, significantly younger than she had appeared upon the *Enterprise,* not to mention a stern-looking humanoid who bore an uncomfortable resemblance to himself. *One of Q's little jokes,* Picard theorized, recalling that the true appearances of the Q had been translated into images his human mind could comprehend. *Should I be flattered or insulted that Q keeps casting me as the heavy hand of authority?* He suspected the latter.

The remaining new arrivals were unfamiliar to him. One was a pale-skinned male, holding his crested bronze helmet against his breastplate, who looked about the same age as the young Q, with straight blond hair combed back away from his brow. He appeared nervous, looking back and forth among his fellow Q for support. The fourth newcomer, somewhat older than the others, had sad eyes, accented by mournful pouches, and a philosophic manner. "Good old Quinn," the original Q said beside Picard. "May he rest in peace."

The Q quartet raised their arms at their sides and coruscating beams of blue-white energy leaped from their fingertips, connecting with the outstretched hands of their associates to form an incandescent fence around 0 and the other malefactors, or, more accurately, a living quincunx with the young Q at its center. The brilliant beams crackled with unleashed power. Picard could not help feeling trapped, even though he knew that the hunters were not even aware of his presence.

The archaic armor donned by the Q only made them look more formidable. The scintillation of their discharged energy reflected off polished bronze helmets, cuirasses, and greaves. Crescent-shaped plumes of thick horsehair crested the Corinthian-style helmets that partially obscured their deceptively human features. Short, double-edged swords hung on their right hips, held on by a leather belt or baldric. While realizing that the historical costuming was largely an illusion created by Q, Picard had to admit that the ancient armor seemed more appropriate to this primeval conflict than, say, the plum-colored Starfleet uniforms he and Q now wore.

"You cannot hide from the Continuum," said the Q who could have been the captain's twin. Picard recognized his double's voice as that which had boomed from the heavens earlier. Apparently the spokesman for the Continuum had deigned to make a personal appearance after all. "Do not resist our judgment."

No, Picard thought, rethinking the matter. Not a spokesman, but a judge. An imperial Roman judge. A quaestor.

"Yes, Q," his future mate urged, resembling an Amazon in her martial regalia, "give up this lunacy before it's too late. You've gone too far this time."

"It's for the best, Q," said Quinn, more in sorrow than in anger. "I know you meant well."

"That's right," the blond Q added, attempting a not terribly convincing smile. Picard guessed he was a friend and contemporary of Q's. "Hey, I misplaced the entire Deltived Asteroid Belt once, but it all turned out okay in the end."

Unlike the rest of the tribunal, who seemed to have Q's best interests at heart, the quaestor had no patience with the erring youth and his dubious acquaintances. His Picardian expression was deadly serious. "Q is our problem and will be dealt with accordingly. The rest must be banished forthwith."

Penned in by the power of his peers, young Q rose to his feet. His simulated Adam's apple bobbed sheepishly as he opened his mouth to speak. *What course will he take now?* Picard wondered. Would he surrender without a fight?

0 made the decision for him. "Never!" he cried, firing a blast of searing energy from his hands at the immense dilithium crystal beneath them and triggering a matter-

antimatter explosion that flung them all, through countless layers of liquid and vapor, out of the gas giant's majestic atmosphere into the icy vacuum of space. Picard felt himself being propelled at incredible speeds, like a quantum torpedo fresh from its launcher tube. Agonizing G-forces yanked the flesh of his face tightly against his skull as he achieved escape velocity from the gravitational sway of the Brobdingnagian planet. He was unable to halt or even control his headlong flight through the Detrian system. *Blast you, Q,* he cursed as he rocketed helplessly. *You could have warned me.*

Finally, after several endless moments, some sort of metaphysical friction, or perhaps the cushioning effect of numerous quantum filaments, curbed his momentum and brought him to a stop somewhere outside the solar system he had just been forcibly expelled from. To his annoyance, he found Q waiting for him, looking none the worse for wear. "My, I had forgotten how exhilarating that was," he observed. "Hope you enjoyed the ride, Jean-Luc."

Picard gave Q a withering look. "Never mind me," he said darkly. "What happened to 0 and the others?"

"Look behind you." Q shook his head glumly and affected a pained expression. "I'm afraid it's turned into something of a free-for-all."

The battle was fought on a cosmic scale. As Picard looked on from what he prayed was a safe distance, colossal figures strode the stars, hurling entire planets and suns at each other. Millennia passed in what felt like seconds as the war against 0 wreaked havoc on what Starfleet would later name the Alpha Quadrant. Picard tried to take it all in, but it was impossible to do more than glimpse fragmentary snapshots of the unthinkable devastation:

The gleaming plate armor of The One, more appropriate to the Age of Chivalry, clashes anachronistically with the Roman war gear of the blond Q, who has reluctantly hidden his face behind his plumed helmet. Determined to resist capture, He saps the energy of a nearby star, turning it against His foe. On the third planet orbiting that sun, the days grow ever colder, forcing an unsuspecting people to cope with the incidental consequences of a conflict beyond their understanding. . . .

The android Ruk stood upon a snow-covered hilltop on Exo III, watching as massive drilling machines carved a cavern into the face of a granite cliff. Many such caverns were being dug these days, as his Creators sought to escape the freezing conditions upon the surface by seeking shelter deep beneath the planet's crust. He and his fellow androids would join the Creators underground, serving the Creators as they always had. There would be many changes in the days to come, as both androids and the Creators adapted to their new subterranean existence, but Ruk was confident that he would continue to function effectively regardless of any unexpected alterations in the parameters of his existence. Had not the Creators programmed him to adapt and survive?

An icy wind blew flakes of frozen moisture against the angular planes of his face. His dermal sensors recorded that the external temperature was several units below the freezing point, but he did not feel the cold as a Creator might. His massive body was immune to pain or discomfort. His heavy feet sank deep into packed layers of snow and permafrost that would never ever thaw.

No one knew, not even the finest minds among the Creators, why the sun had grown steadily colder year after year. None knew how to reverse the process. All the Creators could do was burrow toward the planet's core in search of the warmth they needed to survive. Ruk admired their resolute determination to outlive the fading sun. The Creators were teaching him an important lesson.

Nothing was more important than survival.

(*) thrives on war, so war it incites, feeding on the chaos it creates to find the strength it needs to fend off the scholarly Q with the sad eyes, whose metaphorical spears rain on (*) without cease. On yet another world, caught unbeknownst in the midst of the celestial war, it discovers a people whose mental gifts, and towering ambitions, leave them ideally suited to its purposes. . . .

"But, Sargon, are you absolutely sure this is necessary?" Thalassa asked. "Isn't there some other way?"

Sargon considered his wife's plaintive entreaty. It was indeed a lot he was asking of her, of all of them, but they had no choice. His eyes swept over the austere lines of the hastily constructed vault. Row upon row of steel niches ran along the opposite wall, stretching the entire length of the futuristic catacomb, each niche holding a single translucent globe. All but two of the spheres glowed from within, holding the psychic essences of valiant comrades. One of the remaining globes awaited Thalassa.

"It is the only solution," he said solemnly. "According to my calculations, the forces unleashed by the war will soon rip away the entire atmosphere, rendering our world uninhabitable. Only by storing our minds in these receptacles can we hope to preserve some vestige of our population and culture."

"But to live without bodies of our own? And for how long?" She stared in anguish at her own hands, memorizing the fragile complexity of the flesh and bone she soon must sacrifice forever. "It's horrible."

Sargon nodded. "Perhaps it is the price we must pay for our terrible arrogance." *The coming cataclysm is no one's fault but our own,* he thought. *We dared to think of ourselves as gods and look what has become of us.*

"Speak for yourself, Sargon," a sardonic voice requested. Henoch strolled toward the elderly scientist and his wife, smiling. The representative from the Northern Coalition smiled more than any man Sargon had ever met; it was one of the reasons he distrusted him. "I take no responsibility for the precarious position we now find ourselves in. Perhaps you should have said as much to your own generals, before they challenged our claim to the borderlands."

Sargon frowned, resisting the temptation to strike out at the foreigner with the power of his mind. "You are here as a gesture of peace," he reminded Henoch, "in hopes of future harmony among our people. Do not abuse our generosity by baiting me with your self-serving propaganda."

Henoch shrugged. "I suppose it is rather too late to argue politics at this point. If I did not think the war unwinnable by either side, I would not have joined you here today." He scratched his chin speculatively. "Funny, though, how quickly the conflict escalated, almost as if powers beyond our ken were somehow pulling our strings, setting us against each other."

You seek to blame anyone but yourself, Sargon thought, wondering once more whether it was wise to include Henoch and a handful of his followers among those whose consciousness would be stored in the receptacles, against the far-off day when they might live again. He did not care for Henoch, whose affable charm barely concealed a scheming nature, but he and his people were part of the society

Sargon had worked so hard to preserve. To exclude them from this final chance for salvation would be an act of selfishness and paranoia comparable to those that had doomed their world. *For better or for worse, he is one of us.*

An explosion upon the surface, several miles overhead, shook the vault despite its reinforced steel walls. The war was drawing nearer and growing more intense. "It is time, my love," he told his wife.

"I am ready," she said bravely and approached one of the dormant spheres, securely tucked away in its recess. For the last time, save in memory, Sargon gazed upon the physical form of his lifelong mate and partner, savoring the elegant arch of her eyebrows, the delicate tips of her pointed ears. Then she laid her palms upon the curved shell of the receptacle and closed her eyes in concentration. "Until we live again," she said.

A bluish glow flared within the sphere only an instant before a bright red nimbus spread over her body. Sargon wanted to look away, but could not, standing by passively as the scarlet energy consumed every trace of Thalassa's corporeal remains, leaving not an atom behind. Only when her body had been completely disintegrated, her life force transferred to the interior of the globe, did he lower his face into his hands and sob.

From a technical standpoint, it was not necessary to destroy the body while transferring the mind, but practically there was no better alternative, lest the underground vault become a charnel house. Judging from the sound of the battle being waged above, soon there would be no one left to dispose of the bodies of those whose thoughts and memories now resided within the receptacles. *Forgive me,* he thought to the glowing globe that held his wife's spirit. *Forgive us all.*

"So you actually went through with it," Henoch observed, inspecting Thalassa's receptacle before wandering over to the last empty sphere visible within the catacomb. "I insisted upon being the last to go, just in case there was trickery afoot, but seeing that you were genuinely willing to sacrifice your own wife to this farfetched scheme, I suppose I might as well trust you one crucial step further." He ran a finger over the empty globe, inspecting it for dust. "So how long do you expect we will wait in this underground mausoleum before some wayfaring space travelers drop by to say hello?"

Sargon wished he knew. "Perhaps only a few hundred years. Perhaps forever. The receptacles will preserve our essences for half a million years, maybe longer. Time enough, I hope, for interplanetary explorers to stumble onto the ruins of our civilization, perhaps providing us with new bodies with which to greet tomorrow." If only there had been time to construct android bodies for their dispossessed souls, to provide them with mobility after the turmoil on the surface died out, but the war had come upon them too quickly. Indeed, it was a small miracle that he had succeeded in preparing this vault and these few receptacles before the inevitable catastrophe rendered organic life impossible on this planet for all time to come. "It seems probable that other species will explore the stars, just as our own ancestors did. We can only pray that our alien successors will possess the curiosity and the compassion to free us from our long imprisonment."

"You pray, old man," Henoch responded. "For myself, I just hope that our future bodies, if any, won't be too unappealing in appearance." He laid his hands upon the final dormant sphere, then glanced back over his shoulder, a mocking smile upon his face as always. "Let me guess, it won't hurt a bit."

A moment later, nothing was left of Henoch except a constant glow at the center of his chosen orb. Sargon could not say he missed him. *If I don't hear his voice again for half a million years, then that might be a blessing of sorts.*

Now it was his turn. With a mental command, he extinguished the lights in the catacomb, so that only the collected life force of his fellow refugees illuminated the chamber as he left it behind and entered an adjacent compartment only half the size of the depository he had departed. There a solitary globe, as yet unlighted, rested atop a central podium linked to the most advanced sensor apparatus Sargon could assemble in the face of the mounting hostilities above. Here was where his consciousness would wait out eternity, searching the heavens for the instruments of their deliverance. Unlike Henoch and Thalassa and the rest, whose minds would dwell in dreamless slumber until they were awakened once more, a portion of his psyche would remain aware throughout the centuries, probing the empty corridors of space and sending out an urgent plea for assistance to whatever enterprising beings might someday pass this way.

As he placed his palms against the cool, inanimate surface of the receptacle, and felt his mind flowing out of his body and into the motionless sphere, he wondered how long he would truly have to wait.

The female Q has Gorgan on the run. His seraphic features melt into a hideous mask of bestial fury, only partially obscured by his verdant aura, as he snarls back at his relentless pursuer. Sensing a convenient wormhole, he dives toward that tantalizing means of egress, but some unknown presence within the wormhole blocks his entrance long enough for the Q to catch up with him. She cuts off his retreat with a searing blast of fifth-dimensional fire and he retaliates in kind. . . .

Brightly colored lights streaked the night sky above the western hemisphere of Bajor. Upon a balcony at the top of the highest tower in the temple, the kai watched a burst of chartreuse flame erupt in the heavens, then sputter and die as it traced its way above the horizon. More eruptions filled the sky in its wake, obscuring ancient constellations and outshining the stars. It was as though the Celestial Temple itself was on fire.

"What is it, Holiness?" asked Vedek Kuros fearfully, tugging on the kai's silken sleeve to draw her attention down from the inexplicable stellar pyrotechnics. "Is it the Reckoning?"

The kai shook her head thoughtfully, causing the ornate silver chain dangling from her ear to sway back and forth. "I think not," she said. "The Sacred Texts are very clear that the Reckoning shall not occur until after the Coming of the Emissary." She gave him a playful smile. "You haven't, by any chance, neglected to inform me of the Emissary's arrival, have you?"

"Oh no, Holiness!" the vedek insisted. "How could I? I wouldn't dream of it."

"Calm yourself, Kuros, I was only joking." She reached out to cup his ear and sensed that his *pagh* was deeply troubled by the curious lights in the sky. "The Reckoning is not yet upon us. This is something far different, I think."

The vedek was not alone in his fears, she knew. From her lofty perch high above the sacred city of B'hala, she could see the people gathered in the great square below, their eyes turned upward in awe and terror. Hundreds of Bajorans, from every clan and *D'jarra,* surrounded the monumental stone *bantaca* in the center of the city, perplexed and unnerved by the violent heavenly display, but unable to look away.

The vivid colors of the celestial explosions cast a shifting spectrum of shadows upon the faces and rooftops beneath her. It was as beautiful as it was mysterious.

I must issue some manner of statement, the kai realized, knowing it was her duty to comfort her people in this time of turmoil, *but what can I tell them?* Nothing in the Sacred Texts spoke of such tumult amid the firmament nor hinted when the unnatural phenomenon might cease. In her heart of hearts, she knew that the dazzling portents lighting up the night were not the work of the Prophets, nor even the unholy mischief of the dreaded *Pah*-wraiths. Those powerful beings, both the good and the wicked, were of Bajor. These disturbances, she sensed deep within her own *pagh,* were something different, something alien to them all, but no less dangerous to all who lived.

The strange lights shone on for a thousand days. . . .

The furious struggle between the Q and the forces of 0 attract the interest of other transcendent beings. Some such entities come to investigate. . . .

"Q," Picard asked. "Who are those beings over there?" He gestured toward a quartet of humanoid figures standing silently at the perimeter of the war, looking on with pained expressions upon their faces. Unlike the combatants, they had not assumed the garb of Earth's ancient warriors, wearing instead simple Grecian chitons made of what looked like common wool. Their faces were youthful and unmarked by time. They clasped their hands together before their chests in a meditative pose. Picard was struck by the aura of peace and dignity the beings projected, which reminded him somewhat of the sadly departed Sarak of Vulcan.

"Oh, *them,*" Q said disdainfully. "Those are the Organians. Relative youngsters compared to the Continuum, but still reasonably evolved at this point in galactic history."

The Organians, Picard thought, wide-eyed and astounded. They were semi-mythical beings in his own time, legendary for their historic role in averting a bloody war between the Federation and the Klingon Empire decades before Picard's birth. The Organians had largely kept to themselves since then; Picard had never thought that he might actually see one in person.

Q was considerably less awestruck. "A bunch of upstart, idealistic kids, really. Slackers and layabouts, all of them. Compared to their childish doctrine of pacifism and noninterference, your Prime Directive is practically an incitement to riot."

Picard took Q's assessment of the early Organians with a grain of salt; small wonder Q dismissed a people who practiced the virtues of forbearance and restraint. The Federation of his own time owed a lot to the reluctant peacemaking of these people or their descendants. Still, he could not deny that the Organians of this era seemed content to stay on the sidelines during the Continuum's heated struggle to subdue 0. As he watched the cosmic battle develop, his doppelgänger among the Q plucked a steel-tipped lance from the ether and hurled it at 0 himself, who materialized a disk-shaped shield just in time to block the spear. Deflected, the weapon ricocheted toward the assembled Organians, who merely shook their heads sadly at its approach. The spear vanished only seconds before it would have struck the placid spectators, followed a heartbeat later by the Organians themselves. The four figures dissolved into the emptiness of space, having apparently seen enough of the barbaric melee.

"And good riddance," Q commented derisively. "You know what they say, Jean-Luc, if you're not part of the solution, you're part of the whole god-awful mess."

"Is that so?" Picard asked. "Your younger self doesn't appear to be contributing much to the situation, one way or another."

It was true. The young Q cowered in a desolate corner of space, apart from the others, looking distinctly miserable and conflicted. He squatted in the vacuum, rocking back and forth on his heels, as he peered at the furious hostilities through his fingers as he held both hands over his face. It was a far cry from the preening arrogance Q would display in the future. "It's all my fault," he whispered, although no one but Picard and his older self was listening. "What have I done?"

"Q!" 0 cried, besieged by the leader of the Q, who seemed to have an inexhaustible supply of spears. "Cease your babbling and help me, friend. We're under attack here!"

"Don't listen to him, Q." Always a tall woman, the female Q was nothing short of imposing in her armor. She thrust at Gorgan with her short sword while shouting at Q. The deceptively angelic entity pounded his fists atop each other, invoking his power, but the sword kept cutting closer and closer to his emerald aura. "He's not your friend. You don't owe him anything."

"She's just jealous," 0 insisted, parrying another assault from his grim opponent. His iron shield transformed into a rubber trampoline that bounced the other Q's spear back at him. The quaestor ducked promptly, but the rebounding lance sliced the crest off his helmet. A gigantic crescent of horsehair flew off into a nearby nebula where it would later confound generations of Iconian explorers. "They're all jealous. They envy our vitality, our courage and freedom. They can't stand that we actually have the guts to enjoy our omnipotence as we see fit, that we want to shake things up instead of simply maintaining the status quo. They want to destroy us because we prove how weak and impotent the rest of them really are." Seizing the offensive, he fired at his foe with a crossbow that hadn't existed a second before. "Do you want to be destroyed, Q?"

"No one will be destroyed," the quaestor promised, "if you surrender now." The bolt from the crossbow spontaneously combusted before it could strike home. The young Q looked up hopefully at the quaestor's words, a reaction that did not go unnoticed by 0.

"You might as well annihilate us all," he bellowed as he loaded another quarrel into the crossbow. "What's the alternative? Submitting to the will of the Continuum, condemned to an eternal half-life of dull conformity and anonymity? No, I'd rather take my chances here, and if you're smart, Q, you'll do the same!"

The young Q reacted by throwing his hands over his ears to keep the sound of the debate away from him. He squeezed his eyes shut and let out a mournful howl that could be heard even above the clang of armor and weaponry. *Not the most mature response,* Picard noted, *but strangely in character. Only Q could think that the universe and all its dilemmas would go away if he just ignored them.*

"I didn't know what to do," the later Q recalled. "I felt like unbridgeable chasms had cut me off from both 0 and the Continuum, but that neither side would let me alone. I was lost and alone in the middle of a war."

Like I was, Picard thought with a start, *after Locutus was captured from the Borg, but before Beverly restored my humanity.* He had been isolated, too, neither of humanity nor of the Collective, but an exile from each. *That was not at all the same thing,* he reminded himself hastily; unlike Q, he had not brought that hellish limbo upon himself. Still, he found himself identifying with the young Q more than he liked.

"Where are the other Q?" he asked, eager to change the subject. It dawned on him that he had no idea how many individuals comprised the entire Continuum. Were these four pseudo-legionnaires the sole extent of Q's peers? That seemed unlikely; he had always gotten the impression that the Q's population was as infinite as their abilities.

"Putting out fires, mostly," Q answered. "In case you haven't noticed, this particular donnybrook is producing no end of collateral damage on various planes of existence. A battle between beings of our exalted nature does more than break a few windows, Jean-Luc; why, during a recent civil war among the Q, in your own far-off century, there were supernovas going off all over the Delta Quadrant." He shuddered at the memory. "To be honest, those fractures in the galactic barrier, the ones that your Federation scientists are so keen on, are actually a regrettable aftereffect of that nasty little war."

Now he tells me, Picard thought, although he still wasn't sure what the barrier had to do with 0 and this hard-fought conflict in the distant past. *Why am I here?*

"Anyway," Q continued, "the majority of the Continuum are occupied with patching up the most grievous wounds in the fabric of reality, leaving a few close friends and associates to deal with me personally. In their own inimitable fashion, of course."

Q's explanation sounded plausible enough. Now that he knew to look for them, Picard thought he glimpsed phantom figures scurrying about in the background. They were like shadows, insubstantial silhouettes moving almost too fast to be seen, going about their mysterious errands like stagehands at work behind the scenes of some massive theatrical production. *Are they always there,* Picard mused, spying them only out of the corner of his eye, *or only during a crisis of this magnitude?* Despite all he had witnessed, there was still so much he did not understand about the metaphysical realm the Q inhabited.

"So I see," he said, turning his thoughts to less ineffable matters. "And just how long did this personal matter go on, Q? Strange as this may seem to you, I am anxious to return to my own life at some point."

"If you must know," Q said, "this ugly altercation lasted a mere one hundred thousand years as you reckon time." He nodded toward the celestial battlefield. "Look, the tide is already starting to turn."

His face a twisted mass of lumpen flesh, his shimmering robes reduced to smoking, blackened rags, Gorgan was the first to abandon the fight. His insubstantial form wavered in the void like a mirage above the desert. Turning his back on the female Q and her slashing sword, he fled through space with the armored woman in hot pursuit. Desperate to escape her, he raced back to the very site of the Tkon Empire's destruction, diving into the gaping black hole that had once been their sun, apparently choosing to risk the unknown perils beyond the event horizon rather than face the wrath of the Q. "Coward!" the female Q called out. "Don't let me see you show your hideous face in this multiverse again."

Emboldened by its comrade's escape, (*) retreated from the fray as well. Quinn lowered his sword arm, showing little interest in chasing after the evil entity now that it had been routed. He heaved a heavy sigh, gratefully removing his helmet, as (*) disappeared down the black hole after Gorgan. The hungry gravitational vortex swallowed up every last flicker of (*)'s bloodthirsty light.

"They're just letting them get away?" Picard asked. He knew that neither entity had truly been destroyed. If Q was to be believed, both Gorgan and (*) would later bedevil James T. Kirk in the twenty-third century.

"Without 0, they're petty nuisances at best," Q said with a shrug. "From now on, they'll be forced to lurk furtively in the most obscure recesses of the galaxy, preying like highwaymen on the occasional unwary starship. Nothing the Q need worry about, in other words."

"Your concern for the rest of us is overwhelming," Picard pointed out dryly.

"It's all a matter of scale, Jean-Luc. Haven't you figured that out yet?" Q grabbed Picard by the shoulders and forcibly turned his view away from the insatiable black hole and back toward the sector of space where 0 and The One continued to contend against the Continuum with every weapon at their disposal, apparently undaunted by the desertion of two of their allies. "Now, that pair posed rather more of a problem."

Disdaining symbolic weaponry, The One unleashed lightning bolts from His fingertips. The scent of ozone wafted through the vacuum as the electrical barrage held Q's friend at bay. "Heathen! Infidel!" The One raged, the luster of His golden armor undimmed. Overlapping metal plates covered The One's entire body from the neck down; only His forbidding visage remained uncovered. "Feel the power of My Holy Anger. Quake in terror, O foolish one, as My Mighty Hand strikes you down."

"That remains to be seen," the Q shot back, his blond locks concealed beneath his helmet. His superior tone resembled Q's, although not quite as scathing in its sarcasm. "The Q do not quake."

He ducked his head beneath the upper edge of a bronze, rectangular shield. His cautious stance, crouched behind his protective shield, testified to the intensity of The One's thunderbolts. Although Q had said that the battle was turning against 0 and his allies, Picard saw no sign of imminent defeat where The One was concerned; if anything, the monotheistic monster had the advantage against the opposing Q. Even His burnished plate armor, worthy of a medieval knight, appeared superior to the primitive Bronze Age gear of the Q warriors.

"Curb thy mocking tongue," He declared, advancing on the Q, His fulsome beard framing His stern features like the mane of a roaring lion. "The time of thy chastisement is at hand."

"Not if I have anything to say about it," the Q retorted from behind his shield, whose gleaming surface was now dented and scorched in places. He backed away from The One, holding up his shield all the while. Sparks flew from the battered shield as The One's relentless pace consumed the distance between Himself and His intended victim. "Q! Oh, Q!" the overwhelmed Q called out to his compatriots. "Help me out over here! Better sooner than later!"

Picard had no way of knowing exactly which Q the imperiled entity was addressing, but his cry for help drew both the female Q and Quinn to his side. The sad-eyed Quinn came back to the fracas reluctantly, his expression not unlike the Organians', but his Amazonian companion was all too eager to take on another foe. "There's a black hole waiting for you, too," she taunted The One, placing herself between the oncoming deity and her endangered associate. Her shield blocked bolt after bolt from The One, and she retaliated with an energy blast of her own that stopped The One in His heavenly tracks. Quinn followed her lead, protecting the third Q with his shield while firing a beam of sizzling heat from his free hand.

"Strumpet!" The One cursed, halting where He stood. "Witch!" He beat one gauntleted hand against the molded steel of His breastplate, producing a resounding clang that sounded even in the silent depths of interstellar space. The female Q's attack bounced harmlessly off His chest, while Quinn's heat ray merely caused the fringes of His beard to smoke and smolder. Even with the odds now three against one, He refused to give up, proving Himself a more dangerous and determined adversary than either Gorgan or (*). "Be thou false gods as plentiful as sands upon a beach, yet The One shall vanquish you all. None there is who can stand against The One. Great is My Glory, inescapable is My Severe and Final Judgment."

"Please," the female Q said, rolling her eyes. "Only a Q has the right to be so insufferably full of herself." She glared at Him through narrowed eyes, her classically sculpted jaw set firmly. "Q, Q," she addressed her brothers-in-arms, "let's show this tiresome pretender what all-powerful really means."

Together, the three Q rose from behind their antique shields, uniting their wills against the common foe. The One clenched His metal gauntlets and hurled lightning from His eyes, but the jagged thunderbolts crashed uselessly against an invisible wall that left the row of grim-faced Q untouched by the tumultuous attack. Picard heard a deep, resonant hum rising from where the three Q stood side by side. Even from a distance, he could feel the power swelling between them, growing ever more indomitable as their respective energies came into synch. There was a tension building in the nonexistent atmosphere, like the hush that precedes a storm. The vacuum hummed like the engine room of the *Enterprise* right before it went into warp.

At last, even The One appeared daunted by the trinity of Q. He took an uncertain step backward, retreating from the light, while doubt blurred the rigid imperturbability of His features. "I am My Own Deliverance," he chanted, but His voice lacked the Old Testament certainty of before, "I shall not quaver in My Resolve. I am The One!"

"Oh, lighten up," the female Q said in return.

A dazzling aura enveloped the three figures, uniting them within a single shimmering nimbus of energy. The light was so bright that Picard had to look away, the unexpected blaze leaving dancing blue spots before his sight. He raised a hand before his face to protect his suddenly watery eyes from the glare.

"Pure, raw Q power," Q told Picard. "Lacking in style somewhat, but effective."

An instant later, The One's right leg disappeared. There was no beam or weapon employed, no projectile force or matter penetrated the armor and amputated the limb; it simply ceased to exist, erased bloodlessly from the Q's level of reality. The One stared down in shock at the space His leg had occupied. "No," He murmured, his vainglorious self-worship shaken, "this cannot be." But even as He spoke, His remaining leg vanished, followed by His right arm. His truncated body, encased in the remains of His armor, floated awkwardly in space. "Stop it!" He commanded. "I am The One. I am eternal!"

The Q systematically dismembered Him. They bloodlessly erased His solitary arm, then His armored torso and throat, until all that remained was His bearded head, floating disembodied in space as It screamed obscenities at the heavens.

The severed head, looking like a bust of some forgotten prophet, drifted away from the battlefield, while the cosmos echoed with the sound of His bellicose vows of vengeance. "Perhaps we should delete His tongue as well," the female Q suggested, the light about the trio dimming gradually.

"Let's not be savages," Quinn advised her. "Even the damned deserve to give voice to their torment."

"If you say so," she said, sounding none too convinced. "I think He's a frightful boor who deserves everything He gets."

"Let's just call it a win," the third Q urged, his shoulders sagging forward. "I don't know about you two, but I'm positively tapped out. A mere stellar breeze could blow me away."

He had a point. By now the luminous halo surrounding the trio had faded enough that Picard could once more look upon them directly. He wiped salty tears from his eyes as his vision cleared. All three Q were breathing hard and looked exhausted, although the female Q was doing her best to maintain her customary hauteur. Q's contemporary and chum removed his helmet and Picard saw that his blond hair was pasted to his skull by perspiration. "That was more difficult than I expected," he said. "How ever do lesser species manage to fight wars all the time?"

"I know what you mean," Quinn agreed, leaning forward with his hands upon his knees. Even in the absence of gravity, he acted like he could barely support his own weight. His helmet disappeared in a blink, horsehair crest and all. The bags beneath his eyes looked deeper than before. "Just wait until you're my age."

"This isn't over yet," the female Q chided them, despite her own evident fatigue. The last glimmer of their amplified aura quietly expired, and she strode away from them toward her future husband, still crouching amid infinity, unable to tear his aghast gaze away from the endless clash between 0 and the authoritative Q who so resembled Picard. Both parties in the duel paused barely an instant to acknowledge the brutal defeat of The One.

"You are alone now," the spokesman for the Q intoned. "Your foul creatures fled or undone." Spears and crossbow had given way to crossed swords. 0 and the Q fought with silver blades as everyone from Picard to the miserable young Q looked on. The ring of steel against steel rang paradoxically through the vacuum as the unforgiving Q sought to subdue his foe. An avid fencer himself, Picard saw no flaw in his doppelgänger's technique, although 0 fought back with an undeniably effective mixture of calculation and ferocity. "Abandon this irrational resistance," he demanded. "Surrender to the judgment of the Continuum."

"Never!" 0 swung his scimitar at his opponent's head, only to be blocked by an upward parry of the Q's shining saber. "And I'm not alone. Young Q will come to my aid yet, you'll see!"

Surely the strangest aspect of this cosmic swordfight, Picard observed at once, was that the precise nature of the duelists' blades kept changing from second to second. As Picard studied the fight, critiquing every feint and parry, 0's curved scimitar became a cutlass, then a broadsword, then a Klingon *bat'leth*. Likewise, the Q's weapon of choice transformed sequentially into an elegant épée, a rapier, a Scottish claymore, and a Romulan *gladius*. Regardless of their shape, all the blades appeared constructed of the same indestructible material; although sparks flew when the protean swords met each other, neither blade broke beneath its adversary, no matter how overmatched one might seem when compared to the size or weight of the other. Both blades, after all, were not really made of tempered steel, but were in fact tangible extensions of the duelists' preternatural powers of concentration. *I wonder what this actually looks like,* Picard mused, *from a perspective of a Q.*

"Take that, you draconian dictator!" 0 said, laughing exuberantly. He thrust the point of an Italian *cinquedea* at the Q, barely missing the other's hip. "I defy your despotic Continuum and its suffocating sobriety. Q is the only one of you with any spark of talent or initiative in him. He'll see that, too, after I've destroyed the lot of you!"

There had to be a reason 0 cowed The One and the others, Picard guessed; he had to be the most puissant of them all. The captain wished he knew more about where 0 had come from originally, before Q found him in that interdimensional wasteland. What manner of being was he really? All Picard knew was that 0 was something darker and far more dangerous than the charming rogue he occasionally feigned being. That congenial facade was rapidly slipping away as he hacked and slashed at the Q with a long *katana*. "See, Q," he hollered to his hesitant protégé, "you've no need to fear the likes of these sour-faced spoilsports. Never fear! Never again!"

The female Q had a different idea. Still panting from the exertion required to dismantle The One, she reached Q's side and yanked his hands away from his ears. "Look at me!" she pleaded, throwing away her helmet so she could confront him face-to-face. "Look at them." She compelled him to open his eyes and behold his fellows. "You're one of us, Q, and you always will be."

Hearing her impassioned declaration, 0 scowled and risked glancing away from his intricate duel with the lead Q. If looks could kill, which in 0's case was a distinct possibility, the female Q would have been incinerated instantly. Since that didn't occur, he was forced to resort to other measures. A stray asteroid, consisting of several million tons of solid iridium, passed within his field of vision and, without missing a stroke of his swordplay, he snatched up the asteroid with his free hand, imbuing it with a lethal quantity of energy, and sent it hurling toward the female Q like an assassin's bullet.

"Watch this, Picard," the later Q advised. "You may find it of interest."

Caught up in her efforts to bring the young Q to his senses, the female Q did not notice the deadly asteroid rocketing toward her unshielded head at nearly warp speed. Her future husband spotted it, though. "Look out!" he shouted, pushing her out of the line of fire—which left the accelerated asteroid zooming toward him.

Reacting faster than light, Q ripped open the fabric of space-time, creating a gash in creation between himself and the speeding projectile. The asteroid flew into the fissure, where it traveled backward in time and space until it emerged back into reality on a collision course with the third planet of an obscure solar system countless lightyears, and millions of years, away from the heart of the battle. With Q's power enhancing his perceptions, Picard had no problem recognizing the blue-green orb that the asteroid slammed into with breathtaking force. *"Mon dieu,"* he gasped. "That's Earth!"

"So much for the dinosaurs," Q said, shrugging.

Picard was staggered by the implications of what he had just seen, watching in horror as a cloud of dust and ash enshrouded the entire planet, cutting it off from the warmth of the sun. "You can't be serious," he gasped. "Surely, you don't mean—"

"No use crying over spilled iridium," Q said curtly. He clapped his hands and the catastrophic collision receded from view. "As fascinating as that little sideshow must be, given your provincial roots, we mustn't neglect the main event, especially since my younger self is finally emerging from his morass of confusion, and after a mere one hundred millennia."

Numb with shock, Picard let his eyes wander back to the pitched combat between 0 and the quaestor. . . .

He almost killed Q, the young Q thought in amazement. He could scarcely imagine such a thing, let alone witness it with his own all-seeing eyes. Obliterating the Tkon was one thing; tasteless and excessive and even sadistic, true, but still only affecting one mortal population. But to threaten the immortality of a Q . . . !

And 0 appeared perfectly willing to do so again. At this very moment, he menaced another Q with a sword in each hand, assailing the Continuum's implacable quaestor with a bayonet clenched in one and a *kukri* dagger in the other. The savage intensity of his onslaught was slowly but surely winning out over the meticulous fencing skills of the Q, who clearly lacked 0's gleeful hunger for the kill. The Q fought defensively, wielding a darting saber, but he was beaten backward by 0's vicious blows. The stranger's shapeshifting sword rang against the other's metal cuirass and greaves as he repeatedly slipped past the Q's desperate parries. "See," 0 called to the young Q, "the Continuum doesn't stand a chance. And it's all thanks to you!"

He's right, Q realized. *Q can never forgive me for what I've done, none of them can.*

But maybe that wasn't the point. He had never really wanted the Continuum's approval anyway. Far from it, in fact. All he ever truly craved was the courage to follow his own instincts, no matter where they led.

Driven back by the simultaneous thrusts of a Viking broadsword and an Apache tomahawk, the quaestor tripped over a constellation. He tumbled through space, momentarily out of control, while his weapon slipped from his fingers, evaporating into the ether. 0 pounced on the opportunity; by the time the quaestor righted himself, the point of a sharpened leg bone was at his throat. "Pay close attention," 0 instructed Q, "and you'll see how to deal with opposition. This pallid entity"—he pressed the tip of his prehistoric pigsticker hard enough to spill a drop of luminous silver ichor—"will never dampen our fire again. Never!"

Q glanced about him in a panic. The other Q stood by helplessly, even his formidable girlfriend. He could sense that they were all too depleted to rescue their leader, even if they knew how to extricate him from his perilous situation. "Wait!" he asked 0 desperately, stalling for time while he tried to figure out what to do.

"What for?" 0 demanded, brandishing the primitive poniard beneath the other Q's chin. "Admit it, Q. You've wanted to do this a hundred times before."

True enough, he conceded. There had been times when he would have liked nothing better than to run the Continuum through with an ectoplasmic skewer. He recalled all those occasions in his turbulent childhood and early youth when this particular Q had disciplined and restrained him, imposing odious limits on the young Q's freewheeling imagination. All he needed to do now, Q recognized, was stand aside and let 0 deliver a killing blow that might scare off the rest of the Continuum for an eternity or two. Total freedom, unlimited anarchy, beckoned. He could do whatever he pleased. He could become just like 0. . . .

"I have a better idea," he said.

In a fraction of a second, the young Q traded places with the Q who resembled Picard. Suddenly, the tip of 0's weapon was poised at Q's throat instead, with the quaestor safely out of the way.

Now it was 0's turn to be disoriented. He blinked in disbelief as his mouth fell open. The point of the sharpened bone wobbled in his grip. "I don't understand," he began. "What are you do—"

Q grabbed on to the bone with both hands and sent a powerful galvanic current rushing down the length of the filed tibia into 0's manifested form. The stranger twitched spasmodically as the shock coursed through him, and, for an instant, Q caught a glimpse of subliminal tentacles writhing in pain. His shoes blew off his feet while the ruffled sleeves of 0's linen shirt burst into flames. 0 stared at Q with a look

of anguished betrayal in his bulging blue eyes. "How could you?" he gasped before
his bad leg gave out and he collapsed face-first toward the empty abyss of space.

In a strange, uncomfortable sort of way, Q felt as if he had struck down a part
of himself.

Five

"Handle with care the spider's net,
You can't be sure that a trap's not set. . . ."

The young Q stood in dock before the high tribunal of the Continuum, along with
0 and, disturbingly, the disembodied head of The One. Chained and manacled, 0
crooned to himself, his mind seemingly undone by this latest defeat. He rattled his
chains in time with his demented ditty and refused to look at Q.

Only a few paces away, with neither arms nor legs to fetter, nor even a torso on
which to slither snakelike upon the floor, the severed head of The One had been confined within a sturdy metal cage resting on the floor of the courtroom. His angry eyes,
impossibly alive, glared through the bars of the cage while he ground his teeth together impotently, reminding Picard of those rare occasions on which Data's head had
been detached from his body. But Data had never looked so enraged and vengeful.

"Is this it?" Picard asked. "The end of the war?"

"Almost," Q promised. "All that remains is the disposition of the prisoners, including myself."

The female Q, still armored Amazonian-style, stood guard between the two outsiders and the young Q, ready to defend Q should either of the alien entities attempt
to exact revenge on Q for his betrayal. Her hand rested on the sword at her side. The
two other Qs sat in the jury box, looking on with solemn expressions. They had retained their armor, but removed their plumed helmets out of respect for the court.

Picard's doppelgänger stared down at the prisoners from an elevated seat behind a high black bench. He had exchanged his armor for a Roman toga, and a
crown of laurel leaves rested upon his hairless dome. Recalling the memorable instances in which the later Q had placed Picard (and the rest of humanity) on trial,
the real Jean-Luc found it oddly satisfying to see the roles reversed for once.

No walls or ceiling enclosed the courtroom of the Continuum. Tipping back his
head, Picard could see the entire Milky Way Galaxy spread out overhead. To think,
he mused, that that shimmering spiral of stars and solar systems, a hundred thousand
light-years in diameter, contained the whole of the Alpha, Beta, Delta, and Gamma
Quadrants, holding every species and civilization from the Borg to the Dominion to
countless new life-forms as yet unknown. Even in his own time, Starfleet had explored only a fraction of the galaxy above. It was a humbling thought.

The quaestor brought down his gavel, calling the court to attention. "Enemies
of the Q Continuum," he addressed 0 and The One in as stern a voice as Picard had
ever heard. "You have been accused of malicious mischief and conduct unbecom-
ing that of highly advanced entities."

"I reject your authority," 0 protested, breaking off from his song and shaking
his adamantine chains. "You have no jurisdiction over me."

The One seconded the motion, the jaws of the disembodied head speaking loudly despite the absence of lungs or anything else below them. "All commandments flow from My Wisdom. Thou shalt have no higher laws than Mine."

The quaestor was unimpressed by the prisoners' arguments. "Your access to this plane was done at the sufferance of the Continuum, and at the instigation of one of our less prudent constituents." The magistrate fixed a cold eye upon the young Q, who gulped nervously. Having exchanged his sackcloth robe for prison stripes, Q looked as guilty as he doubtless felt. "This renders the Continuum responsible for your future activities, just as it renders you both subject to our considered rulings."

For better or for worse, Picard reflected, he and the usual Q seemed to have arrived at the tail end of the trial. Just as well, he thought; as much as he enjoyed seeing Q among the accused, he was eager for this odyssey to reach some conclusion. The sooner Q returned him to the *Enterprise,* the less anxious he would feel.

The magistrate rapped his gavel again. "The entity who quite presumptuously calls Himself The One shall be confined to the center of this galaxy until the heat death of the universe or His sincere repentance, whichever comes first. This sentence is effective immediately."

"No!" The One screamed as a glowing blue forcefield surrounded His cage, lifting it from the floor and sending it rushing upward toward the very center of the sprawling starscape above. The living head rocked back and forth within His cage, smashing His forbidding visage against the bars. "Mine is the Power and the Glory and the Will. You cannot lock Me away!" His strident denials faded rapidly in volume as the cage ascended into the sky. Picard watched it rise until its tiny blue glow was lost amid the dazzling panoply of the galactic core.

Of course, he thought, realizing at last who and what this entity truly was. James T. Kirk had reported encountering just such a malevolent force, trapped behind an energy barrier at the center of the Milky Way, during one of the historic early voyages of the *Enterprise*-A. In theory, The One was imprisoned within the core still, even in the twenty-fourth century. *Remind me to leave that particular barrier alone,* he thought, triggering yet another revelation in his mind.

Now the toga-clad magistrate turned his attention to 0 himself. Arrogant and unrepentant, the prisoner waited defiantly in the dock, singing off-key to music only he could hear. His fancy velvet coat, damask vest, and fashionable breeches were soiled and disheveled. His orange-red tresses, once neatly tied, were loose and in disarray, thatches of frizzy hair jutting wildly in all directions. Having lost his buckled shoes in his moment of defeat, he stood barefoot upon a simulated marble floor, his scarred and twisted left foot exposed to view.

> *"A young babe lay asleep in bed,*
> *When a shadow passed his silken head. . . ."*

"The entity known only as 0," the quaestor went on, ignoring 0's self-absorbed singing, "is banished from this galaxy, on every dimensional plane, without hope of pardon or parole."

> *"You bundled him in, and kissed him goodnight,*
> *Trusting that all 'twould be well in the night. . . ."*

"A barricade shall be erected around the galaxy to prevent your return, thus protecting lesser life-forms from your depraved amusements until they are advanced enough to defend themselves against you and your kind."

> *"But ever present, always there,*
> *Too common t'matter, too small for a care—*
> *Heedless of what might befall—*
> *You neglect the spider on the wall. . . ."*

It all made sense now, Picard thought, nodding. The galactic barrier did not exist to hold humanity or anyone else within the galaxy; it was intended to keep 0 out. A galactic quarantine, in effect, with a capital Q.

And a quarantine that Lem Faal's artificial wormhole could undo in a few moments, exposing the Federation and the rest of the galaxy to 0 once more. . . .

0 spat upon the courtroom floor, his spittle eating away at the marble tiles like acid. "You can't be rid of me so readily," he vowed, interrupting his sinister ditty to threaten the court directly. "I'll be back if I have to wait a million years, just wait and see." His head snapped around to glower at the young Q. The female Q started to draw her sword, but 0 only flung words at his onetime protégé. "I won't be forgetting you, Q. We'll meet again, count on it." His angry gaze swept the courtroom; Picard felt a chill pass over him as 0 looked his way, even though he knew the vengeful prisoner could not see either he or the older Q. "I hope you like games, young Q, because I know whom I'm testing next. You, Q, you." He fixed his baleful gaze on Q as he resumed his song:

> *"While the lad is tucked in snug,*
> *It crawls along across the rug. . . ."*

"Enough. The sentence has been pronounced." He rapped his gavel decisively. "Make it so."

> *"Deep in slumber, young dreams sweet,*
> *It works its way beneath the sheet. . . ."*

As with The One, an irresistible force seized 0 and propelled him upward at unimaginable speed, but this time the force aimed the prisoner at the outer limits of the galaxy. "I'll be back, Q," he shouted down at them as his raspy voice grew fainter and fainter. "Oh, the games we'll play, games of life and death and death and death . . . ! How well can a Q die, I wonder. There's a test for you!"

> *"Its legs caressing dimpled chin,*
> *It swiftly pierces tender skin. . . ."*

Cast out of known space, 0 shrank to invisibility somewhere outside the galaxy, in the black abyss between galaxies. Even after he disappeared from sight, Picard could still hear 0 singing madly.

> *"When the spider aims his deadly spikes,*
> *No one spies him till he strikes,*

> Be mindful of this when you kiss yours good-night,
> Beware of the danger that lies in plain sight. . . ."

Then something new and different appeared. Picard watched in wonder as a thin violet cord, neon bright in intensity, stretched around the perimeter of the Milky Way, outlining the entire galaxy like a forcefield . . . or a moat.

Thus is born the galactic barrier, he realized, awestruck at the enormity of what the Q had done. That glowing cordon, the same immense wall of energy that had confronted daring starfarers since time immemorial, was the first line of defense for over one hundred billion stars, and all the planets and civilizations that orbited those stars, from Earth to the Delta Quadrant and beyond. Although it looked like the merest shimmering ribbon from his current perspective, he knew that this same barrier enclosed a spiral cloud of stars more than one hundred thousand light-years in diameter. It was a cosmic feat of engineering that made the Great Wall of China seem like a fraction of a fraction of a subatomic speck in comparison. *Astonishing,* he thought. Just to be present at this epochal moment was almost worth all the aggravation Q had inflicted on him over the years.

0 had been more than simply exiled, Picard also understood, as the full implications of the Continuum's decree sank in. Given the crippled 0's inability to travel at faster-than-light speeds, except via the Continuum, he had been effectively marooned in extragalactic space, over two million years from the nearest alternative galaxy; in essence, he'd been set adrift in a very large ocean with the only shore in sight barred from him forever. Even if 0 set out immediately for the Andromeda Galaxy, he was still going to be alone for a long, long time. Picard almost felt sorry for him; the Continuum's judgment had been unforgiving indeed.

But what of the young Q? Picard had to admit he was curious to see how his own people would deal with the errant Q. *Obviously,* he thought, *whatever they do, it won't be enough to curb his appetite for disorder and chaos.* Picard and his crew could testify to that.

"Q," the quaestor addressed the youth. His oh-so-familiar face frowned in disapproval.

"Yes, Your Honor," Q said, stepping forward. Unlike the departed defendants, no chains or cage restrained him. He was here of his own free will, proving that he had gained a little in maturity since his panicky flight from justice several millennia earlier. Picard admired the youth's willingness to face the consequences of his misdeeds.

"Would that we could dispose of you," the quaestor said mournfully, his expression growing more dour by the moment, "as swiftly and efficiently as the Continuum dealt with your unsavory associates." He sighed and shook his head. "Alas, you are a member of the Continuum and so we are obliged to undertake the daunting, and most likely unachievable, task of your rehabilitation." He nodded at the female Q, standing behind Q in the dock. "Will the bailiff please present Exhibit Forty-two B."

"Certainly," she agreed. Holding out her hands in front of her, she produced a spinning blue-green globe that lifted off from her open palms to take a position between the defendant and the quaestor, floating serenely in midair. "Do you recognize this world?" she asked Q.

He peered at the globe, then shook his head. "Should I?"

"The planet before you," the quaestor informed him, scowling, "is one of several that were damaged during the conflict required to apprehend you and your associates. This world, in particular, was injured by your careless attempt at self-defense near the end of that regrettable altercation."

Picard recalled, if the young Q did not, the diverted asteroid smashing into the Earth many million years in the past, causing death and destruction on a planetary scale. *I still refuse to accept that was really Q's doing,* he thought. That an asteroid had struck Earth in the distant past, causing mass extinctions all over the globe, was a matter of archaeological record. That Q himself had caused the disaster, in a single careless moment, Picard found harder to accept. *That, at least, must be some twisted joke on Q's part.* Or so he hoped.

"Oops?" Q said weakly, wincing at the fierce glare his feeble defense elicited from the quaestor.

"The biosphere of this unfortunate world has been grievously harmed," the magistrate announced. "Your penance is to personally oversee the reconstruction of its environment and any life-forms that may develop therein. Perhaps the rehabilitation of this unassuming world can serve as a model for your own redemption." He regarded Q dubiously. "Probably a lost cause, but who knows?"

Q did not take the quaestor's ruling as well as perhaps he should have. "You want me to babysit some insignificant little planet way off in the middle of nowhere? What sort of punishment is that? It's a complete waste of my abilities and talents. Can't you come up with a penance that's more, well, impressive? Twelve impossible labors maybe, or a hazardous quest that no one else would dare?" He grimaced at the floating orb, his nose wrinkling in disdain. "Nothing so tedious and mundane as . . . that."

That's more like the Q I know, Picard thought. *Supremely self-important even in defeat.*

"Do not question the judgment of this tribunal," the magistrate warned him, raising his gavel. "Be thankful that you were not stripped of all your Q-given powers and privileges, although I would not be at all surprised if it comes to that someday." The Q who looked like Picard rose from behind the imposing height of the bench and removed his laurel crown. "Don't let me see you here again, young Q."

Picard half-expected to see Q escorted out of the courtroom now that the proceedings seemed to have concluded. Instead the whole courtroom, and everyone in it, disappeared abruptly in a flash of white light, leaving the young Q alone with his new charge. His posture sagged gloomily as he inspected the spinning globe with a sour expression upon his face. Continents drifted beneath his gaze, and, from several meters away, Picard thought he spotted a landmass that might someday be France. The arctic icecap crept slowly downward, locking Earth in its glacial grip, then receded northward once more. "What a dump," Q groaned.

"Oh, that's enough!" Picard spun around to confront the older Q. He had seen all he wanted to see. "This is too much, Q. Do you truly expect me to believe that you were placed in charge of humanity—as a punishment?"

"What can I say, Jean-Luc?" Q replied, throwing up his hands. "It was a dirty job, but someone had to do it." He took Picard by the arm and led him away from the young Q and an even younger Earth. The captain glanced back over his shoulder, watching the birthplace of humanity spin beneath the sullen gaze of the young Q, but that unsettling primordial scene was soon lost in a dense, white fog that seemed to form out of nowhere, soon growing opaque enough to conceal all the stars that had surrounded the cosmic courtroom. Picard looked about quickly and realized that he and Q had returned to the same ghostly limbo from which their long journey had begun. He decided to take this as an encouraging sign that their odyssey was nearing its end.

"In any event," Q continued, "you mustn't dwell on that amusing little epilogue, no matter how intriguing. I trust that, by now, you have deduced the real reason why I have taken you on this cheery stroll down memory lane."

Picard nodded soberly. "Professor Faal's experiment. His plan to pierce the galactic barrier with an artificial wormhole." Knowing what he now did, it wasn't hard to grasp the dangers involved. "We could accidentally let 0 back into the galaxy."

"Oh, almost certainly," Q confirmed. "He's surely still out there, no doubt humming one of his obnoxious ditties while he waits for a chance to sneak back into your precious Milky Way." He looked sincerely concerned by the prospect. "I can't imagine several hundred millennia of isolation have improved his personality much."

Picard resisted the temptation to remark about blackened pots versus kettles. From what he had viewed, a legitimate case could be made that 0 was more of a threat than Q; Q had only threatened humanity with extinction on occasion, but 0 had actually carried out his genocidal plan to destroy the Tkon Empire. "Why didn't you just tell me the truth in the first place?" he asked. "You had any number of opportunities to explain why you wanted us to leave the barrier alone."

"Would you have believed me?" Q asked in return.

Probably not, Picard conceded. He'd be extremely reluctant to accept anything, even the time of day, on Q's word alone. Still, he suspected there was more to Q's earlier reticence than the conceited superbeing was now willing to admit. The *affaire de 0* was hardly one of Q's finest hours; no wonder he'd been unwilling to provide Picard with the full story until it became obvious that there was no other way to convince the captain to call off the experiment. *Given a choice,* Picard thought, *I'm sure Q would have preferred to explore my own follies and frailties rather than admit to any imperfections of his own.*

"But wouldn't the Continuum intervene again if 0 broke through?" Picard asked. The swirling white mist was growing thicker and thicker. He could barely see his own hands when he held them up before his face. "Surely the combined might of all the Q would be enough to banish him once more."

"Eventually," Q agreed, "but how soon is the question. Over the aeons, the Continuum has grown more detached and aloof from mortal affairs . . . and preoccupied with its own concerns." He guided Picard through the dense fog, although how he knew which way to go, if directions meant anything at all in this formless shadowland, Picard couldn't begin to imagine. "I alluded earlier to a civil war that recently divided the Continuum. Although peace was eventually restored, in no small part due to my own heroic efforts, rest assured that this has been a time of considerable turmoil and change for the Q Continuum, which now has other things on its collective mind than an interdimensional vandal we disposed of countless centuries ago. Still coping with the aftermath of our epochal civil war, the rest of the Q would also be decidedly unwilling to initiate another armed conflict so soon after our own internecine struggle."

Picard found the whole notion of a Q civil war intriguing and more than a little alarming. He recalled that it was this very war that supposedly caused the hairline fractures in the galactic barrier that had first attracted Lem Faal's attention. Although Q hadn't said as much, Picard would have been willing to wager a Ferengi's ransom in gold-pressed latinum that Q had been responsible for starting the war in the first place.

"To be sure," Q continued, "the Continuum would take note of 0's new depredations in a century or two, but who knows how much havoc 0 could inflict on an unsuspecting galaxy before the other Q took action? It's unlikely your vaunted Federation would still be around to see 0 get his just desserts."

"What do you care?" Picard asked suspiciously.

Q did not take offense at the question, nor at Picard's skeptical tone. "Fatherhood has given me a greater investment in the future of the cosmos. I don't want my son to grow up in a galaxy contaminated by 0."

A valid point, Picard thought. As disruptive as the infant Q had been to the daily routines of the *Enterprise,* the captain could not begrudge Q his concern for his son. "Is that all you're concerned with?" Picard accused. "It seemed to me that 0 was dead-set on revenge against you in particular. Are you sure you're not more worried about your own safety?"

"Enlightened self-interest is one of the crucial hallmarks of a truly advanced intelligence," Q said defensively.

"Regardless of your motives," Picard stated, "you've made your point about the peril of violating the barrier. I have no intention of proceeding with the experiment at this time." He gestured at the featureless miasma that had engulfed them. "I trust this means we can return to my ship with all deliberate speed."

"If you say so."

Abruptly, without any tangible sense of transition, Picard was back on the bridge of the *Enterprise.* To his further surprise, he found himself drifting in front of the main viewer, a few meters above the blue steel floor. "What the devil?" he exclaimed.

"Captain!" Will Riker said, lunging from the captain's chair to his feet.

It didn't take Picard long to realize that there was no gravity upon the bridge. Years of experience in Starfleet alerted him to the unique physical sensations of zero G right away; still, after spending what felt like hours in the abstract realm of the Q, where entities casually occupied deep space with a nary a care in the world, it felt strange to be subjected to such elemental principles as gravity, or rather the lack of the same, once more. *Which probably means I've returned to reality none too soon,* he reflected. "Q," he said, pointing in an irritated manner at the floor, "if you don't mind . . ."

"What?" Q said. Over by Ops, Q was enjoying a reunion with his family. Little q came to a landing within his father's waiting arms. A half-eaten glopsicle bobbed perilously near Q's ruffled brown hair. "Oh, I see what you mean."

Q snapped his fingers and gravity was restored to the bridge, dragging Picard swiftly toward the floor below. Bits and pieces of broken technology also plummeted abruptly, clattering onto the duranium floor. The captain himself landed on both feet with as much dignity as he could muster, then quickly took stock of his new surroundings.

He didn't like what he saw. Even in the alarmingly dim lighting, it was clear that the bridge of his starship had been through a costly battle. Besides the temporary absence of gravity—and Picard noticed now that Riker and the other crew members present, with the notable exception of Q and his family, were equipped with magnetic boots—ominous signs of damage and violent destruction were evident in nearly every direction he looked. The overhead lighting had obviously gone out, so his eyes had to adjust to the resulting gloom as he glanced about the bridge. Flashing alert signals and the glowing viewscreen cast deep scarlet and magenta shadows over the scene. The aft engineering station looked completely devastated by some sort of electrical fire, while bits of ash and lightweight debris polluted the ordinarily pristine atmosphere of the bridge, gradually drifting toward the floor. "The Calamarain, I take it," he said to Riker, who approached the captain with a worried look upon his face. *How long have I been away,* Picard wondered, *and what has become of the ship in my absence?*

"You called it," Riker confirmed. His voice was tighter than usual, as if he were in some pain. He gave Q a dirty look. "Good to have you back, Captain."

"Trust me, you are no more pleased than I am, Number One," Picard said wholeheartedly. He turned around to inspect the main viewer. To his concern and puzzlement, the screen showed nothing but a constant purple glow. "Where are we?" he asked Riker, fearing he already knew the answer.

"Inside the barrier," the first officer informed him. "It was the only way to escape the Calamarain. At present, we are waiting for La Forge to complete repairs on the warp engines before attempting to leave this sector."

Picard nodded. He could get a full report later on; for now, it appeared that, while the ship was definitely in difficult straits, Commander Riker had the situation in hand. "And the wormhole experiment?" he asked with some apprehension.

"Aborted," Riker said bluntly, "after we ran into trouble with the Calamarain." He stepped aside and let Picard take his place in the captain's chair. "Protecting the ship took priority."

"You made the right choice, Number One," Picard assured him, "and a better one than you could even realize." Riker gave him a quizzical look so Picard elaborated, tipping his head toward Q. "I'll give you a complete briefing later, but let's just say that I've learned more than enough about the true nature and purpose of the barrier. Hopefully, that will be enough to satisfy Professor Faal and Starfleet Science."

Settling into his chair, Picard noted that the female Q had apparently commandeered Deanna Troi's seat; it was a bit odd to realize that this was the same woman whom he and Q had just observed several hundred thousand years in the past. He scowled when he saw that the baby Q had left sticky handprints all over the armrest of the counselor's chair, although, from the look of the rest of the bridge, he decided he should be thankful that the command area was intact at all. Taking a quick mental inventory of the bridge crew, he was surprised to see Lieutenant Barclay stationed at the secondary science station and that young Canadian officer, Ensign Berglund, manning the tactical podium. "Where is Lieutenant Leyoro?" he asked. "And Counselor Troi?"

Riker's face warned him there was worse to come. "Sickbay," he began. "The news isn't good. . . ."

Six

Bring down the wall. The wall is all. . . .

Gravity returned to sickbay without warning, but Lem Faal failed to notice. His mind ablaze with new concepts and sensations, he awoke suddenly, his transformed eyes snapping open, to find Beverly Crusher leaning over him, a worried frown upon her face. Surprised by his unexpected return to consciousness, she gasped and stepped backward involuntarily, bringing a hand to her chest.

Faal was disoriented by the familiar surroundings. Sickbay? How had he returned to sickbay? What had happened to him? The last thing he remembered was standing by a turbolift, trying to get to Engineering. *My experiment . . . my work . . . my destiny . . .* Then the power of the barrier had invaded his mind, bringing with it . . . something else. A renewed sense of purpose, along with the strength and the focus to overcome the endless limitations of his decaying body, or so he had thought until he woke here. *I must have collapsed,* he realized, *overcome by the power of the barrier . . . and the voice on the other side.* The voice had spoken to him for months, promising him immortality and infinite knowledge, enough to transcend the disease that was killing him, to overcome mortality entirely. *Come to me, free me, be me.* Faal had followed that voice to the very edge of the galaxy, all the while concealing his true purpose from Starfleet.

Closer now. Close, closer, closest. . . .

"Professor?" the human doctor asked urgently. "Can you hear me? How do you feel?"

He felt like a new being, but saw no reason to explain anything to the doctor. He had evolved beyond her, beyond everyone on this starship. *They must have brought me here,* he realized, just as Picard's crew had interfered with and delayed his mission ever since he first stepped aboard. *They can't see what I see, hear what I hear.* No matter. The ship was still within the barrier; Faal could sense its power all around him. He knew where he needed to be: Engineering, where the equipment necessary to his experiment waited. *My work . . . my destiny.* It was time for the final step, to remove the barrier between himself and the voice.

Bring down the wall. . . .

"Professor Faal," the doctor repeated. She glanced anxiously from his face to the biobed monitor and back again. "Can you understand me? Do you know where you are?"

Engineering, Faal thought. *I have to go to Engineering.* He tried to sit up, but something restrained him. Lifting his head a few centimeters from the bed, he saw that translucent straps held his wrists and ankles to the bed. A longer strap stretched across his chest, further limiting his movement. *Why have they confined me?* he wondered. *Don't they realize how close I am? Close, closer, closest.* He had vague memories of an altercation with the doctor, and with Counselor Troi, but that felt like it had occurred ages ago, to another person, one very different from the being he had become.

Come. Hurry. He could still hear the voice, but now it seemed like the voice was his, almost indistinguishable from his own thoughts. *Bring down the wall. Break through.*

Dr. Crusher saw him inspecting the restraints. "I'm sorry, but it was for the best. I'm not sure you're fully responsible for your actions. It's just a precaution."

He ignored her babbling. The barrier was all that mattered, and the voice. The voice that was both inside him and waiting on the other side of the great wall. *Come. Hurry. Now.* He had to leave this place. Neither he nor the voice, if there was truly any difference left between them, could not wait any longer. *Hurry,* it pleaded and commanded. *Fast, faster, fastest.*

His shining eyes stared at the band across his chest, concentrating his will upon the crude impediment, which began to undo itself as though possessed of a will of its own. *Simple telekinesis,* he observed. *Mind over matter. All that matters is mind.* Crusher made a surprised sound and grabbed for the strap, trying to pull it back into place, but the band resisted her. The straps holding down his wrists and ankles also came free. He didn't even need to touch them; just thinking at the straps was enough. *Release me. Release the voice.* He started to sit up and the doctor's hands pressed down upon his chest, struggling to keep him from rising. "Daniels. Lee," she called desperately. "Help me. He's getting free."

Faal dimly recognized the security officer who had originally escorted him to sickbay, what seemed like decades ago. He didn't know who the other officer was; he had never seen her before. *So many people on this starship,* he thought. *Too many.* He didn't need any of them anymore. All he needed was the voice, just as the voice needed him.

Come. Hurry. Bring down the wall. Release the All. . . .

They tried to help Crusher restrain him, but there was nothing they could do against the newfound power in his mind. With a casual glance, he sent both officers flying away from him. They were propelled backward, limbs flailing, until they crashed into the nearest obstacle. Daniels slammed into a sealed doorway, while the other crew member collided with a metal cart holding a tray covered with medical instruments. Both cart and officer fell over, sending hyposprays and exoscalpels sliding across the floor. On nearby biobeds, injured crew members sat up in alarm, the most able jumping onto their feet and rushing to assist the stunned officers.

"Stay away from him," Crusher warned them all, backing away from Faal as he swung his legs off the bed and onto the floor. He wondered for a second why he was wearing such cumbersome boots when the ship's artificial gravity was very obviously functioning again. He stared at the boots and they transformed instantly into more conventional footwear. *That's better,* he thought. *Better, best, bestow.* The voice had bestowed this power on him, the better to bring down the wall.

"Oh no," Crusher whispered, observing the seemingly magical metamorphosis. He could sense that she was confused and wary. *Best, better, beware.* No fool, she kept her distance as he stood still for a moment, savoring the restored strength and vitality in his limbs. The voice sang within him, filling with power and purpose. *Mind over matter. My mind renews my matter.* He had not felt so robust, so capable, in months, not since the Iverson's had begun eating away at his physical stamina. He felt the power of the voice rushing through his body, eradicating every last trace of disease. *I have defeated death,* he exulted. *I will never cease to be.*

The doctor reached for her combadge, intending to alert Riker and the others, but Faal heard her thoughts before she had even finished thinking them. The shiny golden badge disappeared, transformed into nothingness with just a moment's thought. He glanced around the ward and, just for good measure, removed the rest of the combadges as well. *No more interference,* he vowed. *No more small-minded rules and procedures.* The head nurse, Ogawa, came running in from another ward, no doubt attracted by the clamor of Starfleet personnel slamming into doors and objects, and he consigned her badge to oblivion. *No more delays. The wall is all. . . .*

He started toward the exit; then an apprehensive thought in the doctor's mind caught his attention. He looked past her to where his son lay unconscious upon a biobed.

Milo, he thought. The sight of the motionless boy gave him pause, although he wasn't sure why. He had attained true immortality at last; physical reproduction had become irrelevant. *But my family . . . ?* Peering deeper into the doctor's thoughts, he discovered that Kinya was also here in sickbay, resting quietly in the pediatric unit, her childish mind temporarily deactivated by the doctor's technology.

Milo. Kinya. He stood frozen between the insensate boy and the exit from sickbay. *My children.* Images from the past raced through his memory, coming from someplace other than the voice. The birth of each child, their first words and telepathic outpourings. He saw their entire family together, his wife, Shozana, still alive to share each precious moment. Milo opening a talking gift box on his tenth birthday, the sculpted face upon the ornate container urging him on. The whole family sharing a picnic lunch alongside Lake Cataria, the afternoon sun shining down on them. Little Milo, a few years younger than he was now, lifting up his baby sister for the first time while Shozana looked on, radiantly proud and happy. . . .

For a moment, his purpose wavered. *Hurry,* the voice demanded, but Faal was transfixed by his son's plight. *What will become of him?* Probing the boy's mind, he discovered a power not unlike his own growing within the sleeping child's brain. Perhaps Milo had followed him across the evolutionary threshold, attaining the same paranormal capabilities? Faal found himself both pleased and disturbed by the prospect. This had not been part of his plan; he had resolved to leave such mortal ties behind him forever. *Flesh does not matter. Matter does not matter.* The sunny recollections welling up inside him gave way to the searing image of Shozana as she disintegrated forever upon that malfunctioning transporter pad, demonstrating irrevocably the fundamental frailty and impermanence of humanoid relationships. He could never allow himself to be hurt that way again.

Milo has been gifted, too. He doesn't need a father anymore. Mind is all that matters. Faal turned away from the boy's bed, confident that he was making the right decision. Milo could look after Kinya, too. He had always been good at that, especially since their mother died. Besides, there was another child that concerned him now, concerned the voice. An image came to his mind of an infant, a mere toddler, with incredible powers and an even more astounding heritage. *The child of Q and Q,* the next step in the evolution of the mind. The child of the future. His future. . . .

Goodbye, he thought to both of his children, the children of the past, and left sickbay. No one tried to stop him.

Come. Hurry. Now.

The corridors outside were blessedly free of people. All crew members were at their posts, he assumed. Red alert signals, horizontal in orientation, still flashed upon the walls. Faal walked at an ever-increasing pace toward the nearest turbolift. The last time he had trod these halls, intent on the same destination, he had been near the end of his tether, scarcely able to force his debilitated body to take another step; now he raced effortlessly upon legs that no longer ached with every movement. The closer he came to his destiny, the stronger he felt. By the time he reached the turbolift entrance, he was literally running. He waited impatiently for the door to slide open.

Close, closer, closest.

"The turbolifts are not currently available to unauthorized personnel," an automated voice informed him. "Civilian passengers should report to either sickbay or their quarters."

Of course, he remembered. The blasted red alert. The officious computer and its meaningless protocols had halted him before, but this time he would not be denied. "Open," he ordered the door, his enhanced mind adding force to his command. *No more obstacles.* The bright red door slid open obligingly and he stepped inside. "Engineering," he said, receiving no further argument from the computer. The turbolift carried him nearer to his destiny. *Soon,* he promised the voice. *Soon, sooner, soonest.*

The trip to Engineering took less than a minute. Exiting the turbolift, he entered a beehive of activity. Moving with the efficiency and coordination of a finely calibrated isolinear relay, Starfleet personnel scurried about the massive multilevel engineering center, performing diagnostics and needed repairs on a variety of systems. *Mere specks,* he dismissed them. *Specks inside a shiny, silver bug.* The bulk of their efforts appeared centered around the warp-engine controls, but the crew was also focused on systems as diverse as the subspace field distortion amplifiers and the structural integrity field power conduits. The master situation monitor, featuring a cutaway schematic of the *Enterprise,* highlighted malfunctions throughout the entire vessel, although one by one systems seemed to be slowly coming back on-line.

None of this matters, only the wall. The wall is all.

So intent on their repairs were the crew that no one noticed Faal's arrival at first. He went straight to the chief engineer's office, where La Forge had earlier delegated an auxiliary workstation to Faal. To his relief, no one was utilizing the station as he approached, although Ensign Sutter was hard at work nearby, using a handheld laser wielder to seal the ruptured casing of a waveguide conduit junction. He logged into the computer terminal and called up the parameters for the subspace tensor matrix necessary to create his artificial wormhole. He was surprised and pleased by how easily he could read the complicated display screens; he wasn't even farsighted anymore. *Mind over matter. The mind sees what mere matter cannot.* Providentially, proving the unstoppable inevitability of his quest, the data was still intact, despite all the damage caused by the senseless attack of the Calamarain. The quantum torpedo containing the specialized magneton pulse generator was unharmed as well, and ready to be launched into the barrier as soon as he took over the tactical controls.

Yes, he thought. Mind was all that mattered, but he still needed these machines, at least for this one last task. The voice told him so. The barrier was made of mind as well, and so could not be undone by mind alone. The minds of the Q had made it so. *Curse the Q, curse them all!* Only his wormhole, born of mortal science, could bring down the wall. *Machine against mind . . .*

First, though, he was going to need extra power to generate the subspace matrix via the *Enterprise*'s main deflector dish. With that in view, he began rerouting the preignition plasma from the impulse deck to the auxiliary intake. He and La Forge had already worked out the procedure, back before Captain Picard disappeared and his fainthearted crew lost their enthusiasm for the experiment. *Fine,* he thought, diverting the plasma as planned. *Fine, finer, finest.* This would only take a moment or two.

His efforts did not go unnoticed. Geordi La Forge came running from the matter-antimatter reaction chamber, darting around the tabletop master systems display. "What the devil is going on with the plasma injectors?" he asked loudly, then slowed to a stop as his optical implants spotted the Betazoid scientist at the auxiliary station. "Professor Faal? What are you doing here?" He looked more carefully at Faal. "What's happened to your eyes?"

Says the blind man, Faal thought ungraciously. Not long ago, but before Faal's apotheosis, La Forge had banished him from main engineering after Faal tried to overrule Commander Riker's order to abort the experiment. Despite all that happened to him since, Faal had neither forgotten nor forgiven. *They are all against me. The crew, the Q, all of them.* "I'm doing what I came here to do," he said icily. "What Starfleet Command ordered you all to assist."

What the voice calls out for. . . .

La Forge smacked his palm against his combadge. "Security to Engineering, pronto!" Then he wasted his breath trying to deter Faal by his words alone. "But we can't create the wormhole now," he said, badgering Faal with his timid, trivial objections, "not while the *Enterprise* is still in the barrier, too. We're too close to ground zero to initiate the wormhole even if we still wanted to."

The voice will protect me, he thought, knowing La Forge could never understand. *I am beyond physical danger.* "That's not my concern," he said, turning his back on the cowardly engineer. *The mind is all.* "Computer, prepare to launch modified torpedo, designation Faal-alpha-one."

Ordinarily, a quantum torpedo, modified or otherwise, could not be launched without authorization from the captain or the tactical officer, but control of this particular torpedo, containing the experimental magneton pulse generator, had already been diverted to Faal's personal controls so that he and La Forge could supervise every step of the experiment. *Not that any common computer could stand against my will now,* Faal thought. *My mind is mightier than any mere machine.* The preapproved launch authority only made his task easier.

"Acknowledged," the computer reported. "Torpedo Faal-alpha-one loaded and ready to launch on command."

"Sutter, stop him!" La Forge called out.

Caught by surprise, along with everyone else in earshot, Sutter improvised, aiming his laser wielder at Faal's exposed back like a phaser. "Step away from the controls, Professor. I don't want to use this weapon."

He never had a chance. The metal instrument vanished instantly, leaving him staring in amazement at his empty hand. La Forge was also stunned by this demonstration of Faal's new powers; the circular lenses in his state-of-the-art optical implants refocused on his fingers as he struggled to process this unexpected visual stimulus. Faal sensed the chief engineer's shocked surprise, along with a heightened sense of caution and concern. *Now do you understand?* he wondered. *Now do you comprehend the magnitude of what is at stake?*

To his credit, La Forge did not panic when confronted with the miraculous. "Professor Faal. Lem," he began, stepping toward the scientist slowly while making another futile try at dissuading Faal from his destiny. "Be reasonable. I know how important your work is to you, but—"

"You can't possibly dream how important this is," Faal declared, affronted by the human's presumption. "You never could." He watched in satisfaction as the monitor reported the power transfer complete. "I've been reasonable long enough, while Riker and Q and the rest of you did everything you could to obstruct my plans, keep me from my ultimate triumph and transfiguration." His impatience and irritation swelled when he recalled how Riker had ordered him physically removed from the bridge, taking advantage of his former infirmity and weakness. "No more," he vowed. *Never again, say I.* "Computer, initiate subspace tensor matrix."

A pair of security officers rushed into Engineering, phasers ready. "Stop him," La Forge instructed, pointing at Faal, "but be careful. He's more dangerous than he looks."

Nodding, both officers aimed their weapons at Faal and fired. Twin beams of crimson energy intersected between the Betazoid physicist's shoulder blades, only to be blocked by the invisible forcefield Faal willed into being. The crimson rays ricocheted off the protective shield and bounced back through Engineering, eliciting cries of alarm. The deflected beams triggered explosions of sparks and haze where they met with vulnerable conduits and circuitry.

Fools, Faal thought contemptuously. *Insignificant specks.*

The security team switched off the phasers to prevent further damage, then rushed ahead to subdue Faal physically, but his self-generated forcefield repelled the two officers as well. Psychic energy crackled noisily as their outstretched hands came into contact with his protective field. They yanked back their hands as if burned, then looked at each other in confusion. "Sir?" one of them asked, turning to La Forge for guidance.

Faal couldn't care less about the guards' dilemma. He watched the display panel avidly, his luminous eyes widening in anticipation as the *Enterprise* projected a stream of precisely modulated verteron particles into the weakest region of the barrier, producing a subspace tensor matrix of exactly the correct configuration and intensity. Faal spared a moment to give silent thanks to Dr. Lenara Kahn, the Trill researcher whose pioneering work had laid the groundwork for what he was now about to do, the mind behind the machine. Only a Trill, he reflected, blessed with the accumulated knowledge of an immortal symbiont, could begin to understand his profound and transforming communion with the voice behind the wall, that voice that was now inside him. "Computer, launch modified torpedo. Vector 32-60-45."

"No!" La Forge shouted. He dashed to the master systems table, where he tried to manually override the launch command. His efforts showed up on Faal's monitor and he glared at La Forge in irritation. How long was he expected to endure such small-minded interference? *You have never understood, La Forge. You could never truly see my vision.* With a thought, he deactivated the implants within La Forge's eye sockets, casting the treacherous meddler into darkness. "My eyes! What have you done! I can't see!" A horrified gasp echoed through Engineering as the Starfleet officer groped for the controls with tentative hands, now as blind in reality as he had always been to the true importance of the work. A fitting fate, Faal thought, for so limited and fainthearted an imagination. *You never saw what I see.*

Smiling with cruel satisfaction, Faal tracked the trajectory of the torpedo. *Soon,* he thought. *Soon, sooner, soonest. . . .*

Now.

Seven

Watching Captain Picard keep a wary eye on Q and his family, Riker experienced a distinct sense of déjà vu. As he sat beside the captain on the bridge, gratefully removing his gravity boots, he had a sudden vague recollection of meeting Q under very different circumstances, on a different ship with a different captain. Captain Janeway. *Voyager.* Some kind of trial. . . . He tried to dredge the details up from his unconscious, make the fragmentary impressions cohere, but it was as nebulous and hard to grasp as a half-remembered dream. *That's probably all it is,* he thought, *or more like a nightmare if Q was involved.* He kept his mouth shut, not about to give Q the satisfaction of knowing that he had invaded Riker's dreams.

Excited by his father's return, little q demanded attention. He bounced up and down in Q's arms, waving his half-eaten glop-on-a-stick like a magic wand.

"Good morning to you, little man," Q said sunnily, beaming at his child. Riker felt a peculiar twinge of jealousy; for all his irresponsible ways, Q was obviously a more doting and affectionate father than Kyle Riker had ever been. "Or is it good evening?" Q glanced at Picard. "For the eternal life of me, I never have been able to figure out just how you people manage to tell the time of day in this stultifyingly artificial environment of yours."

"We muddle through somehow," Picard said dryly, unamused by the Q's touching family reunion. No doubt he was concerned about Baeta Leyoro and the other crew members now in sickbay; Riker had brought Picard up to speed on Leyoro's shocking collapse, wishing he could have spared the captain that news. Picard had enough problems to worry about, especially with three Qs aboard and the warp drive still down.

"You're going to spoil him," the female Q scolded, rising from Deanna's seat and stepping around the accompanying computer console. She crossed the debris-strewn bridge to where Q and q cavorted. She wiped her son's messy mouth with a monogrammed handkerchief (inscribed with a stylish "Q") that she drew from thin air. "Look, he's got organic residue and sucrose contaminants all over his face."

Gathered together, engrossed with each other, the Q family presented a surprisingly ordinary portrait of domestic life. *Who'd have thought that Q would turn out to be such a family man?* Riker thought, not quite believing his eyes.

"Nonsense!" Q asserted. "There's no such thing as a spoiled Q." Riker saw the captain raise a skeptical eyebrow at that remark, looking like he was tempted to dispute the claim. The first officer knew just how Picard felt. *The real question is,* he mused, *has there ever been a Q that wasn't spoiled by too much power and not enough accountability?* He was inclined to doubt it. "But why is it so dark in here?" Q asked, seeming to notice the faint lighting for the first time. "Trying to save a few credits on the power bill, Riker?" He shook his head. "No, this just won't do. The place looks like a crypt."

As if on cue, the overhead lights came back on, dispelling the brooding shadows from the bridge. Faint blue tracking lights also reignited along the floor. *Thank heavens for small favors,* Riker thought, refusing to thank Q either verbally or mentally. His command console had previously informed him that gravity had been restored not just on the bridge, but throughout the entire saucer section. *Maybe we're finally starting to get things back under control.*

"Captain!" Ensign Berglund exclaimed at tactical. "According to the control panel, we've just fired a torpedo into the barrier!"

"What?" Picard blurted, spinning around in his chair to face the tactical podium. Riker was caught equally off guard, and even Q looked up in surprise from the babbling toddler in his arms, a puzzled expression on his face.

"It wasn't me," Berglund explained hastily, her pale face whiter than usual. "From the looks of it, the torpedo was launched from Engineering."

Faal, Riker realized intuitively. *The experiment.* Almost simultaneously, Geordi's voice came over the first officer's combadge. "Commander. We have a problem. Lem Faal has just launched the retooled torpedo. He's going to create the wormhole!"

What the devil? Riker thought. Faal had fled sickbay earlier, but security had returned both him and his son to Dr. Crusher in an unconscious state. They were supposed to be out cold, like Leyoro.

"Sickbay confirms that Professor Faal left sickbay after attacking several officers," Ensign Berglund reported. "They say he is armed with . . . telekinetic powers?"

"Faal can *do* things, Commander. Like a Q," La Forge said, unintentionally seconding Berglund's report. His voice sounded shaken, but under control. Riker guessed that the engineer was only giving him the most pertinent details; something else had happened in Engineering, something bad. Had the obsessed scientist harmed or killed a crew member? *First Deanna, now this.* One way or another, Riker intended to see that Faal was put away for a very long time, winner of the Daystrom Prize or not. First things first, however. "Riker to sickbay," he said via his combadge. "Casualties in Engineering."

"Faal has to be stopped," the captain declared, his voice and expression grave. Riker could tell from the captain's manner that there was more at stake than just the safety of the *Enterprise.* "We cannot let the wormhole form, Number One. That is vitally important to the safety of the entire galaxy." He jumped to his feet and strode toward the Q's family tableau. "Q!" he demanded harshly. "Do something. Quickly!"

Still distracted by his squirming, squealing son, Q glanced over his shoulder at the featureless glow on the main viewer. *Can he see something that the rest of us can't?* Riker wondered. "Yes, of course," Q stammered, awkwardly attempting to hand off q to his mother. The child was determined to stay where he was, though, clinging to Q's neck with *jumja*-stained arms while his happy hellos turned into an earsplitting wail of protest. "Just give me a second. . . ."

"Captain," Data reported from Ops. "I am detecting a subspace tensor matrix identical to the one required by Professor Faal's calculations. It is being generated by the *Enterprise* as we speak."

"Shut it down," Picard ordered. The wails of the fussing child added an extra, unwanted level of chaos to an already tense situation. "Do whatever you have to in order to terminate the matrix."

"I am trying, Captain," the android stated, "but the controls are not responding."

"Fire phasers," Picard directed Berglund. "Target that torpedo." If they were lucky, Riker realized, they might be able to destroy the specialized torpedo before it emitted the magneton pulse that would create the wormhole. But what if they failed?

"Captain," he pointed out, "if that wormhole does start to form, we don't want to be nearby. The gravitational flux alone could finish us. Perhaps we should put some distance between us and the torpedo, just in case."

Picard shook his head. "If we don't stop Faal from tearing a hole in the barrier, Number One, it may be too late for the entire Alpha Quadrant." He gave Riker a solemn look, letting the first officer see some of his anxiety. "There's a being on the other side of the barrier, Will. A being that we cannot allow into our galaxy again."

A being? Riker reacted. *Like Q?* While the first officer digested that chilling revelation, Ensign Berglund called out from tactical, her voice cracking. "The phasers aren't doing any good, sir. Something's protecting the torpedo. A forcefield maybe, or the barrier itself. The sensor readings are strange." She wiped the perspiration from her brow. "I've never seen anything like them."

How was Faal doing this? Why aren't Geordi and the others able to stop him? Riker wished now that he had confined the fanatical scientist to the brig the first time he raised an uproar. It was too late now; they were rapidly running out of options. Calling up the missile's trajectory on his own command console, he saw that the torpedo was only seconds from the heart of the barrier.

"Q," Picard exhorted his old nemesis. "You have to do something!"

Successfully prying q off his harried father, the female Q carried the crying child to the starboard side of the bridge, stroking and cooing q in hopes of quieting his tantrum. Free from his son's clutches, if not from the nerve-jangling noise of his shrieks and sobs, Q spun around and faced the shimmering viewscreen. He stretched out his hands before him, as if reaching for the unseen torpedo. His brow knitted in concentration. His fingers flexed as a grunt of exertion slipped past his lips.

"What is it, Q?" Picard asked apprehensively. "What's happening?"

"Something is blocking me," Q admitted. Riker was surprised by the evident strain in the all-powerful being's voice, not to mention a note of genuine fear. "It's him, Picard. He's here."

"Where?" Picard asked desperately. Riker ground his teeth together, wishing he knew more about what was happening. What sort of being could spook both the Captain and Q?

"Here on your ship," Q said, the muscles beneath his face twitching as he sought to exert his considerable powers upon the intractable torpedo, "at least in part. And behind the barrier as well. He's all around us, Picard, flanking me at every turn. . . ."

Perhaps frightened by his father's obvious anxiety, or simply determined to escape his mother's confining embrace, little q teleported away in a twinkling of light. The female Q gaped at her now-empty arms with a look of distress. "Oh no!" she exclaimed and disappeared herself, doubtless in pursuit of her elusive child. Riker was not saddened to see them go, not if it meant two fewer distractions for all concerned, including Q, who seemed to have his hands full at the moment, as impossible as that sounded.

"Captain," Data announced with inhuman calm, "the magneton pulse generator within the torpedo has been activated. The pulse is reacting with the subspace matrix, exactly as Professor Faal's theory predicted." He studied the sensor readings displayed at his console. "I am detecting elevated neutrino levels, indicative of wormhole formation."

"What if we used phase conjugate graviton beams to disrupt the wormhole's spatial matrix?" Riker suggested, remembering that Starfleet had tried just such a tactic to permanently close the Bajoran wormhole near Deep Space Nine. That effort had failed, but only because of Changeling sabotage.

"You might as well throw rocks at it," Q said scornfully, dismissing Riker's plan. His shoulders sagged as his arms dropped to his sides. "It's too late, Picard. We've lost." His voice took on a doleful tone as he exchanged a worried look with Picard. "He's coming through."

"Um, who is *he* exactly?" Barclay asked nervously, voicing the unspoken question in the minds of everyone except the captain and the Q's. *Frankly, I wouldn't mind learning that myself,* Riker thought, but first there was the little matter of a wormhole to deal with.

Picard had reached the same conclusion. "Ensign Clarze," he addressed the conn, "get us out of the barrier now. Maximum impulse."

"Yes, sir!" the young Deltan said. There was no change upon the overloaded viewscreen, but Riker felt the thrum of the impulse drive beneath his feet as the *Enterprise* headed back toward the galaxy it came from. But even at maximum impulse, could they possibly escape the barrier before the birth of the artificial wormhole wrenched apart the very fabric of space-time?

"A massive quantum fluctuation is forming directly behind us," Data reported. "The subspace shock wave, registering 715.360 millicochranes, will strike the ship in approximately 2.008 seconds."

Riker couldn't vouch for the precise accuracy of the android's prediction, but he felt the shock wave almost immediately. The subspace tremor buffeted the *Enterprise,* nearly shaking the first officer from his seat. *Thank heaven for Barclay's psionically enhanced deflectors.* He'd have to commend the hapless engineer for his creativity during a crisis, if the ship didn't come apart first. "Shields buckling!" Ensign Berglund called out, holding on to the tactical podium for dear life.

More shocks jolted Riker as the intense vibrations rattled every bone in his body. His aching head felt like a warp-core breach. Sparks flared at the conn station, nearly burning Ensign Clarze, who shielded his face with his arm. Riker glanced quickly at Picard, who grabbed on to the back of Deanna's chair to keep from falling. The entire ship was quivering like a Vulcan gong right after it had been struck. *Has the captain returned to the* Enterprise, Riker wondered, *just in time to perish with the rest of us?*

"Captain! Commander Riker!" Ensign Clarze shouted over the quaking of the bridge. "The warp engines have come back on-line."

Thank you, Geordi, Riker thought. *And just in time.* "Go to warp, mister. Now!"

Fee fie fo fum, I smell freedom. Here I come. . . .

The scent of freshly liberated neutrinos wafted across the great wall, bringing with it the promise of rescue after oh so many aeons. His pawn within the shiny silver bug, abetted by a piece of his own splendiferous spirit, had done its part at last. He sensed the forbidding fire of the great wall, the same damnable dynamism that had held him back for so long, crumbling beneath the ingenious assault of the clever little beings inhabiting the silver bug. A window was opening, a window through which he would finally be able to slip over to the other side, where an infinity of diversions awaited him, not to mention revenge on the perfidious Q.

Q is for quisling, he chanted impatiently. *Q is for quarry.* He'd hunt Q, he would, enjoying every frenzied heartbeat of the chase, and, at the end of the game, he'd show just as much mercy and understanding as Q had showed him at the moment of bleakest, blackest betrayal. *Q is for quitter, whose questionable quibbles and querulous qualms quashed my quintessential quest and quickened my quiddity to queer and quiescent quarantine.*

Within the barrier, reality twisted and contorted itself, creating a gap that had never before existed. So intent was he on the window that was being carved out of the unforgiving unity of the wall that he barely noticed the tiny silver insect fleeing frantically from the maelstrom it had engendered. Retracting his tendrils, compacting his entire being into a single infinitesimal point of consciousness, he watched and waited until the window opened all the way through to the other side.

He felt exotic solar winds, exhaled by a billion distant suns, blow against his provoked perceptions, inciting him onward.

With nary a nanosecond of doubt or hesitation, he hurled himself into the voracious vortex, diving for deliverance from an eternity of exile and isolation. The empty void of the window was like an ice-cold pond compared with the blazing furnace of cosmic energies that composed the wall. The shock was enough to stop his breath, assuming he felt the need to breathe, but he barreled on nonetheless, eager to reach the other side—where Q would be waiting.

Once before, he recalled, his scattered memory racing backward in time even as the totality of his being rushed back into the galaxy, he had flung himself through another window, the so-called Guardian of Forever. Then, too, Q had been waiting, but to help him, not hinder, not yet. *Oh, those were the days,* he rhapsodized, *days of fire and fun and furor.* He flew past the pierced substance of the wall, the wall that could no longer deny him. *Those days will come again.*

But the window was a fragile one, doomed to dissolve within a heartbeat. Already it was shrinking, squeezing him tightly. The gap was narrowing, the accursed wall encroaching on his escape route at a redoubtable rate. Again he recalled that earlier window, whose graven Guardian had strived so relentlessly to keep him from emerging into the new reality on the other side. For a time, he had been trapped in the window, held fast halfway between one realm and another. Then only Q had been there to pull him through, only Q had saved him, only to betray him when it mattered most.

Q is for quisling. Q is for quitter.

Now he was nearly trapped again, the window narrowing so quickly that he feared he would not be able to squeeze his way through to the other side, no matter how small he made himself, no matter how swiftly he soared nor how furiously he fought against the wall pressing in on him. Now, as before, it was Q that gave him the strength to continue, his hatred of Q and his desire for vengeance that propelled him onward despite the noxious narrowing of the window.

I'm coming for you, he howled into the star-strewn galaxy ahead. *Coming for Q and Q and Q!*

The distant stars were closer now, but the scope of his view was diminishing rapidly, shrinking inward like the pupil of a cyclopean eye dilating in reverse. So close! *Close, closer, closest.* He summoned the remainder of his resources, all that he had not already entrusted to his surrogate beyond the wall, for one final spasm of speed to bring him beyond the boundary forever and ever. The wall tried to deter him, the frictional forces fighting him every inch of the way. Then, all at once, he was free of both wall and window, among the stars he had spied upon from afar. He had made it! Made it he had!

The window snapped shut behind him, shrinking into nothingness, the eternal wall regaining its seamless and sacred solidity, but he did not look back. There was nothing for him there, there never had been, only endless and immeasurable exile. His future, boundless and infinite enticing, lay ahead, like this gorgeous galaxy and its trillions upon trillions of waiting worlds. And Q, of course.

Q is for quarry, quoth I. Q will quake and quiver and quail. . . .

"Go to warp, mister. Now!

In an instant, the *Enterprise* was accelerated at warp speed out of the barrier and away from the wormhole. The bone-rattling shaking subsided and the eerie glow of the galactic barrier, which had filled the viewscreen since Picard's return to his ship, gave way to the reassuring sight of stars streaking past the prow at what looked like warp factor eight or more, faster than the subspace shock wave that had nearly destroyed the *Enterprise*. They'd had a narrow escape, but had they fled swiftly enough to escape 0 himself?

"Captain," Data reported, "according to the long-range sensors, the artificial wormhole has already collapsed. The total duration of its existence was no longer than 1.004 seconds."

"Long enough," Q said glumly, with uncharacteristic directness. "He's here. On the *Enterprise*."

Eight

> *"Little soldiers in a row,*
> *One big puff and down you go,*
> *Bodies, bodies, on the floor,*
> *Sadly you will play no more. . . ."*

The ominous ditty came from on high, echoing all over the bridge. Startled, Riker and the others looked up at the ceiling, searching in vain for the source of the inexplicable crooning. Picard recognized the raspy voice, as did Q, who could not repress a genuine shudder. "I never did like his singing," he said in a transparent attempt to maintain a brave front. For a moment, he reminded Picard inescapably of the in-over-his-head youth Q had once been. He could not possibly be looking forward to this reunion, not after playing such a deciding role in 0's downfall so many ages ago. *I almost feel sorry for him,* Picard thought.

He sat down in his chair and held his breath expectantly. He could not begin to imagine how 0 would manifest himself. Had the immortal entity changed at all over the last five hundred thousand years? What might all those thousands of centuries of banishment have done to him? "Be on your guard, Number One," he said tersely. "This entity is not to be trusted."

But could Q? The thought fleetingly passed through Picard's mind that maybe what he had witnessed in the distant past had been nothing more than an elaborate fiction, an illusion created by Q's vast and limitless power. *No,* he concluded, *that does not ring true.* Although he conceded that Q could certainly create just such a shadowplay if he so chose, Picard knew in his gut that all he had seen had truly happened. 0's crimes had been real, and so was the present danger.

A Q-like flash of light at the prow of the bridge heralded 0's arrival. He appeared in front of the viewscreen, facing Data and Ensign Clarze. The helmsman lurched back in his seat involuntarily while the android merely cocked his head in contemplation of the stranger's miraculous entrance and striking appearance.

"Do you still like to play games, Q?"

Picard barely recognized 0. He looked like a refugee or disaster victim, freshly rescued from some barren asteroid or moon, who had long since abandoned any concern over his appearance. His foppish finery had been reduced to rags and tatters, his shredded green velvet coat hanging like streamers from bony shoulders now a few sizes too small for his garments. Oily, uncombed orange hair, streaked with geriatric shocks of white, spilled over those same shoulders, joining a thick, matted beard through which cracked, yellow teeth bared a skull's unsettling grin. Callused toes, the nails curled and overgrown, protruded from beneath the overlapping strips of fraying damask wrapped around his feet, the left of which remained twisted and distorted. Ancient scars climbed up his deformed ankle, disappearing beneath the torn cuffs of his antique trousers.

The emaciated figure before Picard bore little resemblance to the charismatic ne'er-do-well who had so captivated the younger Q. The present Q stared aghast at what 0 had become. "By the Continuum!" he whispered hoarsely.

The interdimensional exile appeared to have fallen on hard times indeed. *Perhaps,* Picard hoped, *he is no longer as powerful as he once was.* Certainly there was a glint of utter insanity in the figure's gleeful blue eyes that Picard did not recall seeing there before. The wild eyes searched the bridge hungrily, taking in every detail before settling on Q. A string of saliva drooled from one corner of 0's mouth.

"Q!" he proclaimed. "And not just any Q, but my Q, the Q of all Qs!" His manic grin stretched even further, more than Picard would have thought was even possible. Was it just his imagination, or were 0's very features more fluid and mutable than he remembered, as if the crippled castaway could no longer be bothered to maintain a consistent appearance? The bones and musculature beneath his beard and sallow skin seemed to shift subtly from moment to moment. "I told you I'd be back, I did. Are you ready for our game? I know I am."

"What game is that?" Q said warily, keeping his distance. He slowly raised his palms toward 0, just as he had once attempted to fend off Guinan the first time they encountered each other upon the *Enterprise.* He looked ready to defend himself if necessary.

Glancing back at tactical, Picard saw Ensign Berglund reach for her phaser. Catching her eye, he shook his head to discourage whatever she had in mind; he was not about to risk any crew member's life on a futile attempt to take the omnipotent intruder into custody. *Let's see what happens between him and Q before we try anything rash.*

"Why, the only game that matters, Q old Q. The game of life and death, remember?" He pointed a curling yellow fingernail, at least three centimeters in length, at Q, who flinched instinctively even though no lightning bolt or metaphysical death ray leaped from the extended digit. "I'm game if you are."

"More gamy than game, I think," Q said, unable to resist the insult. He wrinkled his nose at 0's wretched and debased appearance.

"Don't put on airs with me, Q!" 0 barked, so vehemently that Q stepped back in alarm. "I knew you when, don't forget." A bolt of energy leaped from his open hand, smashing through Q's defenses as if they didn't exist and knocking Q off his feet. The impact of the blast was enough to make the whole ship lurch downward, throwing everyone forward. Picard grabbed on to his armrails to keep from falling onto the floor of the command area. The inertial dampers restabilized their orientation after a moment, but it was a terrifying demonstration of the power that remained within 0's degraded shell. Picard wanted desperately to intervene, to take a stand against 0's callous disregard for the ship and the crew, but he knew better than to provoke 0 to no purpose. *This is Q's game for now. Let him play the first cards.*

0 paced back and forth before the viewscreen, dragging his mangled foot be-

hind him. "Are your wits as sharp as your tongue, Q? I wonder. You'll need all your wits to play my game. It's time to be tested!" He fired another bolt that sent Q tumbling backward. "Sorry to keep you waiting."

"I could have waited a good deal longer," Q said weakly, climbing awkwardly to his feet. The look on his face deeply concerned Picard; Q looked genuinely surprised. *But is he shocked by 0's actions or his power?* Picard wondered. He could only hope it was the former, given that Q was their best defense against the dangerous entity. *Surely Q can put up a better fight than this?*

"No more waiting! Wait no more!" 0 cackled. "I had to wait for this shiny silver bug," 0 said, spinning around on his good leg to take in the entire bridge. "I had to wait a very long time. Long, longer, longest."

He's lost his mind altogether, Picard realized, a chill running down his spine. What was more to be dreaded, a cool and calculating 0 or a lunatic with the power of the gods? At least the intruder seemed focused exclusively on Q so far; he had yet to even acknowledge the presence of Picard and the others. *We're too far beneath him, I suppose.*

"What a fine, fast bug this is, too," 0 declared. Something wriggled beneath the tattered fabric of his oversized coat. *What in the world?* Picard thought. Peering more closely at the raving superbeing, he took note of various mysterious moving objects coiling sinuously over 0's shoulders and beneath his arms, making their way underneath his ragged clothing. With a start, Picard recalled the spectral tentacles he had sometimes glimpsed flickering about 0's human form during moments of great stress or exertion. He got the distinct impression that the consistency of that human guise had suffered as much as the rest of his appearance. He was almost afraid to guess what was lurking and flexing beneath 0's coat.

"I can use this bug, when I'm through with you, Q. I have places to go, people to free." The quivering tip of some luminous, phantasmal appendage poked from beneath 0's collar and through the unkempt cascade of hair flowing over his shoulder. It wagged back and forth next to where 0's neck presumably was, as if sampling the atmosphere of the bridge, then withdrew back into the concealing layers of hair and fabric. From the startled gasp and nervous gulp behind him, Picard guessed that both Berglund and Barclay had spotted the tendril as well.

"Careful," Q chided him, tugging at the neck of his Starfleet uniform. "You seem to have a bad case of writhing around the collar."

Was that an attempt at courage, Picard wondered, or was Q simply unable to overlook an opportunity to be snide? Knowing Q, he feared the latter.

"Don't worry, Q, I won't forget you." 0 limped across the prow of the bridge until he stood directly in front of the conn. "Just thinking ahead a bit. Remembering a Head I have to go get." He eyed the navigational controls with keen and avaricious interest. "Right," he muttered into his beard. "Ready the rudder. Ready and roaring."

He poked at the controls with a gnarled nail, keying in new coordinates with the speed and assurance of a veteran pilot, treating cutting-edge Starfleet technology like a children's toy. Picard was appalled at how quickly the deranged entity had mastered the intricacies of starship navigation.

"Wait! What are you doing?" Ensign Clarze protested as the ship began to pitch and yaw. Without thinking, he reached out and seized 0 by the wrist.

It was the last thing he ever did. Before anyone even grasped what was happening, a glowing tentacle burst from 0's chest, ripping his soiled shirt front asunder and wrapping itself around the young Deltan's throat. . . .

Nine

"Dr. Crusher, come quickly!"

The holographic physician's entreaty drew Beverly Crusher instantly to the biobed where Lieutenant Leyoro's body rested within the protective embrace of the surgical support frame. She left Deanna Troi, freshly wakened from her cortically induced coma now that the *Enterprise* had left the barrier behind, to watch over the unconscious form of Milo Faal, while Nurse Ogawa supervised straightening up the disarray caused by Lem Faal during his telekinetic rampage. *Thank heaven no one was hurt seriously,* she thought, although the crazed and mutated scientist remained at large, and capable of most anything, or so it seemed. *It must have been the barrier,* she realized; somehow the awesome psionic energy of the galactic barrier had amplified the Betazoid's already formidable mental gifts. *Was this what he was planning all along? No wonder he resisted all my efforts to protect him from the barrier.*

Crusher pushed such speculations aside to concentrate on the patient at hand. "What is it?" she asked the EMH. Had Leyoro taken a turn for the worse? At a glance, her condition appeared unchanged.

"Look," the hologram said, pointing at the monitor above the bed. "Her neurotransmitter levels are dropping dramatically."

He was right. The activity within the unconscious officer's brain was rapidly returning to normal. It was too early to predict what sort of neurological damage, if any, had already been done by her overstimulated synapses, but this was a very hopeful sign. "Did you do anything?" she asked the computer-generated doctor.

"I wish I could take the credit," he admitted, "but I'm afraid not. I was simply monitoring her condition as you instructed." He glanced past her at the ward beyond, where Alyssa Ogawa was retrieving the last of the fallen exoscalpels from the floor. Like everyone else in sickbay, Ogawa had removed her magnetic boots now that gravity had been restored. Another nurse was handing out newly replicated combadges. "What in the name of Starfleet medical protocols went on over there?" the EMH inquired, referring to Professor Faal's spectacular escape. "My programming did not begin to prepare me for any events of that nature."

"Join the club," Crusher murmured, preferring to focus on Leyoro's surprising recovery. What could have triggered this turnaround? The triclenidil, she wondered, or something else? Another thought occurred to her: Perhaps it was simply that the *Enterprise* had finally exited the galactic barrier? The removal of the barrier's direct influence upon Leyoro's artificially enhanced nervous system might account for the sudden diminishment of her symptoms.

"How is she doing, Beverly?" Deanna asked, joining her at Leyoro's side. Crusher noted that Ogawa had taken over the watch on Milo. *Good,* she thought. She wanted to know the minute the boy showed signs of consciousness.

"She's been through a rough time," the doctor told Deanna. Although Leyoro's brain was no longer in danger of burning itself out, the Angosian woman remained unconscious, her face immobile. "I can't say yet when or if she will recover."

Troi rested her hands gently upon the surgical support frame enclosing the stricken woman's torso. The EMH stepped aside to give her a little more room. "I can barely sense her consciousness," she said softly, "it's so faint. But she's in pain, terrible pain."

Trusting the counselor's empathic abilities implicitly, Crusher adjusted the dosage of analgesic being administered to Leyoro by the infusion system in the SSF. "That's better," Deanna reported a few moments later. She gazed at Leyoro's comatose face. "I've barely had a chance to get to know her, and now this. It's so tragic."

"She might well pull through," Crusher assured her. "I don't approve of how the Angosian military tampered with her biology, but their goal was to produce extraordinarily strong and resilient individuals. Survivors." She glanced up at the biobed display, glad to see that the patient's neurotransmitter levels were practically back to normal. She made a mental note to access the medical archives of the Angosian veterans facility on Lunar V as soon as possible, although she doubted that anything in their records bore a close resemblance to what effect the galactic barrier could have on a humanoid brain. "We shouldn't underestimate her innate stamina and recuperative powers."

"Not to mention the considerable talents and medical expertise of certain attending physicians," the EMH pointed out, leading Crusher to wonder briefly whether it was technically possible to turn down the volume on the hologram's self-esteem. He was just a little too much like the real Dr. Lewis Zimmerman, whom she'd had the dubious pleasure of meeting a few years back when she'd temporarily taken charge of Starfleet Medical; his ego had required excess stroking as well, she recalled. *I'll have to ask Data or Geordi about how to adjust the program.*

"What about Milo?" she asked Deanna. "Were you able to sense anything?" Milo Faal had not stirred since his unconscious body had been brought to sickbay by Sonya Gomez and the others, although the psionic-energy readings in his youthful brain were scarily similar to those recorded in his father before Lem Faal fled sickbay amid a flurry of telekinetic violence.

Troi shook her head. "I'm very familiar with the ordinary telepathic abilities of full Betazoids—you've met my mother—but this is something new. I've never sensed anything like it. It's like white noise. I can't even sense his emotions anymore."

Crusher frowned. This didn't sound good. She had to worry if Milo would wake with the same astonishing—and dangerous—powers his father had displayed. *Just one more thing to agonize about,* she thought; it didn't help that the eleven-year-old boy invariably reminded her of Wesley at that age.

How do I treat something like this? she wondered. *I could accidentally do more harm than good.* She was starting to wish she had never heard of the galactic barrier.

"At least his younger sister is fine," Crusher reflected. Little Kinya had come out of her artificial coma with no apparent side effects and was now napping quietly in the pediatric unit. Beverly wasn't looking forward to trying to explain to the toddler what had happened to her father and brother. Part of her was still astounded that Lem Faal could just abandon his children like this, no matter what the barrier had done to his mind. *In a way,* she thought, *that's even more unbelievable than his amazing new mental powers.*

"Why don't I check on little Kinya?" Deanna volunteered. Crusher recalled that the counselor had a Betazoid baby brother about the same age as Kinya Faal. "You have enough to keep an eye on here."

"Thank you," Crusher said, grateful for Troi's assistance during this crisis. Both children were going to need plenty of counseling now that their father had apparently lost his mind. "That would be very helpful."

Giving Leyoro one last look, Troi headed toward the emergency pediatric unit attached to the primary care ward. She had only been gone a few minutes, however, when a startled cry from Deanna electrified Crusher's senses and sent her adrenaline rushing. Crusher raced into the children's ward, Ogawa close behind her, to find Troi backed against a row of empty, child-sized biobeds, her hand over her heart. "I'm sorry, Beverly," she stammered quickly, her face flushed, "but he appeared so quickly he caught me by surprise."

Beverly didn't have to ask whom she referred to. The source of the counselor's startlement was readily apparent atop the counter beneath the pediatric supplies cupboard, his pint-sized legs dangling over the edge of the sleek metal counter. Little q was back, doubtless in search of yet another of Crusher's prescription lollipops. His cherubic face looked more anxious than she had ever seen it before.

"Scared," he confessed sheepishly, although of what the doctor couldn't guess. A pudgy little hand reached out to her. "Yum-yum?"

Then the floor tilted forward violently. . . .

At last, Faal thought. Long-range sensors reported the birth and almost immediate collapse of the wormhole he had created. The transitory nature of its existence did not disturb him; he had not expected his wormhole to last any longer than the ones previously generated by Dr. Kahn and her colleagues. However short-lived, the quantum fluctuation had lasted long enough to serve its purpose— to break through the galactic barrier to the other side. *I did it,* he thought triumphantly. *It I did.* After endless months of planning and striving, after what felt like half a million years, he had succeeded at last.

Now he could turn his expanded mind to even loftier matters. For so long, he had been forced by the limitations of his treacherous flesh to fixate exclusively on one goal, compelled to achieve genuine immortality before death by disease claimed him forever. He had seldom been able to spare one precious moment contemplating what he could do once he attained that immortality. Now, all at once, he had the freedom to find a new purpose in existence, to expand his work to a whole new level of scientific inquiry. *I have evolved beyond mere physical matter. Now my mind can explore the full potential of mind itself. . . .*

The frightened mortals surrounding him, chattering anxiously and cluttering up Engineering, could not appreciate his triumph. They were too caught up in the anxiety and adrenaline generated by his takeover of Engineering, not to mention their foolish Starfleet rigmarole. Even now, Lieutenant La Forge sought to take control of the situation, despite the true blindness into which Faal had plunged him. "La Forge to bridge," he reported, holding on to the tabletop display to keep himself oriented in the dark. "We need more security. Faal is free and dangerous." He shouted a command to his engineering crew, as well as to the first security officers on the scene, whose phasers had proved useless against Faal's inexplicable new powers. "Everyone else, stay away from Professor Faal. Keep at your posts. We still have a job to do!"

Daniel Sutter, a merely competent engineer in Faal's opinion, tried to guide La Forge away. "Sir, you should be in sickbay."

"No," La Forge said passionately. "I'm not leaving Engineering in the hands of that menace. I don't need my eyes to do my duty."

Faal shook his head in bemusement. *Specks. They were nothing but specks.* Even now, the sightless engineer could not see past the petty responsibilities of his post, beyond some routine mechanical repairs. Scanning La Forge's mind in an instant, Faal saw the entire infrastructure of the *Enterprise* laid out before him, from the replicator system to the warp engines themselves. Despite Faal's historic triumph over the barrier, part of La Forge's mind was still worrying about repairing a series of sundered thermal isolation struts, and the difficulties of realigning the off-axis field controller. Faal could have done so in an instant, simply by thinking of it, but why should he bother? He had transcended such mundane chores, even if La Forge and his equally shortsighted servitors had not. *The mind is all that matters now. My mind and the mind of one special child. . . .*

Yes, the child, a voice echoed at the back of his mind, so persuasively that he could scarcely distinguish whether it was his own thought or another's. *The child of Q and Q. The next stage in evolution, beyond the Q, beyond you. . . .*

"Beyond," he breathed softly, recalling the miraculous infant he had briefly observed in the *Enterprise*'s holographic child-care facility. Had not the female Q boasted that her offspring represented a potential advance beyond even the considerable evolutionary development of the Q Continuum? What more suitable subject could he choose for his experiments now that he had transcended his own mortality, achieving a state of being that perhaps rivaled that of the Q themselves? Only he and he alone had the predestined combination of preternatural power and bold scientific imagination to correctly study the unique phenomenon that was the Q child under controlled and rigorous experimental conditions. He had the intellect. He had the ability.

Now all he needed was the child.

He reached out with his mind, searching the entire ship for any sign of the supremely talented toddler. *Where is the child? The child of the mind.* Somehow he knew, perhaps via that voice whispering constantly at the back of his mind, that Q and his family remained aboard the vessel, pursuing their own enigmatic agendas. *The cursed Q, the meddling Q.* All that power and knowledge, he thought rancorously, wasted on frivolous antics and diversions; Q was an embarrassment to immortals everywhere. Faal was surprised at the intensity of the animosity he now felt toward Q. The bitter resentment seemed to course through his soul as surely as the metaphysical might he had absorbed within the barrier. *Damn you, Q,* he cursed, railing against an entity he had scarcely encountered before. *You don't deserve that child.*

His natural telepathy amplified more than he could have ever possibly imagined, he scoured the ship from deck to deck without stirring from his workstation in Engineering. As La Forge and his fellow mortals watched him warily from what they hoped was a safe distance, he located his target in sickbay of all places. *Where Milo and Kinya are,* he recalled, feeling a momentary pang before forcibly shoving the thought away. *Never mind those children. Mind over matter. The child of the mind was all that mattered.* Funny, how his path kept returning to sickbay. What other proof did he require that his destiny was following some mysterious preordained pattern? It was his scientific duty to take custody of the Q child, no matter who might try to oppose him.

That's right, the voice seconded his resolve. *Test the tot. Test him to the breaking point, then probe and peruse the pieces. Test him till there's nothing left of Q and Q. . . .*

The Betazoid scientist strode decisively, on strong and tireless legs, toward the exit. His work in Engineering was done. Now the future, in the unlikely form of a child, awaited him in sickbay.

He didn't even notice when the floor of the corridor pitched forward beneath his feet.

Instinctively, Beverly Crusher reached for q the instant she felt the pediatric unit dip toward the bow of the ship. Granted, the toddler was probably infinitely more indestructible than she was, but years of experience as both a doctor and a mother brought with them protective impulses too compelling to be denied. She snatched the child off the metal counter, holding on to him tightly until the floor leveled out again.

"What was that?" Troi gasped, gripping a biobed to steady herself. Standing in the doorway, Alyssa Ogawa looked equally startled. Beverly assumed that the EMH and the other nurses were monitoring Leyoro and Milo.

"I wish I knew," Crusher said. Was the *Enterprise* under attack again? And if so, from whom? The Calamarain? The barrier? Professor Faal? Q? Something else altogether? There were too many possibilities, she thought grimly, at a time when sickbay was too full already.

Carrying q with her, she peered through a transparent aluminum porthole, seeing no sign of either of the luminescent cloud-beings that had besieged the *Enterprise* earlier, nor any trace of the distinctive glow of the galactic barrier. Judging from the way the stars were streaking past, though, she saw that the ship had gone into warp at some point. *That has to be a good sign,* she thought. *I hope.*

She tapped her brand-new combadge. "Crusher to bridge. Is there an emergency?"

Lieutenant Barclay responded to her hail, indicating that both the captain and Commander Riker, not to mention ops and security, were too busy coping with the latest crisis. *At least Jean-Luc is back,* she thought, the bridge having alerted her to the captain's return. *That's something.*

"There's an intruder on the bridge," Barclay stammered, sounding badly rattled. "Another Q, I think, or something like him. I really don't know much more." She could hear him gulp even over the com line. "Prepare for casualties, Doctor. Barclay out."

Casualties? Another Q? Crusher craved more information, however bad, but knew better than to distract the bridge crew during a battle. This wouldn't be the first time she had found herself holding the fort in sickbay while praying that Jean-Luc and the others would save them all from the Borg or the Romulans or whomever, but that didn't make the waiting any easier.

Not surprisingly, the turbulence and activity had roused Kinya Faal from her nap. The little girl sat up in one of the pediatric biobeds and started crying. Crusher didn't blame her one bit for being frightened. She was feeling more than a little apprehensive herself.

She tried to hand Q's son over to Deanna, intending to calm Kinya personally, but he started to squirm and fuss. "Okay, okay," Crusher assured him. The last thing she needed was two crying kids; Kinya would have to wait a few more moments. "I know what you want." She nodded at Troi. "Deanna, can you get me one of those replicated lollipops from the storage locker? I think he likes the uttaberry ones."

"Actually, his favorite flavor is Baldoxic vinegar," the female Q said, appearing without warning between Crusher and Troi, "but I don't suppose you're familiar with that particular taste treat."

Crusher had never heard of it before and frankly she didn't care. How in the world was she supposed to get used to people just popping in like that? Her heart went out to Jean-Luc when she realized how many times the original Q must have startled him that way; it was a miracle that the captain's blood pressure was as consistently low as it was. "I thought we had a little talk about these surprise appearances," she reminded the female Q a bit testily.

"My apologies," the Q replied with surprisingly little argument. "Darling q just keeps me hopping, you know." She reached out for her child. "Forgive me if I don't linger to chat, but I'm afraid there's been some unpleasantness on the bridge, and I would just as soon see q safely elsewhere."

"What sort of unpleasantness?" Crusher asked quickly, desperate to learn more of what was happening on the bridge. She held on to q in hopes of delaying the female Q's departure for just a few moments. "Who is that intruder?"

"Well, it's a rather long story," the Q replied, a pained expression upon her patrician features. In her Starfleet uniform, she stood several centimeters taller than either Crusher or Ogawa. "A few billion years long, in fact." She paused for a second, placing an elegant finger beneath her chin as she considered how best to summarize the tale. "Let's just say," she said finally, "that an unsavory acquaintance of my husband has made a most unwelcome return."

What exactly did that mean? Beverly wondered. Had the *Enterprise* ended up stuck in the middle of some petty Q feud? Stranger things had happened, especially where Q was concerned. "What sort of acquaint—" she began.

A cry from the primary ward cut off her next question. *That sounded like the EMH,* she thought, anxiously wondering what had caused the disturbance and whether it had anything to do with the "unsavory acquaintance" the female Q had just mentioned. Or maybe Milo had woken up much like his father? Ogawa hurried toward the cry, but Beverly hesitated, reluctant to leave either child alone before she knew what sort of danger might have arrived. More shouts came from outside the children's ward and Troi ran to the doorway to investigate, only to back up immediately when she saw what was coming.

An instant later, Lem Faal appeared framed in the doorway, his eyes glowing with the energy of the galactic barrier, his lean face as cold and expressionless as a Vulcan's. Crusher knew in an instant that he had not returned to sickbay to check on his dormant children.

Faal's icy composure faltered perceptibly when he spotted the female Q standing behind Crusher. "You," he said in evident displeasure. "What are you doing here?"

"I don't believe we've been introduced," the female Q said stiffly. If she remembered Faal at all from their fleeting encounter in the holodeck a few evenings ago, she gave no evidence of it.

Faal eyed her like he might a specimen on a slide. "You don't matter anymore," he told her. "You're no longer the forefront of evolution. You've been rendered obsolete." His luminous gaze shifted from the female Q to the child in Crusher's arms. "It's the child I'm after. The child of the future."

"What?" Before any of the women could react to Faal's astonishing declaration, Crusher felt a powerful force rip baby q from her arms. She struggled to hold on to the child, but it was like trying to hang on to a loose padd during explosive decompression, something Beverly had personal experience of. The toddler was gone, and clutched under Faal's arm, before she even knew what was happening. Snatched from Crusher, q started to cry, but Faal placed his free hand against q's unprotected neck. There was a flash of discharged energy and q's body drooped limply within Faal's grasp, his tiny arms and head sagging toward the floor below.

A sense of horror rushed over Crusher, and she could only imagine what the baby's mother must be feeling. Had Faal just killed q? Was that even possible? At a glance, she couldn't tell if the child was still breathing, if that meant anything at all where a Q was concerned. "What have you done?" she gasped. "What did you do to him?"

"Anesthetized the subject," he clarified, "to prepare it for further testing."

Further testing? Crusher still couldn't believe what she was hearing and seeing. Even with his unearthly new powers, how could Faal knock out a baby Q? *What in heaven's name has happened to him?* she wondered, shocked as much by his psychotic behavior as by his unexpected new abilities. What had changed a noted physicist and father into a crazed stealer of children?

For the first time in Crusher's experience, the female Q's arch and haughty manner gave way to a very human emotional outburst. "My baby!" she cried out in anguish. "q!" Her eyes flashed with murderous hatred. "Give me back my son this instant!"

Faal laughed, remarkably unconcerned by the female Q's maternal fury. "That might have terrified me before, when I was a powerless corporeal being like the rest of them." He sneered in Beverly's direction. "But I'm stronger now, a transcendent being like yourself. Strong, stronger, strongest."

He keeps getting more and more disturbed and irrational, Crusher thought, remembering the soft-spoken Betazoid scientist she had met at the onset of their mission. He had seemed so sane, so normal, then. *It's like there's been a different person growing inside him.* How else to explain those dual brain patterns, as well as his increasingly criminal behavior?

The female Q was not interested in explanations. All she wanted was her child, and to strike out at the being who had harmed him. "Die!" she spat. "Die and disappear!"

She flung out her fingers—and nothing happened. Faal remained as humanoid as before, the anesthetized baby Q still tucked under one arm, his innocuous-looking fingers held out before him like a weapon. Then he did the last thing Crusher expected him to do. He started to sing.

> *"Sweet little baby,*
> *Peaceful you lie,*
> *We'll play some games,*
> *And then you will die. . . ."*

"Oh no," the female Q whispered, her confidence and anger replaced by an unmistakable look of alarm. Beverly could tell that more than just the sinister lyrics of the lullaby had disturbed her. She just wished she knew why.

Ten

Ensign Clarze grabbed on to the twisting appendage with both hands, trying to pull it away from his throat, but the inhuman limb was too strong, seeming composed of equal parts matter and energy. He opened his mouth, either to breathe or to scream, but could succeed at neither. He was being strangled to death upon the bridge of the *Enterprise,* before the horrified eyes of Jean-Luc Picard.

"Q!" the captain shouted at the other immortal, who stood dumbfounded next to Ops. "Save him, blast you!"

Although more solid than the spectral limbs Picard had intermittently spied in the past, this tentacle was not made of flesh as the captain knew it. Lambent veins of azure light, the same hue as 0's wild eyes, coursed along the length of the monstrous extension. It was like a limb of pure phaser fire, or a small child's first crude attempt at a hologram, but clearly no less tangible for all that.

Q blinked in surprise, as if the importance of rescuing one insignificant crewman had not occurred to him before. "As you wish," he said, apparently too unnerved by 0's return to want to debate the issue. Ignoring the radiant tentacle, he extended an open palm at 0 himself. A blinding beam of white light fell upon 0, throwing his ragged shadow upon the viewscreen behind him.

"Ha!" 0 barked loudly. He staggered, but did not fall, before Q's broadside. The white light washed over him, bleaching his image beneath its brilliancy, yet the manic grin on his face did not change. "Not bad at all, not at all bad. Picked up a grain more gumption over the ages, I see."

"I'd hoped to disintegrate you," Q replied, lowering his hand in disappointment. The white light seeped into the folds and crevices of 0's scarecrow-like form, leaving him conspicuously unharmed. "No such luck, alas."

Data, with his superhuman reflexes, reacted next. Springing from his seat at Ops, he dug his golden fingers deeply into the shining tentacle and struggled to pry it loose from Clarze's throat. Amused, 0 stepped back to let the android work, stretching the tentacle taut between his chest and the endangered ensign. No symptom of exertion showed upon Data's impassive features, but Picard knew that Data had to be using every kilogram of strength he possessed. Placed under tremendous strain, concealed servomotors within Data's arms and shoulders whirred audibly. Horribly, that didn't seem to be enough. The tentacle resisted Data's strenuous efforts while it continued to choke its victim, even as Riker hurried to assist Data.

"Security!" Picard ordered. "Phasers on full." Racing around the starboard side of the bridge, Sondra Berglund positioned herself so that Data was out of the line of fire, then unleashed her phaser upon the tentacle where it stretched between 0 and Clarze. A young security officer, Caitlin Plummer, joined Berglund, adding her own phaser to the assault. Parallel beams of crimson energy struck the tentacle, producing a crackling cascade of white-hot sparks, but the luciferous tendril did not come apart. 0 cackled raucously, insanely indifferent to whatever pain the three-pronged attack on his extremity inflicted on him. Smaller tentacles erupted from his shoulders, flailing about alongside his head.

Clarze's eyes bulged from their sockets, his tongue protruded from his wide-open mouth. "Keep firing!" Picard commanded, consumed by fury and frustration. *Couldn't anything stop this monster?* "Q!" he demanded. "You can't let him kill again!"

Q shook his head mournfully. "I'm sorry, Jean-Luc. I tried."

"Then try again, damn you!" Picard refused to give up, even as 0 laughed off the heroic efforts of four Starfleet officers to rescue their comrade from 0's homicidal grasp. He couldn't accept that he had to sit by helplessly again while 0 murdered with impunity. The destruction of the Tkon, as tragic and horrible as it was, had been a chapter out of ancient history, long known to Picard. This was happening *now.*

"What's the matter, Q?" 0 mocked him. "Not up to your game these days? Playing the impotent bystander again? Take a good look, Q. You're next!"

Intent on Q now, 0 released Clarze and retracted his ectoplasmic tentacle back into his torso. The Deltan ensign dropped from his seat at the conn, his limp body crumpling to the floor. Berglund and Plummer switched off their phasers immediately, but, moving even faster, Data had already knelt to check the young man's condition. Picard held his breath, hoping for the best, while the android's fingers felt Clarze's throat.

Data rose without ceremony, letting Clarze's skull lie where it fell. "His neck is broken," he announced gravely. "I regret to say he is dead."

Picard stared in horror at the young helmsman's body, at the deep bruises mottling his exposed neck, the blue cyanotic tint of his lifeless face. He remembered, with bitter irony, that he had assigned the inexperienced crewman to the conn because the captain had anticipated smooth sailing on this mission and it had seemed like a valuable opportunity to give new personnel like Clarze a taste of bridge duty. Now the Deltan youth's Starfleet career had been cut prematurely short, along with any other dreams or ambitions he might have harbored. All thanks to 0.

This one death should not shock me, Picard thought numbly. After all, he had already seen 0 murder trillions, when the sadistic entity condemned the entire Tkon Empire to extinction; intellectually, Clarze's brutal slaying was just one more casualty to add to 0's age-old list of crimes. But it didn't feel that way. "How dare you?" he said, his voice choked with feeling. He rose from his chair to look 0 in the eye. "He was only a boy."

"Bye-bye, boy," 0 sang giddily. "Boy oh boy." He snapped his fingers and Clarze's body stirred unexpectedly. Picard experienced a momentary surge of hope. Could Data have been mistaken? That was practically impossible, but there was Clarze moving again, clumsily climbing off the floor. Riker reached out to help the young man rise, then yanked back his hand abruptly, eyes wide with shock and disgust. Picard understood why when the figure's dead blue face turned toward him for a moment and he saw the emptiness in the fixed, blank eyes. Suddenly, he realized the full horror of what was occurring. Ensign Clarze was quite dead, in fact, but 0 had revived his lifeless body.

With awkward, jerky motions, the animated corpse of the Starfleet officer retook his former seat at the conn. Dead fingers mechanically tapped the helm controls. "There," 0 said smugly, "the boy is back where he belongs. Take us bye-bye, boy."

Even Q looked appalled by 0's latest atrocity. He released another burst of light against his former mentor, this time to even less effect. "By the Continuum," he whispered in hushed tones, "what have you become?"

"And you!" Picard said furiously, turning on Q. "Why couldn't you stop him?"

Looking puzzled and somewhat disturbed, Q contemplated his own empty hand, then peered suspiciously at 0. "I'm not sure," he said finally, three words that Picard had never expected to hear from Q. "He's . . . different now. He's found some new source of power."

"I don't like the sound of that," Riker said, leaving the empty conn and joining Picard. He signaled Berglund and Plummer to back away from 0 slowly before they attracted his attention. Picard didn't like the idea of leaving 0's zombie at the conn, but was not willing to sacrifice another crew member by assigning one to that post.

"Captain," Barclay shouted from science II. "The warp drive is accelerating." Proving him completely accurate in his assessment, the rushing streaks of white upon the viewscreen stretched even thinner, approaching invisibility as the *Enterprise*'s velocity increased by several orders of magnitude. "Warp factor eight point five," Barclay reported.

Is this 0's doing as well? Picard confronted Q again. "What's wrong, Q? You stopped him five hundred thousand years ago. How can he be more powerful now? Explain." Before he could attempt any strategy against 0, he needed to know what was happening.

"I don't understand," Q murmured, more to himself than Picard. "Unless—" An unwanted realization rushed over his features, chilling Picard as he was forced to wonder what dire possibility Q could have possibly failed to anticipate, and whether Q would even attempt to explain. "Oh no."

Before Q could share his fears, 0 turned his back on the conn and strolled counterclockwise around the bridge to where Q waited apprehensively. "The rudder is readied," he declared, "our course is corrected. Ready to play, Q?" The smirk on his face could not conceal the ancient enmity in his eyes. "Quisling. Quitter. Quarry."

Q flinched with each epithet 0 spat at him. "I didn't have any choice," he began, "not after what you did. You went too far, or farther than I wanted to go at least." His faced darkened as he remembered all that happened millennia past, all that he had just relived with Picard. "Besides, the Tkon won! They beat you fair and square."

0's cocky grin devolved into a grimace. "Quell your quibbles, Q, or I'll quash you like the quivering, quarrelsome quadruped you are."

"I should never have let you into this multiverse in the first place," Q said defiantly. "I should have left you to freeze in that arctic limbo where I found you. Which reminds me, I never got a chance to ask: Just how many realities have you been kicked out of anyway?"

"Quack! Quadroon!" 0 clenched his fists above his head and, spiderlike, matching pairs of energized tentacles sprung from his sides, granting him eight limbs in all. Four incandescent extremities leaped forth to ensnare Q within their grasp. Q seemed to welcome the clash, which had been so many aeons in the making; with uncharacteristic violence, he grabbed for 0's scrawny neck with his bare hands and began to throttle his onetime mentor and role model. Picard had never seen Q act so savagely.

For less than a moment, they grappled upon the bridge, 0's glowing tentacles wrapping around Q like coruscating cables, Q's fingers digging into 0's metaphorical flesh, each of them quite intent on squeezing the life out of the other. Then, in a burst of light that left Picard blinking, both figures disappeared from the bridge.

Where did they go? the captain wondered, staring at the empty space that two superbeings had occupied only a heartbeat before. Had that flash been Q's doing or 0's? They could be anywhere in time or space right now, he realized, battling for who knows how long. Was it possible that the dueling entities could keep each other occupied for all eternity, or at least a mortal lifetime or two? There were worse outcomes to imagine, even though he wasn't sure that even Q deserved to be locked in combat with his first and worst enemy until the end of time.

But what if 0 succeeded in destroying Q, as he clearly seemed to have the potential to do? Then every species and civilization could be facing mortal jeopardy. Picard found himself in the peculiar position of rooting for Q. *Better a mischievous imp like Q than the devil himself,* he thought.

In the meantime, he needed to prepare for the eventuality that either Q or 0 or both could return at any moment. He surveyed the bridge, his gaze quickly falling on the abominable sight of the murdered ensign's resurrected body still manning his former post, soulless fingers making minute course corrections to the *Enterprise's* trajectory even as Picard watched.

No, he thought. *Not one minute more.* Until this instance, he had always thought that nothing worse could happen to a sentient being than to be assimilated by the Borg, but this obscene desecration might have disgusted even the Borg Queen. Picard could only pray that no trace of Ensign Clarze's consciousness remained within the undead revenant he had become. "Ensign Berglund," he said coldly. "Give me your phaser."

Taking the type-1 phaser from the young Canadian officer, he clicked the weapon to its highest setting, then fired it directly at all that remained of Ensign Clarze. For a split second, an intense red glow outlined the reanimated body; then the phased energy broke down the atomic bonds holding the flesh and bone and blood together, vaporizing them until not a single molecule remained intact. Picard lowered the weapon to his side, feeling his heart pound within his chest. *0 will pay for this,* he vowed.

"You did the right thing, Captain," Riker said, standing stiffly at his side. "Request permission to take over at the conn."

"Make it so," Picard said hoarsely, grateful for Riker's offer to take the helm under such grisly circumstances.

Riker sat down at the conn, occupying the space so recently filled by Clarze's animated cadaver. "Let's hope Q and that other creature are gone for a long time." His fingertips rested atop the helm controls. "Shall I set course for Starbase 146?"

"Most definitely," Picard agreed. From the looks of it, the *Enterprise* was badly in need of maintenance. Furthermore, he wanted to warn Starfleet of the threat posed by 0 as soon as possible. Returning the phaser to Ensign Berglund, who had resumed her station at tactical, he resolved to contact Engineering next, to get a complete status report on the ship's primary systems from Geordi La Forge. Q had obligingly restored the lights and gravity upon the bridge, but what about the rest of the *Enterprise?* His hand hovered above his combadge.

"Captain," Riker addressed him crisply. The urgent tone of the first officer's voice alerted Picard at once that there was more trouble afoot. "The conn is not responding to my commands."

Blast, Picard thought. This was 0's work, no doubt. "Switch to auxiliary controls," he suggested.

Riker shook his head. "I tried that. I'm completely locked out." His hands marched over the controls decisively, but the hairbreadth streaks rushing past them on the viewscreen revealed that the *Enterprise* was still heading straight along the course set by 0 and his zombie helmsman.

An ominous suspicion stirred within Picard's mind. "What is our heading?" he demanded. "Can you deduce our ultimate destination?"

Riker consulted the navigational display at his console. "As nearly as I can tell, Captain, we're headed directly toward the very center of the galaxy."

I feared as much, Picard mused. "People to free," 0 had said in his ranting, rambling way. 0 almost certainly intended to use the *Enterprise* to liberate The One from his eternal confinement behind the Great Barrier, which surely meant that, unless Q succeeded in exterminating his ancient adversary, he and his crew had not seen the last of 0. Picard realized that he could not possibly let 0 unleash another genocidal superbeing on the cosmos, even if it meant destroying the *Enterprise*-E and everyone aboard. *Let us hope it doesn't come to that, and that 0 cannot immobilize our self-destruct procedure as easily as he took control of the conn.*

There was much he needed to explain to Riker and the others, but first Picard glanced once more at the spot where both 0 and Q had vanished from sight. *Where are you, Q,* he wondered, *and how can we stop the greatest mistake of your youth from wreaking havoc on the future of all who live?*

Eleven

"Gametime, Q! Ready to play?"

The corridors of the *Enterprise*-E were as streamlined and antiseptic as Q had come to expect from Starfleet. To be perfectly honest, he had always been a trifle disappointed by the Federation's sense of design, and this new flagship of Picard's was no exception. He would have gone for something a good deal more baroque or rococo; not as gothic as that dreary Deep Space Nine, but certainly something with a bit more flash and style.

Picard would hate it, of course.

But how had he ended up in this hall in the first place, and where was 0's voice coming from? Only a nanosecond ago, he'd been locked in mortal combat with the deranged entity, their respective powers pitted against each on a dozen different levels simultaneously. He could only assume his involuntary transportation to this unremarkable locale meant that he had lost the first round of their contest.

How terribly galling and unexpected. Q had hoped that the age and experience he'd gained since he last clashed with 0, over half a million years ago, would have given him considerably more of an edge this time around, but, no, he had failed to anticipate how greatly 0's insanity had progressed during his long exile. *His madness gives him the advantage,* he realized, allowing 0 to distort and transform reality, even transcendental reality, in ways that Q could equal only if he was willing to sacrifice his own sanity. He wasn't quite willing to go that far . . . yet.

"I said, ready to play, Q?"

0 appeared at the far end of the corridor. Once again, Q was shocked at how radically the castaway's self-image had mutated since the old days. His torn and shredded clothing testified to millennia of neglect and disregard, while his sallow

complexion and disordered hair reflected the chaotic jumble his mind had become. He was like a rabid beast now, with just enough cunning and depraved ingenuity to make him truly dangerous.

Even more alarming were the murderous weapons he brandished in each of his two hands and four tentacles. Primitive implements of death—a dagger, a phaser, a mace, a boomerang, a flintlock pistol, and a Capellan *kligat*—menaced Q, who had no doubt that 0 had made them real enough, in metaphysical terms, to inflict actual injury upon both mortals and immortals alike.

"Er, what sort of game did you have in mind?" he asked, deciding that it was not entirely prudent to ignore 0's query much longer. He tried to back away unobtrusively, only to discover that something hampered his steps. Glancing down in surprise, he saw that his legs were shackled together by a sturdy length of chain, about half a meter long. "What's this?" he asked indignantly. Try as he might, he could neither extricate himself from the shackles nor wish them away. 0's madness was too strong.

"Just a little something to even the odds. Odd, odder, oddest." 0 tapped his bad leg with his lower left tentacle. "You wouldn't want to take advantage of my innocent, illustrious infirmity, or would you?" He scowled beneath his shaggy beard. "You always had a soft spot for cheaters, a tedious tolerance for treachery. There'll be no cheating this time, Q, oh no. You're playing my game now, by my rules. Rue the rules, you will, the rules you'll rue."

"What rules?" Q demanded. 0's addled mind had left him about as coherent as some atrocious Klingon opera. "What game?"

Malicious glee glinted in 0's pale blue eyes. "Hide-and-seek," he said. "You hide, I seek. I find, you shriek." He waved his grisly weapons like a multilimbed savage. "You can go anywhere on this vast, variegated vessel, but nowhere else, nowhere at all. No Continuum, no cosmos, no craven retreat." His twisting Malay dagger whistled as it sliced through the pressurized atmosphere of the corridor. "Q is for quarry. Run, Q, run!"

"Don't you think this is something of a childish game for beings of our lofty stature?" Q suggested. He tried to transport himself directly to the Continuum, go in search of much-needed reinforcements. *I know I can make the other Q listen,* he thought, belying what he had told Picard earlier. *Never mind all the distractions of the Reconstruction. . . .* But the accursed irons upon his ankles apparently did more than simply inhibit any ambulatory motions. He was bound to this one particular time and place, for better or for worse. Mostly worse. "Perhaps we should just talk things over over a couple of steaming cups of Thasian ambrosia?"

0 responded by firing a warning shot with his flintlock that left a flattened lead pellet embedded in the ceiling above Q's head. The acrid smell of gunpowder filled the air. "No more talk!" he snarled. "Talk no more. I'll count until ten. Take your head start or I'll take your head."

A vivid picture of The One's disembodied cranium popped out of Q's memory like a monotheistic jack-in-the-box. He quickly pushed it back down again. *No more of that,* he ordered his omniscient unconscious. *The future looks bleak enough without dragging the past in as well.*

"One," 0 counted aloud, "thirteen, seven, eighty-four, *pi,* one hundred and eight . . ."

Who knows when he'll actually hit ten, Q thought. *I'd best put some distance between me and that walking arsenal.* Hide-and-seek, was it? Very well, there were lots of places to hide aboard a Sovereign-class starship, and Q knew them all.

He hobbled down the empty corridor, 0's lunatic countdown ringing in his ears. ". . . thirty-two, five, the square root of infinity . . ."

"What I don't understand," Riker said, "is why this 0 can't just blink himself over the galactic core on his own? Why does he need the *Enterprise?*"

The first officer had maintained his post at the conn, for all the good it had done them. The ship remained on course for the Great Barrier at the center of the galaxy, and nothing they had attempted so far had managed to override the coordinates that 0 had fed into the helm controls through the late Ensign Clarze's lifeless fingers. The *Enterprise* was on automatic pilot, and Picard didn't like it one bit. Few things were more frustrating than to lose control of his ship at such a crucial juncture.

"I'm not sure I can explain, Number One, at least not fully." He had done his best to concisely update Riker and the rest of the surviving bridge crew on the nature of the foe they now face. "For reasons I don't entirely understand, no doubt relating to 0's true nature as an advanced energy being, he cannot travel past lightspeed on his own power. In the past, he used the Q Continuum as a shortcut through space, or tried to harness the early Calamarain for his personal transport. Even though he is no longer physically manifest upon the bridge, I can only deduce from our current course that he is somehow still using the *Enterprise* as a means to traverse the considerable distance between the edge of the galaxy and the core."

Riker scowled as he inspected the readout at the navigational controls. "Well, he's getting there as fast as our warp engines will take him. I don't know what he did to our engines, but we're approaching warp nine."

Data confirmed his analysis. "To be precise, we are currently traveling at warp factor eight point eight nine nine nine and climbing."

That was not encouraging news. The sooner they came within range of the Great Barrier, the sooner 0 could use Professor Faal's revolutionary technology to liberate The One from his age-old prison. *We can't allow that to happen,* Picard resolved. He had seen with his own eyes the devastation that The One and 0 could inflict on a planetary, and even a stellar, scale. Perhaps Starfleet Command could assemble a blockade to stop the *Enterprise* from reaching the Great Barrier, even though that would surely deplete Starfleet's resources at a time when the Dominion and the Borg already had the Federation's defenses stretched far too thinly. *That has to be a last resort,* he decided.

"What if we separated the saucer from the stardrive section?" Lieutenant Barclay suggested. Picard was impressed by the sometimes nervous crewman's initiative; Counselor Troi's therapy sessions seemed to have borne some fruit.

"That might work," Picard agreed, "if we could positively determine that 0 was only aboard the saucer section, and that he couldn't simply transport himself onto the stardrive section when we attempted the separation." Besides, he considered, the bulk of the crew resided in the saucer section, not to mention Professor Faal and his children, and Picard was not inclined to leave all those souls to the tender mercies of 0, even if he thought it was at all possible to strand the insane superbeing upon the saucer. "I think we should consider other options as well," he said diplomatically, not wanting to quash Barclay's morale at a time when it was showing genuine improvement.

"First, we need to locate 0 as precisely as possible. If he *is* physically present on the *Enterprise,* as our heading suggests, I want to know where he is and what he's doing." Picard settled back into his chair, uneasy with all the vital questions that remained unanswered. "I wouldn't mind knowing where Q is, too."

His combadge beeped, heralding a message from an unlikely but familiar voice. "Q to Picard. I hope you're listening, Jean-Luc, because this mess you've gotten us into is getting worse every minute."

The mess I *got us into?* That was a singularly Q-like take on their situation, Picard thought, but now was no time to debate who was really to blame for 0's past and present abuses of power. "Where are you, Q?" he asked crisply.

"In one of your cramped and uncomfortable Jefferies tubes, if you must know," Q said. "Who designed these things? A Horta?" A weary sigh escaped the combadge. "Never mind that. The important thing is that I'm keeping 0 occupied so you can devise one of your typically heroic solutions to the problem at hand. But you have to hurry." Q's voice was hushed, as if he were trying hard not to be heard. "I'm not sure how much longer I can keep away from him—I mean, keep him distracted."

Picard had to wonder just how willingly Q had consented to play decoy. Was he voluntarily luring 0 away from the bridge, or was he merely putting a self-serving face on circumstances he was helpless to prevent? "What do you mean?" Picard asked. "What do you need us to do?"

"How should I know?" Q said impatiently. "You're the ones who specialize in triumphing against overwhelming odds. Have Data whip up some technobabble. Tell Counselor Troi to get in touch with her feelings. Let Riker punch someone." Exasperation gave way to desperation in his voice. "Do *something,* Jean-Luc. Don't you understand? He's going to kill me. Probably more than once."

"But why can't you stop 0 yourself?" Picard wanted to know. At the conn, Riker heard enough of Q's tirade to give the golden combadge a dirty look. "You subdued 0 before, when you were younger."

Another frustrated sigh. Picard could practically see Q roll his eyes condescendingly. "Let me try to explain this in terms your primitive intellect can grasp. He's *crazy.* Even the Q recognize a common consensual reality, a certain metaphysical bedrock or foundation that transcends even our own infinite command over time and space, energy and matter. The alternative is utter chaos, and we all understand that. So do the Organians and the Metrons and the Douwd and all of the other truly advanced intelligences. But not 0, not anymore. He's different now. He doesn't recognize any reality at all, on any level, except his own twisted perceptions, which means he's free to distort the fundamental underpinnings of the multiverse to an absolutely unthinkable degree. The observer affects the observed, Picard. Even your own quantum physicists know that. So 0's insanity grants him an insane amount of power. Does this make any sense at all to you, *mon capitaine?*"

"I'll take your word for it," Picard said. To tell the truth, he wasn't sure how much any human could truly understand the subtleties of existence as Q and 0 knew it. So one omnipotent being was more all-powerful than another omnipotent being? *Fine,* Picard thought. It wasn't intuitively obvious, but he could accept it if that was the case, which apparently it was. *I'm sure all humanoids seem equally inscrutable and unstoppable to an ant.* "Can't you offer any suggestions?" he prompted. "What about your wife."

"She has problems of her own at the moment," Q explained, not divulging the source of his information. "Protecting little q takes priority over everything else, even my own—wait, what was that?" Picard thought he heard footsteps in the background, plus a distinctive singsong chanting. *The Jefferies tubes have excellent acoustics,* he recalled. "I have to go, Picard. He's found me somehow. He's getting closer." Q sounded close to panic. "The ball is in your court, Picard. I'm counting on you."

"Q? Q?" Picard tapped his badge, but the transmission was over. Q was on the run presumably, somewhere within the labyrinthine network of access crawlways that ran throughout the entire ship. *He could be anywhere,* Picard realized.

He felt a stab of anger at Q. How dare he place the responsibility for defeating 0 on him? Not that he could have turned his back on this crisis even if Q had commanded him to, but it was typical of Q to make him feel as uncomfortable as possible. "Well, Number One," he said grimly, "it seems both 0 and Q are indeed still aboard the *Enterprise.*"

"Lucky us," Riker commented. His hands continued to manipulate the helm controls, stubbornly searching for a way to regain control of the conn. "Too bad our ship's sensors have never been able to get a handle on Q. Might make it easier to keep track of him."

"Maybe there's another way," Picard said, a thoughtful look coming over his face. "Data, I want you to carefully monitor energy demands throughout the ship. Let me know if you detect any unusual activity that might provide us with a clue as to our guests' whereabouts."

"Understood, Captain," the android acknowledged. He cocked his head in a quizzical manner. "Sir, would this constitute 'whipping up some technobabble'?"

Picard gave Data a wry smile. "I would not put too much credence, Lieutenant Commander, in any of Q's more acerbic remarks."

"I see, Captain. Thank you." Data returned his attention to the console before him. Suddenly, he assumed a more alert posture. "Captain. Commander Riker. I am detecting a dramatic surge in tachyon collisions against the ship's hull."

Tachyons! Picard knew exactly what that foretold, and his fears were confirmed when an iridescent cloud of vapor washed across the screen of the main viewer, accompanied by a thunderous roar that set the entire ship vibrating. The gaseous mass, so very like the conglomeration of vaporous entities Picard had encountered one hundred million years in the past, blotted out the streaking stars upon the screen, even as Picard felt the *Enterprise* drop out of warp.

"It's the Calamarain," Riker stated, speaking aloud what they all understood. "They're back."

Twelve

Pollen tickled the nostrils of his humanoid guise and Q fought against a compelling urge to sneeze, convinced that 0 would hear any nasal outburst from a dozen decks away. Perhaps the hydroponics bay was not such an ingenious hiding place after all.

Flora from all over the Alpha Quadrant and beyond filled the spacious nursery, growing from trays filled with a moist inert medium whose organic content Q preferred not to think about. The shallow trays were stacked one atop the other in parallel rows that permitted an individual to wander, if he was so inclined, between lush assortments of greenery that positively reeked of chlorophyll. It was Q's hope that the sheer abundance of life force would help mask his own energies from 0. He had briefly considered the ship's arboretum instead, but hiding in the woods struck him as just a little too obvious.

Q crouched behind a tray of venomous foliage ranging from the mildly toxic Borgia plant to the lethal cove palm of Ogus III; he found the deadly nature of these particular sprouts uniquely soothing and reassuring. Behind him, samples of Cyprion cactus grew beside a Folner jewel plant and a spray of blooming orange and yellow crystilia. The air was thick with the aroma of flowering vegetation.

His nose tickled again and Q was tempted to materialize a silk handkerchief, but he was afraid that even the most inconsequential use of his powers would register on 0's otherworldly senses. *One more thing to thank 0 for,* he thought resentfully; why, he had even been forced to go to the enormous physical inconvenience of actually *traveling* through the Jefferies tubes to the hydroponics bay, located quite unhelpfully on Deck 11, instead of simply willing himself there. Even though he sensed that he could still teleport within the confines of the ship, despite the burdensome fetters about his legs, there was no way he could bypass three-dimensional distances without producing subspace ripples that would call down 0 upon him like a Vulcan *sehlat.*

How ever did Picard and his sort ever cope with the tedious necessity of physically transporting themselves from place to place? The sheer monotony of it, Q thought, would surely drive him to suicide within days.

Breaking off a ten-centimeter spine from the cactus behind him, Q tried to use it to jimmy the lock on his leg irons. Unfortunately, he was an all-powerful superbeing, not a safecracker, and it seemed hardly likely that there were any veteran criminals aboard the *Enterprise* to whom he could turn for tips. What had been the name of that cutpurse and sneak thief with whom he had consorted three or four millennia ago? The one who stole all those cattle from Sisyphus? Now, there had been a rogue after Q's own heart; too bad he couldn't risk plucking him out of history for a quick refresher course in lock-picking.

At least he had succeeded in contacting Picard via the ship's primitive communications technology. Now it was up to the captain and his dauntless crew to snatch victory from the gaping maw of obliteration as they had so many times before. Q had tremendous faith in Picard; after all, hadn't the somewhat dour humanoid managed to surmount some of Q's most inventive puzzles? Q did feel a tad bit guilty about dumping 0 in Picard's lap, though. Despite what he had implied to Jean-Luc a few minutes before, he had to admit to some small responsibility for the present contretemps. In retrospect, he probably should have leveled with Picard earlier about the true purpose of the barrier, but he could hardly be expected to willingly divulge the imperfections of his youth, especially to so judgmental and self-righteous a lesser life-form as Jean-Luc Picard.

The tip of the cactus spine broke off in the lock, and Q tossed the remainder of the spine away in disgust. That was no good; he would have to think of something else. *What would Jean-Luc do in a fix like this?* he wondered, slightly embarrassed to have to resort to such a demeaning comparison. *How the almighty have fallen,* he brooded, indulging in a few moments of richly deserved self-pity.

A machete slicing through stalks of *Draebidium calimus* interrupted his intro-spection, raining violet petals upon his head. Q scooted back on his rear, impaling his dorsal region upon the sharp spines of the cactus. He let out a shocked and in-dignant yowl of pain before mentally expelling the stinging barbs from his back.

"Tag, you're dead!" 0 leered at him over the decapitated flower stems in the upper tray. "Dead you are." He took aim with his phaser, which was almost cer-tainly set to kill. "I always suspected you were nothing more than a hothouse flower, Q, unable to cope with cold, cruel choices outside the Continuum." He laughed ma-niacally, exposing chipped and corroded teeth. "Prepare to be pruned, petunia!"

Exposed and unarmed, Q grabbed a nearby hypo-atomizer and squirted 0 in the face with concentrated bacillus spray. The madman rubbed frantically at his eyes with his upper tentacles while firing wildly with his phaser. The crimson beam went astray, disintegrating a garlanic seedling and setting a patch of Diomedian scarlet moss ablaze. Then the beam swung in an arc, incinerating some bristly *mutok* cut-tings from Lwaxana Troi's private garden on Betazed before barely missing the top of Q's head. He felt the searing heat of the beam radiate down through his scalp.

With nothing more to lose, Q teleported away from the hydroponics bay, arriv-ing in a flash in a half-filled cargo bay on Deck 21. Molybdenum storage bins were stacked four high along the opposite wall. Clear and meticulous labeling identified their contents as, respectively, thermoconcrete, inertial dampers, driver coil assemblies, and self-sealing stem bolts. Nothing he could possibly have any use for, in other words.

He hurried toward the wide exit doors as quickly as his shackles would permit. He could not afford to linger at this site much longer; that bacillus spray was not going to detain 0 for more than a second or two, and he would surely be able to fol-low Q's fifth-dimensional trail to the cargo bay. Q loped down the corridor outside, scanning his new surroundings for the best possible escape route or hiding place: As he ran, he cursed the fateful moment he first heard 0's ingratiating voice singing through the snow of that frozen limbo outside reality. His close call with the phaser and the machete had shaken him more than he wanted to admit, even to himself.

Must get away, he thought, taking a sharp left at the next intersection. He passed a pair of Starfleet technicians at work repairing a power conduit behind a displaceable wall panel; they stared wide-eyed at his shackled state, but he did not waste a single breath to respond to their shouted inquiries and offers of assistance. There was nothing they could do to help him, not against 0. He had no doubt that 0 had created the cumbersome fetters to be phaser-proof.

Find someplace to hide, he urged himself, *someplace 0 will never suspect.* At any moment, he expected to hear the sound of limping footsteps behind him. He trembled just imagining it. The sensation of genuine fear was not something he had ever had the opportunity to become accustomed to; he hadn't felt so vulnera-ble and at risk since that time the Calamarain had hunted him after he lost his Q-ish abilities. How was he supposed to concentrate on outwitting 0 when he had to fret about being murdered at the same time? It just wasn't fair!

His self-made combadge beeped, and for a moment Q expected to hear Picard explaining the details of some cunning, Starfleet-style plan. Instead his immortal ichor went cold as 0's raspy, singsong voice came over the communications device:

"Say, Q, O Q, whatever happened to that fine, fancy filly you were fiancéed to, once upon a time? She wouldn't happen to be aboard this sleek, shiny ship, would she? Perhaps looking out for some wondrous whelp or another?"

Q, he thought in alarm, *and little q, too . . . !* What could this unscrupulous monster want with them? *Aside from revenge on me, that is.* This was absolutely intolerable; he couldn't allow 0 to turn his perverse attentions to Q's family, no matter what was required.

"Don't tell me you've stooped to picking on women and children, 0?" Q squeezed all the scorn and sarcasm he could muster, which was quite a considerable amount, into every syllable he uttered. "What's the matter, *mon ami?* Hide-and-seek proving too much to handle? Finally find an opponent you can't cheat or bully into submission?" He tsk-tsked into the badge. "What a disappointment. Here I was looking forward to a good, challenging game, but I guess that's not to be. Pity. Why, even these insignificant humanoids have given me better competition than this."

"Run, Q, run!" 0 barked via the badge. Q prayed to the highest power he knew, himself, that his barbs had indeed hit a nerve within 0's chaotic consciousness, enough to make the insane expatriate forget all about Q and q. "You can't fool me," 0 insisted, dashing Q's hopes. "You're as transparent as Time, Q, as obvious as ozone. You think if I go chasing you-Q-you, this wily old wanderer will leave your tart and your tyke alone." A bone-chilling cackle emerged from the badge. "But you're wrong, Q, wrong as Reason. I have them already, or part of me does. . . ."

0 appeared in a flash, only five meters away. The three-sided *kligat* whizzed past Q's ear, lopping off a lock of his hair. "Hide, Q, hide!" he hollered, his husky voice echoing down the corridor. "This game's not over until I say so, unless I kill you by mistake!"

Thirteen

The standoff between Lem Faal and the female Q had drawn a crowd. Nurse Ogawa lingered in the doorway to the pediatric unit, flanked by two security officers summoned to the scene. Their phasers were raised and ready, although they held their fire for fear of hitting the hostage q. Behind them, the EMH stood on his toes, trying to peek over the shoulders of the security personnel. "This is highly irregular," he protested. "Why won't anyone listen to me?"

This is my fault, Crusher thought, staring helplessly at the tranquilized child under Faal's arms. *I should have given q to his mother the moment she appeared, but instead I stalled her in hopes of finding out more about some trouble on the bridge.* Now she still didn't know much more about what was happening elsewhere on the ship, but an innocent child had been taken captive by an insane and potentially dangerous individual who had somehow attained enough power to keep q from his mother.

"I know you," the female Q said cryptically, glaring at Faal with anger and contempt in her eyes. "At least I recognize the part that's pulling the strings behind this pathetic puppet show. The Continuum should have annihilated you, and all your loathsome comrades, when we had the chance. Eternal exile was too good for you."

Crusher had no idea what she was talking about, nor, from the looks of him, did Lem Faal. "You're just trying to confuse me," he accused. Beverly shuddered at his eerie white eyes. "I have a duty to science to study this child, to record his development, test his abilities to the utmost."

Even as he ranted like a mad scientist from some gothic holodeck program, Faal's telekinetic abilities began to reshape the pediatric unit into a laboratory of sorts. The supply cupboards turned into visual display monitors, charting the Q equivalent of brain waves and metabolic functions. The elevated incubator at the center of the ward morphed into a transparent dome about a meter high and another meter in diameter. *Did he intend to cage q inside there?* Crusher wondered. *For how long?* Faal was acting like he intended to experiment upon the Q child for as long as q lived, which was probably forever. Her heart ached at the prospect of an innocent child, immortal or otherwise, treated like a guinea pig, while his mother watched helplessly. *There must be some way to stop Faal without endangering q, but how?*

"Deanna," she whispered to the counselor, who had retreated to the back of the chamber, "take Kinya and go. I don't think he'll stop you." Crusher refused to leave the pediatric unit while the Q child was in jeopardy—this was her sickbay, after all—but there was no reason to risk either Troi or the sobbing little girl. She took care not to refer to Kinya by her full name, lest the female Q get the idea to retaliate against Faal by taking his own daughter hostage. *I hope she's not reading my mind right now,* Crusher thought. Fortunately, the mother Q only had eyes for her child while Troi scooped up the frightened girl and edged toward the exit cautiously, watching Faal with wary eyes.

As Crusher had anticipated, the scientist couldn't have cared less about Troi or even his daughter, paying no attention as the security officers stepped aside to let them pass. She exhaled a sigh of relief. That was two fewer individuals she had to worry about, at least in the short term.

Then, just to make matters worse, the ship underwent another tremendous jolt. Crusher hoped for an instant that the unexpected turbulence would cause Faal to lose his grip on baby q, but he held on to the sedated child as if that were all that mattered to him. Beverly herself had to grab for the incubator to keep from falling, only to yank her hands back as she felt the solid transparent aluminum move beneath her palms like a living thing.

Stepping back from the shapeshifting incubator, while keeping close to the female Q to offer whatever moral support she could provide, Crusher saw one of the security officers speaking hurriedly into his combadge. *Good,* she thought. No doubt he was updating the bridge on the ongoing hostage crisis in sickbay. Crusher wasn't sure what Jean-Luc or Data could do that the female Q couldn't, but she didn't feel quite as trapped and alone anymore.

Then, to her surprise, she heard the unmistakable voice of Captain Picard responding personally to the officer's report. That was good news, no matter how dire things were here, since it suggested that the crisis on the bridge had calmed down for the moment. Had the mysterious intruder been dealt with, perhaps by Q? Beverly was surprised to find herself counting on Q of all people, but she couldn't imagine that Q would permit his own son to be threatened much longer. Between the two of them, surely Q and his mate could overpower Lem Faal, despite whatever uncanny attributes he had mysteriously acquired. *Where are you, Q?* she thought silently. *Do you even know what's happening to your child?*

"Under attack by the Calamarain," Picard's voice explained tersely, "plus an alien intruder of incredible power is loose aboard the ship. Keep on your guard, and do whatever is necessary to protect the children. Commander Riker is en route to take charge of the situation. Picard out."

Then the intruder has left the bridge and could be anywhere, Crusher realized. She knew that Jean-Luc could not possibly be referring to Lem Faal, whose identity was well known, so that meant there were now two highly dangerous individuals at large aboard the *Enterprise.* She couldn't imagine that was a coincidence. Plus the Calamarain had returned as well? Her spirits sank, taken aback by all the threats facing them. Only her faith in Jean-Luc Picard and her fellow crew members kept her hopeful that they would come through these multiplying hazards as they always had before. *We beat the Borg twice,* she remembered.

The incubator had completed its evolution into a high-tech cage. Faal nodded approvingly and his·eyes flared even more brightly for an instant. Suddenly, q was no longer under Faal's arm but deposited within the transparent dome. The female Q rushed to free him, arms outstretched, but flashes of crackling purple energy repelled her eager fingers as soon as they came within a centimeter of the dome. The enclosure was obviously protected by a forcefield, Crusher realized, one capable of withstanding the female Q's maternal might. She pounded on the forcefield with her bare hands, determined to shatter the obstacles between her and her son. Her fists smashed against the forcefield, sparking more flashes of energy, whose violet hue reminded Beverly of the galactic barrier itself, yet both forcefield and dome remained intact. "My q!" the distraught mother cried out. "Give me back my child!"

Faal ignored her heart-tugging plea. "Initiate experimental log," he coolly instructed the surrounding equipment. "File: Faal/hyperevolution. Title: Preliminary Notes on the Onset of Trans-Transcendental Consciousness in the Offspring of Advanced, Multidimensional Life-Forms. . . ."

No longer shielded by the proximity of the unconscious child, he presented a tempting target to the two security officers, who immediately fired their phasers at the seemingly defenseless scientist. Twin beams converged on Faal, who just kept dictating his notes.

". . . subject remains under sedation in observation chamber. In appearance, resembles humanoid infant of Terran ancestry, approximately two years in age. Observation: The population of *Starship Enterprise* is predominately of Terran descent, suggesting that subject's current appearance is a direct response to his recent environment, perhaps even a form of protective coloration. . . ."

The crimson rays bounced off Faal, rebounding back to their points of origin. Phaser beams struck the security team squarely in their chests, dropping them to the floor. Crusher thanked standard Starfleet procedure that weapons had been set on stun; in theory, the downed officers had not been permanently injured. Showing laudable initiative, the EMH began to drag the inert bodies out of the doorway into the primary ward, assisted by Ogawa. She knew she could count on the nurse and the hologram to tend to the fallen crew members as much as was necessary.

Faal appeared oblivious of the incident and its aftermath. ". . . exact chronological age of the subject has yet to be determined," he continued. "Further study is required. . . ." The biobeds along the portside wall of the children's ward started reassembling themselves into an array of scanners and probes whose precise functions Crusher couldn't begin to guess at. What kind of tests could you perform on a baby god? And could any of them actually harm little q? Metal and synthetic polymers flowed like liquid mercury while sophisticated electronic circuitry established new links and configurations.

The pounding and the phaser fire combined to rouse the toddler from his drugged slumber. He sat up slowly, rubbing his eyes, then looked around wildly as he became aware of his surroundings. The density of the transparent dome muffled his high-pitched wails, but there was no mistaking the panic in his eyes as he pounded at the interior of the cage with tiny fists. "Out!" he shouted. "Out! Out!"

"It's all right, sweetie," his mother tried to comfort him, placing her face so close to the forcefield that purple traceries flickered along her profile. "Mommy is here. Mommy's not going to leave you."

Claustrophobia must be especially terrifying to a child who is accustomed to teleporting wherever he wishes, Crusher thought. Her heart went out to the mother as well, their past differences forgotten. Beverly vividly remembered how anguished she'd felt when Wesley had been taken captive on Rubicun III. How could she not sympathize with what the female Q had to be going through?

Baby q spotted Lem Faal and drew back in fear. Somehow he seemed to know that the Betazoid scientist, with his luminous eyes and unfeeling expression, was responsible for his captivity. As small children have done throughout galactic history, q covered his eyes with his hands, evidently hoping that if he couldn't see Faal, then Faal couldn't find him. *Wesley used to do the same thing,* Crusher remembered.

The childish ploy appeared to touch some vestige of mortality within Faal. His expression softened, as if recalling similar behavior on the part of his own children. Beverly hoped desperately for a change of heart as abrupt and comprehensive as the alterations he was imposing upon the pediatric unit. But her hopes for a peaceful resolution to the crisis faded as Faal's lean face froze back into the impassive mask of a detached observer. "Subject's infantile attempt at concealment reveals perceptual errors arising from the immature nature of the developing superconsciousness. Confusion between objective/subjective criteria resembles comparable phenomena in the development of preadolescent primates and equivalent species."

That's one way of putting it, Crusher thought bitterly, both disturbed and offended by Faal's clinical description of a child in distress. Unable to watch q's torment any further, she glanced around the chamber, barely recognizing what had only minutes ago been a state-of-the-art medical facility. The mutated pediatric unit now bore little resemblance to its former self, as transformed in form and function as so much of the ship had been during the Borg occupation several months ago. Illuminated screens presented close-ups of q taken from every possible angle and in a wide variety of formats. Newly created scanners, reminiscent of the docking pylons at Deep Space Nine, loomed over the domed observation chamber like vultures intent on some dying prey. At the center of this intimidating array of technology, the trembling child in his miniature Starfleet uniform looked both out of place and vulnerable.

"Future areas of research," Faal droned on, completely unaware of how horrific the situation looked, "include physiological and behavioral responses to changes in environmental stimuli, including extremes of heat and cold, as well as conditions of absolute vacuum. Also to be explored: the long-term psychological impact of sleep and/or sensory deprivation. . . ."

Beverly couldn't believe what she was hearing. This was like some sort of inhuman medical experiment from the age of Khan Noonien Singh. Less than a meter away, the female Q looked like she wanted to personally dissect Faal himself. Crusher didn't blame her one bit.

"Dad? What are you doing?"

The voice caught them all off guard, even halting Faal's compulsive dictation. Crusher looked to the open doorway, where young Milo Faal stood unsteadily, holding on to the doorframe for support. "Dad?"

His eyes glowed just like his father's.

Interlude

Sickbay? How in blazes did I get to sickbay?

Lieutenant Baeta Leyoro awoke groggily upon a biobed, a surgical support frame pinning her down. Her head felt as if a Tarsian dreadnought had landed on it and her eyes throbbed like a photon grenade. She just hoped whoever zapped her felt a whole lot worse.

The last thing she remembered was being on the bridge. Her head had hurt then, because of that plasma-sucking barrier, but not as badly as it did now. Commander Riker had just ordered her to sickbay, over her vehement objections, and she had been making her way toward the turbolift about as slowly as she could without courting charges of insubordination. Then a white-hot light had exploded behind her eyes . . . and here she was, flat on her back like a damn fatality.

And this was supposed to be a peaceful scientific mission, she recalled. *Hah!* If there was one thing she had learned from a lifetime spent fighting, first for Angosia and then for Starfleet, it was that danger could strike at any moment. The rehabilitative counselors back at Lunar V would call that paranoia, she suspected, and tell her that she needed to overcome such "antisocial" tendencies, but what did any of them know about the life of a soldier? None of them ever had to worry about a Tarsian sneak attack, or be responsible for the security of a starship at the literal edge of the galaxy.

A sickeningly recognizable clap of thunder shook the sickbay, causing miniature warp-core breaches inside her aching skull. *The Calamarain,* she realized, feeling a savage sense of vindication through the pain, which now seemed to extend all the way down to her toes. *I knew we hadn't seen the last of those BOVs,* she thought, using a bit of Angosian army slang. Better Off Vaporized, it meant, although that had proved maddeningly redundant where the gaseous Calamarain were concerned. Still, barrier or no barrier, it was obvious the *Enterprise* was under attack once more.

I need to get back to the bridge. Never mind the pain, she wasn't about to slack off in a med ward while the ship was under enemy fire. Duty called, and she had a responsibility to defend the *Enterprise* to the best of her abilities. *Now, if I can just sit up without my skull exploding . . .*

Her first try went badly. She had barely lifted her head from the padded cushion of the biobed when a sharp, jabbing pain stabbed through the back of her head like a Nausicaan bayonet. Gasping, she let her skull drop back onto the cushion, shutting her eyes against the too-bright lighting overhead. She considered calling for a doctor or nurse, but knew that any medical personnel would just try to talk her into staying put. Probably just as well that nobody seemed to have noticed her return to consciousness yet; she hoped that didn't mean that Dr. Crusher and her staff were coping with too many other casualties to pay attention to her.

Let's try this again, she thought, gritting her teeth. She began to shove the surgical support frame off her, noticing for the first time that she no longer had any feeling in her fingertips. *I don't even want to know what that means.* The exertion caused her head to throb faster and harder, but she eventually succeeded in sliding the SSF up and away from her body. Then came the hard part: sitting up and putting her feet on the floor. The imaginary bayonet jabbed her again, but this time she was ready for it, letting the pain course through her even as she willed her muscles to keep on moving regardless.

Easy does it, she told herself as she slipped off the bed and onto the floor. At first, sickbay swirled around her like a gravitational vortex and she felt her stomach roll over queasily. The dizziness passed, though, and she took a moment to orient herself.

Where are all the medics? she wondered as no one rushed to her side. There seemed to be something going on at the other end of the ward, perhaps in the pediatric unit, but her eyes were too blurry to make out the details. *Doesn't matter,* she thought. The bridge was where she was needed most, directing the fight against the Calamarain.

Despite the disruptor blasts behind her eyes, and the creeping numbness in her limbs, a familiar exhilaration crept over her, giving her the strength to keep one foot marching in front of the other, right through the door out of sickbay. Forget what all those pill-pushers and head-shrinkers back on Angosia said. *"Reintegration into civilized society"* . . . *hah!* This was where she belonged, on the front lines again, doing what she knew best. Fighting to survive.

These Calamarain were a different kind of adversary, to be sure, but they must have their weaknesses, points of vulnerability that the crew could discover and take advantage of. Another thing she'd learned over the course of her career: No enemy was unbeatable. The trick was staying alive long enough to see your victory.

Once she thought she heard a voice calling after her, urging her to return to sickbay, but she didn't look back. She just kept walking.

Easy does it. . . .

Fourteen

"Tag!"

0 appeared sans fanfare atop the bar, kicking aside a row of freshly replicated glass goblets. They crashed onto the carpeted floor of the officers' lounge, shattering to pieces and showering Q with tiny glass slivers that might have stung him inordinately had he not had the wit and the wherewithal to transform them into harmless bits of soft-cooked rice first.

With the ship on alert status, the lounge was deserted except for a single Bolian bartender, who was currently hiding at the far end of the bar. The sky-blue upper hemisphere of his round head peeked over the rim of a bin of fresh ice, gawking wide-eyed at the ragged, scarecrow-like figure who had just materialized upon the bar. *I suppose it really is too much to hope,* Q thought, *that such a timorous specimen will have the fortitude to enforce the dress code around here.*

"Where's this?" 0 asked exuberantly, looking around the empty lounge. "This is where?" He hopped off the bar, his remnant-wrapped feet scattering the grains of rice further. Q could not resist staring in morbid fascination at the scarred and ruined remains of the madman's mangled left foot. "A well-stocked watering hole for wayward wanderers? An excellent choice, Q. I could do with a swallow of spirits. Hunting a heinous hound like yourself is thirsty work, or my name isn't—" He hesitated, his eyes glazing over as if he couldn't quite place his own appellation. "Faal? Q?" He smacked the side of his head and Q thought he heard neurons rattling. His madness would have been amusing if it weren't so unnerving. "0! Now I remember. You're Q and I'm 0 and you have to die. Devils and demiurges, do I need a drink!"

His upper right tentacle snatched a clear, cylindrical decanter from the bar counter. From the bilious green hue of the beverage sloshing within, Q identified it, with a revolted grimace, as Sluggo Cola, the most popular soft drink throughout the Ferengi Alliance. 0 pried open the bottle with his yellow teeth and spit the cap onto the floor. Q watched in amazement as 0 drained off half the bottle. *I thought only Ferengi could drink that dreck,* he thought, *or would want to.* "Ah, that hits the spot it hits." He thrust the bottle at Q. The viscous green brew fizzed when exposed to the air, sending a spray of tiny bubbles out the open neck. "Here, have a quaff on me, Q. Make it last because that's what it is, your last."

"Er, no thanks," Q demurred. If he absolutely had to choose a last drink, he'd prefer something more along the lines of a fine Saurian brandy, vintage 2247, say. "It's all yours," he insisted, pulling back his hands to reject the vile libation. Out of the corner of his eye, he glimpsed the Bolian bartender creep out the closest exit. *That's it,* Q thought, piqued by the mixologist's cowardly desertion. *He's definitely not getting a tip.*

"Drink!" 0 demanded, pointing both a phaser and an antique derringer at Q's head. "You weren't too proud to share a bottle of elixir the first time we met, or so I recall. Drink, Q, drink."

If you'd been drinking this loathsome concoction then, Q thought, reluctantly accepting the bottle, *I might have left you where I found you.* He discreetly wiped the neck of the bottle on his sleeve, eyed the spuming contents doubtfully, then closed his eyes and took a hasty gulp.

It was even worse than he had imagined, both slimy and sickeningly oversweet; he couldn't decide what was most unappetizing, the texture or the taste. Taken together, they made Klingon bloodwine taste like Chateau Picard in comparison. It took all his omnipotence not to gag on the repellent slop. Instead he forced himself to finish off the bottle. *If ever I had any doubts that 0 was a total sadist at heart, this clinches it.*

At least that insufferable Guinan creature was not around to witness his humiliation. Praise the Continuum for small favors! He wondered if Picard had finally had the good sense to dispense with her dubious services and, more importantly, if he would live long enough to congratulate Jean-Luc on his great good fortune if this were indeed the case.

Despite the truly awful nature of the Ferengi soda, he dragged out the last swallow for as long as he could, uncertain what 0 would do once this celebratory drink was concluded. He peered down the length of the bottle at the firearms poised to extinguish his immortal existence. Could he blink away faster than 0 could spray him with phaser fire and/or hot lead? Probably, but he didn't want to chance it. *I need a foolproof distraction,* he mused.

"Fast, faster, fastest," 0 ordered impatiently. His lower lateral tentacles yanked the bottle out of Q's hands so quickly that a mouthful of Sluggo Cola spilled onto the pristine carpet beneath their feet. "That's enough," he said, cocking the derringer and upping the setting on the phaser. "Say goodbye, Q. Don't worry. I'll take good care of that talented tot of yours, see if I don't."

"Watch out!" Q shouted desperately, pointing at the bar. "Behind you!"

0 frowned, giving Q a look of utter contempt. "Oh, now I'm disappointed, Q. Doubly and duly disappointed. That trick was old, old, old before I ever set foot in this great, glittering galaxy." He shook his head while keeping his guns aimed steadily at his onetime protégé. "A bad note to bow out on, boy oh boy. Good thing there was no one to see it but you and me."

Just then, the Calamarain returned with a vengeance. A dense, scintillating fog spread past the wide, panoramic windows of the lounge while a violent shudder shook the hijacked starship from prow to stern. "Smoke!" 0 exclaimed in surprise, taking his eyes off Q for only a fraction of a second. "That stinking, sulphurous, sanctimonious smoke!"

A split second was all Q needed. Humorless and vindictive the Calamarain might be, and sanctimonious, too, but he certainly couldn't fault their timing. By the time, 0 looked back at his quarry, Q was already somewhere else. Transporter Room Three, to be exact.

A single crewman was stationed at the transporter controls. A Caldonian, from the look of his bony forehead. "Halt! Who are you?" he demanded, with admirable presence of mind, when Q materialized without warning upon the transporter platform. He reached for his phaser, but Q had no time to waste with Starfleet security procedures so he simply relocated the Caldonian recruit to the first place that came to mind, namely the bridge. *Maybe Jean-Luc can use an extra pair of hands,* he thought.

Racing the clock, knowing that 0 would be following close behind him, Q hastily reset the transporter controls from about two meters away, programming the console to erase the coordinates as soon as it completed the transfer. With any luck, using the *Enterprise*'s own primitive matter-transmission technology would throw 0 off the trail for a time, at least long enough to give Q a chance to regroup and reevaluate the situation.

But where exactly to beam to? Q hesitated, momentarily stumped. He had already tried the hydroponics bay, the environmental science lab, stellar cartography, a shuttlebay, a torpedo tube, an empty escape pod, Picard's private quarters, the matter-antimatter reaction chamber, the gymnasium, the lounge, and inside Data's cat, but 0 had found him every time and he was running out of ideas. The *Enterprise*-E was larger than the last one, but it wasn't *that* much bigger.

Where next? The arboretum? Sickbay? The deflector dish? Suddenly, the perfect hiding place popped into his mind. And none too soon; even as he programmed the appropriate coordinates into the transporter controls, 0 appeared upon the platform less than a meter away, brandishing his bloodthirsty arsenal. "There you are there!" he cackled. "And no thanks to that fulminating fog that saved you the last time. Smoke and mirrors, that's all it is. Smoke and mirrors, I say!"

They're no friends of mine, Q thought, having no doubt that the Calamarain would be perfectly happy to see both him and 0 destroyed forever; after all, hadn't the gaseous beings been nursing the same grudge for over a million years? Granted, Q was forced to concede, there was something nauseatingly appropriate about their appearance on this occasion. The Calamarain, back when they'd been the Coulalakritous, had been there at the beginning of his escapades with 0, and they had never forgiven him for his own small part in that unfortunate episode, so it was only fitting (in a thuddingly hamhanded and moralistic kind of way) that they be here at the end . . . if the end this be. That their unexpected return had actually worked to his benefit at first he chalked up to pure coincidence, possibly the only force in the universe that was beyond even the control of the Q.

He did not explain any of this to 0. Why bother? Instead he said three little words that Picard and his predecessors had practically worn out over the last century or so. "Beam me up."

Q dissolved into a pillar of silver sparks. . . .

Fifteen

"And thou, all-shaking thunder, strike flat the thick rotundity of the world!"

Lear's immortal words came back to Picard as the Calamarain subjected the *Enterprise* to their tumultuous animosity. The ship pitched and yawed beneath their assault. He gripped the armrests of his chair tightly even as his spine slammed into the cushion padding the back of the seat. Coruscating bolts of lightning arced across the viewscreen, igniting flashes of sky-blue Cerenkov radiation wherever the electrical bursts intersected with the ship's deflector shields.

"Shields down to forty-four percent," Ensign Berglund reported from tactical. Given the destructive barrage directed at the *Enterprise,* Picard thought it was a minor miracle that the shields were holding up as well as they were.

"The extra energy we absorbed from the galactic barrier, and diverted to the deflectors, is fading the farther we get from the barrier, Captain," Lieutenant Barclay confirmed from his own station. "And the standard field generators were badly damaged earlier. Engineering is still conducting repairs."

"I see," Picard said gravely. According to Riker, before he left the bridge to cope with the crisis in sickbay, the *Enterprise* had already endured several hours of such abuse while Picard was away, before the first officer took the ship into the barrier to elude the Calamarain. What's worse, Riker also reported that none of the *Enterprise*'s offensive capabilities had demonstrated any lasting effect upon the living plasma storm, making retaliation all but impossible.

Perhaps that's a blessing in disguise. Knowing what he now did, Picard could hardly blame the Calamarain for their fury against 0 and Q and anyone else who might seem to be associated with them. When last he saw the Calamarain—mere hours ago by his reckoning, a million years past by the rest of the universe's—the sentient cloud of ionized plasma, or perhaps only their ancestors, had been frozen into an inert block of solid matter by 0's unearthly powers, with Q as his unwilling accomplice. The older Q had told him that 0's victims had remained frozen so for thousands of years. If the Calamarain of the present truly believed that the

Enterprise had deliberately liberated 0, as it must have appeared to them, small wonder that they were so determined to exact revenge. *Guilt by association,* he thought, *the hardest kind to refute.*

Riker had attempted diplomacy as well, and to no avail, but Picard believed it had to be worth another try. No matter how damning the evidence against them, which had only grown worse thanks to Lem Faal's unsanctioned breach of the barrier, he had to convince the Calamarain that they shared a mutual foe in 0. *That we protected Q from their wrath years ago cannot help our case,* he acknowledged reluctantly. "Data," he instructed, "initiate a tachyon transmission to the Calamarain."

The Calamarain communicated via faster-than-light particles, not speech as humanoids knew it. When last Picard had encountered them, Q's special brand of magic had permitted him to comprehend their inhuman language. Now, in the absence of Q and his miraculous abilities, he was forced to rely on a translation program newly devised by Lieutenant Commander Data, a program that Riker had warned still had some rough edges. *It will have to do,* he resolved.

Before he could begin to formulate his address, however, he was surprised by the unheralded appearance of a shocked-looking crew member, who appeared suddenly in front of the main viewer. Picard recognized Lieutenant Royel, a junior-grade officer assigned to transporter operations. "Captain? Lieutenant Commander Data?" The Caldonian crewman glanced around the bridge, clearly befuddled by his abrupt arrival. "I don't understand. I was just in Transporter Room Three a second ago, then this strange man appeared out of nowhere. He had a Starfleet uniform, but I didn't recognize him."

"Understood," Picard said, suspecting that he had a better idea of what had occurred than the displaced lieutenant. Picard took this as confirmation that 0 had not yet caught up with Q, and thus an encouraging sign. "I believe you ran afoul of the entity called Q." Royel's eyes widened in recognition of the name; Picard envied the lieutenant his prior lack of personal contact with Q, who had doubtless moved on by now. "You may return to your post."

"Yes, sir." Royel still looked a bit dazed, but ready and willing to do his duty. He headed briskly toward the starboard turbolift.

What did Q want with the transporters? Picard had to wonder. He felt like he was fighting a war on three fronts. The Calamarain without, 0 within, and Lem Faal raising havoc in sickbay as well. The Calamarain presented the most immediate threat to the overall safety of the ship, he decided, so that took priority at the moment. Q would have to keep 0 occupied for the time being, while Riker dealt with the problem of Lem Faal. "Is the translation program still on-line?" he asked Data.

"Affirmative, Captain. You may speak normally."

Picard took a moment to survey the bridge. With the priceless exception of Data, the bridge was uncomfortably devoid of senior officers. Leyoro, Troi, La Forge, Riker . . . all were injured or occupied elsewhere on the ship. At the captain's direction, Lieutenant Jim Yang had taken on the rather thankless job of manning the frozen conn, leaving Ensign Berglund at tactical. Picard had total faith in the young officers, who had all graduated at the top of their classes at the Academy, but, deep down inside, he had to admit to being slightly troubled by the fact that the most experienced officer on the bridge, aside from he and Data, was none other than Reginald Barclay. *At times like this,* Picard thought, *I rather regret that both Worf and Chief O'Brien transferred to DS9.*

Still, there was nothing to be done about it now. "Attention, people of the Calamarain. This is Captain Jean-Luc Picard of the *Starship Enterprise.* Please call off your attack on this vessel. Like yourself, we seek to contain the entity known as 0, whom we recognize that you have a legitimate grievance with. Let us discuss this problem and arrive at a solution of benefit to us all."

The storm continued to rage outside, and Picard feared that the Calamarain would not deign to respond to his diplomatic overture. Then, coming over the com system, an inhuman voice, flat and genderless, spoke for the gaseous life-forms laying siege to the *Enterprise:*

"We/singular am/are the Calamarain. Woe/vengeance to *Enterprise* for bridging moat/restoring chaos. Woe/tragedy to vastness/life entire. Crime/atrocity/madness. Shall not forget/forgive *Enterprise.* Dissipate/scatter/extinguish."

Riker had not overstated matters, Picard noted, when he said that Data's translation program still had some bugs to be worked out. This cryptic and expressionless communication bore little resemblance to the passionate discussions and debate that Picard had eavesdropped upon when he and Q observed the Calamarain in the distant past. Then the Calamarain had struck him as an immense symposium or university, devoted to the life of the mind and engrossed in an endless exploration of the cosmos, values quite in keeping with the highest ideals of Starfleet and the Federation. He heard little such common ground in the cold and somewhat garbled vocalizations emerging from the computer.

Still, the gist of the message was clear enough. The Calamarain blamed the *Enterprise* for releasing 0 back into the galaxy and were determined to exact revenge. How could he convince them otherwise, especially since the accusation was more or less true? He needed to persuade them that defeating 0 here and now was more important than assigning blame for the mistakes of the past. But how to do so, after Riker had done his best and yet failed at the same task?

I have an advantage Will did not, Picard realized. *I know who the Calamarain are and where they came from.* "Hear me," he said. "I speak not of the Calamarain, but of the Coulalakritous. I remember their suffering and understand their anger."

There was a pause, longer than before. Then the artificial voice spoke again, sounding as though it was coming from very far away:

"Who/how calls we/singular by oldest/sacred/hidden name? Who/how/why/where? Explain/illuminate now."

Well, at least I got their attention, Picard mused. The tricky part was going to be using this minor breakthrough to turn their attitude around before they did irreparable harm to the *Enterprise* and all aboard. "I have traveled to the past," he began, deciding that it might be more politic not to mention Q's involvement in that expedition, at least for now, "and I saw with my own eyes what 0 did to the Coulalakritous. It was an appalling crime and he deserved to be punished. But it is even more important that he not be allowed to commit further crimes. Save your strength for the true enemy. Help us against 0 now."

Was it just wishful thinking, or had the thunder and lightning outside subsided to a degree over the last few minutes? Perhaps he was getting through to the Calamarain after all. He prayed that was so.

"Shields down to thirty-seven percent," Berglund updated him, adding yet more urgency to Picard's efforts.

"Why bridge moat/succor chaos?" the Calamarain asked atonally. *"Enterprise* rescue/restore chaos then. Wherefore/how fear chaos now?"

That the Calamarain were seeking to understand the *Enterprise* at all, no matter how suspiciously, Picard took as a very positive development. He only wished he had a better answer. "We were deceived," he said simply. In truth, even now he did not fully understand what connection might exist between Faal and 0, although the Betazoid scientist's bizarre behavior and inexplicable new powers strongly suggested that Lem Faal must have had a secret agenda all along. *Deanna warned me,* he recalled, *that there was something not quite right about Faal.* But who could have guessed he was working to let loose an ancient evil from the dawn of time?

"No/negative. *Enterprise* cannot be believed/trusted. Chaos-haven yesterday/today/tomorrow. We/singular cannot be misled/deterred."

The Calamarain punctuated their unambiguous refutation of Picard's claims with a resounding clap of thunder that set the captain's ears ringing and shook the bridge like a raft adrift upon a surging sea. "Captain," Data stated with admirable composure, "external sensors report increased tachyon radiation against our deflector shields, approximately 69.584 rems along the berthold scale and rising."

"Thank you, Mr. Data," Picard acknowledged, scowling. The Calamarain did not emit tachyons solely to communicate, he knew; they employed the faster-than-light particles as weapons as well, effective against both organic and inorganic matter. Only the ship's crumbling shields protected the crew and the *Enterprise* from the deadly emissions, but for how much longer?

He glanced back over his shoulder at the lighted schematic of the *Enterprise*-E mounted on the wall directly behind him. Blinking amber lights indicated malfunctions on practically every one of the ship's twenty-four decks. If only the cutaway diagram could show him where Q and 0 were . . . !

Orange and yellow sparks cascaded from the secondary aft science station. "Not again!" Barclay yelped, backing off from the console in a hurry. He cast a frustrated glance at the engineering station a few posts away, its surface already charred and melted from a previous conflagration. "Science Two inoperative," he reported dutifully.

"Take over at environment," Picard instructed briskly, filling the position left vacant when Lieutenant Yang took the conn. Obviously, he needed to end this pointless conflict with the Calamarain soon, while there was a bridge left from which to run the *Enterprise.*

It's that old business with Q, Picard realized, silently signaling Data to deactivate the translator for a moment. *The Calamarain don't believe us because we appeared to take Q's side when they came after him nearly a decade ago.* He didn't regret saving Q from a summary execution on that occasion—at least not entirely—but it didn't make winning the cloud-beings' trust any easier. *Some kind of gesture of good faith is required,* Picard thought. *The burden of proof is upon the* Enterprise. *We need to trust them before they can trust us.*

"Ensign Berglund, prepare to lower shields at my command."

"Lower?" Her face blanched, but she quickly composed herself. "I mean, yes, sir."

"Captain," Data inquired evenly. Years of service under Picard made him more comfortable addressing Picard than the ensign was. "Are you sure that is wise, sir?"

"It may be our only chance, Mr. Data," Picard said. Out of habit, he tugged his jacket into place before signaling Data to resume the transmission. "Captain Picard to the Calamarain, in memory of the Coulalakritous." The ancient name had made an impact upon the Calamarain before; it couldn't hurt to invoke it again. "To prove that we mean you no harm, and that we sincerely seek peaceful cooperation with your people during the present crisis, I am prepared to lower our defenses. Please accept this gesture in the spirit in which it is intended, and refrain from taking violent action against us until we have had the opportunity to speak further."

Do the Calamarain even comprehend the concept of a truce? The Coulalakritous that Picard observed in the past had impressed him as a peaceful people, not a warlike or predatory species, although who knew how much their culture and psychology might have changed over the course of a million years? *I guess we're about to find out,* he thought. "Ensign Berglund, lower shields."

"Yes, sir," she said with a gulp. For a moment, he was almost relieved that Lieutenant Leyoro was confined to sickbay. The Angosian security chief would have surely objected strenuously to this particular tactic. *And she might well have been right,* he conceded.

Picard held his breath, his body as tense as an engaged warp coil, as Berglund carried out his command. The first evidence of its effects came when the brilliant blue flashes of the stressed shields vanished from the turbulent display of churning clouds and jagged thunderbolts upon the main viewer. He braced himself for everything from a catastrophic hull breach to the searing pain of radiation burns, but all that greeted his expectant senses was the muted rumbling of the storm as it seemed to hold back the full force of its fury. *Yes,* he thought, elated. The Calamarain were honoring the truce!

"Captain, look!" Ensign Berglund called out. She pointed at the ceiling above the command area, where a glowing mist was phasing through the solid duranium over Picard's head. He rose from his chair, his neck craned back, watching in wonder as what appeared to be an actual portion of the Calamarain entered the confines of the bridge. "Er, is this what you were expecting, Captain?" Berglund asked.

"Not exactly," Picard admitted, although this physical manifestation was not entirely without precedent. Ten years ago, during their previous encounter with the Calamarain, a segment of the gaseous mass had infiltrated the *Enterprise* in search of Q. *Welcome aboard,* he thought wryly.

The shimmering cloud, roughly the size of an adult Horta, descended from the ceiling and began to circulate around the bridge, inspecting its surroundings with evident purpose and curiosity. Lieutenant Barclay and the other officers were quick to make way for the traveling cloud, being careful to give it a wide berth, although the security officer stationed between the port and starboard turbolifts, Ensign Plummer, looked to Picard for guidance. "Shall I attempt to apprehend the intruder, Captain?"

Picard shook his head. He wasn't even sure how to approach the amorphous entity, let alone take it prisoner. "I believe we should think of this as more of an envoy than an intruder," he declared. The cloud completed its circuit of the bridge, then began to hover over the mangled engineering station, emitting a steady hum that reminded Picard of the honeybees in his father's vineyards. "Data, can we communicate with the entity at this proximity?"

"Just a moment, Captain," the android replied. His fingers moved across the operations panel faster than Picard's eyes could follow. "There," he announced less than five seconds later. "The revised algorithms, along with a directive to detect and produce low-intensity tachyon bursts via the inertial dampers, has been downloaded into the primary translation system linked to your combadge. That should suffice, sir, within a 94.659 percent range of accuracy." He shrugged sheepishly. "My apologies, Captain. It was the best I could accomplish under such rigorous time constraints."

Give Data a couple more hours, Picard, *and he could probably compose sonnets in Calamarain.* "This will do, Mr. Data. Thank you." He approached the iridescent cloud, being careful not to make any movements, sudden or otherwise, that might be construed as hostile. He felt a tingling sensation, like static electricity, upon his hands and face as he neared the representative from the Calamarain. *Do they have individual names,* he wondered, *or even a singular noun?*

"Greetings," he said. "Welcome to the *Enterprise.* I am Captain Jean-Luc Picard." Ordinarily, he would offer a hand in friendship but that hardly seemed appropriate given the complete absence of anything resembling an appendage. The vaporous substance of the entity appeared completely undifferentiated; he couldn't begin to tell where its head was, if that term had any meaning at all to the Calamarain. *Hard to imagine,* he thought, *that Q and I actually assumed the form of the Coulalakritous during our voyage through the past.* Already, the experience seemed like a half-remembered dream; his human brain had never been meant to retain the experience of existing as an intelligent gas.

"I am/are of the Calamarain." The voice emerged from Picard's combadge, sounding identical to the inflectionless tones the Calamarain as a whole had employed. "State/propose your intentions/desires."

Small talk was not on the itinerary, it seemed. "The entity called 0, who injured the Coulalakritous in the past, is aboard this vessel," Picard explained. "Can you help us subdue him before he does more harm?"

The cloud hummed to itself for several seconds before replying: "Negative/never. Chaos is too ascendant/hazardous. Condemned/congealed the Coulalakritous. I/we cannot oppose again/ever."

Picard thought he was starting to get a feel for the Calamarain's bizarre syntax, but he didn't like what he believed he was hearing. Although perfectly willing to defend the galactic barrier or punish the *Enterprise* for its perceived transgressions, it appeared the cloud entities were not willing to confront 0 directly. Were they merely made fearful by ancestral memories of their defeat and persecution in the distant past, or was 0 truly that much more powerful than the Calamarain? If so, then all their struggles might be in vain.

"Captain," Data spoke up. "Forgive me for interrupting, but I believe I may have located a clue to the location of either Q or 0."

"Yes?" Picard asked. He recalled that he had asked Data to monitor power consumption throughout the ship in hopes of keeping track of 0's pursuit of Q. He considered deactivating the Universal Translator for this discussion, but reconsidered. *Let the Calamarain see and hear what we are doing to cope with the danger.* Perhaps it would inspire them to action of their own. *I might even settle for a useful suggestion or two,* he thought.

"The EPS power grid indicates that Holodeck Seven is in use," Data reported. He turned from his display console to face Picard. "I find this unusual during a state of red alert."

So did Picard. *That must be Q and 0,* he felt convinced. Who else would be playing games in a holodeck in the middle of a galactic emergency? "Excellent work, Mr. Data. I think you may be on to something." He spun around to face the envoy from the Calamarain, a strategy for survival coming together in his mind. It would take all his diplomatic skills to pull it off, but maybe there was a way to put 0 back in the bottle again, before he could enlist The One to his cause once more.

"Listen to me," he told the swirling cloud of ionized plasma, standing so close to the radiant entity that the minuscule hairs on the back of his hands stood at attention. "I know that 0 hurt you badly long ago, but maybe you don't have to fight him alone. . . ."

Sixteen

"Dad?"

Milo hoped that he was dreaming, that he hadn't really woken up yet, but knew in his heart that this nightmare was all too real. That really was his father, his eyes glowing like a Tholian, getting ready to perform some kind of experiment on a baby in a transparent bubble. Looking more closely, he recognized the baby as that weird Q kid who had popped into the holodeck during their first night aboard the *Enterprise.* A barely healed scab on his soul tore open again as he remembered how impressed his father had been by the Q baby, even as he ignored both him and Kinya. *Figures,* he thought. Even with all that had happened—cloud monsters and the barrier and everything—*that* hadn't changed. Their father still cared about everything except his own children.

"Milo, please come away from there," a voice said behind him. "It's not safe." Counselor Troi placed her hands gently upon his shoulders and tried to pull him away from the doorway. He was very relieved to see that his father hadn't killed her after all, but he didn't want to be shuffled off to some holographic daycare center again. His father had gone crazy, it looked like, and Milo had to find out what was going to happen next, no matter what. "Please, Milo." The counselor tugged insistently. "Come with me."

"No," he said emphatically and, to his surprise, her hands sprang away from him as if burned. *Did I do that?* he thought, astounded. It sort of felt like he did; right when she let go of him he sensed something flow out of him. Like telepathy, but stronger. He *pushed* her away, using a muscle in his head he hadn't even known was there before.

Funny thing, though. Counselor Troi didn't look half as surprised as he was. Scared, yes, worried, sure, but not surprised. He looked into her mind to find out why and, sure enough, there it was. *The barrier.* The galactic barrier had given him amazing new powers, just like it had his father.

Does this mean Dad's not dying anymore? he wondered. He didn't like the image of himself he saw in the counselor's thoughts, with the creepy glowing eyes and all, but maybe it would be okay if this meant that his father had been cured of Iverson's disease. Maybe their family could finally get back to normal, sort of.

The way his father was acting, though, that didn't seem likely. He had glanced in Milo's direction when he first showed up, and for a second Milo had thought he saw a trace of real live interest, and maybe even a glint of approval, in his father's spooky new eyes, but then he went right back to staring at the Q baby like it was the Sacred Chalice of Rixx or something. "Beginning environmental testing," he droned aloud, more boring science stuff like always. "Introducing concentrated zenite gas into observation chamber. . . ."

Zenite? Milo didn't get it. That stuff caused brain damage, didn't it? He watched in horrified fascination as a gray mist began to fill the transparent dome containing the Q baby. What was the point of this? Milo had read all his father's scientific treatises, about the barrier and wormholes and such, and he didn't remember anything about testing zenite gas on alien babies. He felt faintly sick to his stomach.

The baby's mother, whom Milo spotted on the other side of the dome, looked more than nauseated; she looked positively crazed with fear. Tears ran down her cheeks and her eyes were wild. From out of nowhere, she somehow produced the largest phaser rifle Milo had ever seen and fired it directly at his father.

"No!" Milo cried out, but his father just looked annoyed. With a wave of his hand, he created a vortex in the air that absorbed the phaser beam before it reached him. Milo's panicked shout attracted his father's attention, though. He looked away from the Q baby to peer at his own son with new eyes. *In more ways than one,* Milo thought.

Meanwhile, the gray fumes reached the baby's nostrils. He wrinkled his nose and made a face. Then he stomped his feet and the toxic smoke turned into a miniature rainbow that dissolved into a hundred prismatic floating crystals before vanishing entirely. "Oh, good boy, q!" his mother gasped in relief, while stubbornly trying to shoot past the vortex protecting Milo's father. She fired high and low and even attempted a ricochet or two, but his father managed to keep the vortex between himself and the business end of the crimson phaser beam. "That's a very good boy!"

"Interesting," his father noted, talking to himself. "Subject responds to negative environmental stimuli through metamorphic substitution. To compensate for subject's paranormal behavioral strategies, future tests must—" The oncoming phaser beam attempted to bypass Faal's vortex by branching into two separate streams. Faal barely managed to summon a second vortex in time, blocking both forks of the phaser attack, but the effort broke his train of thought. He glared at the mother Q with a look that Milo knew too well: the leave-me-alone-I'm-working look.

"Milo," he called out unexpectedly. "I need your help, son. Use your new powers to keep that interfering woman away from me. Use your mind. Mind is all that matters."

Milo was stunned and excited. His father needed him? For the first time in months, since his mother died really, Dad was paying attention to him again, including him in his life. And all it took was these strange new powers. This was almost too good to be true.

"No, Milo!" Counselor Troi urged him. "You have to get away from here. Your father's . . . not well."

But he's still my father, Milo thought, shoving the counselor away more forcefully, all the way out into the adult ward. The more he used his new powers, the more natural they felt. *I can't let him down now, not when we finally have a chance to be together again.*

"Leave my father alone!" he shouted at the baby's mother. He felt kind of bad about it, since she just seemed to want her baby back, but his father knew what he was doing, didn't he? Maybe the baby wasn't really a baby, but some sort of the shapechanging alien in disguise. Like a Changeling or an allasomorph.

Whatever she really was, the distraught woman paid no attention to Milo, but just kept firing wildly at his father. By now the single beam had diverged into over a dozen separate forks, attacking his father from every conceivable direction. His father had been forced to transform his defensive vortex into a protective bubble that covered him from head to toe. "Please, Milo," he called. "I can't work under these conditions."

There had been a time, Milo recalled, before everything went wrong, that his father had sometimes taken Milo into his lab and let him help out with the experiments. Dad had given him simple tasks to perform, like replicating fresh isolinear chips or entering gravitational statistics into the wormhole simulations, and called him his "best lab assistant." Milo felt an ache at the back of his throat; he hadn't realized until now how much he'd missed that.

The ruby-red phaser beams hemming his father in, crisscrossing each other in their attempts to sneak past his defenses, reminded Milo of the Tholian webs in his favorite computer game, the same one he'd been playing the night he first met the baby Q and his mother. *Well, two can play at that game,* he thought.

With a thought, a pair of miniature Tholian warships popped into existence and flew straight for the woman (if that's what she really was) firing at his father. The diamond-shaped, prismatic ships began to enclose the woman within an intricate energy field consisting of overlapping rays of red-gold light.

At first, the woman looked more irritated than concerned by the web, sweeping the first few strands away with the muzzle of her rifle, but Milo closed his eyes and concentrated harder. To his surprise, he discovered he could still see the entire room even with his eyes shut. He clenched his fists and the severed strands snapped back into place.

Behind him, Counselor Troi pounded uselessly on the soundproof forcefield he had erected in the doorway of the children's ward. Commander Riker stood beside her, scanning the door with a tricorder and shaking his head. The invisible wall swallowed her words, but he could still hear her thoughts in his mind. *Stop it, Milo. This is wrong. Your father is wrong. You'll just make things worse.*

"Please, Milo, don't do this," Dr. Crusher pleaded, echoing the counselor. He had barely noticed the doctor before, standing behind the baby's mother, safely out of the line of fire. Now she eased away from the other woman, seeking safety from the glittering Tholian vessels. "You're making a mistake."

No, he thought desperately. Tears stung his eyes. *You're wrong. You have to be.* Both the doctor and the counselor had argued with his father before. They had insisted that the barrier would harm Milo and his father, might even kill them, but it hadn't hurt them after all; it had made them stronger instead, maybe even cured his father of the Iverson's, which everyone said was impossible. His father had been right then. He had to be right now, too.

Didn't he?

Moving as fast as Milo's racing thoughts, the tiny Tholian ships completed the web around the mother Q, enclosing her completely within a lattice of gold and red strands. "Very good, Milo," his father approved. Milo couldn't remember the last time his dad had actually praised him for anything. "I'm proud of you, son. Proud, prouder, proudest."

Lem Faal added his own strength to the web, so that Milo could feel his father's thoughts pulsing alongside his as they worked together, father and son united at last. There was a strange sort of shadowy tinge to his father's thoughts, like a tone in his voice that Milo had never heard before, but he didn't care, not as long as they were a family again.

The web contracted swiftly, limiting the woman's range of motion. She tried to sweep the strands away again, yet only succeeded in tangling the muzzle of her weapon in the unyielding strings of energy. She finally managed to yank the rifle free, only there was no longer any room to point it anywhere but straight up. The phaser beam shot through a gap in the lattice, ricocheting off the ceiling to continue its Hydra-like assault on Milo's father. "What is this . . . ?" she snarled, frustrated and angry.

Come with me, Counselor Troi begged him telepathically. *Your sister is safe. Let me take you to her. She needs you, Milo.*

Milo's eyes snapped open. *That's no fair!* Milo thought. How could she ask him to choose between his sister and his father? It's wasn't fair at all! He looked over his shoulder at the exit to the children's ward. Where was Kinya anyway? And how would she fit in, now that he and his father had been brought together by the magic of the barrier? They couldn't just leave her alone. They were all she had, and she was just a little girl.

"It's all right, baby," the woman sobbed to her child, her fingers reaching out through the gaps in the web. The anguish on her face tore at Milo's conscience. "Mommy won't leave you."

Milo couldn't help thinking that the baby's mother seemed more worried about her little boy than his father was about Kinya. *Or about me,* he admitted, *before I got these powers.*

"Good work, Milo," his father encouraged him as the web continued to contract upon the hostile woman. She could scarcely poke her weapon through the constricting strands anymore. The multiheaded beam emanating from the phaser rifle dwindled to a single narrow beam as she had to concentrate more of her energy to keep the netting away from her face and body. "Crush her son. Mind over mother. Crush Crusher, too. Crush her. Crusher."

What? Milo blinked in confusion. He saw a look of fear appear on Dr. Crusher's face as she heard what his father said. Milo didn't understand. What had the doctor done, except try to help them? She's wasn't a shapechanging alien monster or anything. Why hurt her?

"Son?" the mother Q said. For the first time, the ensnared woman looked away from Faal and her baby to truly focus on Milo. He was suddenly very scared by the cold intensity of her regard. Nobody (except his father maybe) had ever stared at him with so little feeling or compassion. His mouth went dry and he started to tremble, especially after a crafty smile lifted the corners of the woman's lips. *Please, Dad,* he thought. *Don't let her do anything to me.*

Too late. In a flash, he suddenly found himself inside the web, held tight against the woman, whose right hand was clenched around his neck like a magnetic vise. Her phaser rifle had vanished, and she had her other arm around his waist, even as his own web held him fast as well, the glowing strands of energy digging into his skin like taut optical fibers. *How did this happen?* he wondered in despair. *Nobody told me she could do this!*

"You!" she snapped at his father. "You and the creature inside you. I have a painfully simple proposition for you. You have my son. I have yours. Give me back my baby or I will exterminate your unfortunate offspring posthaste."

To make her point clear, she squeezed Milo's neck until he whimpered. *Help me, Dad,* he thought. He wanted to be brave, but his heart was pounding in his chest and his skin had gone cold all over. He tried to push her away with his mind, the way he had Counselor Troi, but she was too strong for that. Between the netting and her iron grip, he couldn't move a millimeter. *Don't let her hurt me, Dad,* he pleaded.

"No!" Dr. Crusher exclaimed, hurrying up to the woman as close as the patrolling Tholian vessels would allow. "I know you want to get your baby back, but you can't hurt this boy. He's not to blame for his father's madness. He's just a child."

"Don't tell me that," the woman said sharply. She sounded furious enough to kill entire worlds if necessary. "Tell his father. It's his choice to make. A child for a child. A son for a son."

Milo bit down on his lower lip, trying not to cry. *Please, Dad, give her what she wants. Give her back her baby.* Maybe the woman would go away then. He and his father could start all over again, and Kinya, too. He still wasn't sure what his father wanted with the Q baby in the first place, but he didn't want to die for it. *We don't have any choice, Dad. Let her have the baby!*

To his dismay, his father had to think about it. "Milo?" he murmured, and for a second he sounded like the father Milo remembered, even with the weird white eyes. "My son?" Then all the emotion drained from his face and, his neck turning stiffly like a badly programmed hologram, he looked down at the baby in the bubble instead. "No," he said mechanically. "This is the child. The child of Q and Q. The child of the future of the evolution of the mind. . . ." A padd materialized in his hand, and he began tapping out notes, as if neither Milo nor the baby's mother were even there anymore. "Appendix: Some Thoughts on the Relationship Between Advanced Consciousness and Corporeal Manifestation. To be completed following eventual dissection of subject. Compare and contrast to Vulcan concept of *katra* and synaptic pattern displacement in postsomatic organisms. . . ."

Milo's jaw dropped open as a pain as large as Betazed itself crushed his heart. This was the ultimate betrayal. Just when it looked like his father had finally started caring about him again, just when Milo had let himself hope that the bad times and the loneliness were over, Lem Faal chose the Q baby—and some stupid experiment—over the life of his own son! Milo slumped against the woman behind him, held up by the Tholian webbing stretched tightly against him. As he gave up on his father, the web Milo had created, with the help and encouragement of that same false father, began to fade away, as did the two tiny Tholian ships. Despite the absence of the web, Milo didn't even try to break away from the woman's grip. *Go ahead and kill me,* he thought bitterly. *I don't care anymore.*

Instead she shoved him away without a second's thought. "Go," she said brusquely, like she had no more use for him. Milo stumbled across the floor, dazed and uncertain. His legs felt hollow and limp, and he had to grab on to the edge of a tripod-mounted scanner several centimeters taller than he was. Dr. Crusher hurried around the back of the laboratory to throw an arm around him and guide him toward the door. The doctor's efforts barely registered on him; Milo was too numb to notice. *Now what do I do?* he thought, hurt and relieved and bewildered all at the same time.

The baby's mother had no answers from him. Freed from the scale-model Tholian web, she had gone straight to the transparent dome imprisoning her son. "Hang on, little q," she cooed, trying to reassure the anxious toddler. Her voice cracked as she spoke. "Everything will be okay. Mommy will get you out of there somehow."

"Come along, Milo," Dr. Crusher whispered in his ear. "You don't have to stay here any longer."

Milo dragged his feet, unable to look away from the heartbreaking spectacle going on only a few steps away.

The Q baby bounced up and down inside the bubble, reaching out for his mother, his tiny hands pressed against the inner surface of the dome. He looked confused and frightened, mystified by the unyielding barrier between him and his mother. "Mommy?" he cried. "Mommy?"

A new pang stabbed Milo's battered emotions. At least the Q baby, whatever it was and whyever his father wanted it, knew that his parent loved him and wanted to protect him, which was more than Milo could say. He couldn't bear to watch them anymore. *I don't care if they're not what they appear,* he decided. *A baby deserves a mother who cares about him.*

"I'll help you," he blurted.

The doctor tugged on his arm gently. "Milo, I don't think this is a good idea. Just come with me."

Milo wasn't listening. Shaking off her arm, he ran up to the woman who had, only moments ago, threatened to kill him. "Let me help you. You and me. Two against one. Against *him.*" The aching pain in his chest turned into anger and determination. He couldn't let his dad wreck *another* family. "Let's get your baby out of there."

The woman looked down at him, anxiety and fear giving way to hope in her eyes. She scrutinized Milo from top to bottom, weighing his sincerity, then nodded her head. "Yes," she said hoarsely. "I'll try anything."

His father was still tapping notes onto his padd, muttering to himself in what Milo's mother used to call "academese." He inspected the readout on one of the mounted display screens, then keyed the data into his notes. "The subspace dimensions of the subject are highly variable, with little apparent correlation to dimensions of humanoid manifestation. Disparate suggests further lines of inquiry along fourth-dimensional axis. . . ."

"Stop it, Dad!" Milo shouted as loud as he could, using his mouth as well as his mind. No matter what happened next, he was not going to let his father ignore him anymore. "It's over now. All of it."

Lem Faal looked up in surprise from his padd. "Milo?" He spotted the baby's mother standing beside Milo. "What is that irrelevant Q doing free again? I thought I told you to keep her under control."

Don't tell me what to do, Milo thought. *You don't have the right.* The anger poured out of Milo then. He couldn't have held it back if he tried. Months of pain and resentment and crushed feelings hit Lem Faal like the cloud monsters had hit the *Enterprise* before, over and over again. Lem Faal staggered backward, the padd with his ever-so-important notes crashing to the floor. The mother Q added her anger to Milo's, and it felt cleaner, purer than his father's contaminated thoughts had been. Between the mother's relentless need to rescue her child, and Milo's own resolve to end his father's madness, the power they wielded had become an irresistible force. Lem Faal tried to defend himself, vortexes and forcefields and flickering energy pulses springing into existence only to be blown away like cobwebs in a hurricane. He was driven back into a wall of monitors, the manifestations of his power evaporating like mirages. "Mind over matter," he babbled incoherently. "Mind over . . . Milo?"

All at once, the alien glow in his father's eyes was gone. He looked confused and disoriented, clutching his chest as he gasped for breath, which whistled plaintively through lungs that sounded weak and clotted. "Where is your mother, Milo?" he asked. "Where's Shozana?"

He sagged to his knees, then collapsed face-first onto the floor. "About time," the mother Q said without a trace of compassion, "although I doubt that was all of him. That was just a little piece of 0 that found a bit of power to nest in." She spun around and reached out for the transparent dome. This time no forcefield deterred her and the dome crumbled to dust at her slightest touch. Within a second, she had her baby clutched to her chest, stroking his head while she cooed in its ear. "My poor little q! My poor, brave little q!"

Now that it was over, his father crumpled upon the floor, Milo felt thoroughly drained. *At least it's finally over,* he thought. *At last.* He felt like he had lost his real father months ago, the same time he lost his mother. The rest was just a bad emptiness that went on much too long. A little piece of zero, like the mother Q said. A living, breathing hole where a father should have been. He dissolved the forcefield over the entrance and Commander Riker and Counselor Troi rushed into the children's ward. Phaser in hand, the commander knelt to check on his father while Counselor Troi squeezed Milo's hand in hers. "Let's go see your sister, Milo," she said softly, and this time he didn't push her away.

"You really scared me there for a moment or two," Crusher said to the female Q, who continued to stroke and comfort her child. The doctor felt thankful things had turned out as well as they had, thanks to young Milo. "When you threatened to kill Faal's son, I wasn't sure you were bluffing. Remind me not to invite you to our weekly poker game."

"Actually, I prefer contract bridge," the female Q replied, regaining some of her previous hauteur now that the worse was over. She beamed at her smiling child, wiping away the tearstains on his cheeks. Crusher thought q looked none the worse for his captivity. *Never underestimate the natural resilience of children,* she thought. *Especially a Q child.* "Forgive me if I don't stay to tidy up," the Q continued, looking around at the biomedical chamber of horrors that Faal had transformed the pediatric unit into, "but I have a rather important errand to run."

"What about him?" Riker asked gruffly, calling the Q's attention to the prone figure upon the floor. "Are you quite sure he's powerless now?"

"A good point," the Q conceded. Her eyes narrowed as she gave the problem of Faal a moment's thought. Then a very Q-like smirk appeared on her face, preceding a white flash that lit up the ward for a single heartbeat.

When the light faded, the containment chamber had been restored, but now it was Lem Faal, curled into a fetal position, who was confined within the clear dome. "That should hold him for the time being," the female Q declared. "Do feel free to run any tests you choose on him. The more painful the better."

And then both she and q were gone, leaving Riker and Crusher alone in the pediatric unit. Beverly hoped that Jean-Luc and the others were faring as well with the Calamarain and that unknown intruder. One more thing puzzled her as well.

What kind of errand does the female Q have in mind?

Seventeen

"Ugh. What a revolting sensation."

Q's skin still itched from his emergency beam-out; he'd forgotten just how crudely *tactile* primitive matter transporters could be. Still, it beat working up a sweat, he supposed. If he never saw another starship corridor or Jefferies tube for another hundred million years, it would still be too soon.

Nevertheless, here he was. Holodeck 7. Hundreds of alternative environments, and potential hiding places, available at his command. The next best thing to using his Q powers. *Quite ingenious,* he congratulated himself. 0 may have forced Q into this deadly game, but Q wasn't about to make it easy for him.

At the moment, of course, the holodeck was just a big, empty room waiting to be filled with three-dimensional illusions. A stark yellow grid pattern was laid out on the walls, floor, and ceiling, which were a singularly uninteresting shade of black. A pair of red double doors, surrounded by a streamlined archway that looked evocatively like a theatrical proscenium, marked the entrance of the holodeck for those who actually cared to enter via their feet. *Easier said than done,* Q thought ruefully, contemplating the unwieldy shackles about his ankle. He had hoped the transporter would leave the leg irons behind, but 0 had made them more stubborn than that. *I should have expected as much, but who'd expect a lunatic to pay such attention to detail?*

In its bare simplicity, the default version of the holodeck was about the least promising hiding place one could imagine. *But just give a few moments at those controls,* Q gloated, *and it will be a different story.*

"All right then," he addressed the archway, "show me the specialties of the house."

The holodeck controls, which had been programmed to respond to a wide variety of verbal commands, complied by displaying a menu of available programs on a lighted monitor embedded in the right side of the proscenium. He scrolled through the various options, not quite certain what he was looking for, but confident that he would know it when he saw it.

Aikido. *Too strenuous,* he decided.

Altonian Brain Teaser. *Meditation was not exactly what he had in mind.*

Ancient West. *Too rustic, not to mention conducive to shoot-outs.*

Ballroom Dancing. *Crusher's favorite, no doubt.*

Bat'leth Practice. *Left behind by the redoubtable Worf?*

Barclay 1-75. *Too numerous to choose from.*

Bridge Officer Examination. *Please!*

Champs Élysées. *Too French.*

Camp Khitomer. *Too Klingon.*

Christmas Carol, A. *He'd spent quite enough time haunting the shadows of the past, thank you very much!*

Q scrolled through the menu faster, glancing nervously over his shoulder. As brilliant as it was, his transporter trick wasn't going to throw 0 off the trail indefinitely. He might be crazy as a chronal conundrum, but his former mentor had an undeniable talent for showing up precisely where he was least wanted. He raced through the vast array of selections at a feverish clip, examining and discarding options as fast as the display could produce them. **Denubian Alps.** No. **Fly Fishing.** No. *Henry V.* No. **Klingon Calisthenics.** God, no. **Lake Cataria**. . . .

What about that delightfully seedy waterfront dive? he wondered. *With all that cheap hired muscle to throw at 0?* No, wait, that was on Janeway's ship. Would he ever have a chance to drop by *Voyager* again? Only if Picard came through, as was devoutly to be wished.

Moonlight on the Beach. No. **Orient Express.** No. **Rock Climbing.** No. **Romulan Firefalls.** No. **Tactical Simulation.** No.

Q was running out of time and hope when finally, near the end of the alphabetical listing, he spotted something that might suit his present purposes.

The Tempest. From Picard's beloved Bard, no less. Magic, trickery, and deferred revenge, plus an entire enchanted isle on which to elude 0. It was as close to perfect as he was going to find, particularly under the circumstances. Now if he could just call up the program before 0 arrived on the scene . . . !

The sound of a heavy object whistling through the air alerted Q only seconds before a spiked mace would have collided with his skull. Ducking just in time, he pivoted around to see 0 just a few paces away, his archaic pistol aimed at Q once more. "You can't trick a trickster, Q. Tricky, trickier, trickiest. A trick in a nick gives a bit of a kick."

His maniacal blue eyes searched their surroundings. "What's this, Q? This is what? Some kind of aboriginal game room? Very fitting. Fit, fitter, fittest. Good of you to get into the spirit of the thing; too bad the game's almost gone." He grabbed Q's arm to keep him from teleporting away, then cocked his revolver. Fingernails as long as knives dug into Q's wrist. "Any last words, Q? Better make them good ones."

"Yes," Q answered. "Begin program. Act One, Scene One."

The quiet of the holodeck became at once a scene of utter chaos. Q and 0 stood upon the rolling deck of a ship at sea, caught in the fury of a sudden squall. Sheets of cold rain pelted both ship and passenger alike. Sailors and civilians, the latter clad in drenched royal finery, ran about the deck in a frenzy of activity, shouting commands and warnings and heated imprecations at each other. The sky was dark with stormy clouds, not unlike the Calamarain, and the crash of white-capped waves competed with the howl of the wind and the rumble of thunder to drown out pages' worth of theatrical dialogue. Jagged tines of lightning stabbed at the mast and mainsails, threatening to set the tempest-tossed vessel ablaze. "Hang, cur!" a villainous-looking boatswain managed to bellow above the din, directing his tirade at one of the bedraggled noblemen. "Hang, you whoreson, insolent noisemaker!"

I couldn't have put it better myself, Q thought. As anticipated, the abrupt change in venue, not to mention the general tumult, distracted 0 sufficiently that Q was able to yank his arm free from an ectoplasmic tentacle and rush across the pitching, rain-soaked deck to put a sturdy holographic mast between himself and 0's primed firearm. *Thank you, Willie,* he thought, *for an effectively over-the-top opening.* Searching the horizon in every direction, using the electrical glare of a thunderbolt to dispel the worst of the gloom, Q spotted, right on schedule, a verdant island less than a kilometer away, its leafy greenery offering both sanctuary and, more importantly, seclusion. From 0, as opposed to the storm.

"Q! Tricky, tricky Q!" 0 limped after Q, his mangled foot equitably slowing the vengeful madman as much as Q's fetters impeded his escape. He fired his revolver, taking a chip out of the wooden rail beside Q. "Take your tricks to a watery grave, Q!"

Exit, stage right, Q decided, tossing himself over the rail into the surging, frothing sea. For a simulacrum created by shaped forcefields and holographic images, the water was convincingly cold and wet. Almost too convincing, in fact; Q swallowed several mouthfuls of holographic brine before he managed to kick his way to the surface, his head emerging amid a flurry of waves and wind. His heavy leg irons hardly helped him keep afloat, but he trusted that Prospero's magic (and the dictates of the plot) would carry him safely to shore.

Another gunshot, splashing into the water only centimeters from his head, convinced him to give the program a hand by striking out for the island as quickly as a modified breast stroke would carry him. He was sorely tempted to turn himself into a dolphin or a Markoffian sea lizard, but he might just as well fire off signal flares announcing his precise location to his pursuer. There was nothing to be done except paddle along in a humanoid form rendered unfit for this pseudo-environment by several million years of terrestrial evolution. *I tried to tell them that leaving the ocean for the land was a huge mistake, but did they listen to me? Of course not.*

It took longer than he would have preferred, and his arms would have ached had he been genuinely mortal, but time and tide eventually deposited him on a sandy beach unmarred by any trace of human habitation. Climbing to his feet, he brushed the wet sand from the front of his soggy uniform, while a chill slurry of sand and seawater streamed from his hair, running down the back of his neck. *Brrr!* Looking out over the sea, he saw the last vestiges of the squall driving the abandoned ship to a waiting harbor; in theory, the rest of the dramatis personae would be washing ashore anytime now.

Best to get going, he realized. Having not instructed the computer to cast him in any particular role, he remained an extraneous element in this *Tempest,* unobliged to take part in the actual narrative. Still, there was no reason 0 couldn't race ahead of the plot as well, once his scattered mind came to grips with the radically revised playing field. Q wanted to be safely lost in the jungle before 0 set foot on the island.

Facing the sea, across a perilously exposed expanse of sand, the jungle awaited. A thick growth of towering mangrove and banyan trees offered shelter and shadows in which to hide, preceded by hedges of high grass and leafy ferns. He bolted for the overgrown foliage, wishing there were time to erase the sandy footprints he was inevitably leaving in his wake. *I could really use a bushy tail right now,* he thought.

"Q!" a demented voice cried out behind him. "All ashore who's dying ashore!" Q peeked back over his shoulder to see 0 striding out of the surf, his stringy hair plastered to his skull. He looked as though he had walked across the sea bottom all the way from the stormswept brigantine. *Why didn't I think of that?* Q thought, snapping his fingers. *Because it didn't follow the logic of the play?*

Another instance where 0's lunacy, and propensity for cheating, gave him the advantage. *I'm going to have to think a lot crazier if I'm going to beat him at his own game.*

A flag upon a golden pole materialized at the end of 0's upper right tentacle, which jabbed the bottom of the pole into the sand. "I claim this isle in the name of 0 the First!" he proclaimed grandly. The emblem on the flag was a numeral zero that looked like it had been scrawled in crayon, or maybe blood, by either a hyperactive three-year-old or a fugitive from an asylum. Q leaned strongly toward the latter.

"What shall I name this serene and sandy shore?" Q asked aloud. "Q's End? Q-Fall? Q's Just Deserts?" He laughed raucously. "Too bad this isn't a *deserts* island!"

I still have a chance, Q thought. The outer fringe of the jungle was only a few meters away. With little to lose, he used his power to add wings to his feet. Literally. Two pairs of feathered pinions, chafing slightly at the edges of his shackles, propelled him into the sylvan sanctuary at hummingbird speed. A razor-edged boomerang chased him into the trees, slicing off the tip of an emerald frond before returning to 0's waiting tentacle. "Cheater!" 0 shouted angrily. "Cheat and charlatan! Cheat, cheating, cheater!"

Now there's the singularity calling the neutron star black, Q thought as he lost himself in the beckoning wilderness. He leaped over gnarled roots and trickling streams, heading ever deeper into the lush holographic scenery. He couldn't slow down to get some bearings because he could hear 0 crashing through the underbrush behind him, hacking at hanging vines and branches with a machete in each hand and swinging tentacle. "Run, Q, run!" he hollered. "Rotting bones in the jungle are as good as a burial at sea any day. Any day!"

Not exactly Shakespeare, Q thought critically, but the intent was clear enough.

The atmosphere within the tropical forest was hot, humid, and redolent of jungle violets. A dense, green canopy stretched overhead, letting through only shreds of artificial sunlight. Banyan and mangrove, mahogany and teak formed an arboreal maze through which Q ducked and weaved, changing course at random while trying to avoid running into any low-hanging boughs. Thankfully, this unnatural simulation of nature had been designed for relatively easy navigation by culture-seeking Starfleet drones already wrestling with the pitfalls and perplexities of iambic pentameter, so it was not nearly as clotted with underbrush and difficult to traverse as a real jungle would be. Thus, Q was able to make fairly good time, even hobbled by his increasingly aggravating leg irons; alas, the same applied to 0, although Q hoped that the deranged entity was having so much fun hacking and slashing his way through defenseless foliage that he might not realize such strenuous exertions were not entirely necessary. *This is a fantastical romance,* he thought caustically, deriving some small pleasure from his opponent's inferior knowledge of earthly literature, *not a quest for King Solomon's Mines!*

They were not entirely alone within this fictional forest. Monkeys chattered in the treetops while small animals of undetermined nature rustled through knee-deep ferns and creepers. Sometimes he heard the whispered conversation of unseen fairies and spirits, or ran to the lilting music of invisible pipes and drums. *"The isle is full of noises,"* indeed, Q thought. Once he even glimpsed a misshapen humanoid figure, shaggy of hide and webbed of hand and foot, who loped sullenly through the jungle, muttering to himself in verse. Caught up in his own predestined plotline, Caliban remained unaware of Q's uncanonical presence.

It was rather charming, in a lowbrow human sort of way. Q found it encouraging that Jean-Luc Picard, he of the somber disposition and rigid decorum, could find value in something so thoroughly fanciful, and regretted that he was too busy fleeing for his life to fully soak up the atmosphere. *Maybe some other time.*

"I can smell you!" 0 cried gleefully. To Q's distress, he sounded much closer than before. "Smell you I can!" Footsteps behind him silenced the chittering pixies. The ethereal melody wafting through the trees took on a more ominous tone, the rhythm of the drumming keeping pace with the narrowing distance between Q and his foe. *As if his singsong chanting wasn't bad enough,* Q groused silently, *now he has his own musical score!* "Here we go a-Q'ing, a-Q'ing we will go!"

Maybe *The Tempest* wasn't so ideal a setting after all. What he had hoped would be a refuge had turned into a hunting ground, with himself as the live game. *It's these infernal fetters,* he complained silently, chagrined at the cosmic injustice of it all. How could he, the epitome of the unexpected, whose expansive imagination and ever-restless energy had carried him to every corner and cubbyhole in creation, be reduced to shambling through a computer-generated facsimile of a nonexistent fairyland tucked into a single compartment of a dust mote of a starship light-years away from anything resembling true civilization. *This is no way for a Q to die!*

"I can see you, Q!" 0 sounded so close now that Q was afraid to turn around for fear of spying the deranged, multilimbed monster practically on top of him. "See, seen, saw . . . saw you in half, I will! See if I don't!"

With the sickening force of an inescapable cliche, Q saw his life pass before his eyes. Not the whole thing, of course—0 would be able to kill him a hundred times over and still have time to have the Federation for dessert before Q could relive his entire immortal existence—but faces and places from his wild and wayward past flashed upon the viewscreen of his memory, like a kaleidoscopic slide show from the life and times of Q:

The antimatter universe. The heart of a sun. The cliffs of Tagus III. The Guardian of Forever. The Coulalakritous. Gorgan, (*), and The One. The Tkon Empress. The War. The barrier. The dawn of the New Era. Guinan. Farpoint Station. Picard. The Borg. The Calamarain. Sherwood Forest. Vash. Amanda Rogers. Deep Space Nine. Sisko. *Voyager.* Quinn. Janeway. The Civil War. Q. Little q. . . .

The only face he didn't see, the one face he couldn't bring himself to look upon, even in his mind's eye, was the face following close on his winged heels. The face of his greatest folly.

The face that, in a flash, suddenly appeared in his path. A smile like a skull's stretched across 0's weathered features. His ice-blue eyes shone as bright as the supernova that destroyed the Tkon. Snakelike veins wriggled beneath the sallow flesh of his brow, threatening to erupt at any minute. Holographic seawater still dripped from his beard. "Surprise!" he crowed in manic delight. "Now you don't see me, now you do!"

Q's headlong momentum was such that he almost ran straight into 0's outflung tentacles. At the last second he threw himself backward, tripping over the knotted root of a sky-high mangrove. He tried to scuttle away, crablike, only to find that the chain linking his leg irons was caught on that very same root, which wasn't even a real root at all, but a confounded concoction of forcefields and projected images. *Hung up on a holograph, of all things! Talk about adding insult to (mortal) injury.*

"A good game, Q," 0 congratulated him. "Was it good for you?" He turned a machete into an iron spike, which he used to pin the chain to the exposed root, effectively nailing Q to the spot. "But after the best of tests, you end up like the rest. No matter the game, the end's always the same." He yanked a reddish hair from his own bristly beard, then sliced it down the middle with a long silver blade. "But you know that already, don't you? You figured that out a long time ago. Long, longer, longest."

No, Q thought defiantly. *For once, one of your cruel, childish games is not going to end the way you planned. I'm changing the rules even if it kills me.* With his shackles pinned in place, Q could not blink away, so he did the one thing he could do. "Computer, restart program."

They were back on the boat. Thunder pealed in the heavens as the outmatched brigantine yawed hard to port, tossing 0 to one side. His bad left leg could not support the sudden shift in weight, and he fell to the deck like a scarecrow knocked down by the wind. "Hang, cur!" the boatswain cursed the impertinent Sebastian. "Hang, you whoreson, insolent noisemaker!"

With the intrusive root dispatched to the same computer bank as the rest of Prospero's island, the iron spike was wedged into nothing at all. The spike toppled over and rolled away down the deck, freeing Q, who leaped to his feet. He savored the sight of 0, unable to regain his footing, floundering upon the storm-soaked deck, while holographic sailors and noblemen stepped over and on top of him. "Give it up, 0," he gloated, looking down at his sprawling adversary. "You must see by now that I'm hardly the naive young Q you so easily misled before. That was a half a million years ago, and while you've grown crazier, I've grown craftier. A *lot* craftier. You might as well quit now."

"Quit?" 0 sputtered angrily. He crawled across the deck on his hands and knees and tentacles, dragging his twisted leg behind him like a serpent's tail. "Q is for quitting, not 0. Never 0!" His mask of jubilant insanity slipped away, revealing the millennia-old hatred and bitterness underneath. The sheer intensity of his malignant fervor was enough to silence any thought Q might have had of gloating further. He had not seen 0 so angry since the stranger, an exile from realms unknown even to the Q, had stood against the collective judgment of the Continuum. "Enough," 0 spat. "Enough! Enough! Enough!" He slammed his fist down on the wet, wooden deck, so hard that the timbers cracked. "No more tricks!"

In a heartbeat, they went from *Tempest* to tundra. The simulated storm at sea vanished, taking with it all the theatrical noise and tumult that had twice thrown 0 off balance. Nor was there even an enchanted island on the horizon, let alone a sea to swim to safety in. Instead he was alone with 0 in the center of a desolate, frozen wasteland that seemed to stretch on forever.

"How's your memory, Q?" 0 challenged, his breath misting before him. Now that the surface beneath him—once a wooden deck, now a sheet of snow-covered ice— had ceased to roll upon frenzied waves, he levitated off the ice in defiance of gravity, then landed on both feet opposite Q. "This ring a bell? Ring-a-ding, ring-a-ding?"

"How could I forget?" Q replied. A biting winter wind blew flecks of snow against his face while his regulation Starfleet footwear sank into the icy crust. Cold and distant stars shone in the dark sky far above the endless, rime-covered plain, providing only the faintest of starlight. A single burning torch, held aloft in 0's right hand, yielded most of what illumination there was, casting lambent scarlet shadows upon the frosty tundra. Q needed no prompting to recall the bleak, inhospitable icescape where he had first encountered the being who introduced himself as 0. He knew instinctively that this was no hologram. 0 himself had created this arctic limbo from his own obsessed and spiteful remembrances.

Just the same, he couldn't resist trying again. "Computer, restart *Tempest* program. Act One, Scene One."

Nothing changed. The wintry Siberian wasteland remained, appropriately, frozen in place. *I thought as much,* Q admitted with a sigh. Picard's clever little toy had been superseded by a creator of far more dangerous games and amusements: 0.

Q shivered involuntarily. Just from the temperature, of course. He was unquestionably underdressed for this irksome Ice Age environment. That 0 could just stand there, enduring the frigid conditions while wearing nothing more than tatters and rags, was yet more proof of his insanity. *As if any more were needed.* Q indulged himself by summoning a little extra insulation from the ether. *There,* he thought, as the fabric draped upon his frame thickened. *That's better.*

A profound impatience with 0's sadistic notion of fun and games swept over him, dispelling most of his sense of self-preservation, never one of his strongest suits to begin with. Wasn't it 0 who taught him that there was more to immortality than playing it safe? He wouldn't run again. At least not yet.

"No more hide-and-seek," Q said. "How far are you going to go, 0? What form of insane restitution do you require?"

"Listen to you!" 0 snarled. "You sound just like that haughty, humorless Continuum that used to make your life miserable." He spat upon the hoarfrost, which sizzled as energetically as had the metaphorical marble tiles in the courtroom of the Continuum. "I should have known you'd turn out to be just another cowardly, craven, cringing conformist after all. Q is for quitter," he chanted. "Quitter is you, Q!"

A harpoon appeared within his free hand and, ranting all the while, he hurled it at Q. It struck home with brutal force, spearing Q in the leg. His left leg, naturally, now as useless as 0's.

After dodging missile after missile since 0's return, evading blade after boomerang after bullet by the slimmest of margins, Q had been just a nanosecond too slow this time. He dropped, overcome by shock and agony, onto the cold, boreal plain, his falling body carving a deep trench into the snow. *Serves me right,* he thought, clutching his impaled leg and rocking in pain. A stream of his immortal essence leaked out of the wound onto the frozen crust. It looked strikingly like blood. *The big problem with omnipotence is that it leads so easily to overconfidence....*

He felt sure that Picard would agree.

"Always a spear to spare. Never spare the spear, say I." Limping closer to his wounded prey, 0 chuckled and leaned over Q until his smirking face was less than a finger's length from Q, his hot breath fogging the air between them. "Game's over, Q," he said with surprising lucidity. "You lose."

Eighteen

"Lieutenant Leyoro, reporting for duty, Commander."

The Angosian security officer stepped out of the turbolift onto the bridge. Her eyes widened as she spotted Picard standing in front of a dense cloud of radiant plasma, hovering about a meter above the floor. Picard saw Leyoro reach for her phaser, only to discover it was missing from her side. It was hard to say, he thought, what had surprised her more: his return to the *Enterprise* or the presence of the alien entity upon the bridge.

"At ease, Lieutenant," he assured her. "We've reached an understanding with the Calamarain, whose representative this is. Unfortunately, the real challenge lies ahead. At the moment, the true threat is engaged with Q in Holodeck Seven. I was just about to beam directly there, along with the Calamarain."

"Permission to accompany you, sir?"

Picard considered her request. Some manner of security presence was in order, yet he was reluctant to introduce too many potential casualties to the conflict ahead. Ultimately, if his plan succeeded, the decisive role would be played by Q; there was only so much mere mortals could do to turn the tide in a battle between gods. *But that's just what I'm attempting to do,* he acknowledged privately.

"Excuse me, Captain," Ensign Berglund reported from tactical, "Commander Riker reports that the crisis in sickbay has been resolved with only one casualty: Professor Faal." She looked sheepishly at Leyoro, whose post she had assumed. "The Commander also reports that Lieutenant Leyoro has, um, gone missing."

Picard nodded. "Tell the commander and Dr. Crusher that we've located their missing patient." He gave the security chief a concerned inspection. Although hardly at death's door, as she'd been reported to be, she looked distinctly worse for wear. Dark circles hung beneath her eyes, which were shot with streaks of red. "Are you quite sure you're up to this, Lieutenant?"

"Yes, Captain," she said crisply. She walked over to the tactical podium and commandeered Ensign Berglund's phaser. "As head of security, it is my duty to see this conflict through to the end, sir."

Picard recalled the extraordinary physical feats that her fellow Angosian veteran Roga Danar had performed during his stay on the *Enterprise*-D. The man had actually broken free from a transporter beam, a feat Picard had never seen duplicated, before or since.

"Very well, Lieutenant," he said. "I commend your devotion to duty." He quickly brought Leyoro up to speed on his plan, then turned toward Ops. "Mr. Data, is the holodeck still in use?"

The android stared at his console with a quizzical expression on his face. "I believe so, Captain, although present readings are unusual." He sounded as though he could not entirely accept what he was reporting. "As nearly as I can tell, it is *snowing* in the holodeck."

If that doesn't prove that Q is on hand, nothing does. Picard decided to move promptly before either Q or 0 could relocate. "Mr. Data, you have the bridge. Three to beam to Holodeck Seven."

"Yes, Captain," Data affirmed, directing transporter operations from Ops. "Good luck, sir."

We're going to need it, he thought, as the transporter effect washed over him, enveloping Leyoro and the Calamarain as well, *since even if my admittedly improvised plan can be put into effect, the outcome is by no means certain.* There were too many unknown factors, including the daunting question of whether he, or anyone, could get Q to put aside his ego and behave rationally. *That would be a first,* Picard thought dubiously.

He recognized what the holodeck had become the moment his molecules reintegrated at the site. The windblown snow. The endless glacial emptiness. Even the faint gray stars high above. This was a flawless re-creation of that same polar purgatory where the young Q had been unlucky enough to make the acquaintance of 0. The cold, dry air stung his face and hands. A few steps away, her phaser drawn, Leyoro felt the cold, too, the icy wind turning her cheeks red. "Snow, all right," she said tersely, fog issuing from her lips. "Must be the place."

The Calamarain seemed unaffected by the cold. Picard recalled that the vaporous entities had to generate their own internal heat, and in significant quantities, in order to remain gaseous in the extreme cold of deep space. If anything, this environment was probably much warmer than the vacuum-dwelling life-form was accustomed to. *Perhaps someday,* he mused, *if and when the menace of 0 is contained, the Calamarain will permit themselves to be studied by Starfleet.* There was so much that could be learned from so unique a species, just as the Calamarain might benefit from being exposed to the mysteries of humanoid existence.

"Captain," Leyoro said, pointing to the eastern horizon of the vast icefield, "over there."

Obviously, the Angosian government had augmented her eyesight along with everything else. Picard peered into the distance, blinking against the gusts of ice crystals in the air, but all he could discern was perhaps a faint red ember. "What do you see?"

"Two figures," she reported, "humanoid in appearance. They could be Q and that other entity you spoke of. They're confronting each other. . . . Captain, I think we'd better hurry."

Picard paused only long enough to make certain that the Calamarain understood his intentions. "We believe your enemy is nearby, with the other of his kind. Are you with us?"

The voice of the Calamarain, nearly as cold and lifeless as their current setting, spoke via his combadge. "We/singular comprehend/corroborate. Chaos/plural imminent. Approach/caution/imperative."

Was that a warning, Picard wondered, *or a statement of intent?* It troubled him that the entity still declined to draw a distinction between 0 and Q, apparently referring to both as "chaos." That spoke poorly for the only strategy he could devise that might have a chance of succeeding against 0. *I'll have to cross that bridge when I come to it, which shouldn't be much longer.* "Let's go," he said.

Distances could be deceptive in a holodeck, where a generous panoply of illusory techniques were employed to create the appearance of entire worlds within a single chamber. Picard found it difficult to estimate how much ground they had to cover or even how far they had gone. The lack of any landmarks, not to mention the inherent difficulty of trudging through the deeply packed snow, frustrated him. He had to hope that any sort of contest between two ageless immortals would not reach its climax before they had a chance to arrive on the scene.

The Calamarain, who presumably could travel faster through the air than he and Leyoro could on foot, lagged behind them instead. *Perhaps that's what it meant by "approach/caution/imperative,"* Picard speculated. It was becoming increasingly clear that the Calamarain, collectively and individually, did not intend to lead any charge against the forces of chaos, but preferred to let Picard present the first target to their foe. *Rather like negotiating with the Romulans,* he concluded. He just prayed it wouldn't take a martyr or two to bring humanity and the Calamarain together.

As they fought their way through the snow and wind, Leyoro took stock of the simulation in which they were immersed. "Rura Penthe?" she guessed, citing the infamous frozen prison asteroid where the Klingons once exiled their political prisoners.

"Same idea, different dimension," he informed her, reminded, as he had been the first time he beheld this forlorn wasteland, of Cocytus, the ninth and final circle of Dante's Inferno, where the greatest traitors in history were buried in ice forever. *That's undoubtedly where 0 considers that Q belongs. . . .*

Soon, no more than ten minutes at most, the red glow that he could now identify as a handheld torch exposed both Q and 0, facing each other amid the arctic desolation, just as they had over a million years ago, but this time in far less convivial a fashion. Picard watched in disbelief as the debased and demented tatterdemalion that 0 had become flung what looked like a harpoon into Q's upper leg, physically injuring Q in a way that Picard would not have thought possible only days before. Yanking the spear free of Q's metaphysical flesh, 0 raised it high above the wounded superbeing's chest, preparing to deliver the killing blow, as he had to the dying sun of the Tkon Empire. "Stop him!" Picard ordered, his voice carrying through the frigid air.

Leyoro fired her phaser at the harpoon, which stubbornly refused to disintegrate. The energy beam caught 0's attention, though, halting him in midstroke.

"Eh?" 0 contemplated the new arrivals with bemused indifference. "Specks and smoke. Smoke and specks." His gaze swung from the humans to the Calamarain and back again. "Come to pay your last respects?"

"I'm not dead yet, you rhyming monstrosity," Q protested, wincing as he spoke. He looked past Picard and his pained expression turned into one of shock and bewilderment as he spied the Calamarain, following Picard's and Leyoro's sunken footprints across the snow. "Have you gone insane, Picard?" he accused, aghast. "One revenge-crazed arch-foe wasn't enough for me, you had to invite them in this unforgiving fog as well? Have you forgotten that they want to kill me?"

"Take a number. Stand in line," 0 chanted, his fingers wrapped around the shaft of the harpoon, "nobody kills Q until I get mine." He let go of the spear and stepped back, but the weapon remained suspended in the air, poised to impale Q. He winked at Picard and the others. "Want to watch? Watch to want? Watch away!"

The point of the spear descended inexorably toward where Q's heart would be if he had mimicked human anatomy as meticulously as he had created his counterfeit uniform. Sweat broke out on his brow as he used his remaining strength to telekinetically hold back the harpoon, which hung like the sword of Damocles over Q's chest. Picard saw the weapon vibrate from the force of two conflicting wills, but knew that Q, injured as he was, could not hold out against 0's madness indefinitely.

"What is it, Picard?" Q cried out in righteous indignation, while his eyes stared at the harpoon as if it would cost him his life to look away for an instant. His voice held enormous reservoirs of self-pity. "You couldn't turn down a chance to get rid of me once and for all, no matter the cost to creation? Thrown in your lot with the Calamarain and 0 and all the rest who want me dead and buried? I never dreamed you could be so petty. *Et tu,* Jean-Luc?"

"Shut up and listen to me, Q!" Picard barked. "You have to join your forces

with the Calamarain. It's our only choice. Neither of you has the raw power to oppose 0 individually, but together you might be able to subdue him. You have to try!"

Q laughed bitterly as the spear inched closer to his breastbone. "Always searching for the diplomatic solution . . . you're consistent, I'll give you that, Picard. But
you're as stark raving mad as he is if you think that the Calamarain and I can make
peace after a million years of vaporous vendetta. Have you forgotten what I did to
them? What they tried to do to me?"

"Chaos/plural/not singular," the Calamarain stated flatly. "Indistinguishable/
unacceptable. Cannot forget/forgive." The iridescent cloud ascended to the ceiling
concealed by the illusion of an open sky. "Retreat/preserve/remember."

Grunting with effort, Q managed to press back the spearpoint for a centimeter
or two, but what small respite he gained began to slip away within seconds, millimeter by millimeter. "See, Picard," he chided, seizing the chance for one last
I-told-you-so, "the Calamarain can't even be bothered to tell 0 and I apart."

Picard felt his hopes soar away with the departing Calamarain. Nonetheless, he
grabbed on to the spearshaft with both hands and added his own human strength to
the telekinetic dual between 0 and Q. The iron harpoon was freezing to the touch,
and his fingers had already gone numb from the cold, but he struggled against
what felt like twice standard gravity. His arms were aching after only a moment.
His palms and the pads of his fingers felt like they were welded to the freezing
metal. He couldn't pull them away now if he tried. And the worst part was, he
didn't even know if he was making the slightest difference.

"You might as well spare yourself a dislocated arm or two," Q suggested, spit-
ting out the words from a face contorted by the herculean mental effort required to
keep the spear at bay. "0's both gifted and truly insane. An unbeatable combination."

"Sounds like someone I know," Picard grunted. The iron javelin slipped downward suddenly, tearing at the skin of his palms. He held on despite the stinging
pain, renewing his hold on the shaft.

"Flattery will get you nowhere, *mon captaine.*" The harpoon's point dug into
the padded insulation of Q's modified Starfleet uniform. "I'm not nearly unhinged
enough to derail his maniacal momentum. That would take real craziness!"

"And what could be crazier," Picard persisted, "than you and the Calamarain, of
all people, saving the *Enterprise?*" Certainly, the entire venture, his last hope for
saving the galaxy from the ravages of both 0 and The One, was looking more like
a lunatic's fancy with each passing heartbeat. *Who is more insane?* he wondered.
0, or me, for thinking I could stop him?

0 paid no attention to the insignificant efforts of Picard, distracted by the ascension
of the Calamarain. "Smoke and snow. Snow and smoke. Choke, smoke, choke!" His
cracked lips curled downward as he recalled, possibly, the way the Coulalakritous had
forcibly expelled him from their collective being a million years ago. He clenched his
fist at the fleeing Calamarain, then began to squeeze. "Smoke into snow . . ."

Baeta Leyoro had seen a lot of ugly things in her career, but this 0 character
took the grand prize. He looked like a half-mad Tarsian POW crossed with a bioluminescent squid from the pitch-black bottom of some alien sea. This was the
creature that had killed poor Ensign Clarze, and brought the hostile Calamarain
down upon the ship? She was willing to believe it.

But what was he doing now?

His fist was clenched so tightly that his elongated fingernails were digging mercilessly into his own flesh. It was as if he already had the Calamarain in his grasp and were squeezing them into submission.

And maybe he was. The plasma cloud's airborne retreat slowed, then began to reverse itself. The Calamarain dropped toward the snow-blanketed plain, losing altitude dramatically. The cloud appeared smaller, too, and more densely opaque. *He's compressing it,* she realized, hitting on the truth intuitively; somehow 0 was concentrating the free-floating plasma into a smaller and smaller space. She wondered urgently how much longer the Calamarain would be able to maintain a gaseous state under that crushing pressure.

Not long at all, as it turned out. Before her biochemically enhanced eyes, the Calamarain liquefied in midair, raining down upon the icescape like phosphorescent sleet. Leyoro ran to get out from beneath the bizarre precipitation, then twisted around to watch the shower of living liquid crash to earth less than four meters away. But were the Calamarain still alive, she wondered. Could they survive in such a fundamentally different state?

0 was not taking any chances. "Hah!" he hooted, enjoying his triumph. "Smoke to slush! Crush the slush! Crush!" Greenish blood leaked out between his clenched fingers as he continued to squeeze whatever remained of the Calamarain.

Leyoro raced to where the transformed cloud came to ground. She found the Calamarain pooled in a shallow depression in the icy crust. Prismatic reflections on the surface of the puddle made it resemble an oil slick upon the snow, seeping slowly into the frost below. But 0 wasn't finished with the Calamarain yet; as Leyoro watched, the glowing liquid grew thicker and more viscous. Its innate radiance slowly faded as it began to crystalize, freezing solid in a matter of seconds. Its amorphous boundaries congealed, becoming fixed and immobile. Leyoro didn't know a lot about the nature and needs of the Calamarain, but she had to assume that the once-gaseous entity had been locked into a state of suspended animation at the very least, which pretty much sent Captain Picard's long-shot plan straight down the gravity well.

"Smoke to slush to solid," 0 gloated. "Atmosphere to ichor to ice. The smoke never learns. Never learns does the smoke!"

Leyoro got the distinct impression that the ranting monster had done this to the Calamarain before, which might mean that the frozen life-form could still be revived. An idea occurred to her: Once, during the war back home, after her scoutship had been shot down over the south pole of Tarsus, she had used her disruptor to melt the permafrost into drinking water. She had even warmed herself over the steam. Maybe that was the way to go.

She fired her phaser at the Calamarain, not to hurt, but to heal. At first it didn't seem to do any good, but then the hard crystalline edges of the cloud-creature's remains began to deliquesce. The paralyzed alien seemed to absorb the heat from her phaser as fast as she could fire the energy into it. Her weapon, which was no longer a weapon, broke down the crystal lattice into which the Calamarain had been crammed. The solid sheet of plasma residue spread out as it melted, beginning to shine once more with a radiance of its own.

Her rescue efforts did not go unnoticed. 0 glared at her murderously, flinging his torch away in disgust. It landed upon the snow several paces away, sputtering fitfully. "Cheat!" he accused her. "Cheaters, all of you! Cheat, cheated, cheating!"

He didn't charge at her. He didn't need to. Without warning or cause, the phaser in her hand emitted a high-pitched whine that stabbed at Leyoro's ears and filled her heart with dread. *It's overloading,* she realized. *He's doing it somehow.* From the sound of it, she had less than a minute before the phaser exploded in her hand.

She stared desperately at the Calamarain. It had melted almost entirely now, but had not yet attained its original gaseous state. The simmering, shimmering puddle was just starting to come to a boil, barely beginning to evaporate. *I can't stop now,* she thought, urging the process on with the intensity of her gaze. *It still needs a few more seconds.* Bubbles churned upon the reflective surface of the ionized liquid that was the Calamarain, coming to a froth as the heat of the phaser sped up the molecules composing the fluid, sending them farther and farther apart. Incandescent fumes rose from the shallow pool, encouraging Leyoro even as the ear-piercing shriek of the malfunctioning phaser forced her to cover one ear with her free hand. *Almost there,* she thought, so close to success that nothing short of a quantum torpedo could make her stop now; if there was one thing she had learned about the Calamarain over the last several hours, it was that they really were Better Off Vaporized. . . .

The keening phaser erupted in a deafening explosion of searing heat and concussive force that sent her flying backward, landing flat on her back in a snowdrift several meters away from the Calamarain. Embedded in the ice, her face and front scorched and smoking, she felt like she was burning and freezing to death at the same time. The pain was excruciating; it was a wonder that she could even see at all after the blinding flash. *Let's hear it for Angosian medical know-how,* she thought, coughing up blood.

She didn't need a medical tricorder to know how extensive her injuries were. She didn't have a chance. *Funny,* she thought, as her vision blurred and began to go black, *I always thought I couldn't live without an enemy. Never thought I'd end up dying to save one.*

The last thing she saw was the reborn Calamarain rising like an immaterial phoenix from the ice, glittering with all the colors of the rainbow. . . .

> *"Handle with care the spider's net,*
> *You can't be sure that a trap's not set. . . ."*

While 0 sang exuberantly, mocking Q's approaching demise, the harpoon seemed to have a life and strength of its own, pressing toward Q's heart and dragging Picard's frostbitten hands with it. The exhausted captain felt the strain of resisting the spear in his back and shoulders and, most painfully, his arms. *It's ironic,* he thought. *After all the byzantine puzzles and brain-twisting trials that Q has put me through over the years, I end up standing in the snow, breaking my back to keep him from dying at the point of a primitive spear.*

Even the light seemed to be fading with his hopes, as 0's burning brand sputtered and died somewhere upon the barren plain. The miserly stars provided scant illumination, so that the perpetual night leached all the color from the scene, reducing the world to shades of black and gray. Would he even be able to see when the sharpened tip of the harpoon penetrated Q's ribs, or would he hear Q cry out first?

"Heedless of what might befall—
You neglect the spider on the wall. . . ."

Then a light broke through the darkness, shining down on he and Q from directly above. He looked up in surprise and saw the Calamarain, scintillating against the bleak arctic sky like the aurora borealis. But had the cloud entity come to aid them at last, or to witness the long-awaited demise of the hated Q?

"Sacrifice/deliverance. Testimony/trust/gratitude. Sacrifice/obligation."

Sacrifice? Picard heard but did not understand. What did the Calamarain mean? That Q must be sacrificed to win their trust and gratitude? "No," he stated firmly. "We do not make bargains in the blood of others. I will not be party to Q's death."

The Calamarain cast their resplendent light, quite unlike the blood-red glow of O's torch, upon Picard's upturned face. "Misunderstanding/confusion. We/plural grateful/obliged. Sacrifice/deliverance."

"I don't understand," Picard pleaded. He felt that he and Q and the Calamarain were on the verge of a breakthrough that could save them all, if only he could find a better way to communicate. What did the Calamarain want? Who was obliged to whom? What was the sacrifice?

Or who?

Perhaps in answer, the cloud of living plasma plunged toward Q's anguished face, oozing its way past his flaring nostrils and clenched white teeth, disappearing into his agonized body like a genie returning to a bottle. Q fought against the invasive vapor, twisting his head back and forth in a fruitless attempt to evade the iridescent mist that flowed into him against his will. Then his eyes seemed to widen in understanding and he stopped resisting and took a deep breath. As Picard watched, perplexed and anxious, Q *inhaled* the substance of the Calamarain, absorbing the alien entity entirely into himself. The whites of his eyes took on the opalescent luster of the living plasma.

"When the spider aims his deadly spikes,
No one sees him till he stri—"

O's insidious chorus was cut off in midverse when the possessed harpoon suddenly went spinning off through the air, coming to rest in a bank of snow far from Q, who sprang to his feet, his wound healed, his vitality restored. O gawked at him, dumbfounded, understanding little more than Picard. "What the devil?" he asked.

"We/plural/Q are ready/prepared for another game/contest/competition," the revived figure declared. The syntax resembled that of the Calamarain, the voice and the inflections were pure Q. "Do you/singular still like/enjoy games/contests/competitions?"

This was more than Picard had imagined when he first suggested that Q and the Calamarain join forces. Taking him literally, they had merged into a single being, with the power and potential of both. Even O, crazed as he was, appeared intimidated by the prospect. "No," he muttered into his scraggly beard, "one is two is one is two is one. . . ."

All the colors of the Calamarain glistened in Q's eyes as he raised his hand and released a bolt of lightning from his fingertips that crashed into the snow and ice in front of O's rag-wrapped feet. "Tag/gotcha/checkmate!"

Unable to face what Q and the Calamarain had become, O tried to escape, taking off across the snow away from Picard and the Q/Calamarain. At first, he ran on two human legs, but when his crippled foot slowed him down, he fell forward onto his four lateral tentacles and scuttled over the packed snow like a spider. Picard stared in wonder and disgust, until his eyes fell upon a charred and motionless body lying askew upon the ice not ten meters away.

Dear God, no, he thought, feeling a chill that had nothing to do with the wind or the weather. *The sacrifice. . . .*

Unlike Picard, the Q/Calamarain did not pause to grieve. His/their lightning chased after 0, halting his frantic flight with a white-hot thunderbolt that left him sprawled upon the ground. More lightning rained down on him, and as 0 shuddered spasmodically beneath their impact, Picard heard an awe-inducing rumble of thunder that came from outside the holodeck, perhaps even outside the hull of the *Enterprise,* penetrating the created world of 0's polar limbo with its inescapable reality. *The rest of the Calamarain,* he guessed, *surrounding the ship.* Could it be that the fragment of the Calamarain now residing within Q was channeling the collective might of the entire gaseous community, adding the full strength of all the Calamarain to the power of Q?

It was hard to imagine, but how else to explain the undeniable shift in the balance of power that had occurred when the Calamarain merged with Q? As he had hoped, the sum of two infinite powers had indeed proved more infinite than infinity. Conventional mathematics said otherwise, but, as Picard knew full well, there was nothing conventional about the Calamarain or, especially, Q.

Beneath the barrage of transcendental thunderbolts, 0's human guise began to slip away once and for all. Flesh and hair and teeth and eyes crumpled away like powder, until all Picard could see was a writhing mass of otherworldly tentacles that flailed about in agony, churning the packed ice and snow into a swirling haze that thankfully obscured the horrific vision. Then the besieged extradimensional entity began to physically shrink in size, its tendrils retracting and diminishing until all that was left was a tiny wriggling creature about the size of a small jellyfish.

Or a spider.

The Q/Calamarain strode across the tundra, leaving deep tracks in the snow, until it towered over the pathetic specimen. The little multilegged monster tried to scurry away, but it could not outrun the shadow of the Q/Calamarain's upraised foot. The sole of his/their boot hovered over the creature for one ominous moment, and Picard thought he heard an almost inaudible squeal of fear. Then the shoe descended, squashing 0 flat. A single thin tendril, no larger than a hair, stuck out from beneath the shoe, quivering weakly. The Q/Calamarain smiled with obvious satisfaction.

"Game/competition over. We/plural/Q win."

Nineteen

"Well, it's a nasty case of frostbite, but nothing modern medicine can't take care of."

Beverly finished wrapping Picard's frozen fingers in thermal conduction strips, then stepped aside to allow him to stand up and step away from the biobed. His fingertips still felt slightly numb but the doctor's treatment had gone a long way toward restoring their circulation. *If only Lieutenant Leyoro and Ensign Clarze could be restored as well,* he mused sadly. No matter how many times he lost one of his crew, the pain never got easier. He could only note in his log that they had perished in the performance of their duty; he could think of no better epitaph.

Geordi La Forge approached him from the other side of the primary ward, where Nurse Ogawa had just finished a test on his optical implants. "Well, Captain," he said, "I must say you're a sight for sore eyes." Picard was glad to hear that Geordi's implants had not been permanently damaged by Lem Faal's telekinetic rampage. *In the end,* he reflected, *Lem Faal's most lasting victim may well have been himself.*

A broken man, his frightening powers long gone, the celebrated Betazoid scientist, and apparent pawn of 0, now occupied his own biobed not far away. He sat upright, his spine supported by Starfleet cushions, as he stared vacantly before him with eyes that no longer held the lustrous gleam of the galactic barrier. Listening to the man's labored breathing, and observing the feeble life signs reported on the overhead monitor, Picard could not imagine that Faal had much longer to live. *A tragedy,* the captain thought, *but not nearly as terrible as the consequences of his misguided pursuit of immortality.*

Young Milo Faal sat beside the bed, holding his father's trembling hand and speaking to him softly. "It will be all right, Dad. We're going home now, where we belong. You don't need to worry. I'll take care of you."

A curious role reversal, Picard observed. The boy had indeed become more of a parent to his father than a son. He admired the youth's maturity and compassion, especially after all he had heard of the shameful way Faal had neglected and abused his children. Picard could not help holding Faal's various crimes against him; still, given the sorry state to which the scientist had been reduced, he felt certain the man had been punished enough. *He's a lucky man to have a son like Milo.*

Perhaps aware of Picard's thoughts, the Betazoid boy turned to look in the captain's direction. A chill ran through Picard when he saw those unearthly white eyes directed at him. *There's a problem I wish I had a solution for.* The boy had not deigned to use his new powers since subduing his father in the pediatric ward, but Counselor Troi had confirmed that some residue of the barrier's unnatural power, derived from the Q themselves, still dwelt within the mind of this child. *How can I be sure that those powers will not pose a danger to Milo or others?*

A flash of light burst between Picard and Milo, and, for one tense moment, Picard feared that the youth's amazing abilities had been heard from again. Instead, he was surprised and relieved (and surprised to be relieved) that the light had merely heralded the arrival of the entire Q family, all three of them. *Who would have ever thought,* he wondered, bemused, *that I would ever greet the appearance of Q with anything less than dismay?*

As it was, he did experience a degree of apprehension. "What brings you here, Q?"

"Oh, nothing much," Q replied brightly. He patted the head of baby q, happily draped over his mother's shoulder, and strolled over to Picard. "Odds and ends, really. For instance, I thought you might be interested to know that my good wife here has called the recent contretemps to the attention of the Continuum and persuaded them, fractious as they are these days, to undertake an immediate project to shore up both barriers and repair all those worrisome fractures, which have proven to be just too tempting to impetuous and irresponsible species such as yourself."

We're irresponsible? Picard thought, not sure whether to be amused or appalled by Q's gall. Still, if Q wanted to shift the blame for the 0 crisis to humanity, Picard had neither the energy nor the inclination to argue the point. At the moment, that is. "And what of 0?" he asked, addressing the only point that truly mattered.

"Back where he belongs," Q assured him. "If I were you, Picard, I'd persuade your superiors at Starfleet to leave the barrier alone from now on. Even putting aside the problem of 0, the Federation, as well as your assorted allies and rivals, are simply not ready to venture out of the galaxy just yet."

"We may surprise you," Picard said, unwilling to impose an absolute limit on the future of space exploration. That was Starfleet's decision, not the Continuum's. On that point, at least, he remained steadfast. "Still, it is always best to be fully aware of the dangers involved."

"Oh, there are dangers you haven't even conceived of yet," Q promised, a mischievous twinkle in his eye. "Perhap I'll introduce you to them someday."

Don't trouble yourself on my account, Picard thought. He watched with growing uneasiness as the female Q, babe in arms, wandered away. Although Q did not seem to be up to any particular deviltry on this occasion, he saw no reason to encourage their stay. "Is that all?" he asked.

"Actually, there is one more little matter," the female Q said, although she seemed less interested in Picard than in young Milo Faal. She joined the boy at his father's bedside, and spoke to him with unexpected gentleness. "Milo, I think you know you still have a piece of the Q inside you. I'm afraid I have to ask for it back."

"That's all right," Milo said. He looked sadly at the wreckage of his father, perhaps considering all the anxiety and unhappiness that Lem Faal had caused in his thirst for that same power. "I don't want it."

The female Q smiled approvingly and laid her hand upon Milo's inattentively combed hair. Picard saw a soft purple glow sparkle between the woman's outstretched fingers before fading away. More important, he also watched with relief as the eerie white sheen in Milo's eyes faded as well, leaving behind eyes as big and brown and recognizably Betazoid as Deanna Troi's. "Thank you," the woman said. "You're a very well-behaved boy. For a mortal."

And with that, she vanished without further ado, taking her own preternaturally precocious child with her. "Well, I suppose I'll be heading on, too," Q commented. "I'm overdue for a rendezvous in the Delta Quadrant."

"Before you go," Picard delayed him, knowing he would probably regret it, but discovering there was one final question that he could not resist posing. "After all we've been through these last few days, both in the past and the present, could it be that, perhaps, you have finally learned your lesson about the evils of testing other sentient beings?"

Q smiled impishly, looking altogether incorrigible and unrepentant. "But, Jean-Luc, how do you know that this entire odyssey hasn't been a particularly ingenious test?"

And then he was gone, leaving Picard with even more questions than before. Questions with a capital Q.

Epilogue

Begin again. Again, begin and begin. . . .

Behind the wall once more, he howled in frustration. For one brief interval, not more than a tormenting twinkling in the endless expanse of eternity, the galaxy had been his again. Worlds without end had awaited his wicked wiles and wild, wayward will. But then Q had taken it all away. Q!

Ever again. Forever again.

He scratched and clawed and snapped at the wall, which refused to yield to his frenzied need to strike back at Q. The wall was as permanent and punishing as it had ever been, any minute cracks and crevices healed and sealed, leaving him not even a sliver of a window into the great, glittering galaxy he might never see again. A galaxy of smoke and specks and Q and Q and Q. . . .

Forever and ever. Ever and forever. Forever and never.

The voice on the other side, the voice that had come at his call, bringing with it a fleeting fraction of freedom, had gone silent, leaving him alone in the dark and the cold and the eternal emptiness. Had he ever really been free at all? He couldn't be sure anymore. His mind rebelled at the very thought of what had occurred—and what lay ahead. Space was vast and time was long, and all he had now was space and time, forever and ever and ever. It was enough to drive him sane.

A new beginning had ended. His new ending had only begun. . . .

A Look Inside

The Q Continuum

with Greg Cox

Kevin Dilmore: Thanks for sitting down with me, Greg. I hope I don't force you to reach too far into your memory because I'd like to start by talking about your first *Star Trek* novels, *Devil in the Sky* and *Dragon's Honor.*

Greg Cox: Actually, I was just talking about *Devil in the Sky* with someone this morning. A friend of mine finally got around to reading it these umpteen years later.

KD: How did you get involved in *Star Trek* writing?

GC: Well, I've known John [Ordover, one of Pocket Books' *Star Trek* editors] for years. In fact, we were editors at Tor [Books] together. We shared a cubicle, practically. I started writing [media] tie-in books with John Gregory Betancourt when he and I wrote a bunch of Batman stories for some anthologies edited by Martin Greenberg. John had read the Batman stories, and at that point he had moved from Tor over to Pocket for *Star Trek,* and asked whether we would like to do a *Star Trek: Deep Space Nine* book for him. At that time, *Deep Space Nine* was just gearing up, and there was sort of a mad crunch to get as many books as possible in the pipeline so they could launch the book series at the same time as the TV series.

KD: You're kidding? So that was a fast start for you both.

GC: John suddenly needed a whole bunch of new *Star Trek* writers to help get a line of *Deep Space Nine* books off the ground. In fact, we started working on the book before I had seen a single episode of *Deep Space Nine.* I was sent a series bible and the script for the first episode. That's what a lot of us early *Deep Space Nine* authors had to work with. The show had finally come on while I was writing the book, so I got to watch the show a little bit.

KD: I thought it was great that you used your book to link *Deep Space Nine* with the original series by using the Horta as a character.

GC: I have to give credit where credit is due. That in fact was John Ordover's idea.

He actually called me up and asked if we wanted to write a book about Hortas and *Deep Space Nine.*

KD: But that started a trend with your *Star Trek* fiction and its free blending of elements from all of the shows.

GC: You're right, which I guess made me the right person for that, because since then I've been madly tying together loose ends of *Star Trek* continuity. I always end up referring back to the old show somehow.

KD: Is that fun for you to do?

GC: Oh, yeah. In this case, I got to watch [the original series' episode] "Devil in the Dark" over and over again. [laughs] The division of labor on that book was very simple, by the way. If it's on the space station, I wrote it. If it's with the away team, Betancourt wrote it. *Star Trek* is good that way in that you have the story function of the away team on its mission and the B-plot back on the starship or the space station or wherever. We were able to say, "OK, you go off with Kira, Bashir, and Dax and play with them, and I'll stay at the station with Quark, Odo, and O'Brien. And to this day, I feel like I've never actually written Kira.

KD: After writing with Betancourt, you ended up paired with Kij Johnson for *Dragon's Honor.* How did that come about?

GC: This was a different scenario but, again, all roads lead back to Tor Books. Kij at one time was managing editor of Tor Books, so I knew her from way back. Where *Devil in the Sky* started out as a true collaboration for which we truly divvied up the plot to write in a collaborative fashion, *Dragon's Honor* started out as a solo novel by Kij. Then Kij ran into real-life situations intruding on her work, she was no longer going to make the deadline, and I was asked to dive in and help her finish off this book. In my head, I still think of that as "the Kij book" because she invented the characters, the plot and everything, and basically did a detailed first draft of the book. When I came in, I basically did a second draft, rewriting what she already had written. That was sort of an ad-hoc collaboration as a favor to a friend to help finish a book when she had gotten a new job and had to move across the country.

KD: Then next was the *Star Trek: Voyager* book.

GC: Yes. I had done two collaborations, and the collaborations were each fun although they were completely different experiences. At that point, I was nagging John Ordover to please let me do a solo novel. And this ended up being the same situation for me as the *Deep Space Nine* book: *Voyager* in the offing and the show wasn't on the air yet and John suddenly needed to get six or seven *Voyager* books off the ground. In that case, he sent me just a twelve-page bible for the series. I remember writing my outline and starting to write the novel before I had seen a single episode of *Voyager* but just based on that bible, which turned out to be much more tentative than the *Deep Space Nine* thing. A lot of stuff that was in that original [*Voyager*] bible didn't wind up happening in the series. That was the weird thing about writing something like that: You have no idea who the characters are going to be or what relationships might develop or anything. For example, if I had known the Doctor was going to be such fun, I would have given him a bigger part in the book.

KD: Or in the case of *Deep Space Nine,* the friendship that developed between Bashir and O'Brien.

GC: My friend who just read *Devil in the Sky* said this morning, "Boy, Julian is immature and sort of callow in this book." Well, go back and watch the first six episodes or so. He was a bit annoying and immature in those days. He got an infusion of maturity later on in time for the sixth season. But look back at those opening scenes when he's flirting with Dax and seems to have an antagonistic relationship with Kira. I remember that was something that people complained about, the fact that they were so nasty to each other in the book. Go back and watch the pilot. They get off on the wrong foot with each other. At that point, all I knew was that first script, in which Kira and Bashir seemed to not get along and not like each other. We took that and ran with it.

KD: That's what you had to work with then.

GC: Right. The problem with Dax was that I firmly believe that her character was not defined until season two, and we had no idea what to do with her. The reason she had such a small part in that book was that we didn't have much of a sense of her personality from the script or the first few episodes. In fact, I think that John Ordover came back to us and told us we had to put more Jadzia scenes in there. "But we can't figure Jadzia out!" [laughs]

KD: That's a disadvantage when compared to working with the original crew, whom you had kicked around in your head for more than thirty years at that time.

GC: Oh, yeah. They're burned into my brain, and so is the *Star Trek: The Next Generation* crew. With the others, since I wrote them so early on, there is stuff that makes me think, "Oh, if I had known this, that and the other thing, well . . .

KD: So with your fourth book, *Assignment: Eternity,* you hit the last of the four shows at the time. Was it your idea to write a novel for the original series at that point?

GC: Actually, I had been bugging John to write a Gary Seven book for years. This was something I had been lobbying for, and we certainly had been knocking the idea around. I think I even did an early version of the proposal and sent it in to Kevin Ryan, who was John's predecessor at Pocket, but it was passed on for whatever reason. So we went back into the forest a lot to try different ideas. At one point, it was going to be a Picard and Gary Seven novel. I think we did a couple of drafts of an outline for that.

KD: That's an interesting take on things.

GC: And strange but true, at one point John wanted to do a Kirk-versus-Q novel.

KD: Really?

GC: Yes, and I actually did an outline or so for that, but we ultimately decided not to do that. At that point, I rewrote the outline and turned Q into Gary Seven. Ironically enough, I finally got my Gary Seven and Kirk novel. That was a long and circuitous path for it to take.

KD: But waste nothing. If you have an idea that you think is worth exploring, don't just toss it away completely.

GC: Oddly enough, the first idea I had to write something for Pocket Books turned out to be the fourth book I wrote.

KD: Obviously, Gary Seven is a character who really resonated with you.

GC: Yeah, I have very fond memories of Gary Seven. I think that his episode ["Assignment: Earth"] seemed to be crying out for a sequel, it was a pilot for an intended TV series and it was implied that Gary and Roberta and Isis were going to have all of these exciting adventures down the road. It seemed like an obvious hook.

KD: So with those four novels done, you then are offered a big and very ambitious writing project with *The Q Continuum* books. How did that start off?

GC: That was generated partially by John Ordover, who basically thought that *The Q Continuum* would be a great title of a trilogy or a miniseries. He called me up and said, "Greg, how would you like to do a trilogy about Q?" That was as much of a plot as he had. He basically was in love with the title. At first, I remember being sort of intimidated, thinking, "Oh my God, I'm not sure I've got nine hundred pages of Q in me." But I went back and watched all of the Q episodes again. And that was my very first trilogy, which was an interesting experience for me. So I worked up an outline, got it all approved, and I dived into it. And yes, it was a great big chunk of time. I spent a lot of time on the first book. It was a challenge in that I'd never done a trilogy before. The main thing I remember trying to figure out is how much plot I needed. Originally, I overloaded the plot with lots of subplots that didn't end up making it into the finished book. Spreading it all over three books was a challenge.

KD: Would you change anything at this point then?

GC: In retrospect, if I had I to do it over again, I'd give Riker a little bit more to do. He doesn't have enough to do in Book Two.

KD: Book Two was more focused on the Tkon Empire than anything else. It struck me as a look at the machinations of these superbeings on this Job-like race.

GC: Yes. That makes it somewhat odd for a *Star Trek* book, which made me a bit nervous while I was writing it. There were big chunks of the book that don't have Picard or Riker or anybody in it. I extrapolated the Tkon Empire from what basically were five lines of dialogue from [the *ST:TNG* first-season episode] "The Last

Outpost." It seems to be my destiny in *Star Trek* to get entire novels out of two lines of dialogue in [the original series' episode] "Space Seed."

KD: [laughs] But we'll save talk of your Eugenics Wars books for another time. So, justify for the reader your rationale for spending so much time on the Tkon Empire. Why was it so important to these books?

GC: I wanted to show something horrible happening in the past for which 0 and his gang of evil, glowing energy beings were responsible. You don't want a threat to be too abstract, such as "Oh, there's this nasty thing on the other side of the galactic barrier, and boy, it would really be bad if it got through." It's too abstract unless you see it actually doing something so you can get a sense of its capabilities. And I didn't want to invent something new. My philosophy of writing *Star Trek* novels is not to invent a new alien race when there's one floating around waiting to be grabbed. In fact, *Star Trek* is littered with dead civilizations that seem to have imploded at some point. The Tkon Empire seemed a logical place to go.

KD: So in that theme of drawing from existing aliens and beings, did you immediately go to the idea of rounding up these energy beings with the idea of their being on a scale of power equitable with Q's?

GC: That probably was the uniting theme. There is almost this sense that the *Star Trek* universe is full of these weird, glowing balls of energy that do nasty things. I think I had an idea along those lines. One of the discarded ideas for one of the proposed Gary Seven novels involved dragging all of those things into play. But you want something comparable to *The Q Continuum.* At one point, I was going to have Redjac join the evil extraterrestrials, but I decided that it was getting a little crowded and Redjac was one of those things that ended up on the cutting-room floor. I figured that I already had four glowing energy beings that live on fear or whatever. And, if you'll notice, Redjac makes a cameo in the first part of *The Eugenics Wars.*

KD: And they are different kinds of characters. The Gorgan, for example, uses children as his conduits of power. What did you enjoy about writing him?

GC: For all of them, I went back and watched all of the episodes to try and stay more or less consistent with their patterns of corruption. I thought I had Gorgan in character; that's the main thing I remember. I kept trying to make his technique different from the "god-thing" from *Star Trek V: The Final Frontier* and the creature from [the original series episode] "The Day of the Dove." Incidentally, I ended up giving that creature a name because it didn't have a name in the original episode.

KD: [laughs] I noticed that you worked it into a line of Q's dialogue, when he calls it the Beta XII-A entity and says that is the name given to the being in the Starfleet database. That's also the name it was given in the *Star Trek Encyclopedia* [by Michael Okuda and Denise Okuda].

GC: Well, logically, it was not going to call itself the Beta XII-A entity. So I had to come up with a name for it, and Paramount was very nice about letting me do that.

KD: But that's the only reference like that. In the book, you use (*) to represent the concept to the reader. I guess it doesn't matter what you call it as long as the reader knows what's going on.

GC: Given that we're in a book in which one of the characters is named Q and one is named 0, the bar had been raised for weird, extraterrestrial names. The problem is that it has come back to bite me, sometimes. When you find yourself doing a live reading somewhere, sometimes you think, "Oh good God, what have I done to myself? How am I going to pronounce this?" Or worse yet, you get a call from the audio book people wanting to know how to pronounce such-and-such. "Uh, I have no idea. I just typed it."

KD: [laughs] And given what you have to work with—a swirl of colored lights—I think that would have been much harder for you to get a grip on that character's motivation and action. It just sat there and spun.

GC: Again, I just tried to be consistent with its M.O. [method of operation] in "Day of the Dove" and basically escalate things.

KD: And that was your approach with The One as well?

GC: Here, it was a case where I thought it was very logical to revisit the idea because of the nature of the two barriers: The galactic barrier on the rim of the galaxy and the Great Barrier in the center of the galaxy. It seemed that if I was dealing with a creature on the other side of the galactic barrier, I ought to deal with the one on the other side of the Great Barrier, particularly to the extent that the same people who banished 0 beyond the galactic barrier would also be involved with however the god-thing from *Star Trek V* was trapped.

KD: Let's look at the centerpiece of the books, which obviously is Q. What in your mind is the appeal of Q, not just as a writer but as a fan. Why do writers keep coming up with reasons for him to show up on the *Enterprise?*

GC: For one thing, he's very, very fun to write. I was amazed at how easy it was to get into that voice.

KD: And when I read it, I can't help but hear John de Lancie's delivery.

GC: You always want to do a literary impression, if you will, to try and capture the voice of the character. I remember noticing within a paragraph or two that Q was really easy to get into. And yes, it sounded like John de Lancie in my head, too. One of the fun things about Q is that he's got this snarky sense of humor and he allows you to say all of the things that you really want to say but can't. He can make all of these snarky comments about *Star Trek* that otherwise couldn't be made—stuff about Troi's psychobabble or Riker's macho posing or whatever. He in some ways is poking gentle fun at the franchise just to be a little wacky and silly. Lord, he's also easy for scene transitions. You need to get from point A to B? Bang, you're there.

KD: See, you have no worries at all about distances from one barrier to the other.

GC: [laughs] Not when you have Q involved, no. I do remember going back and watching all of the Q episodes, so I could throw in references to them, such as his one and only visit to *Deep Space Nine*.

KD: When he gets decked by Sisko. It was the punch heard 'round the galaxy.

GC: [laughs] I think he makes this snide comment like "Dismal place. I'm never going back." I wanted that to allude to his popping up once and never appearing again.

KD: Do you think that part of the appeal of Q also is his interaction specifically with Picard?

GC: Oh, yes. He and Picard have this weird, quirky relationship. In *The Q Continuum* books, there are great chunks of time when it's just the two of them wandering around in time and space, but that works because we have seen it before. I also try to remember the fact that Q occasionally can be dangerous and has gotten *Enterprise* crew members killed. That's easy to forget about because there are a number of lighter, clown-ier Q episodes. But if you go back and look at [the *ST: TNG* second-season episode] "Q Who," he does, in fact, get people killed when he throws them up against the Borg.

KD: It's an interesting dynamic. There are some moments when he plays the all-powerful buffoon, and others when he borders on malevolence. Do you think Q works better as a comic foil or as a true villain?

GC: Ideally, you want to keep an edge of danger to him. Picard always seems to take him seriously. They may be out palling around, but he knows there's some potential for getting into serious trouble. That's what makes "Q Who" one of the great, all-time Q episodes. Q is funny; he has a great sense of humor, but ideally you want to keep that edge of danger to him as in [the *ST: TNG* series finale] "All Good Things . . . " or "Q Who."

KD: Do you think that [the *ST: TNG* sixth-season episode] "Tapestry" is in keeping with that edge-of-danger premise, too? I'm thinking in terms of his ability to shape history and change Picard's life.

GC: Yes, that is one of the more intense ones, too. I've always thought that you could look at these books as sort of the flip side of "Tapestry." In the episode, Q takes Picard into Picard's past and confronts him with his mistakes. In the books, Q takes Picard into his own past and we get to view his mistakes. Here, it's time for the guided tour of Q's past.

KD: So, do you think that Q and Picard might ever become friends?

GC: I don't know. Picard is always wary of Q; he always sees a potential for things going awry. And Q seems somewhat cozier and more friendly with Janeway, which was, in fact a problem because I never could figure out entirely why he didn't just send them all home. The Q episodes on *Star Trek: Voyager* were fun but to watch them, you had to sort of take away the whole issue of "Q could get them home in five seconds. Why doesn't Janeway really seem terribly interested in this prospect?" They usually would create a threat to distract her when getting home should be number one on Janeway's agenda. If you remember, the episodes always ended with Janeway helping out Q, so why she didn't go ahead and twist his arm a little and have him send them home, I don't know. It was a different relationship even though Janeway can find him just as exasperating.

KD: Maybe Janeway handled Q the way Kirk might have handled Q?

GC: I don't know. I imagine that Kirk would be fairly antagonistic toward Q because Kirk never liked weird, glowing balls of energy coming in and messing with his crew. One of the dangers [of a Kirk-Q story] is that you would end up doing [the original series episode] "The Squire of Gothos" again. Trelane really is sort of like an early draft of Q.

KD: And some of those issues are addressed in Peter David's book *Q Squared*.

GC: I went back and read the other Q books as well as watching the episodes, if only to try and avoid contradicting them. It's not mandatory, but I didn't want to shamelessly contradict anything. I see why we would not want to get too self-referential because then it feels like a closed universe and too club-ish. I would have liked to mention Trelane in my books at some point, but it didn't work out. There were certain subjects that I was told were off-limits in terms of Q's past.

KD: Oh really?

GC: Yes. At one point, I wanted to reveal how he met Guinan for the first time, but Paramount preferred to keep that mysterious for the time being. I think I also was going to bring in Wesley Crusher, who at that point was somewhere off traveling the universe, and again was asked not to deal with that right now. I think there's a throw-away reference somewhere when Dr. Crusher asks Q to keep an eye out for her son.

KD: Yet again, that harkens back to your desire as a *Star Trek* writer to tie up the loose ends that are left dangling. Is that part of the appeal that keeps you going back to writing *Star Trek* books?

GC: Oh yeah. You've got 400 or 500 hours of stuff here in this great, big universe that you can flesh out and make connections. It always seems redundant to invent a new race of energy beings when there's sixteen other races of energy beings already running around the Alpha Quadrant. Besides that, there's sort of a nifty, fannish appeal of "Ooh boy oh boy, I managed to tie that one in."

KD: I know you do a lot of research for your writings. The whole process must be fun for you, especially at that "a-ha" moment when you see something and think, "I can put this over here."

GC: I love looking for loose ends and holes and realizing that they never did resolve what the issue is between Guinan and Q, you know, and that there's room for a book there. I'm bad about it. [laughs] It's gotten to a point where I'm watching this stuff, let's say *Star Trek Nemesis,* and Shinzon mentions that he and his Reman buddies fought in the Dominion War, and I'm thinking "Hmm, book idea. File that away." I've got a file in the back of my head for *Star Trek* loose ends, such as "Whatever DID happen to Geordi's mother, whose mysterious disappearance never has been explained?" You sort of keep these packed away for dreaming books out of one line of dialogue.

KD: There are a lot of unknowns to explore in the printed side of *Star Trek* storytelling.

GC: Speaking of unknowns, and bringing us back to *The Q Continuum,* one problem I had writing was that at that point in the *ST: TNG* series, I did not know who the security officer was on the *Enterprise.* At that point, Worf was on *Deep Space Nine,* and whenever it was time for a movie, Worf conveniently would be dropping by.

KD: [laughs] "Well, what brings you back into this neck of the woods, Mr. Worf?"

GC: "Oh, well, I heard you guys were shooting another movie." [laughs] We just didn't know at this point in the continuity who the officer was; he or she had not been named. I remember asking John [Ordover] just who the hell was the security officer when Worf was not dropping by for vacation. John said, "Go ahead and make someone up, Greg, but he has to be dead by the end of the trilogy." And that's how we dealt with that.

KD: [laughs] Do you remember other potential problems?

GC: I remember living in mortal fear while I was writing the trilogy that *Voyager* was going to run a Q episode that would contradict my entire plot. The third-season episode "The Q and the Gray" was the most recent episode when I was writing the books. That's the one that introduced "Mrs. Q" played by Suzie Plakson. Incidentally, I was not to call her "Mrs. Q." It got very clumsy calling her "the female Q," but contextually I was able to write around it. I have heard some fans refer to her as "Suzie Q."

KD: Very clever.

GC: Yes. So as last seen, Q had gotten married and had a kid. And as far as the trilogy books went, thankfully, *Voyager* left Q alone for a year and a half. So it fits in very nicely. There also was a bit of a problem in that the books were set on the *Enterprise*-E, which at that point I had seen for all of four scenes here and there in a movie. There was a lot we didn't know about the *Enterprise*-E. Occasionally, I'd get a note back from Paramount with something like "There is no Ten-Forward on the ship." Oh, well, that's news to me. I also had a day-care center in the book, but then found out that there are no children on the *Enterprise*-E. I think I invented a holographic day-care center just to keep those scenes alive. That's a difficulty with the weird universe of *The Next Generation* when we see that universe for only two hours every three years.

KD: I'm guessing that can simultaneously inspire and hamstring a story.

GC: It's easiest doing classic *Star Trek* because that's finished; it's done and we all know that. Then again, there's always time travel and they can do the episode where Nichelle Nichols guest-stars on *Enterprise*. My doing *Deep Space Nine* and *Voyager* were interesting because I had to write the books while the show was just starting up and we all were still learning just who the hell Sisko was.

KD: If you had to make a choice, would you be able to pick a favorite crew to write?

GC: I'm not sure. Obviously I'm showing my age, but I always seem to end up going back to the original series and dragging in Hortas or Mugatos or Isis the Cat. But there are things I haven't done yet, pieces of *Star Trek* I haven't touched. I have yet to do a Seven of Nine book because my *Voyager* book was back in the Kes era. Kes is actually on the cover. I think I got one of the last "Kes-centric" novels in right under the wire before she left the ship.

KD: Your strategies just underscore, at least to me, that there's nothing that cannot be blended in *Star Trek* in a good story.

GC: Oh, yeah. Sometimes, it seems very, very logical for it to be blended.

KD: So in all, *The Q Continuum* books remain a good experience for you?

GC: Yes. I think *The Q Continuum* is still the best-selling book or books I have written. It hit the *New York Times* list for a week, which is unprecedented for me.

KD: That's a great indicator of fan response. And I assume that you have gotten positive feedback from readers over the years.

GC: Yes, but it's funny. There are a great number of fans out there who can't remember which Q books I wrote and which ones Peter David wrote. It's very amusing to me when people tell me how much they loved *Q Squared*. And I'm sure Peter David is told a lot how much people love *The Q Continuum*. He's done three Q books; I've done three Q books. I think the two of us are the only people who honestly remember which of us wrote which books.

KD: [laughs] Thanks so much for your time, Greg. It was a lot of fun hearing your take on the Q books.

GC: Thanks. I enjoyed it, too.